A TESTAMENT OF STEEL

A TESTAMENT OF STEEL

Davis Ashura

A TESTAMENT OF STEEL

Copyright © 2020 by Davis Ashura

All rights reserved.

Cover art and design by Andreas Zafiratos

Interior Layout by ML Spencer

Map by Rela "Kellerica" Similä at https://www.kellericamaps.com

Printed in the United States of America

Trade paperback ISBN: 978-1-7329780-8-9

Hardcover ISBN: 978-1-7329780-4-1

First Printing: 2020

DuSum Publishing

Books by Davis Ashura

The Castes and the OutCastes:

A Warrior's Path

A Warrior's Knowledge

A Warrior's Penance

Omnibus Edition (only available on Kindle)

Stories for Arisa (short-story collection)

The Chronicles of William Wilde:

William Wilde and the Necrosed

William Wilde and the Stolen Life

William Wilde and the Unusual Suspects

William Wilde and the Sons of Deceit

William Wilde and the Lord of Mourning

Instrument of Omens

A Testament of Steel

Memories of Prophecies

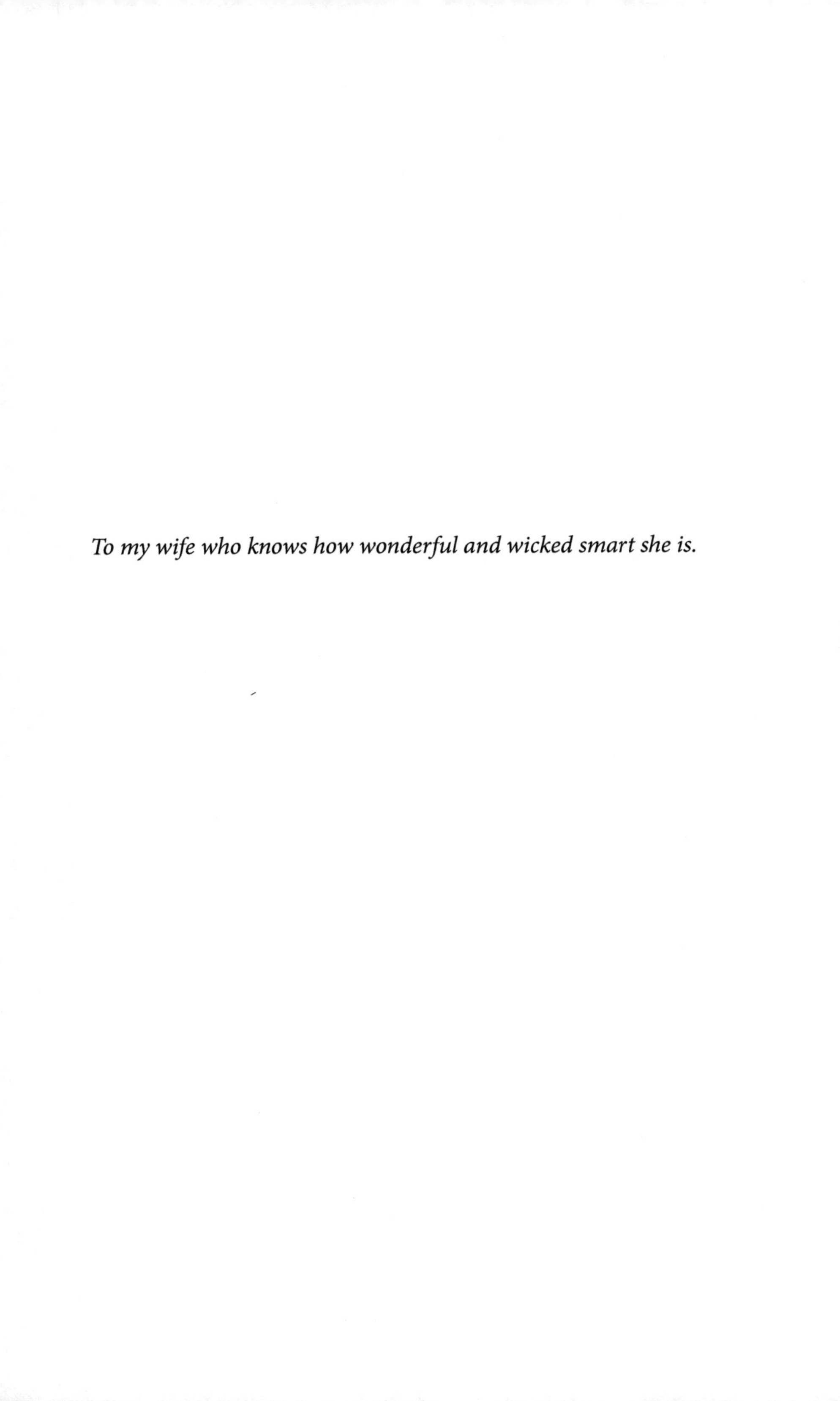

To my wife who knows how wonderful and wicked smart she is.

Contents

Author's Note

I have loved reading since I was in third grade. When I was growing up, it was all *Hardy Boys* and *Nancy Drew*, and from there, Greek and Norse mythology, various biographies, and a bunch of books about horses and animals.

I eventually transitioned to science fiction, especially books by Arthur C. Clarke, Robert Heinlein, Madeleine L'Engle, and Andre Norton. I'm probably one of the few people who remembers *Dolphin Island* by Arthur C. Clarke, and while everyone knows Madeleine L'Engle for her *Time Quartet* series, I more fondly recall *The Arm of the Starfish*.

Those authors and so many more were my heroes, and I wish I could have met them in this life.

The truth is, those books were my childhood escape, and pre-eminent on my Mount Rushmore of most important novels stands *The Lord of the Rings* and *Wheel of Time*. The mystery, magic, wonder, and beauty of those two masterpieces; the sense of a real and deep history; the sheer magnificence and grandeur of those creations . . . those are the kind of books I've chased after my entire life.

I rarely find them, and the older I've gotten, the rarer the finding has become.

So, I sought to write one myself. Hubris, I know, but while this novel is my latest, all along I have wanted to create something of a love letter to *The Lord of the Rings* and *Wheel of Time*. Something from my own heart and mind through words to translate what those two towering series meant to me.

I can't know if I succeeded, but if I have in a single person's mind, then that's good enough.

Davis Ashura

SHAKARAN OCEAN
The WRAITH LANDS
The SUNSET KINGDOMS
Toil
Fare
Crown
Hinane
Bolia
Flail
Shimala
Whip
Elasmara
Purge
Sun
Prune

SHASALA OCEAN
The WRAITH LANDS
The SAVAGE KINGDOMS
Mark
Mahadev
Surent
Apsara
Char
Swift Sword
The Third Directorate
Revelant
N
THE TEMPERANCE OCEAN

1

Time is not the arbiter of what is, what was, and what will be. It is Memory. Without it, falsehoods are believed and truths are discarded. Or so it is thought . . .

The snowtiger had yet to take a name. By now she needed one. She deserved one. She knew herself, understood her place in the world as an individual and had spent the last fifty years in these mountains, hunting and killing whatever prey she required. Already she'd lived decades longer than any others of her kind, and there was a reason for this.

It was centered in her beating heart. A purity she couldn't name. It glistened within her like a stream of water under sunshine. The snowtiger required it in order to maintain herself, and she required it in ever-greater quantities. Instinctively, she recognized the best such sources for what she needed were the strange two-legs who cut trees and yowled nonsense. Months ago, she had ambushed one, a shambling wreck, a creature barely alive. Its meat had tasted putrid, but she'd been so hungry, she'd eaten it anyway.

The rotten flesh had caused her to vomit, and for a time she thought she would die. But she hadn't. She'd lived, and a new type of being, one never before seen, now stalked the Dagger Mountains.

The snowtiger knew none of this. She simply studied her prey, planning her attack.

Cinder Shade would never recall the warning signs that signaled the end of his life.

Why would he? A timeless wind with neither beginning nor end didn't travel the deserts, the wilds, or the highlands and speak of it. Nor did omens split the sky with lightning. Neither did old men, bearded in white, pronounce his prophecy.

Instead, Cinder's doom occurred on a prosaic day. It was a typical summer afternoon in the high plains of Rakesh, dry and sunny, yet cool. A snow-capped mountain range stretched in all directions, a wall of towering gray and white peaks cupping the verdant valley in which Cinder's family lived. The village of Swallow hunkered in this place, and from where Cinder stood, he could see his neighbors and kin farming the stone-strewn fields surrounding the sixty or so homes making up the hamlet.

This was a hard land, shaping and tasking a hard people, folk who defied the chill winds blowing down from the mountainous heights even in the month of Vahasth, summer's deepest warmth. Cinder didn't mind the tribulations thrown at his people, though. It was the lot of humans everywhere to struggle, and this was simply another place to be tested.

In truth, he loved this valley. He loved the peace, the ancient majesty of the soaring aspens and cedar; the night skies filled with shining stars burning like scattered sparks from heavenly fires. He especially loved the lack of elves. Their kind, arrogant and self-centered, lived in all other directions of the compass—south, north, east, and west—but not *here*. Not in Swallow. As Cinder reckoned matters, their presence would have been one test too much. He wouldn't have been able to abide living beneath the scorning heel of those *aether*-loving bastards. Of course, he'd never met an elf, but everyone said they were arrogant assholes.

A hawk cried in the cloudless sky, breaking Cinder from his thoughts. He stared at the raptor, wishing he could fly, a sentiment common to boys, even those who were no longer children but still a few years from manhood. The hawk, a silhouette of grace and beauty, banked on the breeze. That same wind flitted through the surrounding evergreen forest, and the scent of cedar, pine, and aspen lofted on the air. So, too, did mosquitoes, flying torments this time of year. Cinder swatted at them as he hobbled away from the family well, burdened by a pail of water.

Some might have called Cinder handsome given his even features. Nose not too large, smile not too wide, and almond-eyes that weren't too round. Others, though, would have deemed him plain, penalizing him for his clumsiness. It was a clubfoot and an emaciated leg—his right—that made him so. It caused him to sway with every step, leaving him poorly balanced in the way he walked.

But even a clubfooted stumblebum like him was expected to work hard in the warmer months. Warmer being relative. After all, these were the Dagger Mountains, where winter bit deep and lasted long, while summer flitted away as quickly as a pleasant dream and all work was dedicated to surviving the coming cold. Cinder wasn't immune to the penalty of a demanding life. He worked as well as he could, and right now he carried the pail full of water toward the herbs and vegetables in the garden.

His mother called to him, and he halted with a groan, setting down the heavy burden of the water-filled bucket. In addition to a clubfoot and withered right leg, Cinder was also weak. He was short and built like a post rail.

His eyes flicked about, searching for his mother, and he quickly found her. She stood near the chicken coop, steps from the back porch to their log cabin, hands on hips, and a patient, generous smile on her face.

His mother, Inara Shade, had been a beauty in her youth, but the rough life of mountain living had worn her down. Not even forty, her hair was gray, her skin gnarled and leathery, and she complained of a sore back on most days. But time and the difficult elements hadn't worn away her happy spirit or loving smile.

"Only two more pails," his mother said. "Your father says he'll do the rest. Pitch needs your help."

Cinder smiled in anticipation. *Pitch. He was everything an older brother should be. Protective, loving, but most of all, understanding and fun.*

Cinder shouted acknowledgement and glanced to where his father, Onyx, was bent over a hoe. His father was a large man, tall, big boned, well-muscled, and possessing a hearty laugh. His hair remained the same dark color as that of most folk in Rakesh, but his skin was as wrinkled as an apple left out in the sun. Despite his outwardly ancient appearance, Cinder's father could still outwork most of the younger men in Swallow. The only one he couldn't was Pitch, who had inherited their father's stout build and stamina.

Right now, Cinder's father tilled the herbs and vegetables in the garden. The green growths there would add flavor and fragrance to their bland winter fare, which generally consisted of dried meat, potatoes, and barley.

With such thoughts in mind, it was in this timeless moment that Cinder saw an awful portent. His future emerged from the forest, a monster pushing past clinging brambles and pine needles. Cinder's mouth went dry.

A snowtiger. A massive one. This one was larger than a bear. Gray-white fur rippled despite the suddenly still air, and white eyes glowed like lanterns.

Aether-cursed.

All sounds died, the world seemingly holding its breath as the creature gathered itself. It exploded toward Cinder's mother.

Cinder's throat clenched with fear. He couldn't call out a warning, but his mother noticed his horrified gaze. She shifted about, searching for what held Cinder's attention. She screamed at the same time that Cinder's throat finally loosened, and he shouted.

The snowtiger attacked. Cinder's mother had no chance. She brought up an arm to protect her face, but the monster simply plowed through it and bore her to the ground. Four-inch teeth gripped her throat, biting deep. Cinder's mother gave a single anguished cry before she was silenced forever.

The snowtiger rumbled in pleasure, and a faint glow, pale as snow, wafted from the body of Cinder's mother. Her *aether*. Useless to a human, but greatly desired by all other creatures such as elves and dwarves, and even more so by those animals who were *aether*-cursed. It made them smarter, stronger, and longer-lived, but at the price of an abiding hunger, an insatiable need to feast on human flesh. *Man killers.*

The tiger seemed to inhale the *aether*. Its fur crackled for an instant, standing on end before settling down again.

Cinder's father charged from the garden, hoe at the ready. "Run, Cinder!" he shouted. He swung the hoe at the tiger's head.

The beast evaded, growling and lashing out. Cinder's father halted his charge, staring at his bowels trying to push their way through a long set of wounds. Another slash to his legs, and he collapsed. Again, the tiger killed, feasting this time on the *aether* of Cinder's father.

Cinder's mouth gaped with horror. *Seconds.* That's all it had taken. His parents had been killed in the time needed to take a deep breath.

The snowtiger, mouth dripping blood, peered up then, seeming to face Cinder with a terrible smile. It took slow, menacing steps toward him.

Cinder stumbled backward, clumsy with his clubfoot. He lurched away from the snowtiger, who slowly stalked him, apparently certain he couldn't escape.

Which was the truth. There was nowhere close where the tiger couldn't get him.

Cinder's gaze flitted about, and his eyes latched onto the well. A desperate plan formed. He could crawl inside it. The tiger couldn't reach him there.

Cinder lurched faster, but he felt the monster pick up speed. He glanced back, seeing it rush toward him, rumbling. Cinder faced forward, mind tight with terror. Only a few more feet. He threw himself toward the open well, which was little more than a wide hole in the ground. He scrambled inside, trying to make his way farther down.

A searing pain in his forearm made him scream. He felt himself drawn upward.

The tiger had him hooked on a claw, pulling him toward its bloody maw. Cinder punched the creature's foreleg again and again. It snarled, releasing him. He felt the breeze ruffle his hair when the tiger swiped at him one more time. The beast missed, and Cinder plummeted, plunging in an uncontrolled fall. He crashed into the side of the well, his head smacking against the hard stone.

He briefly lost consciousness, regained it, and the last thing he saw was the tiger far above, its massive head shutting out the sunlight as it peered down at him.

He inhaled water and knew no more.

2

"**C**inder!"

The voice came from a vast distance, and the person who heard it couldn't tell who was calling out. Were they even shouting at him? Maybe it was someone else they were trying to reach.

The boy—or was he a man? That, too, he didn't know. He had no recollection of his name or his past. All he knew was one thing: something clogged his ears. *Water.* He floated face down in it, and while his muscles ached and fatigue weighed his limbs, he vaguely understood he couldn't remain like this. He needed air or he'd die a second, final time.

The man—or maybe he was a boy—gathered his energy and spun himself around until he floated face up. He gasped in relief, breathing air now. His eyes crinkled in confusion, focusing on a bright, narrow circle high above. Through it the sky seemed to peer down. Water washed against his sides, and he realized that he lay at the bottom of a well. How had he ended up in such a place?

He blinked as an unfamiliar figure appeared in his bleary vision. It was a young man, fit, strong, and with a rope wrapped around his waist. He'd been lowered down and was holding his position by pressing his back and legs against the opposite sides of the well. The man spoke to him. "Cinder. Stretch your hand. I'll pull you out."

He didn't know who he was, but he knew a friend when he saw one. He inhaled deeply, and with a terrible effort he managed to shift about until he was treading water. He chuckled briefly. At least he could swim.

"That's it, Cinder," the man with the rope around his waist encouraged. "Closer now."

My name is Cinder?

"Reach for me. This is as far as the rope can go."

Cinder took another deep breath, gathering the last remnants of his stamina. With it, he kicked hard against the water, launching himself upward with arms outstretched. An instant later, relief as clean as the well water washed over him when he managed to clasp forearms with the man, who grunted with the effort of bearing Cinder's weight.

"Wrap your legs around my waist and hang on," the man said.

Cinder did as instructed. His legs went around the man, and he found himself facing his rescuer, surprised at how young the other man was. He looked to be in his early twenties, face sporting a wispy beard. Dark hair lay plastered against his head, and almond-shaped eyes peered at him. "Grab hold around my shoulders."

Again, Cinder did as he was bid.

The man stared skyward and shouted. "Pull us up."

The rope went taut, and his rescuer's legs released from where they'd been pressed against the well's wall. They rose in jerky movements.

Cinder could barely hold his head up. Somnolence called seductively to his mind. Lethargy beckoned. His legs loosened.

"No, Cinder," the man shouted. "Just a few more seconds and they'll have us out."

Cinder roused himself, throwing off his fatigue. He could rest when he was dead.

The thought made no sense, and Cinder decided not to explore what it might mean. He had to survive first. Only afterward would he have time to figure out what had happened to him. How he'd ended up drowning in a well. Why he couldn't remember anything . . . He decided the questions could wait a little while longer.

The well's eye grew larger. Only a few more feet, and suddenly he and the man were out. Cinder scrunched his eyes against the abrupt brightness. More hands grasped at him, voices grunting and cursing, tugging at his limbs until he and the other man were settled next to the well's low-lying wall, too far to fall back in.

Cinder released himself from his rescuer and fell over on his side. He opened his eyes, staring at a painfully blue sky, panting and heart pounding, grateful to be alive. He closed his eyes once more, praying to Devesh, thanking him for his life. He also needed to thank those who had saved him. But not yet. Maybe later. When he had a little more energy. Or maybe after a quick nap.

He didn't know how long he lay there, but a hand shaking his shoulder stirred him awake. Cinder started and opened his eyes.

Someone gasped. "*Aether* preserve us," someone whispered. "Look at his eyes."

"White like a zahhack's," another voice said, sounding shaken. "Like a wraith's."

A third person spoke, the man who had saved him. His voice was fierce and protective. "He's my brother. I'll have no curses said about him."

Cinder eyed his rescuer, still not recognizing him but grateful for his defense. He sensed that he needed it.

"Be reasonable, Pitch," the first man said. "We can't let him live. Not when the prophecies and laws say otherwise. He's a cripple anyhow."

Cinder looked at the one who had spoken, a thickly built man, in his forties perhaps. He had the well-muscled frame of a blacksmith or a farmer who tilled his land by hand. His spade-like jaw was clenched in frustration and fear, and he had the same dark hair, wispy beard, and almond-shaped eyes as Cinder's brother, who was apparently named Pitch.

Maybe this older man was another brother? But then why did he seek Cinder's death?

"Enough," Pitch said. "Look at him. Would a wraith steal the life of a club-footed boy? Would it leave him to die in a well, far from the sun? Look at his teeth. His hands. Do you see fangs or claws? He's no wraith, and he's not *aether*-cursed."

"But what about his eyes?" This time it was the second man. Younger than the first, but even bigger, and their similar features left no doubt they were close kin.

"They ain't glowing now," Pitch countered.

Cinder had heard enough. He levered himself upright, struggling to get to his feet. He almost fell over. His right foot was rotated internally, and the leg itself was withered and weak. He managed to stay upright, though. He wouldn't lie down. What these men intended, Cinder didn't know, but if they chose violence, he wouldn't wait for it like an overturned bug lying on its back. He'd die on his feet like a man. He managed to stand, swaying, nearly falling down again.

"But—" the second man persisted.

"No," Pitch cut off the man's protest with a single word and a chopping motion. "I'll hear nothing about it. Not on this day when our parents were slaughtered like a summer sacrifice."

The smell of fresh blood drifted on a vagrant breeze, an iron-rich scent Cinder hadn't noticed before. He did now. His head swiveled, searching it out. He discovered two corpses. A man and woman. Something had savaged them.

Cinder viewed them with vague regret, but otherwise he felt nothing. But he should, shouldn't he? They were supposed to be his parents, yet he didn't know these people. He didn't remember them. He wanted to, though.

The lack of not knowing himself—he didn't even know his own name, not for sure—left him breathless with panic, vulnerable. His mouth gaped empty like his vacant memories. A person with no past was unmoored from reality, and Cinder scoured the recesses of his mind, searching for the solution of who he was, desperate for belonging.

Moments of helpless panic ensued, and yet he discovered nothing.

Someone touched his shoulder, drawing him around. His brother.

Pitch spoke to him, his voice soft and eyes full of sympathy. "Cinder. Did you see what happened? I heard screams, and I ran here fast as I could. Simial and Loke came, too." He pointed to the other two men.

"It was an *aether*-cursed cat," the first man, Simial, said. "Look at the tracks. Big beast. We'll have to hunt it down."

"I ain't hunting no *aether*-cursed that kills men," Loke said. "Leave it to the army. That's their job."

"We ain't cowards here," Simial said.

"There's bravery, and there's foolhardy," Loke countered.

"Was it an *aether*-cursed cat?" Pitch asked.

Cinder realized his brother was talking to him, and he blinked, trying to throw off his confusion, the fugue of his disjointed thoughts and memory loss. "I don't know," he eventually said. "I don't remember. I don't remember anything."

"You didn't see it?" Pitch asked.

Cinder shook his head, ready to explain about his lack of memory.

"He's bleeding," Simial said, pointing.

Where the man indicated, three jagged claw marks ran like windrows along the length of Cinder's left forearm. He hadn't noticed the wounds before, but now that he did, it was as if his awareness of them spurred the injuries to greater fever. They pulsed pain.

"Life preserve him," Loke whispered. "If them's *aether*-cursed, the wounds are already poisoned. The Cripple will die inside two days."

Is that what they call me here? The Cripple?

"They ain't poisoned," Pitch said. "Do you see them leaking black blood? Do you smell rotting meat?" He shook his head. "They're just wounds, I tell you."

"Maybe," Simial said, his voice doubtful. "But what's he mean he don't remember nothing?" He pointed to the dead man and woman. "How can a son not remember something like that?"

Cinder found himself the focus of three sets of eyes. He mentally shrugged. His bewilderment would have to wait. He pushed it to the back of his mind. He had to get through these next few minutes. Then, he could figure out what was going on. "When I say I can't remember anything, I mean that literally. I can't remember a single thing. Until I heard it, I didn't know my own name."

Jaws dropped, and the three men who had saved him shared a nervous chuckle.

"You always were one to spark a good joke," Pitch said.

Cinder smiled faintly. "I wish it was a joke. Can someone tell me where I am?"

All three of them were staring at him, Simial and Loke in suspicion and Pitch in confusion.

Cinder straightened his shoulders. The two big men appeared ready for a fight, but something in him stiffened, not willing to bend or break. He wouldn't go meek for them.

Pitch stepped between Cinder and the two brothers. "You don't remember this place? Our home? Swallow?"

Cinder shook his head. "I don't remember anything."

Pitch's frown deepened momentarily. "It doesn't matter. Whatever happened, we'll figure a way to fix it." His face cleared. "Come on. We'll take you to my home and get you in some dry clothes." He glanced at the corpses of their parents, and his jaw tightened, features relaxing into grief. He blinked back tears, wiping at them. "I'll come back here and take care of Ma and Pa." His voice caught, and he couldn't seem to pull his eyes away from their torn bodies, anguish evident on his features.

Cinder wished he could share the same sorrow. These were his parents, but the man and woman who had been killed here might as well have been strangers. He felt no more than a vague regret at their passing. He actually had a deeper feeling for Pitch, who had clearly loved their parents, aching with grief and yet remaining strong for a beloved younger brother.

Cinder only wished he could reciprocate the feeling. Pitch was a person worthy of respect, and Cinder placed a hand on his brother's shoulder. "I can help with whatever you need done."

Pitch gave a short nod of acknowledgment but didn't say anything at first. "Thank you," he managed, his eyes still shiny with unshed tears and his voice husky with suppressed emotions.

Simial cleared his throat. "We'll take care of it. Loke and me. This ain't the kind of work for kin. You shouldn't see your family like this. Come on. We should go." He gave Pitch a gentle shove on the shoulder, urging him around.

"We'll come back and see to their bodies," Loke added. "We'll bring old Deepak so he can have them ready for the funeral pyre."

Pitch didn't resist, and he allowed Simial to lead him away from the backyard.

Cinder stood momentarily alone until Simial glanced back at him. "You best come along too, like your brother said." His voice was far less friendly than Pitch's.

Having nowhere else to go, Cinder followed. He limped along, realizing only then that he had a clubfoot and an emaciated right leg. He frowned at his arms and legs. He was small, shorter than the men ahead of him as well as thinner. How old am I? Am I a child? He didn't think so. He ran his fingers over his face. A few fine hairs on his chin met his exploration. Not a child.

"I still don't get why his eyes was glowing," Loke hissed in what he must have thought was a whisper. Cinder could hear him clear as a bell ringing across a field.

Pitch pulled up short. "You two best not say nothing about Cinder being *aether*-cursed." His voice came out as a growl.

Cinder still didn't know what it meant to be *aether*-cursed, but now wasn't the time to ask.

Simial held up his hands in surrender. "We'll keep quiet. Shokan's promise." He nudged his brother with an elbow. "Right?"

"Right," Loke agreed with a quick head bob. Cinder caught him staring at him askance. A few seconds later, Loke spoke again. "How come he can't remember nothing?"

Cinder sighed, already tired of their speculation.

Simial scoffed. "Nothing to it. You remember when Rosk Dook got kicked into the side of a barn by his family's bull? He woke up and couldn't remember himself. Maybe that's what happened here."

Loke scratched his faint beard, his head tilted in thought. "Naw. Rosk could remember things just fine, but he was full of crazy talk. Kept going on about how he saw Shokan and Sira. Legends and myths and shit. The boy made no sense."

Cinder wondered if maybe he *had* been hit in the head. He fingered his skull and quickly found a tender spot near his right ear.

Pitch halted again, facing Cinder. "Is that what happened, Cinder? You hit your head?"

Cinder rubbed the tender spot near his ear. "My head's sore where I'm rubbing."

"And he was floating face down in the well when we found him," Loke said. "He must have got himself knocked out."

Pitch gave a slow nod of agreement, his features firming with hope. "Then that's it. You got your bell rung and lost your memories. They'll come back."

Cinder hoped so, but a niggle of doubt told him it wouldn't be quite so simple. Worry surfaced. What would he do here? He was a stranger to these people, or at least they were strangers to him. The worry threatened to take over his thoughts, but he shoved it down, deep into the recesses of his mind where it couldn't distract him. Worry and concern could wait. He had to figure out his place in this world first.

He trudged after the others, and they left the backyard, allowing Cinder a chance to see the village in which he lived. Two strides later, he pulled up short, inhaling sharply at the beauty of the scene. Swallow nestled in a high valley where white-capped mountains soared all around. The jagged peaks towered, shoulders knuckled and gnarled, conveying the kind of permanence only mountains possessed. A cool breeze blew off them, sloping down to the village where it sifted the smoke wafting from various chimneys. The chill wind and the fires in hearths reminded Cinder of autumn, but the green grass and healthy, thigh-high crops growing in straight rows in the surrounding fields told him it was summer.

Cinder paused to study the village. Roughly sixty homes spread out before him, clustered in groupings of twos and threes. They formed the entirety of the hamlet, and all were rough-hewn log cabins, roofed in thatch and wood timbers darkened by tar. Windows covered in a wax film seemed to peer about. Children, lean and strong, played along grassy knolls and amongst lines of evergreens that separated the houses.

Pitch took Cinder along a nearby trail, a narrow mix of gravel and weeds, toward the only other cabin in proximity to where Cinder evidently lived.

A small porch jutted out at the village proper, where dirt roads followed the shape of small hills and hollows, meandering from house to house. Pitch opened the door. "Come on in." He gestured to Cinder. "Shesa is out visiting her sister. We'll get you cleaned up."

Cinder stepped past him, entering a single room that ran the length of the cabin. Little light penetrated the wax-covered windows, and the room remained dark despite the sunshine outside. Details came clear once Cinder's eyes adjusted to the gloom. Directly in front of him, facing a corner hearth, were a pair of heavy rocking chairs. Adjacent to them and to the right, a ladder angled up to a loft holding a bed, while a wooden bench rested against the near wall and faced a chest of drawers.

More details. Beyond the rocking chairs was a small kitchen containing a table and chairs that were rough-built like the home they decorated. A number of chipped dishes rested on planks nailed to the wall. At the rear of the home was another door leading to the backyard.

Cinder paused in his perusal when he realized that Simial and Loke had halted at the front porch. Both men shifted about, Loke rubbing at his head.

"We'll go see to your folks now," Simial said.

"I appreciate it," Pitch said, stepping onto the porch and shaking hands with the other two. After they departed, he came inside and shut the door. He stared toward the home's rear, his gaze distant. A moment later, he seemed to collapse on himself, and a great wracking sob tore through him. His eyelids crushed closed, and his teeth gritted.

Cinder didn't know what to do or say. "I'm sorry." He spoke in a hesitant voice, unsure if his words were welcome.

Pitch shuddered, wiped his eyes and collected himself. "It wasn't your fault." He stepped deeper into the home, making his way to the chest of drawers. He drew out a pair of pants and a shirt and tossed them Cinder's way.

Cinder caught them, holding them out for inspection.

"Get yourself changed," Pitch said. "Then get some rest. I've got some blankets and rolls you can sleep on." He sighed. "We have a long night ahead of us. We'll have the funeral tonight for our folks, and then . . ."

Cinder wondered at the flash of guilt on Pitch's face when he shot a glance his way. Still, his brother's generous gesture and words required a reply. "Thank you, Pitch. I really am sorry for everything that happened."

Pitch seemed on the verge of saying more, but he simply shook his head. "Get some rest."

He left the cabin, and the doorframe shook when he shut the door.

Cinder stared. Without Pitch's warm presence the home appeared darker, but light and shade didn't occupy his thoughts. Instead, the worry he'd shoved aside, roared to the surface of his mind.

The same issues and questions as before threatened to overwhelm him. Pitch, even Simial and Loke—were good folk. Thick and powerfully built, they were clearly farmers. But what about Cinder? What was he? Was he a farmer? What would happen to him? The questions swirled.

He forced himself to take a deep breath and relax. A flash of insight surfaced, and he held still, imagining himself breathing upon it, coaxing it to life like an ember brought to flame against a cold evening.

An instant later, disappointment crashed. The insight disappeared, drowned by the miasma of his uncertain thoughts. He tried to bring it forth again, but it remained lost. Cinder grunted in aggravation.

Thus far he'd held up, pushing past the confusion of not knowing who he was or anything about the world at large. Now all those piling concerns collapsed upon him, and he had an urge to sit down on the wooden bench.

Swallow was a poor hamlet. Memories weren't required to tell him that obvious truth. How would he make his way?

He viewed his body. He was young, less than a man but older than a child. Beyond his withered leg and clubfoot, he was weak, gaunt. He could encircle the bulk of his upper arm with one hand. He couldn't do a full day's labor. He guessed his parents must have been the ones to ensure he had what he needed to survive. With them gone, would Pitch take him in? Could he afford to?

Cinder assessed his brother's cabin. There wasn't much, which meant Pitch likely didn't have enough to support a brother who couldn't do for himself.

Then what? Would he be turned out? It was possible. Strangely, it didn't occur to Cinder to be afraid.

His thoughts still troubled, Cinder found some blankets and a bedroll. He managed to catch a few hours of sleep before Pitch nudged him awake with his boot and a terse, "It's time."

Cinder got himself untangled from the blankets, noticing Pitch viewing him, a question on his face. Cinder guessed at his brother's thoughts. Pitch wanted to know if he'd regained his memories. Cinder answered the unspoken query. "I still don't remember anything."

Pitch's visage closed into lines of disappointment. "Come on, then," he said, leading Cinder outside.

Twilight. He'd slept longer than he realized. Cinder trailed Pitch like a simpleton, merely going where he was told. He had no other choice. He was helpless here. Frustration at his situation welled, but as he had done with the worry, he pushed it down. Now wasn't the time. He needed a clear mind to figure out his next step. His future depended on it. Or at least, so he sensed. His emotions would have to wait until later.

He and Pitch traveled to the village's center. Cinder limped and had trouble keeping up, and he silently cursed his infirmities.

They reached a small, circular area where various paths met at the base of a grassy knoll. There he found Simial and Loke waiting alongside a narrow-shouldered, old man with dark skin weathered like leather. He held a staff taller than his short height. No hair graced his head, and he was bare-chested, wearing only a longyi, white once but tan now. There was also a young woman, long of face and with full lips that seemed like they usually were held in a smile. But not now. Now she frowned and clutched her hands in concern. Cinder figured she was Pitch's wife. Upon a raised bier made from a confusion of kindling and piles of split logs rested two bodies shrouded entirely in white. Cinder's parents. No part of their bodies were visible.

It was time for the funeral.

Pitch gestured to the young woman, who stepped forward. "My wife, Shesa," he said. He then pointed to the old man. "Our priest, Deepak Moral. We hold funerals on the day of death if possible. It is considered auspicious."

Deepak leaned more heavily on his staff, and his head tilted to the side. "He truly doesn't know of us?"

Pitch answered. "He knows nothing. Or at least he didn't when he went to rest." Cinder caught Pitch glance at him in uncertain hope.

"I don't. Truly," Cinder affirmed. "The only thing I remember is waking up in the well, and Pitch hauling me out."

Shesa stepped forward, a warm smile on her face. "Then we shall have to help you relearn what you lost." Her voice was surprisingly deep.

Deepak cleared his throat, and Shesa's smile fell away.

Cinder viewed the priest, eyes narrowed in suspicion. Everyone else knew something, a hidden decision they had made, and the knowledge possibly came from the priest. Cinder deliberated what it might be. He suspected, but—

His suppositions ended, when the villagers arrived, a scant two hundred men, women, and children. Pitch introduced them all, explaining to the other denizens of Swallow about Cinder's loss of memory.

Cinder recalled a few names when the villagers were introduced, but the faces passed in a blur of condolences, heads shaking with commiseration. Sad-eyed children said little, mumbling words of sympathy.

A rapping sound drew Cinder's attention to the bier, where Deepak pounded the ground with his staff. "It's time," he announced. "Twilight. The most auspicious time to send forth our loved ones to Devesh's sublime embrace. May Shokan and Sira guide their steps."

His words spoken, the priest opened a book, beginning a chant sounding vaguely familiar to Cinder, but it was in a language he couldn't understand.

"*Shevasra*," whispered Pitch, who stood on Cinder's left. He held a lit torch, the only light in the rapidly dying day. "It's the priestly language, the language of Shokan and Sira from their original land. Speaking it is said to bring a body closer to heaven."

Shokan. Sira. Shevasra. Important names for the people of Swallow, and Cinder had no idea what they meant. He'd have to learn more than he originally grasped. "Deepak prays?"

Pitch nodded.

"And he reads the prayers from his book?"

Shesa, who stood on Cinder's right, snorted. "*A Warrior's Sorrows*? No. The priests have memorized the important passages, but only Shokan and Sira could read it. They wrote it. It's written in *Shevasra*."

Curiosity roused within Cinder, and he found himself pondering matters beyond his future and lost memories.

Several minutes later Deepak finished, just as darkness settled on the village like a blanket. The priest nodded to Pitch, who stepped forward with his lit torch. Cinder's brother neared the bier where their parents lay and ignited the kindling.

Cinder went to help, but Shesa clutched his arm. "Only the oldest son can set the beacon-fire. Stay and watch."

Pitch circled the funeral pyre, holding his torch to the kindling until most all of it had caught. The fire swiftly took hold then, and Shesa passed Cinder an unlit torch. She held another in her other hand, and

Cinder noticed that the rest of the villagers held one apiece as well, including the children.

"Light your beacon," Shesa said, pointing at the bier.

Cinder went to where she'd indicated. By now the flames crackled heavily, reaching skyward and lighting the faces of all the villagers. The heat was apparent from thirty feet or more and washed outward, ebbing and flowing like the tides from an incinerating ocean.

Cinder drew to a halt when Pitch stepped between him and the fire. His brother held out his beacon, as Shesa called it, and Cinder immediately understood what was required. He lit his torch from Pitch's. Next came Shesa, followed by Simial and Loke.

The rest of the villagers followed suit, igniting their beacons from Pitch's. A sea of flaming torches soon engulfed the burning bier, which rumbled even hotter now. Cinder's eyes widened in wonder at the sight. *Glorious.*

Pitch thrust his own torch skyward and shouted. "Onyx Shade. Inara Shade. Never forgotten! Forever ascending!"

The villagers repeated the words, raising their torches as well, and to Cinder's ears they sounded triumphant. Afterward the folk of Swallow departed for their homes, their steps guided by the fiery torches held in their hands. Cinder watched as the villagers traversed the winding paths, their progress marked by their bobbing torches. A few, however, stayed behind to tend the fire.

His reverie ended when Pitch took him by the elbow. "Come," he said. "We have much to discuss."

By the tone of his voice and set of his features, it was a discussion he didn't want to have. Cinder had an inkling as to the reason. While he lacked his memories, his reason hadn't been stolen. Cinder's future was to be decided, and Deepak followed close behind him. Given the grim line of the priest's mouth and Shesa's once again worrying hands, it was news Cinder wouldn't enjoy hearing.

They walked in silence toward Pitch's home, and Cinder's deliberations led him along a torturous path, one shaped by confusion and distraction. However, he eventually reached a certainty. He couldn't stay in Swallow. The folk here couldn't afford to keep him. Strangely, the notion of leaving this place, his apparent only home, didn't cause him to be upset. In this, his lack of memories was to his benefit.

Simial and Loke also trailed behind them.

When they reached Pitch's cabin, lanterns were already lit, and the hearth contained a cheery, ruddy glow as a fire crackled within. Cinder followed his brother's lead, dousing his torch in a barrel full of dirt set outside before entering the home.

Everyone gathered inside Pitch's cabin, settling themselves in various chairs, which they moved to the front of the home. Cinder, unsurprisingly, discovered himself the focus of their silent, unhappy attention.

Cinder broke the quiet. "I can't stay."

Pitch started. "How did you know?"

Cinder smiled, a smirk with little humor. "I don't recall my life, but I can see. I can think. Swallow is poor. There is no food to spare for those who can't provide for themselves." He was a cripple and was only now coming to grips with what it meant. It might limit his future. It certainly did here, and he didn't know enough—his past or his present—to ensure a better hope for himself.

Pitch appeared abashed. "I would take you in but . . ." He trailed off.

Shesa spoke. "I'm with child. It's a burden we'll barely be able to manage as it is. We can't take on another mouth to feed. Not now."

"It's your weak leg," Deepak said on top of her words. "Your parents both did the work of two. They could afford to care for you. With their deaths, no one else can do for you as they did. I've spoken to the other villagers."

Based on their anxious expressions, they must have expected Cinder to rail and yell, argue against their decision, but he didn't. He merely nodded understanding, contemplative rather than unhappy. "What is to happen to me then?"

The relief from the others was palpable as they shared reassured glances.

Deepak answered Cinder's question. "I'll guide you to Swift Sword.

There's an orphanage there. You're sixteen, too old for a lot of places, but I know the headmaster. He'll accept you."

Cinder wanted to smile. At least he now knew his age. Nevertheless, it was much to take in, and he still had many questions. "What's Swift Sword?" Cinder asked.

"Our capital," Pitch said. "A three-week journey in the summer and impassable in the winter."

"There are no orphanages closer?" Cinder asked.

"There are," Deepak said, "but they aren't of the same repute as the one in Swift Sword."

"Who'll pay for my stay?" Cinder asked. "Surely the orphanage isn't free."

Again, Pitch spoke. "You'll pay with labor for the city's betterment."

"And traveling there is safe?" Cinder recalled the fear Pitch, Simial, and Loke had evinced at the notion of an *aether*-cursed cat wandering the nearby land.

Deepak sat forward in his chair. "I once served in the High Army of Rakesh. Don't let my skinniness fool you. I'm tougher than anyone you're likely to meet. We'll be safe."

Simial and Loke rose to their feet then, and Cinder realized they'd only been present in case he balked.

"It's late," Simial said. "I've got an early morning."

"We all have early mornings," Loke said. "We always do."

Simial grinned and slapped him on the shoulder. "Be thankful. It's the glorious life of a farmer."

Deepak stood as well. "Get some sleep," he said to Cinder. "We depart at first light."

The others left, and Cinder shared an uncomfortable silence with Pitch and Shesa. While he wasn't upset by leaving Swallow, they were. He recognized their unhappiness and turmoil. Ironic. He was the one who had to leave Swallow, but it was they who required comforting. His brother and *vadina*.

Cinder frowned at the odd word. He didn't know what it was, but it had simply popped into his mind. He shook off his vagrant wonderings.

Pitch and Shesa still stared at him in guilty unhappiness.

"I don't blame you," Cinder said, "and I don't hate you, either. You need to take care of yourselves and remain strong for your baby."

Pitch's eyes went shiny again, and he gripped Cinder's shoulder. "You're a good brother." He shook his head. "I wish the future could be otherwise."

Shesa went to worrying her hands again, and tears glistened in her eyes. "We're so sorry about this."

Cinder silenced them with a smile. "Wisdom is the acceptance of what can be done and what cannot. Learning this brings understanding, if not peace."

Pitch frowned. "Where did you hear that?"

Cinder shrugged. "I made it up." At least he thought he did. He didn't know. He yawned then, fatigue once again weighing on his mind. "I think I'll take Deepak's advice. I'm going to sleep."

He climbed into his bedroll while Pitch and Shesa put out the lanterns. He heard them whisper to one another, their tones still upset as they climbed the ladder to their bed.

Cinder, meanwhile, fell into a restless sleep, one leaving him with a residue of uncertain longing when he awoke the next morning.

Pitch was already up. So was Shesa. They had prepared a breakfast of cornmeal and eggs.

"I gathered some of your clothes and made you a pack," Pitch said, holding out a rucksack. "There's bread, dried meat, and some vegetables. I also found the small amount of money Mother and Father managed to acquire. It's yours." He held out a scattering of coins, most of them copper but a few silver.

Cinder refused to take it. Pitch and Shesa were expecting a child. They needed the money more than he did. "Keep it."

Pitch tried to argue. "I'll not have my only brother turned out with nothing."

"You'll need the money for the baby." Cinder pressed his brother's hands around the coins. Pitch had saved his life, taken him in, and offered nothing but loving support despite his grief at the death of their parents. And Cinder? He couldn't remember his brother, his parents, Swallow, or anything of his life here. How could he possibly take the money? "Keep it."

Pitch grumbled reluctant assent, and shortly after, Deepak arrived. He still had his staff, but rather than a longyi, he wore a sturdy pair of dark pants and a thick shirt. "Are you ready?" the bald-headed priest asked.

Cinder nodded, and despite the somber expressions of his *annaya*—he recognized the strange word indicated 'older brother'—and his *vadina*—this one meant 'sister-in-law'—a sense of excitement bubbled inside him.

He and Deepak headed out and a few villagers watched them leave. Cinder heard some of them mutter a word, one Simial had said yesterday, 'zahhack'. It sounded like a curse.

He asked Deepak what it meant.

"It means we need to leave. They think you serve Shet. The proof is if you don't die after a drowning."

"You mean if they think someone is a zahhack, they try to drown them?"

"Yes."

"What happens if they survive the drowning?" Cinder asked, genuinely curious.

"They're made dead. Stoned."

"So you either die by drowning or you die by stoning?"

Deepak grinned. "A stupid test, no?"

Cinder nodded agreement, but he didn't share Deepak's amusement. He didn't fear the villagers killing him. Instead his attention narrowed upon the priest's explanation, which sparked an unexpected reaction. *Shet.* He didn't know that person, but something about the name caused a line of anger to boil in him. His mind filled with fury, and he halted his progress. He saw red, and he glared, not recognizing that his anger fell on the villagers who'd spoken the word 'zahhack'. His lips pulled back from his teeth and he snarled.

The half dozen villagers glowered back. A few more joined them.

Cinder still didn't notice.

"Fool!" Deepak clutched Cinder's elbow, guiding him onward. "You may have courage, but you can't fight the world."

Cinder's awareness snapped back to the here and now. The anger lingered, but he shook his head, flicking away the last of it. *Shet*. What was it about that name that made him so furious? He didn't know. He knew nothing. *Fragging hell.* He growled in frustration. He'd learn about Shet. He'd learn about everything he didn't know. He had to. How else could he make a life for himself?

At another tug on his elbow, Cinder turned away from the villagers and followed Deepak out of Swallow.

3

A long day of traveling followed their departure from Swallow, and it left Cinder's emaciated leg aching. He refused to ask for an easier pace, though. Instead, he gritted his teeth and maintained the clipped gait set by Deepak, who showed no sign of slowing. The old man pushed along the rocky trail leading away from Swallow, his steps steady as a drum, a syncopated rhythm of feet and staff striking stone. He'd glanced back once to check on Cinder's status.

"How you holding up?" he asked.

"I'll make it," Cinder answered.

"Good. We'll have to go fast, like Shet was on our ass. Autumn rains and sometimes snow come early some years. I aim to get you to Swift Sword quick-like and head home before anything blocks the passes." His statements spoken, Deepak faced forward again.

On they went, and Cinder never asked for a break if Deepak didn't offer it first. He had his pride, and he didn't desire the priest's pity. While Cinder couldn't recall his family or his history, he knew one thing about himself. He wasn't a weakling. He was more than his poorly formed body, and he'd push past fatigue, endure pain, and keep

26

going until this trial was complete.

It was with this certainty in mind that Cinder kept to his hobbling gait. The only allowance he made for his discomfort was to fashion a crude walking staff from a long branch lying about when they broke for lunch.

The early afternoon sun beamed down upon them, warming the land against a brisk mountain breeze when they crested a bald, rocky rise. The wind whipped Cinder's long hair, causing it to flop into his eyes, and he made a note to have it cut. He also caught the scent of wood fire mixed with that of cooking meat. His stomach rumbled, and his mouth salivated. Food and rest would be good.

"Do you smell that?" Cinder asked Deepak.

The old man paused. "Smell what?"

Cinder explained.

Deepak grunted. "Good nose on you. We're closing in on Moth, the closest settlement to Swallow. It's a mite larger than our humble hamlet. You'll see." His explanation made, he walked on.

Fifteen minutes later, they came across a set of fields ending at a wooden palisade. An untended gate opened out onto the path upon which Cinder and Deepak journeyed. They passed inside, where Cinder discovered a village twice the size or more of Swallow. However, despite the larger size, there were more similarities than differences.

Beyond the wooden wall, Cinder had already seen the fields stretching in all directions, and gardens and rough-hewn log cabins filled the space within the palisade. All of those features would have been at home in Swallow. The folk here were the same, too. Stout with dark hair and skin and almond-shaped eyes.

A few people called greetings to Deepak, and while the old man never slowed, he did answer back, explaining where he and Cinder were headed. They soon left Moth and its farms behind and entered the shade of a copse of cedar. Cinder halted when two small foxes, kits maybe, flashed from the underlying brush, chasing another of their kind. All three animals halted comically, chittering in surprise when they noticed Cinder. An instant later, they dashed away.

Deepak smiled. "An auspicious sign. Three foxes, a balanced number. It means we should reach Swift Sword without any trouble."

Cinder nodded, heartened somewhat by the priest's words. He needed all the beneficence he could find. He had yet to recover a single fact about his life prior to yesterday, and he worried over the matter. Without awareness of himself, he was at the utter mercy of strangers. They could tell him whatever they wished, and he'd never learn until too late if it was the truth. He didn't want to live in such a powerless fashion.

But what choice did he have?

If nothing else, until his memories returned, he had to trust Deepak.

On they went, Cinder continually gnawing at the gaping emptiness inside, the blank wall where his past began. He chewed at it, hoping to wear away at it and find a sunshine of knowledge on the other side.

"You got to keep up," Deepak shouted, having come to a stop and leaning on his staff.

Cinder started. He'd grown lost in his thoughts and fallen behind the priest. He broke into a graceless hustle and closed the distance.

"Watch where you walk," Deepak admonished. "You go moongazing like that, and you're likely to tumble down a hill."

Cinder took Deepak's advice and followed more closely on his heels. He set aside his concerns as best he could, paying closer attention to the path on which they journeyed. The trail took a sinuous route, passing up and around hills and hollows. It edged along the brink of a cliff, where a fall of a thousand feet awaited the unwary. From there, the path led them to sun-dappled meadows, where songbirds roosted and lovely blossoms, vivid and fragrant, seemed to nod and wave at them under the influence of an intermittent breeze.

Later, they reached a scree hill and slowed to a halt.

Deepak cleared his throat and spat. "We'll stop for the night at the base of the hill." He viewed Cinder with worry. "Don't rush it here. Take your time. You'll fall and crack your fool skull if you don't."

Cinder eyed what awaited him in concern. It would be easy to slip upon this hill of uneven stones and poor footing. He wasn't sure how he'd make it down. After the hard day's travel, his leg ached fiercely, leaving him trembling with exhaustion.

Deepak took no account of his reticence. Without another word, the old man crabbed sideways down the hill. Cinder watched him go, still trying to figure out how he could follow without tumbling down the slope. After several minutes, he spied another path, a slower, circuitous route, but safer.

He inhaled a settling breath and set out. He took one cautious step after another, leaning heavily on his walking staff, inching along, slipping now and again on loose stones. He kept his gaze directly ahead of him, planning each movement. Perspiration covered his brow, stained his armpits, and dripped between his shoulder blades. He sweated as if he'd run a dozen miles.

It took him even longer than expected to reach the hill's base, but in the end, he managed it. A surge of pride lifted his spirits, and he shouted in triumph.

Deepak waited for him with a welcoming grin. He'd already set his tent and had a crackling fire started. "You made it, and with no falls, scrapes, or bruises. Well done."

Cinder shrugged self-deprecatingly. While Deepak's words were welcome, something about them made him feel inadequate. He shouldn't be offered praise for simply walking down a hill.

Deepak must have noticed because his smile dropped away. "Get your tent set," he said.

"Yes, sir."

Deepak leaned on his staff, frowning in confusion. "Why you calling me a lord? I ain't one."

Cinder halted in uncertainty. "I'm not sure. It just seemed like the right thing to say. I'm not supposed to call you, 'sir'?"

Deepak shook his head. "Not unless you think I'm a lord, an officer of the law, or your master, which I ain't."

"Sorry," Cinder said, still confused. The honorific had slipped out without conscious deliberation. "It won't happen again."

"Just get your gear ready. I'll take care of supper."

Cinder set to doing as Deepak instructed, and by the time he finished, the sun hung low in the sky. The last of its light painted the heavens in a rich red transitioning to a burnished orange. A breeze gusted, blustering sharp and cold.

Cinder welcomed the fire's warmth, and he eased himself down. He shook off Deepak's offer of a bowl of stew. He wanted to get his boots off first and massage his sore feet.

When Cinder tugged off his socks, Deepak inhaled sharply in shock or surprise. "Your foot ain't so clubbed no more. It's almost turned out normal."

Cinder viewed his feet pensively. He'd never paid them much attention before this moment. He couldn't detect a whole lot abnormal about them, other than the right one being significantly smaller than the left. He glanced at Deepak, whose eyes had grown troubled.

"You got an explanation for this?" the priest demanded, meeting Cinder's gaze.

Cinder shook his head. "I can't remember what they used to look like. You're certain they look different?"

"I'm certain," Deepak said. "Your mama used to come to me for a salve to help straighten it. It never helped much." After a few more seconds of scrutiny, he shook his head. "Or maybe I'm not remembering it right. Here." He passed Cinder a bowl of stew. "Eat. Today was only the start. We got three more weeks of hard journeying to get to Swift Sword."

A week into their travel to Swift Sword, they ran into heavy rain, which blew out of the heights. It was late in the day, catching them while they walked alongside a gurgling stream. It started as a progression of thick clouds, steadily darkening the sky, and a stark wind moaning a warning, heralding the hard weather's unwavering approach.

Cinder regarded the clouds in worry, figuring they likely bore an icy rain. The sight of one that was lightning-laced caused him to shiver.

He called warning to Deepak, who took one look at the onrushing storm, and in a manner most unpriestly, he cursed loudly. "Come on," Deepak urged. He hastened their steps, searching for a cave or even an overhang in which to wait out the inclement weather. In this, success was with them.

High above the stream, in the surrounding tree-shrouded hills, Cinder spied a small cave, a space appearing little more than an indentation was pressed amongst the rocks. It proved large enough for them to nestle dry within its confines, but not much more.

Cinder stood outside the entrance to the cave, judging when the clouds would arrive. "We've got enough time to gather wood," he decided.

Deepak nodded agreement. "Be quick. Your leg is still weak."

"I know. I won't push my luck," Cinder said. Whatever had happened during the snowtiger attack, the loss of his memory wasn't the only change he'd undergone. His clubfoot was healed, facing forward, straight and true. He also noticed that he had more strength in his emaciated right leg than at the journey's beginning. Possibly some muscle growth, too.

Deepak didn't know what the healing meant, but in no uncertain terms he'd told Cinder it didn't mean he was an *aether*-cursed. "You ain't a wraith," the priest had said, his tone indicating finality.

Cinder appreciated Deepak's support, although he wasn't entirely sure what '*aether*-cursed' meant. Whatever it was, it didn't sound good. He remembered Simial and Loke saying something similar about him when he'd awoken next to the well.

They quickly gathered the wood and hustled into the cave minutes before the rain struck. It pounded their shelter like a cresting wave, but Cinder paid the precipitation no attention. He focused on arranging the kindling and logs for the fire.

Deepak tried to light the wood with flint and steel, but the sparks wouldn't catch. He cursed again. "If we had the *lorethasra* of an elf, this wouldn't be so damn hard. Just a thought from one of them pointy-ears, and the fire would be burning."

Cinder didn't know anything about *lorethasra*, but he understood the use of flint and steel. Shortly after taking them from Deepak, he had the kindling alight, while careful exhalations brought the fire to stuttering life. Small twigs ensured its growth, and larger branches brought warmth to the small cave. The smoke followed a natural chimney out into the night sky.

Deepak grinned, holding his hands toward the flames. "You don't know nothing about yourself or our people, but you know how to take care of yourself."

Cinder had already noticed the same thing. Whether it came to finding the easiest path down a rugged hill, fishing a stream, or setting traps for game to supplement their stores, he knew wilderness skills like he'd been born with them. But according to Deepak, his father had never taken him into the deep woods and forests. No one had. With Cinder's weak leg, such a trip would have been too dangerous. So how did he know so much about living in the wilds? Or was it simply another mystery, like everything else that happened since the snowtiger killed his parents?

He had so many questions. He decided to ask what he hoped was the easiest to answer. "What's a wraith?" Cinder asked.

"I'll tell you if you get supper started," Deepak said.

Cinder agreed to the priest's plan, and he withdrew smoked meat and several wrinkled potatoes and carrots from his rucksack. He also fished out a dented pot and held it under a rivulet tracing its way down the hill's rocky face. When he gathered enough water, he set it on a tripod over the flames. Next, he cut the vegetables, and quickly had a bland stew bubbling.

"Wraiths are humans who can access their *lorethasra*," Deepak began. "They—"

"What's *lorethasra*?" Cinder interrupted.

Deepak sighed. "I suppose I should start at the beginning. *Lorethasra* is something all reasoning creatures possess." He peered intently at Cinder. "Last night we talked about the dwarves, elves, trolls, holders, pixies, and the others."

"The other races of Seminal," Cinder replied. Over the past week, Deepak had started the process of filling in the gaps in his knowledge. Seminal was the world on which they lived, and Swallow and Swift Sword existed in the human nation of Rakesh within the Dagger Mountains. There were many kingdoms and empires spread throughout Seminal's single continent, but the most powerful ones were all elven.

"Right," Deepak said. "*Lorethasra*. It's more commonly known as *aether*. The rishis of Bharat call it *Jivatma*, which is also what Shokan and Sira named it."

A plethora of questions raced through Cinder's mind. *Rishis. Bharat. Jivatma.* He opened his mouth, ready to ask them.

Deepak must have guessed his intent for he held up an admonishing finger. "No."

"But—"

"No," Deepak repeated. "We'll stick with *lorethasra*. It resides within us, like a shimmering waterfall, is what some say. I don't know for sure. I've never seen mine, but those with the right skills can tap into it, source it, and create greatness."

"Our soul," Cinder guessed in a flicker of insight.

Deepak started. "Yes. That's what some believe." He shook his bald head an instant later. "How you know so much and so little . . ." He trailed off.

Another flicker of insight lit within Cinder. "But humans can't source it."

"Correct," Deepak confirmed. "Ever since the *NusraelShev*, the war between the Mythaspuris and Lord Shet, we haven't been able to."

More questions arose in Cinder's mind. It was unsurprising. One of Deepak's explanations usually spawned a dozen more queries. "The Mythaspuris are . . ."

"A story for another time," Deepak said, his tone firm. "Let's stick with *lorethasra* and wraiths. I said humans can't source *lorethasra*, but that's not entirely right. Wraiths can. So can the Bharatian rishis. Both of them kinds are powerful, like all our ancestors are said to have been.

The rishis and wraiths are also far crueler. They use *lorethasra,* but they can't cycle it like the elves and others."

"Why not?" Cinder asked.

"I don't know," Deepak admitted, "but I reckon it's the same reason we can't properly source our *lorethasra* in the first place." He shrugged. "Anyhow, because we can't cycle it, our *lorethasra* becomes dark and polluted. It warps those unlucky enough to source it and leaves them forever hungry for more and more *aether.* They become selfish and uncaring."

Cinder pondered the explanation. There were holes in it, a sense of incompleteness, and he wasn't sure why he felt that way. "Does the same thing happen to the elves and dwarves?"

Deepak snorted derision. "It likely does. It's a certainty that the elves think us little more than animals while the dwarves hold us in contempt."

"Are we at war with them?"

Deepak snorted in further derision. "No. We ever go against the elves or dwarves, they'd crush us without a second thought. The only humans they ever respected, other than Shokan and Sira, were the Mythaspuris because they was the ones who defeated Shet." He seemed to reconsider. "They also respected Mede. Or better to say they feared him. He kicked their asses when he forged his empire."

"Mede was a hero?"

"Mede was a monster. He forged an empire, and the cost was millions slaughtered."

So many names, terms, and unknown words. Cinder's mind whirled. So much to learn or maybe relearn. "So what is our relationship with the elves and dwarves?"

"The dwarves we ignore, and they ignore us," Deepak said. "The elves of the Yaksha Sithe we honor by serving in their army. They don't care for us much even then, but *I* fought alongside some of them because it was the best way to protect our folk from the *aether*-cursed monsters that stalk our world." He gazed penetratingly at Cinder. "The snowtiger that killed your parents isn't the only kind of creature we have to fear. There are many others, many worse, like the damn spiderkin. But only an elven warrior can kill those eight-legged bastards."

Their conversation lulled, and after supper Deepak settled in for the night. Cinder stayed awake, though, staring into the flames and thinking about what Deepak had told him. Seminal was a hard world, and humans survived on the hard-bitten charity of other races that held them in active dislike or contempt. It sounded unjust, and Cinder rankled over the unfairness of the situation.

Injustice.

Cinder stared into the night then, staring at the twin moons rising, one pale ivory and the other burnished gold. He didn't know their names and he shook his head at his ignorance. *So much to learn.*

He crawled under his blankets then, falling asleep within minutes.

He strolled down a residential drive of stately townhouses. A median of grass and leafy elms split the road into two narrow lanes, and the broad branches of the trees arched over both sides of the street, providing shade and a sense of security.

A tall woman, blonde-haired and with a reddish undertone to her skin, paced beside him. He couldn't see her face.

They left the neighborhood and entered a green jewel of a park, where grass-covered hills and wildflower fields merged seamlessly with blue lakes and ponds. During the day, the waters sparkled like rainbows, but now, with the coming of night, they glistened, shimmering under the ivory light of the moon. A number of elderly men of every Caste sat at a group of tables placed beneath a cluster of oaks. They played chess. Firefly globes with muted hues of rose, gold, lavender, or violet, hung above the men, suspended from the broad branches of the thick trees. Beyond the collection of oaks, a scattering of black lampposts was the only source of light amongst a winding web of gravel trails. There, couples took a final stroll before heading home.

Deeper into the park they went, to the empty places where their footsteps echoed upon stone and wooden bridges arching over the numerous streams and rivulets. He stopped upon one such span. It was held aloft by lichen-covered pillars of heavy boulders. Frogs croaked the coming of the night, and a cool wind carried a hint of sea and rain.

He still couldn't see her face, but he could sense her smile and could sense an unspoken question. "I've never regretted showing this to you."

It was the correct answer. She let him draw her close.

Cinder awoke with a start, blinking. Afterimages of the dream flitted through his still sleepy mind, and with a groan, he pushed himself onto his elbows, squinting into the darkness. He blearily noted the camp he and Deepak had cobbled together last night next to a rushing stream and amidst a small stand of maple and oak. The fire still burned, and his gaze went to it as he tried to recall the fragments from the dream. A city. Was it Swift Sword? Had he been there before? And a woman. A park. What did they mean? He closed his eyes, trying to bring the dream to greater lucency.

A moment later, he sighed in frustration. It was no use. The dream was fading as quickly as he could chase it, vanishing into the night's darkness like a spark from the fire.

It was gone, the last of the images disappeared. Cinder could no longer recall it, but he'd dreamt of the woman before—he knew that much—but he'd never once seen her face or recognized the city in which they strolled. Was it a memory? Or was that wishful thinking?

Cinder couldn't go back to sleep, and he pondered the questions in the quiet stillness of the night, staring at the flames until the sun pinked the eastern sky a few hours later.

Deepak sat up with a mighty yawn and stretched his arms. He clenched his eyes against the sun's glare and rolled out of his blankets. "Sun's up," he grunted. "You up for making breakfast?"

Cinder merely nodded, not much feeling like talking. His thoughts remained on the dream, the upset of not knowing what they meant. And worse, not knowing himself. No recollections of his past, even after three weeks. He set to making breakfast—last night's stew which he warmed above the flames and added some hard rolls to go with it.

"Few more hours and we'll be at Swift Sword," Deepak said.

They'd made good time getting to Rakesh's capital, and for the most part the weather had favored them. They'd only encountered the one storm, which had kept them bound to the small cave. Otherwise the days had been warm, sunny, and uneventful. Even better, Cinder's weak right leg had definitely grown stronger, more muscular and more closely matching his left.

Deepak still didn't have an explanation for what the changes meant, and Cinder didn't want to know. Maybe it was a miracle. Maybe it was magic. As long as it didn't mean he was turning into a wraith—Deepak remained firm on that point—he was happy. Especially after he learned more about humans who could wield *aether*, their tendency toward violence and passionless cruelty and how they were hunted down and killed by all people in all lands, be they ruled by humans, elves, dwarves, or someone else. Whatever the case, Cinder wanted nothing to do with wraiths.

He gathered a bowl of stew and some bread, and after breakfast they packed up and headed out. They traveled the southern foothills of the Dagger Mountains along a broad valley, flat and verdant. Fields of wheat, soybeans, barley, and corn surrounded them. Farmers stalked their crops, searching for parasites, blight, and weeds. A few hailed Cinder and Deepak, who responded in kind.

The two of them never slowed, though. They pressed on, the journey's end impelling them along a road rutted from the innumerable wagons trundling over its unpaved surface. Onward to Swift Sword, which Deepak promised they'd reach by mid-afternoon at the latest. They briefly halted for a lunch of dried meat, the last of their vegetables, and more rolls. Several hours later they crested a hill.

Below them spread their destination. Swift Sword. Cinder took in the view. His mouth gaped in shock.

After the hamlets and villages he'd seen, the city seemed too large. Massive. Cloying. Too much. A wall of black stone rose like a cliff. It surrounded Swift Sword. Black smoke, choking and thick, drifted from innumerable chimneys. Noises. So many sounds arose from the city, even to the distance where Cinder stood. Shouts, curses, laughter, all of them forming a din.

Other impressions made themselves known. Tree-covered hills shaped Swift Sword's growth, but they did little to constrain the city's size, which pushed out in all directions, except to a large forest directly east, which abutted the blue waves of the Sentient Sea.

Cinder's eyes widened. *The sea.* He'd never imagined a blue so bright, like a cloudless sky under the brightest sunshine.

"Let's head down," Deepak suggested. "But keep a firm grip on your possessions. The city's rotten with thieves."

They set off down the hill, stopping at a heavy, wooden gate where guards questioned all those who wished to pass inside. It didn't matter if it was a local farmer driving a wagon laden with crops or wealthy merchants, who appeared bored of the entire matter. All who wanted inside had to halt. Deepak spoke a few words to the guards, and while he did so Cinder noticed the soldiers patrolling the wall. He found himself silently approving their ready postures.

Moments later, they passed through the gate and he tried not to gawk at what he saw. From a distance, Swift Sword had been a plethora of sounds and sights. From within, it was a cacophony. Constant motion. Continuous sounds. Barefoot children running among puddles and along cobbled roads. Smells of every sort. Meat charring on a grill. Bread baking. Burning incense. Women dressed in rags calling out lewd offerings. A stench of effluent underneath it all.

A half-dozen hard-bitten men, armed and armored, scowling and barking at those around them.

Cinder scrutinized the presumed warriors, their weapons, their armor, their bearing, and found himself unimpressed. Their weapons appeared poorly cared for. Their armor fit poorly, and they prowled about with an unearned arrogant strut.

"Don't make eye contact with them," Deepak warned. "They're mercenaries seeking fortune in whatever battle they can find." He spat. "Scum. They cause more wars than they solve."

Cinder could believe it.

They left the mercenaries behind and made their way down a clogged side street, ignoring the vendors hawking food, weapons, and everything in between.

Deepak stopped at a crossroads, peering about and muttering to himself. His face cleared a second later. "I know where we are. It ain't too far from here."

They traveled on, Cinder holding tight to his possessions as Deepak had counseled. A half-hour later, they halted at a building taller than its neighbors, three stories in height and surrounded by an old stacked-stone wall, ivy- and moss-covered. A wooden gate barred their passage, and on the lintel hung a placard, an image of a woman holding flames in her hands, and a name: *Our Lady of Fire.*

His new home. Cinder viewed the building in antipathy, unsure of the welcome he'd find within. Something about the notion of orphanages didn't inspire much hope.

Deepak rang a bell hanging next to the gate.

Minutes later, a boy about Cinder's height but thicker of build, answered. "What can I do for you gents?" His gaze flicked suspiciously from Cinder too Deepak.

"I'm here to speak to your master," Deepak said. "I have a new entrant for your home."

The boy grinned, a nasty smile, malicious. "A new entrant, eh? Come on in. I'll fetch Master Choff. He'll get you sorted out." His grin flashed wider, obviously mocking when he faced Cinder. "Welcome to *Our Lady of Fire.*"

4

The boy had a punchable face, especially with his ill-intentioned smile. Smarmy and smug, and Cinder recognized the sneer's purpose. It was the grin of someone who promised bullying.

Fragging jackhole.

Cinder glared at the boy, fists clenched, and stepped close. "You think something is funny?"

The smirk slowly slid from the boy's face. His eyes flickered to Deepak, and a sickly expression took hold. "Nothing funny here," he muttered. "Come with me." He spun around, head down and shoulders hunched.

Cinder and Deepak trailed after him.

"Oh, yes. With that attitude, you're sure to make lots of friends," Deepak whispered, his voice deadpan.

Cinder shrugged. "I don't need friends like him."

"No, but you also don't need enemies." The priest's mouth twitched into a frown. "You cannot fight the world. Remember?"

Cinder understood and appreciated Deepak's advice, but he also knew that if he backed down at this, their very first meeting, the boy and his fellow bullies would show him no mercy. As he reckoned matters, it was better to let them all know he wouldn't be pushed around.

Deepak called to the boy. "What's your name, son?"

The boy paused long enough to draw himself up proudly. "Stard Lener of the Errows Tribe."

"Well, this here's Cinder Shade of the village of Swallow. Maybe the two of you could get to know each other. Maybe you could show him around."

Cinder appreciated Deepak's trying to help him become friends with the boy and decided to play along. "Nice to meet you, Stard."

The boy didn't answer, his silence serving as an eloquent conversation killer.

Cinder mentally shrugged. *So be it.* He might have stirred up a hornet's nest with the bullies, but he couldn't make himself care. Besides, he didn't like bullies, no matter how young.

As they progressed toward the orphanage, Cinder studied Stard and startled when he realized the boy was possibly his own age or even older. It didn't seem right. The boy *felt* younger but based on his wispy mustache and hint of a beard, he was likely older.

They entered the main building, where they ascended a flight of stairs, their footsteps echoing on black, slate tiles, and came to a poorly lit hallway paneled in dark wood. Several windows opened onto the courtyard, but the light they provided did little to illuminate the darkness. They reached a wooden door, dark like the paneling. It barred further passage, and a fine line of light bled under the sill.

Stard knocked loudly. "We're here. Master Choff."

Cinder eyed the closed door, trying to guess at the nature of the man behind it.

His musings ended when the door opened, and a tall, stout man peered out at them. He wore dark pants tucked into brown boots, and a white shirt that threatened to split when he set meaty hands to his hips and inhaled heavily. "What do you want?" He wore an impatient expression on his bearded face.

"Choff," Deepak said. "You've gotten right fat. You're big as a cow."

The large man glowered momentarily, but recognition soon creased his face with a grin. "Rat? That you? You got yourself skinny and decrepit. What thievery are you doing now? Selling teenage boys?"

Thievery? Cinder shifted his gaze between Deepak and Master Choff. Clearly, they were old friends, and the priest had apparently once been something other than a holy man. He wondered what it might have been.

Deepak grinned at Master Choff. "No more stealing on my part. I'm straight as an arrow now."

Master Choff snorted. "And Shokan will take a dump in my privy."

Deepak wore an affronted expression, a hand held over his heart. "I've done reformed. I'm a priest now."

Master Choff snorted. "A priest? You're shitting me."

"Devesh's truth."

Master Choff chuckled and scratched his beard. "Well, Sira punch me in the gut. I never figured you'd go religious on me." His gaze sharpened. "Or get so damn old. Rakshasa's balls, man. What you been doing with yourself?"

Deepak leaned on his staff, his air becoming pious. "The mountains mold a man. They whip away any weakness."

"So does drink."

Deepak dipped his head. "That too, but I don't drink none." He gestured Cinder forward. "But I also didn't come to rehash old stories. I heard you're running an orphanage, and I got someone who needs a home. You got room to take him in?"

Again, Master Choff scratched at his beard. "Place is tight, but I can take him."

"His parents was killed three weeks ago. An *aether*-cursed cat."

Master Choff grunted. "Bad luck, that."

"Worse, he can't remember a thing about himself. Says he didn't even know his name until his brother told it to him."

Master Choff started again. "Devesh's truth?"

Deepak nodded.

"That's right strange," Master Choff said, stroking his beard.

Cinder had heard enough. He didn't need Deepak and Master Choff talking about him like he wasn't standing right in front of them. It was time to take ownership of his future. He thrust out his hand. "My name is Cinder Shade."

Master Choff shook hands with him. "Pleased to meet you. Mine is Master Choff. Not Choff, like old Deepak here said, but Master Choff. We ain't friends. I'll give you shelter and food, but you work for it. We clear?"

Cinder simply nodded, not intimidated in the least by the large man. As he figured things, Master Choff was someone who had started an orphanage, ran it, and took care of those who couldn't care for themselves. He had a kind heart, but he also didn't want his charges to take advantage of that. "Crystal."

Master Choff's face screwed up in confusion. "Crystal? The hell does that mean?" His gaze sharpened. "You funning me, boy?"

"Not at all."

Master Choff took in Stard, who still stood there. "You got work waiting, or you need me to find something to keep your idle hands busy?"

"I was just getting back to it, Master." Stard bobbed his head and dashed away.

Master Choff chuckled. "More likely getting back to chasing a piece of tail."

Deepak brow creased. "I was told you run a clean orphanage. You let your boys run wild?"

Master Choff held up his hands. "'Course not. But you know how boys is. Certain age, all they can think about is girls, getting in their skirts. Them oats get sowed whether I allow it or not."

Deepak grunted acknowledgment.

It was strange. Cinder knew what Deepak and Master Choff were talking about. Boys and girls. Growing up. Discovering each other. Sowing oats. But he hadn't once thought about girls since waking up in the well. Maybe it was because he was too focused on his lack of memories and learning the history of the world, knowledge everyone else took for granted.

Deepak rapped the floor with his staff. "I truly wish I could stay longer, Choff, but you know how it is. Weather waits for no one." His mouth twitched into a smile. "Not even holy priests."

"You really got to get going so soon? I got a room for you. Rest and leave in the morning."

Deepak hesitated. "I don't want to burden you."

Master Choff guffawed, his large belly shaking. "If you didn't want to burden me, you wouldn't have brought me this boy." His laughter settled. "And it ain't no burden, especially if you feel like making a donation or some such."

Deepak dipped his head. "Of course."

"Let's get the two of you settled then," Master Choff said. He gestured to Deepak. "Stay here. I'll see to your boy first."

Cinder followed Master Choff down a flight of stairs.

"You're a quiet one," Master Choff noted. Cinder realized he was being addressed. "The quiet ones is the ones who cause the most trouble. You a troublemaker?"

"No, sir."

They exited the stairs and entered a narrow corridor containing a pair of doors on opposite sides of the hallway, both of them open. Cinder poked his head through one and discovered a long room, currently empty. It stretched the length of the entire floor. Six cots, all of them neatly made and fronted by a single foot locker, took up most of the space. A set of windows allowed sunshine to beam inside.

The room on the other side of the hallway was different in only one way. It had murals on the walls, scenes of the sea, of waterfalls and sunsets, mountains and happy trees.

Master Choff spoke. "This here orphanage has four dorms, two for girls and two for boys." He steered Cinder away from the room with murals. "That one there is for young boys." They entered the plainer one. "This here is for the older lads. There's two more dorms upstairs, on the same level as my own rooms. Those is for the girls." His face grew stern. "Don't go up there. Hear?"

"Yes, sir."

"Good. Then choose a bunk that's not claimed. They're the ones without blankets. Get your gear put away in a foot locker." He kicked one in demonstration.

Cinder set his rucksack on an unoccupied bunk. While he sorted out his belongings, Master Choff spoke again. "Deepak speak true? You don't remember your life?"

"I woke up in a well. That's the first thing I remember. I didn't even know my name until my brother told it to me. I didn't know he was my brother until later."

"That's a right sad story," Master Choff grunted, sounding empathetic. "A body needs to know their past if they want to live a right life. How much you know about the world?"

"I know about *lorethasra*. *Aether* as some folk call it. *Jivatma* as it's spoken by the Bharatians and the wraiths."

"Well, that's a start. What about history? You know anything about how the world came to be?"

History was what Cinder wanted to learn more than anything else. Not just his own, but also his nation's and the world's. Maybe then he'd finally be able to make sense of his place here. "I don't know much about history," Cinder answered.

"Well, it's a lot to cover, so you'll have to read about it." Master Choff scrutinized Cinder. "You can read, right?"

Cinder worried over the question. Could he read? In all his travels, he'd never thought about it. "I don't know." It was an unhappy discovery, another nail in the coffin of his sad state of existence.

"Well, there's plenty of books at the orphanage. Pick one up and see if you can reckon what it says. That'll answer your question one way or another."

Cinder hated the idea of being illiterate. It struck him as a terrible disability. "If I can't read, is there someone who can teach me?"

Master Choff nodded. "Of course. Me. I give instructions on letters and numbers to all those who spend time under my roof. And speaking of living under my roof, forget what I said to Deepak about sowing oats and such. This be a religious home. I don't abide promiscuity or drugs. No alcohol neither. We honor Shokan, but even more we honor Sira. It's why the orphanage is named what it is. Sira. *Our Lady of Fire*. She's holy. Understand like?"

Cinder nodded. "Crystal."

Master Choff frowned at him. "You said that before. You best explain your meaning before I get to believing you're mocking me."

Cinder blinked in surprise. He hadn't expected his light-hearted joke to evince such antipathy, and he quickly explained. "Crystal is short for crystal clear. It means like it's a perfect window. There's no distortion when you look through it."

"Hunh." Master rubbed his chin, lost in thought. "That's an interesting shorthand." He viewed Cinder pensively. "For someone who doesn't know history or himself, you talk pretty educated." A moment later he threw off his reverie. "I'll go over the rest of the house rules later. For now, head on down to the kitchen. Ask for Riner. He's a soft-spoken lad. He'll have some work for you to do before dinner."

The snowtiger licked her paws clean. She'd taken down an elk, feasting to her fill. Jackals and vultures circled the kill, waiting for their chance to eat. Like a regal queen, she paid them no attention. They could wait their turn until she was finished with her grooming.

Once satisfied, she moved on from her kill, and the scavengers immediately moved in. They attacked the corpse in a raucous frenzy of screeches, caws, barks, and growls. She ignored their noise. She was a queen, and queens didn't pay heed to their lessers.

The snowtiger padded across the meadow in which she'd taken down the ungulate, avoiding the bloody pools blanketing various flowers and grasses. The elk hadn't gone down easy, and a month ago, the snowtiger wouldn't have even attempted such a hunt. A month ago, however, she had managed a meal of a different kind. Two humans in a small village, and their delicious *lorethasra*.

It had taken her weeks to ingest and incorporate the magnificent feast, purifying and condensing what she'd consumed. Weeks of her body wracked by weakness and agony, and her mind a welter of confusion. Immediately after making the kills, the pain had started as burning embers igniting her stomach. She'd fled, trying to escape the torment, but no shelter was to be found. She'd run and run and run, ever onward, whipped by the torrents of fire blazing through her veins, pausing only now and then to drink water that burned like lava as it passed down her throat.

At last, the pain had lessened, day by day, it diminished until it finally retreated. The weeks without food had left her famished, but the stolen *lorethasra* had also achieved other changes. The snowtiger had grown. In every way, she was more. Larger, stronger, faster, and most importantly, smarter.

The snowtiger knew herself. She knew enough to want a name. In addition, she understood how her body had to adapt to the higher concentration of *lorethasra* she now possessed. More purification and condensing was required. Who knew how long it would take? However, what she did know was this: if she killed another human and stole their *lorethasra* prior to the work's completion, it would see her dead as well.

Patience was required, possibly years of waiting as she now measured time.

The snowtiger yawned mightily. Her belly full, she needed a nap. Before falling asleep, the snowtiger stared heavenward, vast thoughts filling her mind. What were the puffy, white things in the sky? Where did darkness come from?

She also wondered at the boy she'd nearly killed at the village. She was glad she hadn't. If she had, the excess of *lorethasra* would have ended her. She smiled to herself. Another time then. She had tasted the boy's blood, knew it and him. She had his scent and no matter where he went in the world, she could find him.

And when she was ready, she would find and finish the boy. Before she fell asleep, she closed her eyes and stared inward, at the shifting brilliance, the stream of purity. It sparkled brilliantly in places like a jewel.

The snowtiger smiled. *Brilliance.* It was a good name.

5

The next day, Deepak left to return to Swallow. Cinder saw him off and afterward, he tried to settle into *Our Lady of Fire*.

It wasn't easy. With no memories to guide him, he didn't know so much about the normal ways in which people interacted. He didn't get the jokes the other boys told, the cultural touchstones they took for granted or how to answer their questions about his history. He didn't know, which was the answer he was forced to give to everyone who asked about his past.

Weeks after arriving at *Our Lady of Fire*, Cinder still struggled to attain his bearings. He kept to himself, doing his work and learning about the strange world in which he'd been thrust. A lot of the information came from Riner Strain, a boy who was several years younger. The two of them worked in the kitchen.

Riner was a quiet lad, gentle and shy, which meant he was easy pickings for the bullies who shared their dorm room. It also meant the only place where Master Choff could keep him safe was in the kitchen. There, under the watchful eye of Cook Nestle, he could spend his days unaccosted.

However, he wasn't so safe at night.

Alone in their room and with no one to look after him, the bullies, Jarde Linger and Stard Lener, tormented Riner. It was never anything physical. Instead, they resorted to cruel and cutting observations about the kitchen boy, his rotund build, his soft-spoken manner, his bookish demeanor. But words were often the most potent of weapons.

Occasionally, it was something humiliating they did to Riner. Too often Cinder heard the boy cry into his pillows, and empathy for him welled. It couldn't go on. Riner deserved a life free of fear and suffering, and Cinder decided to help in whatever way he could. He would confront Jarde and Stard on Riner's behalf.

However, he'd have to be careful about how he approached the situation. He couldn't simply intercede against the bullies without preparation. That way might end in disaster. They outnumbered Cinder. Jarde and Stard in his room, and Jam Koner and Fone Paner amongst the younger boys. They were all Errows, a tribe that had emigrated to Rakesh several centuries ago.

Taller, lighter of skin, and rounder of eye, rumor suggested they'd originally come from the Sunset Kingdoms, members of Holy Mede's last conquering army. Over the past one thousand years, they'd forever emigrated south and east, moving their entire insular tribe and culture. Prior to Rakesh, they had lived in Gandharva. However, their prophecies drove them on. It was said that they waited for Mede's rebirth, ready to serve him as fiercely as their ancestors once had.

In Rakesh, the Errows had suffered racism and bigotry, shunned by most everyone else, and banned from holding any position of power. It was a difficult set of decades, ones that hardened their hearts. The Errows held onto their historical humiliations, clutching them close as precious gems, even now when they were now counted as the wealthiest members of Rakesh society.

Still, some things never changed. During their migration, others had mockingly referred to the Errows as *Errogs*, a word meaning "stupid" in the old language of *Shevasra*. The insult stuck. Despite their riches in Rakesh, it was what most people named the Errows—but only behind their backs.

The Errows, though, had taken ownership of the derisive term and referred to one another by it. It was a name only members of the tribe could use. Anyone else who dared speak it risked a beating, a frequent threat when it came to the Errows. From what Cinder had seen, those of the tribe were quick to anger and take insult.

With those thoughts in mind, Cinder waited for Riner to finish dressing. Last night had been the worst so far. Jarde, the leader of the Errows, had mocked the boy unrelentingly, and Riner had cried again. This morning he wouldn't look up from where he stood buttoning his shirt. It was early; the sun had yet to rise. Thankfully, Jarde and Stard had already left, tasked with gardening or some other work. The other two boys who also shared their room, Klam Tarn and Pent Lork, had also departed.

"You can't help me," Riner said, still not looking up, his voice soft. "I can tell you want to. Don't bother. You'll only get hurt. Stay out of it."

Cinder didn't answer. Maybe Riner was right. Maybe he should mind his own business. Maybe . . .

But he wouldn't.

He couldn't. Defending the defenseless, protecting the innocent. It felt intrinsic to who he was, part of the fabric of his being. He had to help Riner.

He didn't say any of this to the other boy, though. Riner had his pride, and if he knew what Cinder intended, he'd probably grow angry about it, humiliated afresh at his perceived weakness.

"You better hurry," Cinder said, making his voice uncaring. "We'll be late."

"I'm ready."

They hustled down to the kitchen, where Cook Nestle reigned. She was a large, big-bosomed woman who carried herself with a gruff demeanor that hid a caring heart. Cinder could see she loved Riner, doing her best to keep the young boy close so he could avoid the bullies and their attention.

"You lads best hustle. We got lots of cooking to do," she said when they arrived.

Cook Nestle had them stirring eggs, chopping potatoes, and mixing water with oats. They quickly readied breakfast for the orphans and staff, which they served as a buffet on a long table in the kitchen. Everyone entered through one door, received a single serving of eggs, potatoes, and oatmeal, and exited out another into the dining room.

One of the earliest arrivals for breakfast that morning was Coral Strain, Riner's sister who was several years older than Cinder. The siblings were of similar height and shared the same dark-haired, dark-eyed features of those native to Rakesh, but Coral was slim where Riner was heavy. Pretty—her smile sparkled—where Riner was plain and forgettable. Brave where Riner was diffident and faltering in his courage. Coral also possessed an intense air, the possessiveness of a mother wolverine. Rumor said that she would move on from the orphanage sometime in the next few months, and it was clear she worried for her brother. Concern lit her features when Riner wouldn't meet her eye.

Cinder stood close, passing out food and listening in on their conversation.

"What happened?" Coral asked.

"Nothing."

"You need to tell Master Choff. Ask him to move you, maybe up with us."

"With the girls?" Riner scoffed. His jaw briefly clenched. "No. Besides, nothing happened, so there's nothing to tell. Leave it alone."

"Riner . . ."

"There's others waiting, Coral," Riner said, skimming his eyes at the line.

Jarde and his crew of Errows waited close by. He and Stard were tall like everyone in their tribe, with blond hair, light-colored eyes, and rangy builds. Jam and Fone, the younger Errows, eleven and twelve, had yet to achieve their growth, but what they lacked in size they made up for with lickspittle smiles and mocking demeanors.

Jarde tapped his foot in impatience. "Hurry up. Me Errogs and me don't have time for this shit. Shove on."

Coral glared at the bully, unmoving. "Don't you dare speak to me like that, you scum."

"What's the matter?" Jarde smirked. "Your little sister, Riner, need you to stick up for her again?"

"Brother," Coral snapped. "My little brother. And I know what you and your *Errogs* are, what you do to him."

Jarde's humor evaporated like water hitting a hot skillet. Fury took its place. "What did you call me?"

"You heard me. Errog."

Violence threatened. Cinder could taste it. He eased out from behind the table, glad that the last of his limp was gone. He clutched a sturdy metal spatula. There was no chance he'd let the bullies hurt a girl.

Jarde's face went ugly. He lunged at Coral. Cinder slammed the spatula into the side of Jarde's head. It made a lovely, hollow sound when it struck the bully.

Jarde cried out, falling away. Here came Stard. Cinder backhanded him with the spatula. Stard's lip split, and he clutched his bleeding mouth. Jam and Fone came next, shouting in anger. Cinder sidekicked Fone in the thigh, and an uppercut with the spatula to Jam's jaw put the younger boy on his ass.

Jarde came again, fists at the ready. "Drop the spatula and let's have a go," he snarled.

Cinder held onto his makeshift weapon. "You're a real hero," he mocked. "Four of you against one girl."

Jarde made to respond, but Master Choff was there, getting between the two of them. "What in the name of Sira's tits is going on?" he roared. "Someone better answer before I put my boot up all your asses."

Cinder didn't flinch from the master's anger. He affected an indifferent pose. "A little misunderstanding," he said. "The Errows were voicing their displeasure with the eggs."

Master Choff gaped at him for an instant. He then faced Jarde. "Is that right? You didn't like the eggs?"

Jarde glowered at Cinder, who gave him a friendly smile and wave, knowing it would further anger the bully.

Jarde scowled a moment longer. "I guess," he said, his voice reluctant.

"You guess?" Master Choff scoffed. "Is that a 'yes' or a 'no'. Because if it's a 'no' and the two of you were trading punches, I'll have a sparring square set up right now. You and Cinder can go at it proper." He glanced from Cinder to Jarde, mouth set in an angry line.

"I wouldn't mind a sparring square," Cinder said. "It'll be fun learning to fight."

He smirked when Jarde hesitated. Like all bullies, he backed off when challenged. *Coward.*

"Naw," Jarde said, shrugging in a bored manner. "As scrawny as the new boy is, it wouldn't be fair."

"You don't have to worry about me," Cinder promised him.

Jarde shook his head. "You ain't worth me time." He gathered his Errows, and they gave a stiff nod to Master Choff before leaving the kitchen.

Master Choff faced Cinder. "You are scrawny," he said, his gaze grazing him up and down, "and you've made yourself an enemy. You step careful."

Cinder appreciated the advice, but it wasn't necessary. "I can handle Jarde." He didn't know where his confidence came from, but certainty coursed through him. Besides, hadn't he already handled Jarde and the Errows?

"I hope so, boy," Master Choff said, his voice ominous. He moved off, and Cinder watched him go, still unafraid of what was to come.

Someone had to stand up to Jarde, and he didn't regret he was the one who had done so.

Coral moved to stand at Cinder's side. "Thank you," she said, giving his hand a quick squeeze.

Cinder glanced up when he noticed someone standing at the entrance to the dining hall. It was Coral. She paused in the doorway, appearing unsure. Cinder raised his eyebrows in question. "Is there anything I can do for you?"

Coral's hesitation ended, and she paced into the room. "I wanted to thank you for protecting me at breakfast. Jarde . . . I'm not sure what he would have done, but it's likely best I didn't learn." She paused. "I also need a favor. It's about Riner."

Cinder glanced to the kitchen entryway. He couldn't see Riner or Cook Nestle, but he could hear them, their voices muffled. They were busy cleaning the dishes after an uneventful lunch. Jarde and his fellow Errows hadn't said anything during that meal, simply taking their food without any sort of acknowledgment.

"What about Riner?" Cinder asked, although he had an inkling what Coral would ask.

His guess proved correct. "You don't look it, but you're strong and brave," she said. "You stood up to Jarde. Riner could use your help. Other than me, no one here has ever defended him. But I can't be with him all the time."

"What about Master Choff? Can't he evict the Errows?" It was a question Cinder had puzzled over ever since coming to the orphanage.

Coral jeered. "Can he protect Riner at night when he's alone with those two?" She deflated a second later. "Master Choff does the best he can, but he can't press too hard. *Our Lady of Fire* receives too much money from the Errows to help care for their orphans. It's how the orphanage remains open. If Master Choff evicted Jarde and Stard, those funds would be gone. He can't risk it."

Cinder leaned on his broom. "You want me to protect Riner?" He'd already planned on doing so, but he wanted to hear for certain that it was actually needed.

Coral nodded. "I'll be leaving soon enough. I have a place as a woman's maid, and if I'm lucky, as a singer, too."

A maid, Cinder could understand, but a singer? How did someone make money singing? He didn't know, and now wasn't the time to find out. He had other questions, ones to do with Riner, but he had to take care in how he asked them. Too blunt, and Coral would become defensive. "If you don't mind me saying, Riner seems frightened all the time. Do you know why?"

Coral offered a bitter laugh. "Because he's been bullied his entire life. Jarde and his friends aren't the first people who've been cruel to him. It started with our parents. Before he died, our father was a renowned warrior, a graduate of the Third Directorate, in fact. He served with distinction in the Yaksha army. Our mother was a brilliant singer. Beautiful, too. She once gave a performance to Empress Sala of Yaksha Sithe. Riner is neither a brilliant warrior nor a wonderful singer, and I'm guessing it was a bitter disappointment for them. They told him he was worthless, both of them, on so many occasions that he began to believe it. He still does."

Cinder took in the explanation, silent and unable to say anything at first. Cruel didn't begin to describe what Riner had endured. No child should bear such measure of hardship, especially from his mother and father. Anger at Riner's parents and pity for the boy warred in equal measure within him. How could someone treat their child so brutally?

Cinder's jaw clenched, and he realized he was grinding his teeth. He made himself relax, exhale a breath he'd been holding until he was able to speak again. "I see."

"You do?" Coral asked, a hopeful note to her voice. "Riner will be all alone. He needs someone to look after him."

"And you want me to be that someone?" Cinder was touched by the trust she was showing him, but he needed to know more. "Why?"

"Because I saw how you handled yourself against Jarde and the others this morning. You aren't big, but you moved like you knew what you were doing, like you'd been in a fight before." She shook her head in disbelief. "You also had a limp when you first arrived. I guess whatever injury you had must have healed."

Cinder shrugged, not bothering to correct her mistake. He still had no explanation for how his clubfoot and withered leg had healed. No one did. Not that he'd asked around. He knew not to. Asking would invite difficult questions, and who knew where that might lead? The people of Rakesh thought anything to do with *lorethasra* was entirely in the province of the elves, and if a human demonstrated such talents, they had to be a wraith. And wraiths were killed on sight.

Cinder was simply glad he no longer limped and that all his limbs worked as they were supposed to. However it had happened—whatever mystery or miracle—was fine by him.

"Plus . . ." Coral trailed off, and her face reddened. She took a settling breath. "Plus, you're kind. Riner tells me about you. He says you're a good person, and I can tell he's right. I can see it in your eyes. You *are* a good person."

That's what Cinder had been hoping to hear. Not necessarily the part about being kind or good. He didn't yet know himself well enough to say one way or another. But he was glad to learn that Coral had more in mind in choosing him than simply taking the first person she'd come across who was handy with his fists.

"I'll protect him," Cinder said.

Coral beamed gratitude, her eyes welling. She gripped his hands, leaning forward on her tiptoes to kiss his cheek. "Thank you."

"Ah. Here we are. Hickory Square," Master Choff said. "Where we get fresh produce in our little section of Swift Sword."

Cinder followed the line of Master Choff's pointing finger. A pair of roads demarcated the area in question, which wasn't a square so much as a long rectangle, two sets of brick and stone buildings facing one another across a long grass lawn. Dew glistened under a vibrant sun. Flowering shrubs peppered the corners and several lines of red-leafed maple trees provided shade as a crowd of people hustled about. The statue of a farmer, a rake slung over his shoulder, stood guard at the other end of the square. Tables holding an assortment of vegetables and goods sheltered beneath canvas tents while vendors hawked their wares.

Cinder crossed the road, keeping close to Master Choff as they made their way to the square.

Master Choff approached the closest vegetable stall, a glint of anticipation in his eyes. He all-but rubbed his hands in glee. Then he began haggling over the prices. It was the same with every stall they visited. Master Choff would proclaim the vegetables too expensive, less costly last week, or somehow imperfect. The vendor would counter with exclamations regarding the price and perfection of his vegetables. Eventually they'd end at an agreed upon price halfway in between what the vendor initially asked and what Master Choff stated he was willing to pay. In this way, they wandered about, picking out tomatoes, okra, turnips, and beets.

Cinder carried the vegetables in several rucksacks, hands gripping tight and shoulders aching from the unaccustomed weight. He considered asking Master Choff to take some of the weight. It only seemed fair. As big and burly as Master Choff was, he'd have no trouble carrying the groceries. In the end, he decided against it. Master Choff might see his request as a form of laziness.

Nevertheless, Cinder wanted to groan when he saw their next stop. The vendor sold potatoes. Potatoes were heavy.

"Why did you ask me to come with you?" Cinder asked after they left the potato vendor. "You seem to have everything well in hand."

Master Choff clapped Cinder with a meaty paw, nearly knocking him off his feet. His bearded face split into a grin. "Would you rather be at *Our Lady's* and have Jarde and Stard rake you over the coals?" His grin disappeared, and he wagged a finger under Cinder's nose. "Don't think they forgot what you did to them."

"Is that the real reason you brought me out here? Or did you merely need a pack mule?" Cinder ducked aside for a fast-moving man dressed in quality pants and shirts who appeared to have a lot on his mind.

Choff laughed. "Sure. A pack mule be mighty useful," he agreed. "But, no, that isn't the reason I brung you out here."

Cinder waited for Master Choff to explain himself.

However, Master Choff was busy haggling with the rice vendor.

Minutes later, he had a large sack thrown across a shoulder. "Let's go. That's everything on Cook Nestle's list."

They crossed the road, avoiding rickshaws, wagons, and carriages. Master Choff threw out a meaty arm, holding Cinder back when a group of five rough-looking men strutted by. They wore swords on their hips and swaggered. *Mercenaries.* Cinder remembered Deepak's warning about such individuals. The one in the lead said something crude to a passing woman, and the other four catcalled her. The woman hustled away from them, which only spurred the mercenaries to bray even louder at her.

Master Choff muttered an oath under his breath after the mercenaries had pushed on. "Scum," he said as an aside to Cinder.

Once more they headed back to *Our Lady of Fire.*

"I didn't bring you with me to Hickory Square to be my pack mule," Master Choff said, resuming their prior topic of conversation. "I wanted to get you out of the orphanage. Get you away from Jarde and Stard. I wanted you to see a bit of the city." He gestured broadly at the cramped streets thick with traffic, the various aromas—some savory, others rank—and the shouts of people making their way through their life here. "What do you think?"

Cinder didn't answer at once. Instead, he recalled the mountains and valleys he'd crossed on his way to Swift Sword. He recalled a dream. A vision of a city of uncommon grace and elegance, buildings resting like setting stones upon an emerald chain of nine hills overlooking a sapphire sea. In comparison to what he'd seen and what he imagined, Swift Sword came off as rather poor. He was wise enough to keep such thoughts to himself. Master Choff clearly loved his home. "It certainly has an energy to it, don't you think?"

Master Choff smiled, his expression distant. "That it does." After a moment, he shook off his reverie. "I also wanted to thank you for taking Riner under your wing. Coral mentioned you'd promised to look after him. The boy is going to need it when she leaves the orphanage."

Cinder wasn't sure how to respond to Master Choff's statements. He had never expected praise for protecting Riner. Wasn't it what most people would do?

They cut across an alley strewn with refuse and a few homeless poor, who lay on the ground, eyes closed and muttering to themselves. Several were missing limbs.

Master Choff's face went tight with sorrow. "Army veterans," he explained. "We don't do enough to support those who gave everything they had for our safety."

"Is there no work for them?" Cinder asked after they exited the alley. "I know they're injured and lame, but surely the city fathers could find labor for some of them. Isn't work its own reward? We all need a purpose in our lives, and those poor men don't have any."

Master Choff viewed him askance. "You talk like someone a lot older than you look."

"It's still the truth."

"It is, but not for those men in the alley. They got no hope. The things they saw battling zahhacks, seeing their brother warriors killed. It's addled their minds. Their kind are broken. They do everything in their power to forget. Drink. Opium. Anything to quiet the memories."

Memories. How ironic. Cinder was desperate to recover his memories, and these men would do anything to forget theirs.

Life and the world was an odd place of contradictions, but one thing Cinder knew: he wouldn't trade places with those men. They had a desperately sad lot, trapped by terrible memories and were never able to live past them. Cinder reckoned it must be like living with a personal rakshasa. A demon who knew all the triggers to cause anguish.

"What do you think the rich ought to do for them kind?" Master Choff asked.

Cinder didn't know and said so. "But it's a sin to overlook those in need."

"Sin." Master Choff shook his head as if in disgust. "Priests talk like that. Deepak, now that I think on it." Cinder also noticed a slight smile of approval on the master's broad face.

"What are you reading?" Cinder asked Riner. He'd wandered into Master Choff's study during his time off, searching for the other boy.

Once a week, all the orphans were given most of the day off to do whatever they wished, time when they didn't have any work requirements.

Today was one such day for him and Riner, and the younger boy always took it here in Master Choff's study, a room containing a large desk, several armchairs, and a lead-lined window bracketed by a set of oak bookshelves that were dark with age. They held an assortment of books, covering topics like history, language, the science of *lorethasra*, and also tales of adventure. *Diptha* bulbs lit the space, and Cinder noted a number of weapons—a sheathed sword, a pitted axe, and a dented mace—hanging from the rafters.

The armaments seemed to call to him, and he eyed them in quiet speculation. He wondered what it was about instruments of death that so interested him. His gaze took in the weapons, and he pondered. Had he always had a fascination with weapons? Or was this a new interest? Perhaps it was because he was so physically weak—scrawny like Master Choff had mentioned—and he thought a weapon would make him strong?

He considered the possibility, but only for a few seconds. That wasn't it. It was something else, something he couldn't name, especially the swords. He traced their lines like he'd seen some older boys eyeing Coral when she wasn't looking.

He shook off his ruminations. He wasn't here because of swords or any other weapons.

He was here for Riner.

After his talk with Coral several days ago, Cinder had tried to get to know Riner better, but it was difficult with their hours filled with work. Then at night, they were too tired to do much more than collapse on their cots.

At least Jarde and Stard left them alone, taking a more careful approach after Cinder's unexpected resilience when he'd fought them off. They were nowhere in evidence now—their time off never corresponded with Riner's. Cinder suspected it was another way Master Choff managed to give Riner opportunities to have safety and happiness. In addition, while Master Choff's study was open to all the orphans, the Errows never spent any time here. They used their free hours in other pursuits, apparently believing that learning and education were unimportant, a view not held by the rest of their tribe.

Upon hearing Cinder's question, Riner glanced up from his reading, likely his favorite hobby. The boy liked books, and he'd once admitted how he enjoyed losing himself in the stories found within them, to pretend he was more than he was, other than who he was, someone stronger and better. Not in so many words, but the gist of it had been there.

"I'm reading about the prophecies of Shokan and Sira," Riner answered.

Those two. Cinder's brows knitted. He'd heard their names many times during his month at *Our Lady of Fire*, but he'd yet to learn anything of significance about them.

"Any chance you can tell me about them?" Cinder asked.

Riner held a suspicious expression. "Why?"

"I don't know much of anything," Cinder said. He tapped his head. "My memory's not right, remember?" He slid into an armchair and faced Riner. "People talk about Shokan and Sira all the time, but I have no idea who they were. I know Sira was a woman, but what about Shokan?"

Riner closed the book, a plump finger holding his place. "Shokan was a man. He is said to have been the finest warrior who ever lived."

"Even better than Mede?"

"Mede was a general, possibly the greatest of all time, but he wasn't a warrior," Riner corrected.

He took on a professorial tone, and in another life, Cinder realized the boy would have done well teaching at a fine school. 'Universities' were what they were called.

"Regardless, while Mede could inspire an army, Shokan could inspire a world, the downtrodden and the oppressed. He *did* inspire a world. His first world, the one he and Sira saved before coming to Seminal. We are meant to follow his example."

So far Riner's explanation didn't make any sense. Cinder said so. "That doesn't really tell me much."

Riner blinked. "Then maybe we should start at the beginning. Thousands of years ago, millennia before the Mythaspuris and the *NusraelShev*—"

"The what?" Cinder interrupted. Would there ever be an end to all these new terms?

"The *NusraelShev*, the Disastrous Submission, in the old language of *Shevasra*." Riner waved his hands. "Never mind. It's for another time. Let's stick with Shokan and Sira, the Blessed Ones." He cleared his throat. "Suffice it to say that Shokan, the Lord of the Sword, and Sira, the Lady of Fire, last strode the land thousands of years ago. They were said to have direct communion with Devesh." He paused then, peering intently at Cinder. "You know about Devesh, correct?"

Cinder nodded. "The Lord of Creation. Our Heavenly Maker."

"Yes. Now imagine the being who created all of this." Riner gestured broadly, indicating everything about them. "And imagine two people, a husband and his wife, who communed directly with our Creator."

Cinder tried to, but he couldn't come up with anything more than a vague sense of power.

Riner spoke on. "Together Shokan and Sira possessed abilities and strength beyond measure."

"I take it they were more powerful than the elves and dwarves?"

Riner snorted derision. "The elves and dwarves are sloths next to Shokan's and Sira's lightning-swift power."

Cinder hid a smile. Riner certainly had a way of describing these *Blessed Ones*.

"And they required their great power," Riner continued, "because they had great enemies, deadly evil who tested their might and goodness."

"The god Shet and his Titans."

Riner's mouth curled a sneer. "The false god and his Titans. Shet was nothing more than a powerful *asrasin*, a human who gained great puissance and fancied himself divine." He smiled in satisfaction. "Shokan and Sira proved him wrong. They defeated him. Crushed him utterly. Cast him adrift in time until the Mythaspuris finally destroyed him."

Cinder considered Riner's story. "So in summation, Shokan and Sira were humans in direct contact with Devesh?"

Riner nodded. "Correct."

There was much to take in. "I still want to know about these Mythaspuris," Cinder said, "but what happened to Shokan and Sira?" It was the missing element to Riner's story.

The younger boy shrugged. "No one knows. They defeated Shet and then they disappeared, lost to human knowledge. We have prophecies, though." Riner grew more excited. "There's one from Gandharva, *the Lor Agni*. Some people in Rakesh believe in it, too. It states that during humanity's greatest test, Shokan and Sira will arise once more, ascending like phoenixes to reclaim their lost glory. They'll usher forth a heaven on Seminal."

It seemed like the kind of story to make the young believe in the innate goodness of the world, a tale of evil gods and brilliantly loving people to defeat them. Cinder didn't believe it. It was too naïve and far-fetched. He didn't say it to Riner, though. The boy clearly loved his stories of Shokan and Sira and telling him they were a children's fable would only insult him.

"Is there a copy of *the Lor Agni* here?"

Riner's expression fell. "Only a polluted one. You'd have to go to Gandharva or Yaksha for a proper version."

Cinder shrugged. It didn't sound important anyway. "Then maybe you can tell me about the Mythaspuris sometime."

"I'd be happy to." An instant later, Riner wore an unhappy expression. "I know what you're doing. What Coral asked you to do. To look after me so Jarde and Stard don't hurt me anymore." His face went red with embarrassment or humiliation. "You don't have to."

Cinder smiled. "Of course I do. Don't your stories about Shokan talk about how he defends the persecuted? Aren't we supposed to follow his example?"

Riner reluctantly nodded.

"Then how can I step aside when I see someone abused? Whether Coral spoke to me or not, I'd want to help because that's what we're meant to do: help those who need it, serve as brothers to those who require it." With the statements spoken, Cinder realized their truth. They resonated deep inside him, a flickering light in the depths of his mind, a silvery pool of water, still and perfect. A coruscating wall of blue-green lightning shrouded the view, and the image in his thoughts faded when Riner spoke.

The other boy still sounded unhappy. "I know you're right, but I still don't like being so weak. I wish I could fight."

Cinder shrugged. "And I don't like my amnesia. We both have our disabilities. Maybe you can teach me what I don't know, and I can defend you until you don't need me to anymore."

Riner smiled as he held out a hand. "Deal."

6

A week later, the sun was streaming through the windows of Master Choff's study, lighting the place to a warm brilliance. Nothing appeared amiss. All was as it should be. The books stood upon the shelves, lined up in even rows like soldiers ready to carry out their orders. The unoccupied desk hunkered within the center of the room, the general in charge of the study. However, despite the martial notions by which Cinder imagined the area, a gentle quiet and the comforting aroma of paper filled the space. They argued against the idea of an occupying army.

So, too, did Riner's presence. Currently, the young boy sat on the couch, head bent over a thick book. *As usual.* Cinder smiled and momentarily watched Riner from the doorway. The boy was no soldier or warrior, and if life was kind, he'd never become one.

Cinder cleared his throat, gaining Riner's attention. "What are you reading?"

Riner didn't take his attention off the page as he silently lifted the book in his hands so Cinder could read the title. Cinder squinted his eyes, trying to decipher the ornate lettering. *The Medeian Scryings.*

"You're reading a biography about Mede?" Cinder guessed.

Riner set aside the book, leaving a finger to hold his place. "Not entirely. *The Medeian Scryings* are a religious text. They supposedly describe Mede's philosophical beliefs and how a moral man should comport himself."

Cinder frowned. He didn't know much about Mede, not having a chance to read much about him. What little he'd learned was that Mede had once been a prince of Parn. He'd inherited his father's throne at the age of nineteen and promptly declared war on the other Savage Kingdoms, conquering the entirety of them in five years. Following that, he had consolidated his holdings, but not content with his conquests, ten years later, he had ridden to war again, sweeping ever westward. He defeated every force sent against his own. Not even the warriors of the various sithes or crèches—doing their best to stand athwart Mede's destiny—could halt his progress. The warlord had drowned the northern world in an ocean of blood and savagery, only stopping his conquests when he'd reached the Sunset Kingdoms. He declared his universal war over when he walked his horse into the Shakaran Ocean.

What kind of morality could such a man teach anyone? More likely the *Scryings* would simply pardon violence enacted against the defenseless.

Riner must have noticed Cinder's antipathy. "The *Scryings* don't make much sense," he said. "I've read the book twice now, but it seems so . . ." He appeared to struggle to find the right adjective.

"Blood-soaked?" Cinder guessed.

"Vapid," Riner said. "Mede was a brilliant strategist, but his writings don't touch on his wars. They're a remarkably shallow amalgamation of various other religious traditions. Mede doesn't understand them, and he includes these contradictory aspects into his writings."

Cinder took a seat across from Riner in a facing chair. "In what way?"

"Let me see." Riner thumbed through the book. "Here's one from Sutra 19 verse 12: *O Divine Follower! Deceive thine enemy and know that all sins are forgiven.*" Riner flipped through the pages. "But then there's this from Sutra 85 verse 7: *Those who lie are sent to the Realms, the accursed final Hell where they shall be as the playthings of the Rakshasas.*" Riner lifted his attention from the book. "Two sutras. One telling us lying is acceptable in some circumstances and another one telling us we're doomed if we do."

"Or maybe they're incomplete," Cinder said. "Maybe some of what Mede meant to convey was lost to history, or the definition of the words he used has changed over time." In his mind, it sounded logical that the meaning of a word might change over time. A simple word like 'stick' might have had a vastly different denotation a thousand years ago. It might have described an experience only understood by those who had shared and lived them.

"Maybe," Riner said, sounding unconvinced. "But *the Median Scryings* are supposed to be Devesh's own words, given to Mede during a set of trances when he rode his horse west. He said—"

"What was the name of his horse?"

"His horse?"

"Every mythic figure has an equally mythic steed." Cinder grinned. "Every work of fiction I've read so far says so. Shokan and Aia. Sira and Shon."

"Mede's steed was named Pale. He named the horse after the thousands of bloodless corpses he left in his wake."

Cinder grimaced. *Disgusting.* "So, in summary. Mede was a genocidal lunatic who fancied himself imbued by the voice of the Lord? Is that about it?"

"His father inspired the conceit," Riner said. "It is said that on his deathbed, Mede's father, Fileep of Parn, told him: *'Heed my command for Devesh inspires these words. My son, ask for thyself another kingdom, for that which I leave is too small for thee.'* Legend says that Fileep died upon speaking the words."

Cinder rolled his eyes. "That sounds about as likely as *the Median Scryings* being the inspired words of Devesh."

Riner shrugged. "Maybe," he said. "Probably," he allowed after a moment of consideration. "But the last verse in the last sutra of the

Scryings says that Mede will be reborn one day. *He'll come from the land of the sun's dying, birthed in blood and bathed in the tears of his enemies."*

"Charming," Cinder muttered. "By *'land of the sun's dying'*, I'm guessing they mean the Sunset Kingdoms."

"That's what most people who believe in the *Scryings* say," Riner said. "There is also a version of the book that alters the final verse. It still talks about the land of the sun's dying, but it also says that the risen Mede will act as the herald for Shokan, the Deathless Hero."

"Shokan? I thought he was dead."

Riner shrugged. "No one knows for sure if Shokan is alive or not," he said. "Prophecies also speak of his return, remember? More importantly, the version of the *Scryings* I mentioned is considered sacrilegious to most Medeians. It's probably best if you never mention Shokan in their company."

Cinder snorted. "Why would I? Besides, Shokan is a dumb name for a hero."

Days became weeks, and Cinder shivered as he hustled to get home. Clouds scudded across the sky, threatening rain and providing a gloomy harbinger of the coming autumn weather. A chill wind blew, and Cinder shivered once more.

"Damn weather," Master Choff muttered. He trotted at Cinder's side, both of them burdened with burlap sacks filled with produce. The orphanage headmaster's broad face was red and his breath strained as he struggled to keep up with Cinder. "There's nothing as bad as a cold rain."

Cinder shared the sentiment, and he glanced at the gray weather in worry. He didn't want to get soaked and catch a cold.

Blocks from home and with no rain falling, Master Choff slowed them to a walk. "I think we can make it the rest of the way without running."

Running? Cinder did a double-take. They had been moving at a fast walk. It wasn't even a jog. Cinder kept his observation to himself. Master Choff was old . . . Well, he was middle-aged, but given his girth, it was the same as old, and it was clear he was no longer used to physical exertions.

They entered the courtyard to *Our Lady of Fire*, and Cinder noticed a paper mâché sculpture above the front entrance. It wasn't easy to discern the nature of the creature depicted, but from what Cinder could ascertain, the imagery was of an upright being with the body of a wolf and the tail of a scorpion. He'd seen similar, newly set out monsters meant to guard other doors throughout Swift Sword.

"What is that?" Cinder asked.

Master Choff's gaze went to where Cinder pointed. "It's a zahhack." They entered the orphanage's foyer and made their way to the kitchen.

Cinder stared at Master Choff in confusion. "I thought zahhacks were servants of Shet."

"They are." Master Choff didn't have time to explain further.

They entered the kitchen and found Cook Nestle standing in front of a large pot resting on the wood-fired stove. She had one beefy hand on her hip and the other stirring what smelled like mutton stew. She halted her work when they entered. "Did you get the beets and corn?" she asked.

Master Choff withdrew the named vegetables from the burlap sacks, displaying them for her.

Cook Nestle grunted, taking them in hand. "These should thicken the stew just right. Too much water otherwise." She began peeling and chopping the vegetables.

"Where's Riner?" Cinder asked.

"Cleaning the washrooms," Cook Nestle said without turning around. "Can you two store the rest of the vegetables in the cellar?"

"Of course," Master Choff agreed.

The headmaster usually did what Cook Nestle asked, and Cinder followed him down the steep wooden steps leading to the cellar. A dank aroma greeted them. The headmaster held aloft an oil lantern since *diptha* bulbs were too expensive to waste in the cellar. Master Choff placed the lamp on the lip of a dust-covered shelf, and the light displayed brick walls encasing a space barely large enough for two people. Cinder crossed the perpetually damp dirt floor and reached a row of shelves lining two sides of the cellar. A set of barrels squatted on the wall opposite the rickety stairs.

He set to storing the vegetables. "You were saying about zahhacks," he said to Master Choff, resuming their prior topic of conversation.

"It's a tradition. *Holiva.* The middle of Devasth, the holiest month of the year. Two days of feasting, but only after sunset." Master Choff said. "It's a holiday unique to Swift Sword. At summer's end, we set a zahhack on the lintels of our front doors. It's meant to ward off other monsters and evil creatures."

Cinder tried to piece together why the people of Swift Sword would post zahhacks on their front doors. It didn't make any sense. "I thought zahhacks were evil."

"They are," Master Choff said with a shrug. "I know it sounds strange. Using evil to ward off evil, but somehow that's the tradition."

It still didn't make sense, and Cinder found the entire situation confusing. The truth was that whenever he heard the word 'zahhack', a shiver went down his spine and an ember of anger breathed to life. He hated the name 'zahhack'. He hated their depictions. He didn't know why, and he couldn't imagine celebrating or feasting with one of them looming over his shoulder or standing outside on his home's lintel.

His lip curled at the notion.

"Maybe you'll find the Days of Deliverance more to your liking," Master Choff said. "It's held at the same time every year in every part of the world. The third week of Kev, late spring or early summer. A five-day celebration. It rings in the end of the *NusraelShev.*"

"And there aren't any zahhacks?"

"Course not," Master Choff scoffed. "We're celebrating the end of them, right?"

"Glad to hear it," Cinder muttered. He still couldn't imagine why anyone would make zahhacks part of a religious tradition. It was nonsensical.

"Zahhacks aren't even the worst of Shet's creatures," Master Choff continued. "Not even the Titans. The worst are—"

"Demons?" Cinder guessed.

"Demons?" Master Choff wore a puzzled frown. "Everyone else calls them rakshasas, but they aren't zahhacks. Shet didn't create them. He called them to our world. They come from the Realms of the Rakshasas, or at least that's what the priests say."

Cinder smiled, remembering the only priest he really knew. He missed the scrawny, old man. "You mean like Deepak?"

Master Choff snorted a chuckle. "Don't remind me. I can't believe that scoundrel got himself remade as a priest. It doesn't seem natural. When I knew old Deepak in the army, he wasn't very holy." For a second, Master Choff's eyes went distant with remembrance. "Anyway," he said, returning to the here and now. "It's necrosed who are the worst of Shet's monsters. You best pray you never encounter one of them."

Cinder didn't know about the necrosed. He'd never heard the name before, and it didn't sound particularly frightening. Nevertheless, like all things related to Shet, this word also inspired a kernel of anger. In addition, a vision bloomed in his mind. He imagined a tall, gangly creature, hairless and pale as snow. Its arms hung to its knees and its fingers were tipped with the claws of a bear. An albino with dark eyes blazing malice and promised cruelty.

Despite its horrific features, an unexpected emotion drifted to the forefront of Cinder's thoughts. Pity, sorrow, and a strange longing.

The next time he had a day of rest, Cinder chose to spend it in Master Choff's study and read more about the zahhacks. He didn't like their names and didn't like thinking about them, but if he wanted to learn the ways of the world, he had to be willing to make himself uncomfortable. Besides, his discussion with Master Choff from the other day had him curious, and thankfully, the headmaster had a primer on zahhacks.

He settled into his favorite chair in the study. Sunshine beamed through frost-covered windows, the light scattering into rainbows and painting the floorboards in vibrant hues of red, orange, green, and purple. As usual, Riner shared the room, reading on the couch. Coral was supposed to stop by later as well. Today would be one of her last ones at the orphanage. She was moving on to work as a lady's maid in the next few days.

Cinder hadn't forgotten the promise he'd given Coral. He'd look after Riner when she left.

An hour passed, Cinder and Riner reading in silence, neither of them breaking the quiet.

"I knew I'd find you both here," a familiar voice spoke from the doorway. Cinder glanced up. Coral stood highlighted in the doorway by a beam of sunlight. She'd let her hair out of its ponytail, and it softly framed her features. Cinder inhaled sharply in appreciation, hoping she didn't notice. She looked ethereal standing in the light. A warm smile lit her features. He'd never noticed the dimples crinkling her cheeks.

"It doesn't take much to guess where I'd be," Riner said, moving to rise. Cinder quickly followed his lead. "I'm always here on my days off."

Coral nodded. "Of course, but how about him?" She indicated Cinder. "I knew I'd find him here, too. I say that's impressive reasoning on my part."

Cinder tilted his head in question. "Why? You know I like to read."

Coral chuckled. "Of course you do. You're like Riner. You're always wanting to know as much as you can about the world."

Cinder grinned. "When I don't know all the things everyone else takes for granted, it's rather important."

"Rather important," Coral teased. "My goodness, you like using expensive words when cheap ones will do."

Cinder laughed. "Or maybe *ghrinas* simply don't know words with more than two syllables."

Coral's amusement dimmed. "What's a *ghrina*?"

Cinder found himself frowning in confusion. He didn't know. What *was* a *ghrina*? Was it a word peculiar to Swallow? An image blossomed in his mind. *A woman, blonde hair curtaining features Cinder knew would be lovely. He had seen her before, and she whispered a word in a laughing tone. "Priya."*

"Cinder?" Riner was saying.

Cinder blinked, and the vision popped like a soap bubble. Only a bare residue was left to remind him what he'd seen. Who was the woman?

"Cinder," Riner repeated. "Are you all right?"

The image of the woman disappeared, and he couldn't recall the slightest essence of it. "What?" he asked, still distracted.

"I asked if you were all right. You went . . ." Riner waved a hand ". . . somewhere else."

Cinder's thoughts refocused, and he smiled. "I'm fine. I was just confused by what I'd said."

"You mean about *ghrinas*?" Coral asked.

Cinder nodded, continuing to smile. "I have no idea what it means."

"You don't have no idea of nothing," spoke a voice from directly behind Coral.

She started, an expression of alarm on her face. She spun about and took several quick steps deeper into the room. Four people, the Errows, followed her into the study, fanning out.

Cinder moved in front of Coral. "What do you want?"

"We were coming in for some learning," Jarde said. "You don't mind sharing the books with me and me Errogs, do you?"

Fone had moved to flank Cinder to the left while Jam flanked him on the right. Stard drifted until he stood at their backs, directly behind Riner. Coral's brother had gone pale and trembled.

The Errows threatened violence. Cinder recognized the danger he, Coral, and Riner were in, but fear didn't touch him. Neither did indifference. He knew enough to worry, and that was enough. His heart tripped faster, and his eyes flicked right and left, pretending concern at keeping Jam and Fone in his view. In reality, he was scanning for anything he could use as a weapon. A pen would do. Could he grab a sword? It wouldn't have an edge, not this long without sharpening, but even as a club, it would do.

Better, though, if he didn't have to fight at all. "It's all yours," Cinder said to the Errows. "We were just leaving."

Jarde blocked the exit. "Stay. You don't have to leave on our account." He grinned, nasty and brutish. "We'll entertain one another."

Cinder shrugged, working for a nonchalant pose. "I appreciate the offer, but as I said, we were just leaving. The room is yours."

Jarde's smile fell away. "What? We not good enough for you?" His features and eyes hardened. "We smell bad?" His focus shifted to the other Errows. "Which of you boys didn't shower today?"

The other Errows laughed, their voices low and menacing. They eased forward, tightening the circle.

Cinder sighed. He let his shoulders relax, rolling any stiffness out of them. *So be it.* "Master Choff is going to be furious if we make a mess in his study," he said, trying one last time to get the Errows to see reason.

"You'd do best not to worry none about his feelings," Jarde said. "You best worry about yourself."

"Yeah," Stard added. "The only mess in here is going to be you and the coward."

"And the girl," Jarde said. He addressed Coral. "I didn't forget what you called us. Errogs, you said." He cracked his knuckles. "I don't care none if it's a pretty girl who says it. You speak that word, and you get a beating."

"What you boys doing in here?"

Cinder breathed out in relief. Now it was Cook Nestle who stood in the doorway. The Errows started and shared guilty expressions.

"You have tasks to get to," Cook Nestle said. "You best see to them. Master Choff didn't give you leave to waste time in his study."

"We were just having a talk with our friends," Jarde said, his voice oily.

"I'm sure you were," Cook Nestle said, her tone flat and unamused.

"Now get on to your work. Your Errow patrons don't pay for you to be lazy."

Jarde bowed mockingly to Cook Nestle. "Yes, mistress." He gave a sharp jerk with his head. "Come on, boys. Best leave before the mistress here gets a wrong notion about us."

Cook Nestle didn't move as he tried to exit. She eyed him in antipathy. "You realize who does your cooking, right? You realize what I might get a notion to put in your stew?" Her gaze wandered to Riner. "Or who else might get a similarly bad notion?"

Jarde stiffened in startled realization.

"That's right." Cook Nestle snorted in derision. "Now he starts to use that useless lump of a head for some thinking."

Jarde shot Cinder and Riner an angry glare, a promise that this wasn't over, but for now, he departed the study without another word. The other Errows followed silently in his wake.

7

A week after the run-in with the Errows, Coral left the orphanage, assuming her position as a lady's maid. It had been a sad leave-taking, and Riner had been broken-hearted for days after. Cinder missed Coral, too. Her generosity, wit, and intelligence. Plus, she was beautiful.

On an evening several days after her departure, Cinder worked alongside Riner, the two of them alone in the kitchen. They cleaned the last of the dishes and plates after supper. Cook Nestle generally left once the food was served since she had her own family to see to. By the time Cinder and Riner got to the washing up, the sun had long since set. The days were growing shorter. True autumn had arrived and winter's chill breath would soon close in. A hard frost had already patched the ground that morning.

Cinder shuddered. He hated the cold, something he intuitively knew about himself without realizing the how or why.

Thankfully, while the *diptha* globes illuminating the kitchen provided no warmth, the room remained comfortable, retaining the heat from earlier when the oven had been used to cook the meat pies served at supper. A few murmurs and creaks came from upstairs every now and then, but otherwise the orphanage was quiet.

"Do you want to learn to fight?" Cinder asked.

Riner didn't glance up from where he dried the dishes. "Who would teach me? You? Do you know how to fight?"

Cinder thought about the question and realized he didn't know the answer. He'd made the offer to Riner without thinking it through. Could he actually fight? He wasn't sure, but maybe? Sure, he'd handled himself well enough against Jarde and the other Errows during the rumble at breakfast a few months ago, but he'd been armed and they hadn't. And while it had only been a heavy, metal spatula against the four thugs, a weapon was still a weapon.

"I don't know," Cinder finally answered. "I think I can." A moment later his voice firmed. "I'm sure of it." Once more he didn't know where the confidence came from, but as had other convictions on prior occasions, it felt right. He'd explored the topic as best he could, during those other times scratching at the obstinate blank wall indicating where his memories and life began. He wanted to know what lay on the other side, but so far he'd achieved and learned nothing.

"I'm not much of a fighter," Riner said. His shoulders hunched. "My father tried to teach me, but . . ." He swallowed heavily, appearing on the verge of tears, and Cinder turned aside, using the pretense of putting away some dishes until the other boy could regain his composure. Several seconds later, Riner spoke again. "He said I wasn't any good. He didn't think I ever would be."

"Well, that's where he's wrong," Cinder said.

Riner faced him with a startled expression, like a rabbit seeing a fox guarding a field of carrots, a bounty directly past a terrifying danger. "What do you mean?"

"I mean your father wanted you to enroll in the Third Directorate." He made a note to ask someone what that was. "You may lack the abilities to make it there, but it doesn't mean you can't learn to fight. You can always learn, and when we're done, you'll be plenty good at defending yourself against people like Jarde. That's all you're ever likely to need, right?"

Riner nodded, still uncertain. "I guess so?" he said in his soft-spoken, too often hesitant, manner. "But when could you teach me? We work all day, and there's no time at night."

"What about our time off?" Cinder asked. "Once a week we can spend a few hours sparring."

"Will that be enough?"

Cinder wasn't sure. "It'll be slow learning," he allowed. "But then again, it takes a while to read all the books in a library. I'm guessing the only way to get it done is to start. What do you say?"

"I think . . . I'm not sure." Riner seemed lost in thought as he put away the last of the plates. Cinder waited on him, remaining quiet until the younger boy appeared to reach a decision. Riner slowly turned around. "Yes. I'd like that." He smiled, a wide grin of happiness and hope, a rare expression on his normally somber demeanor.

Cinder made another mental note. He needed to find a way to get Riner to smile more, to have greater joy in his life, especially since his sister had moved on from the orphanage now. He spoke to Riner. "We'll start next Aden, the first day next week, when we're free."

Riner smiled wider.

Early in the afternoon of the next Aden, Cinder and Riner went to a square sward of grass near the orphanage. Many such fields existed throughout Swift Sword, a green space to break up the clutter of chimneyed buildings belching smoke, the wagons clattering along macadam roads, and the clangor of industry meant to maintain the city.

Many squares had grand titles and a grand history, named in honor of the heroes of Rakesh, but not this one. It was an untended sward in a poor and remote district of the city. A cluster of low-lying buildings, many separated by alleys, curled around the square, and evergreens—cedar, spruce, and fir—broke up the expanse of grass. The trees provided shade in the city's mild summer, but with the seasons having bent toward fall, an early lacing of snow decorated their boughs.

A wind sighed then, stealing Cinder's misting breath, and he cursed.

He'd bundled up with an extra layer of clothing and donned a thick coat, but the chill still managed to nip at him, icing his hands and face. He hated the cold, reckoning that whoever he had been before he lost his memory, that person surely must have been made for warmer weather than what was found in Rakesh. It also didn't help that Riner and the few other folk present in this less populated part of the city wore nothing more than long-sleeved shirts and light jackets. Nevertheless, they seemed perfectly comfortable.

Riner all but bounced over to an unoccupied place in the square, an area separated from the few merchants who had stalls along the sward's perimeter. They sold flour, dried meat, and other sundries.

"Is this a good place?" Riner asked.

Cinder cast his eyes about the area the boy had chosen. The ground was level. There were no trees to obstruct their movements, and no one else was nearby. "It's perfect."

Riner literally danced in delight. "What do we do first?"

Cinder grinned at the boy's barely contained excitement. "We stretch," he said. "Follow my lead." He had Riner bend over and touch his toes.

Well . . . at least Riner bent over. His protruding belly prevented the toe-touching part. Next they sat on the ground, legs pressed together and straight before them. They leaned forward, again touching their toes, Riner trying more than succeeding. More stretching: their necks, shoulders, arms, hips . . . All their muscles.

Riner's breath puffed in the cool autumn air. "Is this the exercising part?"

Cinder held in a chuckle. "Not yet. We're still stretching."

Riner's face fell. "Oh."

"Well, look what we have here," an unwanted voice mocked. Jarde, and with him were his sycophants, Stard, Jam, and Fone.

Cinder noticed all four had roughly carved cudgels. His eyes narrowed, and he immediately rose to his feet, stepping between the Errows and Riner. "What do you want?"

Jarde tapped his cudgel into his hand, a nasty grin plastered on his face. "What do we want?" He glanced back at his fellows, sharing a menacing laugh. "The boy wants to know what we want. What do you say, Stard? What do *you* want?"

Stard appeared eager, leaning forward, eyes wide and bright. He licked his lips. "I want to see his blood."

Cinder's heart pounded. He glanced about, searching for a weapon. A stick, a rock, anything. His eyes darted about, but he came up empty. *Shit.* There was nothing he could use.

He pushed aside his disappointment, focusing on the now. Fear didn't touch him. *The Errows want a fight? Fine. I'll give them a fight. All they can handle and then some.* Cinder took deep breaths, readying himself.

"Jam," Stard barked. "What do you want?"

Jam smiled, an evil expression on such a young face. "Blood's good. That and the coward squealing."

"The coward's blood, too," Fone added. "And broken bones."

Jarde turned about. "See, that's not too much to ask, is it? We'll just beat your asses bloody and break some bones."

Knowledge surfaced from the depths of Cinder's mind, a piece of advice he couldn't recall learning. *When no choices are left, the wise warrior does the unexpected. He attacks.*

Jarde continued. "Maybe then you'll learn not to fuck with—"

Cinder was on him, arms going around the bully's waist. He strained to lift Jarde in the air, but his spindly arms were too weak to complete the maneuver, which would have ended in a body-slam. He had to release the hold, choosing to lace his hands around Jarde's head, bending it low, and ramming his knee into the Errow's face. Once, twice, three times. Jarde collapsed.

"You bastard!"

Cinder didn't know who shouted. He saw a blur in the periphery of his vision. Cinder tucked his head. He was too slow. He took a blow to his shoulder. Pain bloomed. He rolled away from another strike, tumbling upon and across Jarde. He landed on his hands and knees.

A cudgel clubbed him between his shoulder-blades and he sagged. A kick to the midsection lifted him off the ground, and he tried to roll away. Thoughts became incoherent, but he knew he couldn't stay prone like this.

"Hold him up," Jarde snarled, nose dripping blood. He'd gotten back to his feet, and while he swayed a bit, he held his cudgel tightly. "I'm going to work him over good."

Stard yanked Cinder to his feet and placed him in a rear headlock. The Errow didn't have it tight enough. Cinder worked on instinct. He rammed an elbow into the other boy's midsection. Stard spat an oath, but he didn't let go. He merely shifted to avoid another attack.

An instant later he cursed anew. *Riner.* He was attacking Stard.

"Get that fat fucker off me!" Stard shouted.

Riner cried out when Jarde struck him hard in the back. A follow-up blow, and Riner fell over, poleaxed.

Stard retained his grip, and Cinder knew he only had seconds to free himself. He tugged against the other boy's hold.

"Damn, he's a slippery mother," Stard said. "Someone help me—ah!"

He shrieked when Cinder snapped his head back, hammering it into Stard's nose. A welcome crunch accompanied the blow. Blood sprayed, splashing on the back of Cinder's neck.

Stard's hands went to his broken nose and he dropped his cudgel. Cinder ducked low and grabbed it. Time slowed. He sensed a strike coming at his head. He rolled away. He rolled again and found himself at Fone's feet. He slammed his cudgel against one of the younger boy's ankles. Fone howled, hopping around in pain.

He sensed another attack coming, once more from behind. Cinder tried to evade. A hard thud to his forearm caused his fingers to go numb. Another blow struck his jaw. Pain exploded. His upper lip split. His vision blurred and he nearly dropped his cudgel. He spat blood.

"Herd him to me," Jarde shouted.

Don't drop the cudgel, was Cinder's only thought.

Another incoming attack. Instinct saved him again. Cinder deflected the strike with his cudgel. He deflected another blow and stumbled away, seeking distance. He parried another strike, sensing it rather than seeing it. He swung wildly, trying to clear the space about him.

Jam cursed.

Cinder's vision steadied and he saw the younger boy in front of him, arm cocked. Jarde was rushing forward.

Cinder blocked a fourth blow from Jam. The younger boy overbalanced. Cinder punched his cudgel into Jam's stomach. The young bully grunted, breath blasting out with a whoosh. A flying knee to the forehead put Jam on the ground, moaning and unable to rise.

Jarde slid to a halt, his face pale. He viewed Cinder in alarm. "Wait a second now. Hold on. You bested us. There ain't no call for no more fighting. You learned us. We're done."

Cinder didn't listen. Bullies couldn't be reasoned with, not until they were broken. And he'd break this bully. He advanced on Jarde, who threw his cudgel at Cinder and missed.

Stupid to throw away his weapon.

Cinder launched a backswing with his cudgel, aiming it at the other boy's thigh. Jarde twisted and tried to hunch low. He ended up taking the blow on his hip. A cudgel-fired uppercut cracked Jarde in the armpit and he fell to the ground, crying out.

Cinder followed him down, wrapping his legs around the other boy's abdomen. He stared at his fallen foe, calculating whether to offer him mercy. His eyes went to Riner, who was only now stumbling to his feet. He moaned once before promptly falling over. Cinder looked to Stard and the two younger Errows. They remained out of the fight, moaning in pain.

And Jarde, the one who'd inspired them, he'd barely taken any damage. He hadn't yet learned his lesson.

Cinder's heart hardened. His decision made, he clinically hammered one elbow after another into the bully's face. The Errow tried to defend, blocking with his hands. Cinder worked around their interference, smashing Jarde's mouth, fattening his lips, and opening deep lacerations on both cheeks. A final blow blasted into the bully's forehead, and Jarde's arms went limp. His eyes rolled upward.

Cinder let off and climbed to his feet. He stared at a groaning Jarde, pity for the beaten bully arguing with the fury at what he'd been forced to do. He hadn't wanted to hurt the Errows. *All men should be as brothers.* A drifting idea floated through his mind.

Riner groaned, limping to his side. "What do we do now?"

"We go home," Cinder said. He addressed Jarde. "You ever come after me or Riner again, I'll break your arms and snap your legs. Nod if you understand."

Jarde managed a single head bob, and Cinder left him lying on the ground.

He and Riner hobbled on their way, but the pain started to overcome him. His shoulder and arm throbbed, a soreness like . . . well, like they'd been hammered by a cudgel. His balance also felt iffy, and several teeth were loose in their sockets. He spat out more blood, wondering if he'd broken his jaw. He worked it around. It hurt plenty, but he didn't think so.

He and Riner staggered away from the Errows, pausing at the edge of the green sward when they were halted by traffic from one of the roads abutting the square.

A passing guardsman, gray-haired and with a thick middle, hailed them. "You the two louts been causing the ruckus I heard about?"

Cinder shook his head. "No, sir." He pointed to the Errows several yards away, who were slowly tottering to their feet. "It was those four. We were just on our way home."

"Where's home?"

"*Our Lady of the Fire.*"

"The orphanage run by Choff?"

Cinder nodded.

The guardsman eyed him in suspicion. "And what? On the way back you bashed your faces into a couple of cudgels?"

Cinder managed a grin. Sometimes a smile smoothed over rough feelings. "Would you believe we were climbing a tree and fell? We must have hit every branch on the way down."

The guardsman shook his head, unamused and disgusted. "Boy. I ain't blind. I saw some of what happened. I was standing right here. Get on home. I might have some more questions later on if those four have something different to say about the why of your brawl."

"Yes, sir," Cinder replied.

The line of orphans quickly noticed Cinder's and Riner's presence when the two of them joined the others for supper. It was later in the day following the scuffle against the Errows. The injuries they sported inspired wide eyes, pointing fingers, and wild gasps of speculation. Voices murmured excitedly and whispers carried past hands cupped around mouths.

Cinder straightened, doing his best to ignore their rumormongering. He hid a wince as a throbbing pain lanced through his shoulder and down his arm. It was the least of his injuries. His mouth hurt the worst, lips swollen from when Jam had hit him with his cudgel. Meanwhile, Riner slouched low, hunching his shoulders and ducking his head.

Master Choff arrived then. He took one look at their appearances and a forbidding frown took hold of his features. His arms crossed, reflecting his displeasure. "Do I need to set up a sparring square?"

The pain and inflammation from Cinder's mouth made it hard for him to speak, but he managed to answer. "No, sir."

More excited whispers and titters occurred when Jarde, Stard, Jam, and Fone shambled into the kitchen. They looked even more battered than Cinder and Riner.

Cook Nestle viewed them all with a solemn shake of her head and a clear expression of concern.

"What happened to you lot?" Master Choff asked Jarde and the Errows. He waited expectantly for an answer while the line of orphans paused in their whispered conjectures, listening in on the conversation.

Cinder glanced at Jarde and his Errows in challenge, but they wouldn't meet his eyes. They kept their gazes firmly fixed on the ground, clearly miserable and in pain.

"You're sure we don't need a sparring square?" Master Choff asked when no one spoke up.

"No, Master Choff," Cinder said, maintaining his challenging gaze at Jarde. "I think I taught those who needed instruction everything they needed to learn. It's finished."

Master Choff addressed Jarde. "That true? You got your schooling?"

"Yes, sir," Jarde said, his voice a whisper. "We learned our lessons."

"Good," Master Choff said with a nod. "Then the matter is settled." He faced Cinder. "See me after you eat."

"Yes, sir."

Supper turned out to be a hearty potato soup with a chunk of meat for each orphan, along with a hunk of hard bread. Cinder sat on a bench taking his meal, bracketed between Riner and a younger boy who kept eyeing him in awe. Afterward, Cinder limped up the stairs to the top floor, where Master Choff had his rooms. He knocked, entering after a voice from within ordered him inside.

Master Choff faced the door, seated behind a desk. A pair of *diptha* globes in the far corners provided a dim light. They illuminated a map of the world hanging next to the room's only window. Dark paneling lined the walls, and a few bookshelves held Master Choff's private collection of biographies and history.

"You wanted to see me, sir?" Cinder asked.

"Close the door."

Cinder did so.

"I was visited this afternoon by an acquaintance of mine. We served in the army together. Got out the same time. He said he saw six boys brawling in the square nearby. He described them, and he also said what happened. You want to speak up on what he might have told me?"

"I'd say he saw four boys approach two others with cudgels in hand and ill intentions on their faces."

Master Choff smiled fleetingly. "He didn't put it in such flowery terms, but that's about the gist of it. He also said that one of the boys, a scrawny shit, put the others down even though he was unarmed. Kicked their asses proper. But once he had the leader down, he worked him over, but not too much. Showed an admirable restraint given what those other four might have done if the roles were reversed. Controlled. My friend was impressed, and that don't come easy."

Cinder didn't know what to say. It sounded like Master Choff was applauding his actions. "So, I'm not going to be punished for defending myself? For defending Riner?"

"I don't reckon you need punishing," Master Choff said. "I got something worse in store for you. My friend is planning on speaking to someone else we know, Master Lerid, a master of the fighting arts. My friend plans on recommending you to him, have you test for the Lerid's school. See if you have what it takes to become a true warrior. Maybe even make it into the Third Directorate, if you're good enough."

Of all the things Cinder had expected to hear, a chance to become a warrior had been far down the list. Until now, all he'd cared about was figuring out who he was, his place in Swift Sword and Rakesh. That, and learn the world's lore and history.

Now, with this unexpected opportunity, excitement lofted his spirits as high as a soaring eagle. *A warrior.* He smiled, his pain momentarily forgotten. A true warrior meant he'd have a chance to join Rakesh's army, a high honor. And the Third Directorate . . . He'd read about it. Only the best of the best went there, trained by elven warriors who knew all that could be known of the sword or any weapon. Some of the instructors there were ancient masters, possessing hundreds of years of life and experience.

Cinder inhaled deeply, hope swelling. "When do I meet Master Lerid?"

"Tomorrow." Master Choff barked laughter. "But don't get your hopes up. As slim-pickings as you are, you've got a donkey's chance against a dragon to impress Master Lerid. As for the Maker's Tournament, that's a mountain too high for any orphan to scale. You'd be going against those who've spent years training for a chance to get into the Third Directorate."

Cinder understood the steep odds he faced. Maybe he couldn't win this Maker's Tournament. Maybe he was scrawny and weak, like Master Choff said. Slow, too. But that didn't mean he'd always be this way. Training and hard work could carry a person far in life, especially when married to deep desire. And Cinder deeply desired the chance to become a warrior.

He'd never known of this passion until this moment, but now that he heard the call of the sword, he couldn't shut it out. It spoke to him, a crystalline certainty in the depths of his heart and the marrow of his bones.

8

The morning after his fight with the bullies found Cinder standing in front of an unfamiliar building. He checked the slip of paper in his hands. On it, Master Choff had written the address to *Steel-Graced Adepts*, the school where Master Lerid trained his handpicked students. He glanced again at the paper, and then at the building, checking it one last time. He nodded to himself. This looked to be the place. The sign above the lintel had a warrior contorted in some fantastical position, sword in hand.

As for the building, it was a white-washed, brick structure, two-stories tall with a peaked roof tiled in terra cotta. Blacked-out windows faced a quiet street, and on the other side of the road was one of Swift Sword's many grassy squares. From the forge next door came the ringing of a hammer on steel while on the side opposite wafted the smell of fresh bread from a bakery. Cinder's belly rumbled although he'd eaten breakfast only an hour ago.

He checked a nearby clock-tower and breathed out in relief when he saw he wasn't late. Cinder had left the orphanage early, and it was a good thing he had. The two-mile journey to the school, a distance normally covered in thirty minutes, had taken him forty. It was his left hip and knee. He'd twisted his leg during the brawl against Jarde and the rest of the Errows, and those injuries vied with his shoulder for what hindered him the most.

He checked the clock again, noting he had a few more minutes before his appointed meeting. Curiosity beckoned, and he glanced up and down the street.

He was in a wealthier part of Swift Sword, one closer to the bay, and the distant cry of gulls carried on the wind. He saw the mast of a ship in the harbor peeking above the rooftops. He also noted the folk already out: a farmer riding a wagon laden with vegetables; a trio of workers, young men—brothers, maybe—tired in appearance and wearing rough clothing and old boots. Heading in the opposite direction sauntered a wealthy couple dressed in fine linens, smiling and whispering to one another.

And on the other side of the street, Cinder saw her. An elven woman. His attention lit on her like a raptor's. He'd never seen an elf before, had only heard stories of them, and he couldn't help but stare. She was tall and strongly built but still possessing feminine lines. The tips of her pointed ears were barely visible through the richness of her honey-blonde hair. She was also armed, a sword on her hip and a cased bow and arrows on her back.

The elf glided away from Cinder, her back to him, but something caused her to pause, and she glanced over her shoulder in his direction. Cinder's heart tightened. She was striking, beautiful with a reddish cast to her skin. Green eyes glinted as she beheld him. Her eyes went to the sign proclaiming the martial academy. She briefly smiled at him, dipping her head in his direction as if acknowledgment before striding off.

Cinder stared after her, fascinated as she walked away. Her cloak swayed with every step she took, languid like a gown. How could someone so martial be so feminine and beautiful? Were all elves so tall? And were all their women also warriors? He watched until she took a corner and was lost to view.

Even then, his thoughts lingered on her, and the drowned thread of lost memory stirred. He kept still, urging it to rise to the surface. *Come on,* he silently urged.

But it didn't, and no matter how hard he tried to bring it to light, it remained hidden.

He grunted in annoyance. His recollections and questions were apparently meant for another time. Right now he had testing to complete with Master Lerid, and it wouldn't do to make him wait. Cinder took a final moment to straighten his clothes. He inhaled a settling breath and rapped on the door.

Seconds passed.

A lean man, gray hair in a neat bowl-cut, answered the door. He had the same bearing as the elven woman, that of a warrior. More impressions. Dark clothing—a hemp shirt and trousers—and sturdy half-boots that looked comfortable.

"Can I help you?" the man asked.

"My name is Cinder Shade. I was sent by Master Choff to see Master Lerid of *Steel-Graced Adepts.*"

The man's eyebrows climbed. "You were the one sent? You're injured. You can barely stand. How will you possibly demonstrate any skills?" He appeared annoyed.

Cinder didn't let the man's agitation upset him. "You are Master Lerid?"

"I am."

"I'm not at my fittest, it's true, but a warrior will oftentimes have to fight in spite of being injured."

"What do you know of being a warrior?"

Cinder quirked a grin. "Very little, but I hope to learn much more. Will you test me?"

Master Lerid smiled. "You're a bold one. I like that. Come in."

Cinder followed Master Lerid into a large, empty room. A pair of *diptha* globes lit the space, banishing all shadows. A heavy mat, black and made of a soft material, padded the floor, and paneling of white wood covered the walls, including the blacked-out windows.

"The other students are in the back, stretching," Master Lerid explained. "I was waiting closer at hand for your arrival. We'll test you here. But before I do, tell me about yourself."

Cinder paused. It was a broad question, and he wasn't sure how to answer. "What do you wish to know?"

"Start with where you're from."

"I'm from the north, a village called Swallow," Cinder answered. "I don't know much more about my personal history beyond that."

Master Lerid continued to wear a querying expression.

"Did Master Choff mention my amnesia?"

"He did not."

Cinder mentally sighed. He was tired of discussing what had happened to him, but it seemed he would have to do so once again. However, some information, he kept to himself, such as the information about his healed clubfoot and withered right leg.

"Interesting," Master Lerid said after he finished. "And you've never held a sword?"

"Not that I know of."

"What happened with those bullies? I heard some of the story, but I want to hear your version."

Again, Cinder explained his role in yesterday's brawl.

"Interesting," Master Lerid repeated. "Why didn't you hurt Jarde worse? You could have made it so he could never hurt you again."

"Because . . ." Cinder tried to answer, but his voice drifted into silence. Why hadn't he hurt Jarde more? He could have, but would it have been right? He didn't think so. Jarde's actions hadn't been so awful as to require a potentially lethal response. "Because hurting him further would have been disproportionate. It would have been wrong. More importantly, I believe all of us deserve a second chance, even bullies." Once more, Cinder was struck by the rightness of his words. They felt like a proper description to how he wanted to see the world.

All men should be brothers. A floating idea he recognized as a truth.

"Interesting." Master Lerid apparently liked the word.

The swordmaster smiled again, a warm expression somehow more fitting to his features than his prior frown. "You showed an admirable restraint, even if others might label it simplistic or naive." He clapped his hands, apparently ending any further discussion. "If you're ready, I'll be the one to test you. We'll do light sparring only. No weapons, since you've never had training with one. We'll see how well you are at unarmed combat."

Cinder did some quick stretching, thankful the walk to *Steel-Graced* had already done a good job of working out some of the stiffness in his hip and shoulder. He took his stance, knees bent, arms up, hands fisted.

"Shall we begin?" Master Lerid asked.

"Yes, sir."

Without preamble, Master Lerid shot a punch. The man was fast. Cinder's surprise nearly cost him a blow to the face. Thankfully, muscle memory or instincts took over, and at the last instant he ducked and slid to the left. Master Lerid didn't chase him. Cinder took the brief reprieve to study his opponent.

Master Lerid had both reach and strength on him. Which meant Cinder had to stay out of range and pick his moments on when to engage.

Again, Master Lerid shot a punch. This time something in his stance gave away his intentions. *A feint.* Cinder didn't bite on it. He shifted and leaned away to the right before the expected side kick connected with his abdomen. Cinder circled his opponent, who shifted slowly, keeping in front of him.

Master Lerid snapped off a one-two, a straight right and left, ending with a front kick. Cinder twisted at the torso, taking the punches on his shoulders. He grunted when one of Master Lerid's blows landed against his injured arm. The front kick he smoothly evaded. He pulled back, wanting distance from the larger man's reach.

Master Lerid stalked him. Four punches this time—a jab, a right and left cross, and a right hook—all of them faster than before.

Cinder saw the blows coming, but he didn't know how to evade them. He desperately backpedaled. Another jab from Master Lerid. Cinder barely got his face out of the way, darting to the side.

Master Lerid halted his pursuit, a disappointed expression on his face. "Running isn't what we teach. At some point a warrior has to engage." His words spoken, he pressed forward, cutting off Cinder's escape, trapping him along the wall.

Cinder's mind went blank with confusion, and he worked off simple instinct. He threw a right cross. It missed. He sent a left uppercut. Master Lerid leaned away from it. Cinder ended his flurry with a side kick, one Master Lerid easily checked.

None of his punches had landed, but Cinder didn't care. They did what he'd wanted, which was to give him a chance to push away from the wall.

"Somewhat better," Master Lerid said, not coming after him immediately.

Anger flared at the master's half-hearted compliment. Cinder saw an opening then, and he darted forward, throwing a right jab.

Too late. A ruse!

Master Lerid slipped the jab and fired an overhand left. It clipped Cinder in the temple and stars sparkled in his vision. He stumbled away.

"But you're slow," Master Lerid said.

On they sparred. Cinder did his best to defend, bobbing, weaving, and slipping. The fight went on. He took a few more punches on his arms and thighs. Several to the face, also. He was soon every bit as sore as he had been yesterday and imagined this was what it must feel like to be a lump of meat pounded flat.

Master Lerid finally called a halt to their sparring, and Cinder's arms immediately fell to his side. He couldn't lift them anymore. Sweat covered his face and torso. He gulped deep breaths of air, and his heart pounded. By strength of will alone, he prevented himself from sagging, remaining upright.

"You did well," Master Lerid said. He circled around Cinder, studying him as a farmer might a horse he was considering purchasing. "Better than I expected for someone so scrawny and slow. Good form early on. Not so good when you're tired."

The words were mostly kind but could also be interpreted as somewhat mocking. Cinder locked himself in place, keeping his head held high. He wouldn't show weakness in front of the master, not even now.

Master Lerid nodded. "You also have heart. Heart you can't teach." He stopped his circling, standing directly in front of Cinder. "You'll do. I'll let Master Choff know."

Cinder didn't dare hope. Not yet. "Does this mean you'll train me?"

"Yes."

Cinder wanted to shout for joy, but he figured it might be too boisterous a display. He settled for a happy grin. "Thank you, Master."

"A few more items," Master Lerid said. "You'll have to leave the orphanage. You'll no longer be available to earn your keep there."

Cinder's elation faltered. "If I can't stay at the orphanage, then where will I live?"

"Here. You can clean and cook as required. It'll save me from having to hire a servant."

"Yes, sir." A thought came to Cinder then, and he frowned in unease. *What about Riner?* Without Cinder around, would the bullies harass the boy again? It seemed likely.

"Something troubles you?" Master Lerid asked.

"Yes, but it isn't your concern, Master. I'll attend to it myself."

"Will it impact your ability to train?"

"No, sir."

Master Lerid gave a sharp nod. "Then I'll see you tomorrow. You have the day to complete your affairs at Master Choff's."

"I'll need three weeks," Cinder blurted.

Master Lerid's eyebrows rose. "Three weeks? Why so long?"

Cinder thought quickly. "I'll need that much time to heal. I'll be no good to you until then." It would also give him time to figure out what to do with Riner.

Master Lerid scrutinized him through narrowed eyes. He shrugged a moment later. "Three weeks then."

It turned out Cinder didn't have to worry about Riner's future. Several days after the fight against the Errows, Jarde and Stard were claimed by a powerful clan from their tribe. They were then promptly inducted into Rakesh's army and were gone and forgotten from *Our Lady of Fire* inside of a week.

Cinder thought it a near miraculous ending to Riner's troubles and he said so to Coral, who came to visit one evening after supper. During the day she worked as a maid to Lady Wenthern, the wife of a retired general.

Lady Wenthern wasn't actually nobility, but her title was one given to the spouses of those selected for lifetime appointments to Rakesh's legislative branch. Half of those positions went to retired army officers while the other half were chosen by wealthy members of the mercantile class. However, the true power in Rakesh's government lay with the judiciary, which was entirely composed of shrewds. They were members of the priestly caste, expected to serve as the nation's holy justices and judges. *Shrewds.* They were the ones who decided which edicts passed by the legislature were acceptable, and the chief and most holy justice—known by the common folk as the chief justice—also served as the head of state and had full veto power over the legislature.

Cinder thought Rakesh's system of government didn't rightly reflect the will of the population, but at least it wasn't something idiotic like a monarchy. In this the nation had modeled itself after Gandharva, and together they were the only two human-dominated political unions that didn't have a king or a queen or similar autocratic form of government.

As for Coral, she had previously visited *Our Lady of Fire* on multiple occasions, and during those other calls she had explained her work situation. It didn't sound too bad. Coral only had to serve as a maid eight days out of the ten in a typical week, and during the other two, she was free, including on most evenings. She spent them apprenticing with a musician, where she took voice lessons. Her master believed she could make a profession from song. Coral was pretty enough to capture an audience's interest and had the requisite lovely voice to keep their attention.

Other times, such as now, she chose to visit Riner.

Her brother was currently helping with the dishes while Cinder swept and cleaned the dining hall, a task required after every meal. Orphans were a messy lot.

Cinder wasn't sure why Coral had decided to wait with him instead of with Riner, who was finishing in the kitchen. Maybe it was because she didn't want to get in her brother's way.

"It wasn't a miracle that sent Jarde and Stard away," Coral said in response to Cinder's comment.

"What was it then?" Cinder asked, using a broom to sweep the crumbs and debris littering the floor into a more manageable pile.

"It's because when the Errows settled in Rakesh, one of the requirements expected of them was an agreement to supply the army with a certain number of soldiers."

Cinder quickly figured out the rest on his own. "And because the leaders of the tribe don't want to send their own children, they volunteered Jarde and Stard?"

"Exactly." Coral lifted her legs out of the way when Cinder went to sweep underneath the bench on which she sat. Her ankle-length dress swished, revealing a flash of her calves.

In a modest society like Rakesh, the exposure of any part of a woman's legs above the ankle was considered indecorous. Instead of embarrassing Coral by pointing it out, Cinder simply kept on sweeping, pretending not to notice. "A sad result for Jarde and Stard, but a good one for Riner."

"A *very* good one for Riner, especially since you're leaving."

Cinder paused his sweeping and glanced at Coral. "When I was gifted the opportunity at *Steel-Graced Adepts*, Riner's situation had me worried. I didn't know what would happen to him when I left. I'm glad it worked out for him the way it did."

"Which is also part of the reason I'm here tonight." Coral rose to her feet. "I wanted to thank you personally before you left the orphanage."

"You don't have to thank me. I simply did what was needed. It's like what Riner's always saying about Shokan and Sira. We're called to help those in need in whatever way we can."

Coral stepped closer, into his personal space. Cinder held himself still. While her closeness made him uncomfortable, as when he'd seen her calves, moving away might cause her unnecessary embarrassment. Besides, he liked standing near her. A strange notion came over him, a desire to hum a tune.

Coral tilted her head up to meet his gaze. Her dark eyes appeared depthless. She was beautiful, and Cinder's heart beat faster. "You still have my gratitude," she said. "You always will."

Cinder had to work moisture into a mouth suddenly gone dry. "Thank you. I appreciate it, but—"

Coral placed a finger against his lips. "There are no 'buts'. You're the one who protected Riner, which means you're a good man, Cinder Shade."

"And you're a lovely woman, Coral Strain." Cinder mentally gaped, horrified by what he'd just said. A lovely woman? Where had that come from? He tried to recover. "I'll be sure to check up on Riner when I have time."

Coral offered him a slow smile. "Maybe I'll check up on you, too." She squeezed his arm before stepping past, her shoulder brushing against his as she entered the kitchen.

Today was Cinder's last day at *Our Lady of Fire*, and it also happened to fall on his time off. Riner wasn't so lucky. He had to work in the kitchen, and as a result Cinder had a day free of obligations but no one with whom to share it.

Cinder decided to explore Swift Sword. In the nearly three months since his arrival in the capital he hadn't done much more than occasionally walk back and forth to *Steel-Graced Adepts*, where he'd start formal training in the morning. Otherwise he hadn't seen much of the city. He'd spent most of his free time learning as much as he could about topics everyone else took for granted. The various human and elven cultures, theology, and philosophy.

In addition, he had yet to recover his past memories and at this point, he doubted he ever would. He reckoned his true awareness of himself might always begin on that fateful day nearly four months ago when Pitch had saved him from drowning in a well. *Four months.* A short span in which to measure his supposed sixteen years of living.

At least the world wasn't so confusing any more. Cinder understood what he wanted from it and how to obtain it. He wanted to become a warrior, and the path to reach the destination of his dreams started tomorrow.

Today, though, he planned on seeing the sea. He wanted to stand on the shores of a wide-open expanse of water. He wanted to soak in its restless power, feel the constant breeze, the endless surf that promised a grim reckoning for those who didn't recognize the supremacy of the waves and wind. Seeing and feeling all this would help him remain humble, and for reasons he couldn't put into words he thought a modest decorum was important.

To reach the harbor and the sea, Cinder took a well-traveled road. It passed close by *Our Lady of Fire*, and he shared it with a plethora of people. Merchants on their wagons, pedestrians carrying out their various tasks, and rickshaws transporting the wealthy.

Vendors alongside the roadside offered simple snacks such as samosas, pakora, and tikka. The heady scents and aromas contrasted with what Cinder knew of the fare in Rakesh's mountainous interior. There, in places like Swallow, the food tended to be bland with nothing more than salt and herbs to offer flavor. But in Swift Sword, matters were different. Here, under the influence of the Yaksha Sithe—elves apparently liked their food savory—an appreciation of spices had taken hold.

It wasn't a surprise. Rakesh tried to model itself after Gandharva, but it answered to Yaksha Sithe, the powerful empire of elves that surrounded their nation on all sides. In many ways, the elven empress Sala Yaksha was the true titular ruler of the human nation rather than the chief and most holy justice. It was said that whenever the Yaksha Sithe sneezed, Swift Sword developed pneumonia and the rest of Rakesh got a cold.

Cinder couldn't recall the kind of foods he had liked before waking up in the well, but nowadays he liked his food every bit as spicy as what the elves preferred. Too bad he didn't have the money to purchase any of the tempting food from one of the roadside vendors.

He paused when he reached a square. Centered within it was a granite statue, a man holding aloft a sword. He stood upon a large plinth and a plaque proclaimed the sculpture to be a representation of Holy Mede, the World Conqueror. The figure was missing an arm, and his face was a broad smear, all the features worn down to an indistinguishable nub by wind, rain, or vandalism. Maybe all three.

Near the statue's base clustered a number of poor, their clothes ragged and bedraggled. A few had open wounds on their faces or wore heavy wrappings on their arms and legs.

Lepers.

Everyone shied away from them, and Cinder would have as well, but just then, an unexpected sight held him frozen in place, and his eyes widened in shock.

A tree walked toward him. He stared in gape-mouthed amazement, and it took him a moment to understand what he was seeing.

Not a tree. A yakshin, a tree maiden. She stood more than twenty feet tall, covering several yards with every stride. Bark encrusted her limbs. Gray moss resembling hair hung from her head and draped low over her nut-brown eyes. A thick projection extended from the center of her face. Perhaps it served as a nose. If so, Cinder reckoned the thin slit below the growth must be her mouth.

He tried to recall more about what he knew about yakshins. They lived in Shalla Valley, somewhere in the Dagger Mountains, sheltered in an inaccessible rift between a cluster of towering peaks. In it was a forest, one only the most penitent and holy could visit and where a single species of tree grew, the ashoka tree, a hardy evergreen. In its centuries-long life, the ashokas produced only two flowers, a highly-prized white one containing a rich concentration of *aether*, and a red blossom that eventually grew into a yakshin.

Tree maidens were also said to be bearers of good tidings. In Rakesh, a common image upon the lintels of temples and homes was of a yakshin standing upon a fallen tree-trunk with her hands holding aloft the branches of a budding ashoka. Most yakshins remained at Shalla Valley, but a few traveled the world, journeying unmolested while they searched for a forest or tree worthy of their service. No one dared harm one of them. To do so risked the worst of curses. In addition, like elves and dwarves, yakshins were woven, beings created by *aether*. In this case, born of a tree rather than the union of a male and a female.

Although if that were the case, were they truly maidens? Why couldn't they be tree men? For instance, this one wore no clothing and there was nothing to indicate she was female.

Cinder's scrambled thoughts came to a stop when the yakshin spoke to him. "Would you grace me with your name?" Her voice was lilting and undeniably feminine, answering one of Cinder's questions even as she asked one of him.

Cinder tried not to gape again. Of all the things he might have dreamed to see today, a tree maiden wasn't one of them. He had only wanted to view the sea, something prosaic and common. Not meet a yakshin. He had a sense of disbelief while answering her question. "Cinder Shade."

The yakshin tilted her head in thought. "A strange name. It suits you not. Do you have another?"

Cinder shook his head, his disbelief not easing in the slightest. "No. It's the only one I know."

He noticed a small crowd had gathered close by, likely listening in on his conversation with the tree maiden. Yakshins weren't common anywhere, including Swift Sword. They likely attracted attention no matter where they went.

"Your roots stretch deeper than my vision pierces, into mists I cannot penetrate. I wonder what it means." The yakshin tsked. "You are a mysterious one, Cinder Shade."

"I'm sorry," Cinder replied, not sure why he was apologizing. He had no idea what the yakshin was talking about.

The tree maiden smiled. "There is no need. You cannot tell what you do not yourself know."

Cinder's curiosity piqued. Talking to a yakshin was surreal, but he was growing more comfortable with her. She had a kindness, a patience he found disarming. "What don't I know?"

"Your true name," the yakshin said, "and your true past." She smiled, a finger thrusting into the air. "I have it. Your name among my people shall be Maynalor."

Cinder frowned. *Maynalor? What did that mean?*

He asked the yakshin, and she laughed. "Telling would give away the gift of mystery. You must learn the meaning on your own." She bowed low then. "May soft rains grant what you are missing." With that, she strode off, people scrambling to get out of her way.

Cinder noticed those who remained gathered in the square eyeing him in speculation. He didn't like the looks on some of their faces, hungry, predatory, and desirous.

It would be best to return to the safety of the orphanage. On the way back and for the rest of the day, he kept replaying the brief conversation with the yakshin in his mind. He realized only later that he'd never learned her name.

9

The day after his unexpected meeting the yakshin, Cinder arrived at *Steel-Graced Adepts*, excited and happy to get started with his training. However, he first needed to be shown his room by one of the other students.

"Drop your things off here," said Sash Slice. The apprentice-warrior was a year younger than Cinder and resembled a whip: lean, fast, and sinuous in how he moved. Cinder wished he had an ounce of Sash's grace and lethality.

He ignored his envy, though, burying it beneath a desire to work, and glancing around his new home. His room at the school was basically a closet under the stairs, barely large enough to contain a cot, a *diptha* lamp, and a locker smelling of mothballs to store his clothes. Nothing else. Unfinished planks of wood formed the floor and unpainted cinder blocks comprised the walls. In that moment, someone descended the stairs, which groaned with their every step.

The room was noisy, too, it seemed.

Cinder considered the space. Claustrophobic, dimly lit, loud with creaking stairs, and the risk of splinters from an unfinished floor.

Excellent. He didn't mind. While the dorm at the orphanage was nicer, it wasn't a place where he could become a warrior. This was, which made all the difference in the path he wanted to take.

"What do you think?" Sash asked, his smile challenging. "Bet it's not as nice as the orphanage."

"It'll do," Cinder replied.

"It better." Sash stepped closer, standing within inches of Cinder, eyes intense. "You're new here but know this. We're all aiming for greatness. You best not slow us down. You do and we'll break you. Master Lerid won't care about it neither." He snorted. "Fact is, he'll probably help us toss your worthless pieces on the street."

Cinder met the other boy's gaze, making sure he didn't blink. Sash might or might not be a bully, but he was without a doubt aggressive. Cinder had seen it when the apprentice sparred, and he knew he couldn't show weakness to the boy by dropping his eyes. More importantly, he would have to watch Sash. Young apprentice-warriors like him didn't always have full control of their weapons, be they fists, feet, or swords.

"You're currently ranked third in the school," Cinder said, eyes still locked. "Before next spring, you'll be fourth." It was an empty boast, but so what? Sometimes a simple threat was all it took to encourage a bully to look elsewhere for a victim. Cinder inched forward, close enough to smell the breakfast eggs on Sash's breath. He didn't care that he had to stare upward to meet the taller boy's gaze. "I won't slow you down, but you better not try to hold me back."

Sash features furrowed in a sneer. His jaw clenched and unclenched. After a few seconds he stepped away with another snort of derision. "Just keep up. Come on. The masters are waiting."

"What kind of training are we doing today?"

Sash left the closet-under-the-stairs and answered without turning around. "Do I look like your momma? Master Lerid will tell you what you need to know. Now shut up."

Cinder closed off any further questions. There would be no point in asking them of Sash. However, he made a mental note. There would come a time when he was as good as Sash or even better—he forced himself to believe the words—and he'd remember how the boy had treated him. There would be a reckoning if Sash's attitude toward him didn't change.

The two of them went outside, exiting onto a breezeway that ran the length of the back of the building. Before them stood a broad court-yard enclosed by a brick wall, which would have come up to the thighs of the yakshin Cinder had met yesterday. A strip of grass surround-ed a flagstone floor that might have served generations of apprentice warriors. A line of *diptha* lanterns hung from ropes stretched from one side of the courtyard to the other, looking like strange fruit. More lights were mounted on the long, gray stones capping the brick wall.

The other apprentices had already gathered in the courtyard. Cinder had met them before. Other than Sash, there were four others. They stood in a loose knot in the center of the courtyard.

The oldest, Dorr Corn, a stout young man, offered Cinder a friend-ly smile. Next to him was the finest apprentice at *Steel-Graced*. Bones Jorn, tall, with a tremendous reach and a cocky smile that was well-earned. Cinder had seen him fight. He was every bit as fast as Sash but far more powerful. Next was Mirk Bassang, a year older than Cinder at seventeen. While he ranked the lowest amongst the apprentices, he worked twice as hard as any of them. In a fight he could go for hours and remain fresh. Finally, there was Gorant Sin Peace, who was the same age as Sash. Gorant had a lisp and tended not to speak much. He was thicker than Sash, almost as fast, and would have made a tre-mendous warrior except for his timidity, his unwillingness to push to victory.

Cinder acknowledged the apprentices with a shallow bob of his head. The others in the courtyard included the school's two masters and the one journeyman. They waited in the far corner. To them Cinder offered a deeper bow, slapping his hands to the side of his thighs and bending low at the waist until his head was parallel with the ground.

Sash whispered a final warning before departing. "Don't screw up."

Cinder's mouth curled in annoyance. *Jackhole.*

He smoothed his features when Master Jine Kole and his son, Journeyman Faine Kole, approached. The older of the two masters was a tall man who didn't smile much. He had a white beard and white hair, both of which he kept trimmed short. His blue eyes, a reflection of his partial Errow heritage, were rounder than the norm. In addition, like Master Lerid and everyone else at *Steel-Graced*, he wore tan, loose-fitting cotton or hemp clothing that allowed ease of motion.

His son, on the other hand, was of medium height and build, and had features typical of those from Rakesh. He was in his early thirties and Cinder had heard he had served two tours in Rakesh's army, a total of eight years. He smiled much more readily than his father, but there was a determination to him, an essence that spoke of his Master Jine's parentage. "Friendly and focused" was Cinder's interpretation of the journeyman.

Master Jine gestured and Cinder followed him along the breezeway, where they halted at the corner of the courtyard. "Today is your first day. You'll not be training." His words fell as blunt as a hammer.

Cinder bit down a surge of disappointment. More watching wasn't what he had in mind. After three weeks waiting to heal, he was ready to go.

Master Jine continued. "After the morning's session, go see the cook. He'll tell you the duties required for you to earn your tuition and room and board. You'll help with the cooking and cleaning. Understood?"

"Yes, sir," Cinder replied.

Master Jine left without another word.

Cinder watched him depart, annoyed he wouldn't start his training today. He startled when Journeyman Faine slapped him on the shoulder. He'd forgotten the man was still there.

"It's going to be all right," Journeyman Faine said with a smile.

Cinder blinked. "Excuse me, sir?"

"Call me Faine, not 'sir' and not 'journeyman,'" Faine said, still smiling. "Come on. I know Master Jine told you to observe but you've done enough of that. Let's get you sorted out."

They left the courtyard and re-entered the main structure housing

Steel-Graced. While they walked, Faine explained the rules of the school and what was expected of the apprentices.

"In this house we train for battle," Faine said. "We train warriors."

Cinder presumed nothing less. "Master Jine says I'm to cook and clean to earn my tuition. What about the other apprentices? How do they afford their tuition?"

"The others are luckier than you. They were picked out early from clans or families wealthy enough to supply martial tutors to their young. Those who thrive are given sponsorships to cover any tuition or special training they might need. Some might have private instruction their entire lives while others join a martial academy. All of Rakesh's finest warriors follow this path."

Cinder intuited a further positive outcome for the other apprentices. "They're exposed to more than one style of fighting." It would make them far more formidable, possibly beyond what he could hope to gain from learning at *Steel-Graced* only.

"Got it in one. Every day we'll train, even in the bitter cold of winter. But Master Lerid also likes it if we learn to craft. I make watches." Faine's posture straightened, and he held an aura of suppressed pride. "They're some of the finest timepieces in Rakesh and Gandharva."

"You make watches?" Cinder asked in confusion. "Why? And what about me? Will I have to make a watch, too?"

"Not at first, you won't," Faine said, "but you'll have to make or do something creative. As to why I chose watches, that's easy. Have you ever examined a watch? Examined the mechanisms inside of one? They're very fine. Working at that level teaches a person patience *and* precision. A good set of skills for a warrior to have, no?"

It made a kind of sense, although Cinder remained ambivalent about the notion of watchmaking. Still, if that's what it took to become a warrior, then he'd do it. He'd make the best damn watches anyone had ever seen.

"As for the training itself, we have a motto at the school: *steel sharpens steel.* It means while we're all in competition with one another, we also do our best to help someone who needs it. Doing anything less is a quick way to get yourself on the school's shit list."

"What about the Third Directorate? I heard it's the finest elven martial academy. How does someone earn a place there?" Cinder asked. It was a question he'd asked of Master Lerid, but thus far, he hadn't received a satisfactory answer.

"How old are you?" Faine asked. "Sixteen?"

Cinder nodded.

"Kind of small for your age, aren't you?" Faine noted. A moment later, he offered up a knowing smile. "And you're hoping to be ready for next spring's Maker's Tournament?" His next words dashed Cinder's hope. "It won't happen. You won't be ready. Not this year, not next, or the year after. I wouldn't expect a chance try for the Maker's Tournament until you're twenty at the earliest. Four years, and even then there are no guarantees."

Four years. Disappointment weighed on Cinder's mind, causing his shoulders to sag. Some people had a profession they were lucky enough to learn early on in life—smithing, baking, tailoring—but he hadn't learned of his calling until a few weeks ago. The sword, mastering its use, protecting those who required it. He wanted to get on with the journey of becoming a warrior worthy of the name, but it seemed he had years to go before he could even be considered proficient.

"I know what I'm telling you doesn't make you happy," Faine said, "but think about what you're asking. All of us here have been training since the time we could first pick up a sword. I held my first blade when I was two." He squeezed one of Cinder's shoulders. "Whatever Master Lerid saw in you, there's no way to overcome that lack of experience. Not in one year or three years. Only in a lifetime."

The words were a cascading avalanche, and they might have crushed Cinder's hopes, but he forced himself to focus on the positive. He was at *Steel-Graced Adepts.* He knew what he wanted to do in life. He'd make it to the Third Directorate, and he'd do it faster than Faine thought possible. He had to. The Third Directorate. Becoming the finest warrior possible . . . nothing would deter his hopes and goals.

Faine clapped him on a shoulder. "Don't worry. You'll be able to help train the actual entrants. That's probably the best you can hope for." He pulled up short. "We're here."

They arrived at the kitchen, a cramped space full of skillets, pans, spices, cutlery, a butcher-block table, and a wood-fired oven.

Lording over it all and currently stirring a fragrant stew within a giant pot was a large, red-faced, bald man. He wore a stained apron, which stretched heroically over his ample belly. Sweat beaded on his forehead, and he scowled furiously at whatever was in the pot. Cinder had met him on a few other occasions, receiving a few terse replies when he tried to make conversation.

"Meet Morr Snyth," Faine said by way of introduction. "He's our resident chef, sorter of all problems, keeper of the keys, and—"

"—wiper of your asses," Morr finished with a grumble. "What do you want?"

Faine grinned. "This is Cinder Shade."

"We've met," Morr said.

Cinder held out his hand in greeting. "Nice to meet you on a more formal basis."

"Great to meet you, too," Morr said with a distinct lack of enthusiasm as he shook Cinder's hand. "Now that we've gotten the formalisms out the way, let me tell you what I need from you. You'll help me make breakfast and prepare lunch. That means you're up an hour before dawn. Don't be late." He leaned forward, peering intently. "You don't want to get on my raspy side, you hear?" He leaned back. "Next, you train after breakfast. Then lunch, and afterward we get supper started. You also get the added joy of helping me clean the kitchen and whatever else needs doing. More training in the afternoon, then more cleaning afterward. Any questions?"

Cinder shook his head. It sounded straightforward. Busy as hell, but straightforward. "None."

"Good. Then I'll see you after lunch."

"I think he likes you," Faine said, smiling or smirking—Cinder couldn't figure out which—as they exited the kitchen.

Cinder glanced back, somewhat overwhelmed by the gruff set of instructions Morr had tossed his way. "I hope so."

Faine laughed, clapping Cinder on the shoulder. "You'll be fine. We'll make sure of it."

Cinder didn't know what he meant. "Sir?"

"I'm not a sir," Faine corrected. "What I meant is we won't let you screw things up for yourself. It's what we are here. Brothers, and brothers look out for each other."

After breakfast the next day, Faine handed Cinder a practice sword.

The other apprentices were spread about the courtyard, standing within square areas twenty feet on a side and marked off by lines of bricks. Everyone else sparred under the watchful eyes of Master Lerid and Master Jine. The clash of wooden weapons sounded like some strange, atonal music, the beating of a clacking percussion instrument. Dust motes drifted in the morning air as sunshine beamed inside the courtyard. The day was unseasonably mild. Autumn held sway and winter would soon beckon in a few more months, but this blast of resplendent warmth might likely be summer's last gasp.

Cinder loosely gripped his practice sword, twirling it to gain an idea of its balance. The blade was a slender piece of wood, tan like the clothes he wore and straight all the way to the tip with a cross-guard. It also possessed the same shape, length, and heft as the double-edged swords favored in Rakesh. Or at least, that's what Cinder had been told. He didn't know for sure. This was all new to him.

"You ever hold a sword before?" Faine asked, breaking into his thoughts.

"No. This is my first time."

Faine grunted. "Then I guess we'll take it slow. But no worries. The practice blades we use are made of wood, but as you can see, they have the size, shape, and heft of a real sword." He swirled his practice blade with practiced ease. "Thankfully, the worst you can expect is a bunch of bruises."

Cinder's brow furrowed. A memory surfaced, like a dolphin momentarily cresting the waves. It faded, but in its wake a question rose. "Are there any kind of practice swords that don't just leave bruises?"

"You mean in Rakesh?"

Cinder nodded.

"No. This is all we got, and this is all we need. The elves are said to have something called a shoke. Their practice blades. They named them after Shokan. It's supposed to be some kind of blue-purple wood but shiny like oil. I've never used one, but when you're hit with a shoke, I'm told it feels like an edged weapon cut you down. Strange thing is there's not nearly as much of an injury. You'd think there would be. It's still made of wood, after all. But mostly it's just the pain for a few seconds. The elves say it teaches honest effort."

It also sounded like it made a lot more sense. Transient pain with no debility? A person could train harder that way. "Why don't we use shokes?" Cinder asked.

"Because only elven craftsmen know how to make them. Now shut it. It's time to work."

Cinder cut off any further questions, and excitement bubbled in his chest. He had to take a cleansing breath to settle his nerves. *Finally. I'm starting on a warrior's path.* He got his blade into position. "I'm ready."

"I wasn't asking." Faine attacked.

Cinder found himself immediately disarmed. He stared, disheartened. His practice weapon lay in the dirt. Faine had won in one move, and Cinder couldn't even tell how he'd done it. He replayed the brief fight and still didn't know what had happened. *Damn it.* He'd expected to do better than to immediately lose his sword.

Frustration swirled in his mind although he recognized how useless the feeling was. This would probably be the first of many such defeats. He might as well get used to it.

At least Faine hadn't hit him with his sword. Cinder wouldn't have a bruise to show for his first defeat. He would simply have to improve over time. He concentrated on that future, trying to rid himself of disappointment.

Cinder bent to scoop up the blade, prepared to reset and go at it again.

"Stop!"

Cinder stared at Faine in confusion, unsure why the journeyman sounded so angry. He let his weapon's tip droop.

"You want to know what you did wrong?"

"I lost. Isn't that wrong enough?"

"Of course you lost, you idiot. It's your first time holding a blade. Why did you lose? What did I do to win?"

Cinder once again replayed the sparring match in his head, and he still couldn't see what had happened. Faine had simply moved too fast. "I don't know," he finally said. "One moment I was holding the sword, the next moment I wasn't."

"It's because you got your blade set, and I never told you to. In *Steel-Graced*, the moment you get your weapon ready, the fight's on. Next time let me guide you."

"Yes, sir."

Faine scowled.

Cinder had forgotten. Faine didn't like being called 'sir'. "I'm sorry. It's a habit."

"Then break the habit," Faine growled. "Also, you held the blade like it was some kind of scythe. That won't do." Faine gripped his practice blade. "Hold it like this." He squared his shoulders, bending at the knees. "And this is the proper stance for a beginner. It's stiff, but it's stable."

Cinder mimicked him.

Faine nodded approval. "That's it. Now, let's try again. Focus on my hands. The blade moves too fast. Watch my shoulders. That's where you'll see where I might be going. Same with the hips, but that's for when you can actually hold onto your sword. Set yourself."

Cinder did as he was told. This time the sword felt more natural in his hands.

Faine fired off a diagonal slash. "Here's the attack." He stepped back and angled his practice blade. "Here's the parry." He took a step forward again. "The counter." *A thrust.* "Three moves. Practice those. I'll call them out."

The practice blade and stance felt right, and Cinder quickly fell into the rhythm of the simple pattern. "Attack. Parry. Counter. Reset." Within minutes he no longer had to pay strict attention to what he was doing. It was like his muscles already knew what was expected of them, as if they had long ago developed a memory of this simple maneuver.

Cinder's mind drifted, and he considered how to attack and maintain position so an immediate parry wasn't required. He imagined what to do after a counter, to strike again rather than reset. *If I angle the sword, it might allow a follow-up slash.* Ideas flitted through his mind. He couldn't tell if any of them would work or not, but he had a strange assurance they would.

Faine stepped closer, and Cinder managed not to stumble when the journeyman blocked his attack. He shifted automatically into the parry he'd been practicing during the past few minutes, deflecting Faine's diagonal slash. Cinder countered; a thrust the journeyman easily turned away.

"Reset," Faine said, "and again."

Cinder attacked. Faine parried and countered. Cinder blocked and shifted to his own counter.

"Reset," Faine called.

Again they went at it, on and on, sparring in a dictated pattern, each of them parrying and countering the other's attack.

Attack.

Clack.

Parry.

Clack.

Counter.

Clack.

Reset.

Faine continued calling out the words throughout their sparring, but he subtly increased the pace. Cinder initially kept up with the faster speed, but it didn't take long for his breathing to grow ragged. His slender frame and lack of endurance did him in.

"Halt," Faine ordered.

Cinder stopped, hunched over at the knees and sucking in great gasps of air. All the while he made sure not to let his practice sword touch the ground, not even the tip. It struck him as sacrilegious if he allowed it.

Faine slapped him on the shoulder. "You did pretty good for your first time. Go get some water. Get your breath back and we'll go at it again. I'll show you a fourth move."

Cinder went to the water barrel hunkering in the corner, knowing it was full since he'd made sure of it earlier in the morning. One of his kitchen duties was to ensure the barrel never went dry. Once a day he was expected to lug buckets of water from the neighborhood well, which was situated next to the bakery a block down from the school.

Cinder withdrew a full pitcher and drank deep but not his fill. While the water tasted delicious, mineral-fresh and cool, and he was parched, he also didn't want stomach cramps.

How do I know drinking too much cold water can cause a thirsty person to develop stomach cramps?

He figured it must be common knowledge that had carried past his amnesia. Cinder let the pitcher fall into the barrel and returned to Faine.

"Here's a follow-up attack you can use after the counter," Faine said.

He demonstrated the maneuver, and Cinder silently celebrated. Earlier, when he'd mused about what attacks to string together following the counter, Faine's move had been one of them. He'd guessed right.

"What are you smiling about?" Faine asked.

Cinder told him.

"Then you'll have no trouble figuring out your foot placement. Set yourself." Faine called out the tempo. "Attack. Parry. Counter. Follow-up. Reset."

Cinder flowed from one stance to another, the sword feeling more natural in his hands with every passing moment. His stuttering steps became more certain.

He was soon panting again, however, and Faine called another halt. "Take a break. No water. It's time to toughen up. Get your breath."

Cinder forced himself upright. Bending over, gasping like a fish out of water, wasn't how he wanted the other apprentices to think of him.

He waited for his heart and breathing to settle, and while he did, Faine spoke. "Is it true a yakshin talked to you the other day?"

Cinder didn't know why Faine was bringing up the strange meeting with the tree maiden. "I did. She called me Maynalor."

"Maynalor. *Someone of interest with a secret.* That's what the word means in old *Shevasra*," Faine mused. "You're an odd one."

Four weeks—a full month—into Cinder's time at *Steel-Graced* and he used every spare moment grinding away at his training. He pushed himself harder than anyone, spending hours after the other apprentices were gone for the day, pushing himself, struggling to make up the distance between his abilities and his desire.

At last, some of his tireless work was paying off. He was finally finding his footing, able to do the required training, be it calisthenics, sword forms, or unarmed sparring. He could do it and no longer fall over from exhaustion.

Barely.

"Break!" Master Lerid shouted.

As one, Cinder and the other apprentices finished their exercises and rose to their feet.

They had been going at it for an hour this morning. Nothing but stamina-building drills on the square across the street from the school. First had come slow stretches and forms meant to increase their balance and their core strength. After that, their instructors had them transition from a wind sprint, to a set of push-ups ending on an explosive leap, and finally a dragon crawl the length of the grassy square.

A minute break and they repeated the cycle.

A few residents of Swift Sword had paused to observe the apprentices, calling out encouragement and making bets on who would finish the exercises first. They hooted laughter at the one who finished last, which was Cinder. It was always him.

While he had a chance to recover, Cinder made himself take deep, regular breaths. Controlling his breathing would serve better at helping him recover his wind than panting like a dog. Control would also allow him to eventually become the equal of the other apprentices, who were currently only merely winded from the morning training session. Nevertheless, sweat beaded on their faces, dripped down their necks, and collected on the collars and armpits of their shirts.

Cinder's shirt, on the other hand, was utterly soaked. It was wringing wet and would need washing after today's training. A breeze, which carried autumn's chill, caused him to shiver, but he ignored his discomfort. It was unimportant.

"We're done here," Master Lerid said. "Follow me to the courtyard."

Cinder trailed the other apprentices as they followed the masters and Faine back to *Steel-Graced.* They entered the courtyard where they did most of their training. There they discovered an ancient man waiting for them. He sat in repose, limber enough to sit cross-legged on the ground, feet resting on the opposite knees. In appearance, he resembled a more ancient version of Master Jine. His skin held the aspect of wrinkled rice-paper and a rim of wispy, white hair ringed the crown of his age-spotted head.

"Get some water," Master Lerid said to the apprentices, "then gather here. We have a special guest today."

Cinder joined the apprentices at the water barrel. They apparently knew the old man seated at the center of the courtyard, and they spoke in excited tones.

Gorant fairly bounced on his feet. "Last time he was here, I finally realized what I'd been doing wrong."

"Which was probably everything," Bones scoffed.

Gorant scoffed right back. "Says the man who couldn't stop singing his praises when he first met him."

Curiosity itched at Cinder, and he stared at the old man. *Who is he?*

Minutes later Master Jine called to them. "Gather."

The conversations broke off and the apprentices quickly took cross-legged seats in a semi-circle around the ancient man. Curiosity continued to prick at Cinder.

"This is Master Sharn, the artist who taught me," Master Lerid said by way of introduction and also answering Cinder's unspoken question.

Master Sharn opened his eyes. Cataracts dulled previously dark eyes, but a sparkle of joy still seemed to fill them. "Lerid is correct. I was the one who instructed him, and in this way, I am also your teacher." He smiled then. "A simple query. Time robs all of us of our martial abilities, but with Devesh's grace we hold onto the most important aspect of ourselves. It is also our greatest weapon. Who can tell me what it is?"

Dorr, Bones, and Mirk must have heard the question in times past because they shared a knowing grin. Sash and Gorant, on the other hand, frowned in uncertainty. They leaned close to one another, muttering possibilities. Cinder silently pondered the question on his own. *What was the greatest weapon a person owned?*

The silence stretched until Sash spoke up. "Our hands. It's how we can still craft *and* fight."

"Our feet, so we still have motion and a productive life," Gorant said.

They were both wrong, and it didn't take the seniors chuckling to tell Cinder so.

"Our minds," Cinder said after a few further seconds of consideration.

The older apprentices cut off their laughter, and Cinder discovered himself the focus of Master Sharn's attention.

"Why do you believe so?" the ancient master asked.

"Physicality is a gift, but it is still directed by the mind," Cinder said. "So long as the mind is undamaged, so is one's will. No matter how broken the body, any person who can reason can remain dangerous."

Master Sharn smiled wider, clapping his hands. "Well done," he said. "I will now tell you why I'm actually here. It isn't to simply ask you questions." The other apprentices chuckled at this. "As you know, next summer, two of you will represent this school in the Maker's Tournament. If we're fortunate, both will win a place in the Third Directorate. It is the academy where the finest warriors in all Seminal are forged and tempered. You must train hard, focus intensely on your bodies, but do not forsake your minds. Will and desire can overcome many obstacles. It can transform a poorly endowed person into a dangerous individual, an average warrior into someone of repute, and the truly gifted into a legend."

Cinder shifted in embarrassment. He wasn't average or gifted. In fact, compared to the other apprentices he was poorly endowed. He wasn't nearly as fast as Sash or as consummately correct in his technique as Gorant. He lacked Mirk's unending stamina, Dorr's completeness, and Bones' overwhelming talent. What did he really have?

"All of you are talented in some way or Lerid wouldn't have chosen you," Master Sharn said, reducing some of Cinder's fears about his relative worth. "Focus on your talent, refine it, strengthen it, but never lose sight of your weaknesses. On them you should work equally hard, if not harder."

Sash nodded his head vigorously in agreement.

"But there is one matter, one weakness, none of you can overcome," Master Sharn said. "No one can."

"We can't cycle *prana*," Dorr said.

"Exactly," Master Sharn said. "*Prana*. Or as it is also called when quiescent, *lorethasra*. Without that ability we cannot open our Chakras. No matter how swift our swords, an elf will always be faster. No matter our strength, a dwarf will always be more powerful. We may have greater skill than the woven, but without *lorethasra* we cannot overcome the handicaps which hobble our species. We will always be unbalanced warriors."

Cinder had a dozen questions. Deepak had told him some of this during their journey to Swift Sword, and since then he'd read as much as he could about the topic: *aether* and *lorethasra*. Deepak had said they were two names for the same thing, but he was wrong. There was a difference. *Lorethasra* resided within a person while *aether* was part of the world without. Also, while Deepak said humans couldn't cycle their *lorethasra* and as a result, it became polluted. So how did this relate to *prana*? Cinder didn't know, and he raised a hand, wanting to ask more about it.

"Yes," Master Sharn said, giving him permission to speak.

"What is *prana*?"

"Ah. A good question." Master Sharn glanced around. "Anyone care to tell him?"

The other apprentices grumbled under their breaths, but none of them appeared ready to speak.

"No?" Master Sharn chuckled. "You're wise not to answer for no one knows the nature of *prana*. Is it merely another word for *aether* and *lorethasra*? The elves and dwarves say 'no.' Same with the trolls, the yakshins, and the holders. But none of them can tell us what the difference actually is. Some claim *prana* is the same substance that Shokan and Sira labeled *Jivatma*, but the Blessed Ones aren't around to tell us. Maybe the Mythaspuris could have explained it but they, too, are absent."

"What about the rishis of Bharat?" Cinder asked. "Aren't they humans who have opened their Chakras?"

Master Sharn frowned. "So they claim. They're certainly the most powerful members of our race, but they are also insular and unkind with their gifts. Opening one's Chakras is supposed to bring a being more in tune with Devesh's desires. The Lord is said to be generous and loving, neither of which can be said about the rishis. They have always been far more dedicated to their own wants and needs."

"Then why are they so powerful?" Bones asked.

"I don't know the nature of their strength," Master Sharn admitted, "but I have my doubts it's related to an ability to cycle *prana*. I don't think any human possesses that ability, and it leads me to a truth you must embrace. All of you are weak in comparison to the other races on Seminal. You always will be. But you aren't lesser beings. *We* aren't lesser beings. We are the equal of any woven in the only way that matters, in Devesh's eyes. We have the Lord's grace. Remember that unalterable fact. No matter how high you rise in the ranks of Rakesh's warriors, you aren't a better person, a more worthy individual, than the baker next door or the boy cleaning a horse's stall. We are meant to be servants, not lords."

His statement struck Cinder like a hammer striking a gong. The phrase resounded inside his core, echoing a truth he had once recognized but forgotten. *Servants, not lords.*

The awareness left him wondering how much other wisdom he must have once learned from his parents or Pitch that he'd later forgotten with that fall down the well. His deceased memories. What other kernels of deeper meaning had been lost to the casualty of amnesia?

10

Weeks of training at *Steel-Graced Adepts* passed by as swiftly as the sweep of a sparrow's wings. Then squalled in winter, lashing in with a wreckage of hail, snow, and harsh gusts of a bitter wind. Trees shed the last of their leaves and icicles sagged like stalactites from the eaves. In the storm's wake there remained a ragged, ill breeze.

The wind brought a deeper chill to the already frigid morning air of the courtyard behind *Steel-Graced Adepts*. There the apprentices sweated, sparred, and trained under the tutelage of their masters, who corrected form, posture, and decisions. The students slipped now and then on the paving stones, but it was no more than usual since Cinder and Morr Snyth had cleared the previous night's snowfall during the dark hours of the morning, collecting the white powder into piles which they left along the yard's perimeter.

Cinder still sparred against Faine, not yet able to offer any benefit to training against the other apprentices. He listened to the journeyman explain the rationale for his latest failure.

Faine mimed a movement. "You shot a thrust, but you stayed on the center-line. It left you overextended. All I had to do was sidestep, a simple slash, and it was over." He demonstrated. "When you commit to a thrust, you have to be prepared for the counter. It's coming."

Cinder knew this, and he shoved down a scowl, annoyed at how Faine was telling him what he already knew. By now, after two months of training, he understood the basics.

He must not have hid his irritation very well because Faine cut off his clarification with a glower. "What? You think you know everything? I'm wasting my time and yours by teaching you?"

"No, sir," Cinder quickly answered.

He liked Faine. The journeyman had always treated him fairly, spending extra time teaching him forms and the underlying principles of *why* a warrior might move in certain ways. The last, the deeper instruction of balance and feints, of the usage of traps and setups, had opened Cinder's eyes to the possibilities of combat. The knowledge also helped him bridge the gap between his innate understanding of movement to a more technical familiarity of how to make that instinctual perception more effective.

In essence, combat as taught at *Steel-Graced* was akin to a physical version of chess, with similar planning and strategy. Sparring occurred in all dimensions, required all the senses, and had a host more variables and potential outcomes than moving pieces on a board. Cinder had years to go to make sense of it all. He knew that now.

"Then what?" Faine demanded. "Because you look like you've eaten a sour apple and it's pissed you off. Which means I'm pissed off."

"I was trying something new, but it didn't work," Cinder said. "My thrust was a feint. I knew you'd slide and slash. I didn't overextend. I wanted you to think I had. If I was faster, I would have reset, blocked your counter, disengaged, and swept around to take you in the side."

Faine's scowl smoothed away. Surprise took its place, then deliberation. After a few seconds, he gestured. "Show me."

They resumed their postures prior to Faine's winning slash.

"It went like this," Cinder said.

They slowed their movements. Cinder shifted out of guard, leaning his weight forward and easing into a thrust. Faine followed along in what he recalled of the exchange.

"You had more weight on your back foot," Cinder said. "It wasn't much, but it was why I thought to try the thrust."

"You're sure of this?" Faine asked, surprised anew. "You remember seeing that?"

"I saw it, but it wasn't like I processed the information in my mind first. I saw your balance, recognized an option, and I went for it."

"You saw me shift my balance to my back foot," Faine pressed. "In the middle of sparring? You wouldn't have enough time for that kind of an observation."

"I saw the opening," Cinder persisted, "and I got the thrust off in time. My problem was your counter. I couldn't get back to guard quick enough."

Faine closed his eyes. He seemed to murmur to himself. His eyes opened. "Sonofabitch. You're right. It would have worked if you were faster."

"But I'm not," Cinder said, sullen at himself. His body, beefier since coming to *Steel-Graced*, wasn't beefy enough. It remained the iron chains restraining his progress. "I'm not necessarily scrawny, but I'm still weaker and slower than what I need to be."

"Sure, but that won't always be the case," Faine replied. He slowly shook his head, seemingly incredulous. "I still can't believe you recognized an opening like that. It had to be less than a split second. *How?*"

Now it was Cinder's turn to be surprised. He figured everyone at *Steel-Graced* could do what he did. After all, they'd been training at combat for years. "I've always been able to see those kinds of possibilities." He corrected after an instant of reconsideration. "At least I think I can. I'm not completely sure, but it was how I fought off the bullies at the orphanage."

Faine eyed him in greater appreciation. "Well aren't you full of surprises?"

Cinder hesitated then, not sure how his next question would be taken. "Can you do what I'm talking about?"

Faine chuckled in a faintly bitter tone. "Only sometimes. Same with the apprentices, except for Bones and maybe Dorr. He might have an inkling of what you're describing. But in reality, the only people at *Steel-Graced* who can predict a fight like that are Master Lerid and my father. But they're masters." He gave Cinder a calculating stare. "That's what you're talking about, you know. A master-level ability."

Cinder blinked in surprise. He had no idea.

"How long have you had this skill?" Faine asked.

"Like I said, as far back as I can remember, but that's not too long." He grinned. "A bit over five months." The length of his memories. "The first time was at the orphanage, but it really only came into focus when you explained the principles of combat. Those conversations gave me a deeper appreciation of what's possible and how to predict what my opponent might do."

Faine exhaled heavily. "Well, you might be skinny as kindling, but with your intuition, you have a chance to go far." He brought his blade up. "Let's see how you do this time."

Winter maintained its stern grip on Swift Sword, and a week after his conversation with Faine, Cinder found himself seated at a table in the room called the Dullness. It was one of the two spaces in *Steel-Graced* given over entirely to apprentices. The first one was the Anvil, the large training hall situated at the front of the building and where they sparred when the weather didn't allow them to work outside.

The Dullness, on the other hand, was where they crafted. It was a cramped room possessing all the cheerlessness of a prison cell. In it were several long tables and benches that took up most of the space. All were pitted, worn, and stained. In addition, an array of acrid stenches—the reek of oil, metal, and leather—filled the space.

Cinder worked in the Dullness alongside several other apprentices—Dorr Corn, Mirk Bassang, and Gorant Sin Peace. It was their rest day, but Bones and Sash had decided to continue training. With it snowing, those two sparred in the Anvil under the watchful eye of

Master Lerid. The sounds of their practice rang through the house. Cinder would have joined them, but he was worn to the nub. His weak body was slowly strengthening, but even after all his training, by the end of the week he had nothing left to give on the rest days.

He might have still pressed on, but in the depths of his mind, a voice of caution warned him against over-exertion. In this, it matched the firm suggestion of Master Lerid who also ordered Cinder to give his body time to rest and relax, heal, and incorporate the week's learning.

As a result, here he was in the Dullness, sitting and staring at an old piece of leather he'd intended to transform into a pouch to hold coins. Instead, his creation reminded him of a tumorous growth. He pushed the leather away with a grunt of disgust. He had neither the talent for leather-working nor the desire to attain it.

"This is a waste," he said, scowling in frustration.

Next to him Dorr Corn, the senior apprentice, had his attention focused on a watch. He apparently had chosen to follow Faine's decision to craft timepieces, and he hummed happily. On hearing the complaint, he cut off his song and lifted his head, glancing Cinder's way. "You're pushing too hard at a task you don't like. Do something else." He pointed to the closet. "Look in there. There's all kinds of materials you might find more to your liking."

It sounded like a better idea than mucking around with the stupid leather. Cinder stood.

"Also, since you're already up, fetch yourself to the kitchen and get me some food," Dorr said with a friendly grin, clearly joking. The senior apprentice was generally a happy person, and Cinder liked him.

"Why should I?" Cinder asked. His gaze went to Dorr's gut, and he made sure the senior noticed. Dorr's belly had a slight but definite bulge. "Besides, it looks like you've eaten plenty."

Dorr laughed, patting his stomach. "This here's padding to protect my innards. It doesn't slow me down any. Now fetch. It's in your contract."

"Get it yourself."

"No. No. No. The newbie is supposed to get us food," Gorant said, his odd lisp making his words difficult to decipher.

"Yeah, mate," Mirk added. "Go fetch before I fetch my boot up your backside."

Cinder shot them all a rude gesture, to which they laughed. While they continued chuckling, he went to the closet, a tall, narrow structure taking up most of a corner and rising as high as the ten-foot ceiling.

Cinder opened the closet doors and perused the interior. He quickly discovered a plethora of useless inventory. A bunch of bent metal, scraps of leather, pieces of wood, broad swatches of canvas, colored thread and ropes, and many unfinished works, such as horseshoes, paintings, and even clothes. Apparently one of the apprentices, either current or in the past, had taken a hand as a clothier.

Nothing of interest for Cinder, though. He kept searching, shoving aside more and more items. He finally saw something in the back corner that piqued his interest, a wooden case. He thought he recognized the shape. It looked like it was meant to hold a musical instrument. His heart beat faster, almost as if he was in the training yard.

He got the case clear of the junk littering the closet. Two clasps held the lid shut, and Cinder unlatched them. He slowly opened the box, feeling like the solution to one of life's great mysteries awaited him. Inside, nestled in soft, red material, he discovered a musical instrument.

Cinder whistled in appreciation. It was beautiful.

A mandolin.

That was what it was called. Until this moment he hadn't known the word. It wasn't the first time unexpected knowledge had come to him. It happened a lot, and he reckoned it was because while he still couldn't recall anything of Swallow or the events of his past, the memories weren't entirely clouded. He simply didn't know what he knew until an event prompted the fresh discovery of old knowledge. In a way, it meant every day was an opportunity for self-discovery.

He carefully withdrew the mandolin. A sheen of dust covered its surfaces, but a quick swipe with his sleeve, and the wood underneath fairly gleamed. The strings had clearly seen better days, but they could likely still maintain their notes.

He returned to the bench next to Dorr, cradling the mandolin and sitting so his back was to the table.

"What do you have there?" Dorr asked, peering over Cinder's shoulder.

"A mandolin," Cinder answered.

He trailed his fingers across the instrument, feeling like it was a priceless treasure. He studied it more carefully. The mandolin was old and marred with stains, but there were no obvious defects in its construction. He gave the instrument a gentle strum and immediately winced at the discordant notes. It was terribly out of tune.

He set to fixing the problem, softly picking at each string and making minute adjustments to the corresponding peg.

"I wish I knew how to play," Gorant said, sounding wistful.

Cinder empathized. Until this moment he hadn't realized how important playing music must have been to his past self. His fingers itched to strum the strings and bring forth a song.

"Can you actually play or you just messing around?" Dorr asked.

Cinder grinned at him. "I have no idea." He tapped his head. "No memories, remember?" However, based on his confident handling of the mandolin, his ability to tune it by ear only, he suspected he probably did know how to play.

Mirk laughed. "Not remembering what you do and don't know must play havoc on your mind."

Cinder chuckled. "It definitely has its moments." He resumed working on the mandolin. Soon each string was tuned to his satisfaction, and he gave the instrument a more vigorous strum. He was pleased when they all kept their proper notes. The mandolin had a nice resonance, and he wondered how long it had lain forgotten in the closet.

"Don't just sit there doing nothing," Dorr said. "Play something already."

Cinder realized he didn't know the names of any songs. He didn't know what to play. Maybe he could . . .

Cinder closed his eyes and let his fingers find their own pattern. He began hesitantly, as if his hands were relearning a skill they had once known but no longer remembered. His fingers picked at the strings until they found a melody. They slowly recalled what his conscious mind couldn't, and his confidence increased. He quickened the tempo.

It was like the sword. Every day Cinder grew surer of his abilities. He was far from competent, but he'd come a long way. Improved strength and stamina might see him obtain even greater gains.

He pushed aside thoughts of combat and focused on the mandolin, strumming and picking, and the music came to life. He played a song, eyes still closed.

The world faded as a vision arose in his mind.

He sat on a bench perched on the edge of a cliff. Below him spread a village, the homes nestled on terraces carved into an escarpment. All about the hamlet washed a wisping river. It tumbled down a set of laddered waterfalls, creating a glory of rainbows.

Beside him sat a woman. He'd seen her before. He'd dreamt of her several times, including on the journey from Swallow to Swift Sword. They'd taken a walk in a park in some faraway city of grace and beauty. She was nearly as tall as he, and she sang now, her voice a confident contralto, in a language he didn't understand.

He played for her and her alone, his fingers moving across the mandolin. He lost himself in the music, in the sensation of hearing her, being near her. He missed her, missed dancing with her.

The song ended, and Cinder opened his eyes, his thoughts troubled. Those couldn't have been memories from Swallow. He'd felt far older in the vision, world weary . . . which made no sense since he was only sixteen.

But it had seemed so real. Cinder could still feel the ocean breeze against his skin. He smelled the jasmine flowers braided into the woman's hair. He could still hear her sing, feel her love.

He shuddered then, upset and concerned for his sanity. What did the visions and dreams mean? Why was he having them?

But he had no chance to consider his questions because the other apprentices were busily clapping their appreciation.

"Absolutely wonderful," Dorr said, grinning enthusiastically.

"Fantastic," Gorant agreed, smiling every bit as much as Dorr.

The senior apprentice nodded. "Winter won't be nearly as bad with you playing for us while we muck around and work."

"It'll sure be better than listening to your humming," Mirk said. "No offense, mate, but you sound like a wounded cow."

"If you ever give up the sword, you might want to think about taking up an instrument," Gorant said.

Cinder clutched the mandolin more tightly. Gorant's sentiments were kind but misplaced. The sword was what Cinder wanted more than anything else. A warrior who protected those who needed it. Plus, he didn't have the skill to play music well enough to make a living from it.

Only one Caste of people did.

The thought had him freshly upset. *What's a Caste?*

Cinder strummed the mandolin he'd discovered in the Dullness almost a month ago, adjusting the pegs to get the strings back in tune. He still had no recollection of when and how he'd learned to play, but he no longer cared. He enjoyed making music and that was enough.

He sat at a table with the other apprentices in the Lonely Donkey, an alehouse several miles from the school. It was the night prior to a rest day, and they'd decided to meet here after supper, as soon as Cinder finished his work in the kitchen.

A number of people had already gathered at the Lonely Donkey, and the waitresses hustled to fill their orders. Most of the patrons were men, regulars. A mix of craftsmen and workers, a lower-class crowd. They sat at round tables stained from countless spills, or at the long bar ending a few feet short of the entrance. They sucked down their beers with a mournful monotony. Trip Badger, the owner, served them, his voice booming. Pipe smoke drifted across the large room. A buzz of voices filled the air, raucous laughter carrying now and then. A cheery fire burned in the large hearth centered along the wall opposite the entrance. It warmed the alehouse.

The other apprentices ordered drinks, and while waiting on them, they discussed the day's sparring. Cinder listened in on their conversation with half an ear. Most of his attention, though, remained on tuning his instrument.

"And I'm thinking I've got Cinder," Mirk was saying, "but then the bugger sweeps my legs, lands in top position, and taps me out like a door closing."

Sash frowned in confusion. "A door closing? What's that mean?"

"It means he kicked my ass," Mirk replied. "Fast. Like he did to Gorant yesterday."

Cinder held back a pleased smile. It had been fun to beat Mirk so quickly in unarmed sparring, a simple transition ending in a front choke. The older apprentice had never seen it coming.

He saw Gorant glance at Dorr. "What do you think?" he asked, his speech impediment slurring his words. "Cinder have a shot at beating Bones?"

Bones chuckled as if the notion was utterly ridiculous. "Hell, no. Cinder's gotten better, but that ain't the same as good. At least not for what I got." He stretched extravagantly, displaying the well-muscled length of his arms.

But the notion *wasn't* ridiculous. Not truly. At least Cinder didn't think so. A month ago he'd started sparring against the other apprentices. He'd quickly improved in all facets of fighting, be it with the sword, in unarmed combat, or in his innate ability to perceive an opponent's position and balance. Every day all his skills seemed to advance.

Nevertheless, he reckoned he'd never reach Bones' level. The other apprentice was too fast, too strong, and just too good. Bones was a genius with his hands, feet, and the sword. He could see the flow of a fight in a supernatural way, impose his will and force openings where none existed. Simply put, Bones was a prodigy.

Cinder wasn't, but he didn't need to be. He was improving, which was enough for now as he figured matters. He no longer went into the sword-sparring sessions expecting to lose. He'd yet to win a match, but he could see the day when he would. It wasn't too far off. It all depended on his body's ability to react to what his mind required.

The door to the alehouse opened and Cinder glanced up from his mandolin. In walked Riner and Coral.

Cinder stood, smiling welcome.

Even after leaving the orphanage, Cinder had kept in touch with the brother and sister. Some of it was because he continued to feel a degree of responsibility for Riner. While the boy no longer risked the wrath of bullies, he still needed help. Someone to teach him to be strong. Not necessarily to fight, but to be firm in who he was and allow no one to steal his dreams.

It was working.

Riner looked to be an entirely different person from when Cinder had first seen him. Gone was the frightened boy he had seen early on during his time at *Our Lady of Fire*. In his place was a slimmed-down, more confident youth. Maybe it was because Coral had discovered a means for her brother to apprentice with a librarian, a worthy occupation for the boy.

Cinder also maintained contact with Coral, and it was easy to understand why. She was a lovely person—beautiful, wise, and caring—and his heart beat a little faster whenever she was around. She still worked as a lady's maid, but these days, she also earned money as a singer. In fact, Coral had been the one to introduce Cinder to Trip Badger, convincing the ample-waisted owner of the Lonely Donkey to allow the two of them to perform here. Cinder accompanied Coral on the mandolin while she sang, and their busking brought him a much-needed source of income.

Cinder hugged Coral and Riner when they reached his table. "It's good seeing you."

"It's good seeing you, too," Coral said, kissing his cheek. She smiled warmly and took his hands, fingering the calluses on his fingertips. "You've been practicing."

"Only when I'm not too tired from training," Cinder said with a chuckle, removing his hands from hers.

"You look bigger," Riner said to him. "Taller, too."

"Eating lots of food and exercising all day will do that to a person," Cinder replied. "What about you? How have you been?"

Riner shrugged, but a proud smile lurked at the corner of his mouth.

Cinder grinned. "I think that's the answer I was hoping to hear." He guided Coral and Riner to the table and introduced them to the apprentices, all of whom stood and dipped their heads to Coral.

"Any *special* friend of Cinder's is a friend of ours," Bones said, his grin a tad short of a leer.

Cinder wanted to smack him. First, it wasn't true that Coral was his *special* friend, and second, even if she was, it wasn't right to make her uncomfortable over the possibility.

Coral merely rolled her eyes at Bones, obviously not missing the intent of the apprentice's near-leer. "I don't know about *special* friends, but Cinder *is* my friend. A good one." She tilted her head in challenge. "What about you? Do you have a special friend? Or does your right hand serve that unhappy task?"

The table roared while Bones blathered about how he had *many* special friends.

"Well, he does have two hands," Mirk said.

Again, the table burst into laughter.

Cinder broke off his chuckling. "Shall we?" Cinder asked Coral, pointing to the raised platform set up on the far end of the alehouse.

"I'd love to." Coral addressed the apprentices. "It's been a pleasure, gentleman." She gave Bones an unrepentant wink.

Cinder led her to the stage upon which rested a pair of stools. He set the open mandolin case in front of them, using it to hold whatever money the crowd felt like offering. Coral warmed up with a few scales while he limbered his fingers.

Someone extinguished several of the *diptha* lanterns lining the walls, and the room dimmed. The crowd slowly hushed as they realized what was happening. Cinder played the opening bars, a hypnotic melody. His fingers strummed and plucked the strings.

Coral waited a few measures, feet tapping to the rhythm. She began singing. Her lyrics told the story of a man wishing to marry a woman. Her reply was that he had to prove his love. Only then would she love him in return. He begged and pleaded for her to reconsider.

Cinder picked up the pace.

The woman demanded ever more extravagant tasks. The man tried to do what she wanted, but in the end, he failed. She showed him the door, telling him never to darken her front stoop ever again.

The tempo slowed. After months and years of heartache, the man recovered. The tempo increased. The man dusted himself off and fell in love with a neighbor's daughter. Cinder played more softly now, slower. Coral's singing became a whisper. The woman was left alone, tired and loveless.

It was a bitter song, but the audience didn't care. They clapped and cheered anyway.

Cinder and Coral played another song, kept on going, a dozen more. The hour grew late, and the pile of coins at their feet grew. After a final tune, they bowed to the audience, who clapped and whistled appreciation. The patrons resumed drinking or left the alehouse altogether while Cinder and Coral collected their earnings.

Cinder noticed Coral smiling broadly at him, and she drew him into a brief hug. "Same time next rest day?"

Cinder nodded. "Only if you're free."

"Of course." She and Riner left.

The apprentices approached then. They congratulated Cinder on his performance, and most of them left.

Bones remained behind, though, something evidently on his mind. "I was joking before, but you know you could do a lot worse than that woman. Think about it." His observation made, Bones made his exit.

Cinder had already thought about it. The truth was he liked Coral. She was smart, warm, and funny. A wonderful person.

His breathing deepened, but while imagining a future with Coral, the voice of a different singer entered his mind, a blonde-haired woman, and an unfathomable longing filled him. For the thousandth time, he pondered the same unanswerable question. *Who is she?*

11

A little more than three months after his entrance to *Steel-Graced*, Cinder was much further along in unarmed combat than he was with the sword. He had yet to land a touch on any of the apprentices with a practice blade. They remained too skilled, too fast, and too strong for him, but every day he closed the distance, learned something new. It helped that Cinder continued to work harder at his craft than anyone else. Every night after everyone else went home, Cinder would retreat to the Anvil where he trained late into the evening, defending against imagined attacks, correcting errors, and striving to perfect his form.

There was no other way to accelerate the trajectory of his growth, and every day, he hoped his hard work would show.

This morning, like all the other mornings, it hadn't. He sparred against Sash. Practice swords. As usual, both of them wore thick padding to protect against the wooden blades, and Cinder sweated despite the cold, winter air. His breath steamed.

So far, Sash had worked him pretty good, landing touches half a dozen times already, and Cinder needed a breather. While waiting for his heart to settle, he watched Master Jine train against his son, the latter seeking to advance to second-level journeyman. Two more rises in rank and Faine would reach first-level master status. The other apprentices trained as well, circling one another, crashing together in the sparring squares. Bones sparred against Gorant, generally crushing him.

If anything, Bones was even better now than he had been when Cinder had first arrived at *Steel-Graced*, and he continued to improve every day. Cinder shook his head. How much farther could Bones possibly advance? In Cinder's eyes, he was already a near perfect warrior.

Sash interrupted his observations. "Time's wasting, boy. Let's go."

Cinder grimaced, but he returned to their training square. He took a few seconds to study his opponent, scrutinizing Sash's posture, the angle of his weapon, the placement of his feet, anything to help him determine what might be coming. Sash didn't take it easy on him. No one did—Cinder had the welts to prove it—but Sash seemed to take a special pleasure in pushing and punishing him.

Without warning, Sash attacked. Cinder's eyes widened in surprise, and he gave ground. A few passes, and he settled into the match, initially holding his own. Three strokes later, he missed a parry and the whip-fast apprentice managed another touch. A slap against Cinder's arm. Even through the padding, it stung.

Cinder cursed.

Sash smirked. "Why are you even here? I've seen a baker's boy do better than you."

Cinder glowered. It didn't help that Sash needled him constantly about his lack of skill, about how he was wasting everyone's time at *Steel-Graced*. He was tired of it, but several factors kept him from giving in to Sash's scorn. First, Master Lerid didn't seem upset with Cinder's level of progression. In fact, he seemed happy with it. Second, Master Sharn's words about dedication and focus drove Cinder onward, inspired him. And finally, Faine had recently told him how it had taken Sash over a year to reach Cinder's current level of skill.

"I'm getting nothing out of this," Sash said.

"Well, I am." Cinder brought up his practice blade. "Ready?"

Sash snorted. "Sure. Why not?" He lunged. Cinder dodged artlessly, and Sash pressed him, staying in the pocket. "I'm more than happy to kick your ass all damn day."

He landed another touch, and Cinder went down. The blow had landed against his lead leg.

Sash smirked wider. "And there's nothing you can do about it."

Cinder clenched his teeth, wanting to shout his frustration. He glared at Sash, who continued to grin in mockery.

The wise warrior controls his emotions. His passions are bound to his needs. The sentiment whispered in Cinder's mind, sounding like an aphorism. He didn't know where he'd learned it, but it sounded right.

Cinder closed his eyes and sought to center himself. He took deep breaths, focusing on his lungs, imagining the anger draining from him, down his head, into his chest, his abdomen, and legs. It emptied out of him into the ground. When his anger was gone he opened his eyes, rose to his feet, and met Sash's arrogant visage. "Again."

"Why should I?" Sash demanded. "It's a waste of time."

"Because the other apprentices are working, and you've got nothing better to do."

"Give it up. You're hopeless."

"I don't quit." Cinder spoke in a matter-of-fact tone. "Come on." He held his arms out. "I can do this all day."

Sash ground his teeth. "Fine."

Cinder set himself. His heart beat slowly and steadily. His breathing came easily. His vision narrowed upon Sash. He saw nothing else.

Sash dashed forward, faster than before. Cinder slid to the side, avoiding a lunge. Sash recovered and slashed. Cinder parried and shifted off the center line. His concentration remained entirely on the other apprentice. The moment stretched, timeless yet ephemeral. A sensation washed over Cinder. His mind opened to a flash of understanding. He more precisely deciphered Sash's posture, the lean, the bend, the thrust, the parry . . .

Here comes a feint.

Cinder didn't fall for it.

This time a thrust, recovery, and a rapid sequence of testing slaps and more feints.

Cinder defended.

Sash stepped back, surprised.

An overhand strike, a horizontal slash, recovery, lunge.

Cinder evaded, parried, readied himself, and parried again.

On it went.

Cinder kept up with the far faster apprentice but eventually his body failed. His stamina had improved but not enough. He gasped for breath. The practice sword weighed heavy. His legs wouldn't respond in the way he required, leaving him slow as a slug.

Sash attacked again. Cinder tried to parry but was a split-second too slow. The blow slammed into his abdomen. He crumpled, falling to his knees, struggling to breathe. The wind had been knocked out of him. His stomach rebelled. He tried not to vomit while also trying to draw air into lungs refusing to work correctly.

"Not bad," Sash said.

Cinder glanced up and met the other apprentice's grin. For once Sash's face wasn't full of sarcasm, annoyance, or active malice. It was friendly. He even had a hand held out to help Cinder rise to his feet.

"You had me working. Think you can do it again?" Sash asked.

Cinder's stomach settled, and he took a cleansing inhalation. His lungs worked again. He took Sash's proffered hand and slowly clambered to his feet. "Only way to learn is to give it another go." He settled into a stance, practice sword at the ready.

Sash attacked.

Cinder defended. The understanding from his prior engagement remained. He could predict many of Sash's moves, blocking or evading as required. But once more, it was his weakness of body that let him down.

A slash slammed home against his thigh. A mite harder than a mere touch. Cinder smiled in spite of the pain. He limped, rubbing at the ache. He'd have a bruise on his thigh.

"What's so funny?" Sash asked.

"Nothing," Cinder said, still reveling in the perceptive leap he'd achieved today. By utilizing his knowledge, increasing it, he would have a chance to become a warrior worthy of the name.

Just as importantly, by improving himself, he could help the others achieve their dreams. *Steel sharpens steel.* The Maker's Tournament was still almost six months away. Dorr and Bones, *Steel-Graced*'s likely representatives, would need everyone's assistance.

Cinder was determined to be of use.

Cinder's sparring match against Sash left him limping for most of the remaining week, but by the time of his next rest day, it was fine. Thankfully so, since he planned on visiting Riner at *Our Lady of Fire*.

He hadn't seen Riner, Master Choff, or Cook Nestle in a few weeks, and on a cloudy morning, he hiked over to the orphanage.

The wind whipped about, swirling icy fingers through his hair and wiggling chilly streamers through narrow openings in his coat. He hunched his arms close to his body, noting that the cold weather hadn't seemed to have driven anyone else indoors. The streets remained clogged with many recent arrivals. Several merchant caravans from Gandharva, a large convoy of ships hauling down from the Savage Kingdoms, and a mercenary company, the infamous Red Flags, a unit nearly a legion strong. All of them had shown up in the last few weeks.

The Red Flags had come down from the northern territories of the Dagger Mountains where they'd taken on a commission from the Yaksha elves and spent the summer battling zahhacks. With the contract complete, they planned on shipping out with the Savage Kingdom vessels in a few days. Their intent was to raid the Wraith Lands for precious *aether* items. Elves, dwarves, and rishis paid a fortune for such treasures.

Cinder wasn't sure why, but it had something to do with purifying *lorethasra* or opening Chakras. He wasn't clear on the matter.

Maybe Riner would know.

As Cinder neared *Our Lady*, the neighborhood became poorer, a proliferation of sordid gambling casinos, alehouses hunkering like mushrooms, and scantily clad women and men leaning over second story railings and calling scandalous yet desultory offers to passersby.

Such establishments were rare around *Steel-Graced*, and Cinder noticed the number of mercenaries loitering about those houses of ill repute, glaring and strutting about as if they owned the city.

Like flies to dung.

Swift Sword was looking forward to being rid of the Red Flags. The mercenaries were bored, and with nothing else to do, they often picked fights wherever they went. Ten days into their stay, and the city watch was overwhelmed. The jail was overflowing with Red Flags, and there was no place left to put them. As a result, the watch had taken to housing them on the Savage Kingdom ships with strict prohibition to remain aboard until the vessels left Swift Sword's harbor.

Cinder crossed the street to avoid a passing group of Red Flags. He remembered Deepak and Master Choff's advice about mercenaries.

Minutes later, he reached *Our Lady*. He entered the grounds and went straightaway to the kitchen. It was after breakfast. Riner and Cook Nestle should be cleaning the dishes and prepping for lunch.

He found the two of them exactly where he expected. With clouds providing minimal light, they had the *diptha* bulbs turned up. Riner cleaned the dishes while Cook Nestle chopped potatoes on the butcher block island.

"Need any help?" Cinder asked.

Cook Nestle smiled his way. "You'll never hear me turning down free labor."

"Do you need me to prep the food?" Cinder asked. "Or would you rather I swept the dining hall?"

"I'll take care of the dining hall," Cook Nestle said. "You prep the food. That way, you two boys can catch up." She gave further instructions on what she needed done.

Cinder gave Riner a brotherly hug after Cook Nestle left. "It's good seeing you," he said. "How's Coral doing?" He tried to make his voice nonchalant, but he recalled the last time he'd seen her. A few weeks ago. He also remembered Bones' advice.

Coral truly was a wonderful person, and Cinder would be a fool to turn her down. Assuming she was interested in him in the same way. After all, maybe she wasn't. He frowned. Maybe she only thought of him as a friend, as someone who had helped her brother. Wait. Did that mean she thought of *him* like a brother, too?

Cinder didn't know, and his knitted brows furrowed more severely, lost in speculation. But Coral didn't smile at him like she smiled at Riner.

Did she? He didn't think so. Or maybe she did. Or maybe . . .

He cut off his thoughts, realizing they were rambling. He realized Riner had told him something, but he'd missed it. "What was that?" Cinder asked.

"I said she's doing well, and she asks about you, too."

Cinder's heart tripped a little faster, and butterflies fluttered in his stomach. Coral asked about him? He tried not to smile and failed.

"I'll tell her you asked after her. I'm sure that'll make her happy."

Is that a sly grin on Riner's face? "No need," Cinder said quickly. "Just tell her I said 'hello.'"

Cinder took up Cook Nestle's knife and began peeling and chopping potatoes. He changed the topic. "I finished the *Medeian Scryings*."

"What did you think of it?"

Cinder rolled his eyes, making sure Riner noticed. Reading the *Scryings* had been a chore. Boring, venal, and self-important were only the beginning of how he felt about the book. "I think there might be a nugget of wisdom in all those pages, but it's hidden beneath a mountain of bullshit."

Riner laughed, the sound open and free rather than diffident and shy like it had been when Cinder had first met him. "Don't say I didn't warn you," Riner said.

"There was one thing I ran across," Cinder said. "*Jivatma*. According to the *Scryings*, it's the same thing as *lorethasra*, but a more complete description of a person. That's not what I've read in other places. Everywhere else they're considered synonyms."

Riner nodded. "The rishis call it *Jivatma*. So did the Mythaspuris, or at least I think they did. Neither explain why, and the only ones who probably could are—"

"Shokan and Sira," Cinder guessed, smiling wryly.

Riner grinned.

"Speaking of those two, I also ran across something else in the *Scryings*. It says that *Jivatma* is the soul. Ever heard of that?"

Riner stared off in the distance as if lost in thought. "I don't think so. I've heard *lorethasra* called the soul, so I guess it makes sense that *Jivatma* would be the same thing." His vision sharpened. "Where did you read it?"

"An early sutra. Don't ask me which one, but the verse made a comment about how *Jivatma* infuses life into the body and impels the mind. Later on there is a separate reference to *lorethasra*."

Riner wore the faraway expression once more, clearly thinking the matter through.

Cinder waited.

A few seconds later, Riner's awareness returned, and he sighed, sounding disconsolate. "You realize what this means?"

Cinder shook his head.

"I don't remember that verse." He wore a look of misery. "I'll have to read the *Scryings* again."

"A horrible fate," Cinder agreed with a chuckle.

Cinder had a good visit with Riner and Cook Nestle. He also had time to talk to Master Choff and let him know how he was doing at *Steel-Graced*. As a result, his visit to the orphanage took longer than he intended, and he ended up leaving late in the afternoon.

A light rain had begun during his time at *Our Lady*, and he tightened his coat. The precipitation did what the cold weather couldn't; it drove people indoors. The streets were relatively free of traffic, and Cinder made good time on his way home to *Steel-Graced*.

Several blocks from the academy, he noticed nine Red Flags, easily identified by a large, flame-shaped red patch on their coat-sleeves. The mercenaries were a disparate group. Some were clean-shaven, a few had beards, a couple had scabby-looking scruff, and their hair length varied as much as their features and their build. However, other than their red patches, another common finding was their seedy, dissolute appearances.

And right now, the Red Flags looked like they were facing off against Dorr, Bones, Sash, Gorant, and Mirk. A fight was in the offing, and the street was quickly emptying. Folks rushed away from the two groups, flicking fearful glances over their shoulders. Cinder distantly noted faces peering through the windows of the surrounding buildings.

He quickened his pace, calculations racing through his mind. *How best should he approach the Red Flags?* It looked past time for mediation. He made a choice, deciding to approach at a perpendicular angle to the two groups. He remained quiet, making sure his boots didn't slap against the ground. His gaze narrowed. He wouldn't announce his presence until the last instant. He'd attack the Red Flags from behind.

Fairness in a street fight is for fools.

A calm settled over him, the stillness of a winter-frozen field. His adrenaline pumped, but he controlled it, maintaining focus. A wash of sound, a breaking wave rushing across a sandy beach. A distant light gleamed, calling to him. A pond, mirror-sheened, perfectly reflective glimmered into view and faded.

The Red Flags grinned. A few cracked knuckles.

"You don't belong in Swift Sword," Dorr said. "Crawl back and find whatever whorehouse you call home."

"And I'm sure we'll be finding your mothers spreading their legs in there," a bald Red Flag said, pate gleaming. "We'll be sure to give them our best." He thrust his pelvis, and his fellows brayed.

Cinder accelerated, anger rising. Throughout the city's alehouses, the Red Flags had chased off patrons, bullying them and the wait staff. Cinder hated bullies.

The two groups came together in a clash of knuckles, knees, and anything they could bring to hand.

The world seemed to brighten. Sounds hardened. Time slowed.

Cinder roared his fury, launching into the fray. He tackled two Red Flags who were battling Bones. He took them down and immediately surged to his feet. The ground was a terrible place to be in a fight. He frontkicked a rising Red Flag in the face. The mercenary face-planted. A rush of air heralded a punch. Cinder ducked and gave ground. The punch missed his head. He faced a burly Red Flag, one wearing braids.

A stupid affectation.

Cinder twisted to avoid a punch, leaned in to grab a handful of braids, and threw the Red Flag over his shoulder. The mercenary landed with an explosion of breath. Cinder dropped to land an elbow to the man's temple. The Red Flag was out of it.

Once again, Cinder was on the ground. This time, he didn't have a chance to get to his feet. A Red Flag loomed over him. A battering ram of a kick had Cinder groaning. He vomited his lunch and struggled to breathe. His ribs were bruised if not cracked. He covered up right before another kick landed. A boot-tip got through his defenses. The kick slammed into his cheek, opening it up. Another kick cracked into his skull. Cinder's vision went black for an instant.

A cry of pain, and the attack eased.

Cinder stumbled to his feet. Close at hand, Dorr was intent on hammerfisting a downed Red Flag into unconsciousness. Blood flowed, distorting Cinder's vision, but he saw a mercenary, a skinny knife-wielder stealthily approaching Dorr from behind.

Cinder shouted a warning and raced forward. His shout caused the Red Flag to halt. The mercenary's head came up, and his eyes widened. Cinder tackled him. The knife went flying.

A mad scramble. The Red Flag was good. He landed on top.

Cinder managed to grab onto the mercenary's wrists, controlling the other man's hands. He got a foot on a hip and pushed, reversing their positions. Cinder straddled the Red Flag. He let go of a wrist and cracked the mercenary with a heavy elbow. A scalp wound opened. Another elbow. The Red Flag's eyes rolled. His arms momentarily went limp. The mercenary wasn't out of the fight yet. Awareness returned to the Red Flag's eyes. Cinder put him out with a final elbow.

He glanced around, searching for another opponent. Two more Red Flags swayed on their feet, facing off against Bones, Dorr, and Mirk, who wore bruises and cuts but appeared far fresher. *Where are the other Steel-Graced apprentices?* Cinder quickly found them. Sash was laid out, and Gorant was trying to get to his feet but kept falling over.

A total of six Red Flag were either unconscious or out of the fight. *Wait. Weren't there nine of them?*

"Asshole."

A fist crashed into the side of Cinder's head. *There* were *nine.*

Cinder crashed over, turtling. Punches rained down, but only a few got through his defenses. Thankfully, the Red Flag was incompetent. Cinder took most of the blows on his shoulders and arms. He ignored the blood pouring down his face, the blurred vision from his aching head and got to his knees in stages. He accepted more blows on his shoulders, taking a second to gather himself. Once ready, he shot toward the Red Flag. He grabbed the mercenary's lead leg, powering forward. From there, he rose, driving the mercenary backward. Cinder lifted, and the Red Flag cursed as his feet left the ground.

Cinder slammed the mercenary to the bricks. The man's head bounced against the unyielding surface, and he went out.

Once again, Cinder was on the ground. A really terrible place to be in a fight, and he'd done it three times now. He groaned, staggering to his feet. Thankfully, he had nothing else to worry about because by now the Red Flags were out of it. Only one of them still stood.

It was the one who had spoken to Dorr about whorehouses. The bald mercenary waved off Bones and Dorr as they approached him, hands fisted. "Enough," the mercenary cried. "You win. We're done. Let me just get me men before the watch shows up."

Dorr stepped ahead of the others, getting directly in the face of the

Red Flag. His hands remained clenched. "I'll want all your names and the names of your commander," he said. "I'm passing them on to the watch. Go back to your ships. Stay there and don't disembark. Next time you fight the *Steel-Graced Adepts*, you won't walk away from it."

The mercenary merely nodded and set about the work of gathering his fellow Red Flags.

As for Cinder, while the thrill of victory might eventually come over him, right now all he could focus upon was his aching body. Everything seemed to hurt, and he dearly hoped there wouldn't be another fight with the Red Flags. Once was enough.

12

"**E**nd!" Master Lerid shouted.

As soon as he heard the release from the exercise session, Cinder immediately flopped at the waist. His hands went to his knees and he gasped, struggling to breathe. Following the brawl against the Red Flags, Cinder had spent most of the past two weeks recuperating from his injuries. He hadn't been able to afford to see a physician like the other *Steel-Graced* apprentices, so his body had to heal on its own.

Devesh-damned mercenaries. He had finally achieved a level of ability where he could hold his own against the other apprentices, and then this happened. Rest and recuperation. He had lost most of his hard-won strength and stamina, and the regular drills had him once again panting like he'd never done them before.

He took a last shuddering breath. There was no use whining about it now. *Push past the pain.* It was his private mantra. He'd get back what he'd lost and then some. He pushed off his knees, straightened with a long exhalation, and worked to control his breathing. *In through the nose. Out through the mouth.* No gasping. Deep, steady breaths.

The other apprentices exited the yard, laughing and joking, and

Cinder watched them, envy stirring in his heart. If he had the coin or a wealthy clan to support him, he could have seen a physician and purchased the *aether* tablets to heal his injuries. He wouldn't then be so far behind.

He quickly snipped off his whiny thoughts. He didn't have the coin, so there was no purpose in wishing for it.

Once his heart settled to a normal pace, and his breathing came more easily, he glanced around the yard. This was his home, the place where he'd truly come alive, and it was a hard place, but he loved it.

The sun hung low in the sky, and shadows stretched across the yard. The day was warm for this time of year, and his sweat quickly dried. A cool wind tousled his hair. The late day breeze carried a touch of dryness mingling with the smell of woodsmoke drifting from the many hearths throughout the neighborhood. It also wafted the aroma of fresh bread from the bakery next door. Cinder inhaled the delicious smell, his stomach growling. All the resting and recovering and training had him ravenous.

"Hold a moment," Master Lerid said.

"I have supper to attend, sir."

"Faine can do it. I already asked him," Master Lerid said. "Sit. We should talk. I have matters to discuss." He pointed to a pair of stout chairs in a corner.

Cinder hissed in discomfort as he sat down. His thighs and buttocks burned, the joyful ache of overwork and greater strength to come. Squats into jumps had that effect.

"You're recovering?" Master Lerid asked.

Cinder grimaced, rubbing at the front of his thighs. "I'm coming along."

Master Lerid eyed him for a few seconds, neither of them speaking. "You're probably thinking about how much further along you'd be if you could have afforded *aether* tablets?"

"Am I so obvious?" Cinder asked with a grin.

"I saw you staring at the other apprentices," Master Lerid said. "It wasn't hard to deduce. Besides. You're a terrible liar." He smiled, taking the sting out of his words. "You'll want to work on that. Sometimes a lie is required."

"Sir?" Cinder asked, confused.

Master Lerid waved aside the question. "It's of no importance. I wanted to explain something to you. I could have purchased *aether* tablets for you. Master Jine thought I should."

"Master Jine? Why?" Cinder didn't think the elder master liked him very much. He had a curtness when speaking to Cinder, a tone in his voice not present when he spoke to the other apprentices.

"I could have, but I didn't, and I want to explain why. By healing naturally from the injuries, it'll inure you to pain. It'll teach you to work around it, fight on even when your body tells you it can't go on. You'll also be stronger in the end for it." He shrugged "Plus, *aether* tablets won't be available in the field when you're serving in the army, whichever army that might be."

Cinder frowned. "Your statement implies there might be more than one army who accepts my application." As far as he'd reckoned matters, the Army of Rakesh would be the only one in which he could enlist. Prior to his injuries against the damned mercenaries, he had a fond, faint hope of entering the Third Directorate. Now, not so much, at least not this year or next. He'd lost too much time healing, and he'd keep on losing time while he recovered his strength and stamina.

He also recalled Faine's statements when Cinder had first joined *Steel-Graced Adepts.* The journeyman had said Cinder would never make it to the Third Directorate. He'd started his training too late. He'd be years in acquiring the skills necessary to compete in the Maker's Tournament, but by then, it would be too late. The Third Directorate didn't admit humans who were older than twenty.

"There are many armies a warrior of Rakesh could join," Master Lerid said. "Any of the Savage or Sunset Kingdoms would be glad to have you. Same with the Gandharvan Federation or Yaksha Sithe, it-self." He rapped the table. "We may not have the skills and abilities of the woven, but the men of Rakesh are the finest human warriors in the world. It is our pride and our calling to serve honorably and fight without fear." His eyes glowed with intensity. "That is what it means to be of Rakesh. Never forget it."

Cinder was somewhat taken aback by his master's fervor. "I'm sorry, sir. I didn't mean to overstep or insult you." While he offered an apology, it was half-hearted because he still didn't understand what he had said or done to cause his master to speak so forcefully.

"You didn't overstep or insult me," Master Lerid said. "I only want you to truly know your worth. Right now, I think you measure yourself far too low. You have a strange gift, a rare ability to decipher your opponent's plans with a single glimpse. You also have a rapidly improving skillset. You're improving by leaps and bounds, faster than anyone I ever expected to train. It's astonishing." He shook his head, an air of disbelief on his face. "I know you won't get a swollen head by what I'm saying. The truth is you're too humble in your reach."

"Yes, sir," Cinder replied. He acknowledged his master's words while confusion continued to ripple across his mind. He had never thought he was being too humble when evaluating his abilities. He thought he was merely accurate.

Master Lerid chuckled. "I can see you either don't believe me or you don't understand what I'm saying." His smile faded, and he leaned forward in his chair. "Continue training and working as you've been doing. Improving, never cease in your desire for perfection, and you can reach the Third Directorate." Again his eyes glowed intense. "And I mean by this year."

Cinder closed his eyes and breathed deep. Master Lerid's words set fire to his fading hope. The words were everything he needed to hear. He would continue to heal. He would continue to train. He would continue to perfect himself. He opened his eyes, smiling in raptor-like anticipation. "Yes, sir."

A month following the brawl against the Red Flags, Cinder was finally healed of the last of his injuries, and he and Coral walked along a busy boulevard in the heart of Swift Sword. They were several blocks north of the docks, and the stench of drying fish drifted on a vagrant breeze now and then, polluting the air. The sun hung high in the sky, an unseasonably warm day. Spring was coming fast—or at least he hoped so. The weather was made worse by the thick crowd sharing the street with Cinder and Coral. The heavy traffic clogged and congested the avenue, making it difficult to make forward progress. In addition, the cacophony from the multitude of conversations required Cinder and Coral to shout at one another in order to be heard.

"You should have at least let me pay for your meal," Cinder told Coral.

They had just had lunch at Rozero's Place, and the meal hadn't been cheap. It didn't matter that the restaurant wasn't likely to be mistaken for a fine dining establishment. Rozero's Place didn't have waiters in starched uniforms speaking in hushed, calm voices. Everything 'no, sir' or 'yes, madam' or 'of course, sir'. Rozero's Place was an eatery catering to tradesmen and their families instead of the wealthy. But for someone of meager means like Cinder, even moderate meant it would have drained most of his money.

Coral had paid for both of them.

"Consider it my treat for everything you did for Riner," Coral said, having to speak directly into Cinder's ear in order to be heard over the surrounding crowd.

Cinder didn't think her generosity of coin was a fair trade for what he'd done for her brother, but it was also an argument he couldn't win. They'd already gone over the matter on several prior occasions and nothing he said would change Coral's mind.

Coral must have noticed his disagreement. She graced him with a crooked grin, amusement clear in her features. "Did you have enough money to pay for both of us?"

Cinder didn't bother answering. She knew the answer. He had enough coins but only barely.

Coral chuckled at his lack of response, nudging into him with the length of her body. "When you have the money, you can pay then.

How about that?"

Cinder nodded agreement. "It's a promise."

They kept walking, Cinder wasn't exactly sure where. "Where are we going, by the way? The playhouse?"

Rather than their normal evening busking on his day off, Coral had asked him to accompany her to a play. Cinder had asked about the cost, and when she breezily named a number, he made sure to save enough money to purchase a ticket.

Instead of answering, Coral tucked a hand into the crook of Cinder's elbow and guided him into a relatively quiet alley. Small piles of garbage lay shoved along the sides of the narrow lane, and a rat scampered away at their approach. The stench of drying fish was replaced by a sewage reek of urine and feces. Cinder didn't like the gloom within the alley, and his senses heightened. This had the trappings of a place where good people found themselves robbed.

"It's safe during the day," Coral said, apparently picking up on his increased vigilance. "It's only at night you should avoid this alley."

Cinder didn't know if she was right, but some of his worry faded when he noticed three well-dressed women saunter in their direction. The two groups had to hug the walls of the alley in order to pass one another.

"See," Coral said.

Cinder grunted acceptance of her assessment, but he continued to let his eyes flit about, searching for danger.

Coral chuckled. "I see what you're doing."

Twenty feet later, they exited the alley and joined another street, one as busy as the one they had just left. They journeyed through another equally shady backstreet, took a left turn and then a right, and were soon striding along a road lined by townhouses and well-maintained shops.

"It's right here," Coral said, smiling in excitement, an extra bounce in her step.

They came to one of Swift Sword's many squares. Tall bushes lined the perimeter of the park, creating a green wall that provided privacy and serenity for the grassy interior. A pair of paths broke the symmetry of the shrubbery and intersected at the base of a centrally placed live oak. The moss-covered tree towered over the square, shading a small crowd gathered around a middle-aged man standing atop a low platform.

He wore a half-smile, one shadowed by a dark, luxurious mustache. His bright clothing had clearly seen better days, and he clasped his hands behind his back as he seemed to gaze patiently at or beyond the crowd.

Coral drew Cinder to a halt, and they faced the man.

"Why are we here?" Cinder asked. He glanced at the others gathered around.

It was a group of well-dressed individuals. Their clothes were fine but not overly so. These were upper-class folk, but they weren't wealthy.

"This is the play," Coral replied. An instant later, she waved aside her answer. "Well, not really the play, but it's what I wanted you to see." Her smile brightened. "You'll see."

A surprise, then. But what kind? Cinder took a closer examination of the man on the stage whose bearing spoke of patience, of waiting for the attention of those gathered here to settle. *A performance rather than a play.* Then there was the man's vibrant clothing . . .

Cinder smiled in recognition. "A gleeman."

Coral was still grinning, and she clapped her hands, pleased and excited. "Yes. His name is Tomas Linimer. He's quite famous. My vocal instructor knows him. I spoke to Tomas yesterday. He has a story to tell. I think you'll like it."

Tomas lifted his arms, calling for quiet. Once the crowd silenced, he began speaking, his voice rich and sonorous, a timbre at odds with Tomas' appearance. His voice should have belonged to a much bigger man. "Sapient Dormant and Manifold Fulsom," Tomas said. "Names that shine brightly. Names given to the moons above. Names of the leaders of the Mythaspuris. The legendary men who cast Shet into a deathless sleep. But who were they before they became myth?" Tomas offered a sly smile. "Wouldn't you like to know?"

The crowd called encouragement. A few folk tossed coins into the hat at Tomas' feet to spur the gleeman on.

Tomas tilted his head in acknowledgement of their generosity and spoke on. "Before Shokan and Sira were lost to memory, mystery, and myth, Sapient and Manifold were their finest friends and their most powerful servants. It leads to an obvious question: from whence did the Mythaspuris truly arise? After all they came to *our* aid thousands of years after the deaths of Shokan and Sira. So where were they and what were they doing in that long interval?" Again came the sly smile. "Does no one ever wonder? Perhaps this will give you a hint." His voice took on a more serious note, one matched by his mien. *"After sailing across an immensity of sealess stars, the Mythaspuris came to Seminal, and we celebrated the sun. The kingdoms of our home were a dark place with a dark, distant star. A pallid realm."* The gleeman gazed about, letting the crowd soak in the statement.

Tomas had clearly quoted a work, but Cinder didn't know which one. He hadn't read much about the Mythaspuris, and he made a silent promise to correct the oversight.

After pausing for several seconds, Tomas continued. "Long have I pondered those words, written as they were by Manifold Fulsom himself. Long have I given thought to their meaning, and I am not the only one." He thrust a finger in the air. "Many have also wondered at this mythical homeland of the Mythaspuris. Where is it? Across the vast and trackless Shakaran Ocean or the equally endless Shasala Ocean?" While he spoke, Tomas strode the length of his small platform, hands clasped behind his back, head bowed and brow furrowed as if in deep consideration.

Cinder found himself captivated by Tomas' story. Not by the content since the gleeman hadn't yet said much, but more by the notion that a vast mystery waited to be unearthed. A secret story about Sapient's and Manifold's unknown past, one Tomas would reveal and deliver to those collected here, the select few.

The gleeman reached the end of the small platform, and he spun on a heel, strode the other direction, and stopped once he was centered on the stage. He again faced the audience. "I have my own beliefs about the place from whence Sapient, Manifold, and the Mythaspuris hailed." He smiled warmly, arms open as if to hug the audience. "However, you are kind folk, and I won't dare harden your hearts with my strange notions. Instead, allow me to tell you a story, one which may shed light on my odd suppositions."

Cinder sucked his teeth, unsure where this was going.

"Long ago, in a far distant place was a young man, Wilm Wile," Tomas said. "A simple man was our Wilm Wile, possessing an abundance of friendship and fellowship and not a care in the world. He 'wiled' away the days of his life."

Cinder groaned at the awful pun, and he wasn't the only one.

Tomas chuckled at the response. He picked up the story again. "Our Wilm was fortunate in his friends and family, but disaster eventually found him. And like it so often does, it came in the guise of a beautiful woman. Saranna was her name, and Wilm was beguiled by this charming deceiver." Tomas' voice carried an ominous note. "In time, Wilm found himself lost and trapped in a strange land, the realm of Sin. There, he was captured by the king who ruled this kingdom, a terrible tyrant who called himself the Servant. Worst of all, the author of Wilm's tragedy was none other than the king's beautiful daughter, Saranna. It was she who betrayed Wilm to her father."

None of this came as a surprise to Cinder. In every story he'd read, it was the beautiful woman—usually wise in the ways of the world—who betrayed the young man, the unknowing naïf. Others in the crowd must not have been as well-read because they gasped in shock. Cinder rolled his eyes at their surprise. *Don't they pay attention to the stories?*

Tomas continued. "Wilm was enslaved in Sin for an endless time of toil. He struggled in this cruel realm, fighting to stay alive. It was truly awful. A generous young man who had previously possessed a life full of love and happiness was now bereft of all friendship. Worse, his only companion during this time was his greatest enemy, the person he hated above all others: Jayak Riddle, a man enslaved alongside him.

"Then, in the darkest hour of his slavery, faith lifted her lovely head and brought him hope." Tomas' features shifted with the mood of his story, transitioning from furious betrayal to helpless sorrow to rising optimism. "And like it so often does for the most fortunate of men, it came in the guise of a beautiful woman. Saranna. The voice of Lord Devesh reached her hollow heart, filling it with his singing light. Saranna repented of her evil."

Cinder made a noise of surprise. He hadn't expected this twist.

"She recruited a mighty warrior to help Wilm and Jayak escape Sin. And Wilm's friends and family hadn't been idle during his imprisonment. A man and woman of uncommon wisdom came to them." Tomas nodded. "Yes. I speak of the Blessed Ones. Shokan and Sira. They developed a bold plan to free Wilm."

Cinder had a guess as to how the rest of the story would unfold, and he placed a private bet.

"On the day of Wilm's departure from Sin, when he enacted his mad plan to escape from slavery, he spoke to Shokan and came to understand solemn truths. Wile had to forgive his enemy, the man he hated above all others, Jayak Riddle. Wilm made this man his brother. And Wilm forgave Saranna, too. More he freed her from the bootheel of the Servant's tyranny. Later, in a land of lush plenty, they wed."

Tomas bowed his head, as though overcome by the emotion of his tale. He addressed the audience again. "How did such miracles come to pass, you might ask?" Tomas didn't wait for an answer. "It is because the highest ideals that we are taught of Devesh are to forgive and to love. Wilm forgave, and he loved and he was made whole and happy." Tomas smiled broadly. "Ponder what I said and consider the place from which Sapient and Manifold set sail. Dark kingdoms. Pallid realms. Think of how they must have ended up in such a place for they had prior been boon companions to the Blessed Ones."

Coins rained into Tomas' hat, and the crowd cheered, although many appeared confused. This hadn't been a humorous tale or one meant to send their pulses racing with excitement. It had been a story meant to provide a lesson, but Cinder couldn't imagine what it might be. The names, though—Wilm and Saranna—struck a note of familiarity. Maybe before his memory loss he'd heard the tale. He reckoned that to be the most likely explanation.

"I'll be at Whalet House all week to provide further entertainment for those of curious bent," Tomas said after his performance.

Cinder wished he could hear more from the gleeman. Unfortunately, even water at Whalet House, likely served in a crystal decanter, was more than he could afford to spend.

"Thank you for bringing me here," Cinder said to Coral as the crowd disbanded.

"You're welcome." She eyed him quizzically. "Do you know what he meant about how the story of Wilm relates to the Mythaspuris?"

"I have no idea."

Coral chuckled. "Good. I'm glad I'm not the only one."

After listening to a few more stories from Tomas, Cinder dropped Coral off at the home where she worked and made his way back toward *Steel-Graced Adepts*. It was getting late, and the sun stood only a few fingers above the horizon. The day's unexpected warmth had given way to a cool evening. The smell of moisture promised a snowfall to come, while an intermittent breeze tugged at Cinder's clothes now and then. Folk hurried about, rushing to get home before dark. Others traveled in small groups, shouting in voices filled with laughter and excitement. They were obviously readying for a night out with their friends.

Cinder frowned when he noticed a group of five men heading his way. All of them wore the uniforms of the Army of Rakesh, gray trousers tucked into black boots and dark-blue shirts. He also recognized two of the figures. *Jarde and Stard.*

His heart sank.

It was too late to avoid their attention. Jarde had already nudged Stard's shoulder, speaking to him while pointing Cinder out.

For a second, Cinder closed his eyes in disbelief and disgust. *What did I do to deserve another brawl so soon after the last one?* Maybe Devesh would allow him to walk away from this one. Or run away. As long as he didn't come out with any serious injuries. Five against one was bad odds, and it wasn't worth it to test himself against Jarde, Stard, and their friends.

Cinder kept the group in view, but he gazed about, searching for a way to escape.

"Hey, Cinder!" Jarde shouted. "Hold on there. We've got words. We want to talk. That's it."

Cinder could always run, but the notion of scampering away from a pair of bullies like a scalded dog didn't sit well with him. Plus, Jarde's words didn't sound belligerent. Strangely enough, they sounded entreating, and with all the people wandering the streets, he hoped the Errows wouldn't be stupid enough to start a fight given all the witnesses.

His decision made, he folded his arms, waiting to find out what the Errow wanted.

"Heard you got into *Steel-Graced Adepts*," Jarde said, oddly friendly. "That's impressive as hell. Congratulations."

Cinder started in surprise. Jarde sounded earnest in his admiration. He remained alert, however. The Errows had never given him reason to trust them.

Stard chuckled and elbowed Jarde in the ribs. "Yeah. At least we got our asses handed to us by a right badass."

The other three soldiers with them had hung back, but they rustled to life on hearing this. They faced Cinder with renewed interest.

Cinder held off from taking a step away from the soldiers. If they were friends with the Errows, he didn't figure they would be the honorable sort. However, retreating prompted the notion of weakness and weakness would invite an attack.

"You kicked their asses?" a tall, beefy soldier asked Cinder. He wore a friendly smile. "That sounds about right. Those two are about the sorriest sack of Errow grub to ever enter the Army of Rakesh."

For a wonder, Jarde didn't take offense. "And this ugly one is the only person in all Rakesh who a dwarf would pity for his looks."

Some of Cinder's concern dissipated. None of the soldiers appeared ready for a rumble. Instead they spoke to one another in the teasing fashion of young men who were good friends.

Jarde must have noticed. "You were probably thinking we wanted another go at you," he said with a grin. "That's not it."

"The thought crossed my mind," Cinder said. He relaxed further, although not entirely. While he currently felt more and more comfortable in the presence of Jarde and Stard, it didn't mean he liked them.

"I can understand why you might think that," Jarde said, "but we saw you, and me and Stard had the same inkling."

"Which is?"

"We wanted to thank you," Jarde said.

Cinder blinked. Of all the things the Errows might have said, a statement of gratitude was the last thing he expected to hear. "Thank me? Why?"

"Because you kicked our asses and didn't rat us out," Stard answered.

"Plus, by kicking our asses, we ended up sent to the army," Jarde added. "Army discipline was the best thing that ever happened to us."

"If you don't mind me saying so, we're much better people than we used to be. In some ways, it's all because of you."

"You're welcome," Cinder said, perplexed by the shape of the conversation. It hadn't been what he'd expected. The apparent change of heart in the two Errows . . . he still didn't believe it. "If you really feel that way, why don't you apologize to Riner? He was the one you hurt the most."

The two Errows shared a look of uncertainty and possible shame.

"We thought about it," Stard said, "but we're not sure we should. He might be better off if we never step foot into his life again."

"We weren't good to him," Jarde said.

Cinder blinked in surprise. What was going on? Bullies couldn't become better people. He would have wagered every last coin on that fact.

And yet . . .

Jarde and Stard appeared repentant, a demeanor Cinder would

have never expected to see from either of them. Maybe bullies *could* change—stranger things had happened—and maybe they even understood that humbly asking for true forgiveness was one of the hardest acts in life. The only thing harder might be offering it.

"No, you weren't," Cinder agreed, speaking to Stard, "but if you ever want to set things right, you'll want to talk to Riner."

"I suppose so," Jarde said. His troubled expression cleared slightly. "We didn't mean to keep you so long. Have a good night."

The soldiers said their farewells and left with glad laughter.

Cinder watched them leave in bewilderment. Jarde and Stard seemed to be utterly transformed. They weren't anything like the bullies he'd known at *Our Lady of Fire*. He shook his head in disbelief. Who could have guessed that two people with such loathsome personalities could become persons of worth?

Maybe that was the point of Tomas' story about Wilm and Saranna. She had betrayed him and had the courage to ask for forgiveness and received it. Perhaps even the worst of us are worthy of Devesh's mercy, and if so, what does it mean for how we should treat one another?

13

A winter wind rattled the shutters of *Steel-Graced Adepts*, and Cinder grimaced. Last week's warm weather had taken a turn, but thankfully, the cold didn't penetrate the kitchen where Cinder was cleaning a few final dirty dishes, utensils, pots, and pans. The oven continued to bleed heat, warming the space, and he remained comfortable. He swept the room one more time and gave it a last look-over. *Good enough.*

He could finally take his meal. Cinder turned down the *diptha* lamps and gathered his mug of water and the plate he'd already piled high with chicken, brown rice, and spiced lentils. He set them down on the table in the narrow room where everyone normally had their meals. Large, gray blocks of stone formed the walls, giving the space the claustrophobic presence of a cellar, a sense heightened by the dim lighting.

At least it was quiet. The only ones left at the school were Mirk and Gorant. From the hearth room next door, Cinder could hear them conversing. The other apprentices had gone home earlier in the day while Masters Lerid and Jine had personal matters to attend. As for Morr, Cinder had no idea what he was doing. Probably off drinking with friends.

Cinder took a seat, groaning in gratitude. It was after supper, and following a long day of training interspersed with hours of cooking and cleaning, he felt like an overheated dog on a muggy, summer day. All he wanted to do was lie down and sleep.

Before that, however, he needed food. Lots of it. He tucked into his supper. First, he finished off the chicken and was in the midst of working through the rice and lentils when Mirk and Gorant wandered in.

"We are heading off," Gorant said in his inimitable strange accent. "See you in the morning?"

"Of course," Cinder replied, smiling slightly. "I'm always here."

"The son of a mother probably trains in the middle of the night," Mirk said. "That's how he's gotten so damn good so damn fast."

Cinder continued eating the rice and lentils. Ever since he'd become aware of his unique ability to recognize his opponent's likely decisions based on their posture and positioning, he'd made himself focus on that talent. He exercised it every day, although his focus remained on perfecting his sword forms and strengthening his body. Still, his unusual skill had served him well so far. As a result of his work, he could now defeat Gorant and Mirk on most occasions and Sash sometimes. As for Dorr and Bones? Not yet.

But soon.

"That is not what I heard," Gorant said in reply to Mirk's statement.

Mirk quirked a grin. "What? That he doesn't train in the middle of the night?"

"I don't train in the middle—"

"I know that," Mirk said to Cinder, rolling his eyes. "I was joking. Everyone takes things so bloody literally."

"I heard a different reason for how he has gotten so good," Gorant said.

Mirk perked up. "Oh? What's this? Speak on, man. What did you hear?"

"Faine said our skinny friend can predict the outcome of a fight. All he needs is to see someone's stance."

Mirk scoffed. "What's so impressive about that? *I* can do the same thing. I've heard you can, too. Same with Bones and Dorr."

Cinder kept quiet. According to Faine, Mirk was wrong. Not everyone could do what Cinder could. It was a master-level skill but pointing it out would likely strike the others as arrogant, a trait he disliked.

"Not like Cinder," Gorant said. "We can tell if someone will fall, whether they're in position to counter, feint, those kinds of things. Cinder sees more. Faine says he sees through feints and traps. He knows by blade position, stance, and balance alone what the next strike will likely be, and what will come after his counter."

Mirk stopped scoffing. "I thought only the masters could do that."

Gorant gave an eloquent shrug as if to say, *"Maybe so, but I'm only telling what I heard."*

"I thought it took decades to learn what you're describing," Mirk said.

"It does," Gorant replied.

Cinder finished his food and drained his water. He went to the kitchen and cleaned his plate and mug while Mirk and Gorant continued discussing his ability.

When he returned, Mirk gazed at him in inquiry. "Is this true?"

"It might be," Cinder said. "But it's meaningless if I can't use the information it provides. I'm slow, and no one feels the sting of my blows."

"Oh, piss off," Mirk said with a chuckle. "Stop your whining." He clutched his hands together as if in prayer. His voice rose an octave and a quavering mockery entered his tone. *"I'm slow. No one feels the sting of my blows."* He growled, "Shut up. You've got a miraculous gift there. No wonder you keep kicking our asses."

"He is right," Gorant said. "I would take a skill like yours over Sash's speed. So would Sash. Do not underestimate its worth."

"Were you born with it?" Mirk asked.

Cinder hesitated. "I don't know. Maybe."

"Well, don't go complaining about nothing no more," Mirk said. "I'm off."

He and Gorant bundled up and left.

After they departed, Cinder went to his room—the closet-under-the-stairs—and gathered his coat and mandolin. He left the academy, as well. With a rest day tomorrow, he had plans to meet Coral and Riner tonight.

Cinder entered the Lonely Donkey, mandolin in hand, relieved by the sudden warmth. Snow fell outside, dusting his hair and clothing.

Last week's warm spell had lifted his hopes for an early spring, but the current cold snap dashed those optimisms. It also let him know something about Rakesh's winters: they bit down with frigid teeth and didn't easily let go. The freezing weather had started with an icy rain, damp and uncomfortable, that transitioned into inches of snowfall during the afternoon and evening. The crippling cold had driven most folk indoors. No one lingered outside, and only a hearty few, like Cinder, traveled the darkened streets.

Cinder let the door to the alehouse close and pressed deeper inside, away from the wretched cold. His wool coat—a hand-me-down from Faine who could no longer fit into it—kept his torso warm but his fingers felt as stiff and cold as frozen steel. It wouldn't do. He needed his hands to play the mandolin if he wanted to earn a bit of extra money.

Cinder rubbed at his hands—he didn't have any gloves—blowing warmth into them as he stepped deeper into the Lonely Donkey. He called a greeting to Trip and a few patrons he'd gotten to know during his times at the pub. He recognized their faces, but didn't remember their names.

He was terrible with names.

Cinder smiled to himself. Or maybe he was just terrible with anything related to memory. The recollections from his prior sixteen years of life remained a blank slate and likely always would, but it no longer bothered him. He had come to accept it, moving on and creating a new life for himself in Swift Sword.

He gazed around the alehouse, searching for Coral and Riner.

Smoke wafted through the room, obscuring his view. A fire burned cheerily in the large hearth. The alehouse was crowded tonight, a large gathering of folk hoping to share warmth and fellowship during winter's last month. On a more selfish level, for Cinder it also meant a greater opportunity for tips from the patrons.

He smiled in anticipation.

He saw Coral then, sitting alone at a corner table with two mugs in front of her. Riner was nowhere in evidence. Maybe he was using the outhouse.

Cinder went to her.

Coral wore sensible clothing, a long coat over a thick, blue dress reaching down to black boots. Sensible, but the clothing gave her the appearance of having donned a sack. She'd left her hair untied, though, letting it follow the soft curves of her face. Doing so transformed her from merely pretty to lovely.

Cinder smiled. Coral *was* lovely.

"Riner won't be joining us tonight," Coral said, smiling to him, her eyes crinkling and dimples showing. "He has extra chores today. I hope you're not too disappointed."

Cinder paused in the act of sitting. He and Coral alone again? He didn't know what to make of it. Was it intentional on her part? Not that he was complaining. He liked Coral. She was wonderful; smart, easy to talk to, and she made him laugh. She was also lovely, and he sensed she liked him, too, but was it only as a friend? He still wasn't sure, and he didn't want to risk their relationship over his possible misconceptions.

Cinder lowered into the chair, forcing aside his considerations. "How is Riner?"

"He's well," Coral answered. "He sends his regards." She pushed one of the mugs to him. "I ordered for you."

Cinder took a sip. *Warm cider*. He sighed in appreciation.

"How are you doing at *Steel-Graced*?" Coral offered a teasing smile. "Are you still the prodigy your friends say you are?"

"I don't know about being a prodigy, but I'm starting to keep up with them."

"You're always too modest," Coral said, resting her chin on folded hands. She captured his gaze with her dark eyes, which sparkled in amusement. "Answer honestly. Are you keeping up or catching up?"

Cinder considered her question. In his five months at *Steel-Graced* he had gone from barely able to do the physical drills, much less the sparring, to regularly defeating Mirk and Gorant. He recalled his conversation with them. "Catching up." He couldn't hold back the smile of pleasure.

Coral clapped her hands, seemingly delighted. "At last. He accepts the truth."

The door to the Lonely Donkey opened and a blast of cold air followed. It continued to flow like a freezing river, the icy wind never letting off, and Cinder twisted around in his seat to face the entrance. Whoever had entered the alehouse was standing at the front door, leaving it wide open.

Cinder glowered until the door finally closed. "I hate winter," he declared.

Coral's brow lifted in disbelief. "Oh, my. Just then you sounded like a whining child. Don't tell me the prodigy is afraid of a little cold."

"I'm not afraid of the cold. I just don't like it."

Coral chuckled. "I'm sure that's all it is."

One of the waitresses, a new one, someone Cinder had never before met, came to their table. She carried a tray containing a bowl of stew and a hunk of bread. She set the food in front of him.

Cinder leaned back in his chair, throwing Coral a surprised look.

"I know you probably had dinner at the academy, but you're always hungry, so I ordered for you." Coral shrugged. "And don't worry about me. I already ate."

"How much do I owe you?" Cinder asked, indicating the food and ale.

"Nothing. Consider it a gift from a friend."

Cinder eyed her in skepticism. He didn't like owing anyone anything.

"Really. You don't owe me anything," Coral urged. "It's a gift. Eat."

Cinder relented. "You treat me too well."

Coral twirled a thick strand of hair around a finger, smiling her crooked grin. "No less than you deserve."

Cinder had no response to her statement. Was there an offer in what she had said? One of the other apprentices, someone like Bones who had a way with women, might have been able to tell him. He decided to treat Coral's statement as nothing more or less than friendship. It was safer that way.

He tucked into his food, finishing the stew in record time. At *Steel-Graced*, meals were consumed quickly. The apprentices took an inordinate joy in stealing one another's food. It was an amusement played by a simple rule: finish your meal and anything still on anyone else's plate was fair game.

"What do you want to play tonight?" Coral asked while he wiped the bowl with the last of his bread.

"I thought we'd play something lively. Something to get the blood pumping."

"You don't think people are already warm?" Coral asked, waving herself as if she was overheated. "With the fire and all the bodies, it's a right summer's day."

Cinder frowned in confusion.

Coral wore another teasing grin. "Or did you mean you need to get *your* blood pumping? Weren't you just complaining about the cold?"

Cinder laughed, enjoying her gentle teasing. "Not anymore. I'm fine."

"Good. Then let's go." Coral held out a hand, drawing Cinder to his feet. "It's time to play." She walked ahead of him, leading him by the hand to the small stage opposite the bar. She glanced over her shoulder. "Try to keep up."

14

It was another full month of ongoing discipline and training until the calendar finally marked winter's end. However, when spring arrived, it entered as a lamb rather than a lion. The days remained cool, but at least the gray-bellied clouds had been swept away and replaced by beaming sunshine.

Unfortunately, this early in the day—a few hours after dawn—the sun didn't offer much warmth. Cinder's breath plumed in the frigid, dry air, and he waited alongside the other apprentices in the courtyard for Master Lerid to tell them what he wanted for the morning sparring session. The world held still and quiet, although Cinder knew others were up and working. For instance, the baker and his family next door. The delicious aroma of bread baking set his mouth to salivating.

His mind drifted. At least the cold no longer bothered him so much. After six long months of training outdoors, he was now inured to winter's lack of charm. Plus, the stretching exercises they did prior to sparring helped keep him warm.

He only wished Master Lerid would let them get to the sparring part. Standing around would only give the chill a chance to penetrate their clothing.

Master Lerid finally spoke to the assembled apprentices. "The Maker's Tournament is in three months, in Devasth, summer's holiest month. Train hard. The ones who will represent the school have yet to be fully determined."

It wasn't entirely true. It would be Bones and Dorr. Despite Cinder's increased status, he had a long way to go to reach them. They would be the ones who represented *Steel-Graced's* honor in the Maker's Tournament.

As for Cinder, he had recently surpassed Sash in the school's rankings, and the younger apprentice hadn't taken the loss in status well. He'd groused about it for a week, constantly pestering Cinder for a rematch. Sash had lost every time.

"For the morning session, we'll pair up, but there will be some alterations," Master Lerid continued. He surprised Cinder with his next words. "Gorant will face Sash. Bones versus Faine. Mirk will train with Master Jine, and Dorr against Cinder."

Cinder shot Bones and Dorr a speculative assessment. Those two generally faced off with the masters or each other while the other four apprentices sparred against one another.

"I'll observe," Master Lerid said. "Take your places."

Cinder went to a square, still surprised that he'd be facing Dorr. The older apprentice saluted him with his practice blade. Cinder did the same.

"Cheer up," Dorr said. "You look like someone stole your precious jewelry."

Cinder realized he was scowling. "It isn't that. Why did Master Lerid pair me against you?"

Dorr laughed. "You haven't noticed? You give Mirk and the others all they can handle. Master Lerid wants to send you into the deep waters." He rolled his shoulders. "I'm the deep waters."

Until Dorr pointed it out, Cinder hadn't really thought of it that way.

"Don't let it go to your head," Dorr added. "You might be a prodigy or a flash in the pan. Whatever it is, it hasn't been decided yet."

A prodigy? Cinder didn't think so. Bones was a prodigy. Cinder simply had a special gift of perception, one he hadn't earned.

"Let's see what you got," Dorr said.

Cinder automatically bent into his stance. Maybe he wasn't a prodigy, but he outworked everyone else. He always had, and he always would. To his way of thinking, that was better than being a prodigy. But hard work alone didn't give him enough satisfaction. He wanted to know how far that hard work had carried him. *Yes. Let's see what I can do.*

Dorr settled into his own posture. A pregnant second passed. "Go."

They carefully paced forward at the same time, getting in range of one another's blades. Dorr sent out a questing slash. It wouldn't come close. Cinder didn't bother parrying. Another flick from Dorr. Another.

Dorr was trying to get a sense of distance and maybe Cinder's timing.

Cinder didn't give him any extra information. He shifted away from Dorr, keeping his distance rather than blocking the probing thrusts. He let the play of his opponent's stance, sword position, and grip wash over him. His innate understanding told him what would come. Dorr had his weight forward.

A lunge.

Cinder readied to counter.

Dorr exploded forward, a straight thrust aimed at Cinder's heart.

Cinder was already moving. He slid to his right, but prior to sending his counter, Dorr corrected, using his impeccable timing and balance to adjust and defend. Cinder retreated. Again came Dorr. Cinder fell into the pattern of the swords, letting it guide his movements. He fought without a need to think.

Months ago, even weeks ago, he couldn't have kept up with Dorr's speed, couldn't have parried his strength. Truthfully, he could barely do so now. His arms and legs had a greater density of muscle, but they remained thin and weak compared to the other apprentices.

Nevertheless, despite his physical limitations, Cinder was strong enough to do what was needed, fast enough to defend.

But that wasn't the kind of warrior he wanted to be. In his heart, Cinder was a predator.

He attacked.

He parried a horizontal slash, pushed aside a thrust, countered with a thrust of his own. Returned to center when Dorr shifted minutely. Cinder sent a stabbing feint. Dorr didn't bite. Cinder sent another one.

Dorr, with his years of experience, still didn't take the bait. A third stab, but this one wasn't a feint. Dorr cursed and fell back gracelessly, off balance.

Cinder's instincts guided him. He didn't over-commit in his aggression. He recognized what Dorr had to do, and the senior did it. He swung sweeping slashes to gain distance. They were powerful blows, but slow. Cinder slammed home a block. Dorr twisted, barely keeping from being spun about. Cinder's momentum carried him into a side kick, which crashed against Dorr's thigh. His opponent's leg buckled. A short step forward, and Cinder landed an overhand chop. It landed against Dorr's forearms, and the senior's sword fell from his hands.

Cinder's awareness of the world resumed. Adrenaline surged. He wanted to shout in victory, but he managed to limit his celebration to a triumphant grin. It wouldn't do to rub it in. Still, he'd beaten Dorr, a feat he never expected to accomplish so soon.

"Shit," Dorr growled. He massaged his forearms, which likely stung. "When did you get so fast?"

Cinder continued to grin. "I've been taking lessons in speed from Sash."

"You can't teach speed, idiot." Dorr bent to retrieve his practice weapon.

"Maybe not, but you can learn timing."

"Timing?" Dorr mused. He grunted eventually. "A well-timed blow beats quickness for sure," he said, "but you still have to deliver it." He shook out the leg Cinder had kicked. "Best two out of three."

Dorr didn't win the next fight, and it became best three out of five.

Then best five out of nine. Dorr finally overcame Cinder, winning the contest in a best six out of eleven. By then, Cinder's arms had the strength of wet noodles, weakness ate at his legs, and his stamina was long since spent. While he lost the final two matches against Dorr, he also didn't care. Of greater significance was the fact that he'd won five.

It was a step in the right direction for a journey measured in months, years, and decades.

Another month passed and another rest day arrived. This was a special one because it landed at the end of the Days of Deliverance, the celebration heralding the end of the *NusraelShev*. It had been a vibrant, happy holiday for most folk, but for Cinder—with no family in which to share the fellowship of the festivities—he had spent the days training; shadowboxing, practicing his forms, or his working to improve his strength and stamina.

Some of the apprentices—Cinder, Bones, and Gorant—had decided to get together afterward, and they met at the Lonely Donkey. The windows of the alehouse were wide open, letting in the warm, spring weather. A bustling trade occurred. Most tables were full. Same with the bar. After winter's harsh weather and resultant doldrums, folk wanted to celebrate with a pint or three. Trip appeared happy as a dog with a stolen shank of meat. For some reason, a fire still roared in the large hearth.

Cinder was the last of the apprentices to arrive, mandolin in hand, since Coral might be able to make it tonight. He hadn't seen her much recently, only a quick lunch with Riner during a day off three weeks ago.

They were both busy, Coral with her work as a maid and apprentice singer, and Cinder as a warrior-in-training. In fact, he trained harder now than ever before. While his body remained a shade thicker than scrawny, it no longer limited his ability to push himself. As a result, he spent every spare moment—including on his rest days—sparring against whoever was willing.

A secret desire, one he didn't dare voice, had crept to life, lurking in the corner of his mind like a hidden promise. He wanted to enter the Maker's Tournament. Not in four years like Faine had once told him, but this year. He was close.

Dorr stood ahead of him in the rankings at *Steel-Graced*, but not by much. The older apprentice was more skilled, but Cinder's understanding of combat erased most of that advantage. Then it came down to will.

Lately whenever they sparred, it was a toss of a coin as to who would win. The outcomes affected each apprentice in an opposite fashion. For Cinder, it bolstered his confidence, but for Dorr, it whittled at his.

Cinder knew it, and he took no pleasure in the fact. He respected Dorr, liked him tremendously, and would be forever grateful for the older apprentice's guidance. However, he also wouldn't let up. The Third Directorate called to him in ways he didn't understand. He had to get there. The Yaksha elves. They were said to be the finest warriors in the world. They were also the only ones who could train Cinder to the level he wanted to achieve. He didn't simply want to be a good or great warrior. He wanted to be the best. Period.

What that meant, and why he needed it so badly, he wasn't sure. Nor did he worry about it. Cinder had never expressed this desire to anyone, not even to Coral. She'd likely consider such a pursuit the height of pride.

"Your girlfriend coming?" Bones asked, a cocky grin on his face. He had his feet propped on the table.

"She's not my girlfriend," Cinder corrected. "Just a friend."

"A special one, right?"

"Didn't you say that to her once?" Cinder asked. "She asked about your special, right-hand friend, remember?"

Gorant laughed, and Bones chuckled too, but Cinder noticed the annoyance in his eyes.

"Well, if she's not your special friend, why don't you send her to Dorr? He's been feeling bad since you keep beating him. He could use a woman's touch to take care of his troubles." Again came the cocky, mocking grin.

Cinder didn't like it. His decision to seek greatness might be considered arrogant, but Bones *was* arrogant. In all their sparring, Cinder had not yet come close to defeating him, and Bones let him know it. He was like Sash in how he treated others. Constant needling and diminishment. Humor laced with contempt. It had only gotten worse as Cinder improved. It was Bones' way. He was only cutting and cruel to those who threatened his position. He used to speak that way to Dorr, but not anymore—which in some ways was a form of flattery aimed at Cinder.

"I think there's trouble brewing," Gorant whispered under his breath. "Look who just walked in."

Cinder twisted about to face the entrance, where four young men slowly paced into the alehouse. Two were short and thickly muscled, one lanky, and the final one was built much like Bones. They all moved in the same way the apprentices of *Steel-Graced* did, deadly grace mixed with leashed violence.

They were warriors, but Cinder didn't know them. "Who are they?"

Bones was no longer smiling and was uncharacteristically serious. He had his feet off the table. "Apprentices from *Jasmine Water*. We don't like them much. The one in the front is Wark Nil, their second best. The others aren't too shabby, neither."

From Bones, that was high praise.

Cinder eyed the arrivals, especially Wark. He was taller than the others, bulkier of build, and about the same age as Bones or Dorr. His dark hair gleamed nearly blue in the lamplight. A mustache curled around his mouth and extended to his chin.

One of the short *Jasmine Water* apprentices noticed them. He smiled, nudging one of his fellows.

Cinder didn't want trouble, but he could see it coming in the pleasure glinting in the eyes of the *Jasmine Water* students. He rose to his feet, fully facing the other apprentices as they approached. Chairs scraped the floor behind him as the others stood up a beat later.

Cinder cut off Wark, who had eyes for no one else but Bones. He hoped to defuse whatever was about to happen. "It's good to meet fellow apprentices. Why don't you have a drink with us?"

Wark flicked him a contemptuous glance. His mouth curled as if he had stepped in something foul and only now smelled it. He leaned to the side, peering past Cinder, gaze focused on Bones. "Is that what happens at Steel-Graceless Novices?" he asked. "They train you to be kiss-asses?"

"That's funny, coming from someone like you," Bones said. "Isn't that what you *Water* lovers do? Flow like water. Accept the contact, and absorb it good and hard? Well I got all the hardness you need." He thrust his pelvis.

The alehouse had gone quiet.

Cinder wanted to groan. He shifted slightly, preparing for what he knew was coming. He distantly noticed Trip desperately striving to reach them.

Wark reddened with fury. "You're going to eat those words." He stepped toward Bones, who didn't back down.

Advice scrolled through Cinder's mind, teachings not from *Steel-Graced Adepts. Be aware of your surroundings at all times. Mark your enemy. Know their location. Anything at hand is a weapon.*

Wark had his attention riveted on Bones. His mistake.

Cinder grabbed his pewter mug and back-swung it against the side of Wark's head. The *Jasmine Water* student went down. His fellow apprentices shouted in outrage. They focused on Cinder. He dashed the remaining ale in the mug directly into the eyes of one of the two shorter *Jasmine Water* apprentices. He fell back with a cry. The other short apprentice received a crescent kick from Bones and dropped like he'd been poleaxed.

Wark wasn't out of it yet, though. He got to his knees, struggling to get back to his feet. He shook his head, blinking heavily, blood pouring down his face from where the mug had cut him. Gorant laid him out with a right cross to the jaw.

The *Jasmine Water* apprentice who'd received ale in his eyes surged at Cinder, but his lanky fellow caught him, holding him back.

"I'm going to kick your ass, you bastard!" the short apprentice said.

The one restraining him whispered in his ears, likely explaining the vastly changed odds. The ale-doused apprentice struggled a second more. He finally gave a sharp nod of agreement to his fellow *Jasmine Water*, jerking himself free of the other one's hold.

He continued to glare at Cinder, who met his rage with as much calm as he could muster. More advice. *The wise warrior remains calm in the face of fury.*

Cinder controlled his breathing, shedding his remaining anger with every exhalation.

"We aren't going to forget this," the ale-doused apprentice said. "You suckered Wark. *He* won't forget this." He pointed at Cinder, placing his finger less than a foot from Cinder's nose.

Cinder slapped the finger away. There was calm and then there was stupidity. No chance he'd let an opponent put a potential weapon within striking distance of his face.

The short apprentice made to rush him again, but once more his fellow held him back. In this, the lanky one showed wisdom. The fight was over and the *Jasmine Waters* had lost.

"You're done," Cinder said, making his voice flat and threatening. "Get your friends out of here."

"Watch your back," the ale-doused apprentice warned, his features grim with promised vengeance. "Bones won't be there next time."

"Frag you. Bones wasn't needed this time."

With a final venomous glare, the two *Jasmine Waters* gathered their fellow students, who'd awoken by now, and shuffled out the door. They muttered darkly the entire time.

Trip finally arrived from the other side of the bar. "Nothing broken. Thank Devesh." He exhaled heavily, relieved. "You gentlemen all right?"

"We're fine," Cinder answered.

"Good." Trip faced the other patrons. "A round on the house," he shouted. His statement was met with applause. Everyone soon resumed their prior conversations.

"You didn't have to do that," Bones said after Trip left, clearly annoyed. "I could have taken Wark."

Cinder shot Bones a glower of annoyed disbelief. He'd put down Wark, ended a fight before it got started, and Bones was mad at him? *Idiot.* "You're welcome," Cinder said, not bothering to hide his sarcasm. "We won, Trip's bar wasn't destroyed, and none of us got hurt. I don't see the problem."

"The problem is I don't need protection," Bones growled. "Next time, don't get in my way. I fight for my own glory."

Cinder had heard enough. His simmering anger flared to life. He got in Bones' face. "If that's what you think fighting is about, then go join a mercenary company or become a gladiator. We're meant to be warriors, and true warriors don't fight for personal glory. We fight for victory, and the safety of those entrusted to our protection."

Bones glowered. His jaw clenched.

Cinder didn't back off. He stood unmoving and glaring. Inches away, craning his neck to meet the other apprentice's gaze, the warrior who had always wiped the floor with him.

Trip, sensing another fight, tried to intervene, but his mediation was unnecessary.

Bones broke eye contact, smirking as he usually did. "You're a brave little shit, I'll give you that."

Cinder rolled his eyes. Fine. Bones didn't want to fight him, but he also wanted to get in the last word. He always did against Dorr. He wouldn't do so this time. There were important truths to tell. "And you're a privileged, arrogant prick," Cinder said. "That's a bad combination, brother. It'll get you in trouble one day."

Bones stood straighter, swelling with pride. "Trouble? I was born to bring trouble."

"Maybe so, but none of us can handle everything this world throws at us on our own. We need our brothers."

Gorant spoke, sounding confused. "Why do you keep speaking of us like brothers? We are not related."

"In battle, all men are brothers," Cinder said. He'd heard that some-where. An image flitted across his mind, maybe imaginations from a story he'd read. In it, he saw four warriors in a hopeless battle against monsters, their backs to a cliff.

"Brothers." Bones said. He surprised Cinder with the approval in his voice. "I like that."

Cinder's anger dissolved in the face of Bones' agreement. He grinned. "Then, brother, you won't mind paying the bill for tonight's drinks?"

In the nine months since Cinder's arrival at Swift Sword, much had changed for him, and as he measured matters, all of it had been for the better. Lost, confused, and without purpose, he had started a new life. He had found a profession that spoke to him, one which echoed in his heart. He had made friends he truly cared for in Coral, Riner, and the apprentices at *Steel-Graced*. He had discovered a path forward, a jour-ney on which he'd already taken the first steps. He had even discovered a talent for music.

He was where he belonged, certain of himself, and driven by a fu-ture he wished to attain.

He didn't like the thought of losing any of those things, so his heart weighed heavy when he found out Dorr was leaving *Steel-Graced*. The senior apprentice had accepted a posting in the Army of Rakesh, sign-ing on as a lieutenant based on his blade skills and knowledge. He'd made the decision some time during the past week and no one could talk him out of it.

It was Cinder's fault. Several weeks ago, he'd surpassed Dorr in abil-ities, and every day since, the gap between them had only widened. As matters stood, the senior apprentice was no longer one of *Steel-Graced*'s entrants into the Maker's Tournament. It was to be Cinder and Bones. Master Lerid had only recently made the announcement.

The decision validated all of Cinder's hard work, but in the privacy of his thoughts, he hadn't thought it would be enough, not so soon. Still, here he was, attempting the Third Directorate after less than one year of training. An impossible achievement. In fact, had Cinder read of such an account, he would have labeled it the stuff of dreams, a fantasy.

He only wished his success hadn't come at the cost of a friend's dream. Dorr had decided to leave *Steel-Graced* shortly after Master Lerid's announcement.

"You could try for the Third Directorate next year," Cinder suggested to Dorr. Guilt roiled his stomach like acid, especially because he knew he wouldn't have done anything differently. Even knowing then what he knew now, he couldn't—wouldn't—give anything but his best effort.

It was a rest day, and he had asked Dorr to meet him at the Lonely Donkey for lunch. It might be one of the last times they saw one another, and he had things to tell Dorr, things best said in private. He didn't want to say them during the raucousness of tonight's leave-taking party, which would include the other apprentices.

The Lonely Donkey was empty right now, quiet but for a few Sunset Kingdoms merchants whispering in the corner. Their waist-length beards gave them away. Otherwise, the alehouse lay dimly lit. The fire in the hearth had long since grown cold. Spring was soon to transition to full summer. Trip Badger was nowhere in evidence. Instead his son, Fill, a man several years older than Cinder, stood behind the bar, wiping down pewter mugs and hanging them on pegs projecting from the ceiling.

Dorr took a swig of ale. "I don't think so," he said in response to Cinder's suggestion.

"With me and Bones gone, you'd be a lock. If I'd never shown up . . ."

Dorr smiled, gentle and forgiving, and the acidic guilt roiling Cinder's stomach lessened slightly. "Don't worry about it," Dorr said. "You only taught me a lesson I should have learned last year when Bones galloped past my best work. I'm good, but I'm not a genius. Those are the sort of warriors you'll be facing in the Maker's Tournament:

geniuses. *You're a genius.*"

What an odd statement. To be labeled a genius . . . it sounded silly, like proclaiming oneself an artist.

"What are you going to do about Coral if you make it to the Third Directorate?" Dorr asked.

"I don't know," Cinder admitted. He liked Coral. He liked her a lot, but if he made it to the Third Directorate, how could he ask her to wait for him? Three years at the Directorate and even more in Yaksha Sithe's Imperial Army. It was too much to ask, especially if all Coral felt for him in return was mere friendship.

"Don't let her go," Dorr advised. "She's a special one. And she likes you." Another swig of ale. "That doesn't happen all the time."

"I know," Cinder said, and he did. However, he also didn't want to talk about Coral any more. "Why did you join the army?"

"Because it's necessary. Danger is all around Rakesh. We don't have to worry about the wraiths. They're way up in the far north, but there are the zahhacks, Shet's woven." Dorr's mouth curled. "There's trouble everywhere, and we can barely hold it off."

Cinder frowned. Dorr's explanation didn't match with what he had read about Rakesh's situation. "I know about the zahhacks, but don't the Yaksha elves protect us?"

Dorr laughed, a bitter sound. "Sure. But only if we do what they say. We might as well be their vassal state, and you and I living as nothing more than their vassals. I'm hoping to make a mark to lighten that yoke some."

It was a worthy goal, one made by a man of honor. It was so like Dorr.

"I asked to meet you today because I wanted to thank you," Cinder said. He kept his eyes pinned on Dorr, wanting his senior to know the depth of his gratitude. "You've been an inspiration to me, the way you treat the younger apprentices, sharing your knowledge, your skills. You could have kept your wisdom to yourself, but you didn't. Your generosity is why I'm where I am. I couldn't have achieved what I have without you."

Dorr chuckled. "Look at that. You're making me blush." He was doing nothing of the sort. After a little bit, Dorr grew serious. "Listen. I didn't do anything you wouldn't have figured out on your own. Learning the sword and martial artistry is in your blood. Just make me one promise." He offered a predatory grin of anticipation. "Wipe that arrogant smirk off Bones' face. Maybe not this year, but some year. Kick his ass."

"I'll do my best," Cinder replied, but his thoughts were distracted. There was one final matter he needed to take care of. "Can you look in on Coral and Riner for me, if I make it to the Third Directorate?"

Dorr's smile gave way to a grave nod. "I will. At least as best as I'm able. I may not always be in Swift Sword."

"I understand. But you'll look in on them? Make sure they're doing well?"

"You ought to speak to her before you leave," Dorr advised. "Tell her how you feel."

"I don't know how I feel," Cinder said, which he knew wasn't true. Cinder liked Coral. He admired her courage and caring, and his heart ached for her, for both of them because Cinder couldn't stay in Swift Sword.

A distant calling, a ringing bell, egged him onward. It overcame the feelings he had for Coral, undoing any ties to her, Swift Sword, or Rakesh. He wished it didn't, and the journey he vaguely viewed began with the Third Directorate.

Dorr gazed on him pityingly. "You really are a damn fool letting a woman like that go."

Cinder sighed. "I know that, too."

"Are you nervous about the Maker's Tournament?" Master Lerid asked. He sipped a cup of hot chai, a soothing blend spiced with cinnamon sticks, cardamom pods, and ginger. Master Lerid had a cup of it every evening.

Cinder sat with him in the quiet dining hall. It was the night following Dorr's leave-taking from *Steel-Graced*, and they shared a table, the *diptha* lamps turned down for the night. No one else was about. Master Jine and Faine were out for the evening. Same with Morr. As for the other apprentices, they had left several hours ago, directly after supper. Cinder had already cleaned the dishes and swept the floor of the dining hall where he and Master Lerid sat, both sipping steaming cups of chai while having a conversation.

Cinder considered his master's question. He *was* nervous, and he said so. "But I'm not afraid," he explained further, pausing to collect his thoughts. "It's more that I'm aware of the Tournament's importance. It could change everything for me."

"It could," Master Lerid agreed. "And yet, placing too much emphasis on it won't help you achieve what you desire."

Cinder frowned, unsure what Master Lerid meant. How could he achieve what he wanted without the Tournament and the Third Directorate? "I don't understand," he said after several moments of quiet reflection.

Master Lerid set his tea on the table, and his eyes focused on Cinder. "If you win a place at the Third Directorate, you will receive the finest training in Seminal. You'll have a chance to earn *aether* infused creations and become a warrior everyone else holds in awe." Master Lerid held up a cautioning finger. "But also consider this. What if you don't win a place in the Third Directorate? Will you give up your dream of becoming a warrior?"

The question didn't require thought, and Cinder immediately shook his head. "Of course not."

"Why?"

"Because becoming a warrior is what I was meant to do," Cinder answered. "Protecting and defending others is my calling."

"And could you not do so even without the Third Directorate? Are those who serve in the Army of Rakesh less worthy of the name 'warrior'?"

Cinder understood now what Master Lerid meant. "You're saying that whether I win a place at the Third Directorate or not, I will always want to be a warrior. I can still become a warrior." It was the exposure of a simple truth. "I shouldn't let one failure change the course of my life."

"Exactly." Master Lerid smiled. "It pleases me how I never have to spell out my lessons for you." He took a sip of his tea. "There is one other matter to discuss, however. Your self-confidence. We've spoken about this before. You worry too much about your weaknesses and never grant yourself approval for your skills. Belief in yourself, confidence that you will win is also critical. You focus too much on your faults." He shrugged. "Besides, you should know by now. There is no such thing as a perfect warrior."

"Except for Shokan."

Master Lerid smiled in amusement. "Shokan was a legend, but in this matter, I think the legends lie. And even if they didn't, you and I both know there will never be another like him." Another sip of tea. "At any rate, what I meant was that you need to be more aware of your strengths. Lean on them. Don't let doubt cripple your actions."

Cinder considered Master Lerid's advice. He did tend to concern himself too much over what he'd done wrong, believing himself less skilled and able than anyone else. He needed to have greater certainty in his abilities. Sometimes the line between victory and defeat could be measured by the width of a warrior's confidence.

An odd question rose to the forefront of Cinder's mind. "If I go to the Third Directorate, will I be able to defeat an elf?"

Master Lerid chuckled softly. "Why do you ask?"

"Elves are supposed to be the finest warriors in the world."

"They aren't. That accolade belongs to the holders, but the elves are certainly better than any human warrior."

Holders hunted zahhacks, could battle a necrosed—the most powerful of Shet's creations—unassisted, but otherwise Cinder knew nothing about them. He made a mental note to rectify his ignorance. For now, he had other questions. "So, there's no way to beat an elf? Is Master Sharn right? They're too good."

Master Lerid paused before answering, mouth pursed in thought. "In every battle, the outcome is unknown, but there are always likelihoods. In this case, even if you gain all the attributes you desire, you will likely never be able to defeat a true elven or dwarven warrior. Since you bring up Master Sharn, you remember what he said about their *lorethasra*?"

Cinder nodded. "Some folk say it's our soul, one possessed by all reasoning creatures. The woven can touch it, but humans can't. It grants them skills."

"Yes." Master Lerid took up the explanation. "And by doing so, by sourcing their *lorethasra*, the woven can make themselves mighty. For elves, they gain an innate sense of the world around them along with improved senses and speed. For dwarves, it's about improved balance and power. For trolls, it's the ability to Judge." He shook his head. "Those aren't abilities a human can easily overcome." He offered a single bark of laughter. "Some elves are even able to cast ranged attacks made of fire or other elements." Master Lerid peered over the rim of his teacup. "You know about the elements?"

"Earth, Fire, Water, Air, and Spirit," Cinder responded. "Those are the Elements which make up *lorethasra*." He'd read a book on the matter a few days ago, although other than naming the Elements, the author hadn't been clear on what one could do with them. He'd named and described them in a circular fashion. Sulfurous Fire, hissing Air, rustling Earth, and washing Water. What did that mean? "In nature, Spirit is absent. It's only Earth, Fire, Water, and Air."

"Exactly," Master Lerid said, sounding surprised.

"Has any human ever touched his *lorethasra*?" Cinder realized the answer was probably 'no', but what about the Mythaspuris? They had been human, and they could touch their *lorethasras*. Same with their descendants, the rishis of Bharat. Why couldn't other humans do the same thing?

"Of course," Master Lerid said.

Cinder's hopes surged.

"But not on a consistent basis."

Cinder's hopes crashed.

"From what I've read, when a human touches his *lorethasra*, it's during times of danger. Otherwise, we lack the ability."

Cinder pondered Master Lerid's answer, but he couldn't help but hope and wonder. What if a human *could* touch their *lorethasra*? What might they be able to do?

Shortly thereafter, Master Lerid said 'good night' and retired to his quarters, and Cinder went to his room as well, the closet-under-the-stairs. He lay on his small cot, *diptha* lamp turned up to light the small space and a book propped on his lap. He always liked to read a novel before going to bed.

Reading let him forget his troubles and questions.

Tonight, he'd chosen *A Gleeman's Travels*, a set of fables about a wandering minstrel, Kal Thomlin, and his amusing anecdotes about the various empires and nations in which he journeyed. He had a particularly biting wit when it came to the elves, puncturing their overly developed sense of importance. One story in particular about an elf, a kebab, and a camel set Cinder to laughing.

15

Two weeks after Dorr left, in early Devasth—the year's holiest month—it was time for the Maker's Tournament. The annual competition was held at Swift Sword's coliseum, and while the arena could accommodate several thousand attendees, generally every seat was needed. The Maker's Tournament was the most popular event held in Swift Sword. It was far more widely regarded than the fighting exhibitions occasionally held between rival mercenary companies or the single-elimination contests amongst gladiators. The Maker's Tournament was the competition meant to highlight the city's martial pride, a chance to see their finest apprentice warriors test one another's mettle.

Of course, many wagered on how those same applicants to the Third Directorate would do against the gladiators. Most thought the victors of the Maker's Tournament would be hard pressed, and Cinder thought the same. He'd seen the gladiators train. They fought in the city's famed circuses for fame and fortune, but the source of their inspiration meant nothing regarding their skill. Gladiators were dangerous, and Cinder respected their abilities. They had earned every bit of

185

their notoriety. In fact, Swift Sword's various promoters continually sought to match a human Third Directorate graduate against the city's gladiatorial champion, but so far no one had been able to book such a match.

Cinder realized his mind was drifting. He needed to focus on the here and now. The gladiators and the Third Directorate were unimportant. Cinder took a deep breath and concentrated on his surroundings.

He sat next to Bones, the two of them seated amongst a cluster of competitors. These were the sixteen participants in the Maker's Tournament. They had helmets resting at their sides, wore heavily padded clothing, white and unmarked, and all of them were twitchy. They waited in restless silence, deep in the heart of the coliseum, crowded in a windowless space. Upon three of the room's four walls hung paintings of the great warriors from Rakesh's history. Cinder briefly wondered if any of those gathered here would have their image grace this place. The final wall was given over to three doors, the only entrances and exits from the room.

Cinder noticed a flat glare emanating in his direction from Wark Nil and Brow Cowl, the apprentices from *Jasmine Water*. He glared back. *Frag them.* They ought to focus on what was to come instead of wasting energy being angry. *Jackholes.*

The *Jasmine Water* apprentices weren't the only ones glowering warily at others, though. Other combatants did, too.

Tension knotted the air.

A tall, middle-aged man entered the room through the centermost door. He strode with the bearing of a warrior, marching rather than walking. Master Carnil was his name. He wore dark clothes, gray half-boots, and a sword at his hip. Master Carnil went to the lectern at the room's head. "Attend," he said, his voice commanding.

Cinder gave Master Carnil his full attention. The other participants did the same, all of them intense and ready.

"I know you've likely heard the rules many times already," Master Carnil said, "but we will still go over them a final time."

Cinder thought the master's last-second instructions unnecessary, but he listened closely anyway.

"As most of you know," Master Carnil continued, "the masters in charge of the Maker's Tournament inspected the city's four martial academies last week. We also carefully examined those chosen to participate in the Tournament, including any apprentice warriors who have been privately tutored and are thought to be highly skilled. You know this, yes?"

A ragged bobbing of heads answered his question. The latter apprentices to whom Master Carnil referred were the children of wealth and privilege, the at-large entrants to the Tournament.

"Good," Master Carnil said. "We spoke to you about what is to occur but let us review. From our observations, you've all been ranked from first-to-worst."

Again, this something Cinder already knew. He was low ranked for the Tournament, fifteenth. It meant that in his first match, he'd have to face the warrior ranked second. Thankfully, that wouldn't be Bones. His fellow *Steel-Graced* was ranked first overall.

"The goal is simple," Master Carnil said. "Win two matches and enter the Third Directorate. Continue winning and you'll earn coin to spend however you see fit. Any questions?"

No one spoke.

Master Carnil surveyed the room. "Excellent." He gestured about himself, indicating the space in which they waited. "This is the staging room. When called to fight, the higher ranked opponent will take the left hand door to reach the arena. The lower ranked takes the right. You'll fight in a large sparring circle—not a square—thirty feet in diameter. Master Jarvid will judge this year's Tournament. His word is final. There are no appeals. To win a match, you have to earn four points. A *'fatal'* blow counts as two points, a *'non-fatal'* one as one point. Two fatal touches, four non-fatal ones, or one fatal and two non-fatal blows wins. Leaving the ring counts as a non-fatal touch."

Cinder fingered the practice sword strapped to his waist. Black ink lined the edges. There would be no mistaking when someone was hit with the sword. It would leave a readily seen mark on their clothing.

"Those who lose won't return to this room. They are free to re-join the members of their school or family," Master Carnil further explained. "Those who win *will* return here and wait for their next match. We want all the combatants to have no prior knowledge of the skills and weaknesses of the other participants. Once we're down to only four, you'll be seated in a special area reserved for the finalists. Understood?"

Again, no one spoke.

Master Carnil clapped his hands a single time. "Fine. Then prepare yourselves. I'm sure the city officials will soon finish their welcoming speeches. Shortly after, we'll begin the Tournament."

Minutes passed, an immeasurable time of tedium and nerves.

Cinder stood. So did some of the other participants. By silent accord, none of them spoke to one another, including those from the same school. They fanned out, stretching or pacing in small bubbles of privacy. The tension in the air never eased.

A boy dashed into the room, entering through the center door. Everyone stopped what they were doing and waited to see what would happen next. The boy whispered in Master Carnil's ear, who nodded.

"It's time," Master Carnil said, even as the boy dashed out. "The first against sixteenth. When the winner returns, it will be the second against fifteenth."

Bones and one of the students from a wealthy family exited without a word.

Cinder didn't know what to do. He stood still after Bones left, waiting and hesitant. *Now what?*

He knew he should focus on his own match. After all, he was to face one of the privately trained participants, someone of high caliber given his ranking, and he knew nothing about him. He should concentrate on that fact.

But he couldn't manage it. While he knew what he should do, knowing and doing were two different things. His mind wouldn't focus. He kept musing about how Bones was doing.

Seconds later, the crowd roared. Bones and the other apprentice must have reached the arena floor. More shouts and announcements, and then the crowd quieted. Another roar.

The match must have started.

Cinder stared at the ceiling, as if he could pierce the heavy stone blocks and see the action above. Two more roars quickly sounded from the crowd, and minutes afterward, Bones returned, a triumphant grin plastered across his face. He hadn't even broken a sweat.

Cinder smiled in happiness for his fellow *Steel-Graced*. It would have been a travesty and a tragedy for someone of Bones' ability not to make it past the first round. "Congratulations," he said, and meant it.

"Save it. You're up next."

Cinder didn't need the reminder. It was finally happening. His first match. Until this moment, even after Bones had exited the staging area, the Maker's Tournament had seemed distant and illusory. Now, the reality of the situation crashed upon him. Butterflies filled his stomach. An entire kaleidoscope of them.

Cinder took to pacing, hoping to burn off the nervous energy.

The call came, but before he could leave, Bones intercepted him. His voice was intense and urgent. "Make Master Lerid proud."

Cinder took in Bones' exhortation, and the words calmed him somewhat. "I'll do the best I can."

"Do better," Bones growled, softly punching his shoulders. "Fight and win. Fight for all of us."

Cinder's anxiety lessened. Adrenaline pumped an urgency into his veins, an angry desire that rushed through his body. He wanted this. He needed this. He clenched and unclenched his fists.

Bones leaned into Cinder until their foreheads butted. "Go get it. This is your time. Kick some ass. What are you going to do?"

"Kick some ass," Cinder barked.

"What are you going to do?" Bones shouted, directly in his face.

More adrenaline. "Kick some ass!" Cinder shouted back. Bones' exhortation filled him with a savage energy, the demand for wanton destruction. The other participants were staring, but Cinder didn't care.

"Hell, yeah! Go get some!" Bones again punched both of Cinder's shoulders.

Cinder gave a final incoherent shout. He smacked his face several times. It woke him more fully. A final shout, and he was ready.

Only then did he exit the staging room, entering a curving tunnel. It was dark and otherwise empty, and his footsteps echoed. As he marched forward, he focused on his match, visualizing the fight, imagining his first moves, the counters he'd need, the openings he'd force. Over and over. Starting from the beginning to the end, and every time he won.

A light ahead guided him to the tunnel's far end, where it opened onto the floor of the arena.

Believe you're a champion and you will *be a champion.* Cinder didn't know where the notion came from, but it sounded right.

He stepped out of the relatively quiet tunnel, into a bedlam of noise and abrupt brightness.

The audience roared, and Cinder slowly spun, gazing in wonder. *So many people in one location.* They cheered, shouted, stomped their feet. It was like being touched by lightning, and Cinder held his arms out, closed his eyes, and soaked in the energy. The cheers went on and on.

He opened his eyes then and took in more details. He stood at the base of a bowl. It was about one hundred feet wide, and his opponent stood on the opposite side. Tiers of bleachers soared all around. To his right was a private area, a raised pavilion, roofed and holding a dozen men and women. It leaned out to shade several rows below it. It was where the shrewds, including Chief Justice Tomain Ravien, would watch the Tournament.

Cinder had never seen the chief justice before, but he reckoned it was the old man standing at the front of the private box. Cold eyes accentuating an ascetic, fierce set of features gazed at the world from amidst a sea of wrinkles. A long, white beard hung to the middle of his chest, and he wore white robes decorated with gold thread, an assortment of gems, a golden torc, and a tall, white, pointy hat.

Cinder also noticed another man standing near the pavilion. He was clad similar to Master Carnil in dark clothing. Master Jarvid, apparently. A lean warrior, stoop-shouldered with age but still tall. He was the judge for today's matches.

The chief justice lifted his hands, and the audience quieted. He spoke then. His voice had a surprisingly reedy quality. "Two more of our glorious sons fight for the high honor of winning a place in the Third Directorate," he said. "First is Garlin Fairsent, scion of house Fairsent, and Cinder Shade, representing the *Steel-Graced Adepts*. The rules are simple and I won't belabor them." He now addressed Cinder and his opponent. "Approach."

Cinder did so. He scrutinized his opponent while making the short walk to the chief justice's stand. Garlin was older than him by a year or so, bearded, and also much taller, just a few inches shorter than Bones. His simple, white clothes fit well on his frame, which was neither muscular nor overly lean. He'd be fast and powerful. A difficult opponent.

For a moment, the two of them stood shoulder-to-shoulder in front of the chief justice and, as one, knelt to him.

"Rise and bow to one another," the chief justice ordered. They did so. "It is time for one of you to earn your glory. For the other," he quirked an unexpected grin, "perhaps next year. Take your marks, and may Devesh keep you from harm."

Cinder and Garlin entered the sparring circle, which was marked by a ring of low-lying stones. A red square indicated where Cinder was to stand, a blue one for Garlin.

Master Jarvid entered the circle, going to the center. He called them to his side. Cinder kept his attention on Garlin.

"You know the rules," Master Jarvid said. "All weapons are legal. All attacks, other than attempted maiming and eye-gouging, are legal." He held up a cautionary hand. "But victory is determined by your blade alone. Any questions?"

Cinder maintained eye contact with Garlin the entire time, who did the exact same. Both gave the briefest shake of their heads.

"Then get your helmets on and go back to your marks."

Cinder did as instructed, cinching the leather helmet under his jaw. He walked backward, still maintaining eye contact with Garlin and studying his opponent, searching for weaknesses, any clue as to what he intended. Garlin clenched his scabbard in his left hand and tapped at the hilt of his sword with his right. He paced minutely, shifting his weight from one foot to the other. He gave every indication of preparing a hard, fast attack. Or was it anxiety that had him twitching?

Cinder thought it the former. If so, timing would be critical, especially if Garlin was as fast as his rank suggested. Several options skated through Cinder's mind. He settled on one.

Master Jarvid held up a hand. "On my command, you will fight." A pregnant second passed. "Fight!"

Garlin did as Cinder expected. He burst out of his stance, sword aimed like a spear. Cinder stepped forward and to his left, waiting for Garlin's momentum to carry him past.

It didn't happen.

Garlin slammed to a halt.

A feint! Dammit! Cinder was already committed to an angled slash. He had to carry through. Garlin parried and immediately countered. Cinder had no option but to roll away. He lost track of his opponent and swung wildly to clear space. He had to get back to his feet. A flicker of movement to his side. A practice blade slammed into his ribs. Cinder's breath exploded with a whoosh.

"Break!" the master shouted. "A kill for Garlin. Two points. Sheath your weapons and resume your marks."

Cinder cursed, rubbing at his chest and glad for the padding under his clothes. Without it, he'd likely have a few bruised or broken ribs. He flushed as he went back to his mark. He'd lasted all of a handful of seconds. Embarrassed didn't begin to describe how he felt. He heard the crowd hooting at his poor showing and he did his best to ignore their jeering. He found Garlin's superior grin annoying, but he set aside that emotion as well. He reached for calm, imagining himself a winter lake, cold and still. His breathing steadied. His heart slowed. The flush left his face.

He studied Garlin anew. Once more, his opponent twitched, giving the impression of repressed energy, that he'd explode forth. A greater awareness then settled over Cinder's eyes, a deeper perception of how Garlin truly stood, his balance, the narrowing of his eyes. It was another feint. He'd try the same move as before, more cautiously though, in case Cinder recognized it.

"Fight!"

Garlin charged, not quite as fast this time. Again Cinder slid forward and to the side, moving with greater certainty and swiftness. As before, Garlin slammed to a halt, but he was too late. He was over-extended. Cinder's blade came down on the back of Garlin's thigh. His opponent lost his footing and fell.

"Break!" Master Jarvid shouted. "A kill for Cinder. Two points. Sheath your weapons and resume your marks."

The crowd jeered, this time at Garlin, and he no longer smiled. Instead, he scowled angrily while limping back to his place. He winced with every step.

Cinder eyed Garlin skeptically, and his improved understanding told him it was another feint. Garlin wasn't seriously injured. He only wanted to lull Cinder into a false sense of security.

"Be ready," Master Jarvid said. Another pregnant pause. "Fight."

Garlin moved forward hesitantly, as if his leg were truly injured. Cinder paced forward, not taking the bait. They tested each other then, flicking out with their swords, thrusts and parries. Garlin continued to limp, pretending a weakness to draw Cinder in, who didn't bite on the ruse. More testing.

Garlin finally gave up his limp and pressed harder.

Cinder let him. He needed a better gauge of his opponent's true speed. He wouldn't commit himself to an attack until he had it.

Garlin sent a questing jab, followed by a quick thrust. Next, he stepped forward, his blows faster now. Cinder struggled to keep up. He had no chance to counter. Garlin wasn't quite as strong as Bones, but he was at least as quick. Cinder sought to retreat but found himself cut off by the edge of the ring. His hands stung from parrying Garlin's heavy attacks. He fought to free himself and gain space, but to no avail. Garlin was always there, too close.

Cinder missed a parry. A diagonal slash would have slammed into his shoulder, a fatal blow. Instead, Cinder stepped out of the ring before the attack landed.

"Break!" Master Jarvid shouted. "Point to Garlin. Three points-to-two. Another touch of any kind from Garlin, and he wins the match. Resume your marks."

The crowd cheered wildly, clearly enjoying the match.

Cinder paid no attention to their cries. His confidence sagged, but he wouldn't let bleak thoughts of losing break him. Garlin would have to earn his victory. He'd know he'd been in a fight when this was over.

"Fight!"

Garlin charged, and Cinder met him in the middle. They clashed, and their wooden blades echoed. Garlin didn't bother with probing attacks. He went full bore. Cinder kept up. It was his innate sense of movement and placement, of timing and angles that guided his motions. He and Garlin separated. An instant later, they slammed together again.

Another moment of separation.

A stirring rippled deep in Cinder's mind, like a great pool of water, perfectly reflective and smooth but walled away by crackling flickers of blue and green. Cinder grimaced at the distraction, and he pushed it aside, willing the image to fade to the back of his mind.

As soon as he did, the world unexpectedly seemed to brighten. Sounds came clearer. Time scattered to a slower pace. His understanding of what Garlin intended heightened.

With a rush, time resumed.

Cinder answered an attack. He parried a slash, slipped a thrust, and hammered a vertical slice into Garlin's extended arm.

"Break! Two points and the win goes to Cinder!"

For an instant Cinder didn't recognize the enormity of his accomplishment. Seconds passed until he realized he'd won. Then he shouted in jubilation, holding up his sword and screaming his victory. A deafening cascade of approving roars, stomping feet, and clapping hands came from the crowd. In the moment of his triumph, Cinder noticed his despondent foe. Garlin stood alone, blinking back tears. His head hung low.

Empathy for him welled in Cinder's heart. He went to Garlin and hugged him close. He spoke into his ear while the crowd continued to cheer. "I'm sorry, brother. You're an amazing warrior. You'll go far. Next year, you'll make it to the Third Directorate. I know."

Garlin pushed him away, a bitter smile on his face. "Too bad I had to run into *you* this year."

Cinder opened the door to the staging room and found himself engulfed in Bones' enthusiastic hug.

"I knew you'd win," Bones said, grinning like a fiend. "Easy as stealing pie from a baby. One more win, and we're in. Third Directorate!"

Cinder laughed, enjoying this version of Bones, who was generous with his praise and joyful for another's success. "It wasn't easy, but I got it done."

Bones clapped Cinder around the back of his neck, giving him a brief shake. "Get something to drink. They've got meat samosas, but don't eat too much. It'll slow you down."

"I won't," Cinder said, not needing the advice, but also knowing there was no reason to say so.

He left Bones' side and went to the wall opposite the one with the doors. A table had been set up there, and upon it rested a clay jug full of water, glasses, and a number of the aforementioned samosas. Cinder was parched. He poured himself some water, drank it, poured himself another, and sipped at this one. He also collected several meat samosas. He took his drink and food to an unoccupied chair and collapsed onto it.

Bones sat nearby, legs stretched out, eyes closed and apparently sleeping or merely resting.

A boy, the same as the one who had announced Bones' and Cinder's fights, entered the room through the center door. He ran to Master

Carlin, whispered in his ear, and dashed out.

Brow Cowl, the top-ranked *Jasmine Water* apprentice, exited by the left-hand door. A student from one of the other schools went to the arena by the right-hand one. Minutes passed. Cinder continued sipping at his water and nibbling at the meat samosas, enjoying the potato-and-beef mixture. All the while he replayed his fight against Garlin in his mind. He reviewed every blow he'd received and every counter he'd offered. How he could improve as a warrior.

Part of his ability to understand an opponent's likely next step also allowed him to recall in vivid detail every aspect of his fights and sparring sessions.

Cinder continued to rest while the other apprentices and students were called for their turns in the arena. The room slowly emptied. He noted that both Brow and Wark won their engagements. The two of them would have a chance of making it to the Third Directorate. No surprise there.

Cinder had asked his masters about those two. They were good. Currently, they sat in the same row as Cinder and Bones, several chairs away, eating samosas and drinking water. The *Jasmine Water* apprentices no longer glared at Cinder. Instead, they scrutinized him, seemingly trying to decipher who he was.

Maybe it was time to bury the hatchet. Cinder considered the matter, but in the end, he decided against it. He still had at least one more fight ahead of him. It might be against either of those two. He'd seek them out and try to make peace once they were done with the Maker's Tournament.

One of the privately trained warriors re-entered the staging room. His had been the last of the first-round fights. He went straightaway to Master Carlin and hugged him. The older man smiled proudly and whispered encouragement.

The final eight had been determined. Cinder only knew four of them.

Master Carlin resumed his place at the lectern, rapping it to gain everyone's attention. "The other masters have seen all of you fight.

You've been re-ranked, one through eight. In round two, it will be just like round one. Whosoever is ranked first will battle the eighth, second will face seventh, and so on. Get some rest. Relax as best you can. We'll start again soon enough."

Cinder did as Master Carlin suggested. He rested, focusing on the fight to come. Now that he better knew the size and scope of the sparring ring and recognized the rules more definitively, he could more accurately visualize his possible opening moves, the counter that might be thrown his way.

Believe you're a champion and you will *be a champion.*

A half hour later, the call came. The second round was to commence. Bones against one of the private students, an older apprentice. Seth Jothan was his name. He was taller than everyone except Bones. His light skin and almond eyes announced his mixed Rakesh and Errow heritage.

"Good luck," Cinder said before Bones departed.

"Save it for yourself," Bones replied, his tone gruff. His attention was elsewhere. He curled his mouth at Seth, eyeing him like a tiger viewing a trapped gazelle.

Seth stared back at Bones, features impassive, but Cinder noticed the doubt hiding in the depths of his eyes.

The two apprentices departed the room, and it was left to those remaining to wait on the outcome. Cinder passed the time by limbering up for his next fight. The other students did the same. While he stretched, Cinder again visualized his coming contest, always making sure to believe himself the victor.

His musings were interrupted when Bones returned. He wore a smile of triumph. It hadn't been as easy this time. Sweat actually beaded on his brow. However, no lines marred his white uniform. He hadn't given up a single point yet.

"How did it go?" Cinder asked.

"He had some tricks up his sleeve, but nothing I couldn't handle," Bones said, his tone dismissive.

"Glad you made it through." Cinder left Bones' side then. He had his own match to worry about.

He resumed pacing. Shortly thereafter, his name was called. He was the seventh-ranked combatant. His opponent was Brow. Cinder stared at him, aggression rising. He wanted to beat the *Jasmine Water*. It didn't matter how, as long as he got it done and as long as he won. They left the staging room together, neither saying a word.

Again, came the winding tunnel. Part of Cinder wondered if the path from the left hand door was any different and whether he'd ever see it. He entered the arena to loud cheers. Cinder inhaled deeply, closing his eyes, soaking in the sensations, forcing himself to think of nothing but victory.

After a few words from the chief justice, Cinder strapped on his helmet and took his mark in the sparring ring opposite Brow. Master Jarvid still served as the judge, and he quickly reviewed the instructions once more.

Cinder breathed deeply, filling his lungs and exhaling heavily. In and out. His perception of Brow's intentions came more easily. The *Jasmine Water* apprentice was shorter than him, built more like Dorr. He'd be strong but not as fast as Bones. Cinder formed a strategy.

"Fight!"

Cinder went on the attack. He didn't bother testing Brow. He went flat out.

Brow defended smoothly. He slid out of the way, parrying easily. His technique was perfect.

Perfection, though, wasn't always enough. Brow's focus on a perfect form made him vulnerable to someone who moved nearly as well but put more power into his attacks. They ranged throughout the circle. Cinder continually pressed his opponent.

There!

Brow countered a vertical swing but was slow in his recovery. But Cinder didn't take immediate advantage. Instead, he shot forward and aimed a horizontal slash. Brow parried. The move left him over-balanced. He never saw Cinder's elbow until it crashed into his jaw.

Brow went down like a sack of potatoes. Cinder stabbed his practice sword into his opponent's chest, directly over his heart. Of course it didn't penetrate, but it won him the points.

"Break!" the master shouted. "Two points for Cinder."

Brow got to his feet, groggy and unsteady. He promptly fell over on his butt.

The master gave the *Jasmine Water* apprentice a few minutes to recover. When it was clear he was still wobbly-headed, he called the fight. "Victory for Cinder Shade by means of his opponent being unable to continue."

Cinder boggled, and a sense of disbelief washed over him. He'd won? He'd made it into the Third Directorate?

The awareness of what he'd achieved fully crashed over him.

He'd won!

Cinder screamed his triumph. He was going to the Third Directorate! It was a feat he had always dreamed of accomplishing but not so soon, certainly not a year ago when he first arrived in Swift Sword. Cinder exulted, wanting to share his joy. He searched the audience and quickly located the members of his school. They cheered him on, every one of them on their feet, grins plastered on their faces. Cinder raised a triumphant fist, and they shouted even louder.

Once more, he was presented to the chief justice and the arena in general before being allowed to return to the staging room. When he walked in, Bones gave him a glad cry of relieved surprise. Wark viewed him in anger and shock.

After sharing a brief hug with Bones, Cinder went to the table in the back, gathered some more water and another samosa, and took a seat far from the other apprentices. His excitement had faded during the walk back to the staging room. He still had matches ahead of him. He wasn't done, and he didn't want to talk to anyone.

None of the others did, either.

The tension filling the room at the beginning of the day had transformed into a brooding mix of aggression and hunger for victory.

The remaining warriors were called for their contests, and soon enough the final four was set: Cinder, Bones, Wark, and Depth Knarl,

Master Carnil's privately trained apprentice. Of them, only Bones had an unmarked uniform.

Cinder took a longer examination of Depth. He had a wiry build that suggested speed. Short, too, but still many inches taller than Cinder. He'd be a hard one to beat. Cinder realized that the same could be said of all of them. After all, they were the ones bound for the Third Directorate.

Now that the initial two rounds were complete, Master Carlin directed them through the central door where they exited into a wide tunnel, this one brightly lit with an abundance of *diptha* lamps. A number of corridors emptied into the hallway. Through them Cinder caught glimpses of the stands directly on the level of the arena floor. They were seats for the wealthy to watch the Maker's Tournament. Some of those same rich folk congregated in the tunnel through which Cinder and the others passed. They wore expensive clothing and spoke encouragement to the remaining participants. To Cinder they seemed to assess the apprentices with the calculation of a merchant measuring flesh. Their gazes left him feeling like a lump of meat.

Master Carlin spoke while they marched. "You'll be seated in a special space marked out for the four of you. At this point ranks are immaterial. You'll face one another by random draw. It remains a single elimination."

They arrived at a cordoned-off area directly adjacent to the pavilion where the chief justice watched the Tournament. Cinder hadn't noticed it until now, but the aroma of roasting meat permeated the air. His stomach growled. It had been a long day, and all he'd eaten were several samosas.

The four apprentices climbed a handful of steps and reached four identical seats, red-cushioned and comfortable. No one else sat anywhere closer than twenty feet, but it was still close enough for Cinder to hear the buzz of conversation.

Unsurprisingly, folks were wagering on the Tournament's outcome.

Cinder searched the stands, locating the members of *Steel-Graced*. He nudged Bones, indicating their masters and fellow apprentices. The *Steel-Graced* contingent sat several rows back and in a different aisle. Cinder and Bones pumped their fists their way. The *Steel-Graced* contingent shouted back in reply, still excited and overjoyed, obviously proud of what Cinder and Bones had accomplished. Behind them sat Coral and Riner. Master Lerid had obtained tickets for them. Riner simply beamed, while Coral blew him a kiss.

Cinder responded with what he knew was a sickly smile. Now wasn't the time to brood over his uncertainty about Coral.

Bones wasn't the first to be called to fight this time. It was Cinder and Depth Knarl.

"Good luck," Bones said.

Cinder didn't bother responding. He needed luck, but he also had to hold onto the notion that he was so good he didn't need it.

Believe you're a champion and you will *be a champion.*

He entered the arena floor, striding alongside Depth. Neither of them spoke as they made their way toward the pavilion where the important members of the government viewed the proceedings. Cinder listened with half an ear as the chief justice explained the final fights and the prizes for the winners. Those who lost in this round received a hundred coppers, enough to rent a nice flat for four months. The second-place warrior received five silvers, the equivalent of five hundred coppers, and the overall winner of the Tournament was gifted twenty silver coins.

Money, however, wasn't Cinder's motivation. Neither was glory. He'd already achieved his goal by making it to the Third Directorate. Anything more at this point would be the sugar on top of the pie.

He glanced askance at Depth, studying him for any weaknesses. Depth had two black lines marring his white outfit, one that cut across his left shoulder and another to his right chest. Neither appeared to have left him the slightest bit injured.

Cinder's ribs, on the other hand, still ached from his first fight.

He continued to do his best to scrutinize Depth, but the man was inscrutable, his affect flat. A flicker of memory simmered in the background of Cinder's mind. It was as if Depth's unreadable emotions reminded him of someone he might have once known.

The chief justice wound down his speech, and Master Jarvid called them to their places. The rules were unchanged.

The world beyond the sparring circle faded. Cinder's awareness centered on Depth, who still held a bored demeanor. *No.* That wasn't right. He simply maintained a bland air, like no thoughts or emotions stirred inside his mind. Cinder's perception of posture and balance couldn't seem to unlock the man's mysteries. He was utterly indecipherable. The notion troubled Cinder. If he couldn't reckon Depth's plans, he might not be able to beat him.

The master shouted. "Fight!"

Depth went from unmoving to shooting across the training circle in less than a blink. Cinder barely had time to get his sword in place. He parried, managing to push Depth offline at the same time. Depth's expression never wavered. He remained rooted in an unexpressive affect.

Here he came again. Cinder shifted to the right, moving away from the edge of the training ring.

Depth followed, cutting him off. His lateral movement and speed were every bit the equal of Sash's. He attacked in a swirl and twist of his practice blade. Again, Cinder defended, deftly holding him off. *Devesh, the man is fast.* They separated.

Depth gave him no time to reset and collect his fragmented thoughts. He strode forward, his blows faster. Doubt crept into Cinder's mind. Depth still gave nothing away. His balance was steady. He never shifted unnecessarily, was never over-extended. His technique was as good as Gorant's and Brow's but married to a ferocious aggression those two lacked.

Another exchange. An abrupt slap to the front of Cinder's right thigh caused it to collapse, and he fell to a knee.

"Break!" the judge shouted. "Two points for Depth. Return to your marks."

Despite the padding, the strike had hurt. Cinder shook out his leg, trying to get rid of the lingering ache. The discomfort remained, and he tried to hide a limp as he resumed his position. More doubts surfaced. He fought a genius, one almost as good as Bones, and Cinder only had one good leg under him.

He wasn't afraid, however. Only frustrated and upset. He breathed deeply, reaching for his center and seeking calm.

"Fight!"

Cinder stepped toward Depth, intending to take the fight to him. Depth met him in the middle of the sparring circle and quickly took control of the match. He pressed forward, and Cinder gave ground.

A glimmer in his mind's eye. *The pond again.* Cinder shook his head, and it dissipated. He barely restored his attention before Depth was on him. Cinder awkwardly parried a simple thrust.

Another glimmer, and again the silver pond formed, reflective of a cloudless, summer sky. Blue and green lightning surrounded it.

Cinder scowled. *Not now.* He didn't need this distraction, and he tried to force away the image of the pond, pushing against the wall of lightning.

Cinder hissed in pain, his mind feeling aflame. The lightning-laced wall burned like fire.

A blur in the corner of his vision. At the last moment, Cinder noticed a horizontal slash, and he rolled clumsily underneath it. He couldn't fight like this. He artlessly dodged another attack. Depth halted, confusion on his face, likely unsure as to the cause of Cinder's poor form.

Cinder took the momentary pause to put distance between himself and his opponent. As Depth edged forward again, the silvery pond finally weakened and waned. Less than a second later, it was gone, and Cinder could finally concentrate on the fight at hand.

The world slowed. Sounds heightened. Images sharpened, and he saw Depth about to land a killing blow to his abdomen. He would have no chance to evade. He would lose, but it didn't mean he was defeated.

Cinder adjusted his practice sword. A rising slice hammered Depth's bicep. At the same time, a horizontal slash crashed into Cinder's abdomen.

Cinder went to his knees, groaning in pain. Depth swore loudly. He clutched his arm close to his side.

"Break!" the judge shouted. "Simultaneous strike. Two points apiece. Depth wins four points to two."

Cinder rose to his feet with a grimace, angry with himself. He'd lost.

The crowd cheered wildly, but Cinder didn't hear their roars. His abdomen vied with his sore ribs and throbbing thigh for what hurt most. None of that compared to the agony of defeat. He glanced to where the *Steel-Graced* members sat. Master Lerid clapped his hands in Cinder's direction. All of the *Steel-Graced* contingent did. They stood, applauding wildly. It eased the sting. He and Depth were presented to the chief justice, with the other man declared the winner.

They made their way back to Bones and Wark, who were already headed for the arena floor.

"Good try," Bones said to Cinder as they passed one another.

Cinder grunted acknowledgement before flopping into his seat, still frustrated. He'd been so close. If not for the strange pond distracting him, he might have—

He sighed. No. That wasn't it. Depth was the better warrior today.

Depth settled next to him. His prior emotionless demeanor was gone. Disbelief filled his voice. "What the hell did you hit me with? A mace? Shit. I think my arm might be broken."

Cinder was instantly contrite. He had wanted to win, but not at the cost of truly injuring his opponent. "Sorry about that."

Depth rolled his shoulder and moved his arm about. "Forget it. It's not broken," he said. "It's going to sport one hell of a bruise, though."

On impulse, Cinder held out his hand. "My name is Cinder Shade."

Depth took his hand and they shook. "Depth Knarl."

"Pleased to meet you, Depth. What do you think about Bones and Wark?"

"My money is on Bones."

"You can't bet on him. He's from my school. I already put my money on him to win the entire Tournament."

Depth viewed him askance. "Then you're going to lose when Bones faces me."

Cinder grinned, warming to the other man. "No bets for now, but when we get to the Third Directorate . . ."

"Deal," Depth said with a laugh.

The bout between Bones and Wark went about as expected. Bones overwhelmed Wark with a combination of speed and efficiently applied brutal power. He still hadn't given away a single point during the Tournament.

Depth folded his arms, chewing the inside of his cheek. "Hunh," he eventually allowed. "Maybe it's a good thing we didn't bet on me and Bones."

He was right to worry. After a brief rest period, Bones defeated him four points to none.

16

It was one week after the Maker's Tournament. A week of hectic, non-stop work where everyone in the city seemed to want to meet, greet, or just talk to Cinder. There were the city's political powers who needed *only a moment of his time*, wealthy patrons who sought to attach their name to his, and visitations from various religious functionaries, wanting to ensure his righteous moral state.

Cinder's hours had been full, but there was also all the shopping. He had to purchase an ungodly number of supplies for the Third Directorate. At least four trousers and shirts, including one set good enough for a formal ball, the instructional volumes needed for his various classes, a number of empty book-ledgers, and writing instruments to jot notes in said ledgers. It was a large list of items, and without his winnings from the Tournament, he couldn't have afforded them.

And two days from now he'd set sail for Yaksha Sithe and the Third Directorate. So much mystery to both. The beginning of a great journey, and like many voyages of discovery this one would start with a number of leave-takings. Cinder had already bid Riner farewell, promising to write to him whenever he could. Same with Master Choff and

Cook Nestle at *Our Lady of Fire.*

Now it was time to talk to Coral. Cinder should have spoken to her directly after the Maker's Tournament, but he'd been unable to find the time or the courage. As a result, their talk was long overdue.

Today, he finally had the hours to talk to her, and they strolled through a park near her place of employment. Both of them wore light clothing, and the day was fine. It was Devasth, summer's holy season, and the warm weather sustained the green life covering the land. Cherry trees lined the park, wearing clouds of pink blossoms. The trees bloomed twice a season, in early spring and now, in the deep days of summer. Same with many of the various shrubs, such as late-flowering azaleas and rhododendrons, which were similarly garbed with fragrant blossoms. Their perfumed aroma wafted on a mild breeze.

Other couples walked the park, and Cinder had a startled awareness. Did others view him and Coral in the same way? As a couple?

Cinder glanced at Coral. Saying goodbye to her would be different and much more difficult than any other farewell. It was a gut-wrenching realization. Coral wasn't merely another friend. One day, she might become someone far more special to him.

One day.

Unfortunately, the future wasn't the present, and he didn't think he could ask her to wait for him. It wouldn't be fair. He was destined to become a warrior of the Yaksha Sithe, meant to live a life of uncertainty where he might never return to Swift Sword. How could he ask Coral, or any woman, to wait for him in those kinds of circumstances?

He had to leave her.

An uncertain quiet had fallen over them, and Cinder noted a stiffness in the way Coral carried herself. He had to tell her the truth, and he wished it didn't have to hurt so much.

"I'm leaving for the Third Directorate in two days," Cinder said. "When I graduate, I'll enter the Yaksha Army. They say the humans who join have a high fatality rate."

Coral halted, facing him fully. She wore a frown bordering on the edge of a scowl. "I know all this. Why are you bringing it up now?"

Cinder's stomach hollowed with anticipatory dread. He really didn't want to have this conversation. "Because I can't make any promises to you. We haven't spoken of the future. I think we should."

"The future is unwritten," Coral said. "There are no lyrics to sing of it. You are planning for what might never be."

"But the future will happen whether we want it to or not," Cinder argued. "We should talk."

Coral nodded. "You're right. We haven't discussed the future. And we haven't because you don't owe me an explanation or an apology for what you think will happen. *I'm* the one who owes you. You saved Riner."

In Cinder's estimation, only Devesh's grace saved a person. "I helped Riner. I didn't save him."

Coral disagreed. "You saved him. Without you, he wouldn't have a chance for the life he does now."

"Maybe."

Coral gazed at him, an inscrutable expression on her features. It seemed like she traced the lines of his face. She shifted the course of their conversation in an unexpected direction. "I guess I shouldn't expect a tiger to enjoy a cage, and Rakesh must sometimes feel like a cage to someone like you. I think that's part of what you want to say. That and one other thing."

"And what do you think that is?" Cinder asked.

"Dying," Coral said, facing him. "But that can happen to any of us at any moment. An orphan knows this better than most. But I choose to live without fear. I choose to live with hope for a good future. Otherwise, why even bother waking up in the morning?"

Cinder felt the same way. "I want the same things, to live the same way."

"Then why are you talking to me about dying? What do you truly fear?"

While he considered what to say, it surprised him how much taller he was than she. When he'd first come to Swift Sword they had been closer in height to one another. Now she came no higher than his forehead. He peered into her eyes, which were alert and steady, still unable to respond. Fighting, sparring, training . . . all of it was far easier than telling Coral of his fears.

"Do you love me?" she abruptly asked.

"Yes," Cinder replied without hesitation, although he wasn't certain it was the truth. He wanted to love Coral. It was beyond stupid not to. She was a wonderfully beautiful person, and any man would count himself lucky to have a chance to win her heart.

Nevertheless, while Cinder knew he *should* love Coral, his heart remained steadfastly unsure. He wondered if his lack of certainty was because of who he was. Perhaps his dedication to a warrior's life left no room for love. And maybe that needed to change. Eventually, though. Right now, he *had* to become a warrior. The desire to do so seemed to oblige him to set aside any hopes for a family or a wife, at least in the near term.

He recalled an image then, one from a dream: *a lush city, beautiful and elegant.*

Coral glanced his way. "Are you all right?"

"I'm fine, and I'm sorry," he said, feeling like he was failing Coral in some fashion.

"Don't be." Coral grinned. "You just told me you love me." She looped her arms around his neck and drew him in, kissing him softly on the lips. Their first kiss.

His skin grew warm, and his heart soared, beating like he'd run a mile. He held her close.

She broke the embrace, still smiling. "I love you, too, and I will wait if you ask. But you have to ask." She chuckled gently, when his face fell in chagrin. "I think you feared to ask me to wait more than anything else."

Cinder nodded, glad for her insight and wisdom. "I didn't think it was fair, not with how my life might end up."

Coral put a finger to his lips. "We already talked about that. Let it go. Come back to me. That's all the promise I need to hear from you."

"I'll come back to you," Cinder said, praying he could keep the vow, but privately guilty and uncertain if telling her these things was the right thing to do.

An instant later, a tide of emotion swept aside his worries. He didn't know if he loved Coral, but he knew he could. After he'd finished his work as a warrior, the same dedication he'd made to the sword, he could make to her and their life together.

"Thank you for being so wise," Cinder said, embracing her in return and grateful that she understood.

Coral smiled at him, tears in her eyes. "Promise me one other thing. I've heard the Third Directorate hardens a person's heart. Don't let that happen to you."

"I promise."

Coral viewed him, her eyes luminous. She kissed him again, a soft press of her lips against his. "Goodbye, Cinder."

She left him then, returning toward the manor house where she worked, wiping at her eyes.

Cinder watched her leave, his heart heavy, her final admonishment echoing in his mind.

A tall-masted ship, the *Whispering Tanned Fox*, was Cinder's destination. It would carry him, Bones, and the other two apprentice warriors to the Yaksha home island and the Third Directorate. Today was the day they would set sail. Accompanying Cinder and Bones were the other members of *Steel-Graced Adepts*, including Dorr, who smiled as proudly as a father holding his newborn son. The other apprentice warriors who'd won their way to the Third Directorate were similarly surrounded by those from their schools. They trailed behind Cinder and Bones since *Steel-Graced* had pride of place. Bones, after all, had won the Maker's Tournament.

Strangely, no family attended any of them. It was something to do with a curse. In times past, families had voyaged with the students to the shores of Yaksha proper. A century ago, however, tragedy had struck. Three such journeys in a row had ended with terrible ship-wrecks and all souls aboard lost to the cruel sea. Since then families said their farewells in private celebrations in the night prior to the departures.

But because Cinder had no family in Swift Sword, he'd spent his last night in quiet meditation at *Steel-Graced*, the only home he knew. After a generous meal hosted by his masters and attended by Faine and Dorr, Cinder had returned to his room-under-the-stairs. A vague desire had urged him to seek private contemplation.

He'd sat alone in his small bedroom last night, staring at the sword Master Lerid had commissioned on his behalf. Double-edged, long, lean, and deadly. A basket hilt to protect his hand. Near perfect balance.

"It isn't your final sword," Master Lerid had said when he'd given it to Cinder last night. "You must pay for that one on your own, earn it with blood and sacrifice."

"An insufi *blade," Cinder had said, recalling the word from the depths of his otherwise blank memory.*

"That is one way to obtain the weapon made for you and you alone," Master Lerid had said. "An insufi *weapon is given as part of an* Upanayana *ceremony. But it is only granted to students who the masters at the Third Directorate consider sublime."*

For some reason that hadn't sounded right to Cinder. He thought the *Upanayana* ceremony was a religious observance, one performed by everyone. Apparently, he was wrong, and he'd let the matter lie. He'd gone to his room and prepared himself as best he could for what was to come. *Yaksha Sithe and the Third Directorate.*

Today, the morning had dawned in an auspicious fashion, sunny and warm. Cinder and the others had gathered at the academy be-fore traveling to the docks where sailors and fishermen congregated, shouting loudly. The morning catch of fish had been left to dry on the docks, and the stench carried on the stiff breeze blowing off the sea. It mingled with the smell of brine. Gulls cried, flying about Swift Sword's docks.

"We're here," Master Lerid said.

They stood at the gangplank leading to the *Whispering Tanned Fox*. Cinder gazed at the ship. The crew bustled about, loading cargo, prepping sails and lines, and getting the vessel ready for departure. Despite its wide berth, the ship had an elegance, an indication that it wouldn't merely wallow in the water. It likely had speed enough to out-sail most pirate vessels, but that ability wouldn't be put to the test on the trip to Yaksha Sithe's home island. The Sentient Sea was free of pirates. The elves ensured it. Their lean vessels patrolled the waters of their dominion, surging like sharks on the hunt and killing pirates wherever they were found.

Cinder had never seen one of those fabled elven ships, but he hoped to when he arrived at Yaksha proper.

Once again the excitement of journeying to a new place swept over him, and he grinned with joy.

Master Lerid surprised him then by placing his right fist in the palm of his left hand and bowing low at the waist to Cinder and Bones. "Honor your house, honor your school, and honor yourselves. Follow these principles and they will see you to success. Good luck to both of you."

Master Jine wished them well on their voyage as well. "Grow. Learn. Master. Teach. Do this and your life will have meaning."

Faine smiled as he offered his own deep bow. "I know you will not bring shame upon yourselves or your school." He paused, quirking his head to the side. "Well, maybe Bones will, but one out of two isn't bad."

"Faine!" Bones said in mock-dismay.

Faine merely chuckled.

Next came the apprentices. Cinder shared a hug with all of them.

"Show those prancing elves what a *Steel-Graced* warrior can do," Mirk encouraged.

Cinder promised he would. He stepped away from his *Steel-Graced* family. It was time to go. Part of him mourned those he was leaving behind—his mind drifted to Coral—but joy and eagerness quickly subsumed his sorrow.

He gathered his rucksacks full of belongings and ascended the gangplank, trailing after Bones.

The captain met them on deck. He was a tall man, heavily built and possessing rounder eyes than was the norm for Rakesh. His fair skin was freckled, and a blond mustache drooped around his mouth. His eyes and coloration indicated that he was either from the Savage Kingdoms or the northern portions of Gandharva.

"Third Directorate apprentices, eh?" the captain said without preamble. "You'll share a room with the other apprentices." He led them to a room with four bunks. "Choose which is yours and stay out of me hair. Me sailors have work to do."

He left, shutting the door firmly behind him.

Cinder placed his rucksacks under a bed and sat on it. Bones did the same. They had a few minutes alone before the other apprentices were to arrive.

"You ready for this?" Bones asked, sounding oddly anxious.

Cinder had never before heard that tone from his fellow *Steel-Graced*. Bones had always been cocky to the point of arrogance. Now he sounded unsure. What was wrong with him? Or was his bravado all for show? Cinder had heard of men like that, the ones who barked the loudest in order to hide their fear.

Cinder viewed Bones with raised eyebrows. "Something bothering you?"

"Of course not," Bones said. A nervous chuckle exposed his lie. A few seconds later, he spoke again. "We'll be training with dwarves and elves. Both of them have advantages over us. Dwarves are strong. Elves are fast. And with *lorethasra*, they're both stronger *and* faster than we are." A bitter cast stole across his face. "We're weak." He stared at the floor, despondent.

All this, Cinder already knew. But there was nothing to be done about it, and he didn't know what to tell Bones. In the end, he could only come up with one way to possibly ease Bones' fears. "You're right," he said. "We are weak, but that isn't going to stop us from overcoming the elves and the dwarves."

Bones' despondency lifted somewhat. He raised his head, viewing

Cinder in hopeful curiosity.

"In war, all men are brothers," Cinder said, the words feeling like an old recitation of an unalterable truth. "And in battle, it isn't the individual who counts. It's fighting as a unit, as a company, as a brigade that's more important. It's why a human, Mede, managed to carve his way across the world, all the way from the Savage Kingdoms to the Sunset Lands. He defeated every elven and dwarven army sent against him. Why?"

"We aren't Mede," Bones said.

"Are you sure?" Cinder asked. "We can fight for one purpose, fight with and for everyone else in our unit. That's how Mede won. Why can't we do the same?"

Thoughtfulness replaced the bitter defeat on Bones' face. "Maybe."

Cinder squeezed Bones' shoulder, hoping to infuse confidence. "We can do this, brother," he urged.

Bones broke into his typical grin, sure and mocking. "You don't have to take it so seriously, *brother*. I was funning you."

Cinder rolled his eyes, abruptly annoyed. "Then consider yourself on your own."

Bones' grin faded. "No. It's fine. We should do what you said." A beat later. "Brother."

17

The journey from Swift Sword to Yaksha Sithe's capital of Revelant was scheduled to take the *Whispering Tanned Fox* and its crew roughly three days. However, until the ship left dock, Captain Swell wanted Cinder and the rest of the inductees to the Third Directorate to remain in their shared cabin. He didn't want them getting underfoot while his sailors were getting the vessel ready for the open sea. Thankfully, several hours after they left Swift Sword's harbor, Captain Swell finally let them out of their cabin, but before he allowed them to leave, he repeated his admonishment to stay out of the way of his sailors.

Cinder, for one, was grateful for the open air. During the few hours he and the others had spent in the cabin, the small room had been pervaded by a strained quiet, one entirely due to Wark Nil. The *Jasmine Water* apprentice was someone Cinder was quickly discovering was a jackhole of the first degree.

Shortly before they set sail, Cinder had tried to reconcile with Wark. His payment for his attempted peacemaking? An increasingly hostile set of grunts followed by a growled warning to stay out of his way and not talk to him.

Cinder shut his mouth and returned to his bunk.

Bones lying on his bunk, chuckled. "You sure all men are brothers?" He tipped his head toward Wark. "That there is an asshole." He made no attempt to keep his voice quiet.

Wark, of course, heard, and he surged to his feet, glaring at Bones. "What did you say?" he demanded, hands clenched.

Bones didn't bother standing. He laced his fingers behind his head and yawned in Wark's face, like the *Jasmine Water* apprentice wasn't worth the dirt on his boots. "You heard me. Fuck off."

Wark continued to glower, but he didn't challenge Bones. Instead, he settled grumpily into his bunk with a muttered oath. No one else wanted to talk afterward.

Cinder glanced one time at Wark, who had his eyes closed, pretending to sleep. Cinder shook his head. *Fragging idiot.* Didn't he realize what was coming? They were bound for the Third Directorate. They would soon enter an academy where the masters and non-human students were their superiors in every measurable way: faster, stronger, more durable, and longer-lived. If the apprentices from Rakesh were to have any chance of success, they had to work as one, fight as one, and have everyone pull as one. They truly needed to be as brothers.

Wark was apparently too stupid to realize it.

As a result, when Captain Swell let them out, Cinder bolted for the door. He was the first one to leave. Given the stifling tension and closed quarters, the cabin had felt like a prison. Cinder went straight to the railing and breathed in the briny air, closing his eyes and exhaling his frustrations with Wark. Five breaths he took before opening his eyes and taking in the sights.

Gulls still trailed the ship, but of Rakesh nothing could be seen. All around the vessel was the vast Sentient Sea, the waters an indigo color that troubled him for some reason. The sailors worked the rigging and the sails, calling out or acknowledging orders. They clambered the lines with the sure-footedness of a scurry of squirrels, barely pausing when the ship crested a wave and lurched downward, which it did over and over again, rolling and rocking in an unpredictable fashion.

Cinder's stomach didn't appreciate the heaving movement, and he remained by the railing, clutching his stomach. *Seasickness.* He imagined Captain Swell wouldn't appreciate vomit on his clean deck. Cinder breathed in through his nose and out through his mouth, hoping to settle his nausea.

Bones and Depth joined him at the railing. Wark was nowhere to be seen.

"You sure got out of there like an arrow," Bones said. "What's the hurry?"

"Didn't feel like being in the same room as Wark," Cinder replied. He kept his eyes locked on the horizon, willing the nausea to recede.

Depth stiffened. "Look."

Cinder peered over his shoulder and inhaled sharply. A pair of elves, both men, exited from below deck. One was blond, and the other auburn, and both were impossible to age. They could have been anywhere from twenty to two hundred. Elves aged slowly. The two men wore tailored clothing, thick gray shirts, and dark colored pants. In contrast to their effeminate handsomeness, they moved with a martial grace that left Cinder envious. He noticed the swords strapped to their waists, and it set him wondering if these two might be instructors or fellow students at the Directorate.

The elves came their way.

"You are destined for the Third Directorate," the blond one said rather than asked. "I am Sinu Lome." He gestured to the dark-haired elf. "This one is Linwon Waine."

Linwon bowed. He was taller than Sinu—but still inches shorter than Bones—and more thickly built, although both elves were still relatively slender.

Cinder held out a hand. "Cinder Shade," he said by way of introduction. He shook hands with the elves, both of whom gave him an extra measure of firmness. Cinder hid a grimace. It seemed the stories of elven strength weren't exaggerated.

Bones and Depth introduced themselves also.

Linwon spoke. "My cousin and I were unworthy of admittance to the Third Directorate. Perhaps you would be willing to spar with us. Show us your human prowess." His eyes glinted, a mocking smile curling the corners of his mouth.

Cinder didn't like the elf. Bones was cocky, but Linwon's expression was something else entirely. Linwon had to crane his head to meet Bones' gaze, but the bent-neck posture did nothing to soften his proud, haughty bearing or the hunger lurking in his eyes. Cinder quickly deciphered the expression. Linwon wanted to humiliate them. And he likely could.

Wisdom dictated that Cinder find an honorable means to decline the offer.

Wisdom be damned.

Cinder plastered a bright smile. "We'd be happy too."

Depth grunted. "Speak for yourself." He clutched his gut, and his face had a green cast. "My stomach wants to crawl out my mouth." He lunged to the rail and vomited.

Cinder watched Depth get sick. In truth, he wasn't feeling much better, but the short conversation with the elves had helped him forget his abdominal difficulties. Unfortunately, Depth's vomiting reminded him of his own nausea. "Excuse me," he said to the elves. He went to the railing, hunching over it, keeping his attention on the horizon, and doing his best to hold down his gorge. *Breathe in through his nose and out through his mouth.* His heart raced. He hated vomiting. The world around him faded as the entirety of his attention went to the queasiness threatening to upset his stomach.

Strangely, the vision of the perfectly reflective pond seeped into his mind just then. He'd noticed it before during the Maker's Tournament, and as before, he couldn't view the image clearly. A cloak of blue and green lightning surrounded the water.

Cinder grimaced in confusion, unsure what he was seeing, not that he cared. The seasickness was of greater concern.

He forced away the vision of the pond as best he could and focused instead on his breathing exercises. Those always calmed him.

The distracting vision slowly faded, and the breathing exercises started to work. The nausea reduced from a boil to a simmer. His heart rate slowed. The nausea reduced even further, and Cinder sighed in relief. *Thank Devesh.*

He could see again, focus on the world around him, and he glanced about. He scowled in annoyance when he noticed Bones lounging nearby. His fellow *Steel-Graced* appeared unaffected by the ship's motion, and he casually leaned back, elbows resting on the railing, the utter picture of nonchalance. He viewed the elves with crossed arms and a bored expression.

"Perhaps another time," Sinu said. "When your human stomachs aren't so overcome by the sea's motion." His mouth twitched, flashing into a mocking smile. "We forget. Not everyone has the constitution of one hailing from the Blessed Race."

Linwon bowed, and the elves departed.

Cinder gritted his teeth. *Blessed Race. Is that what the elves called themselves?* Arrogant pricks.

"Those two could use a punch in the face," Bones said.

"You said it," Cinder said by way of agreement. By now much of his nausea was gone, and the image of the pond popped like a soap bubble. He noticed Wark loitering nearby.

The former *Jasmine Water*, edged their way, glancing sidelong at Bones and Cinder. "I heard your conversation with those two. It's a good thing you didn't agree to spar against them."

Depth continued to hang over the railing, and while he no longer vomited, he was also in no position to reply. Bones grunted at Wark's words. He crossed his arms and stared at nothing in particular.

Cinder took the initiative. He hoped Wark was finally letting go of his anger. "Why's that?"

For a wonder, Wark answered in a civil tone. "Have you ever seen an elf actually train?"

Cinder shook his head. The motion caused the nausea to flare, and he spun about, facing the water, focusing on the horizon, breathing in through his nose, out through his mouth.

"You're about to get your chance," Bones said. "They have their practice swords."

Once again, the deep breathing calmed Cinder's stomach, and he turned around.

Sinu and Linwon had cleared a small area on the deck. They held wooden practice blades, dark like walnut and glistening with an oily sheen.

"They're using shokes," Bones said.

The elves bowed to one another and exploded forward. It was the only way to describe their movements. They shot forth like arrows, and their blows cracked with the staccato cacophony of rain hammering a tin roof. Cinder followed their swaying strikes and parries.

The elves swept apart, paused, and went at it again. Another series of blows. Sinu took a slash to the arm, and he grunted in pain. The elves broke apart.

"A clever move," Sinu said, shaking out his arm.

Linwon dipped his head in reply.

Sinu inhaled deeply. A golden light flashed about him, disappearing too quickly for Cinder to fully register if it had been real or merely a trick of the light. The smell of pine and the tinkling of wind chimes rang out, and he glanced about, looking for the source of the scent and sound. He frowned, unable to locate whatever had rung out. Did he imagine it? Maybe it was pine from the ship's wood, and the ringing was something due to the sailors.

He mentally shrugged and returned his attention to the elves.

"Devesh, they're fast," Bones breathed in awe. "Master Jine always used to say that one elven warrior is the equal of three of us. I think he overestimated our worth."

"It's only because of their *lorethasra*," Wark said. "Without it, they're no better than us."

"Well, they have it and we don't," Bones complained.

"Which is why it's a good thing you didn't spar against them," Wark said. "We need to stick together at the Third Directorate."

Cinder viewed him in shock, mouth agape. It took him several seconds to overcome his surprise. "What changed your mind? You weren't so friendly down below."

Wark shuffled his feet like a boy caught sneaking candy. "About that. You need to understand. Brow's a good friend of mine. He taught me everything I know, in some ways even more than our masters. He's like a brother, and I had to leave him on the docks today. It broke his heart when he lost to you."

Cinder grunted. "I know how you feel. I ended up taking the place of my senior in the Tournament. He's a good man, but good men don't always win."

"But hard ones do," Bones said.

Revelant. It was a lovely word, and the city exceeded the glory of its name. Cinder gazed at the elven capital, lost in wide-eyed wonder as the *Whispering Tanned Fox* pulled into a deep harbor and settled next to the dock.

The morning light glinted off the waves, and rugged hills—treed and green—cupped the water like an emerald crown. Shelves of gray granite pushed out from the foliage, rising like stony sentinels. More rocks formed the wharf, appearing as nothing more than an outgrowth of the crusty ledges. Cinder stared at the sights, and it took him a moment to realize the extent of the large city nestled amidst the slopes and stone shelves. The buildings were sculpted to accentuate the curve of the hills and the gentle grace of the swaying trees. Roofs, high-peaked and tiled in terra cotta or shimmering silver, served as a counterpoint to the generous greenery.

The vast beauty of Yaksha Sithe's capital stole Cinder's breath. There was so much to see and absorb.

Strangely, the majesty sparked a vague memory, a reminiscence of a place he perhaps once read about, a city on the water, larger than Revelant and nestled amongst nine hills. The memory disappeared, and Cinder shook off the lurking thoughts. He wanted to focus on

Revelant, which was so different from Swift Sword. Rakesh's capital made little-to-no accommodation for nature's grandeur. For instance, in Swift Sword, the wharf jutted into the harbor like a set of grasping fingers, broken-nailed and arthritic, and the homes and buildings might have been designed by a distracted child. The most graceful aspect of Rakesh's capital were its squares. Those could be lovely, but none of it was like this.

Cinder was broken from his examination of Revelant by Bones.

"Beautiful city, isn't it?" Bones said, a hitch in his voice indicating repressed awe.

Wark and Depth stood nearby, listening in.

"Yes, it is," Cinder agreed.

Cinder threw off the last of his reverie when Captain Swell called them to his side.

"Come with me," the captain ordered. He led them down the gangplank to where a slim, red-haired elf wearing a gray coat and blue slacks waited.

The elf spoke, his tone prim. "I am Ruom Shale. The masters sent me to guide you the rest of the way to the Third Directorate."

Here was the elf who Master Lerid promised would take them on the last leg of their journey.

Captain Swell blew out his mustache and addressed the elf. "I turn them over to you, then." Next, he turned to Cinder and his friends "I hope you boys have safe travels. Look me up if you're ever in Revelant. I'll buy you a beer." With that, he went back to his ship.

Taking his place were Linwon and Sinu.

The blond elf, Sinu, spoke. "Good luck on your studies. Though we can never claim the honor of graduating from the Third Directorate, I am sure you four will uphold the academy's high standards."

"Yes," Linwon added. "I'm sure you will do as well as your kind can."

Sinu and Linwon shared a smirk as they departed.

Ruom cleared his throat. "I see you've met Sinu and Linwon. The cousins—those two—did not attend the Third Directorate, but they blossomed later in life. If you were lucky enough to see them spar, then you witnessed true excellence, even for those of the Blessed Race. Both have earned *insufi* blades. Come along now."

Cinder wanted to view the city—every turn of his head seemed to bring forth a new wonder—and he could have gazed on it for hours. Ruom, however, had other ideas. The elf had a carriage waiting, one with blackened windows, and he had them stow their luggage and addressed them. "We find your kind do best if you travel straightaway to the Third Directorate in as quick and uninterrupted fashion as possible. We'll take Sun's Passage Road and should arrive at the academy in three or four days. We'll camp in designated areas as required, but I'm afraid there will be no time to see the city or island itself. We're off."

Before anyone could speak another word, Ruom quickly shut the carriage door, ascended to the driver's seat, and they were soon trundling along.

Cinder tried to peer through the windows, but all he could see were a few vague outlines of people and buildings. He sat back in dejection. "Well, this is going to be a boring mess."

The others grumbled their agreement.

Three days of travel passed in monotony. The only breaks to their tedium were when they paused to eat and camp.

Their journey ended several hours into the morning of their fourth day on Yaksha proper when Ruom opened the door. He wore a bright smile on his face. "We're here."

Cinder was the last to creak his way out of the cramped carriage. The days spent locked within like a prisoner had left the back of his legs and butt numb and lifeless. Other parts—his shoulders, back, knees, and neck—were stiff and aching. He groaned when he stepped onto level ground, stretching out the tightness and working circulation into his numb areas.

Pins and needles persisted as he took his first view of the Third Directorate.

If Revelant was a city melding gracefully amidst stone, sea, and trees, then the Third Directorate was where a set of rugged buildings hunkered like an obdurate fortress at the base of a broad mountain pass. They conceded nothing to the unforgiving mountains that soared in the near and far distances. Lichen colored the shadowed walls, red bricks, and gray flagstones of the blocky structures, not softening them in the slightest.

The carriage had pulled into a courtyard next to a stable, and a pair of young elves got busy unharnessing the horses. To the left, an arched doorway, tall and wide, allowed a view of the gravel path upon which the carriage had crunched after passing through the now-closed gates of the Third Directorate. Directly ahead, Cinder viewed a grassy square where the statue of an indistinct figure stood centered. There was an odd sense of motion to the sculpture.

The wind gusted then, and Cinder shivered under its unexpected chill. Devasth, summer's holiest month, currently warmed Swift Sword and Revelant, but here, the sun struggled to penetrate a thick blanket of gray clouds scudding across a cold sky, and a sporadic drizzle fell.

It was an unhappy omen, and disquiet rustled within Cinder. He didn't like this weather. It stirred unhappy memories.

"Gentlemen," Ruom pronounced, interrupting his troubled thoughts. "Welcome to the Third Directorate."

Ruom's gait was as prim and proper as his speech, and he walked them through the grassy sward Cinder had earlier seen. He paused in front of the statue, which was thick with verdigris. "This square is the Quad," Ruom said, "and the statue is the real reason for the Third Directorate's founding. We guard against his awakening."

No one spoke to ask the questions Cinder reckoned they were all thinking: *Guard against a statue? Why?*

He stared at the figure, who stood on a tall, broad pedestal; a square, black block rising higher than Cinder's height. The person depicted was similarly large—titanic, in fact. He was handsome to the point of beautiful and appeared life-like. It was as if the arrogant smirk on his face had been frozen in the midst of becoming a mocking sneer.

Overall, the pedestal and statue rose as high as the yakshin Cinder had met in Swift Sword, and the man seemed to gaze at the world from his lofty heights, his eyes fairly shining with a cruel intellect.

"This is the center of the Third Directorate," Ruom said. "Ironic that *he* is housed at the locus."

Cinder's breathing came heavy and deep. He couldn't take his eyes off the statue. Hatred for the figure came to a quick boil. "Who is he?" he rasped.

Ruom didn't immediately answer. "That unrest you're all feeling is to be expected," the elf said. "This is Garad Lull, one of Shet's Titans."

Bones eyes snapped toward the elf. "You mean a statue of Garad Lull."

"No. I mean the actual Titan. When he was defeated by the Mythaspuris, he was frozen to the state you see now."

"That can't be," Depth breathed in shock. "The Mythaspuris, Shet, and all the rest aren't real."

Ruom sighed. "If only that were the case. Unfortunately, in this you are wrong. Shet and his Titans were all too real." He pointed. "You can see one in front of you. Garad Lull, in a sleep akin to death. He and his master will never awaken. They were put to eternal rest by the Mythaspuris, but they live on, although few believe it." He gestured again. "But here is your proof. Garad's presence at the Third Directorate is well-known throughout the world, and yet no one believes us when we say this is the actual Titan. Not even when they learn he breathes once a day, every day at noon."

Cinder rocked on his heels. *Garad Lull.* One of Shet's actual Titans. Garad Lull, the immortal evil who had battled alongside Shet against Shokan and Sira. Their war had occurred thousands of years prior to the Mythaspuris, on a distant world whose name was long forgotten. Garad was considered the master of treachery and seduction, the one who had tricked some of Shokan's and Sira's greatest allies into willingly transforming themselves into necrosed.

How can this be the same being?

"Your questions about Garad, the other Titans, and Shet will be answered during your coursework," Ruom said. "Let us continue. We have other things to cover." He sauntered on.

Cinder followed the elf, gazing about his new home. To their right were the stables, and to their left was a broad set of stairs leading to a long, rectangular building fronted by a columned portico. An entablature depicted scenes of a crowned elven woman dispensing justice. As for the building itself, it was four stories in height and made of red brick. Ivy covered much of its face, and what mortar was visible wore the dark stain of years-long exposure. Tan stone lintels and aprons housed regularly spaced mullioned windows, which opened onto the Quad.

Directly ahead of them, however, was their destination, a three-story building, similar to the one on the left, but smaller in scale, including a far smaller portico. It had two entrances, both facing the Quad, and Ruom took them to the right-hand one.

They entered a foyer floored in a honeyed oak. The walls had a soft caramel color and were decorated with a number of paintings depicting humans and dwarves standing in heroic poses. A large chandelier hung from a tall ceiling, and warm *diptha* bulbs lit the entrance. Several upholstered chairs, red and gold, huddled around small tables along a windowed wall. On the side opposite the seating, a large rug fronted a floating staircase that angled past a large landing. Directly past the foyer, Cinder spied a darkened hallway.

"For most of the next two years, this is your home," Ruom announced. "Krathe House, *Vanquisher's House* in *Shevasra*."

A well-built young man, features typical of those from Rakesh, exited the darkened corridor on the far side of the foyer. "Are these the Firsters?" he asked Ruom.

"They are," Ruom answered, "and since you're here, I'll leave them in your hands." The elf addressed Cinder and the others. "This is Cor Garwing, a third year. He'll show you to your quarters. I'll see you again tonight when the General-Commandant makes his formal welcome." Before Cinder could even thank him, Ruom exited the foyer.

"Your rooms are upstairs," Cor said. He led them up the floating staircase and spoke while they climbed. "Your year is on the top floor during your time here. The middle floor is for the second years, and the bottom is for any third years who might be on campus."

Cinder gazed about, absorbing his new home.

The stairs bifurcated as they ascended, bracketing floor-to-ceiling mullioned windows facing the Quad. They reached a final landing at the top floor and entered a common room containing a half-dozen scattered tables and chairs resting beneath *diptha*-fueled chandeliers. One sofa faced a large hearth, which was currently cold. To the left of the fireplace extended a corridor, and along its length were a number of open doors. A quick glance told Cinder that each one opened into a dorm room, a private space for each student.

"We have a few maids to tidy up washrooms and such," Cor explained. "That's it. Otherwise, you're expected to keep your floor and rooms clean." He peered at them intently. "You are expected to maintain yourself and your rooms. The elves will not be happy if you don't."

"How many others are going to be staying here?" Cinder asked.

"Traditionally, there are seven humans and five dwarves in each class," Cor answered. "The rest should arrive later today."

"And the elves?" Bones asked.

"Seven of them, and they stay in their own part of the House." Cor glanced at Cinder and the others. "Do you think you can sort yourselves out? Each of you has your own room. Claim one. The commandant, General Arwan, will address all of us at supper for your formal welcoming ceremony. When it's time, I'll take you to it."

18

After Cor left, Cinder went down the hallway and entered a random dorm room. He discovered a bare-walled space that contained a cot, a wardrobe for his clothes, and a wooden desk and chair. Thankfully, it was larger than his closet-under-the-stairs at *Steel-Graced Adepts*. He put away his belongings and went to the room's single window. The mullions were dark with age and verdigris and the glass sagging and distorted with age. They allowed a view of green hills soaring in the near distance, rugged mountains towering further out, and closer at hand, a lichen-covered, walled courtyard. Cinder did a quick assessment and realized his room was directly opposite the Quad.

He studied the courtyard. A gravel path traced a winding line amongst flowers and shrubbery. A couple of benches were discretely placed next to a small pool of water, in the center of which gurgled a tiered fountain. The courtyard was otherwise empty.

Cinder returned to the common area. He found his fellow Firsters regathered there, discussing what was to come, their expectations, and fears. Even Wark took part. The *Jasmine Water* apprentice had warmed up during the short voyage to Yaksha.

An hour or so later, voices rose from the staircase as Cor guided three more humans to the common area. Quick introductions were made. Two were Gandharvans, Joria Javsheck and Ishmay Sensow, and the other was a Rakesh apprentice-warrior, Rorian Molinking, from the mountains.

"We're finally here," Ishmay said. He was a tall, lanky man with sandy-brown hair and hazel eyes, a color Cinder had never before seen in a person. He appeared to take the measure of the room. "Who's the best here? Because you're second now."

Cinder took an immediate dislike to the Gandharvan's attitude.

So did Bones, who bristled. "So that's how it's going to be? First thing you do is talk us down."

"I'm only talking the truth," Ishmay replied. "No need to hide that, is there?"

"You keep believing that when all of us whip your ass," Bones said, stepping forward.

Ishmay didn't back down.

Cinder got in between them, hoping to defuse the incipient argument. He held up his hands, bracing Bones and Ishmay apart. "We're all here for the same thing. Steel sharpens steel. Whoever is the best will only have to fight that much harder to defend our people."

Joria joined Cinder. "He's right," he said. "We shouldn't fight each other." The other Gandharvan had a slim build like Sash's and a lean face topped by a mop of sandy-brown hair. Like Ishmay, he, too, had round, light-colored eyes, blue in his case—another hue Cinder had never before seen. Despite his calm words, an air of repressed intensity lingered about Joria.

Ishmay smirked at Bones but settled down.

"Cor said we should choose a room," said Rorian. He'd been quiet until now, hanging in the back. "Maybe we should do that first and get to know each other later?"

Cinder assessed the mountain Rakesh, who had an appearance typical for someone from their country. He spoke in a measured fashion, and his eyes appeared sleepy. Yet underneath his unhurried demeanor, Cinder discerned a ferocity equal to Joria's. Rorian was a warrior.

The new arrivals took Rorian's advice and scattered to claim a room. Shortly thereafter, they regathered in the common room, sharing stories of their training, their achievements, and their travels. By unspoken accord, Bones and Ishmay stayed on opposite sides of the room.

"Hold on now," Joria said to Cinder. "You aren't lying about your training, are you? You've only had one year of combat instruction?"

"One year," Bones confirmed. "I was there when he first stepped into *Steel-Graced.*"

Rorian murmured, "A singular talent then to come so far, so fast." A speculative gleam lit his dark, almond-shaped eyes.

Cinder shrugged off their praise. "We're all talented, and if we fight for one another, there's nothing we can't do. That's all that matters."

"In battle, all men are brothers," Wark said. His words surprised Cinder. He hadn't realized the other man had actually been listening to him.

"What does that mean?" Ishmay asked.

"It's what Cinder's always going on about," Depth said. "We're supposed to be a band of brothers."

"It's the truth," Cinder said. He refused to show embarrassment about what he so fiercely believed, no matter how naive others might think it.

Ishmay snorted, but whatever he might have said was cut off as more voices arose from the stairs.

Cor re-entered the common room, and on his heels stomped five dwarves.

Cinder's head jerked in surprise. The dwarves rose no taller than his forehead, but they were each twice his width. All had thick beards hanging down to their chests, and their long hair was plaited in braids.

"I leave you to sort out your belongings and rooms," Cor said to the dwarves. He next addressed the room in general. "I'll be back in a few hours. The welcoming ceremony starts soon."

After Cor left, one dwarf put fists to his hips and gazed about in a commanding fashion. He was taller than the others, blue-eyed and the only one with a reddish beard. "Who's in charge?" he demanded.

"No one," Cinder replied. "We haven't learned how we're to be organized." He approached the dwarf, hand held out. "I'm Cinder Shade."

The dwarf flicked a glance at the proffered hand in thinly veiled disgust. "Dwarves don't shake hands." His voice was a deep rumble. "That's an elven way of showing respect. A coward's way."

"It's what humans do," Ishmay said.

The dwarf's mouth curled. "Like I said, a coward's way."

"Sriovey," one of the other dwarves cautioned, naming their apparent leader.

Sriovey glared at the one who had spoken.

Cinder recalled something he'd read about the dwarves. They hugged one another on first meetings. He held out his arms. "I'm Cinder Shade." He drew Sriovey into what he intended to be a brief embrace.

The dwarf didn't let him go, though. He held Cinder tight, squeezing him hard.

Cinder squeezed back, gritting his teeth when Sriovey's grip further tightened. His ribs creaked, but still he held on. There was also a test that went with the hug. The pain built. Cinder found it hard to breathe, but he maintained his grip, feeling it was important to repress any weakness in front of Sriovey.

The dwarf finally released Cinder, stepping back with a grunt of approval. "I'm Sriovey Surent of Surent Crèche," the red-haired dwarf said. "You did well. I reckon if I squeezed a mite harder, I'd have broken your ribs." He tilted his head toward Cinder in assessment. "I think you'd have held on even then. Strong work." He broke into a pleased grin and gestured to the other dwarves. "Introduce yourself to my band here."

Cinder wanted to do nothing more than sag with relief, but he remained upright. *No weakness.* He also recalled something else of dwarven culture. Whoever controlled a conversation was the acknowledged leader of a group. "You first," Cinder said, indicating his fellow humans.

Sriovey's friendly demeanor became surly.

"You were the one to step out of the embrace first," one of the dwarves softly said to Sriovey. He was the same one who'd spoken earlier.

Sriovey frowned at the other dwarf for an instant before giving a sour scowl of acknowledgment. He went to the other humans, introducing himself with a hard hug. Cinder was glad to see Bones and Ishmay blanch in Sriovey's iron grip.

Cinder went to the dwarves.

"Derius Surent," said the one who'd chided Sriovey. He was the most heavily built of all of the dwarves. His hug would likely hurt worse than Sriovey's.

Cinder braced himself for another bone-crushing embrace. Thankfully, he only received a brief hug, more of slapping of the arms across each other's back.

Derius smiled at Cinder. "Relax, friend." His voice was even deeper than Sriovey's. "I won't try to break you. Sriovey already did that. He failed, so we don't need to waste our time. We know you have courage."

The remaining three dwarves followed Derius' example.

"Nathaz Surent," said the next dwarf in line. Unlike Sriovey, the other dwarves had brown beards and soft brown eyes. Nathaz was no different, but he carried himself like someone who could bite off a person's head for looking at him crosswise.

A laconic dwarf introduced himself next. "Jozep Surent. It's good to meet you." The dwarven man spoke in a deliberate fashion, slow even. He and Rorian could have held a contest on who appeared the most bored or unimpressed by what was going on.

"Dorcer Surent," said the next dwarf. It seemed all the dwarves spoke in basso tones. "We're going to have a good time here. I just know it." He grinned wide.

Cinder couldn't help but smile back in response. Dorcer had a grin to put a person at ease.

The introductions made, Cinder addressed the room, wanting to impress the unity he felt they needed in order for them to flourish at the Third Directorate. "We're strangers to one another now, but it won't always be like that. It shouldn't be. We need to work together, build each other up, fight so all of us succeed, a band of brothers."

"He's going on about fraternity again," Bones whispered to Wark and Depth in a voice meant to carry.

"You think he'll ever talk about anything else?" Wark asked.

Cinder strove to hold onto his patience.

"Fraternity is a good thing," Sriovey agreed, "but dwarves only share brotherhood with our own kind."

"Not always," Derius said. "We once shared peace with everyone."

"Now's not the time," Sriovey warned.

"Peace is a dwarf's highest calling," Derius persisted in an obstinate fashion.

"Not now," Sriovey ordered, glaring at the other dwarf, who quieted.

Cinder glanced at Sriovey, wondering what he didn't want said out loud.

Minutes later, any chance to ask was gone when Cor arrived to take them to the welcoming ceremony.

Anya Aruwen, princess of the Yaksha Sithe, watched from the commandant's office as the newest additions to the Third Directorate, the humans and dwarves, marched forth from Krathe House. The third floor of Firemirror Hall, the building where most classroom instruction at the Directorate took place and the administrators had their offices, offered an excellent view of the students as they approached. The windows in the room took up most of a wall, and Anya stared through their diamond-shaped panes.

The humans and dwarves trailed the first-year elves, all of them traversing the Quad and headed for the welcoming ceremony. It was to be held in the banquet hall, here in Firemirror Hall. The humans in particular seemed so young, which was to be expected. They *were* young, all of them not much older than children as elves measured matters. Had she ever been so new to the world?

It was unlikely. Anya's soul felt ancient. It *was* ancient.

A lock of her honey-blonde hair escaped its ponytail, and Anya tucked it behind a pointed ear. The ear was rounder than typical for elves, which was yet another reminder of her unique heritage. She was taller than the rest of her kind, too—men or women, including the noble castes—and strongly built rather than possessing the waif-like stature of those considered truly lovely, such as her sister. Most distinctive of all, Anya's eyes were emerald-green, a rare, off-putting hue since every other elf had eyes that were either sky-blue, stormy gray, or coal-black. As a result, she was told her gaze could be somewhat distracting, if not disturbing.

Her husband, however, had loved the color of her eyes. Why had Devesh been so cruel as to take him from her?

Anya folded her arms across her chest, setting aside the old pain. There was a reason for her differences, one which explained how she had managed to become the first and only woman to graduate from the Third Directorate, but that reason no longer mattered. She was of the Yaksha Sithe, and that was enough.

"What do you think of our new students?" asked General Sylve Arwan, the commandant of the Third Directorate.

Anya didn't need to turn around to know that he sat at his desk, an oak monstrosity overflowing with papers. She heard him shuffling through the mess. The bookshelves lining the walls were similarly untidy. They held a plethora of books, maps, scrolls, and assorted oddities, such as stones the commandant found interesting; notes written to himself, and a number of weapons, some rusted and broken. In other words, junk. It had always been the case with the commandant. He enjoyed keeping broken relics of the past, items a sane person would discard.

The commandant left his desk and stood at her elbow. He was an older elf, in his late three hundreds, blond hair streaked with white. "Other than your brother, do any of the incoming Firsters strike you as superlative?"

Anya smiled in amusement at the comment. It was an old joke. Decades ago, when Anya had entered the Third Directorate, the commandant had been one of her instructors. As the only woman to ever matriculate into the academy, he had asked what objectives she had for herself. Anya had answered that she wanted to become a superlative warrior, and three years later, she had achieved her goal.

"My brother is skilled," Anya said, "but I would not classify him as superlative."

"He isn't up to your standards then?"

Anya chuckled. "He will not bring shame to the family, if that's what you're asking. He'll do well."

"I'm sure he'll do better than that." The commandant touched her elbow, indicating for her to sit in one of the two high-backed chairs facing the desk. "Have some tea before the festivities." He gave a bleak chuckle. "I know how much you love the pomp and circumstance to come."

Anya was about to follow the commandant when she caught sight of one of the humans, possibly younger than the others, short and more slightly built. He walked like a typical boy on the cusp of manhood, clumsy at times despite his martial training. And yet, when his limbs moved in proper alignment, he walked with a feline grace, one her own kind might have envied, like a tiger stalking through the weeds.

The commandant paused on his way to his desk. "You see something?"

"A human," Anya answered. The boy entered the hall and was lost to sight. "The way he walked . . . He had a way about him, a subtle grace."

"I've seen other humans with the same," the commandant said, his tone dismissive. "It won't help them. They lack the ability to source their *lorethasra*. They will be forever limited."

"Some can source *lorethasra*," Anya said. "Not often, but I've seen them do so in times of danger."

"It's a good thing it's only during times of danger. Could you imagine if it were otherwise? A world in which humans could use their *lorethasra*?" The commandant shuddered.

Anya could imagine such a world. She dreamed of it often, and it left her considering her past. Even after nearly four score years, some memories never faded. She remembered the name by which she'd first been known, the husband she had fiercely loved and who had loved her in return. Why did he have to die? His name always escaped her recollection, and all she knew of him were fragments of songs, times from when he played the mandolin and she sang, a walk through a lovely park at night. The moon reflecting off a pond as they stood on a bridge, and he kissed her.

She couldn't recall his name or his features, but she remembered their love, fierce and depthless. In addition, the memories taught her a brutal truth: she would never again love another, and she didn't want to. Even taking a lover seemed wrong. Her fragmented remembrances of her husband were enough.

"It's time for the welcoming ceremony," the commandant said, interrupting her reverie. "Hold your nose. You know how much the humans smell."

Anya laughed. "Their aroma still bothers you? I would have thought you would have gotten used to it by now."

"How can I? It's impossible to ignore."

"You say they stink, but I know the truth." Anya flashed a smile. "You don't like their smell because you like it too much. Most every woven feels the same way."

The commandant scowled. "I'm just glad the humans can't source their *lorethasra*. They'd be too dangerous, otherwise."

The banquet hall of the Third Directorate was a high-ceilinged rectangular space filled with five long tables. Four of them were positioned lengthwise—one for each year and another for visiting warriors and various instructors teaching at the academy. The fifth table rested on a dais and ran perpendicular to the others. It was where the administrators and masters in charge of the Third Directorate sat during formal events such as the welcoming ceremony.

The delicious aroma of spiced foods suffused the air, and Cinder's stomach growled. He was starving and hadn't eaten all day.

Chandeliers shaped like wagon wheels and ringed with dozens of *diptha* bulbs illuminated the space while a final few beams of the western sun at twilight beamed a shimmering curtain of gold through a tall bank of windows. The sunshine illuminated the many murals of elves standing in martial poses that decorated the wall opposite the windows. Cinder figured the paintings were of famous warriors from history, but he didn't know any of them.

The instructors and commanders of the academy filed into the room through a pair of doors behind their table. The entrances bracketed three banners. The central one had a fiery golden crown on a field of red—Yaksha Sithe's flag—while the other two were black banners. The right-hand one contained a simple symbol, a silver aum, and the left hand one, a stylized eagle clutching a sword.

A final officer entered, and everyone stood, including the Firster elves. Cinder belatedly rose to his feet alongside his fellow first-year humans and dwarves. He cursed under his breath. He hadn't known he was supposed to stand.

The officer who had just entered had to be General Sylve Arwan. Master Lerid had described him. An elf in his late middle years, powerfully built for his kind, fit and straight, streaks of white through otherwise russet-blond hair. Blue eyes peering at the students.

The general smiled, holding out his arms. "Please be seated. I am General Sylve Arwan, commandant of the Third Directorate. I bid all of you welcome." He faced the fourth table, the one given over to the instructors and visiting warriors. "For some, you return to a place where you first earned renown." He scanned the third-year table. "For others, you ready for your final year and your greatest Trial." His eyes swept to the second years. "Then there are the middle students. Caught between mastery and newness."

The commandant's attention came to the Firsters. He smiled more broadly, his gaze settling on the elves who sat at the chairs closest to the commanders. Cinder noticed the seating arrangement was the same for the other two years as well: elves to the front and humans and dwarves to the rear.

The commandant's eyes eventually roamed the rest of the Firster table, briefly resting on the humans and dwarves. "Finally, we have a new first-year class," General Arwan said. "To you, I offer a most hearty welcome. You have much to learn. Your seniors will explain your class schedule, and your masters will become well known to you as the year progresses." He chuckled. "I'm sure you'll learn from them *quite* well. On to business, before we eat. This is a military academy. We mean to forge you into warriors. You are already gifted. We will make you great. Some of you might become superlative." The commandant glanced at a striking elf woman seated next to him, smiling briefly in her direction.

Cinder had noticed her straightaway and wondered who she was. One of their instructors? She had honey-blonde hair and green eyes, and an undeniable physical presence. She was strongly built for an elf, and beautiful, with a diamond-shaped face, high cheeks, and full lips. Cinder was drawn to her, but he also realized it probably wasn't a good idea for him to stare at her so raptly. It was said that elven men didn't appreciate their women being ogled by those not of their kind.

He also had a guilty remembrance of Coral. Only a week away from her, and he was staring at another woman.

The commandant continued. "In order to join the legends you see honored on the walls around you—" He pointed to murals of elven warriors gracing the room. "—you must know the past. The Third Directorate was founded shortly after the *NusraelShev*, the great war between the Mythaspuris and Shet. Many now believe those battles were simply the fables of another age but take one look at the Quad and you'll see Garad Lull, one of Shet's Titans. You'll know I speak the truth. Our academy was founded by Swan Yaksha, daughter of the great Koran Yaksha, our first empress, who guided our people through that terrible war. Since our founding nearly three thousand years ago, we have been dedicated to one proposition: to train the world's finest warriors. And this we do. You are now matriculated into this grand legacy!"

Thunderous applause met his words, and Cinder's heart swelled. He was now part of a vast tapestry stretching back thousands of years. He was a member of a carefully cultivated fraternity whose only criterion was a desire for greatness.

On spoke the commandant. "And one thing we've learned during these millennia of training and teaching is that the best way to forge a warrior is to test the iron from which he is made. That fire and hammer is stoked and applied by the men seated next to you." He paused momentarily, giving time for the Firsters to glance at one another. "It is said," the commandant continued, "that steel sharpens steel, a phrase first reputedly spoken by Shokan, the finest human warrior in history. While he might not have fared as well in today's world since Shokan lacked *lorethasra*—"

Cinder's jaw clenched in annoyance at the insult. "Elves," he muttered.

Ishmay heard his softly spoken word and nodded in agreement. So did some of the other humans seated nearby. Shokan was the finest warrior of all time, period. Those were the legends spoken of him in Rakesh, Gandharva, and all human nations. Cinder didn't like hearing him portrayed as anything less.

"—but such a flaw isn't important compared to what he taught us. Shokan taught of honor, of fraternity, of protecting those who require it. Thus, we live by his creed. *Mastha par iti krathe lomon pa.* It has become our own creed, the motto of the Third Directorate. *To cultivate perfection and vanquish foes* as it was said in old *Shevasra*. That is our great charge as given by Empress Swan, and it is a duty in which we have not wavered in all these long centuries and millennia. We will not fail. We will do as Shokan advised. *Steel sharpens steel.* And you will be sharpened. Do not doubt it."

More cheers erupted.

The commandant held up his hands, calling for silence. "I've spoken much, but do not fret. Dinner will shortly be served. Before the meal, a declaration. In order to know if steel has sharpened steel, there must be a measuring stick. At the end of the year, you'll be competing against your fellow students. The Grand Melee. We hold it during the early part of the Days of Deliverance. It is a chance for you to display your skill and will in armed and unarmed combat, archery, horseman-ship, and tactics and strategy. The winners earn great prizes and glory. The losers earn a chance for glory next year." He glanced around the room. "Or not."

Many of the elves chuckled when they heard this, but Cinder no-ticed the humans and dwarves of the more senior classes did not.

He had a realization. The seating arrangement in the banquet hall was determined by rank in the class, and the elves held all the top spots.

Not this year. Cinder was determined to see the elves defeated, even if all he managed was to pull a prank on them. He remembered a fable about four young men who attended a military academy. The House of Fire and Mirrors was its name. In the story, they had tricked the several hundred members of a rival military school into holding up placards that when placed together, spelled out in huge letters: *We are jackholes.*

He wondered how difficult it would be to pull off something like that here.

When she slumbered, she knew some of her truth. Her name was Jessira Shektan, born Jessira Grey. Sira to some, and she rolled over in her sleep as a familiar dream took her.

"We have a few minutes until they arrive," Shokan said. "Chandragupta already left."

Sira glanced at her husband. He appeared relaxed, but she noticed the tightness around his eyes. No one else would have seen it. Her in-sight might have derived from their decades-long shared life together as husband and wife, but it wasn't the only explanation. It was also their Jivatma, *linked as it was. And yet, their vast sum of years was not reflected in their appearance. Both of them remained youthful, and a stranger might have counted them in their twenties.*

"What do you think he'll do with himself?" Sira asked, referring to Chandragupta, their visitor out of time from Pataliputra.

"Hopefully something worthy of his empire."

Sira hoped so, too. When they'd first encountered him, Chandragupta had been a person of violence, a bandit in his youth and a conquering emperor in his later years. It was strange how he'd turned to peace. Sira hadn't believed he would. After all, Shet hadn't, and the difference between the so-called god and the emperor had seemed merely a matter of scale.

"You were wrong about Chandragupta," Shokan said, knowing her thoughts even when she didn't speak them. Their bond of understanding, first forged on Arisa, had only grown stronger over time.

Sira smiled. "And since it so rarely happens, we should mark the occasion." Shokan didn't respond, but she sensed his amusement. Her own trailed away when she scanned the surroundings. They were here for an unamusing matter.

Nearby stalked Shon, her Kesarin, all twenty-five tawny feet of him. Standing, the giant cat overtopped her by a foot, and she wasn't a short woman. Size, though, wasn't a Kesarin's greatest attribute. It was their speed. They moved too swiftly for even a Kumma like her husband to handle. Kesarins were the unchallenged rulers of the Hunters Flats from Sira's first home. They went where they willed, and few could hinder their progress.

Thankfully, they preferred to remain on their verdant plains, rarely venturing from them. Only a few ever had, such as Shon and his older sister, Aia, who had chosen Sira and Shokan as their humans.

The Kesarins prowled restlessly, alert to danger, and while they had far keener senses than she did, Sira continued to study her surroundings. She didn't trust this meeting or the place in which it was to be held. The jungle meadow, the saha'asra in which she and Shokan waited, was too convenient a place from which to launch an ambush. Around them soared towering trees, broad limbs and leaves shadowing the ground, and deep within their embrace came the raucous cries of monkeys, birds, and other animals. The intermingled stench of detritus, mold and a cloying sense of decay filled the air, which otherwise lay pregnant and unmoving, tense like Sira's shoulders.

No, she didn't like this meeting even while she understood its importance. This was to be a parlay, a brokerage of peace. The war amongst the asrasins *had already stretched far too long. Shet's forces would most likely lose, but the denouement yet beckoned, a final battle which would be a shattering catastrophe for both sides. The winners would be hard pressed to find reasons to celebrate their victory. Sira and Shokan didn't want to see such an ending for those they had come to love.*

Thus, this meeting. It was meant to define the terms of Shet's surrender, his capitulation and emigration to Seminal. There, while he'd find little succor—Antalogore waited for him—at least it was an opportunity. He could survive.

**I'm hungry,* Shon muttered, speaking in Sira's thoughts, another talent of the Kesarins.*

**Quiet,* Aia admonished.* *Now is not the time to behave like a silly kitten. Danger lurks.* *The calico Kesarin lifted her snout.* *I can smell something coming.*

Sira instantly straightened, growing more alert. She conducted Jivatma. Her senses heightened. Her vision grew more acute, sounds more discernable, smells sharpened.

A foul stench filled her nostrils. A necrosed.

A creature, powerfully built and perfectly proportioned, pushed through the jungle's encumbering undergrowth. Shocking red hair crowned a handsome face while pale eyes, cold and cunning, peered at them. His hands ended in the claws of a bear. It was from him that the stench arose. Grave Invidious. The first necrosed.

"My master sent me to ensure you were alone," Grave said, his voice mellifluous.

His master was Shet, the so-called god of the mahavans.

Shon roared suddenly, his cry panic-filled. He raced toward her.

Another stench filled Sira's nostrils. It came from behind. She tried to spin around to face it, but sharp claws raked her back. She collapsed to her knees. Pain and disbelief crowded her thoughts but foremost was a feeling of folly. How had another necrosed approached them so closely and managed to remain undetected?

Shon bludgeoned something away from her while Aia went after Grave.

Sira conducted more deeply from her silvery pool of Jivatma. *The pain receded, and she hissed in relief. She Healed herself as best she could, closing the wounds so they no longer poured blood. Next, she took a deep inhalation, gathering herself, and with a single lunge, she forced herself off her knees and onto her feet. The tearing pain of her wounds caused her to groan. She swayed a moment, and Shokan reached out, steadying her.*

He had his sword bared. Lightning crackled along its length. His eyes were white with the Wildness. He spared her a glance, one filled with love and fury. He'd kill whoever attacked them or die trying. Of that, she was certain.

From behind them came the sound of battle as Shon and Aia fought a pair of necrosed, Sapient Dormant and Grave Invidious. No longer hindered by the element of surprise, the Kesarins could easily handle those two.

"We need to flee," Shokan said, not taking his eyes off the surrounding jungle. "The anchor line here only connects to the Web of Worlds. Can you open it?"

"Yes." Sira reached for her Jivatma, *spooling out the necessary threads of Fire, Earth, and Spirit without thought and attaching them to the corresponding Elements of the anchor line. The connection complete, the most doleful of bells rang out, shattering the air. Tree limbs swayed. In front of Sira, a black line, thinner than a leaf on end, split the air. It rotated, exposing a wide doorway floating a foot off the ground and swirling with rainbow hues.*

The anchor line to Seminal. Right now, it might be their only route to safety.

"Did you really think I would surrender?"

Shet.

Sira spun about, flinching at the stabbing pain in her back. Shet and several of his titans pressed out of the jungle. They towered over her, each close to ten feet in height. Shet, Garad Lull, and the two female titans, Liline Salt, and Rence Darim, the so-called IllWind.

The battle between the Kesarins and the necrosed waned.

Shet smirked. "None of you will live to see another sunset."

Sira's gaze darted about. Wait. Only four titans? Where were the other three?

Aia and Shon howled in agony. Their anguished cries spurred Sira. She reached deeper into her Jivatma *and disregarded her pain. As one, she and Shokan attacked.*

19

After the welcoming ceremony, Cor guided the first-year students back to Krathe House. He also briefed them on their daily routine. It was to consist of an early rise where Cor would lead the humans on a five-mile run while the dwarves were led by one of their own. Afterward would come breakfast at the cafeteria, a low-lying building adjacent to Krathe House. Following the meal would come several hours of Weapons Training, an hour of Tactics and Strategy, and then lunch. Next would be Unarmed Combat followed by Archery, Equitation, and an hour on History. It was a long day, and it didn't always end with supper. Cor promised there was usually an hour of daily study as well.

The schedule repeated every four days until the students earned a rest day.

"Eat hearty whenever you can," Cor advised at breakfast. "You'll need all the food you can get."

The morning following, Cinder took the senior student's advice. After running five miles, he was starving, especially since he had pushed himself hard, not wanting to come in last. He had succeeded, but only barely. Only Joria finished behind him, while the others well ahead of him. The dwarves had completed their run even more quickly. Of course, the bandy-legged woven had the advantage of *lorethasra*, so it wasn't a surprise.

Nevertheless, everyone—humans and dwarves alike—were famished after the run. They hunched over their bowls and plates, stuffing down the food like it might run away. There was a reason for this. Not only had they run five miles, but these were growing young men, including the dwarves who Cinder learned last night were all in their mid-twenties. The Firster elves were apparently in their late forties.

Speaking of the elves, Cinder glanced around. He hadn't seen them all morning. Even now they were absent, and he frowned, speculating where they were.

Sriovey must have picked up on his perplexed gaze. "What's bothering you?" the dwarf asked.

"Where are the elves?"

Sriovey snorted. "Don't worry about them. They're fine. They're too good for our kind anyhow. They think they're faster, smarter, and smell better than the rest of us."

"Not the smell part," Derius said. "At least not humans. All woven like the way humans smell."

Cinder's brows raised in surprise, and he glanced to Sriovey for confirmation.

The red-haired dwarf nodded agreement. "It's true," Sriovey said. "Your smell is soothing. We like it."

Cinder frowned in perplexion. *How odd.*

After breakfast, everyone—humans and dwarves alike—exited the banquet hall and went to their class on Weapons Training. It was held on a square field north of the Quad and the main buildings of the Third Directorate. The Cauldron was its name, and it was a large meadow framed by a split-rail fence. Rings of stone created further delineations—sparring circles, each one thirty feet in diameter. Some of them were paved with large flagstones and others by trampled grass. The morning sun blazed from a cloudless sky, but a gentle breeze kept the weather cool and dry.

Earlier in the morning, Cor had mentioned that the Third Directorate rarely got hot in the summer, but winters could be ferociously cold.

At the field, the Firsters met their instructor. Master Absin Morewe, an older elf, white-haired and with a face weathered and leathery in appearance. He had clearly spent many years or centuries exposed to the sun. According to Cor, Master Absin had served in the Yaksha Army, achieving the rank of colonel, and prior to his retirement, he was said to have been an absolute demon with the sword. Time, though—as it did to everyone—wore away his skills, but it didn't wear away his knowledge, and once he mustered out of the army, he'd transitioned to the Third Directorate.

Master Absin held a switch in his hand and lightly rapped it against his thigh. "Hurry and attend," he shouted as the Firsters approached. "Line up here." He waved the switch to a general location in front of him. He introduced himself and took a quick roll call. "Now that's out of the way, it's time to see how much work we have in front of us." He gestured at the field in general. "This is the Cauldron. This is where you will be made into warriors worthy of the name."

Cinder straightened and tried not to smile in excitement. *Warriors worthy of the name.* Music to his ears.

Master Absin pointed to a barrel that contained a number of wooden practice swords. They had a purple hue and glistened like they were covered in a film of oil. Cinder reckoned they were shokes. In another barrel were similarly gleaming wooden hammers, likely meant for the dwarves.

"These are shokes," the master said, confirming Cinder's guess. "Choose one. It doesn't matter which. We'll have you fitted for a more personal weapon as the year progresses and I have a better idea as to what would be most suitable for you." He gestured to the other barrel and called for the dwarves. "The same applies to you."

Cinder approached the barrel of swords, getting there before the others. He didn't want to be left with what everyone else didn't want.

He quickly sorted through the shokes and found one seemingly right for his build and reach. He stepped away from the other students and took a few practice swings. The shoke had the shape of a longsword but utilized a crossguard rather than a basket hilt.

The others quickly got themselves sorted out as well.

Master Absin addressed them. "Let me see what you can do." Cinder found himself the focus of the master's attention. "Since you were the first to claim a blade, you also have the pleasure of going first." He had exchanged his switch for a shoke, and he pointed to a training circle. "If you will."

Cinder's heart rate picked up, hammering the rhythm of his nervous energy. He took a second to center himself, to control his breathing. It wouldn't do for excitement to mar his first sparring session in the Third Directorate. Once his breathing and heart rate were settled, he stepped into the indicated training circle. He focused on Master Absin, who faced him from roughly twenty feet away, wearing a look of equanimity. Cinder tried to divine what the master might intend, but not even the slightest hint was present in the elf's pose and demeanor. In this, Master Absin buried his plans more deeply than even Depth.

The Master brought his shoke to the ready. "Begin."

Cinder took a defensive posture. He thought it best to take the fight slow.

Master Absin did not. He immediately engaged with Cinder, sending out probing thrusts. The elf increased the pace. Cinder kept up, defending and staying off the center line. He kept his lead foot outside Master Absin's, increasing the angle and distance the elf had to cover. He parried a slash, countered with a lunge, backed off from an overhand. So far, it wasn't anything Cinder hadn't seen or couldn't handle.

Confidence growing, he wanted to know just how good the Master was. He pressed forward. Master Absin moved aside and blocked as needed, but he didn't counter. He seemed content with defending. Cinder pushed harder, and Master Absin kept up, no strain on his face.

Cinder realized the elf was far faster than he was showing, stronger and more skilled, too. It quickly became evident that Master Absin was as far above Cinder's skill as Cinder was above a raw novice. It was a humbling experience. Worse, in the few minutes of their sparring, Cinder's ability to gauge an opponent's weakness and likely angle of attack proved inadequate. Master Absin was always perfectly composed, smooth as water in how he moved, giving away nothing.

"Break," Master Absin barked. "You have some skill. You might do. Step aside now."

Cinder did as instructed and left the training ring. He watched in amazement as the master tested the rest of the Firsters. No one came close to landing a touch on him, and he didn't bother landing one on them. It was a sign of how sublimely talented he truly was. He didn't need to demonstrate his superiority with a touch. He demonstrated it by holding them off without any effort.

While the others sparred against Master Absin, Cinder wandered next to Bones. "He's something, isn't he?" He lifted his chin in the direction of the master.

Bones held a stark expression of worry. "Are they all like that? The ones on the ship and now Master Absin. Are we really so incompetent compared to them?"

Cinder understood the reason for Bones' concern, although he didn't share it. As he considered matters, a team of fairly good fighters was better than a group of phenomenal individuals. "Sinu and Linwon were a lot faster than us, but they weren't as skilled as Master Absin," he said. "We'll never match their speed, but we can still overcome them by working as a team."

"I'm not sure," Bones said, appearing despondent. Ever since he'd witnessed the elves sparring, how they conducted *lorethasra*, Bones had sounded like this, doubtful and his self-confidence shaken.

Cinder tried to lift him up, hoping to spark a fire inside his friend. "It's our first day. Don't give up on me so soon."

Bones' brow rose. "Give up on you? What makes you think I'm fighting on your behalf?"

"You're not, but you are my brother, and I won't let you quit, not because of one sparring session. You'll get better. You'll get stronger and faster, too. We all will. We're still young and have a lot of growing to do."

Bones grunted, and Cinder couldn't tell if it was in agreement or a way to indicated he didn't' want to talk about the matter any longer.

Cinder mentally shrugged and dropped the matter. Their conversation fell silent, and they focused on the ongoing sparring. Soon it was Bones' turn to be tested.

Eventually, everyone had a chance against Master Absin, and when it was over, he called for their attention. "Line up!" he shouted, waiting a few seconds for the students to get themselves sorted out. "You did well enough for your first day." Master Absin had his switch in hand again. "I want to tell you something. I'm naturally faster and stronger than all of you because I'm a fully-grown man. None of you are. You have years more to reach your peak, but when you do, then you will be able to keep up with me. You can all become so much more than you believe."

Cinder straightened, his chin coming up. Master Absin's words were a direct reiteration of what he'd been telling Bones only seconds earlier.

He nudged his fellow *Steel-Graced*, getting his attention, lifting his brows as if to say, *"See. What did I tell you?"*

Bones nodded understanding. He had heard. Hopefully it meant he would finally let go of his doubt.

"In addition," Master Absin continued, "we aren't training you to be foot soldiers here. You won't become masters of polearms or learn how to fight in close-in formations with shields and short swords. We'll certainly cover the basics on those areas of combat. But the focus of our attention will be turning you into warriors and commanders, mostly as rangers, cavalry, or fast infantry."

Master Absin directly addressed the humans then. "Courage cannot be taught, and none are more courageous than the weakest who refuse to quit in the face of adversity. My kind—the Blessed Race—believes your kind is weak, but we will make that weakness your strength. You will grow, never waver, and fight for one another."

"Yes!" Cinder shouted, hoping the others would join him. Battling as a unit. That's what the master was talking about.

"It is as we say here. The creed of this academy!" Master Absin shouted. "Say it with me. *Mastha par!*" Cultivate perfection.

Every Firster, human and dwarf, shouted back. "*Mastha par!*"

"*Krathe lomon!*" Vanquish foes.

"*Krathe lomon!*"

"Remember these words," Master Absin said, still focused for the most part on the humans. "It is who we are and what we do." He turned his attention to the dwarves. "As for your kind, you knew who you once were. Bringing peace to those in need. Soothing their hurts."

Cinder's ears perked. He hadn't heard this about dwarves.

"But that isn't why you're here," Master Absin said, turning away. "I've never known true peace, and I don't need soothing. I need men who can fight. I need men who can bring war. And I'll teach you how."

The dwarves shouted enthusiastically.

"A final note." Master Absin held up his hands, calling for quiet, and once again, he spoke to the humans. "My kind and the dwarves can lean on *lorethasra* to make us faster and stronger. You cannot." His switch went silent, resting against his thigh. He gazed narrow-eyed at the students, seemingly lost in thought and yet, intense at the same time. "So you believe, but it is not entirely true. There are many accounts of humans who have sourced their *lorethasra* during dire emergencies, and there are also records of some who did so at will."

Startled conversation broke out, the humans hopeful, the dwarves troubled.

Humans could conduct their *lorethasra*? It was impossible. Everything Cinder had read about the topic said so, but Master Absin appeared to be saying otherwise. Cinder found himself holding his breath, waiting on the master to more fully explain himself.

"It isn't easy," Master Absin said. "Amongst elves and other woven, we source our *lorethasra* and cycle it as needed through our *nadis*. It is then more correctly called *prana*. But first, the *lorethasra* must first be purified. We do so by inhaling and exhaling through the correct nostril. Learn how to do this, purify your *lorethasra*, and perhaps you will find yourself able to source the smallest part of it during a dire need. The greatest human warriors, men such as Mede and his Immortals could do so. It made them mighty."

This, Cinder had read about, but until today, he'd eschewed the claims. He had thought them the fanciful dreams and aspirations of those who wanted the world to conform to their wishes.

"To source and purify your *lorethasra*, you will do thus, as an elf does." Master Absin settled on the ground, seated cross-legged, each foot on the opposite knee, and his eyes shut. He closed his left nostril with his left thumb, the other fingers stretched straight up. His right hand rested on his right knee, thumb and first finger forming a circle and the other three fingers straight. "Do this an hour a day, and perhaps you will learn to source your *lorethasra* and begin the cycle of purification."

Cinder memorized everything about Master Absin's positioning. If there was truth to what he was saying, Cinder was determined to learn it.

Tactics and Strategy, the class after Weapons Training and prior to lunch, was held in Firemirror Hall. It took place in a second-floor classroom where a wall of windows provided a view of the Quad, other buildings of the Directorate, and beyond them, the hills and mountains surrounding the academy. Seven sturdy, rectangular tables, each with three chairs, faced a desk where the master was to sit. He hadn't yet arrived. Behind the instructor's chair was mounted a large, square slate tablet. A blackboard was what it was called.

Cinder entered the class alongside his cadre of Firster humans and dwarves. They spread out, chatting and taking whatever chair they felt like. Cinder sat next to Bones.

Seconds after they settled themselves, the first-year elves sauntered in. They had their own schedule, and Cinder hadn't seen them since breakfast. As one, the elves sniffed in annoyance, and their mouths curled as if they smelled something rotten.

One of them introduced himself. He was a blond-haired elf with dark eyes. "I am Riyne Coushinre." He pointed to another elf, this one also blond but blue-eyed and with a seemingly haughty sneer lurking at the corners of his mouth. "This is Estin Aruyen, a prince of Yaksha Sithe. It is customary for humans and dwarves to stand and bow when your betters arrive." He folded his arms, sounding and appearing utterly serious.

Cinder didn't like Riyne's attitude. "We are men of Rakesh," he told the elf. "We stand for those worthy of our respect, but we bow to no one."

"Damn right," Bones said.

"Gandharva feels the same way," Ishmay said.

"As do the dwarves of Surent Crèche," Sriovey added.

Estin chuckled. "I told you it wouldn't work," he said to Riyne. "They're barbarians. They don't know the meaning of the word 'civilization.'" He addressed the other elves. "Find a chair. We're running late." Taking notice of his own statement, he sat next to Dorcer and Jozep.

A dark-haired elf, tall and thickly built for his kind, squeezed in next to Cinder. He had bright, blue eyes. "It was interesting what you said to Riyne. He can be somewhat presumptuous."

Cinder viewed the elf in confusion. His words were open and friendly; no hint of the customary arrogance Cinder had come to associate with elvenkind.

The elf winked, apparently picking up on Cinder's surprise. "Some of us don't think we're the absolute pinnacle of Devesh's creation."

Cinder chuckled. "I'm Cinder Shade."

"Mohal Holwarein of House Holwarein." They shook hands.

Bones introduced himself as well.

There was no time for further conversation because in walked their instructor, Master Nuhlin Genhim. He was a middle-aged elf with straight black hair, startling blue eyes, and an unkempt, distracted manner, and according to Cor, he had never actually served in Yaksha's Army. Instead, Master Nuhlin had spent most of his life studying deeply in many fields, including history, war, music, and poetry. He was said to be a genius, and as their initial class with him wore on, it quickly became apparent how true that was. Master Nuhlin had an exhaustive knowledge of various conflicts the world over, be they low-level engagement or large-scale battles, and an understanding of what did and didn't work during those events.

Unfortunately, his ability to translate his deep knowledge into material the students could easily use proved somewhat lacking. Master Nuhlin had an unfortunate habit of repeating himself, losing his train of thought, and grinning wildly at nothing in particular. He used the blackboard, writing wildly with a piece of white chalk, and covering the large slate with a plethora of utterly indecipherable drawings and abbreviated words.

Cinder had brought one of his empty ledgers to the class along with a quill, but within minutes, he set down his writing instrument. Master Nuhlin's lecture was a wild, disorganized affair, and the hour passed interminably. A handsome wall clock, one Faine and Dorr would have appreciated, marked the slow crawl of time.

It eventually rang out the end of the hour and the beginning of their freedom.

Thank Devesh.

Everyone—humans, elves, and dwarves—surged to their feet and rushed to the door.

"I expect a description of the Battle at Sage's Field done by your first break," Master Nuhlin said as the students stuffed their way through the classroom's only exit. "Along with an explanation of how the commander could have more effectively defended the chokepoint with cavalry."

Cinder groaned in dismay—not at the work, but at the thought of finding the necessary information. He might be able to discover it in one of his bound textbooks, but it likely wouldn't be enough. He'd have to search the library, wherever that was.

A worry for later. It was time for lunch, and his stomach rumbled.

Cinder walked in the center of his fellow humans as they headed toward the cafeteria. The Firsters dispersed into small, separate knots, ones consisting entirely of their own kind.

"You should not walk ahead of us," Riyne shouted at the dwarves. "This is the Third Directorate of Yaksha Sithe. It should be the elves who lead, and the rest who follow."

Sriovey halted, spun about, and waited on the elves to approach him. The rest of the dwarves stood at his back, while several of Riyne's compatriots moved to support him.

"Your mouth is making promises your fists can't ensure," Sriovey said. "It's going to get you in trouble, boy."

Estin pushed past Riyne and sneered at Sriovey. "You think I'm afraid of you? I'm an elf of Yaksha Sithe. I fear no dwarf."

Cinder didn't know if Estin and Riyne were truly that conceited or truly that stupid, but whatever the reason for their attitude, it needed a swift adjustment.

He pushed to stand next to Sriovey, wanting the dwarf to know he had support. The other humans joined him as well, intermingling with the dwarves. Sriovey eyed him askance and dipped his head in acknowledgment.

"You might want to rethink your odds," Cinder said. "We won't bow to you, rise for you, or pretend you're better than us."

Estin brayed, pointing at Cinder. "Observe. A monkey speaks! The animal husbandry texts will have to be rewritten."

Fragging asshole. Anger stole rational thought, and Cinder surged at Estin. He was brought short by a hand gripping his elbow.

"Easy, Hotgate," Sriovey said. "He insulted the dwarves first. We'll deal with him."

The rest of the elves fanned out behind Estin and Riyne. Violence threatened.

A golden-haired woman swept into their midst. Anya Aruyen, the princess of Yaksha Sithe. The commandant had introduced her last night, and right now she scowled, clearly furious. "Is there a disagreement that needs settling?"

Estin quickly backed away from Anya, while Riyne's face went white.

"No, your Highness," Riyne said. "No disagreement."

Sriovey stepped away from the angry princess, too. Rumor stated Anya was perhaps the finest warrior alive, male or female, elf or otherwise.

"Yes. A simple misunderstanding," the red-bearded dwarf said.

Cinder found himself the focus of Anya's ire. He'd failed to step back, and he now stood on an island alone, facing her fury by himself.

"And what of you?" Anya demanded. "Do you have something to add?"

Cinder caught Riyne snickering and Anya tapping her foot in impatience. He blurted out his first cogent line of thinking. "Riyne was mentioning how in the Third Directorate, the slow give way to the quick. The dwarves walk swiftly, and Riyne is rather slow." He paused a beat. "But not just with his feet."

Riyne scowled, but a small smile possibly flickered across Anya's face, too quickly for Cinder to be certain. "I see. Well, if that's the case, then I believe you don't need my chastisement." She faced Estin, glaring at him. "Although it goes without saying that the Third Directorate is a place for warriors to become brothers." Her glare became hotter. "Any member of the imperial house should know this."

Estin blanched, but defiance continued to crackle in the back of his eyes. At least he was smart enough to keep quiet.

Anya took in everyone with a sweep of her eyes. "All you Firsters better learn this lesson and learn it fast."

Cinder managed not to duck his head in shame.

"Get to lunch." Anya ordered before marching off.

A chastened group of Firsters made their quiet way to the dining hall. No one much felt like talking.

As they walked to the cafeteria, Cinder recalled what Sriovey had called. "Why did you call me Hotgate?" he asked the dwarven leader.

Sriovey grinned. "As angry as you looked, it sounded right. Hotgate. Piss you off, and a door opens to fire."

Cinder slowly smiled. *Hotgate.* He liked it.

Wark interrupted their conversation. "The princess . . ." He trailed off. "She's something." His voice was filled with admiration.

Estin heard him. "Don't talk about my sister. You do, and your face meets my fist."

Lunch came and went without further incident, and afterward, the humans and dwarves shared Unarmed Combat. It took place in the same field as the morning, the Cauldron.

Waiting for them in the center of a training ring was an old elf. Master Jovick Sonsen. His wizened face and cataracted eyes referenced a truth about his black hair, which boasted the sheen of shoe polish. Master Jovick colored his hair. Cinder had learned that the master had served in the Army of Yaksha, joining as a commoner with no noble connections. Despite this deficit, he had risen to the rank of captain. Thirty years he'd served in the army. Afterward, he'd retired to a small village in the Dagger Mountains and became a vintner. Fate, however, wasn't kind. His wife and family were killed in a spiderkin raid, and with nothing left in his life, he'd come to the Third Directorate, determined to teach the next generations of warriors.

Master Jovick spoke to them. "We'll get to work in a bit, but you should know we won't be doing much today." He spit to the side. "Truth is, you're all probably wrung out like wet clothes on a line. You're no good to me right now. You'll have to get stronger, and then I'll teach you true." He paused a moment, barking out a question. "What's the first rule of combat?"

"Win by any means," Cinder said, the answer coming automatically. During his time at *Steel-Graced Adepts*, he'd thought long and hard about what true battle meant.

"Correct," Master Jovick said. "We aren't talking about your friendly sparring matches. We're talking about the nasty blood-and-piss of war. You are expected to kill, to feel your enemy's innards slice open, to smell their breath in close quarters, taste their fear, look into their eyes when they die. You kill them. That's the expectation, and mark my words, gentlemen, they mean to kill you back. In order to win, you better make sure you're the one who's still breathing at the end and not them. It's a simple rule. Hold fast to it. Don't forget it." He clapped his hands a single time. "Next question. What weapons can you use to defeat your enemy?"

Cinder knew this answer, too. "Anything you can put your hands on."

"Correct again. Anything is a weapon. Even a simple piece of wood. Stab a man in the throat with a stick, and he dies. A rock can bash a person's brains in." He offered a crooked grin. "This is where you scrappy humans excel. You have no qualms about killing in what we elves call a dishonorable fashion. It's what makes you such useful soldiers. You're willing to get your hands dirty when dirty is needed."

"What about the dwarves?" Jozep, the intense appearing dwarf, asked.

"What about them?" Master Jovick asked. "From what I've seen, dwarves tend to follow where humans lead."

Sriovey and a couple of the dwarves scowled.

"Whine all you want, but it's the truth," Master Jovick said, dismissing the muttered complaints. "Let's do some work."

He had the Firsters split off into pairs, generally a human against a dwarf, each of them in a training circle.

"This is wrestling only, so no punching, no eye gouging, no attempts to maim, no shots to the privates, and if your opponent calls quits, you let him go." He addressed the dwarves. "You runts listen right. We all know how this could go if you want it to, but that isn't what *I* want. So do as I say. No *lorethasra*, and don't hurt anyone. Any questions?"

As a group, the Firsters shouted "No, sir!" The humans far less enthusiastically than the dwarves.

"Good," Master Jovick said. "On my signal, then."

Cinder faced Derius, the massive dwarf, who was seemingly wider than he was tall. Cinder didn't like his chances wrestling the man. He had an inkling that the moment Derius got ahold of him, it was over.

"Have at it," Master Jovick yelled.

Derius exploded forward. Cinder circled to his right, wanting to maintain distance. He needed to gauge the dwarf's speed and gain an idea of his reaction time. Derius tracked him. Cinder tried to move left, but the dwarf cut him off.

An instant later, they were engaged. Cinder tried to get a single leg takedown. He managed to latch his hands around Derius' left leg—his lead leg—and heaved. It was like trying to uproot an oak.

Derius didn't move an inch.

Cinder felt arms go around his abdomen. Derius grunted, lifting explosively. The world spun, and Cinder was suddenly facing the blue sky. His feet had left the earth. He had an instant to panic. His back slammed into the ground. The air exploded from his lungs, and he struggled to breathe.

A moment later. "You alright, Hotgate?" Derius asked, his face a picture of concern.

It took Cinder several seconds to get enough breath to speak. "No. I'm not alright," he eventually got out. He groaned. His ribs ached from when Derius had squeezed them.

"You want to go again?" Derius asked.

"Not really," Cinder said. He rolled over on his side and got to his feet with a sigh. "I suppose we should, though, shouldn't we?"

"I'm not sure what I'm supposed to learn from tossing you around," Derius said darkly. "You're too weak for me. I hate when the strong abuse the weak."

Cinder managed a grin. "I'm not sure I like being thought of as weak. I'm stronger than I look."

Derius eyed him doubtfully. "I don't think so."

Cinder called him forward. "Try me." He had no illusions of how another session against Derius would go, but he also understood the importance of trying to impress the man. Cinder was weaker than the dwarves, but that didn't mean he wasn't worthy of their respect. "Let's go," Cinder said.

They locked up. Cinder twisted and turned, darted laterally and abruptly changed directions—anything to keep Derius from locking his hands. It worked for a few seconds, and Derius grunted in surprise. He followed up with a driving double-leg takedown.

Once again Cinder slammed into the ground, back first again. At least this time, the air wasn't blasted from his lungs. Derius held out a helping hand. Cinder took it and was yanked to his feet.

"You've got the right instincts," Derius said. "You just don't have the strength to do what you want."

"The story of my life," Cinder muttered. "Again?"

Derius shrugged. "If you can take it, I can dish it out."

Cinder didn't want to keep going but walking away wouldn't teach him what he wanted to learn. "I can take it."

Derius grinned. "Good man."

20

After Unarmed Combat, the humans and dwarves went to separate classes. The humans had Archery, while the dwarves had a course involving close-quarter combat in narrow confines. The dwarves were notoriously near-sighted, but they were unmatched in street-fighting and battling in low light environments.

Cinder found himself missing the dwarves' rough-and-tumble nature as he walked in what he hoped was the direction of the archery range. They had received vague instructions from Cor, their third-year prefect, as to its location. West of Firemirror Hall was what he had said.

It wasn't true.

Instead directly west of Firemirror Hall lay a broad lawn pebbled by a cluster of stone cottages, which housed the senior-most instructors and visiting dignitaries.

Cinder and the others had halted when they ran across the cottages, and a brief discussion on what to do next ensued. Cinder thought they should head north, and they pressed on. Shortly after, they discovered the archery range. It was actually northwest of Firemirror Hall.

They halted there, at a sun-dappled field where various man-shaped, wooden targets were set upon frames to hold them upright. A small shed, roofed in thatch, stood forlornly off to the right, and around and behind the targets were bales of hay, probably meant to catch stray arrows. Beyond the range rose the swell of a hill, topped by a small oak. The trunk was curved slightly such that the foliage leaned over a small boy, seated and leaning against the tree while reading a book. The endless blue sky stretched beyond the bucolic scene.

Cinder momentarily wondered who the reading child might be—probably the son of a staff member. The majority of his attention, though, was focused on the other people gathered at the range. When he saw who it was, he muttered an oath.

Elves.

Bones saw them too, and he cursed out loud, as did Ishmay and Joria.

"Devesh-damned elves," Depth muttered. "I guess we've got another class with them."

"And I'm sure they'll show us up," Wark said. "You know what they say about elven archers? How they can put an arrow through a gnat's ass."

Cinder scoffed. "A gnat's ass? No one says that."

"Yes, they do," Wark protested.

Everyone laughed at him.

"They really do say that," Wark persisted.

The chuckling continued, and the tension lightened.

"Do gnats even have asses?" Rorian asked.

No one had time to answer the inane question. They had reached the elves.

"Did you pretty lasses get lost?" Riyne asked. "You need us to hold your delicate hands next time?"

"We're men," Cinder replied, "but it's good to know with whom you prefer to hold hands."

Riyne reddened, glaring hotly, and Estin held him back.

Cinder rolled his eyes. What an idiot. An inference about preferring men to women had the fool offended?

Another elf, blond-haired and older—their instructor—stood several paces away. Like most elves, he was slim, but in his case it was amplified to a whipcord narrowness. It was as if he mirrored one of the strings threading his bow and possessed nothing but straight lines. "Cut that shit out," he said to Riyne. He addressed Cinder. "And shut the hell up." He spoke to all of them next. "You scat-brained jackasses better listen clear. None of you dipshits are worth my time right now. You do what I say, and *maybe* I'll be able to make something of you."

Cinder found himself subconsciously straightening. So did the others, including the elves. The older elf was obviously their instructor. Master Serwil Opturund. From what Cinder had learned, he had been a captain in the Yaksha Army. After serving under Master Absin, their sword instructor, he had retired to a village in the northern Daggers. It should have been a restful time for Master Serwil, but ten years after resigning from the army, his village had been overrun by zahhacks and his family slain. A story similar to Master Jovick's. Years later, Master Absin somehow convinced his broken-hearted captain to join him at the Third Directorate and take up instruction in archery.

"I've got enough bows for all of you," Master Serwil said. He indicated the small shed. "Go inside. Gather a bow, a string, and a quiver of arrows. Don't fight over them. None are nicer than any other."

Cinder joined the others and entered the shed. The humans and elves formed separate lines, and within they discovered a well-kept room. The air was dry, and a single *diptha* globe lit the space. Hanging on three of the walls rested a plethora of recurve bows, none of them stringed. To his left, Cinder found a set of shelves upon which rested neat rows of quivers holding arrows and waxed leather bags containing linen strings.

He waited his turn and chose a bow at random along with a quiver.

Outside, Master Serwil had them stand in a single row behind a white, chalk line. He silently observed them, waiting until the last person exited the shed.

"Go ahead and string your bows," Master Serwil said. "I trust you know how to do this much."

Again, he waited while the students strung their bows.

Master Serwil spoke. "These are composite bows, useful on foot or on horse. The core is bamboo. The back is made of sinew, the belly of horn, and the layers are held together with animal glue. Keep them dry. They don't like moisture. Now. Let's learn to shoot properly." Master Serwil joined them behind the white line. "Many of you probably think you already know how to use a bow. Scat that. At the Directorate, you're all beginners. First thing is the stance. Mimic what I do. Feet shoulder-width apart. Bend your forward knee. Only a little. Don't lock it. Back straight. No arching. Torso perpendicular to the line. Eye the target." He withdrew an arrow from his quiver.

They hadn't done much archery training at *Steel-Graced*, but so far, none of this was beyond what Cinder already knew.

"Nock the arrow," Master Serwil said. "Eyes on the target." He paused. "If you drop an arrow or—Devesh save you!—if it falls out of your hands and rolls away, leave it until everyone on the line is done shooting. Next is the draw. There's the pinch draw, the thumb draw, and the three-finger draw. I prefer the three-finger draw. Watch." He placed his index finger above the arrow and the middle and fourth below, all three on the string to the level of the first joint. "Grasp the bow firmly, not tightly. Relax. Especially your shoulders when you bring the bow up. Find the target. Relax. Elbows parallel to the ground. Stay relaxed. I've said it three times now. *Relax.* A good archer isn't like a swordsman. There is no explosive tension and movement. This is about relaxation and concentration."

Cinder paid more attention. Relaxation wasn't something he had been taught at *Steel-Graced*. Always before he'd gripped a bow like it was a sword. His stance had been wrong, too, at least as far as his elbows were concerned.

"Also, when you draw, use your shoulders and your back," Master Serwil said. "It's not about your arms. Expand your chest. Your wrist stays flat on the drawing. The string remains centered on the bow. Find your anchor point. Release your fingers and let the string jump forward by itself."

He released the arrow, and it whistled, a high-pitched whine. An instant later, it thudded into the target, a center mass hit.

"Spread out and have at it," Master Serwil said. "I'll monitor and advise."

A shuffling of feet and mutterings ensued. Cinder eventually found a relatively open space. The closest students were six feet on either side of him.

He didn't start shooting straightway, though. Instead, expected failure and presumed embarrassment kept him from nocking an arrow. This was relatively new to him, and in previous attempts at using the bow, he had found himself utterly lost. He generally hit a target by accident more than intentionally.

He observed the others who were soon aiming and firing with smooth regularity. The humans weren't having a bad showing. Most had some training in archery, and their arrows usually found the mark.

However, their results were nothing compared to what the elves achieved. Cinder watched them in envious admiration. Their arrows almost always hit the target, knotting in tight clusters, striking nearly every time in areas which would have been lethal.

Cinder shook off his wonder. *Enough.* The elves provided him a measuring stick. Nothing more. Their skill with the bow was not said to be due to *lorethasra* but due to hard work and dedication. Well, he could work hard, and he was most assuredly dedicated.

Cinder took a stance at the line, focused on the target, and remembered to relax. He inhaled deeply, and exhaled slow and controlled, blowing out tension. He nocked an arrow and made himself unclench his shoulders. *Elbows parallel to the ground.* He drew smoothly. *Relax.* He sighted the target. *The head.* A quiet settled over him. The voices of the students faded. The shifting wind, rustling across grass and through leaves, stilled, no longer distracting. That same breeze would push his arrow to the left.

Cinder minutely adjusted his aim. Less than a second had passed since he drew. The target seemed to loom in his sight. He saw nothing else but the head, the area between the eyes.

He let loose the arrow. It whistled, whining before slamming to a stop in the center of the target's head.

The strange focus guiding Cinder's use of the bow popped like a soap bubble. The world resumed in a wall of sight and sound.

"Well done," Master Serwil said, arms folded and addressing him in a dispassionate tone. "Do it again."

Cinder nocked another arrow. He aimed, but this time distractions abounded. The other students, conversations, the sweat on his brow, the sun beaming heat. He tried to focus, but the target wouldn't center. He fired the arrow anyway.

It whistled five feet over the target and into a bale of hay.

"Keep trying," Master Serwil said. "Remember to relax and work at it. It's a skill like any other."

Cinder took Master Serwil's advice to heart. He'd outwork everyone if that's what it took to achieve his goals. He wanted to at least equal, if not surpass, the elves.

The rest of the class in archery passed by in a blur, and Cinder never again recaptured that sense of oneness with the bow, the singleness when his focus beamed unwavering onto the target. Nevertheless, he improved. The simple act of learning the proper stance and more importantly, relaxing his muscles, allowed him to achieve greater success than he had ever before known. He hit the target nearly half the time in that first class, an achievement he never would have expected from such a simple alteration to his approach.

After Archery, it was time for Equitation, another skill Cinder lacked. Thankfully, the elves had a different class, and they departed. Cinder was glad for it.

He'd heard their mocking comments during Archery. It was so childish, and while Cinder had easily disregarded the supposedly cutting comments from the elves, the others didn't. They found the insults grating, and it caused them to mutter their own jibes. Worse, the humans faltered in their concentration, and as a result their performance at the archery range suffered.

Master Serwil had put a quick stop to it by taking the elves to task, but it didn't matter. Cinder knew that while Estin, Riyne, and the others might have been abashed by Master Serwil's rebuke, their arrogance remained undiminished. It was easily distinguished by their scornful visages.

At least he wouldn't have to put up with their worthless insults during Equitation. Cinder was nervous about riding a horse, and he didn't want to waste any more energy dealing with the elves.

"You'll be alright," Bones said, apparently noticing his anxiety. "You did fine in Archery, and I know how much you sucked eggs at it back at *Steel-Graced*. This is going to be the same thing."

Wark entered their conversation. "Aren't the horses here from Devesth, of Yavana stock?" He leaned closer as if telling them a secret. "They're supposed to be high-strung. I've heard even experienced riders call them hell horses."

Cinder winced. It was true about the kind of horses they would be riding, but he hoped the reputation of the Yavanas was overblown.

"Good job, jackhole," Depth said, nudging Wark.

"What?" Wark protested.

Depth rolled his eyes. "You know Cinder hasn't ridden much, and here you go telling him he's about to get on a hell horse."

"Oh."

"What's a jackhole?" Rorian asked Cinder. "You've said it before."

"It's a portmanteau," Cinder explained. "Parts of two words fused into one. Jackass and asshole."

"I've never heard it before," Rorian said. "Did you make it up?"

Cinder opened his mouth but realized he didn't know the answer. Where had he first heard the word? Maybe in Swallow, a part of his lost memories? "I don't know," he eventually allowed.

"I like it," Ishmay declared.

Bones snorted. "That's because it reminds you of your mother."

"Naw. It reminds me of your sister."

"Hey! Sisters are off limits," Bones protested.

Ishmay didn't have a chance to respond. They had reached the stables.

It was a long structure, framed in tall wooden planks set upon a base of red bricks. Left of the stables ran a breezeway, and next to it was a large, fenced field where a number of horses munched grass. To the right were various paddocks of varying size, mostly made of dirt and sand. Several nearby smaller buildings huddled around the stables. From one came the ringing of a hammer striking iron. *A farrier.* The other structures were probably where the veterinarians worked or meant to store tack.

As for the main barn, the doors were thrown open and a long corridor extended through the heart of the building. A line of stalls ran on each side of the hallway. A hayloft took up most of the second story along with rooms for those who worked in the stables.

A black-haired, gray eyed elf of middling years stood facing a paddock. Master Halin Dorund, the Master of the horse. Or at least Cinder guessed it was him. He matched the appearance Cor had described for the elf in charge of the horses, including the limp on the right. The result of a long-ago battlefield injury.

Currently, Master Halin's attention was occupied by a white stallion within the paddock. A young elf was attempting to tie a rope to the horse's harness but was having no luck at getting it on. Every time he closed with the animal, the stallion darted away with a flick of his tail and what sounded like a laughing nicker. The horse was obviously having fun with the elf, who finally threw the rope down in disgust.

The stallion pranced within inches of the young elf, seemingly proud of himself and high-stepping past.

"I don't know what to tell you," the young elf said to the master. "He's a rakshasa in the form of a horse."

Master Halin spat out the straw he'd been chewing. "What a waste. The stallion might be special, but he bids himself untrainable and unteachable."

"Maybe that's why the Devesthians sold him to us for so little. Even as a purebred Yavana, they knew he was useless."

"He's not useless. We can still breed him. He could improve our native stock some."

"But their kind doesn't breed true here," the younger elf said. "The only way to breed a proper Yavana is if they're foaled and raised in Cord Valley in Devesth with the dam and sire both Yavanas. Anything else gives us a fast, smart animal, but not as fast or smart as a true Yavana."

"I know, but what else can we do with him?" The master turned about and faced the students, unsurprised. "You're here. Good. I'm Master Halin. Tell me your names, one at a time."

After taking the informal roll call, Master Halin indicated the horse. "As you can see, we're having a bit of trouble with this hellion, which is as good a description as any for this breed of horse. How many of you have ridden a Yavana?" He scanned the students. No hands went up. "How many of you have experience riding a horse?"

This time every hand but Cinder's and Rorian's went up.

The master nodded. "Forget everything you ever learned. Most of you will have a horse of Yavana stock but not a true Yavana. Only the pre-eminent riders and graduates of the Directorate are graced with Yavanas. They're to horses as an eagle is to a sparrow. They're bigger, faster, and stronger than a normal equine. See for yourself."

The white stallion was easily seventeen hands tall, perfectly proportioned, and rather than the bulky build of a plowhorse, he had a stature that promised both speed *and* strength. Cinder also saw intelligence gleaming in the horse's eyes as he seemed to assess the students who observed him.

"Most importantly," the master continued, "they're smart. Intelligent and willing to learn. Some riders claim to even hold conversations with them." He mock-glared at the stallion. "Though they can also be as stubborn as mules. They don't let just anyone ride them. It takes a special touch to earn their acceptance. That's what we'll teach you here. How to ride properly so if you're lucky enough to have a Yavana as a mount, you'll not fall off and get yourself killed."

Cinder heard the words, but there was a mystery in the stallion's posture, in the canted position of his head, the question in his eyes. The horse seemed to call him forward, wanting something of him. Cinder stepped beyond his fellow Firsters, drawn to the animal.

The master broke off his instruction when Cinder approached the paddock's railing.

"What are you doing there?" he heard Master Halin say, his voice faraway.

He paid him no heed. His attention was on the white, his eyes locked on the horse. *What do you want?* Cinder didn't move when the stallion confidently stepped forward and halted a few feet away. The horse rested his large head on Cinder's shoulder.

Cinder started when a perception came to him. It emanated from the horse, a language of feelings rather than words.

You promised to return. You never did. The stallion snorted and nudged Cinder's chest, irritation evident. *I waited a long time.*

Cinder stroked the stallion's forehead, rubbing at the forelock.

Don't make me wait so long ever again. The white snorted again and trotted off.

Cinder broke from whatever had him spellbound. He blinked in confusion. The horse hadn't really spoken to him, had it? No. It couldn't have. Horses didn't talk. Besides, until today he'd never met the stallion, not even in Swallow. He couldn't have.

"Well bite me in the ass," the master said.

Cinder realized everyone was staring at him.

"He's never been so gentle with anyone." Master Halin slapped Cinder on the shoulder. "It looks like you get to be the one to help educate that rakshasa."

The final class of the day, General History, took place in the same room as the one in which they'd taken Tactics and Strategy. This one also included all the Firsters: humans, elves, and dwarves. The sun lingered over the western horizon, and as a result, its light no longer poured into the room. Nevertheless, the space remained bright.

The illumination was the first thing Cinder noticed. The second was less appealing.

The elves had already arrived, and they sat at adjacent tables, four at one and three at the other. They glanced to the doorway when Cinder and the others entered the classroom. Not surprisingly, Riyne's mouth formed a sullen curl of distaste.

Cinder disregarded the elf. The supercilious jackhole wasn't worth his time or his trouble. He and the others settled themselves at the remaining tables and waited on the instructor.

Riyne continued to stare at them, his dislike obvious.

Mohal, the elf who had sat at Cinder's table during Tactics and Strategy, noticed Riyne's antics, and he shook his head in rueful apology.

Nathaz jutted his chin at Riyne and cursed. Cinder was discovering the dwarf tended to curse a lot. "Ignore the asshole," Nathaz said. "Fucking prick."

"Do you kiss your sister-wife with that mouth?" Sriovey asked.

"What the fuck is a sister-wife?" Nathaz asked. "Besides, I'm not married."

Cinder laughed, as did the others.

"I'm thinking he was teasing," Jozep said.

Riyne continued to stare their way, but now he was joined by Estin.

"You have a problem?" Bones asked them.

Estin answered. "Yes. It's the humans who think they're worthy of the Third Directorate."

"And yet they *are* worthy." In strode their instructor, Lieutenant Capshin Sonsing, the aide-de-camp to General Arwan. He was of early middle years, trim and fighting fit, and hair still black. He wore the uniform of the Third Directorate, gray shirt, dark blue slacks, and black boots. A pin on his left breast, a silver eagle clutching a sword—the Directorate's symbol—indicated his status as an officer, and his rank was denoted by the pair of stripes on his left shoulder, each decorated with a single gold star. He continued to address Estin. "And as a prince of the realm, you should know this. If not, you soon will."

Estin settled into his chair, a mulish clenching of his jaw indicating how little he cared for the lieutenant's admonishment.

The lieutenant went to the desk but rather than take a seat, he remained standing, his bearing military-straight. "You are not in your proper seating assignments. Let us take care of this now." He called instructions, indicating where he expected each student to sit.

Cinder ended up sharing a table with Derius and an elf with curly, brown hair—wild like brambles—and eyes of similar hue. The sensation of forest and moss clung to him.

Cinder introduced himself, and the elf spoke his name, without hesitation and without a trace of conceit. "Cariath Gelindun."

Lieutenant Sonsing rapped a fist on the desk. "Now that's settled, let's get to work. This is General History. You will have this course—" His mouth quirked. "—or this 'curse', as some of you will likely name it, for the entirety of your time at the Directorate. In the first year, we will focus our attention on Yaksha Sithe. We will also spend time on the Gandharva Federation, Rakesh, and Surent Crèche. Next year will come the other political unions, although in an admittedly cursory form. It is the *curse* of our time that one would require several elven lifetimes to truly learn and understand the history of our world."

Cinder raised his hand. "Will we discuss the rishis?" He hoped their history might provide some insight into why they were so powerful. They were humans after all.

"Yes," the lieutenant said, "but that is for year two. Let us get started with year one. Take notes. This information will be on your mid-term exams."

A scramble ensued as everyone quickly fetched ledgers and pens from their satchels.

"*Porash nazah loni, telemarr rul*," the lieutenant said once the students were settled. "It's *Shevasra*. Can anyone other than an elf translate the phrase?"

Cinder wracked his memories. The phrasing and the words . . . they sounded familiar, but he couldn't recall why.

Jozep, the happy but intense dwarf, raised his hand and was called on. "The literal translation is *peace want you, war prepare.* Or more properly, *if you want peace, prepare for war.*"

Lieutenant Sonsing nodded. "Exactly. It is the adage which most closely embodies the spirit of Yaksha Sithe and was first spoken by our illustrious founder, Empress Koran Yaksha. She said it after combining what were then disparate elements into a nascent empire. With those words and her iron will, she forged a sithe of remarkable endurance and power. Yaksha was first founded in 453 SR, hundreds of years prior to the *NusraelShev,* the Disastrous Submission, and we survived those terrible centuries of war. Yaksha endured, and she endures. We possess an unbroken lineage that continues to this day with our beloved Empress Sala Yaksha, only twelve generations removed from our founding. Can anyone explain why we have been so successful and long-lived?" The lieutenant didn't pause in his lecture and answered his own question. "Because we live and breathe the spirit of the phrase I mentioned earlier. It is our sithe's creed. We want peace, but we are ever prepared for war." The lieutenant paused then, peering at the room with flinty eyes. "If you learn nothing else in this course, master that aphorism, understand it completely, and you'll have a chance to succeed."

Porash nazah loni, telemarr rul. Cinder played the words in his mind. *If you want peace, prepare for war.* It was an elegantly spoken truth, an obvious one, and Cinder reckoned it was information probably not unique to Yaksha. Other nations and unions likely made the same connection, the one in which perceived weakness invited attack, especially from those without scruples. He broke off his ruminations when the lieutenant began lecturing again.

"As I said, Yaksha Sithe was founded in 453 SR, *Sapro Ran,* the time before the *NusraelShev.* Given our current year of 3024 SY, *Sapro Yan,* the time after the *NusraelShev,* the sithe is obviously old, the oldest of all political entities in Seminal. The sithe has outlasted Shet, the

Mythaspuris, the supposed final followers of Shokan, and humans like Mede who fancied themselves gods. We have persevered." His voice ended on a ringing note. "The why is almost as important as the how, and that is what we will learn during the first few months of this course."

Lieutenant Sonsing paced. "Let us step back further in time. Let us go to the age prior to Koran Yaksha. Originally, this island was a simple place, like all proto-sithes, it was a place of nature, where our forebear elves maintained a natural order and built beauty and fought for survival against the zahhacks of the time. They did so on their own, unsupported and without allies. It was the pressure to survive annihilation that allowed Empress Koran to rise. Without her, the elves of Yaksha would have died. Koran taught them a different path, an imperial path." Here, the lieutenant smiled. "Ironically, Koran might not have meant for her imperial line to continue. Her first name, 'Koran' was one the Empress adopted, an affectation she chose. It means 'final' in *Shevasra*. It is thought that Koran meant for herself to be the *Final Yaksha*. Her daughter, Swan Yaksha, clearly felt otherwise. When Koran fell during the early years of the *NusraelShev*, it was Swan who conceived the continuation of her dynasty. It was she who established the boundaries of the empire. We are the elves of the south. Our borders extend through portions of the northern half of the Dagger Mountains, wrap around Rakesh and push out into the wilds of the Gilded Peninsula and the Gold River. Then, of course, there is Yaksha proper." Lieutenant Sonsing opened his arms, indicating the world at large. "The island itself is separated from the mainland by the Sentient Sea, which serves as our greatest defense. Because of it, we can more easily maintain our preparations for war while striving for peace. We are able to have equitable trade with other nations, such as the Gandharva Federation for their material goods and industry or Apsara Sithe for the special grasses that allow us to make fine pottery and even more finely crafted weapons." The lieutenant clasped his hands behind his back. "We will delve more deeply into those matters. But before we do that, I want an essay by the end of the week on the history and meaning of the phrase I earlier mentioned." His eyes went to the elves, lingering longest on Estin. "Perhaps you will even prove how you are worthy of this grand institute."

21

The evening following his first classes Cinder wanted to search out the library. Everyone else was gathered in the common room, slumped in their chairs and couches, holding desultory conversations, and appearing completely worn out. Cinder didn't know if anyone would want to come with him to the library, but he felt like he should ask anyway.

"I'm beat," Bones said.

"Same," Rorian agreed. "I'm ready to fall asleep."

Cinder glanced in the direction of the dwarves; brows raised expectantly. They shouldn't be too tired. They were dwarves after all, supposedly able to work from sunup-to-sundown and have enough energy to go drinking afterward.

His hopes were quickly dashed.

"Forget it," Derius said. "I want to take a nap until tomorrow morning. But bring back whatever you learn, Hotgate, and I'll praise you to the jeweled depths."

"Yes. Share it with all of us," Sriovey said by way of agreement.

Cinder viewed the dwarves in surprise. They appeared no less worn

276

out than the humans. "I thought you were supposed to be stronger than us," he said to the dwarves. "Aren't you supposed to be able to train or fight for days without rest?"

"Train and fight, yes," Sriovey said. "Read and study, no." He was crashed out on the couch, eyes shut.

Cinder shook his head in disbelief. He felt the same fatigue weighing upon his limbs, but unlike the others, he couldn't afford to sit here and rest. He had to find the information required by Master Nuhlin. Plus, he remembered what Riner had said long ago about the book of prophecy from Gandharva. *The Lor Agni.* He wanted to read more about Shokan and Sira.

Those thoughts in mind, he exited Krathe House, entering the Quad where twilight had settled upon the Third Directorate. Streaks of orange and red blotted the sky, and bats soared, dipping and twisting. From the stables came the sound of work. A few folks were still up, getting the horses settled.

Cinder studied the paddocks and barn, peering as if he could see through the wood and brick cladding. His thoughts went to the white stallion. *Did I really hear him speak?* He figured not, but the entire situation struck him as bizarre.

It was another on a long list of personal oddities. His complete loss of memory. The inexplicable healing of his clubfoot and withered leg. His strange abilities with the sword, and his even stranger recollections of a lovely city and a lovelier woman. And now this.

There was a mystery to it all. He sensed it, but no matter how much he racked his brains or studied various texts, the mystery was no closer to being solved. It remained indecipherable.

He could have asked for help in his research—two minds were generally better than one—but he didn't dare. It wouldn't be wise. If nothing else, his readings had taught and continually reinforced a simple truth: the mystery of his existence smacked of a deep use of *lorethasra*, and only rishis and wraiths exhibited such talents.

Both were equally despised, and in the case of wraiths, killed on sight. No effort was ever made to speak to a wraith, to learn what drove their actions. They were simply slain.

Cinder shook his head. No. He couldn't tell anyone.

He realized he had crossed the Quad during his ruminations, and he noted several older students heading his way. He dipped his head to them in respect, but they were lost in deep conversation and never acknowledged his gesture. Instead, they passed him by, their footsteps crunching across the gravel paths of the Quad.

Cinder shrugged and entered Firemirror Hall.

It didn't take him long to discover the library. It was a secondary structure attached to the main building and reached by means of an open breezeway. The hours were posted outside the entrance: open from early in the morning to several hours after sunset.

Cinder pushed through a pair of heavy brass doors engraved with the imagery of books and scrolls and rocked to a stop.

Before him stretched a long, rectangular space, currently unoccupied and filled with tables. Chandeliers of *diptha* bulbs illuminated the area, and on all sides around the seating rose several stories of shelving. All of them groaning beneath the weight of an assortment of books. A musty smell and a sense of bated breath or pregnant quiet filled the air. To Cinder's right, a set of staircases rose to the upper levels. To his left was a desk where an elderly, bespectacled elf sat, head bent toward a book.

Cinder's gaze flittered around the library, and he tried not to show his dismay. *So many books.* He might be better off asking the old elf at the desk for some help.

From directly behind him, a voice spoke in a confident contralto. "You appear lost."

Cinder started and spun about, finding himself face-to-face with Princess Anya. Since her welcome intrusion into a brewing argument this afternoon, he'd learned a little more about her. She was the second child of Empress Sala, and unlike any other woman of her station—royalty or nobility—she had opted for the military life, the first female member of the imperial house to do so. In fact, she had been the first woman to ever graduate from the Third Directorate, period, and at the top of her class, no less. After finishing her courses at the academy, like other highly skilled graduates, she had become a ranger. However, Anya worked alone. She apparently enjoyed the solitude while she scouted the rugged terrain of the Dagger Mountains, killing zahhacks and wraiths as the need arose.

Maybe she'd been the one called to put down the *aether*-cursed snowtiger who had killed Cinder's parents. He considered asking, but with her standing so close, questions about his parents or her work as a ranger were shoved far from the forefront of his mind. Instead, his thoughts were taken up by the pressure of her presence. He found it hard to speak or breathe.

Anya was taller than him, striking and unforgettable. Her depthless eyes held the hue of emeralds, promising the secrets of a forest. She wore a ranger's camouflage clothing, a scabbarded sword slung across her back, and a brace of knives on her hip. Even in the Third Directorate, she went armed. Cinder wondered if she ever relaxed.

He managed to rein in his racing thoughts and nodded in respectful greeting. "Your Highness."

"Simply Anya will do," she corrected, in a cool voice.

Cinder's response to her slipped out without conscious thought. "Of course, Simply Anya." The moment the sentence left his mouth, he wanted to smack himself. How could he be so stupid? Teasing someone so far above his station? And a royal elf, no less.

Thankfully, his worries proved unnecessary.

Anya's lips curled into a gentle smile, and her eyes crinkled with amusement. "You are a bold one, aren't you?"

Cinder let out a breath he didn't realize he was holding. "Maybe so, but I'm a bold one who's lost."

"And your name?"

"Cinder Shade. It's a pleasure meeting you." He shook hands with Anya. She had a firm grip, and her hands were callused.

"What are you looking for?" Anya asked.

Cinder explained.

"*The Lor Agni*," Anya mused. "*The Hidden Life* or *the Hidden Flame* in *Shevasra*. We elves don't give the prophecy much credence. In fact, it's safe to say that we consider it nearly sacrilegious."

Cinder blinked. Sacrilegious? Did he really want to read something the elves disliked so much?

Anya strode off. "We have several copies in the section where the religious texts are housed," she called over her shoulder. "Come along."

Cinder didn't respond at first, surprised by Anya's no-nonsense attitude. He eventually got going and trailed the princess up a flight of stairs. The faintest touch of cinnamon drifted along the breeze of her passage, likely from her perfume. Again, his mouth proceeded faster than his judgment.

He mentioned the cinnamon, and she came to an abrupt halt, frowning at him.

"It smells nice," he quickly added.

"It isn't perfume," Anya said. "It's part of who I am." She pursed her lips. "You have an excellent sense of smell. Most elves don't notice my natural scent. And certainly, no humans ever have." She set off again, a stiffness in the set of her shoulders. It hadn't been present a few seconds prior.

Cinder must have offended her, and he chided himself. He didn't know what it was about his observation that bothered her so much, but he vowed to keep his mouth shut from now on. He wouldn't try again to make her smile, and he would definitely shut off any overly familiar comments. They were clearly unwelcome.

They paced between a long set of shelves on the second floor, and the musty aroma of old paper became more pronounced. Dust covered many of the books.

Cinder glanced at the titles. He recognized some of their names, but he hadn't yet read many of them. The books here were religious texts; explanations of *Median's Scryings*, translations of *Revelatory Dreams*, copies of *Forever Triumphant*, and various volumes of *Crèche Prani*. There were others, too.

"Here we are," Anya said. She withdrew a leather-wrapped book from the shelves. "You would be wise to peruse this here rather than ask the librarian to allow you to check it out. It would lead to less questions."

Cinder silently agreed. Less questions given his past was good advice.

He handled the slim volume. It was more like a booklet, something he could easily read in a few hours. "Where can I find out about the Battle at Sage's Field?" It was his primary task for coming to the library.

Anya chuckled. "You can't. The battle never happened," she said. "Master Nuhlin enjoys his pranks, and he always pulls this particular one on Firster humans and dwarves. He tells them to write an essay about the Battle of Sage's Field. They spend a week in a panic, scrounging around for any information on a battle that is entirely fictional. It comes from a humorous play, *Coronation of a Fool.* It's about an elven man who wants to become an emperor." She leaned in toward Cinder, seemingly to impress her next words. "Elves have always been ruled by women, by empresses. Not men. It has always been thus. However, this man who would be emperor eventually wins his way to the throne. He overcomes his foes at the Battle of Sage's Field, but during the conflict, he is emasculated. Thus, while he takes the throne, in a sense, he is no longer a man."

Cinder laughed. "I'd like to see that play. I have a feeling my past self enjoyed theater."

"What do you mean?"

"I don't remember my life prior to a year ago," Cinder said, going on to explain about the *aether*-cursed snowtiger.

"A grim tale," Anya agreed.

Cinder merely grunted in reply. He didn't want to talk about it any further. *Less questions.* He once again fingered *the Lor Agni.* "Why do elves consider this sacrilegious?"

"Because the final set of verses, the *Denthera—the Time of the Great Wielder* in *Shevasra*—says that Shokan and Sira will return during a time of Seminal's greatest need. Despite their reputation, they are only human. From the perspective of my kind—the Blessed Race—we have to ask: what can Shokan and Sira do that we cannot?" She shook her head. "There are also other things the book claims, all of them clearly impossible. Shet rising. The coming of the Hydra of the Realms, whatever that is. Things of that nature."

Cinder sighed in disappointment. It sounded like a typical prophetic text. Vague warnings of doom, impossible evil rising, a slender thread of unlikely hope, a ring or sword to save the day . . . Nothing to get alarmed by and certainly nothing to earn the opprobrium of sacrilegious. "Is there anything worth reading in the text?"

"Certainly," Anya said, "but those are items you'll have to learn on your own." She smiled, a ray of sunshine through a cloudy day. "Enjoy your reading."

She left him then, and Cinder watched her departing figure, his mind focused on her rather than the book in his hand.

Anya paced through the Third Directorate, headed back to her quarters in Firemirror Hall. No one else was about, and her boot steps echoed through a quiet corridor. *Diptha* bulbs in their wrought-iron chandeliers were turned down for the evening. To her right, a bank of windows allowed a view of the Quad and a tidal wash of moonlight. To her left, doorways opened into darkened classrooms, and along that same wall were hung a number of portraits, images of famous academy graduates. Most were elves, but there was also the occasional human or dwarf.

Anya marched down the corridor and took a right, climbed a flight of stairs, and reached the floor where some of the masters and visiting dignitaries were housed. Rugs lined the wide oak flooring, softening her boot steps. Here, a soft illumination arose from crystal chandeliers, a type of lighting that always struck Anya as being out of place in a school baptized for combat.

As she strode toward her room, Anya's thoughts remained fastened on the Firster she'd met tonight. *Cinder Shade.* A common surname for the Dagger Mountains, and yet his visage proclaimed him as being from somewhere else, somewhere not entirely from Rakesh. It was subtle, but his skin was not the same hue as most of his countrymen. It was a darker shade, more like tea touched with milk. His eyes were rounder, too. He might have a touch of Errow in him.

She couldn't rightly tell his ancestry, but what struck her more forcefully than his appearance was his sense of smell. He'd noticed her cinnamon scent. Only her closest family—parents and siblings—noticed it. No one else. Not even friends or cousins.

So how had Cinder? *Why* had Cinder? Perhaps it had something to do with his mixed heritage. Maybe it gave him some hidden insight beyond the norm. It certainly wasn't because he was a Pureblood. If anything, those folk had fewer gifts, but it didn't stop them from wanting to preserve their racial purity.

It was strange. Some human tribes believed so deeply in the purity of their ancestors that they demanded all their members share a common physical appearance, be it skin tone, eye shape, or hair color, and they wanted their descendants to have the same.

Such a notion had never sat well with Anya, and it didn't do so now. She hated such closed-minded thinking, which wasn't surprising since in another time, she'd been known as a *ghrina*, an abomination. She couldn't fully recall those parts of her past. It was from a long-lost portion of her life, an era of faded memories, of years of joy and happiness and love. It hurt to think about them.

She set aside the burden of remembrance, focusing again on Cinder Shade. She liked the boy. Unlike most humans, he wasn't afraid of her, wasn't overwhelmed by her status as a royal elf. He was even willing to tease her, something few men of any sort dared. Cinder had courage, and something else. Something more. Anya had an impression that Cinder's soul held the obdurate heart of a warrior intermixed with a generous spirit.

Or more likely she was intuiting more virtues than he actually possessed. She smiled to herself, imagining what her older sister, Enma, would make of him. It wasn't hard to guess. Enma shared Estin's antipathy toward humans. Anya, on the other hand, was known to favor humans, believing in their possibilities.

Some elves claimed her views unseemly, but Anya didn't care. She had never brought shame to her family and house. She had never acted in an indecent fashion toward a human, be they man or woman. She was simply willing to see them as potential friends.

Anya reached her room and entered. She turned a handle on a pair of nearby *diptha* lamps, using the stored *aether* within the bulbs to bring them to life. The room slowly brightened, and she took stock of her quarters. A bed, larger than what was afforded the students, crouched in a corner. A dresser and mirror to the left, her own washroom, and a window on the right looking out over the surrounding mountains where she always felt more at home and at peace.

As she stared at the shadowed peaks, the need to travel surged through her like a tide. She didn't fight it. In her decades of life, she'd learned to trust her instincts. When they told her she'd spent enough time in Yaksha proper, then it was time to leave, time to return to the continent and travel the Daggers.

She'd leave in the morning, return to Revelant and see her parents and tell them of her plans.

Several days of hard travel later, Anya arrived home at the capital. It had been a taxing ride, but with the presence of the manned mission houses roughly every twenty-five miles, she had been able to switch horses several times a day.

During her ride to Revelant, the desire to travel had become an insistent itch. She needed to see the world. The deeper mountains of the mainland called to her, a recognition of a bygone past when snow-capped elevations, cavernous crags, and verdant fields overlooking a teardrop shaped lake formed the boundaries of her vistas, and she was content. Where a city carved into the slopes of one particular peak—a dead place now—called to her soul.

My soul.

All at once, Anya felt older than her ten decades. She had felt the burden of her years during her recent time at the Third Directorate, when she was surrounded by students who seemed like children. But it was much more acute in moments such as this, when she more fully recalled her history.

She finally reached Revelant just after sunset, entering through the western gate. From there, she went to the imperial compound—Taj Wada—a number of buildings set amidst a cluster of high hills, laddering up a set of slopes and flattened areas. Some of the structures were given over to the various potentates and mandarins who helped run Yaksha and too often seemed to believe they could better administer the far-flung sithe without her mother's direct intervention.

Anya approached the palace grounds of Taj Wada where the main entrance was protected by a towering gate and a gilded wrought-iron portcullis. In addition, a blocky wall of gray granite, taller than a yakshin and ten feet thick, surrounded the entirety of the grounds. Overlooking the road leading inside and bracketing the gate stood a pair of towers. From their topmost heights flew Yaksha's flag, the symbol a fiery crown on a field of red.

Anya nodded greeting to the half-dozen warriors standing to either side of the entrance. There were more stationed upon the ramparts and within the compound itself. She passed into the gate, through its long tunnel, and exited into the grounds where a long lawn stretched ahead of her like a green banner. A long pool of water split the grass and on either side of it, matching rows of palm trees ran like lines of soldiers. In the distance, Anya spied a set of stairs. They led deeper into the compound, rising toward the palace itself.

She halted her progression then, gazing at the white marble structure. *The palace.* It glowed in the light of the twin moons—white Dormant and golden Fulsom. She'd spent most of her life here, and while it would be generous to name the place a home, those were the feelings it stirred. The soul of her, though, longed for a cozy three-room abode carved into the heart of a mountain. Her first true home. Or even a flat in a city that was glorious enough to put Revelant to shame, the place where she'd so joyfully loved.

Anya tsked, annoyed by her cloying recollections of the past. It was long gone and the people who brought them to life were all dead. She couldn't even remember their names or faces. She forced aside her feelings and thoughts. She'd come here to speak to her mother and father.

The road leading from the main gate bifurcated, and on either side, it led to where the administrators had their own buildings, some of which rivaled the main palace in terms of luxury. Ahead, however, the road continued, transitioning into a brick path running parallel to the lawn and depositing visitors on the steps leading to the palace.

Anya took the right-hand path, riding past a koi pond. A wooden bridge spanned the water and a small gazebo rested at the crest. Another turn sent her past a rock garden surrounded by wildflowers. She took several more right- and left-hand turns before reaching the stables. A wide-eyed boy, pointed ears peeking over a tousle of hair, took the reins to her horse. Anya didn't recognize him. He was likely new to the palace.

"I'll see to your mare really well, your Highness," the boy said in a voice full of awe.

Anya smiled. "Thank you, child. What's your name?"

"Enmen, your Highness."

"See she gets an extra helping of oats."

The boy promised he would.

Anya set off to see her family. She climbed several sets of stairs, took an ivy-covered passage through more gardens, and eventually arrived at the palace where she entered through a servant's entrance. From there she slipped into one of the main halls. Despite the late hour, the broad corridor, wide enough for five people to walk abreast, remained flooded with a soft light. The illumination arose from the many crystalline chandeliers suspended from the barrel ceiling. Wooden ribs the color of teak curved down to meet white-washed walls upon which hung various portraits and tapestries. Soft rugs, plush enough to lie upon, softened the dark marble floors and quieted Anya's booted steps.

At the intersection of two hallways, she came to a groined vault and a large mural. It captured an image of the Mythaspuris caging Shet, chaining him in the deep, black depths of a mountain's darkest heart. Leading the Mythaspuris were the brothers, Dormant and Fulsom.

Anya paused, absorbing the imagery. Rustlings in the depths of her fallow memories troubled her. It felt like Dormant and Fulsom should be something other than brothers, that their true past was a mixture of horror and terror. Were they really the ones who had led the glorious Mythaspuris?

She didn't know. All she understood of the Mythaspuris was that from them arose the insular rishis of Bharat. *Rishis.* Their name was a byword for selfish and cruel, and yet they were undeniably powerful. It was said that the rishis, the so-called Upright Ones, had each opened four Chakras.

Anya doubted it. Humans—no matter their supposed heritage—didn't have that kind of power, not when the wisest elf known could only claim the opening of two Chakras.

She left the intersection and its depiction of Shet's imprisoning and continued on to where she reckoned she'd find her parents. She ran into a number of servants finishing up tasks for the evening, and they bowed to her. She acknowledged them with a distracted wave but pressed on, drawing ever nearer to the private apartments of the imperial family.

The hallway narrowed, and the ceiling height lowered to a more personable scale. The lighting softened further as well. In these private areas, the Yaksha elves had no reason to impress any visiting dignitaries. In these places, Anya and her family could relax.

She soon arrived at her mother's study. Light bled from beneath the sturdy mahogany door, an oval seamlessly set into a frame. The craftsmanship was impeccable. It was nearly impossible to tell where the door ended, and the frame began. In addition, upon the lintel was carved Yaksha Sithe's symbol, the fiery sun.

Anya centered herself with a settling breath and knocked on the door.

"Come in," a voice called. Her mother, Sala Yaksha.

Anya entered the study, a square room lined by chocolate-colored bookshelves containing neatly racked books. Her sister and heir to the throne, Enma, sat on a couch in front of an unlit fireplace. A mess of books was spread out on the coffee table before her. Seated in a nearby armchair was their father, Avan Aruyen. To Anya's right waited her mother, Sala Yaksha. Anya and her siblings had taken their father's surname since by tradition and law, only one elf at a time could claim the sithe's actual name. The empress sat behind a massive desk with snarling dragons carved into the legs.

Anya took in more details. A pair of ladders allowed easy access to the higher bookshelves. Facing the entrance was a broad window. During the day, it offered a view of a lovely walled garden just outside, but for now, all Anya could see was her reflection.

Anya's gaze went from one family member to another, automatically searching for any changes. It was an old habit.

Her focus began with her sister. Enma's blonde hair—a whiter hue than Anya's honey-gold locks—was in its typical braid. Her sister was six decades older than Anya's roughly one-hundred ten years and had an immeasurably more difficult nature. Prickly, prideful, and far too often petty. Enma took offense for the shallowest of reasons. For example, when it first became apparent that Anya was the taller sister, Enma wouldn't speak to her for a month.

Yet it was undeniable that Enma was smart, capable, and charismatic when needed. If she could ever rein in the baser aspects of her personality, she might one day be worthy to sit upon Yaksha's Sun Throne. Enma gazed at Anya, her dark eyes neither welcoming nor unwelcoming. Neutral. It was often the best Anya could hope for.

Next, Anya went to examine her mother. The empress was an unprepossessing elf of middle years. Her hair remained blonde, the same shade as Enma's, although perhaps Sala's had lost some of its luster. It was where the similarities ended for a certain warmth emanated from their mother's dark eyes. In addition, Enma was beautiful. Their mother was not. Handsome was the kindest that could be said about her. Nevertheless, it was Sala's sense of presence, her ability to command a room that set her apart from all other elves. At times, she could be a force of nature.

Anya's focus next went to Avan, her father, who sat in an armchair adjacent to Enma's couch, a book in his hand. He was a dark-haired elf in his late middle years, his three hundreds, and his blue eyes remained bright with curiosity. Her father was originally from Heliar Sithe's imperial family, and several hundred years ago, Avan had been auctioned off to marry Yaksha's heir. He'd quickly found his footing in Yaksha, although he cared little for the day-to-day running of the sithe. Rather, he spent most of his time healing—he was one of the finest physicians in all of Yaksha. He had also mastered aspects of crafting, such as furniture, gardening, and even bladesmithing. In fact, the *insufi* sword strapped to Anya's waist was of his creation.

Anya's mother stepped out from behind her desk. She moved to meet Anya, drawing her into a hug. "We didn't expect you home for several weeks."

Anya embraced her mother. "I had a longing."

Her mother reached forward, tucking a stray lock behind one of Anya's ears. She smiled knowingly. "Let me guess. You have a longing to travel."

Anya smiled in return. She should have realized her mother would understand her plans. "You know me too well."

"You didn't come to see your family?" Enma asked, her tone unnaturally sweet and innocent.

"Be kind," their father admonished. He stood, moving to hug Anya as well. He had a smoky aroma clinging to his clothes. He must have been working the forge. "Where do you plan on going?"

"Not far. The southern Daggers. I haven't been through them in several years."

"When will you be back?" her mother asked.

"More importantly, when will you give up this ridiculous pose of a warrior?" Enma demanded.

Anya closed her eyes, praying for patience. Sometimes she wanted nothing more than to punch her sister.

"That isn't how I would phrase the question," their father began.

Anya opened her eyes, hoping her sudden surge of anger didn't show. She was expected to find a husband at some point—likely in the next fifty years—but until then, she was supposed to take on a series of lovers, temporarily locking their interests to those of the imperial family. Enma certainly did the latter, enthusiastically so as far as Anya could tell. But Anya couldn't do the same. She remained a maiden. Something in her cringed at the thought of a strange man's touch. In her past life, she had been married, and she still longed for her dead husband. *Why did he have to die?*

"You have responsibilities to the sithe," Enma said, rising to her feet. "Responsibilities only a princess of the blood can perform. Let another ranger handle the southern Daggers."

"I know my responsibilities," Anya snapped at Enma.

"Then act upon them," Enma snapped back.

Their father held up his hands in a placating fashion. He spoke to Anya. "I understand some of your reasons for wanting to escape the city, but Enma is right. You *do* have responsibilities."

Enma nodded. "It is far past time that you grew up."

Anya's gaze shot to her sister, fury cresting. Something in her anger must have finally penetrated Enma's self-righteous attitude. Her sister took a sharp step backward.

Her mother spoke then. "Your responsibilities as a ranger are not insignificant," she began, "and I know you won't shirk your duties here when it's time to come home. How long will you be staying?"

"A few days at most," Anya said. "However long it takes to book passage to Swift Sword."

Her mother smiled brightly. "Then you'll have time to tell me about the new Firsters at the Third Directorate."

"There are many who speak approvingly of Riyne Coushinre," Enma said.

"He's from Yaksha proper, is he not?" their father asked.

"Yes. He and Estin are friends," Enma explained. "His brother is Lisandre."

"Lisandre?" their father said. "Isn't he the one who earned an *insufi* blade within a decade of graduating the Directorate?"

"The same," Enma said. "He may also garner the title of *Sai* in the not-too-distant future."

Anya kept quiet. Lisandre was also the one who many expected her to take as a lover. Handsome, charming, and a skilled warrior. She could do much worse, but she had no interest in Lisandre. In some ways, it was to both their detriments.

"They say Riyne has an equal chance for greatness" Enma spoke to Anya, a civility to her voice. "What do you think of him?"

"He may be special," Anya replied. She went to explain her observations of the Firsters. While she spoke, her thoughts settled on Cinder. *How did he notice my cinnamon scent?*

22

Months at the Third Directorate passed in a blink. Months spent in training, sparring, learning, and studying. The depths of autumn soon blanketed the Third Directorate in days of damp dreariness, but for a few glorious weeks, the weather shifted to resplendent. Crickets chirped their last songs for summer's final remembrance, and a pleasant breeze filtered through the windows opening into the Firsters' common room at Krathe House. It brought in the night's fragrances of flowers from the garden in the back, and both moons beamed their light.

The fireplace was unlit, and Cinder hoped it wouldn't be needed on a regular basis for a few more weeks. He didn't look forward to winter's questing fingers and icy touch.

The common room was crowded this evening. Rorian and Ishmay were in a corner, writing a history paper due tomorrow. They should have been done by now, but they'd procrastinated and would likely be awake late into the night. Joining them was Derius. He was done with his essay, but he'd kindly volunteered to help the two humans.

Everyone else was scattered around the common room, relaxing and laughing softly. The humans and dwarves had overcome their early aversion, and during the months spent so far at the Third Directorate, they'd managed the miraculous: they'd bonded. So much so that they even played together. Currently a mixed group engaged in euchre, a card game popular in Surent Crèche. The dwarves had taught it to the humans. It was an easy game to play, and Cinder liked it. Paying attention to what cards were played helped, but it wasn't entirely necessary, definitely not so much that conversation couldn't be had.

Right now, though, Cinder had another interest in mind. His mandolin. Since coming to the Third Directorate, he'd rarely had time to play. Every day, there was so much to do—breathing exercises as taught by Master Absin, an hour of extra practice on his sword forms, and then his regular coursework. He was proud of how well he was doing. He was keeping up with all of it.

He grimaced a moment later. He was keeping up with everything but equitation. There, he was falling behind. The cursed white stallion. The horse barely let him ride, and they were rapidly losing ground to everyone else. The stupid animal liked to play too much. Or maybe he was just stubborn. Or stupid. Or stupidly stubborn or vice versa. Whatever the reason, if the horse didn't pick up the pace soon—

Cinder cut off any thoughts of his discontentment with the stallion. He could worry about the horse some other time. Tonight, he wanted to play music. So far, he'd pushed himself hard at the Directorate, and he deserved an evening off. It would be tonight, a relaxing evening of music.

First, the mandolin needed tuning. He tightened a key, bringing a flat string closer to the note it was meant to hold. He smiled as he worked, remembering a time when a string had snapped in the midst of playing at the Lonely Donkey. He and Coral had been busking, and the hard twang had rung out, ruining her lovely soaring note. She'd laughed with him over the matter.

Cinder sighed. He missed playing with Coral, and guilt arose at how little he thought of her these days. Perhaps it was all the work he was expected to complete. He liked to think—hoped, in fact—that was the reason.

"Does Hotgate actually know how to play that thing?" Sriovey asked the room at large.

Cinder glanced at the dwarf.

"He knows how to play," Bones answered.

"Because right now it sounds right awful."

"He's got to get it in tune," Bones said.

"Does he know any good work songs?" Sriovey persisted. "I don't want none of those stupid human songs about long lost love and such. I want something with a kick to it."

"Maybe you could let me tune the mandolin instead of whining so much," Cinder said.

"Yeah," Bones said to Sriovey. "Maybe you should dig into a large pile of shut the hell up."

Sriovey laughed. "You dumbass."

Cinder smiled. During their initial few weeks, Sriovey had been at odds with every human in the Firster class. He'd mellowed over time, going so far as to form friendships with those for whom he'd initially felt nothing but apparent contempt. Then again, Cinder wasn't sure what Sriovey had actually felt toward humans when they'd first met. The dwarf had mellowed too easily, and Cinder wondered if some of Sriovey's irritability had been some kind of ruse.

Nathaz wandered over to Cinder's side just then. "You torturing a fucking cat over there?" he asked.

Cinder didn't think Nathaz could say a sentence without cursing, but he didn't comment on his observation. Instead, he kept his head bent over his instrument. "Is every dwarf this impatient or only the ugly ones?"

Nathaz grinned. "There's no such thing as a handsome dwarf. Haven't you realized that by now?" For a wonder, he didn't curse.

Cinder smiled. "Yes. I guess I'm starting to figure that out." After a few more minutes of work, he had the mandolin in tune and gave it an experimental strum, pleased by the notes it produced.

"Is it ready?" Sriovey asked.

"It's ready."

Sriovey clapped his hands and addressed the room. "Everyone, listen up," he shouted. The room quieted. "Our wise and illustrious leader, Hotgate—"

"When did Cinder become our leader?" Ishmay asked.

Cinder wondered the same thing.

"When I said he was," Sriovey growled. "My vote's the only one which counts. Now shut up while Hotgate graces us with a song."

While waiting for him to begin, the Firsters jeered, laughed, and clapped. Some gave mocking opinions about Cinder's ability to play the mandolin, and he shook his head at their jesting ridicule. These were some of the pre-eminent warriors of their various nations, but in the end, they were also young men, and young men the world over liked nothing better than to tease their friends.

There was only one way to get the Firsters to settle down. Cinder loudly strummed the mandolin, all open strings. The loud notes penetrated the room, and the Firsters quieted.

Now he could play.

Cinder stretched his fingers, knuckles cracking, and began a song he had learned during his time in Swift Sword. He worked the strings of the mandolin hard, trying to capture the sound and energy of the tune. With the lyrics, the song told the story of a hearty band of warriors from glaciers in the north. They traveled on longships from a place of harsh winds, journeying toward new lands, intent on conquering. The song had a pounding, driving sound, especially when percussion was added, but even on just the mandolin, some of the song's energy must have come through.

When he finished, the prior jeering was replaced by an eruption of applause.

"Play another," Ishmay called.

"Are you done with your history paper?" Cinder asked.

Ishmay scowled.

"I thought so," Cinder said. "I'll still play, but you need to get your work done."

Ishmay grumbled. "Yes, illustrious leader." Despite his sarcastic tone, he went back to work.

Cinder played another song. It was something he'd found in the library, a song about Shokan and his legendary home of Ashoka.

"What was that?" Sriovey asked after he finished.

Cinder explained.

Sriovey's face grew melancholy. "My people believe that we'll only remember peace when Shokan remakes us."

Cinder had never heard that before. He waited in silence for the dwarf to say more.

"It's from the *Crèche Prani*. It's our most deeply held and revered religious text, but some fools think of it as nothing more than a historical document. It claims the dwarves will regain what we lost when we set aside the sword and take up the hammer."

Bones spoke. "But dwarves already fight with hammers."

"I know," Sriovey said. "It doesn't always make sense. Religious texts are like that."

"Dwarves fight with war hammers," Cinder said, "but there's another kind of hammer. It's the kind used in the forge."

"It still makes no sense," Sriovey grumbled.

Cinder agreed, but nevertheless, he still made a mental note to read the *Crèche Prani*.

The next song he played was about riding through a desert, his only companion a nameless horse. The tune reminded him of the stallion, and he made another mental note, this one to figure out how to tame the white. Either that or move on to a different horse. He couldn't keep on wasting time with the obstinate beast.

The resplendent weather which had started last week persisted, but the morning was still chilly. Cinder's ears had gone numb, his nose ran, and his breath steamed as he stood inside the white stallion's stall. The familiar scent of horse, hay, and droppings clogged the air. The stable hummed with the activity of young elves taking care of their charges. Otherwise, it was relatively quiet. The other students in Cinder's class were already outside, mounted and gathered in a nearby paddock, taking instruction.

Meanwhile, Cinder was still inside with the white.

He had yet to name the beast. Maybe he should call him 'Pest' or 'Useless'. The white shuffled about and chose that moment to swish his tail in Cinder's face. A playful light gleamed in the stallion's eyes; one Cinder recognized.

Oh, no you don't.

Cinder gripped the animal's halter, forcing the stallion to meet his gaze. He had to get the beast to understand what he needed and playing around wouldn't do. Not for either of them. Not today when Cinder was expected to have the white saddled and ready for a ride.

It was a task about which he had grave doubts. The stallion didn't like to be ridden, only rarely allowing Cinder to sit astride him during a slow walk through the training paddock.

They were falling far behind the others, who had hours of experience in the saddle by now. Some were even learning to shoot a bow while astride a horse. A few had even gone so far as to take part in planned maneuvers, the work of cavalry units.

Cinder, on the other hand, had learned none of these skills. It was an unacceptable circumstance for both him and the white.

It had to change. Master Halin was growing impatient. Either Cinder rode the white regularly, or he would have to take another horse, and the stallion would go to stud, permanently locked away in a small pasture and the stables. The horse would never again have a chance to run like the wind.

Cinder tried to get the stallion to understand the serious nature of their situation.

The white snorted in his face, flickering saliva on Cinder's chin.

Cinder grimaced. *Stupid horse.* "We have to show we can work as a team." He again forced the stallion to meet his gaze. "Do you understand what I'm saying?"

Cinder rolled his eyes at his foolish question. Of course, the white couldn't understand him. He was nothing more than a horse. It didn't matter that Cinder had imagined hearing the stallion's thoughts on their first meeting. Ever since then, he had yet to understand anything intelligible from the animal, and the white clearly didn't recognize anything Cinder wanted from him. The horse remained resolutely dumb, mute, and obstinate.

It wasn't to say that Cinder couldn't decipher some of the stallion's intentions. He could, but most of them seemed to center on playing or trying to bite him.

As if in demonstration, the horse bent low, and Cinder shoved aside the stallion's snout. The horse's teeth closed on empty air. *Idiot animal.* The white snorted in what Cinder recognized was his form of laughter.

Cinder couldn't help it. He chuckled in reply.

The white's actions were never malicious, but there was a time to play and a time to work. Right now, they had to work.

Maybe fear might motivate where logic and appeal hadn't. Cinder recaptured the stallion's head. "They might geld you. Do you know what that means?"

The stallion nudged Cinder in the chest, offering what sounded like a doubtful snort.

"They will," Cinder said. "Either that or you'll go to stud."

A happy wicker.

Cinder rolled his eyes. "You'll be kept in your stall all the time. You'll only be allowed out to breed or when you need grass. A small pasture will be the limits of your world."

The stallion snorted again, this time in agitation. Thoughts seemed to whirl in his rolling eyes. He settled down after a few seconds, and a regal expression took hold on his long face. *I will allow you to ride,* he seemed to say.

Cinder stared at the white. Could he trust the beast? The stallion jutted its chin at the saddle hanging over the stall door and pawed at the floor.

Well then. . . maybe he did understand.

Cinder fetched the saddle, and with mild trepidation, he laid it and a blanket across the stallion's back. The horse remained still, and Cinder tightened the cinch and quickly got the reins in place.

Minutes later, everything was finished. The white was saddled and ready to go. Cinder led the stallion from the stable and into the paddock. The horse's heavy hoofbeats clunked against the hard dirt floor.

They exited the stable and entered the paddock where Master Halin was waiting for him.

The master sat astride a gelding, and his brow lifted in astonishment when Cinder led the stallion outside. "Devesh take me, but I never thought you'd get that rakshasa saddled so quickly." The master's eyes narrowed. "Think you can mount him?"

Cinder eyed the stallion, who stared back at him with equanimity. *Can I?*

The stallion hoofed the ground.

Cinder wanted to take that as a 'yes', but he didn't trust the white, especially since he'd never before acted so tame. Cinder took a deep breath. *Better to find out now than later.*

He got a foot in one stirrup and vaulted into the saddle. The stallion snorted once when he landed, but otherwise remained still and calm.

Cinder's heart unclenched slightly. "Good boy." He stroked the stallion's neck and withers.

Fastness, a voice might have whispered in his mind.

Cinder started. Had he really heard the voice? Maybe he had. Two times couldn't be a coincidence, could it? *Fastness. The stallion's name.* Then again, Cinder knew his mind wasn't exactly normal. No memories of his past and all. So, maybe it *was* just his imagination, but it also didn't matter. Fastness was a good name for the stallion.

Master Halin viewed them with surprised suspicion. "What did you do to him? That devil of a horse has never been so gentle."

"He and I had a talk," Cinder said, continuing to stroke the white's neck and withers. He ran his fingers through the stallion's long mane and made a note to trim it. "His name is Fastness."

Master Halin grunted. "Fastness. It suits him." He got his gelding turned around. "Follow me. I'll have you and Fastness working out in one of the training paddocks. You'll learn how to ride and maybe train your pet rakshasa in how to be a proper warhorse."

Cinder patted Fastness' neck. "Learn quickly and we get to run. You want that?"

Fastness neighed, trotting after Master Halin.

More weeks passed in a blur, and Cinder and Fastness continued their training. Their progress had initially been slow. They both had so much to learn, and none of it came easy, but most of it was because the stallion was willful. Fastness always wanted to do things his way and in his time. It had taken a lot of patience for Cinder to get the horse going in the right direction, but once he did, they started making up some of the lost ground.

Of course, Cinder felt like he always had ground to make up. So many things to do and not enough hours to do them. Riding, archery, studying, the sword. Not to mention the breathing exercises. In the months since Master Absin had taught humans how to breathe in order to conduct their *lorethasra* and cycle their *prana*, Cinder had done so every night without fail. And every night without fail, he had failed. He couldn't conduct *lorethasra*, was nowhere close to learning how, and the inability frustrated him.

Why couldn't humans touch their lorethasra? In many ways, it was the question that drove him onward.

Such a disability hadn't always been the case. There had been ancient human nations existing prior to the *NusraelShev*. They were said to be the most powerful political entities of their era, a time in which some scholars claimed there were no such things as imperial sithes or crèches. Only humans dominating a world at peace.

Everything changed with the rise of Shet, the ancient god who destroyed Shokan, Sira, and his original world, and if not for the Mythaspuris, he would have destroyed this world, too.

So what had happened? In their daily sparring with Master Absin, Cinder had witnessed what the dwarves could do, and what humans couldn't. He wanted to know why. What curse caused such a lacking in his species?

"Are you going to the library?" Jozep asked Cinder, breaking into his thoughts. The dwarf held open the front door to Krathe House, heading in while Cinder was heading out.

Autumn's coolness carried inside: the sharp air, crisp like a tart pear, and the smoky fragrance of wood fires in a chimney. The lovely weather starting a few weeks ago was gone, but winter's icy breath had yet to carry down from the surrounding peaks. The *diptha* globes were turned down for the night, and the foyer held a restful quiet. Every now and again, the silence was disturbed by a raised voice from one of the upper floors.

"What do you read there?" Jozep asked.

Cinder paused, taking in the dwarf's confused innocence, and couldn't help but smile. Though Jozep was his elder by eight years, he always struck Cinder as being younger. Only during their sparring matches did Jozep's intensity shine forth. Otherwise, he had a charming naïveté to him, a light-hearted silliness that left everyone smiling.

"Weren't you coming from the library yourself?" Cinder asked.

Jozep bristled, but in him it was as if a young boy was caught doing something naughty. "No."

Cinder kept a smile off his face. The dwarf likely *was* coming from the library where he'd probably been holed up in a cubby, reading a romance novel. It was an enjoyment the other Firsters might have mocked but didn't, since all of them felt protective toward Jozep.

Cinder didn't press the dwarf. "I like to go to the library and do research on Shokan," he said in answer to Jozep's earlier question. He didn't want to fully explain his interests in the ancient human warrior, though. He had bonded with the dwarves, become friends with them, but who knew how they would react to his line of research. Some might support him, but more likely he'd face sarcasm, ridicule, or worse, knowing condescension. *"Of course you can uncover the truth about your species that no one has been able to learn in millennia.*" Cinder thought it best to keep his research private.

"Shokan?" Jozep said. He stepped inside, letting the front door close. "Did you know many of our wisest dwarves think he was the creator of our kind?"

Cinder's interest perked. He knew Shokan was important to the dwarves, but this was a story he hadn't yet come across.

"We don't speak of it much," Jozep continued. "We don't like to be reminded that humans might have come first. Your kind might have created mine. All the woven maybe." He theatrically pressed a shushing finger to his lips, eyes shining with humor. "It's a secret. Don't tell anyone."

Cinder smiled. "I promise to keep quiet, but is it true?" He'd never heard about such a relationship between woven and humans.

"I don't know," Jozep said with a shrug. "But it's why we honor humans. Because of Shokan. He was a human, and many of us think he created us. It's why on Tympany, I pray to Devesh and make sure to honor Shokan."

"Tympany?"

"It's the first evening of the first day of every month. It's when we pray for deliverance. Dwarves, I mean. It's a private matter. At home it ends with a long supper served with azalea-flavored water."

"And you're sure it's the same Shokan from history?" Cinder asked, not masking the doubt in his voice. It sounded too unlikely. Shokan—if he had ever existed—was said to have lived ages prior to the *NusraelShev*, and that great war had taken place three millennia ago. "Who kept those records?"

"We did," Jozep said. "Or at least our wisdoms did. My mother is one. She says her sister wisdoms didn't write the stories down, though. It's an oral tradition."

With every statement Jozep made, more questions arose in Cinder's mind. "Sister wisdoms? Are they all women? And what are they exactly?"

Again, Jozep theatrically placed a shushing finger to his mouth.

"That's another secret. I'll tell you some other time. If Sriovey says I can. Enjoy your reading." He went to the stairs, ascending to the Firster quarters.

Cinder watched him go, feeling like he'd learned so many new things since coming to the Third Directorate, and yet somehow remaining ignorant.

After his brief talk with Jozep, Cinder hustled across the Quad to the library. He blew on his fingers the entire way, trying to keep them warm. The night was colder than he expected with the last of autumn's warmth likely soon to break down into winter's ill chill, but thankfully, it was a short jaunt from Krathe House to Firemirror Hall and the library. He wondered if he'd actually learn anything of use this time.

Thus far, his research hadn't yielded anything of benefit, although it did confirm what he'd long suspected: humans knew very little about *lorethasra*. Most of what had been explained to him during his time in Rakesh had been either incomplete or full of falsity.

Meanwhile, every book and tome he inspected at the Directorate confirmed what seemed a law of nature: only the woven possessed the ability to conduct *lorethasra*. Only they could use it and develop abilities forever denied humans. For instance, when the wielder conducted it upon themselves, they could alter their actual essence. They could make themselves faster and stronger. In other circumstances, *lorethasra* could be connected to the world at large, and thereby create far more powerful and widespread weaves. Every woven had their own particular skills.

The explanations of how they managed this spawned dozens of questions. Why were elves, dwarves, trolls, and holders called woven? And what was *aether*, the substance to which *lorethasra* was sometimes linked? From what Cinder ascertained, it was apparently an invisible substance permeating the world, traveling along phantom underground rivers, a force felt rather than seen. However, some texts described places of power, lakes filled with what appeared to be the clearest water but was, in fact, poisonous and burned like acid.

Cinder often considered these questions.

His reveries ended when he reached the library. He halted in the entryway, soothed by the scent of old paper and the quiet hum of muffled conversation. A number of students sat at desks, reading under the bright lights of the hanging *diptha* chandeliers. It wasn't the sights, sounds, and scents alone that caused him to pause, though. It was the sight of so much knowledge gathered in one place. His shoulders involuntarily hunched. He knew so very little of the world.

A cleared throat broke into his ruminations. "What can I do for you?" asked Master Molni Cirnovain, the head librarian, smiling in welcome. Master Molni was many centuries old, his hair white, his posture stooped, and his mien wrinkled.

It still struck Cinder as odd to see an elf with wrinkles. He went to the front desk where Master Molni was situated in his typical location.

Cinder had gotten to know the old elf as a result of his frequent visits to the library, and he smiled in return. "You know me," he answered, approaching Master Molni. "Same as always."

The old master chuckled. "Why am I not surprised? You and *lorethasra.*"

"I found a text the other day," Cinder said. "It suggested that there was a time when the use of *lorethasra* was called *Asra*, the Beautiful Craft in *Shevasra*. It also said the finest practitioners of the beautiful craft could condense their *lorethasra*. Have you heard of anything like that?"

Master Molni's brows furrowed, his dark eyes lost in thought. After several seconds, he shook his head. "*Asra* is a rarely used term these days. It's fallen out of favor. There are also references to *asrasins*, but they were all human. As for what you say about *lorethasra*, I've not heard of anyone condensing it, but it wouldn't surprise me if the rishis could manage it. They are the greatest masters of *lorethasra*."

"Even though they're human?"

Master Molni smirked. "So they like the world at large to believe."

His wise eyes crinkled in humor. "It isn't true. The ancient rishis bred with elves or some other humanoid woven in times past. It was the only way for them to access their *lorethasra*."

Cinder's mouth gaped in shock. "Really?"

"Really."

Cinder shook his head, still shocked. "What a bunch of hypocrites. Claiming to be human descendants of the Mythaspuris and their greatness, but really descendants of some unknown woven. Why do they lie?"

Master Molni shrugged. "Because they're liars and it's what liars do. They lie about their power and intent. Is it really so surprising that they lie about their origins?"

Cinder supposed not, but the information was still disappointing. "What about cycling *prana*? Why do it?"

"That's a complex answer." Master Molni harrumphed. "I'm not surprised you haven't read about it in all your studies. Left untended, *lorethasra* tends to become polluted. Therefore, it needs to be cleansed both by breathing and by a beating heart. And once cleansed, it is usable. It is sent through a Chakra where all aspects of it are purified and strengthened and sent coursing through one's *nadis*. Or if a Chakra is not open, directly into one's *nadis*. Those in such a state are required to focus upon their *lorethasra* and attach corresponding weaves of Fire, Air, Water, and Earth to *aether*. That is what it means to cycle *prana*." Master Molni shifted in his chair, seemingly pleased and embarrassed at the same time. "Pardon my ramblings, but I have devoted a number of decades studying *lorethasra*."

"I see." And Cinder did. He had spent hours and hours reading various books throughout the library, but maybe he would have been better served by simply talking to Master Molni. He said as much.

"Perhaps," Master Molni said, "but you also needed a certain fund of knowledge in order to ask useful questions. Until then, you needed to do your own research. Learn what you could. Only now do you know what you don't know."

Cinder smiled. "And now I know enough to explore my ignorance?"

"Exactly." Master Molni wore an answering grin. It softened his seamed face, making him appear youthful.

Not for the first time did Cinder wonder about the master librarian's age. How many centuries had he actually seen? He didn't think it proper to ask, though. It would probably break some kind of elven taboo. Instead, he continued with his original line of questioning. "Why can't humans touch our *lorethasra*?"

Master Molni's mien grew thoughtful, his gaze distant. "It wasn't always so. The histories you've read have obviously told you that." He tapped his chin. "Something occurred after the Mythaspuris defeated Shet. Until then—if the records are to be believed—it is clear that humans wielded *lorethasra* in ways we can only imagine."

The master librarian's explanation coincided with what Cinder had thus far learned. Humans had once wielded powers vastly greater than those utilized by today's woven. Then had arisen Shet. To counter his power, the Mythaspuris had arrived from somewhere else, and the *NusraelShev* had started. The long decades or centuries of conflict had led to Shet's defeat and the sharp, hard fall of humanity. The war's end also coincided with the ascension of the elves and other woven.

Master Molni shifted in his chair, discomfited for some reason. "Most of my people think those kinds of stories to be fables. They don't believe them. In their eyes, humans have always been our lessers."

"They would mock you for what you're saying?" Cinder guessed.

The elven master smiled. "Let's not tell them and find out."

Cinder grinned in reply. "Were they linked?"

"Were what linked?" Master Molni asked, and Cinder realized he'd spoken aloud.

"The end of the *NusraelShev*, the rise of the elves and other woven, and the fall of humanity?"

Master Molni shrugged. "It's possible. It's certainly a logical explanation. Something was done to humanity, likely by your own ancient forebears, possibly by the Mythaspuris themselves." He shook his head. "In all my decades and centuries of searching, I've yet to discover what it was. There are no records from that time to tell us."

Cinder exhaled in frustration. "And you know of no place to search."

Master Molni didn't immediately answer. "There is one location where you may learn the answer you seek." He held up a cautionary hand. "I urge you to never visit that wretched place. It is the last home of the Mythaspuris. Mahadev." He said the name like a curse. "Should you dismiss my advice, you will find none but ghosts and fiends haunting the city's ruins. Anyone who enters that blighted place can never leave. It is a tomb for the dead. Leave it to them."

Cinder glanced to the side when Sriovey flopped onto the sofa next to him.

"Jozep said you wanted to learn more about our culture," the dwarven leader said.

It was late in the evening, and Krathe House was quiet, including the Firster quarters. Everyone else in Cinder's class had retired to their rooms, either tucked in for the night or studying on their own. The common room was darkened, the *diptha* bulbs turned low and the fire banked. It still popped occasionally, but otherwise the coals glowed red under a mound of ashes.

Cinder had only returned to the dorms a few minutes ago from his time spent in the library. Since his discussion a few days ago with Master Molni about Mahadev, he'd read everything he could about the mythical city of the Mythaspuris.

So far, he'd discovered very little in the way of useful information. It was as the old master librarian had said. Only the dead called Mahadev home and any who dared disturb their restless slumber were never heard from again. There was even an account of the Tenth Tiaxis from Mede's old empire of Shang Mendi entering the city. The Lost Tiaxis was what it was called. It had been in pursuit of a large horde of zahhacks, which sought to hide amongst Mahadev's endless fogs. Both forces were forever lost to time, neither emerging from the dead city.

Cinder also recollected his discussion with Jozep from several days past about wisdoms in dwarven society. The young dwarf had said he wasn't allowed to speak about it. Only Sriovey could.

"That's right," Cinder said to Sriovey's comment. "Will you tell me about your people?"

"It depends on what you want to know," Sriovey said, his manner neutral, neither willing nor unwilling.

"Jozep mentioned some people called wisdoms. There isn't a lot about them. What do they do?"

"Wisdoms are our wise ones, the ones who keep our history. They know truths the rest of us have forgotten." His demeanor firmed. "They are highly respected."

It was not much more than what Jozep had told him and what Cinder had gleaned from his readings. "Jozep made it sound like the wisdoms are all women. Is that true?" Which was incongruous since men led the dwarven crèches; not the women. As a result, Cinder couldn't figure out the status of the wisdoms.

Sriovey's mouth twitched in a fleeting expression of annoyance. "Jozep shouldn't have told you that."

"He didn't," Cinder said, not wanting Jozep to get in any trouble. "I guessed at it. Don't blame him because I'm—"

"Too curious for your own good?" Sriovey's demeanor transitioned from annoyed to sour.

Something about wisdoms clearly made Sriovey touchy, and Cinder didn't think it wise to push the matter. "We don't have to talk about dwarven culture anymore."

Sriovey waved aside his words. "It's fine, but instead of answering all your questions, I'll tell you what I'm allowed." He cleared his throat. "Our people are a contentious bunch. I think everyone knows that. We have to be if we want to survive the harsh mountains and the harsher zahhacks, especially the goblins, ghouls, and necrosed." He stared into the embers. "Some think we're *too* contentious."

His tone didn't indicate whether he shared that opinion.

"The wisdoms say we weren't always so," Sriovey continued. "They say we once lived in small villages, deep in the heart of the mountains, protected and at peace." He snorted in disbelief, as if the notion was utterly ridiculous.

Cinder kept silent, letting Sriovey talk without interruption.

"We no longer live in small villages," Sriovey said, "but we still live in the heart of the mountains, in powerful fastnesses. Roads and great bridges connect our far-flung keeps. We have forged powerful nations. We are feared and respected." His mouth pursed. "But it's never enough. Our warlords strive for ever more power and territory." Sriovey stared once more at the embers, his voice a whisper. "It is never enough."

Cinder had never expected the dwarven leader to tell him so much about his people. Nor had he expected the antipathy Sriovey apparently felt about how his people lived their lives. A propensity for violence and war—those were the issues, the undercurrents Sriovey didn't mention, but which clearly caused him pain.

It was a sore topic, and Cinder carefully edged his way around it. "What happened to your people?" he asked. "You used to live in small, peaceful villages."

Sriovey laughed bitterly. "Shet happened. The zahhacks happened. The world happened. Who knows? If you haven't noticed, Seminal is not a place for the faint of heart. This world requires men willing to commit ugly acts."

Cinder accepted Sriovey's statements without disagreement. They were obvious. "Life on Seminal forced the dwarves to give up their peaceful ways?"

"Yes, and according to our wisdoms, it wasn't easy. It isn't easy. At least for most of us." He ended in a mutter. "For some, it's become too easy to find the pulse of anger."

Cinder eyed Sriovey in surprise. To the rest of the world a dwarf was considered the epitome of troublesome and easily angered. "What are you saying? That you have to work to get angry?"

"You didn't know? Most of the time we only pretend to be angry. It keeps other folk from bothering us too much."

Cinder reasoned his way through what Sriovey had said. He parsed everything he knew, and logic led him to a single conclusion. "You were once a peaceful people. Events conspired to force you to violence, to find a means to protect yourself. Your wisdoms maintain the notions of your mythic past—"

"It's no myth."

Cinder dipped his head at the correction. "And in your holy text, the *Crèche Prani*, there is a reference to '*reclaiming that which was lost.*' It's talking about peace, isn't it?"

Sriovey nodded. "I take it you read our prophecy."

"I did," Cinder said. "I read all the holy texts. I'm still unclear on one matter in the *Crèche Prani*. Dwarves want to reclaim the peace and protection they once enjoyed. Who protected you before all this? Shokan?"

"You'll laugh, but yes, and our wisdoms say he had help. They were called magavanes."

"Magavanes?"

Sriovey slapped the sofa's armrest. "Magavanes were men and women. Humans. *Asrasins.* You'll have to learn about them on your own. Go read about them in the library. Consider it penance for getting me to speak so openly about my people." He peered at Cinder, uncertainty on his features. "Don't tell anyone what I said. I told you more than I should have."

"As far as I'm concerned, you didn't say anything." Cinder made a locking motion around his mouth.

Sriovey stood with a grunt. "A man who knows how to keep a secret. I knew there was a reason I liked you."

23

The elven masters at the Third Directorate generally trained against one another in the morning, a few hours after breakfast when the Firsters had Tactics and Strategy. Cinder had never witnessed their sparring, and he itched to know how good they really were. What abilities did conducting *lorethasra* grant them? He already knew it gifted them speed and strength, but what other powers did they gain from it? The dwarves could use *lorethasra* to control terrain, shake the earth, open small holes in the ground, that sort of thing, but what about the elves?

A month following his conversation with Sriovey, the Firsters had the day off, and Cinder decided to go to the Cauldron and find out for himself just how good elven masters truly were. There, he found roughly twenty elves stretching and limbering up.

The sun hung high overhead in a blue sky. Clouds puffed, and Cinder's breath plumed with every exhalation in the early winter morning air. A soft breeze flitted fingers through his hair. It also carried the lingering aroma of the grilled meat the staff was preparing for lunch. The delicious scent wafted from the kitchen all the way to the field. Cinder inhaled in appreciation, stomach rumbling although he'd eaten breakfast only a few hours ago.

He observed those gathered at the Cauldron. In addition to the students and instructors, there were members of the Yaksha Army who spent time at the academy for specialized tutoring. Most were already good warriors, but they sought to achieve greatness. In the Directorate, they could find the means to attain their goals. Some even pursued the rarified rank of *Sai,* an ancient honorific from the time of Shokan. From what Cinder had read, only a dozen elves currently held that title.

Cinder kept to himself while observing the elves, hanging in the background. He didn't want to get in anyone's way. He noticed most of the elves currently at the Cauldron bore an *insufi* sword, a matte-black weapon that was highly prized. Harder and more limber than steel, the blades maintained their edge without sharpening and were nearly indestructible.

Insufi swords were only granted to the best of warriors. Their forging took years, requiring a special grass—*sathana* grass—which only grew in Apsara Sithe, in a single shadowed river valley. In its natural state, the tough vegetation grew to over six feet in height and was capped by a brilliant orange, feathery tassel.

After harvesting, a weaver took stalks of *sathana,* braided them tightly, and infused them with *aether.* From there, the mass of grass formed a soft, spongy bar, a process that took months. At that point, a bladesmith took over. More months of gentle baking was required to extrude every last drop of water from the *sathana* bar.

Then came the shaping, a slow progression of heating, gentle hammering, folding, and refolding, over and over again. It was another months long task until, eventually, the bar was ready for its final shaping, which was followed by a careful glazing with a thin, translucent layer of black ink. A last heating in a kiln, and the blade emerged with a matte-black finish oozing menace.

Cinder snapped out of his reveries.

The elves were ready, torsos protected by leather gambesons and a few bore shields. Over their heads, they strapped on large, open-faced, leather helmets. *Governors.* In this case, rather than offering simple protection, their helmets reduced the amount of *lorethasra* each elf could conduct, limiting them to non-lethal attacks. The warriors further buckled straps under their chins and snapped large flaps to protect the front of their necks. In all ways, they were kitted out like any typical Firster.

The elves then broke into pairs and entered the training circles.

Cinder found his head snapping from one sparring session to another. The elves . . . They moved swift as the wind, fluid as water, graceful with their parries, thrusts, and slashes. Some jumped ten feet or more in the air, vaulting over their opponents. They even vanished momentarily from view, a strange kind of camouflage.

How does anyone defeat such power? Cinder couldn't reason it out. A human army facing a force of elves would surely be destroyed en masse. And yet history indicated Mede was victorious over every foe he faced, destroying them all.

How did he do it?

Cinder scowled, ridding himself of the distracting thoughts. He'd come here to watch the elves, to learn what he could of their capabilities.

He focused on Master Absin and the elf against whom he sparred, Lisandre Coushinre, Riyne's older brother and already a warrior of repute. If Cinder didn't already know of Lisandre, the elf's tall, powerful build would have readily declared his noble status. His long, black hair was pulled into a ponytail, displaying his peaked ears.

In Cinder's time at the Third Directorate, he'd discovered the elves had an interesting assessment of beauty. It related to the height of their ears. The taller the ears, the lovelier or more handsome was considered the elf. Unsurprisingly, the nobles tended to have taller ears than the peasants, and Lisandre was certainly handsome.

Lisandre flowed when he moved, smooth as a dancer. He was to the other elven warriors as they were to Cinder.

He and Master Absin circled one another for a few seconds, careful and cautious. They eventually came together in halting steps. Master

Absin sent a questing slash. Lisandre blocked. They circled one another. Lisandre thrust, defended, and strangely, he held a blue whip, like a cord of water, coiled around his off arm. From where Cinder sat, he swore the whip sounded like waves crashing against the shore. A flick of Lisandre's wrist, and the whip snapped out, fast as thought and cracking like lightning.

Master Absin made a motion, and the whip disintegrated into a fog.

Lisandre charged. The fog dispersed around him. He was on Master Absin as swiftly as the whip he'd momentarily wielded. The two engaged. Cinder could tell Master Absin was fighting off his back foot. The older elf parried, his face tight with concentration. He slid to his right, circling, trying to gain distance. Lisandre didn't allow it. He pushed and pressed Master Absin toward the edge of the training ring.

The earth beneath Lisandre shook, and he disengaged. Now it was Master Absin who charged. Despite his age, he moved every bit as swiftly as the younger warrior. Again, they traded blows, and as before Lisandre gained the upper hand.

Cinder's mouth gaped at their speed. He couldn't keep up with their movements. He only knew of their contact based on the cracking of their shokes.

Master Absin disappeared. Lisandre leapt into the air, five feet straight up, trailing mist. The fog swirled toward the younger elf, the impression of a fast-moving object cutting through it. *Master Absin's shoke.*

Lisandre landed. A horizontal slash, and it was over. Master Absin re-appeared, clutching his side and grimacing in pain. He bowed to Lisandre, who bowed in return.

They spoke to one another, and Cinder's attention drifted to those others who were training. His initial impression of supreme speed and control was reiterated by the rest of the elves. He watched them use their shields like fans, redirecting blows rather than taking them straight on. Envy burned. The Firsters were still learning to use shields, and they were nowhere near as good as these elves.

And none of these elves were as good as Lisandre, who had finished his conversation with Master Absin.

The two resumed sparring.

Cinder continued to watch, and questions drifted in the back of his mind. About Lisandre, Master Absin, and the elves in general. Mostly about how impossible it seemed for a simple human warrior to reach elven heights of skill and abilities.

But he was determined to find a way. He had to. Humans were weak, and the powers of the world knew it. Zahhacks, *aether*-cursed, wraiths; they exploited that weakness.

After witnessing the elven sparring session, Cinder wandered back to Krathe House, his thoughts circling to what he'd seen. The elves . . . He couldn't get over their speed and strange ability to fade out of sight. Blending, they called it. It wasn't a perfect camouflage, but nevertheless, when properly utilized, it could be devastating. Then there was their control of the earth. Weaves or braids—terms to describe *loreth-asra* connected to the world at large—to trip an attacker. He had spoken to a few of the elves after their sparring session, and they referred to a similar control of fire, air, and water.

Cinder frowned. Taken as a whole—their skill, speed, and abilities—it was no wonder elves so readily mocked human warriors. His mind distracted, he wasn't paying attention to his surroundings and wandered toward the Quad, not noticing until too late the person moving to confront him.

Riyne.

Cinder cursed.

No one else was nearby. He and Riyne were alone on a brick-paved path near a far corner of Firemirror Hall. Twin rows of red maples lined both sides of the walkway. The trees provided shade as well as cover, hiding this part of the Quad from the surrounding buildings.

"I heard you wanted to see the elven masters train," Riyne said with a smirk. "Well, you've seen them. Maybe now you won't act so proud."

Cinder eased away from the elven noble, wanting to keep his distance. He forced himself to meet Riyne's eyes, although he subtly searched about for a weapon in case one was needed. "They are better warriors," Cinder allowed, "but they aren't my betters. In battle, all men are brothers."

"But some are the older, wiser brothers. Others the younger, weaker brothers, forever shadowed by the glory of their *better* elders."

Cinder knew he shouldn't push the elf. He wasn't good enough to hold his ground against Riyne, not after seeing what elves could really do. It would be best to hold his tongue.

But Cinder hated bullies and braggarts. He ignored the part of him advising quiet. "I saw your older brother at the Cauldron. Didn't he earn an *insufi* sword ten years after graduating from the Third Directorate? He's considered one of the geniuses of his generation. I've heard he might even achieve the title of *Sai*."

Riyne's jaw clenched. "How do you know about my family? Don't speak about them."

"I asked around," Cinder said. He egged Riyne, recognizing the foolishness even as he did it. "What does that say about you to be younger to someone so accomplished?" Riyne reddened. "It must mean you're weaker and will forever fall in his shadow."

Riyne burst forward.

Cinder found himself held aloft by the lapels. He gasped. He had barely registered Riyne's movement. The world whirled. Cinder realized Riyne had thrown him. An instant later he crashed into a tree and slumped to the ground. His back ached from where he'd struck the maple. He'd have a bruise there. Many bruises.

He groaned and made to rise.

His breath exploded out of his lungs. Riyne had kicked him in the chest.

"No one told you to stand up," Riyne growled. "Stay down."

Cinder would do no such thing. He glared at the elf. "Go frag yourself."

Another kick, this one to the gut. Cinder's stomach heaved. He tried not to vomit. Again, his stomach heaved. Cinder threw up his breakfast. More heaving. He vomited again. A final spit, and it was done. At least he managed not to get any of the mess on his clothes.

Cinder's stomach and chest hurt worse than his back. Once he was done throwing up, he glared at Riyne who smirked down at him. Didn't the fragging bastard know any other expressions?

"Take instruction from this," Riyne said, staring down his nose. "Remember this pain and humiliation. No one will care what I did to you because I'm an elf, a member of a noble house, and you're nothing but a dirty human. A dirty human lying in your dirty filth." He scowled in disgust. "Stay down there and don't ever think to challenge me again, not with thoughts, words or deeds. It will end badly for you, worse than this small lesson."

Cinder refused to remain on the ground while the elf towered over him. He made to stand, knowing another kick was coming, but this one came at normal speed. He blocked it with his forearms.

Riyne's crotch. Wide open, unprotected, and inches away. Cinder hammered a punch straight into the elf's groin.

Riyne collapsed with a high-pitched shriek.

Cinder levered himself upright. "I will take instruction from this," he told the elf, who turtled in apparent agony. "I'll remember the pain and humiliation. As will you."

Riyne gathered himself, rising to his feet, teeth clenched in pain. "This isn't over," he promised, his voice dire.

Cinder nodded. "I would expect nothing less." He turned his back on the elf. It was a gamble. He hoped the elf remained too injured to pursue him. If Riyne did come after him, there was no telling what kind of beating he'd try to deliver.

Thankfully, the elf didn't follow, and Cinder continued on his way. He headed toward Krathe House, maintaining an erect posture, head held high and shoulders square. All the way until he turned a corner and Riyne could no longer see him. Only then did he hunch over from the throbbing pain aching across his torso, back, stomach, and chest.

As he hobbled back to Krathe House, he realized that Riyne was right. This wasn't over. If the elf wasn't an enemy before, he was now. So be it. Bullies needed to be confronted, but until he could better protect himself, he would have to be careful. He'd have to watch out for Riyne. The elf would want revenge.

At the Cauldron, a group of figures practiced, their breaths pluming as they sparred against one another. Their shokes cracked a tympanic rhythm.

Cinder was one of the warriors. It had taken him several days to recover from his encounter with Riyne. Only then was he able to go full out again in his training. But during the entire time, he continued to train harder than anyone else, spending extra time with his breathing exercises and with the sword.

Such as now. He worked alone at the Cauldron, focused on his craft, dedicated to improving himself. At the moment, he practiced the very same sword forms taught to him by Faine, the journeyman at *Steel-Graced Adepts*. It felt like he'd learned them years ago, and by now, he could complete the movements in his sleep, the four steps—attack, parry, counter, defend. They were critical to maintaining good habits.

The scent of seared meat and fried vegetables from the recently completed supper lingered in the air, carrying on a vagrant breeze that mingled with the aromas of wood fires burning in hearths. No doubt, the crackling flames in fireplaces would provide warmth and a cheery light given the shortened days and cold nights. For now, the sun lingered a finger's-breadth above the horizon, its last brightness beaming across a darkening sky. Shadows pooled in the shallow hollows of the Cauldron, inky fingers grasping for the light. *Diptha* globes fought the darkness, providing large pools of illumination, but they couldn't banish the cold.

Cinder ignored the world around him. He didn't allow the cold to cause distraction. His focus remained inward, on his slow, deliberate motions. Every movement had to be precise. After a few minutes, his muscles loosened, and only then did he increase the pace. All the while he concentrated on his actions, retaining their precision. *Timing beats speed. Precision defeats power.*

More minutes passed. His speed increased. The exactness never faltered. He wouldn't allow it. His shoke blurred.

Cinder finished a complete set of movements in the space of a single breath and halted, finally satisfied. However, when he recalled the morning's sparring session, the pleasure faded. He'd gone against Rorian, and the mountain-apprentice had surprised him. Rorian had slipped in an attack. He'd hunched low when he should have parried and countered by launching in a leap and ending on a rising thrust.

Cinder had taken an aching blow to the abdomen, but the pain hurt less than the knowledge that his intuition had failed him. He'd never considered that Rorian could come at him in such a way. Leaving his feet? Madness.

Unfortunately, it hadn't been Cinder's only loss of the day. Later on, Bones had smashed him apart in a half-dozen different ways. So had Ishmay.

However, his lack of success against those two was not due to a faltering in his intuition but because of a simple lack of speed, coordination, and recovery. Cinder just wasn't fast enough or strong enough to face Bones and Ishmay. It wouldn't always be the case. He was closing the gap against those two with every passing week, having added both height and bulk during his time at the Third Directorate.

No. It was the loss to Rorian which burned in his craw. His intuition could still fail him, and warriors could surprise him. As Cinder reckoned matters, it meant he needed more training against a greater variety of opponents. Doing so should gain him an increased flexibility of expectation, an improved consideration of his options.

Hence, he was here tonight. He usually spent an hour every evening working on his forms, but from this point forward, he also hoped to spar against one of the elven masters. He'd fail against them. Of this, Cinder had no doubt, but mastery came from overcoming great failures rather than achieving mediocre success.

And Cinder intended on becoming a master. The desire to improve wasn't to simply be the best. It was an innate desire to succeed because it was necessary. As Sriovey had once told him, Seminal was not a place for the faint of heart. Plus, after his run-in with Riyne, Cinder had another reason to improve as rapidly as possible. He needed to find a means to bridge the gap between himself and the elf. *Humans are weak.* He remembered Riyne's statement.

However, Cinder didn't know if any of those here would be willing to grant him a match. After all, he wouldn't provide them much of a challenge. Cinder glanced around, wondering who to ask.

While doing so, he again reviewed his sparring session against Rorian. This time, he understood the counter required to defeat the mountain apprentice's gambit. He practiced it immediately, quickly realizing other, better options. *A diagonal, downward counter, a kick to the solar plexus, and a slash to the chest.*

He worked alone, determined to defeat Rorian's attempt next time.

Master Absin wandered over, interrupting his practice. "You're thinking on how to defeat Rorian."

Cinder completed his counter, delivering a slash to an imagined foe. Only then did he straighten and face his master. "How did you know?"

The old elf, white hair shining in a halo of light from the *diptha* bulbs, smiled, and his face crinkled in a web of wrinkles. The dim lighting did little to hide his weathered, leathery appearance. "I've taught the sword many decades longer than you've been alive. Your counter is ideal for Rorian's maneuver." His eyes slitted in consideration. "I'm guessing that's not the only reason you came here tonight."

Cinder smiled. There was no hiding his intentions from Master Absin. "No, it's not," he said. He hesitated then, unsure how to ask the question at the forefront of his thinking. *How does a human defeat an elf?* He had trouble believing Master Absin would tell him. Why would he? The master was himself an elf. He wouldn't be likely to divulge such information.

Then again, why else had Cinder come to the sparring session tonight? He opened his mouth, about to voice his question.

Master Absin spoke first. "You're wondering how to defeat a certain noble elf."

Cinder started.

Master Absin chuckled. "A truism the world over is that young men cannot keep a secret. They like to gossip, and gossip grows wings."

"Someone saw our fight?"

"Someone might have seen it, but it was Riyne who bragged about it. He claimed to have *taught a dirty human the meaning of humility*. Given how stiff you moved in the past few sessions, I'm guessing his disagreement was with you?"

Cinder nodded, scowling. Just what he needed. The elves laughing at him behind his back. Then again, he didn't require their good opinion, but it grew tiresome dealing with their derision. Besides, Cinder remembered Riyne crying in pain when he'd punched him. "Is he making this claim to everyone?"

"He is."

Cinder cursed under his breath, deliberating on his options. He needed more information before making any kind of decision. "What happens next?"

"Nothing," Master Absin said. "Riyne hasn't mentioned who he fought, and the person he claimed to have beaten hasn't come forward to contest his assertion."

"And if that person did come forward?"

"He could challenge Riyne. It would be a sparring match if he chose, or he could leave it to the administration to deal out the punishment." He said the last as if it was actually an option.

Cinder wanted to smirk. Hiding behind the administration would confirm every poor opinion most of the elves had of him. He'd brand himself a coward. No, he had to handle this on his own. He looked Master Absin in the eyes. "Can you teach me to defeat an elf?"

Master Absin hesitated. "It's possible you could learn how to do so, but highly unlikely. You'll have to suffer for your victory. You can't defeat us any other way. We're too fast and too strong. But pain is our greatest weakness, and your only hope."

Cinder's brow knitted in confusion. "I don't understand."

"Humans can tolerate pain far more easily than we can. We feel pain more deeply than you. Accept however much pain you can handle whenever you train. Maybe then you'll have a chance to administer it."

Cinder remembered the other night when he'd struck Riyne in the crotch, and the resultant high-pitched scream. The blow must have hurt, but Riyne's reaction had seemed extreme.

Accept a blow to give a blow. That's what it sounded like Master Absin was telling him. Cinder nodded to himself. Yes. He could do that.

He then recalled the heavy strikes Riyne had landed, kicks too swift for Cinder to even see, and his confidence faltered.

His determination, though, did not. "You'll help me, then?"

"I will," Master Absin said. "Just one thing. Take some time off and enjoy yourself. Life isn't all about work."

"Work is how we define our lives."

"And pleasure makes that life worth living. Take your next rest day off. Go see the city. I'll only train you if you do." Master Absin sounded unrelenting in his requirement.

Cinder exhaled heavily. He hated being told what to do. Worse, he hated having to take the time off to do something that sounded so frivolous. He had so much to accomplish first. Nevertheless, in the dimmest part of his thinking, he knew Master Absin was right. He needed to relax and enjoy himself. "Yes, sir."

24

A few days after his conversation with Master Absin, the Firsters had the day off and Cinder did as the elven weapons master suggested. He visited Certitude, the city nestled several miles west and down the valley from the academy. With him went Bones, Ishmay, Depth, and Sriovey.

Extending from the academy to the city was a sinuous, cobblestone road, the Whileaway Path. It was wide enough for two wagons to pass one another, and it followed the curves of various hills and hollows. In addition, the Pantheon Forest wrapped the Whileaway in an assortment of maple, oak, and chestnut. This time of year, with winter calling, the tree limbs were bare, the weather had turned cold, and a lingering fog quieted the land.

Cinder wore his Third Directorate uniform, a gray shirt under a blue coat, dark blue slacks, and black boots. A bronze pin—a stylized eagle clutching a sword—was pinned to his left breast, the academy's symbol. He was glad he'd decided to wear the jacket. The cold weather had never been his friend.

Cinder listened with half an ear as Bones and Depth got into an argument about whether one of the Yavana horses of the Devesth, the finest equines in the world, could outrun Aia, Shokan's mythical steed.

"It has to be the horses," Bones said. "You've seen how fast Cinder's white runs."

"Sure," Depth agreed, "but how do you know how fast Aia might have been? No one does."

"That's not the point. I read once that a Yavana stallion once made the Lessek Run in under twelve hours. There's no way any other land animal could do that."

Depth disagreed. "Aia could. She was supposed to be, I don't know, huge. The fastest creature ever."

Ishmay interjected. "Except for her brother. What was his name?"

"Shon," Cinder supplied. By now, he'd all-but memorized the stories of Shokan and Sira.

"Right. Shon." Ishmay said. "He was bigger and faster than Aia. Giant cats."

"Kesarins," Cinder corrected. "That was what they were called. Shokan and Sira rode them as steeds."

Sriovey nodded. "Both were twenty or twenty-five foot from their head to tip of their tail and a little over a thousand pounds." He barked laughter. "Could you imagine facing such a creature? I'd wet myself."

Bones scoffed. "That's impossible. No predator is that big."

"Well, look at this," a voice called out from behind. "A dwarf and four humans. There's a joke in there somewhere."

Cinder winced. He recognized the speaker. *Riyne.* The world's biggest pain in the ass. Cinder stuffed away his annoyance and put on a grin. Maybe a pretense of happiness would confuse the elf, throw him off his insults, and he'd move on. Or maybe it would annoy him. Either would be fine as far as Cinder was concerned.

"Riyne. What a pleasure to see you," Cinder said.

With Riyne was Estin, who eyed Cinder and his friends down his nose and through hooded eyes filled with contempt. "He seeks to be courteous," Estin said, addressing Riyne. He sighed theatrically. "I suppose this means you'll have to be courteous in return."

"He's only a human. I fail to see why we have to show him even the pretense of courtesy."

Sriovey spoke. "Because you are supposed to be civil beings, and civil beings behave civilly to one another. Or are noble elves unable to accept those who are different?"

Riyne continued to scowl. "Do not delude yourself." He indicated himself and Estin. "*We* are civil beings." He pointed to Cinder. "*He* is a human. It is the opposite of civilized."

Cinder didn't know why Riyne was so bigoted toward humans. How could he feel so strongly about an entire race? Especially one in which he clearly had limited direct knowledge. Riyne was from a noble house on Yaksha proper and there weren't many humans who lived on the island. The few who did were all in Revelant. Perhaps his lack of exposure to humans had something to do with his racism.

By this point, however, Cinder had given up trying to learn the reasons for Riyne's ongoing intolerance. It wasn't his job to explain civilized modes of behavior, not after what Riyne had done to him. Besides, even Anya had warned Riyne to curb his ways, and if royalty couldn't convince him to rethink his bigotry, he didn't know what would.

Cinder faced the white-haired elf, edging into Riyne's personal space. "You have a problem with my kind. You should settle that problem now before it gets you in trouble."

Riyne smirked. "Beating you would be child's work—"

"Who said anything about fighting?" Cinder harbored no delusions that he could defeat the elf in a fight. "You're a bully and a coward. I understand you elves have a word for that: *naaja*. You are honorless."

Riyne's dark eyes bulged. "How dare you! You cursed *ghrina*. *Naaja* is not a word to lightly throw around."

Cinder smiled in the face of the elf's anger. "And yet you haven't denied my claim." He flicked a glance to Sriovey. "My friend has been too kind to state it in so many words but consider what it means to be civil and offer no civility." Cinder quoted from *Forever Triumphant*, the religious book that guided elven society and morals. "*'Let not your heart grow cold to those who are different in views for in this you em-brace certitude, which is entirely* Devesh's *province.'"* When he had first read the words, they had reverberated within Cinder, ringing a truth he felt like he was re-learning.

Riyne's mouth opened and shut as he apparently struggled to come up with an adequate rejoinder. Estin viewed Cinder in narrow-eyed speculation.

"We'll see you in town." Cinder gestured to Bones, Ishmay, and the others in his group. "Let's go."

Ishmay snickered softly, but otherwise none of them said anything as they left Riyne and Estin standing seemingly rooted on the road to Certitude. Cinder smiled at the metaphor.

"That mouth of yours is going to get you in trouble one day," Ishmay said to Cinder.

"Isn't that what Sriovey's always saying?" Cinder asked.

"Plus, you think too much," Depth added. "Anyone ever tell you that?"

Cinder grinned. "Trouble I can handle. I'll just shove Sriovey in the way. He'll take care of it for all of us."

"Ugly enough to scare off a zahhack," Bones said.

Sriovey grinned. "I'd still be prettier than your sister."

"Hey! Sisters are off limits," Bones protested.

The rest of the walk into Certitude passed uneventfully. Cinder and the others never again caught sight of Estin and Riyne, who must have returned to the academy.

The curtain of clouds from earlier in the day moved on, allowing sunshine to burn off the afternoon fog. The road flattened as they approached the city, and Cinder had his first view of the place. In the distance, set upon a hill and overlooking Certitude, rose a building of gray stone and tall spires. *Duchess Cervine's palace.* It soared from amidst a large copse of evergreens, never overwhelming the landscape but melding with it.

Closer at hand, broad fallow fields surrounded a large number of low-lying homes and other buildings. They were slope-shouldered and huddled within a large grove of maple and oak. Much like the palace, the buildings served to highlight the trees rather than draw attention to themselves. The structures were constructed of brick, stacked-stone, or woven wood and had roofs thatched in grass, wildflowers, or a mix of the two. Narrow brick-lined paths wended amongst the homes, and a number of elves wandered about the curving roads.

Like Revelant, Certitude's health and beauty highlighted the poverty found in Swift Sword. Cinder reddened, ashamed of how poorly his people treated the less fortunate.

"The restaurant is over here," Bones said. He led the way to an unremarkable building, which appeared no different than the others. One wall consisted of a bank of windows, their lintels and frames green with moss. Smoke trickled from a single chimney, and laughter leaked past its curved, brick walls.

Cinder entered a white-washed room, bright with the sunshine beaming inside. Carved chandeliers sporting a plethora of *diptha* bulbs provided further light. Thick beams supported the ceiling. To the left, a fire burned cheerily in a hearth. Straight ahead stood a small bar and a door leading to what was likely the kitchen. A scattering of elegant tables provided seating. They were round and had legs carved into the shapes of fantastical creatures, such as unicorns, dragons, and griffins. A handful of elves were already present and seated in the restaurant.

One of them stood and met them at the entrance with a smile. "Hello, fellows. It's good seeing you again." He faced Cinder. "I'm Quire Shoal. And you are?"

"Cinder Shade."

"Welcome to the *Silent Reverie*, Cinder." He gestured to a table near his own. "Have a seat. Come. We have a wonderful chicken stew, if you're hungry."

Cinder and the others settled themselves at the indicated table.

"So, what do you do here?" Cinder asked.

"We drink," Bones answered.

"And listen to the gossip about the outside world," Depth said.

"And talk about a whole lot of nothing," Ishmay added.

"You basically waste time," Cinder said, grinning. "Sounds perfect." By now, he'd come to accept Master Absin's advice. He *did* need to take off more time. Without rest, he would eventually break.

They soon had bowls of chicken stew and tankards of ale in front of them. They ate and drank, discussing the training they'd undergone during the past week. Most of the talk centered on the spiderkin.

"We're supposed to get training against them soon," Ishmay said.

Depth grimaced. "I'm not looking forward to it. I hate spiders." He rubbed his arms. "Damn eight-legged monsters. Makes my skin crawl just thinking about them."

"I think everyone feels that way," Sriovey said, his voice dry. "Spiders and snakes. They both move unnatural like."

One of the elves seated alongside Quire, twisted about in his seat. "Afternoon gents. Name is Heloin. Speaking of unnatural, any of you hear about Genka Devesth?"

Cinder and the others hadn't. He was also surprised by the elf's willingness to talk to them, a quartet of humans and a dwarf. In this, he seemed more like the elves who worked at the Third Directorate. They didn't put on airs, either.

Heloin twisted about further, facing them full on. Despite his graceful movements, neat attire, and clean features, there was the sense of farmer about him. A steadiness to how he spoke and moved that relayed a relationship to the land. Plus, he lacked the elegant clothing worn by the more prosperous sort. His ears weren't as peaked, either.

Heloin cleared his throat. "Well, Genka is the ruler of Devesth, a small no-account kingdom in the Sunset Kingdoms. Only good thing to come out of the place is their horses. Anyway, until a few months ago, no one outside those parts even knew Genka's name. We didn't need to. He was from the back end of nowhere." The elf warmed up to his story, eyes glinting. "That's where we were wrong. Genka is a conqueror. He's already taken Parnesth, Barnesth, and Loseth and all the lands in between those benighted cities. Word is he's arrowing straight and true for Kalesth. He says he means to unite the Sunsetters."

Cinder didn't know much about the Sunset Kingdoms. He'd never had much need to read about them.

"He won't do it," Quire said in a voice of quiet assurance. "No one can unite those fractious folk."

"I agree," Sriovey said. "The Sunsetters may breed the world's finest horses, but those people are nothing but barbarians. They'll stay united just long enough to slit this Genka Devesth's throat and fall back to infighting by day's end."

"I don't know about that," Heloin disagreed. "He convinced Parnesth's ruler, Vel Parnesth, to fight at his side. Vel might be a barbarian, but he's no fool. He's got a reputation as a clever thinker."

"Then they'll slit *Vel's* throat, and then Genka will be done," Bones said. "Sriovey is right. The Sunsetters can't be ruled. They never have been."

"Yes, they have," Heloin said. "Mede conquered them. He ruled them, and they only fell apart when he died."

Sriovey rolled his eyes. "That was over two thousand years ago. And after Mede died, what did they do? They fell right back into barbarism."

"Don't the Sunsetters follow a version of the *Median Scryings*?" Quire asked.

The Median Scryings were said to have been transcribed by Mede, dictated directly from Devesh. Cinder had read it. Riner had convinced him to do so, but to him, the book provided a veneer of justification for savagery while offering contradictory advice on moral living. He seriously doubted Devesh would countenance what the *Scryings* allowed.

"They do," Heloin said, smiling wider in anticipation. "Now you know why Genka might be trouble."

"Why is that?" Cinder asked in confusion.

Heloin rubbed his hands. "Because the version of the *Scryings* followed in the Sunset say that Holy Mede will return, and the first thing he'll do is unite the Sunset Kingdoms. He'll conquer them by the sword, and after that, the world." He leaned back in his chair. "The Sunsetters might be barbarians, but they're also religious fanatics. They'll sweep through the Trendil Mountains on Genka's command and bring war to the rest of us. It'll be a disaster."

"And he's close to uniting the Sunset Kingdoms?" Cinder asked.

"I don't know," Heloin said. "He still has a lot of free tribes to bring under his control, but as for cities, he's close. There's only Zomesth and Quoresth left and he'll have control of all the major cities."

Sriovey had gone pale. "Devesh save us if that happens," he intoned, his words sounding like a true prayer.

"Devesh save us all," Heloin said. "If he conquers the Sunsets, he'll bring war to the world."

Quire scoffed. "Let him come." He glanced at Cinder, Depth, Bones, and Ishmay. "No offense, but you're only humans, and so is this Genka. The dwarves of the Trendil and Aurelian Crèches will crush him if he comes against them. And if not them, then he'll die when he comes against the Blessed Race. Shima Sithe is a powerful empire."

Cinder wasn't so sure. While humans were clearly weaker than the other races, they also outnumbered everyone else. And humans were far better strategists and tacticians. That fact was obvious from Master Nuhlin's class. Every engagement he had them study involved a human force overcoming an outnumbering foe. It didn't matter if the enemy was another human army or one consisting of elves or dwarves, somehow the humans pulled through.

"Is Genka using cavalry?" he asked Heloin. He reckoned he knew the answer, but he wanted confirmation.

"He's a Sunsetter. Of course, he's using horses."

Bones scoffed. "Quire's right, though. Horses won't do him any good when he has to engage the dwarves in the Trendil Mountains or if he makes it to the Shima Sithe."

"Horses were invaluable to Mede when he conquered the northern world," Cinder reminded Bones. "He never had an overwhelming force numerically, but it's like Master Nuhlin explained. It isn't who has the most warriors. It's whoever has the most effective force at the point of the attack. And who chooses that point. If you can bring overwhelming force to bear on the ground of your choosing, the enemy will fall."

Cinder doubted Heloin knew the first thing about war, but the elf was nodding agreement the entire time. "And if Genka is strong enough to conquer the Sunsets, he isn't someone to take lightly," Heloin said.

Cinder shouldn't have been surprised, but the day off he'd spent in Certitude turned out to be greatly beneficial. It allowed his body to rest, but more importantly, it allowed the same for his mind.

As a result, he was able to attack the next week of his training with greater dedication and concentration than ever before. He saw tremendous gains in all aspects of combat, except one: the bow. He was the worst amongst everyone involved in the course. For whatever reason, he couldn't find a way forward with the weapon. He didn't know if it was because of excess stiffness in his stance, a lack of focus, or some combination of the two mixed with nervousness. Whatever the case, without a consistently correct form, Cinder's use of the bow was seriously lacking. He might never master the weapon, and the very notion of failure set his teeth on edge.

What made the situation even more frustrating was how well he'd done in his first practice session. The very first arrow he'd fired had been sent unerringly into the dead-center of the target's head. And now?

He snorted in derision. Now he only managed to strike the entire target a little more than half the time.

Today promised to be an extension of his frustrations. He had no reason to believe he would do any better than before.

He snarled. *Failure.* He was coming close to accepting and expecting his failure at the archery range. It was an attitude that simply wouldn't do. He had to snuff out those thoughts. He couldn't allow failure to take a seat in his heart. He *would* succeed. Cinder visualized the next shot, aiming at the target, imagining the arrow striking directly where he focused.

He stood with the other Firsters at the archery range. Clouds gathered to the east. The wind gusted now and then, blowing across the range and challenging everyone's skill. The air was cold and dry. The trees stood naked of their summer foliage, limbs bare and spindly.

Cinder let loose the arrow. He scowled when the shot went wide of the target. He hadn't accounted for the wind.

"Cinder, a moment of your time," Master Serwil said.

Cinder released the tension off the string. The bow drooped, aimed downward.

"Over here. Off the line," Master Serwil ordered. As usual, his tone was brusque.

Cinder didn't know what he'd done wrong. He took several long, backward strides off the line, not wanting to distract the other students. Only then did he go to Master Serwil. "Sir?"

"I can see you're getting frustrated with your lack of progress," Master Serwil said. "It's making you sloppy, seizing up, and going backward instead of forward. Do you have any notion of what I'm saying?"

"I think so, sir," Cinder replied. "I'm pressing instead of relaxing."

"And I said relaxing was the key in using a bow. My first lesson. I've mentioned it to you since then, too. Anger, frustration, excitement can be useful motivators. They get the heart racing, the blood pumping, fill your body with power and energy." He leaned toward Cinder, bringing greater gravity to his words. "But they must be controlled. In the heat of battle or during practice, a wise warrior reins in those emotions and remains calm."

Cinder knew all this. When he sparred with a sword, he always sought a calm center. It allowed him to think and plan more clearly, to react more smoothly and correctly. Archery was the same. He needed to let his darker emotions—anger and frustration—flow through him. He had to breathe them out when using the bow.

But thus far, desire and achievement were proving to be two different things.

"I understand, sir," Cinder said.

"Back to the line then. Focus only on the target. Don't set an arrow until you're ready. You'll know when. Your form is fine. So are your eyes. All you need is to ignore your emotions."

Cinder bowed and resumed his place at the line. He focused on the target. Doubt bubbled in the back of his mind, and he breathed deep. In and out like Master Lerid had taught him at *Steel-Graced Adepts*. *In and out. In and out.* The doubt receded. So did frustration and anger. His mind calmed. The target steadied in his vision. His concentration bore down upon it.

He nocked an arrow, smoothly lifted the bow to the ready, and drew. His eyes never left the target. In and out went his breaths. His emotions fluttered away. He felt a breeze build. It would push the arrow to the right. An adjustment to his aim. *Release the string.*

The arrow shot toward the target, whistling like a strange bird. Cinder's focus remained on where he aimed. The arrow hammered into the target's head, a few inches right of center. Almost exactly where he'd intended.

Cinder exhaled in relief. He smiled, pleased and overjoyed. Until this moment, he didn't realize how much his confidence in archery had sagged. Maybe now, he'd rebuild some of his lost surety and start improving.

He nocked another arrow, but he didn't draw. He narrowed his gaze on the target, aware of his breathing, intent upon it. It was again as Master Lerid had taught him. *In and out.* The excitement of success lessened. His vision tightened. *In and out.* The hope and need for mastery of archery drained away. *In and out.* His mind emptied of emotions, not just the darker ones, but all of them. Excitement, joy, anticipation . . . He let them all drain away. His mind was at rest. The target loomed. *In and out.* He raised the bow, drew, and released.

The arrow slammed home, dead-center of the target's head, directly next to his earlier shot.

Cinder allowed himself another smile of victory, but he wasn't done yet.

In and out. He nocked another arrow. *In and out.* Focus on the target. *In and out.* Draw. *In and out.* Release.

The arrow whistled away, slamming into the throat of the target.

Since relaxing had allowed Cinder to progress with all aspects of his training, he took off the next several rest days as well. Especially because he understood what he and the other Firsters were expected to face. *Spiderkin*. Cinder wanted to be fresh for when he fought the horrors.

The encounter took place on the morning following a rest day, and he and the rest of his Firster class—the humans and dwarves—shuffled into a dimly lit space in the basement of Firemirror Hall. There, they discovered a broad room, yards across and deep with a dirt-covered floor. Dull *diptha* bulbs offered scant illumination. Masters Absin and Serwil awaited them, standing next to a black, circular doorway leading into a separate unlit room. The secondary space was as small as an alcove.

"Today, we train against our most ancient and deadly of foes," Master Absin began. "You know little about the spiderkin, but they infest the Dagger Mountains. More than any other creature, race, or nation, the spiderkin are the single greatest cause of elven deaths. They are our enemy, and when we encounter them, we kill them without mercy or question. We will teach you how."

Master Serwil took on the explanation. "The most dangerous of the spiderkin are their elders. Some are truly ancient, hundreds of years old. They grow larger, smarter, and more dangerous as they age. Some are bigger than a wagon, their chitin harder than steel. Those we avoid. When they reach such a size, they become cunning, deceitful, and far too deadly for any of us to defeat. Thankfully, they live deep in the mountains, rarely venturing forth from their territories. It is their young you have to worry about. Every year, they spread their webs, forever threatening our distant villages. It is those spiderkin we will teach you to kill." His gaze sharpened, his manner intense, which was typical for him. Only when practicing with his bow did Master Serwil relax. "Pay heed," he continued. "These are the lessons that may see you live or die."

Cinder straightened.

Control through calm. The apropos aphorism echoed in his mind, dredged from the recesses of his peculiar memories.

Again spoke Master Absin. "We call them the spiderkin because that is what they resemble: giant spiders. What they call themselves, we don't know, although they do have a language. They are intelligent and can speak to one another in a chittering fashion. However, they are also savage and territorial. They rarely work together in large units. Their favored strategy is to swarm and overwhelm, and their lack of coordination is the only reason we of the Yaksha have been able to defend our homes against them. If they chose to come against us as a true army, they would roll over our outposts, fortifications, villages, and cities in a tidal wave of eight-limbed horrors. They might sweep all the way to Swift Sword."

Cinder rocked on his feet. Until today he'd never paid the spiderkin much attention. He hadn't realized what a threat they represented.

"The males amongst the spiderkin are small," Master Serwil said. "They are the size of large dogs and are slow and stupid. Their chitin is weak enough for a sword or arrow to easily penetrate. They are of limited danger. It is the females who will prove your deadliest foes. It is they who become intelligent. They start out the same size as a male and are similarly weak, slow, and stupid. But once they reach the size of an elf, they are likely of similar intellect. Then they become deadly. One-on-one against a spiderkin, only the dwarves among you would survive, and that barely. Which leads me to the most important lesson for today." He peered about, intensity roiling off him. "Never place yourself in a position where you must fight a spiderkin on your own."

Cinder had a question, and he raised his hand. "If they are like spiders, do they also see in nearly a three-hundred-sixty-degree arc?"

"They do," Master Absin said. "In almost all ways, they are like spiders, with all the advantages that entails. They even produce webbing strong enough to trap a horse."

Cinder racked his brain, trying to remember what he could of spiders "Does the webbing come from their abdomen?" he asked. "And are they weakest if they're tipped over?"

Master Absin smiled. "You're getting ahead of yourself. Let's train. Pair up."

In the time since Cinder had arrived at the Third Directorate, he had made a point to spar against every other Firster, including the dwarves. He wanted exposure to as many different combat styles as possible. He did the same thing when it came to fighting in groups, and again, it was for the same reason. As a result, he teamed with Joria, the younger and least skilled of the Gandharvans.

Joria grinned at Cinder, his blue eyes crinkling. "You ready to kill an insect?" His sandy-brown hair flopped over his eyes, and he blew it out of the way.

Cinder chuckled. "Spiders aren't insects." He clapped the slim Gandharvan on the shoulder. "But sure, let's go kill one of them."

Master Absin went to the black doorway and patted it. "This is Misery Gate, and these chevrons . . ." He pointed to a number of strange markings carved into the doorway, ". . . will take us to the Foe. All will be made clear when you pass through the gate." He manipulated the markings and quickly stepped to the side. He ordered everyone to do the same.

Cinder watched as the symbols on the doorway slowly came to life, glowing golden. An instant later came a flash of light followed by an explosion of something with the appearance of bubbling water. It was a cone as wide as Misery Gate itself. The liquid blasted twenty feet into the room before settling down to fill the black doorway with a watery, mirrored film.

"Come with me," Master Absin said. He passed through Misery Gate and disappeared with a plopping sound.

"After him," Master Serwil ordered.

Cinder followed on Depth's heels, passing through the watery film. The moment he did so, an icy chill penetrated to his bones. His teeth clenched, and his body spasmed.

He stumbled when he exited, discovering himself standing on a circular field of low-lying grass and wanting to throw up.

"Move aside for the others," Master Absin ordered.

Cinder held down his gorge by the barest of margins and did as ordered. He hunched away from the gate, and once his stomach was settled, he took in the world around him.

The Firsters stood in a small glade. The sun stood at its zenith, pale and wan, as if smoke obscured its light. They'd left the Third Directorate in the morning. Towering evergreens surrounded them, and mountains loomed in the distance. Cinder frowned in confusion.

Where are we?

Everyone eventually arrived with Master Serwil bringing up the rear.

"This is the Foe," Master Absin said. "We believe it was created by the Mythaspuris, but we don't know how. We only know how to use it. Opening Misery Gate brings a person here, to this glade, the place we call the Foe. It isn't part of the real world. Here, one can take severe damage, even die when training against the spiderkin, but those injuries and fatalities are all a trick of the mind. It's akin to the pain of a shoke, temporary but with no lingering after-effects. You'll see what I mean." He stepped aside.

A hissing noise came from the forest. Trees swayed as something large pushed past them. The hissing grew louder. Cinder's focus heightened, and he stared at where the sounds emanated. Out shambled an eight-legged monster. Dark as dried blood, it hissed and chittered, coming to a halt. Twin fangs like swords waved in warning.

As one, the Firsters stiffened. A ripple of unease coursed through Cinder, and his hand shot to his shoke. It was only made of wood, but it was also the only available weapon.

"Hold," Master Absin said. "It is only a sparring simulacrum powered by *aether*. It can't produce webbing, but otherwise it perfectly mimics the physical abilities of a spiderkin and will respond appropriately to your shokes and arrows."

"It's best to attack it from a distance," Master Serwil said. "Now look closely. You'll see they have eye clusters directly above their fangs. Use arrows to blind the creature and your task becomes easier." He offered a bleak smile. "But this is the Third Directorate. We don't take the easy route. You'll fight the spiderkin in close quarters." Master Serwil pointed at the spiderkin. "Their legs are a weak point. So is their abdomen. For this one, as big as it is, a sharp sword can shear through their legs or stab into their abdomen. Anywhere else, the chitin is too tough, except for a thrust. Your sword will otherwise simply bounce off." He held up a cautioning finger. "A final word of advice. Attack the creature from different angles. Force it to choose one foe while the other attacks."

"Will our shokes work against them?" Cinder asked.

"The magic of the Foe ensures they will," Master Serwil said. "Any blow you land will have the power of sharpened steel rather than wood."

Master Absin barked. "Bones and Ishmay. You're first."

As usual, Bones and Ishmay had paired up. In spite of their initial hostility, the two had become fast friends. They were the best human warriors amongst the Firsters, and they always chose to partner with one another.

The two of them held a short, hushed conversation. Then they split apart and approached the spiderkin. The creature hissed and hustled their way, a mass of blurring legs. Bones and Ishmay responded smoothly, separating further. Ishmay went right and Bones to the left. They reached the spiderkin at the same time.

Bones attacked first. He slashed at a leg. The spiderkin defended by parrying. It spun about again, blocking Ishmay now. Again came Bones. The spiderkin continued to defend. It blocked and countered, twisted about to take on each human as needed, slowly giving ground.

Cinder recognized its strategy. "It's trying to draw you closer!" he shouted. "Move apart. Come at it from the front and the back."

Bones and Ishmay didn't listen. They both tracked down the spiderkin, but in the process, they ended up directly in front of the creature.

Ishmay missed a parry, and a leg slammed him in the chest. He cried out, flung ten feet away. Blood spurted from his chest. He didn't get up.

Cinder gasped, drawing his shoke and moving toward the spiderkin.

"Hold!" Master Absin shouted.

Cinder did as ordered, but tension knitted his muscles. Bones was alone against the monstrosity. His worry eased when he saw Ishmay flicker. The blood and gore disappeared, and he got to his feet, uninjured.

"That was awful," Ishmay said, pale and shaken.

"Stay out of the fight," Master Serwil ordered. "It killed you."

Bones did his best to fight one-on-one against the spiderkin, but seconds later, a fang got him in the thigh. Another punched through his gut, and he was dead. Blood pooled about his corpse.

Again, just like Ishmay, seconds later, he rose to his feet, uninjured. He and Ishmay commiserated, trembling and leaning on one another. Both wore expressions of lingering terror, seemingly ready to cry. Master Serwil draped an arm around their shoulders, drawing them close and speaking softly. They nodded their heads to whatever he was saying.

Cinder viewed Bones and Ishmay, studying them for any hidden injuries. They appeared fine. "How?" he asked Master Absin.

"How do they die and come back to life?" Master Absin asked. "We don't know. It's part of the magic of this place, the Foe." He wore a sadistic smile. "And since you seem to know what you're doing, you and Joria are next."

Face that horrible monster? Die but not really die? Cinder sighed. He had wanted to be next anyway. *Best get on with it.* Cinder stared at the spiderkin, seeking any weaknesses the masters might have failed to mention. He didn't see anything obvious at first, but when he recalled how it had reacted to Bones and Ishmay, an idea formed. He addressed the masters. "Are we allowed to use shields?"

Master Absin smiled, thin and pleased. "A good idea, but this is the Third Directorate. A shield is too easy. No shields. Not yet. Not until you know how to use them properly."

Cinder scowled. *Of course.*

"I come at it from the left? You come from the right?" Joria suggested.

"Yes, but fifteen feet apart," Cinder said. "Let me get to it first. I want you hanging back, just out of range. I'll engage it with two attacks. Then you enter."

Joria eyed him in doubt. "You sure?"

"I don't have a better plan. Do you?"

Joria shrugged. "Let's see what happens."

Cinder and Joria slowly approached the spiderkin from several yards wider than Bones and Ishmay had attacked. The spiderkin waved its fangs as if to urge them on.

Cinder gave a sudden shout. Some spiders hunted by vibrations. Maybe the yell would disorient the creature. It paused its motions when he cried out.

Cinder rushed forward during its moment of apparent confusion. The spiderkin quickly recovered, easily blocking a diagonal slash and a follow-up thrust aimed at a joint.

Joria arrived, and the spiderkin spun to defend against him.

Cinder shouted again. Once more, the spiderkin hesitated. He took its short-lived lapse to shift toward its rear and attacked a hind leg. The spiderkin never had a chance to defend. The rear leg audibly cracked. The creature cried out like a living being in pain and gave ground.

Joria moved to re-engage.

"Wait," Cinder ordered. "We come at it from the same distance apart. You shout this time and stomp the ground. I'll attack it first again."

Cinder eased toward the spiderkin. Before his plan could take shape, the creature charged him.

He was suddenly confronted by a mass of swiftly moving limbs. Instinct took over. He blocked a front leg thrusting at his head.

A mirrored pool formed; the same one he'd seen during the Maker's Tournament. But this time there was no sheet of blue and green lightning. Cinder retreated a few steps from the spiderkin. The water called to him, and he reached for it, hesitant and unsure. It must have reached for him as well because in a rush, it washed into him, surging through his mind.

The world of the Foe snapped back into focus. Everything was more real, sharper, clearer . . .

Cinder had no more time to think about the pool or his heightened senses because here came the spiderkin. Cinder defended against the creature, startled at how smoothly he moved against the monster. His attacks and defenses were effortless and swift. He parried blows, evaded fangs, and nimbly evaded a leg meant to trip him. While celebrating his success, an unseen limb slammed into his abdomen. It ripped raggedly across and through his stomach, and the blow flung him a dozen feet through the air.

He crashed to the ground, screaming in pain. The wound had ripped deep. The ropes of his intestines pooled in his hands. He gaped in horror, vaguely noting how Joria fell to the spiderkin a second later, head crushed to a pulp.

The world went dark. The agony disappeared, and the glade returned. Cinder blinked in uncertainty. The pain was gone. His abdomen was whole. No ropes of intestines spilling out. Everything was as it had been before he had challenged the spiderkin. There was no sign of injury.

He shuddered, horrified by what he had experienced. The agony. He rubbed at his abdomen. The pain had been so real. *His intestines.* He'd felt them. He'd died. The world had gone black.

Cinder closed his eyes, trying to hold back the tears.

The Foe was a place of nightmares.

25

Thankfully, their horrific encounter with the spiderkin wasn't to be repeated any time soon. Master Absin let them know that they wouldn't face the creatures again for another couple of weeks. Until then, they would simply resume their normal routine and gain experience until they were ready to have another go against the eight-legged monstrosities.

Afterward, Cinder had re-dedicated himself to his training, pushing even harder but wise enough to give his mind and body a chance to rest, no matter how much it chafed. Occasionally it still felt like he was wasting his time, sitting around doing nothing, but whenever he allowed his body to recover, he performed so much better the next week. So, despite his irritation with the matter, he continued to take the rest days off.

Most of them, anyway.

It was now a month since he'd entered the Foe, and Cinder stood at attention alongside his brother Firsters upon the fields of the Cauldron, waiting for Master Absin to go over today's session. The elf, however, appeared in no hurry to do so.

Clouds like lacunae of cotton littered a vibrant blue sky. The early winter sun beamed brightness, causing the frost-slick grass to glisten. However, the sunshine provided little warmth. The mountains of Yaksha proper ringed the academy like a crown, the gray granite similar to tarnished silver and the white peaks a kind of opal.

Cinder stood ninth in line, his ranking amongst the Firsters. The dwarves held the first five spots. Then came Bones and Ishmay followed by Depth and then Cinder. Next were Wark, Rorian, and Joria. Nervous sweat gleamed on all their brows, and the air held still, pregnant as if in honor of the day, and it was a special day. Today was the halfway point of their time in their first year at the Third Directorate.

"We have something interesting in mind for you today," Master Absin said. "Thus far, I have been the one to determine your ranking in your class. Today, you have a chance to earn a new ranking. The onus is on your shoulders." The white-haired elf stared from one Firster to another as he paced along the line. "The rules are simple. It's a one-on-one competition, best two out of three wins the match."

Cinder shared an eager smile with Depth and Rorian.

"Shokes and anything else you can think of are allowed," Master Absin continued. "But no eye gouging or knees to the groin. The lowest ranked warrior . . ." His gaze landed on Joria, the slim Gandharvan who stood at the end of the line, ". . . is allowed to challenge the man directly ahead of him. If he wins, he takes the higher ranked spot and can challenge the next warrior. If he loses, the higher ranked keeps his spot and is now allowed to challenge the next warrior ahead of him." Master Absin ceased his pacing. "Any questions?"

No one spoke.

"Then we'll begin."

The Firsters gathered around a dirt-floored sparring circle. Joria immediately challenged Rorian. They bowed low to one another, and the match began. It was fierce. The two Firsters were closely matched, but in the end Rorian proved successful. Unfortunately, the bout took a lot out of him, and he lacked the stamina to challenge Wark.

Wark, on the other hand, grinned at Cinder. "What do you say?

Why don't we finish what we started in that alehouse in Swift Sword?" He referenced the long-ago time when they'd gotten into it in the Lonely Donkey, but no hint of malice touched his voice. By now, Cinder counted Wark as a friend.

They took up positions in the sparring circle, shokes in hand. Master Absin stood as the judge. A breeze gusted, swirling Cinder's hair. He made a note to have it trimmed. He took the last few seconds before the bout's beginning to study Wark, who stood on the opposite side of the circle.

A hint of a smile, a twitch now and then, lingered on the other man's mouth. He held the shoke, tip pointed at the ground and shoulders loose and relaxed. Too relaxed. He wasn't taking the match seriously.

Cinder held himself expressionless, disappointed at Wark's lack of gravity. A plan quickly formed. Wark liked to work at a distance. He wasn't as good at close-in fighting, something at which Cinder excelled. Maybe Cinder could overwhelm Wark with a flurry of attacks. He could get in tight, slam home a fist or knee and end the fight.

Master Absin shouted, "Fight!"

Cinder rushed Wark. He aimed a thrust like a dagger. Wark's eyes widened, and he clumsily slapped aside the attack. Cinder didn't give him room to breathe. He pressed the action, keeping Wark in front of him. He sent a rising diagonal slash. Wark parried, but it left his abdomen exposed. Cinder took the opening, landing a heavy knee against Wark's stomach.

His fellow Firster's breath went out with a whoosh. He collapsed to his knees, head bent low and groaned.

"End!" Master Absin called out. "Point to Cinder."

Wark remained on the ground, still hunched over in pain.

Cinder squatted next to him, feeling bad he'd hit him so hard. "Are you all right?"

Wark glared at him. "I always forget how tricky you are with your knees and fists."

"Sorry about that."

Wark sighed, the pain apparently subsiding. "Never mind. It's what

I get for treating this like a lark. You didn't. Something to learn from you, I guess."

Cinder stood and offered Wark a helping hand. "Come on. I've still got another point to win off you."

Wark chuckled, rubbing his stomach. "No thanks. I'm done after that liver shot."

"Are you withdrawing your challenge?" Master Absin asked Wark.

"Yes, sir," Wark answered.

"Then the win goes to Cinder."

The wash of victory didn't touch Cinder. He wouldn't allow it. Not yet. Not when he had more work to do. "I challenge Depth."

Depth rose to his feet, shaking his head and grumbling. "Let's get this done."

Cinder studied the other student, whose wiry build had filled out some since their arrival at the Third Directorate. If anything, it made Depth even more lethally fast and deadly. But he no longer had the greater reach. Cinder was surprised when he realized the two of them were the same height. When they'd arrived at the Directorate, Depth had been half a head taller.

Nevertheless, his fellow Firster retained the near-inscrutable manner as when Cinder had crossed swords with him in the Maker's Tournament. His flat affect and posture gave away little hint of his intentions.

But little wasn't the same as none. Since coming to the Directorate, Cinder's ability to predict possible outcomes had improved. Depth bounced on the balls of his feet. He grasped his shoke more surely than if he were planning on merely defending. He would attack, a shot across the circle with a horizontal cut followed by an attempted smash with the hilt.

Cinder wasn't afraid of the attack. He was inches taller and many muscled pounds heavier than he had been in the Maker's Tournament. He was fast enough to counter Depth. Skilled enough, too. When he and Depth sparred against one another, it was a guess as to who would win, but in the past week, Cinder felt like he was gaining a slight advantage, maybe the nose of a snail. At least he hoped so.

Master Absin stood to the side of the sparring circle. "Be ready," he called.

"Make this more interesting?" Depth asked. "Whoever wins has to buy drinks next time we're in Certitude? I'm heading there in a week. Need a new uniform for the duchess' Winter Gala."

"Deal." The agreement made, Cinder's attention tightened on Depth. The world beyond the sparring circle held no importance. Sounds faded. He took passing note of a stray wind. His breathing deepened. His heart beat faster. Motion slowed.

"Fight!"

As expected, Depth launched forth like an arrow. Cinder waited a split second. *Now.* He slid to the side, shoke ready. Depth was fully committed to his attack, and he desperately sought to correct. Cinder slammed down a vertical blow. It drove Depth's shoke into the ground and left him off-balance. Cinder followed with a diagonal slap. The edge of his shoke smacked Depth's left arm at the bicep.

"Break!" Master Absin shouted. "Point to Cinder."

"Damn it, Cinder," Depth complained, rubbing his bicep. "It's the same arm as before."

Cinder winced in sympathy. The Maker's Tournament when he'd landed a blow against Depth's bicep. The same arm and the same location. "Sorry, friend," he said, feeling bad for his fellow Firster. The hit had to hurt.

Depth shrugged. "Forget it. It happens."

"Are you ready to continue?" Master Absin asked.

"I'm ready," Depth said.

"Ready," Cinder replied.

"Take your marks."

Cinder resumed his position in the sparring circle, and so did Depth.

Once again, Cinder watched his opponent. Depth's shoke was held at the ready, but he favored his left arm. In addition, based on his stance, he was planning on a slower approach this time.

Cinder would do the same, but when the opportunity presented itself, he'd attack.

"Fight!"

Cinder shuffled forward. Depth sidestepped to his right. Cinder moved to cut him off. They crept closer to one another. Depth's grip on his shoke tightened. He took several steps forward. Cinder held his ground. A thrust was coming.

Depth shot forward. Cinder parried the expected thrust. Defended against a follow-up second thrust. He circled to Depth's left and sent a horizontal counter. Depth blocked but winced when their shokes connected. The blow to his bicep from earlier must be bothering him. Cinder continued to circle, keeping his lead foot on the outside of Depth's left leg.

Cinder sent a questing thrust. Depth slipped it, not bothering to block the blow and sent a counter. Cinder easily parried and came back with a downward strike.

Depth set his shoke, parrying the blow aimed at his right leg. Again, he winced. He was also slow to recover.

Cinder committed to a thrust. It hammered home against Depth's chest, who stumbled away, groaning in pain. Cinder empathized. Even with the protective gear they wore, the strike had to hurt.

"Break," Master Absin said. "Point and victory to Cinder."

"You all right?" Cinder asked Depth, who rubbed at his chest.

"You didn't break any ribs if that's what you're asking," Depth said. "But, shit, that's going to leave me a pretty bruise."

"If you aren't bruising . . ."

"You aren't trying," Depth finished, citing one of Master Absin's favorite sayings.

"Congratulations on your victory," Master Absin said to Cinder. "You have choice of challenge."

Cinder looked toward Ishmay. The Gandharvan shifted on his feet, appearing altogether too enthusiastic. While Cinder had confidence against Depth, Ishmay was a different matter. He wasn't at Bones' level, but he wasn't far below. Cinder wasn't ready to take him on. "I'm finished."

Master Absin addressed Ishmay. "The choice of challenge is yours."

Ishmay grinned in anticipation. "I want Bones."

Bones shook his head. "You're asking for an ass-kicking. I won't be taking it easy on you this time."

Bones proved true to his word. He quickly demolished Ishmay, leaving the Gandharvan limping and sporting bruised ribs.

Anya unsaddled her gelding, undid his tack, and brushed him down. The horse, a palomino, snorted and twitched, but otherwise he kept his focus on the oats she'd set aside for him. While he lipped his food, she continued to brush him, working out dirt and burrs. He deserved the care. He'd traveled many miles with her, and she liked him. He had a gentle, inquisitive nature, which she found charming. Plus, she had always favored palominos. For whatever reason, their tawny coloring struck her as beautiful.

One final brush, and she was satisfied. *Done.* She returned the brush to the tack.

As she strode through the darkened stable—she had reached the palace at night—she drew on gloves to ward off the chill. Winter retained its firm grip upon Revelant, and spring was several months away. She looked forward to it, the sudden fragrant rush, a warm breath banishing the cold and bringing life to the world.

Until then, Anya didn't mind the winter. She loved it—the snow, the pluming breath, and the sharp cold to shock a person awake. Winter also reminded her of the home of her heart, a place of lofty peaks, snowy passes, and a teardrop-shaped lake caressing a set of holy fields. She blew out at an exhalation. Yes, she loved the winter, even Revelant's pale imitation of that chilly season. Here, winter touched Yaksha proper with only the mildest of icy fingers.

Not like the Third Directorate. Now *there* was a proper winter.

Anya made her way to the palace, quickly climbing the stairs leading upward. She took a familiar servant's entrance, and from there entered the public hallways where the *diptha* lamps were dimmed for the evening. Her footfalls echoed. No one was about, but a few tired servants and several roaming guards on their rounds. They bowed as she passed, and she reciprocated their signs of respect with a quick dip of her head. She might have inquired about their families or their personal lives since she knew all their names, but these men and women were on duty. They didn't have time to chit-chat with her.

In addition, Anya wanted to talk to her mother. She had troubling information. Soon enough, she reached her mother's study. Light poured out from beneath the oval door, and she knocked.

"Come," her mother's voice ordered.

Anya opened the door and found her mother seated at her desk. No one else was about. Anya entered the study, shutting the door behind her.

Her mother stood with a welcoming smile. She stepped past her desk and approached; arms open for a hug.

They embraced, Anya folding her mother into her arms. It never failed to surprise her how much smaller and frailer the empress felt. Or maybe it was because Anya was so tall and powerfully built, even for one of the noble caste.

"You're worried," her mother said, after pulling away. "What happened?"

Anya explained. "I left Yaksha proper, and at the garrison in Shansa, I gathered a troop of ten scouts."

"Shansa? I thought you were staying south."

Anya shrugged. "I felt a calling to the eastern bounds of Rakesh, so I went there." She frowned. "There were many more zahhacks prowling about than usual. Every species. Necrosed, unformed, ghouls, goblins, vampires even. The spiderkin were also bolder than usual." She rubbed her arms, goosebumps rising. "It's as though a presence stirs them to life."

"Can this have anything to do with this warlord in the Sunset Kingdoms, Genka Devesth? Everyone is talking about him. Remember,

Mede stirred the zahhacks, too. They swarmed after him like a swarm of bees, knowing him to be a grave enemy."

Anya stared at the fire burning in the hearth, contemplating the question. Could it be Genka? She hadn't considered him as the cause. If so, it would ease her mind. As soon as Genka fell, maybe the zahhacks would return to their normal state.

Her lips pursed.

Perhaps, but a warning in her mind suggested otherwise.

"You don't believe it has anything to do with Genka," her mother said.

"I'm not sure. It might." She hesitated. The necrosed she'd killed at the last. His words made no sense. What had he meant to say? She wasn't sure if she should mention it.

Her mother must have noticed her vacillation. "What is it?"

"One of the necrosed said something: *the burning one comes.*" Anya glanced at her mother, hoping she might have insight into what the creature meant.

"The burning one comes?" Her mother frowned, thinking. After a moment, she shook her head. "I don't know what that means."

It was too much to hope her mother would know, and Anya sighed.

Her mother silently peered at her, as if trying to puzzle out a mystery. "Was there anything else?"

"As I said, there was a presence."

"What kind of presence?"

Anya rubbed her shoulders. "I don't know. I've never before felt its like. Even now, I can't tell if it was real or just my imagination. It was gone like the wind. I had no chance to focus on it."

"What about the other rangers? Did they feel the same as you?"

"No. They never noticed anything amiss, except for the number of zahhacks we encountered." She forced a grin. "At least there will be a half-dozen less necrosed and five less tribes of unformed roaming the Daggers."

Her mother barked laughter, a note of scorn in her voice. "Yes, thank goodness a princess of Yaksha risks her life to kill the corrupted."

Anya ducked her head, cursing her stupidity. She shouldn't have joked about killing the zahhacks. While her mother allowed her to maintain her status as a warrior and a ranger, the empress didn't like to hear about the battles in which Anya engaged. It made her afraid for her daughter. The truth was that Anya's mother would vastly prefer it if Anya followed in Enma's path, the traditional circuitous route to adulthood taken by most elves. The empress would also be overjoyed if her youngest daughter took a lover or two.

Anya lifted her head, forcing herself to meet her mother's gaze. "Evil needs to be contained if it can't be changed. Killed if it can't be contained."

Her mother's lips pursed. "An odd saying. Is it one you created?"

Anya didn't know. The aphorism had sprung to her tongue without thought. Perhaps she had read it? Or was it a phrase from her elder years? Maybe said to her by the man she had once so fiercely loved? "It doesn't matter," Anya finally said in answer to her mother's question. "Regardless of the source, it contains the truth."

Her mother made a noise of agreement. "Yes, I suppose it does." She paced to her desk, appearing distracted or lost in thought. "If what you saw and sensed is true, then we must keep our eyes sharp. Who knows if this is anything of real concern or merely a set of coincidences."

Anya thought it more likely to be the former. "The Daggers . . . the bones of our world groan. Seminal changes."

"As you say." Her mother's distracted air vanished. "Now that you're home, what are your plans?"

"I'll rest for a few days before going to the Third Directorate and checking on Estin. I think I'll stay there through the spring and the Unitary Trial."

"So, no lovers then?" her mother asked with a wry half-smile. She waved aside Anya's protest. "Never mind my words. You are young. Choose as you will for now. I know when the time comes, you'll accept duty's burden."

Anya remained quiet. Would she do what was required of someone of her station? Take a lover? She wanted to believe that she would, but she had no desire for one, much less a husband. She suspected her attitude would never change.

Her mother smiled. "And I know you have a fondness for those youth and their training."

"Enma says it's a weakness."

"It's not," her mother declared. "I wanted to train there myself when I was young." Her smile faded. "More importantly, if the bones of the world truly stir . . ." Again came a wry smirk, this time containing a faint barb of disbelief. Her mother thought Anya was letting her fears get the best of her. ". . . we'll need the warriors of the Third."

Anya chose to overlook the subtle mockery. "Then visiting the Third will give me a chance to gain their proper measure."

"Fair enough." Her mother waved her toward the door. "You're tired. Get some rest. We'll speak more in the morning."

Anya bowed to her mother and left the study. As she strode toward her rooms, her thoughts went to her brother and Riyne Coushinre, the reputed best of the Firsters, better than Estin. In this, he apparently followed in the footsteps of his brother, Lisandre.

She flushed at the thought of Lisandre. She'd served under him during her third year at the Directorate, and afterward, he made plain his interest, seeking her out as a lover, but she'd turned him down. In the years since, his interest had never waned. If anything, it had waxed, and he even spoke of love. Unfortunately for both of them, she felt nothing but respect for Lisandre. How much easier would it be if she *could* take on a lover or better yet, accept a husband?

She dismissed notions of matrimony, focusing again on the Firsters.

She wondered how the dwarves were measuring up. They had one, Sriovey Surent of Surent Crèche, the son of the famed Stipe. He and another, Derius, were said to be formidable. As for the humans, they likely couldn't even beat a single spiderkin, but they had their uses.

Anya left Revelant several days later, and it took her two days of hard travel to reach the Third Directorate. She arrived late in the evening, well past supper, and the academy's grounds were quiet and darkened by the time she arrived. Sapient shone overhead, the moon's light ivory and cool. It matched the cold, crisp air, and her breath fogged in front of her. A ragged wind rustled now and then. The only other sound was the lonely clopping of her palomino as she guided him toward the stable. Throughout the buildings of the academy, she spied a number of lighted rooms, but on the grounds themselves, no one was about. Folk were awake, but they were wise enough to stay indoors on this cold evening. They likely huddled next to their cheery hearths. The smell of wood smoke permeating the air expressed this.

Anya inhaled deeply, smiling in warm remembrance. She loved these kinds of nights. Quiet, serene, and with the soothing scent of crackling fires burning in hearths. They reminded her of her childhood in the mountains during her first life. She exhaled heavily. As always, thinking about her past recalled her family's fiery deaths, and the ongoing absence of her husband. *Why can't I see his face or know his name? Or my true name?*

She pushed aside the memories with an irritated shake of her head. The past was dead. Only the present and the future mattered. She got to work then, quickly unsaddling the palomino, brushed him down, and got him settled in for the night. She patted his withers as she left him there, his nose buried in the trough.

Cinder's white Yavana stallion stuck his nose over his stall door as she passed him by. Fastness was his name. He whickered softly at her, seemingly asking her a question. She paused next to his stall but made sure to step no closer. She'd heard too much about this horse, his by-now legendary predilections for pranks, and his stubborn refusal to let anyone saddle him, much less ride him. He should have been named 'Trouble'. It continued to astonish her that Cinder, a human with no prior experience handling a horse, had been the one to tame this Yavana.

Fastness whickered again, and she viewed the horse in speculation. What did he want? The stallion's eyes lingered on her coat pocket where she had an apple tucked away. He whickered louder.

Anya chuckled in amusement. Fastness was apparently a spoiled beast with an excellent sense of smell. She withdrew the apple and allowed the stallion to take it from her palm. She softly stroked his forehead while he munched away at the fruit. He nudged his nose deeper into her hand, and she rubbed his forelock.

"I've got to go, young man," Anya said a few seconds later.

He snorted as if he understood her and withdrew deeper into his stall.

Anya chuckled again and left him and the stable. She carried her belongings to her room and deposited them next to the front door. Her bed looked tempting and fatigue should have been dragging at her limbs—the final leg of the journey to the Directorate had been long—but a restless energy stirred within her. She couldn't sit still and wasn't ready to call it a night. She paced back and forth, considering what to do.

She came to an immediate stop when a peculiar idea glided into her mind.

The Foe. She generally didn't fight the spiderkin so late in the hour, much less when so tired or troubled, but . . .

The odd notion firmed in her thoughts. *Yes.* Perhaps a few matches against the spiderkin would work out her excess energy? Maybe that's what she needed.

The decision made, Anya strapped on a shoke and left her rooms. She trotted down a few flights of stairs and reached a pair of age-darkened, plain wooden doors. Behind them was the room housing Misery Gate and the Foe.

In the depths of winter were found the wickedest nights of the year. It consisted of days as short as a baby's nap, and nights as cold as a killer's heart. On one such evening, a few weeks after raising his rank, Cinder found himself pacing the common room. He wasn't ready to settle in and end his work. Ever since he'd started taking off a rest day every now and again, he had nights like this—nights when a driving desire to test himself bubbled through his veins like a boiling stew.

But test himself against what?

Cinder didn't know. Everyone else was in their rooms, and the Firster area was quiet this evening. No one around to offer advice. The Cauldron would be similarly empty at this late hour and reading held no appeal.

What then?

An idea snapped into being.

The Foe. Yes. He could face off against a spiderkin simulacrum. He nodded to himself. In his first few attempts against the spiderkin, he'd utterly failed. He couldn't accept his losses. He needed to learn how to defeat the creatures.

His decision made, he quickly fetched his shoke, a helmet, and thick padding and exited Krathe House. He trotted across the cold grounds of the Quad and entered Firemirror Hall, which was never closed, and made his way to the basement.

He reached Misery Gate and stared at it, examining the strange black stones, which formed a ring, the unlit chevrons, and the hulking immensity of the device. Once it was activated, the Foe would come to life, and Cinder would step into that strange half-world and face spiderkin. Pain, and death.

Was he willing to do so?

Cinder didn't take long to ponder the question. The answer was 'yes'. It would always be 'yes'. No matter the cost, he would accept it. No matter the burden, he would bear it. It was necessary. The deep-seated yearning to make himself into a warrior worthy of the name had no identifiable rationale. It simply was, an urge driving him, but he felt sure it wasn't an accident. There was a purpose and a reason. He just hadn't discovered it yet.

Cinder viewed the Gate for a moment more before reaching for the chevrons. Thankfully, utilizing the Gate didn't require *lorethasra*. It only required proper placement of the chevrons. He adjusted the symbols, shifting them into place like Master Absin had taught him. He chose one of the lower-ranked spiderkin warriors. A moment's hesitation, and he twisted the dial to the right. *Let's try a mid-ranked spiderkin.*

The Gate activated, and Cinder stepped through the watery film, entering the dimly lit world of the Foe. A chittering sound soon reached him, heralding the spiderkin's approach. The creature already neared the glade, and Cinder took the final few seconds to adjust his helmet and padding.

The spiderkin pushed into the glade.

Cinder stared at the monster, recalling when Master Absin had defeated a spiderkin by himself.

"Watch," the elven sword master had said. He had engaged, moving in a blur. A clatter of shoke against the creature's limbs. Master Absin's strikes had come too quickly for Cinder to clearly observe.

One of the spiderkin's legs had buckled.

Master Absin hadn't let up. He slammed home a thrust to a joint where a leg met the creature's body. It, too, went limp. Seconds later Master Absin had the spiderkin prone and unable to move, most of its limbs broken.

Cinder couldn't fight like an elf, but he could fight better than he once had. But was he good enough to defeat a spiderkin? It was a question he wanted answered. He also realized that coming down here tonight offered another opportunity, and he stepped away from the spiderkin. As he knew it would, the creature halted its forward progression. It would only attack if he did. Otherwise, it would leave him alone.

Mortal combat and terrible testing were what the Foe offered. But it might offer even more.

His *lorethasra*.

It had come into being on a few other occasions. A pool of silvery water. A distraction was what he had thought of it at the time, but just like Master Lerid had once told him, his *lorethasra* might appear to him during times of need. In addition, he'd read an account. The mirrored pond was how a few accounts indicated the Mythaspuris saw their *lorethasras*. Plus, whenever Cinder had seen his own, the world afterward had been different. Sharper, brighter, and time moved more slowly, a balm to his apprehensions.

Since then, Cinder had tried again and again to draw his *lorethasra* forth and failed every time. This despite his endless hours of meditation and sparring. But he wasn't ready to give up. He wasn't ready to accept that his *lorethasra* would forever remain a dream and not a reality.

Which was why he had entered the Foe. Maybe there was an unknown nature to the world beyond Misery Gate, one in which humans could conduct their *lorethasra*.

There was only one way to find out.

Cinder reached for his *lorethasra*. An instinct guided him, determined his breathing, showed him how to reach deep into his heart and mind, search with his inner eye, and find—

There it was. Astonishment nearly cost him, but he concentrated and relaxed at the same time, allowing a winter-clear pool of water, perfect in all ways—his *lorethasra*—to slowly take shape. The vision of it filled his mind, centering his thoughts. *Calm.* Cinder exhaled in relief. Again, instinct guided him, and he reached for his *lorethasra*. The moment he dipped his figurative fingers in it . . .

Anya opened the doors to Misery Gate and prepared herself for the battle to come. Her breathing deepened, and her heart rate quickened. Her hands twitched with the need to draw her shoke. However, when she neared the Gate, she realized the Foe was occupied. She grimaced in disappointment. Who was using it this late at night? Anya adjusted the chevrons, smoothing away the gate's normal watery image to a perfect clarity. She was curious to see who was battling the spiderkin.

Cinder Shade.

The spiderkin he was set to face was large, and her frown deepened.

It was too much for him. She checked the chevrons. She wasn't wrong. Cinder had the Foe set for a single opponent, but one of a mid-level skill. The spiderkin he had chosen was beyond his capabilities. A Firster elf or dwarf could defeat such an enemy, but not a human.

An infusion of energy filled Cinder to overflowing. It saturated his muscles, and he wanted to kick down the walls of the world. He vibrated with the intensity of staying still. The world of the Foe brightened. The soft creaking and chittering of the spiderkin sounded louder. He scented dirt and wood, aromas he hadn't noticed before in this strange half-world.

Cinder set himself, shoke rising into position. The spiderkin clicked and chittered its way forward, maw opening, fangs forward, and its front two limbs poised.

Cinder edged sideways, striving for control, but the smells and sights were too much. His senses burned, and his muscles twitched. He couldn't hold back any longer, and he rushed the creature. He moved faster than he ever had before. He had an instant of amazement at his closing speed.

Then he attacked.

Anya stepped forward, shocked at Cinder's attack. How was he moving so fast? *Was* he moving so fast? Or might it be a mirage from the distortion produced by Misery Gate?

Anya didn't know, and the only way to find out was with a closer view. She pressed through the watery-film of Misery Gate and entered the Foe.

Cinder bent backward at the waist under a swiping foreleg. He backflipped and met a thrusting fang with a parry. Again, came a sweeping leg. Cinder leapt onto it, kicked off, and vaulted over the spiderkin. He slashed at a mid-thorax leg-joint in passing. He landed, his back to the spiderkin. Disturbed air inspired him to roll forward. Another leg slashed across where he'd been standing.

He sensed a stabbing fang and blindly blocked it. He rolled away, came to his feet, parried a thrust from a foreleg. The spiderkin charged. Cinder stood his ground. At the last instant, he slid to the side and slashed out. He severed a leg. Dark blood spurted, and the spiderkin keened, high-pitched and ululating.

The creature spun about, legs sweeping outward.

Cinder backed off. The spiderkin chittered at him, louder now, furious. It circled, and Cinder methodically matched its movements. The spiderkin darted forward. Cinder parried a thrust. He gave way to a slash, slapped aside a follow up stab. The creature rushed forward, seeking to overwhelm him with its mass.

Too slow.

Cinder darted out of range. His *lorethasra* continued to power his movements, although he noticed the pool was visibly smaller than before. He had to end the battle quickly. Cinder shifted right. The spiderkin followed, keeping him directly in front of it. Cinder zigzagged; left-right-left. His rapid movements threw the creature off balance, and Cinder arrowed toward it. He stabbed into the monster's maw, and using the shoke as a lever, he launched upward. He landed on the simulacrum's back. A single stab where the head met the thorax, and his attack penetrated the creature's chitin. A killing blow. The spiderkin cried, harsh and ringing before going limp.

Cinder wanted to shout his exuberance over his success, but soft applause drew him out of his joyful reverie.

The elven princess, Anya, stood at the entrance to the Foe. She wore camouflage leathers, a sword at her hip, and had her honey-blonde hair in a neat braid. "Well, done," she said, her voice warm and a pleased smile on her face. "I don't think I've ever seen a human move so swiftly. You moved almost as fast as an elf."

Cinder jumped off the spiderkin and approached the princess. "I thought you went to the Daggers."

Anya nodded. "I did, and now I'm back."

He supposed he should be overwhelmed and awed by her majesty, but those feelings had no hold on his heart. Instead, a greater desire took shape. He wanted to see Anya smile again.

"By almost as fast, do you mean I'm quicker?" Cinder asked. "Because I'm not sure about the others, but Riyne certainly is slow."

Anya quirked an eyebrow. "I have known Riyne since he was a child. I have seen him spar. He is anything but slow."

Cinder shook his head. "That's not the kind of slow I meant."

"What other kind of slow is there?" Anya's face registered sudden understanding. "Oh." Repressed mirth was evident by the shine of her eyes and the way her lips thinned. "I see."

"You're allowed to laugh," Cinder said. He wasn't sure why he dared speak to her in such an informal manner, but he didn't think she would mind.

"I'll laugh when you tell me how you moved so fast."

Cinder pretended perplexion. "Why would you laugh then? How I moved so fast isn't funny."

Anya chuckled. "You are irrepressible, aren't you?" Seconds later, she sobered. "How did you move so quickly?"

Cinder answered without thinking. "I conducted my *lorethasra*. Then again. I'm human, so would it be *Jivatma?*" He shook his head. "Whatever it was, I conducted it." He immediately wanted to smack himself. He probably should have kept that to himself.

"*Jivatma?*" There was an edge to Anya's question, and Cinder wanted to cringe. He really should have kept what he'd done to himself. "Where did you hear such a word?" Anya asked.

"I read it. In *the Lor Agni.*" He prayed she would let the matter drop. The less questions from her, the better.

His prayers must have been answered because Anya's easy-going manner recovered. She smiled. "*Jivatma* is an old term, but it is a human one. It's probably best if you didn't use it here."

"Yes, ma'am."

Anya chuckled. "Ma'ams are middle-aged women. I told you to call me—"

"Simply Anya." He hoped she would see the humor in his statement.

Thankfully, Anya laughed. "Not quite what I said, but it'll do." Her mirth diminished. "Will you be attending the Winter Gala? It's in a few weeks."

"The gala of the Winter Lord, right?"

"Yes," Anya confirmed. "Ash, the Winter Lord," Anya confirmed.

Cinder pursed his mouth, recollecting what he knew of the Winter Gala. "Isn't there also a Summer Gala? An honoring of a Gray Lady of some sort?"

"Yes. The rest of the world knows the Winter Lord as Shokan and the Gray Lady as Sira."

Cinder's eyebrows rose. "I knew elves didn't like Shokan and Sira, but it seems a little much to give them such terrifying names. The Winter Lord. The Gray Lady," he scoffed.

"They were terrifying individuals," Anya said. "Consider the power they are said to have wielded. Regardless, for the Gray Lady, her birthday is said to fall in Vashasth, in summer. The Summer Gala. People pray in her name for rain and avoidance of summer's fire, a drought." Her lips quirked into a smile. "A sacrifice is made to a cat of all things."

Cinder laughed. "I always liked cats."

"So do I," Anya said, still smiling. "As for the Winter Gala, it is held at the end of Jevasth—the first month of the New Year in the deepest part of winter—in honor of the Winter Lord, for Ash. The birthday of Shokan when people pray the Winter Lord's sword won't cut short their lives. So, are you coming to the gala?"

"I was planning on it. I just have to get a new outfit requisitioned."

"Requisitioned?" Anya's eyes twinkled with amusement. "A large word for a relatively simple action."

Cinder grinned, glad to make Anya happy. "I like to use large words." He eyed her in challenge. "Elves know the meaning of large words, don't they?"

Anya's brows lifted. "Are you implying I'm uneducated?"

Cinder shook his head. "Not at all."

"Good. Then have your new outfit *requisitioned*." Anya winked. "You might even find yourself a dance partner for the evening." She departed the Foe.

Cinder gaped after her. She hadn't really suggested he dance with her, had she? No. That couldn't be right. She had to be joking. She wasn't serious . . . was she?

His eyes widened in horrified realization. *She was.*

A pit opened in Cinder's stomach. The thought of dancing with Anya terrified him more than the spiderkin.

26

Cinder, Bones, and Depth traveled along the cobblestone roads of Certitude with a definite objective in mind. However, in the elven city, the streets were sinuous, brick-paved tracings. Every turn brought a new vista. Switchbacks wended amongst groves of trees, and in the summer, the overhanging branches would have shaded the roads.

Before reaching their destination, Cinder noticed a well-dressed elf woman headed their way. She was tall, clearly of high caste—a noble— and he shifted to give her a wide berth. Her blonde hair was arranged in an elaborate braid, her tall ears easily visible. She might have been anywhere between his own age to decades older, but her haughty carriage proclaimed a different truth: she considered herself well above their station, and in Cinder's eyes, her overly proud demeanor diminished her beauty.

For this reason, it surprised Cinder when she halted in his path, gaze going to his uniform. She addressed him, her dark eyes assessing. "You are of the Third Directorate, correct?" She continued to speak, not waiting on his reply. "How are you finding your time amongst civilized people?"

Cinder understood her implication. She meant that as a human, he had never experienced life amongst those who were civilized. He was about to reply with a cutting remark, but in the last instant, he reconsidered. In Certitude, there was no such thing as poverty, a sad phenomenon all-too common in Swift Sword. In addition, the elven city had no mercenaries stalking the streets like predators hunting gazelles; nor were there evil folk who drove women and men into prostitution. Certitude was beautiful, the buildings blended amongst a broad grove of trees. The streets were clean and the people healthy and happy. Maybe she had a point. Swift Sword could use a great deal of elven civilization.

"I'm finding it enlightening," he said. "Perhaps one day human cities can be more like the ones of Yaksha Sithe."

She smiled. "What a fine dream. Carry on, young man." On she went without another word.

"That was strange," Bones said.

"That's because elves are strange," Depth said.

Cinder watched the elf woman maneuver through traffic for a few more seconds. "Come on," he told the other two. "We need to order those new clothes for the Winter Gala."

"Are you sure you have enough money?" Bones asked him.

Cinder wasn't sure, but he refused to beg for assistance. If nothing else, he'd become handy with a needle and thread. He could mend some of his older clothing into a semblance of what was required. Still, it would be nice to have new clothes. He'd grown during his time at the Third Directorate and was now almost as tall as Joria but far lankier. "I have enough," he replied, knowing his tone was curt. Bones and Depth were good friends, but Cinder didn't want their help. It made him feel poor.

"Well, I've got a few extra coins saved if you need a loan," Depth said.

"I appreciate the offer," Cinder said, "but I don't need it. The day's wasting."

They pressed on, forced by the crowded, narrow streets to a slow travel. Despite yesterday's snowfall, many people were out today. A clear sky, cloudless and an endless blue, predicted the lack of any further inclement weather. The sun shone bright, melting the snow and leaving puddles like lacunae along Certitude's streets.

As they strode through the city, it struck Cinder how alike Yaksha Sithe's culture was to Rakesh's, at least in some ways. Both were obviously nations, but there was more to it than that. The members of the so-called Blessed Race resided in cities—beautiful ones, true, and without any hint of poverty—but full of industry and homes, any of which could have been planted in Swift Sword. They also farmed large fields and brought their agriculture into markets on wagons pulled by bullocks. In addition, the elves had a productive mercantile class as well as blacksmiths, coopers, farriers, and other artisans who provided goods and services. In all the ways that counted, Yaksha Sithe and Rakesh were more similar than dissimilar.

It surprised Cinder. He would have expected greater differences. According to Lieutenant Capshin, their History instructor, it had once been true. In the ages prior to the Mythaspuris, elves had lived a more bucolic type of existence.

A half-hour later, the traffic thinned, and they reached their destination, *Elegant Weaves*, the tailor shop recommended by Master Absin. The store was owned by an elf who was willing to work with humans.

They entered the shop and were met by the fragrance of uncut cloth and sandalwood incense. Several chandeliers provided bright illumination as did the sunshine pouring through a pair of windows looking out onto the road. Bolts of fabric and lengths of leather were stacked in wooden bins scattered throughout the store. Cinder had no idea there were so many different types and colors of cloth.

An elf—short, rotund, and elegant—stood behind a counter. "I am Master Brance Reaville. How may I help you gentlemen?" he asked, his voice rich and resonant.

Cinder stepped forward and introduced himself. "My name is Cinder Shade," he said. "We're students at the Third Directorate." He gestured to their clothing and spoke for all three of them. "We need new attire for Duchess Cervine's Winter Gala."

Bones and Depth made their own introductions.

Master Brance nodded his head in understanding. "Of course. The Winter Gala. All the finest members of elven society will be in attendance. You will require new uniforms? All three of you?"

"Maybe more than just us," Cinder said. "There are four other humans who likely need new clothing."

"What about the dwarves?" Depth asked.

"They're dwarves. They have their own tailor in mind," Bones answered.

Dwarves were woven, which meant they also had a greater variety of tailors willing to accept them as clients. Another aspect where humans were considered lessers.

Master Brance didn't remark upon this unspoken fact. He stepped out from behind the counter, holding a clipboard and a pen. Hanging loosely around his neck was a long strip of leather bearing regular markings. "Perhaps we shall take your measurements first," he said, addressing Cinder. "This way, please." The tailor guided Cinder to a mirrored alcove. "Take off your jacket and boots."

Cinder did as instructed. He twisted, turned, held his arms out to the side, expanded his chest, held in his stomach. All the while, Master Brance took measurements of his waist, hips, shoulders, chest, and neck, writing them down on a piece of paper.

Several minutes later, it was Depth's turn. After that, Bones.

Master Brance named a price, and Cinder hid a wince. It would take a good portion of his savings.

"I'll have the uniforms ready in a week," Master Brance said. "You'll also want new boots. I can recommend a cordwainer, if you like? Sterias Shawenre. He's two streets away." He gave them the directions.

Cinder and the others thanked Master Brance for his service and left his store. From there, they made their way to the cordwainer's shop. During the short walk, Cinder idly wondered if there might be any work he could do at the Third Directorate to earn some extra coin. Between the clothes and boots, he would hardly have any money left.

As promised by Master Brance, a week later the requisitioned clothes were completed, and they were exquisite. It was now the evening of the Winter Gala, and Cinder readied himself. The day's classes had been cut short, and after showering, he dried off, shaved and got dressed, buttoning his slim-fitting coat and tying the laces to his new boots. The clothes fit him perfectly, and he examined himself in the mirror, admiring the cut.

Cinder was grateful, especially since he'd outgrown the clothes he'd brought with him to the Third Directorate. His original pants were several inches too short, and the shirts were too tight. He'd had to alter all of them on his own, and the work was rough. The clothes from Swift Sword were serviceable but not acceptable for formal occasions.

Unlike this outfit. He tried not to preen while examining himself in the mirror, but he couldn't help it. He'd never worn such fine clothing.

A final glance, and he buckled on the sword provided to him so long ago by Master Lerid. A string was wound around the hilt and knotted at his belt, locking the blade within its scabbard. The elves would provide a weave of *lorethasra* to ensure any weapons brought to the Winter Gala remained sheathed. However, General Arwan, the commandant, had made it clear that the students of the Third Directorate were to go to the Gala with a weapon at their hip.

Cinder polished the bronze buttons holding his gray coat closed, adjusted it one last time, and attached a crimson cloak. He was ready, and not a moment too soon.

Bones stepped into the doorway leading into his room at Krathe House. "You ready?"

Cinder nodded. "Yes. How about everyone else?"

"Everyone but Wark. You know how much he likes to primp."

"I heard that," Wark said from several doors down. "I was ready ten minutes ago."

Cinder chuckled. "I think that's our sign."

He exited his room, shutting the door behind him as was his habit, and went to join the others in the common area. Everyone looked fit, tidy, and trim in their uniforms, even the dwarves, who had brushed and freshly braided their beards and hair.

"Devesh save us, Hotgate. It took you long enough," Sriovey said.

"You could have left without me," Cinder said. "After all, age before beauty."

"Well, we're older, but you sure aren't more beautiful," Derius said. "You look like a carrot, as skinny and tall as you are."

"You look nice, too," Cinder said dryly.

Ishmay clapped his hands, gathering their attention. "You ladies can argue about who's prettier later on. I'm famished. Come on."

The first years set off in a series of grumbles and laughter, exiting Krathe House. They were filled with boisterous energy, excited to see the palace and witness all the elves dressed in their finery. Mostly, they wondered about the food. This was the Winter Gala, and from what the second years had told them, it was the finest feast they'd likely enjoy the entire year.

For young men, food was generally their primary concern. That and women, but at the Gala, they wouldn't run into the latter, at least not the humankind. The Gala was for the highest members of elven society, an occasion for them to prance and preen, to see and be seen, to mingle and gossip.

Cinder had no interest in any of it. The local nobles at the Gala likely wouldn't talk to them, and the humans and dwarves certainly couldn't talk to the women and ask them for a dance.

The conversation amongst the Firsters continued while they marched along the road to Certitude, their breaths blooming in the cold air. The sun hung low on the horizon, highlighting the sky and clouds in pomegranate reds and lush oranges as the heavens transitioned to purple and darkness. The turnoff for the ducal palace wasn't too far off.

Ishmay sidled up to Cinder. "You think they'll have strawberries?" he asked. "I love strawberries."

Cinder grinned at the Gandharvan. "I'll be sure to eat them all and let you know how they taste."

"That's not funny." Ishmay didn't appear amused.

"What does Ishmay want to eat now?" Wark asked, walking a few paces away.

"Strawberries," Cinder answered.

Depth, striding alongside Wark, rolled his eyes. "My sister, Kaylee, used to go on like that about strawberries," he noted. "Of course, she's only twelve."

Ishmay, never one to take teasing well, glowered while the others laughed.

Seconds later, they reached their turnoff, a gravel path lined by twin rows of cedars. Their boots crunched as they traversed a winding, mile-long road. *Diptha* lamps on black posts twice their heights lit their way and brought them to a manicured lawn, one bisected by the gravel path. A tasteful decoration of topiary—unicorns, pegasi, and dragons—held court upon the wide expanse of grass. More *diptha* lamps—strings of lights wrapped through the links of a wrought iron chain—draped the road's edges.

They reached the palace, a gleaming structure of slick, gray stone. Soaring spires reached for the darkening sky. Pennants flew from the towers, and an arching set of stairs drew them toward a pair of doors that were thrown open. The doorway at the top was wide enough to allow the passage of a wagon.

Guards, their greaves and gauntlets shining silver and their cloaks pinned just so, faced outward. They held their spears loosely and at an identical angle.

Cinder shook his head in bewilderment. Their weapons and armor would be near useless in any kind of combat.

A fussy-looking elf stood in the doorway, barring further entrance. He wore a black tuxedo and white gloves and had a self-important bearing. His stiff manner of speech matched his arrogant air, and only after verifying their names and status did he let them enter the foyer. He directed them down a hall where a ceiling lofted twenty feet above their heads and their boots echoed on white marble tiles. Chandeliers lit the way and expensive rugs softened their footsteps. They trailed a line of elves, took a left turn, and reached the ballroom's entrance.

Cinder halted, inhaling sharply.

A wide flight of steps descended several feet into a room vast and large enough to hold hundreds. Above them, fifty feet or more, soared a muralled ceiling—a scene of a forest separating desert and sea. Hundreds of small *diptha* bulbs glowed amidst great crystal chandeliers, causing them to glitter and gleam. The light illuminated the room to daylight brightness causing the gold filigree decorating every surface to sparkle. On either side of the room ran a line of regularly spaced arched, open doorways leading to different parts of the palace such as large alcoves or small rooms where various elves appeared to be in deep discussion or playful banter. Grooved columns with entablatures of tigers and playful monkeys bracketed and supported each doorway. On the far end of the ballroom was a bank of windows and glass doors opening onto a balcony running the room's width. Warming the massive space was a set of fireplaces blazing with logs, each one large enough for Cinder to enter unstooped.

"Food," Rorian moaned, pointing out a table groaning under a plethora of fare.

For whatever reason, Cinder wasn't hungry, and he waved the rest of the Firsters on, holding back while they sprang toward the tables like a pack of starving wolves. Instead, he took his time to descend down the steps and found an unoccupied space along the wall. It was distant from the small orchestra playing a lively tune on the other side of the ballroom.

Cinder closely observed the elves in attendance.

Everyone's clothing made his uniform appear drab. The women wore elaborate outfits, jeweled and lovely, with hair piled atop their heads and left to cascade down to their bare shoulders. The men were attired in brightly colored shirts and jackets along with pants piped in silver or gold. Diamond-encrusted clasps held back their long hair. This included General Arwan, Master Absin, Master Serwil, and Master Nuhlin. All of them wore uniforms, but theirs were of a far finer cut and quality compared to Cinder's.

More details.

Some elves traversed the periphery of the ballroom, speaking and laughing in bright tones. Most, however, danced, men and women in close proximity, stepping in formal measures. Cinder recognized the movements, although as usual, he couldn't remember how he knew it.

Unfortunately, he also recognized Riyne and Estin who presently danced with a pair of lovely elf women.

"You don't appear to be having a very good time," a voice cut into his thoughts.

Cinder turned to the side and found Princess Anya several feet away, her expression amused. She wore a simple, green gown. It fit her perfectly and was the same lovely hue as her eyes. A silver net supported her hair. Her outfit wasn't as fanciful as some worn by other women at the ball, but Cinder thought Anya's was more elegant because of its simplicity. Her only accommodation to her status as a princess were the pair of emerald earrings shining at her ears. That, and a thick gold necklace, which supported an emerald brooch nestled between her breasts.

Cinder probably shouldn't be looking at or thinking about her breasts. Rather, he forced a memory of Coral smiling his way while she sang.

Anya held a pair of silver goblets in her hand and extended one to him. "It's only water, and you'll need it," she said. "The room tends to get warm with all the bodies inside."

Cinder accepted the goblet with a word of thanks.

"So. Are you enjoying the Gala?" Anya asked.

"I can't say for sure one way or another," Cinder said, taking a sip of water. "I only arrived a few minutes ago."

"A fair answer," Anya said. She faced the dance floor and its occupants, arms crossed under her breasts.

Cinder quickly looked away. He definitely shouldn't notice her breasts.

A furrow creased Anya's brow. "We are a lovely race," she murmured, possibly to herself. "But perhaps too soft and frivolous."

Cinder didn't know whether he was being addressed or not, and he held silent. However, Anya's observation agreed with his own, at least about the nobles.

"You agree with me, do you not?" Anya said, facing him again. She arched a single elegant eyebrow in question.

"I didn't say anything," Cinder protested.

Anya quirked a smile. "Your silence spoke on your behalf."

Cinder was about to answer, but he caught sight of the other Firsters. They stood by the food, and to a man they shot him silent pleas of panicked warning, the battlefield equivalent of *'Get out now!'* They likely thought he was committing a major breach in etiquette by speaking to the princess.

Anya followed his gaze and noticed the Firsters, many of whom suddenly found the tablecloths or their food utterly fascinating. The princess chuckled. "I think your friends are worried you might get in trouble for speaking to me."

Bones considered himself a humble man. He wouldn't lie about his skill with the sword or any kind of fighting. He knew he was good, and there was no point in denying it. He was the best human warrior out there, but otherwise he was humble. He knew his place in the world, and he knew enough not to rock the boat and cause trouble.

Cinder didn't seem to have that same sense of self-preservation. The fool kept leaping from one stupid situation into another. For instance, his argument with Sriovey on their first day at the Directorate; never backing down from the elves; or fighting when all hope was lost— Bones had heard how Cinder had won his first battle in the Maker's Tournament. *Pure luck.*

Or maybe it was pure luck *and* overwhelming will. Bones had never met a more determined or dedicated person than Cinder. It was both scary and awe-inspiring.

Whatever the case, Cinder somehow always came out on the other side of his stupid escapades smelling like roses. It was unconscionable. How could someone who continually made one stupid decision after another never pay a price for his stupidity?

Cinder's luck never ceased to amaze Bones, but this time he had really done it. He was talking to Princess Anya, and the fool didn't have the good sense to walk away.

None of his claims to actually know the princess mattered now, not here at the Winter Gala with all these elves around. Cinder could say they were friends. That he'd spoken to her at the library during their first days at the academy when she had apparently shown him the location of a book. Or he could make his claim to have talked to her while they were alone in the bowels of Firemirror Hall a few weeks ago. He could even tell about how she'd teased him about dancing with her at the Gala.

No one would believe him. Not here. Not now.

Bones mentally snorted. *He* didn't believe Cinder. There was no chance any of what he said was true. Cinder blathered on about brotherhood this and brotherhood that. It and training were all he cared about. Sure, he'd grown impossibly skilled as a warrior in an impossibly short time—in the recesses of his mind, Bones knew Cinder would eventually overtake him—but regarding the princess, Cinder had to be a braggart. His claims weren't true, right? They couldn't be. No one spoke to the princess if they didn't have to. She was just so fucking intimidating.

Then again . . .

Bones peered at Cinder, eyes narrowed in assessment. How was he smiling and laughing with her? Was he really that stupid? Didn't he know how his behavior looked to everyone else? Nothing good came from a human talking to an elven princess.

Bones came to a startling realization: Cinder liked the princess. Liked her like a man liked a beautiful woman. He could see it now, and pity rose in his heart. *Idiot.*

Cinder smiled at Anya. "Consider it from their perspective. You are a beautiful elven woman, and not just any beautiful elven woman, but a princess. The daughter of the empress, the woman who holds our lives and the fates of countless others in her hands. From their perspective, you are a terrifying figure."

"You think I'm beautiful?" Again, came the smile of amusement. "Careful. That *will* get you in trouble."

Cinder silently cursed. Why in Devesh's name had he told the princess she was beautiful? Even if it was true? *Idiot.*

Estin had been having a pleasant evening, dancing and drinking with his friends and the lovely women of Certitude. They sought out his company since tonight, he was their prince, not a lowly Firster. He was the most important figure in attendance. No bowing and scraping to the masters of the Third Directorate. Best of all, he didn't see any humans or dwarves in attendance. Their absence made the evening all the sweeter.

But then, like insects carrying disease, they'd scuttled into the ballroom. Hovering like flies over the food. Their presence curdled the cream of his enjoyment. His pleasure soured further when he noticed that arrogant bastard, Cinder Shade, cornering Anya and forcing his conversation upon her.

Anya was too kind to the humans. She allowed them too much leeway, granted them far too much leave to treat her as a near-equal. They should know better. Anya was as far above them as an eagle soaring over pigs in their sty. She was a princess of the realm, second in line for the throne, and they should bend knee to her whenever she deigned to walk amongst them.

Not bray like a donkey in her face.

Estin glowered. Riyne noticed.

"What is it?"

"See for yourself," Estin growled.

Riyne took one glance in the direction of Estin's gaze, and his face instantly reddened. He scowled. "That *ghrina*. He should know better than to talk to our women."

Estin silently agreed, although he recognized the basis for Riyne's outrage.

Riyne was a good friend, but only a blind man could fail to notice the feelings he had for Anya. Not that it would do him any good. Riyne came from a noble house, but he had been born six decades too late. Anya was too old for him. Besides, it was his brother, Lisandre, who held Anya's regard.

Estin continued to glare at Cinder, watching him. His face clouded with fury when he saw the human's gaze possibly flick to Anya's breasts. "This ends now. Come on," he ordered Riyne.

He marched toward Anya's rescue, Riyne at his elbow. Estin intended to drive Cinder off, and if it left the human bloody, then so be it.

He caught sight of Anya's face as she faced the human, speaking to him in a firm tone of disapproval. "Careful. That *will* get you in trouble."

"What kind of trouble has the human caused this time?" Estin asked, arriving with Riyne at his side and apparently overhearing Anya's warning.

"What trouble was it?" Anya asked Cinder with a challenging tilt to her head. "Was it not in denying me a dance?" She addressed her brother. "I mentioned it to him earlier, and now he's trying to weasel out of it."

If he had a shovel, Cinder would have dug himself a bottomless pit and never exited. Either that, or his grave. Either would do. Invisibility would be nice, too. Then he could just slink off unnoticed.

"Really," Estin said, his tone flat as he slowly faced Cinder. "You would deny my sister, a princess of the sithe, this simple request? A dance? It is a blessing she offers, and you would tell her no?" His voice had an angry, disbelieving note.

Cinder felt his face burn. Other elves were starting to stare. In the corner of his vision, he saw the Firsters viewing him with pity. There was no good way out of his predicament. "I didn't think we were allowed to dance with elves."

Riyne snarled in outrage. "If an elf asks you to dance—man or woman—then you dance. Do you understand, stupid human?"

Cinder's embarrassment transformed to anger. He scowled at Riyne, about to say something he might regret.

Anya spoke first. "I can handle one human, gentlemen. Move along."

Estin appeared ready to continue berating Cinder. His mouth opened for a moment before snapping shut. His eyes flickered to Anya, who simply viewed him expectantly. Estin settled down, shoulders rounding like a little boy caught doing something naughty. "Yes, Anya," he muttered. "Come on." He tugged on Riyne's sleeve.

"But—"

"Leave me. Now!" Anya commanded.

This time it was Riyne who was chastened. He and Estin shuffled off.

Cinder watched them depart with a sense of disbelief. He'd seen Anya cow her brother and Riyne before, but it still shocked him how they shrank before her anger. Especially since he seemed to have no fear of her fury. Respect, yes, but not fear. His mind told him he should, but his heart wasn't listening.

Anya was a graduate of the Third Directorate. She was a renowned warrior without equal. She could break him in half, and there was nothing he could do to stop her. However, her fearsome strength didn't matter to Cinder. He wasn't afraid of her, and he realized he didn't want to fear her either.

"I apologize for my brother's behavior," Anya said. "He and Riyne require further schooling in some matters."

Cinder didn't know how to respond. Disagreeing would be a lie but agreeing might be considered too forward. Estin, after all, was her brother, and Riyne a member of a respected family. He chose to disregard her words and held out a hand. "Shall we dance?"

Anya chuckled, slipping her hand into his. "Certainly."

Cinder might not be afraid of Anya, but holding her hand set his heart racing for reasons he couldn't explain. It wasn't desire. It was something else, something he didn't understand.

He halted. Strange memories—

No. That wasn't right. It wasn't strange memories. It was a strange longing for the fleeting *possibility* of memories. Whatever it was, it wisped through his mind, flashing like fireflies, gone too swiftly to allow understanding of what he was seeing.

"Are you well?" Anya asked, peering at him in concern. "We don't have to dance if you feel ill."

Cinder forced a smile. "No. I'm fine."

They joined the dance floor just as the orchestra began a quick melody.

"Do you know this one?" Anya asked.

Cinder observed the other dancers on the floor. They moved more quickly this time. He shook his head. He didn't recognize their movements.

"Follow my lead," Anya said.

She held out a hand, and he took it. Next, she indicated for him to put his arm around her waist. He did so with reluctance. It seemed wrong to hold Anya so close, especially when images of Coral drifted through his mind.

She must have noticed his discomfort. "Relax. You need not fear the opinions of others. You aren't doing anything untoward."

Cinder took a deep inhalation, exhaling slow and controlled through his nostrils. The breath settled his nerves some, but his heart continued to race.

"Ready?"

Anya led them through slow steps, guiding him with voice and subtle gestures. Cinder stumbled about. He did his best not to step on her toes as they made a slow circuit of the dance floor. Anya was a patient dance partner, but Cinder could tell she looked forward to the end of the music. She glowered, biting back an oath when he nearly stomped on her open-toed shoes.

Anya bit back a curse. Cinder was not a graceful dancer. Whatever skill he had with the sword clearly didn't carry over to the ballroom. He'd almost stepped on her toes three times so far. Her gown had evaded his heavy feet by the barest of margins, and she was starting to regret pushing him to dance with her.

It was strange how poorly he moved across the dance floor. She'd seen him fight. Then, he'd been all grace and speed. The quick movements and timing of a dance shouldn't be so difficult for him to learn.

And yet, it apparently was. He danced as well as a hobbled horse.

Then again why had she wanted to dance with him in the first place? It likely had something about the challenging glint she caught in his eyes whenever he spoke to her. She wanted to meet the challenge and wipe it from his face.

It was the most likely answer, although she wished she'd chosen a safer method, one in which her feet and gown wouldn't be placed at risk.

Cinder almost stepped on Anya's toes again. Only a swift withdrawal on her part had saved her foot from getting stomped.

Sweat beaded on his forehead, but an epiphany struck him then. His innate sense of motion, of an opponent's likely movements while sparring, could he use it here?

He tried.

Several steps later, he attuned his awareness, guessing at Anya's next steps. He altered his movements to match hers; when she would bend, sway, step forward or backward, twist and spin.

He fell into the rhythm of the dance. His anxiety faded, and he began to enjoy his time dancing with Anya. A smile replaced her frown of displeasure.

In that moment, a pure pond formed in the core of Cinder's being. His *lorethasra*. It was different from how it had appeared in the Foe. Blue and green lightning warded it off now, but regardless, its appearance at the Gala surprised him. He reached for it, but the lightning caused him to mentally hiss. It burned when he tried to conduct his *lorethasra*.

He pulled away from the pond, considering the matter while he and Anya drifted through several more movements of the dance. Why did lightning guard his *lorethasra*? Cinder didn't know, but he decided to reach again for the perfectly reflective pond. As before, the strange lightning stung him, but the barest essence of his *lorethasra* still entered him, and Cinder's senses expanded. The world came alive. Sounds, shapes, and smells enhanced.

Cinder fell into the rhythm of the music, more fully into Anya's movements. They swayed, twirled, and swept amongst the other dancers, in perfect harmony and rhythm with one another.

Their pace increased, and they sped across the dance floor. The music reached a crescendo. Cinder twirled Anya about, and she ended the motion resting in his arms, in a dip.

He stared into her green eyes, which were wide. A flash of fear might have passed across her face.

Cinder hastily straightened.

Anya flushed. "Thank you for the dance." She fanned herself. "The heat seems to have gotten the best of me. If you don't mind, I need some air."

"Of course," Cinder said. "Do you want me to get you some water?"

Anya smiled. "You're kind, but no. Enjoy the Gala." With that, she hastily dashed away from him.

Cinder lost sight of her in seconds. He didn't know what had her so upset. Once he'd overcome his clumsiness, he thought the dance had gone well.

Hadn't it? Cinder continued staring after Anya. Or had he offended the princess in some way?

With a start, he realized he was still standing on the dance floor, and he quickly removed himself, making his way to where the Firsters remained perched by the food table.

"What did you do?" Bones asked. "The princess didn't look too happy when you finished dancing."

"She looked like a scared rabbit," Rorian said around a mouthful of food.

"I didn't do anything," Cinder protested.

Bones gave him a pitying expression. "Well, judging by how quickly she left you on the floor, you must have done something."

"I honestly didn't do anything."

"Whatever it was," Depth said, "I'm thinking her brother disapproves." He pointed to Estin, who was scowling furiously in their direction.

Cinder's heart sank. "Just great."

Anya stood alone on the balcony outside the ballroom, shadowed and partially hidden by the tall shrubs decorating one corner of the bricked space. Fulsom ruled over a cloudless night, and its golden light highlighted the palace and its grounds in stark illumination. The air held still, no wind to bring a further chill to the cold, and the night was quiet except for the murmuring of couples strolling the gardens below or conversing on the balcony.

Anya breathed out in soft, clouding pants as she sought to wrestle her roiling thoughts under control.

The dance. The memories. They couldn't be true. She wouldn't allow it.

She was Anya Aruyen, and she had long since set aside her past life. She had made peace with the absence of her husband, the loss of her children and family. The other woman who occasionally peered through her eyes was long deceased. Anya no longer reflected on deep questions of existence. She no longer worried what it meant to have fragmented memories. She no longer considered the nature of her reality. Questions about her innate nature. Was she a real person or the delusion of someone else? After all, what was a person if not the sum of their memories? And if that was true, did it mean Anya was fragmented?

She had convinced herself of the unimportance of those questions, and she desperately wanted to believe they were unimportant. Desperately wanted to forget them.

But they persisted, troubling her mind like an unreachable itch, and tonight all the lies she told herself, the ones in which she pretended the loss of her memories didn't matter, were exposed as the falsity she'd always sensed they were.

It was the dance with Cinder. He'd surprised her, initially proving to be an incompetent dance partner and then transforming into someone sublime. But it had been his final maneuver. The simple steps ending on a dip.

The movements had sparked a memory within Anya, one from her first life. She remembered dancing with her long-dead husband, and he'd said her name. "Jessira."

27

Several weeks after the Winter Gala, Cinder was walking back to Krathe House from the library, his mind elsewhere and distracted. His distraction ended when he noticed a monster stalking the Quad. Cinder crashed to a halt, and his hand immediately went to his shoke, which he always had on his person. He only calmed somewhat when he glanced about and realized no one else appeared worried by the creature.

Cinder blinked. *Wait. What am I actually seeing?*

Seconds of observation later, he had his answer. *Not a monster. A troll.*

The woven creature wasn't as tall as the yakshin, but he had a granite presence, an unyielding, stony strength that made him appear as massive as the mountains surrounding the Third Directorate. The being wore nothing but a loincloth and was otherwise garbed in short fur the gray-brown color of bark and had equally rough-hewn features. Beetled brows jutted like a craggy ridge above a nose thrusting forward like an outcropping, and his obdurate jaw was shaped like a spade. Curling horns similar to a ram's flared from his temples. Long, dark hair was collected in a braided ponytail, and he held a staff that was taller than Cinder. The troll used it as a walking stick, and it clacked a steady rhythm with every step he took.

Cinder stared in slack-jawed amazement, taking a few moments to notice the humans pacing beside the troll. Two of them. They were utterly forgettable in appearance, except for their dark eyes, which were rounder than the norm for Rakesh. Otherwise, both had limp, mousy-brown hair, which was cut short, plain features—neither ugly nor handsome—and were of medium height and build. But it was their bearing which caught Cinder's interest. They prowled rather than walked, and both held wary, dangerous expressions. Their hands never left the swords at their hips. Most strange of all, the elves bowed low to them, clearly respectful, possibly even fearful.

Who were the humans? Were they rakishi warriors from Bharat? And what about the trolls? He didn't know much about them. They were said to be givers of justice, and they went where they willed.

In this case, the troll marched directly toward the center of the Quad, to Garad Lull's forever frozen body.

Curiosity got the better of Cinder, and he followed the troll. He wanted to know more about him, especially because a tingling in the back of his mind told him he should trust their kind, befriend them if possible. He also wanted to know more about the humans. Why did the elves seem afraid of them? He cautiously trailed the strange new arrivals.

One of the humans took note of him. "You have a question, boy?" he demanded.

The brusque tone should have warned him off, but Cinder had too many questions. He disregarded the human's glare and introduced himself. "I'm Cinder Shade. I don't know for sure if I've ever met a troll before. I was hoping to talk to one."

The troll reached Garad Lull but paused in his perusal of the Titan. "Let him pass, Breech. He doesn't have a bladed weapon."

"He doesn't need one," the human—Breech apparently—countered. "He walks like one of us."

"A holder?" the troll stepped closer. "He doesn't smell like one. He smells human."

Holders? Of course! Cinder had read an account of them. They guarded the trolls and yakshins, serving as their protectors. Holders were a strange type of woven, a mix of human, elves, and maybe another species. They possessed the physical stature of the former but the *lorethasra* of the latter and whatever else went into their weaving. However, for holders, it went even deeper. They were far greater than the sum of their parts, consummate warriors, said to be even deadlier than the rakishis of Bharat. No wonder the elves appeared cautious.

And right now, Cinder discovered the holders were viewing him with suspicion and wariness. He carefully eased away from them, making sure to keep them in view. Nervousness didn't cloud his judgment, but he still recognized that he might have stepped into a heaping barrel-full of trouble. The holders were in the midst of bracketing him.

"He is not an enemy," the troll said.

"You don't know that," Breech said.

The troll smiled. "And yet I do." He took two strides, covering several yards in the process and reached Cinder. "My name is Maize."

Cinder viewed the holders sidelong for a moment more. He addressed the troll. "Cinder Shade."

"You are a student here?"

"I am."

"My people are Justices. Have you heard of this?"

Cinder shook his head. "I've heard the word, but I don't know what it means."

Maize smiled again. "It's not a surprise. Few do. A Justice is one who ascertains the truth and writes it into the world's *aether*. We do so in such a way that it can never be unknown."

Cinder blinked in surprise. A powerful ability if true, and he had no reason to doubt Maize. After all, it was said that trolls couldn't lie. "What did you hope to learn here?"

"I was called to investigate the Third Directorate," Maize said. "I thought it was something to do with the Titan. Has he seemed different to you than usual?"

Cinder glanced at Garad Lull. What a bizarre question. But, no, as far as he could tell, the Titan was the same as he had always been. He said so.

Maize's regard went to the Titan. "Odd. When I approached him, I thought I felt a brief flight of unusual power wanting to come to awareness. It's gone now."

Cinder grunted, not sure what the troll meant. Garad was a stone-skinned, living statue. Able to take a breath a day at noon. Nothing more. He had no power or awareness.

The troll silently peered at Cinder, and the holders held a nearby position. Their hands remained on the hilt of their swords. Cinder shifted uneasily beneath the uncomfortable weight of their distrustful scrutiny.

"You might want to be running along now," Breech said. "I can see you've got a lot more questions, but we don't have the time or inclination to answer them."

Cinder flicked his gaze to the troll, who stared unblinking at him. The strange visit with the troll was apparently at an end. Cinder bowed to Maize and the holders, straightened, and made to walk away.

"Maynalor," Maize said.

Cinder stopped in his tracks, shocked. *Maynalor.* The word the yak-shin in Swift Sword had called him. *Someone of interest with a secret.*

"Are you him?" Maize asked. "The winds whisper the name. It blows through the boughs of the trees."

"I was once given that name," Cinder said carefully, not sure where this bizarre conversation was headed. He waited for Maize to explain further, but the troll appeared lost in thought.

"Strange power wanting to come to awareness," Maize said, his voice and eyes distant. "I will have to think on this." His mindfulness of the world at large returned, and his gaze sharpened on Cinder. "Love Devesh above all else. Have faith. It is the hardest of hopes, and the only thing more difficult is admitting and repenting of your sins."

By this point, Cinder was completely lost. *What in the frag is the troll talking about?*

Maize's eyes went to Garad. "Faith and steadfastness. Humans once had this in abundance. It will be needed when the storm breaks."

In the days following Cinder's meeting with Maize, winter tore into the Third Directorate with a fresh blanket of snow, ice, and snapping cold. The memory of the troll seemed a long- ago occurrence given the unchanging freezing weather. The garden outside Cinder's room at Krathe House lay fallow, the stream running through it frozen. Snow fell today, a steady cascade of heavy, white flakes.

Cinder sat in the common room, alongside a few other Firsters. A fire blazed in the fireplace, and he viewed the winter outside, especially the falling snow, with antipathy. He was glad he was indoors, some place warm and dry, especially after the past few days.

The Firsters had started training for when they would be sent for the year-end Unitary Trial, which was generally held in the Daggers. Their preparations began last week when they had been sent to the high hills north of the Third Directorate and camped out and drilled in small units. It had been a wet and dreary experience with a blustery wind, cloudy sky, and freezing rain.

Cinder hated it. He didn't like miserable weather. Not one bit. But then again, what could he do about it? Complaining was useless, so he'd shoved down his unhappiness and did his duty as best he could. He was glad to be back at the academy now, although in another month, he and others would head out again. He hoped it would be warmer by then.

Cinder absently plucked the strings of his mandolin while the others discussed their recently completed trip to the hills. Just then a gust of wind tugged at the shutters, pushing cold air into the common room, and he shuddered. *Damn winter.*

"Bones was a git," Sriovey declared. "He just had to go charging against Ishmay and Rorian."

Bones protested. "Come on now. How was I supposed to know no one was supporting me?"

"By looking to the left and the right, you daft prick," Sriovey snapped.

"But Derius was right next to me."

"Hotgate killed me," Derius said. "Didn't you notice?"

"How did Hotgate kill a dwarf?" Joria asked. The Gandharvan twirled a knife, a habit from home apparently.

"I had help," Cinder said. "It was Rorian's idea." He sought to deflect attention and praise to the mountain Rakesh, who currently stood lowest ranked amongst the Firsters.

"We both came up with the idea," Rorian corrected. "We did it at the same time."

"But what about Sriovey?" Bones said. "He was on my right hip."

"Until Jozep got in my way," Sriovey said.

"He was meant to slow you down," Rorian explained.

"And he did," Sriovey confirmed. "I finished him off, but by then you'd gone chasing after Rorian and never saw Ishmay come up on your flank."

"And now I'm expected to remember that Rorian is smart?" Bones challenged. "In the heat of battle?"

"Of course you are," Cinder said. "Or haven't you been paying attention. Rorian's team always wins in small unit drills. He's our best tactician. And Joria's not too far behind."

Jozep had gone to his room, and now he returned to the commons, a tabla in hand. He sat next to Cinder. The two of them were the only two musicians amongst the Firsters. "What do you want to play?" he asked Cinder.

"How about "Will She Dance Alone"?" It was a dwarven love song. Jozep nodded.

"Wait," Bones said, appearing perplexed. "I thought *Cinder* was the tactician."

"Cinder is a good tactician," Derius said, "but he's not Rorian."

"Well, shit," Bones muttered. "It's too much to keep straight. Just show me who to kill, and I'm happy."

Rorian wore a pleased expression. "It's not like I'm Genka, the Sunset Warlord. I heard he's heading for Zomesth as soon as spring arrives."

"As long as he stays in the Sunsets," Ishmay muttered. "I'm not wanting to fight a strategic genius."

"I bet he doesn't slow down until he conquers all the Sunset Kingdoms," Rorian added.

Cinder noticed Sriovey share a troubled glance with Derius. He shrugged. The Sunset Warlord was troubling, which wasn't something he wanted to think about, at least not today.

He got Jozep's attention, indicating for him to set a beat, and they began playing.

"Boo!" Sriovey declared as soon as he heard the first notes. "I don't want no maudlin stuff. Play something happy. Play a drinking song."

Cinder rolled his eyes, making sure Sriovey saw it. "Do you like any kind of music other than drinking songs?"

"Why mar perfection?" Sriovey asked, an unironic portentous expression on his face.

His self-important demeanor was at odds with his normal state, and the room broke out in laughter.

"What?" Sriovey demanded.

Cinder shook his head, still chuckling, but for the dwarf's benefit, he picked out a different tune, a drinking song. Jozep knew it, and he set the new rhythm.

The room was soon filled with the sounds of humans and dwarves singing a bawdy tune about a serving boy and a group of maidens who ran him ragged, the women offering all sorts of outrageous promises they failed to keep.

When Cinder and Jozep finished the song, the others clapped enthusiastically.

"What about 'The Silent Meadow'?" Wark asked once the clapping ceased. "I love that one."

"That's another love song," Sriovey complained.

"No, it's not," Cinder said. "It's a song about heartbreak and loss." He spoke to Jozep, who didn't know the song. "It's like this." He demonstrated the tune, his fingers picking out the opening notes. Jozep quickly figured out the beat, and Wark joined them, singing in his clear tenor.

While they played, Cinder's mind drifted. The image of a blonde woman rose in his mind. He'd seen her before, sometimes in his dreams and other moments like now. She was tall, but beyond that, he couldn't make out her features. Somehow he knew she was striking.

More weeks passed, and in some parts of the world, spring sent faint green shoots as a herald for summer's eventual approach. At the Third Directorate, though, winter continued to grip the land with frozen fingers of icicles and snow, but faint hints suggested the breaking of its frigid siege. Warmer weather would eventually arrive; seen in the longer days, the sunnier afternoons, and the first buds on the trees. The sunshine in particular was a welcome change. Winter at the Third Directorate had mostly consisted of gloomy clouds, a drizzly rain, and a freezing wind.

Currently, though, the weather was warm enough for Cinder to shrug off his coat. He and Bones had the day off and the two of them shared a sparring ring. Others worked in the Cauldron, too—the warriors who came to the Directorate for advanced training, other students, and even the masters of the academy.

Cinder viewed his opponent. Bones remained superlative compared to the other humans of their class. In fact, Cinder felt sure that if Bones had even the slightest ability to conduct *lorethasra*, he would be a match for any dwarf and possibly elf. The former *Steel-Graced Adept* had progressed far under the tutelage of Master Absin. Since coming to the Third Directorate, he had married his unmatched physicality with a perfection of form.

Then again, so had Cinder. A few weeks ago, he had defeated Ishmay. At the time, it had been a surprising outcome, but not anymore. Following his victory, Cinder had continued to regularly win against the Gandharvan. It was a situation similar to when Cinder had first defeated Dorr at *Steel-Graced Adepts*—an initial victory followed by domination. Cinder reckoned that when he next had a chance to increase his ranking, he would take second place amongst the human warriors.

But what about Bones? Cinder wanted to gain a better understanding of just how much farther he had to go in order to match and surpass the best. He felt sure he could do it.

"You sure you don't want no shields?" Bones asked.

"No shields," Cinder confirmed. "I want it like the Maker's Tournament."

Bones eyed him in speculation. "When did you get so tall? First time I saw you, I thought you were a starving rat. Now look at you."

Cinder grinned, pleased to no longer be so small. He was nearly as fully muscled as Bones and didn't have to crane his neck quite so much to meet the other man's eyes. "Call it a side effect of living well."

Bones grunted. "More like eating well." He twirled his shoke. "Let's get to it then."

They were already at their marks, and of silent accord, they began the match. Neither rushed toward the other. Instead, they shuffled forward, edging in stops and starts, shokes pointed straight ahead. Cinder began circling, and Bones matched his turn, taking the center of the ring and remaining relaxed, shoke unwavering.

Cinder mentally shrugged. *Nothing to it.*

He and Bones came together in a rush. Their shokes smashed against one another, the sound an irregular rhythm of clacking wood. Cinder was content to merely defend. He parried a slash, evaded a backhand follow-up, and checked a knee.

Bones smoothly reset before Cinder could take advantage of his opponent's momentary lack of balance.

Again, they circled.

Cinder waited on Bones, but also used the short pause to deduce the other man's plans. He let the skill he'd first manifested at *Steel-Graced* guide him. The instinctual knowledge of balance and positioning that allowed him to predict his opponent's likely decisions.

Bones will rush forward. A downward attack to disguise a kick. Maybe end with an elbow or a smash with the pommel.

Cinder set himself.

Bones dashed at him.

Cinder deflected the downward slash. He slid to the side, easily dodging the kick aimed at his thigh. Bones didn't bother with the elbow or pommel. He simply reset before Cinder could counter.

"You've gotten better," Bones acknowledged. His shoke twirled, a cocky maneuver. "Must be all your practice."

"It's the only way I'll ever get better than you."

Bones grinned. "Keep dreaming."

Cinder noticed a slight bend to Bones' lead knee. A lunge was coming. Which meant Cinder would have to sidestep and counter.

Bones lunged. Cinder was already in motion. He parried, and at the same time, he shifted a single step to the side, twisted his wrists, and aimed a horizontal slash. Bones recovered and parried.

Cinder sent a lazy thrust, a jab really. Bones didn't bother blocking. Rather, he evaded the slow thrust and got in the pocket. He pressed harder now, not allowing Cinder time to recover.

Cinder disengaged, gaining valuable space. He needed to refocus.

Bones attacked. A thrust leading to an elbow. Cinder parried the first and swayed away at the waist from the latter. His motion allowed for a sidekick, one Bones checked. Another thrust from Bones, one handed this time.

Again, Cinder blocked. He darted to the side, gaining more space.

As long as he kept his nerves under control, he was able to keep up with Bones. Cinder snipped off the incipient joy threatening to fill his mind. He still had a sparring match to win.

Bones re-engaged. A circling flicker of his weapon meant to distract. Cinder slapped Bones' shoke aside. Bones went for the circling flicker once more, leading to a lunge. Cinder blocked. Bones over-extended. *An opening.* Cinder's heart raced with hope. He slammed home a vertical slash into Bones' shoulder.

Cinder stood in stunned amazement. It took a long time for his accomplishment to penetrate his shock. He wasn't sure who was more surprised, he or Bones.

He'd never won a touch against Bones before and hadn't expected to do so today. He'd hoped to, wanted to, tried to make himself believe he would but always a worm of doubt sapped his confidence.

Cinder's shock slowly transformed to satisfaction and joy. *He'd won a point off Bones!* It had been difficult but not impossible. He could do it again. Cinder felt sure of it. He also felt sure he'd continue to improve. Maybe when the next ranking challenges occurred, he'd take first place amongst the human warriors, not just second.

Bones was cursing loudly. "How the hell did you get so good?" He rolled his shoulders and reset himself, shoke ready. "Let's see you do it twice. I promise you won't."

He proved equal to his vow, demolishing Cinder in their next five matches.

28

More days sped by, one after the other, and spring sent its first couriers to the Third Directorate—a profusion of wildflowers bobbing in the breeze like lines of dancers. The wind blew warmer now, softer, too, and from the south. No one much felt like spending time in the classroom. Focusing on History or Tactics and Strategy proved a chore. The students wanted to live and breathe the brighter, happier weather, no matter how short-lived for a late frost was still likely. They especially felt the stirring rush to be outside whenever they had a day off. Then they went to Certitude, to have a few drinks, relax, and listen to the gossip.

Spring fever.

Cinder felt it himself, but the gnawing need, the forceful desire to become a better warrior—a great one—kept him trapped at the Directorate. He couldn't argue against his unknown yearning; nor did he want to. Instead, he heeded its advice and trained. It wasn't the entire day—he still remembered to let his body rest—but some of it, the mornings at least. He rotated his practice, spending an hour on archery, then the sword, and finally unarmed combat. For the latter, he

393

generally sparred with Master Jovick or whichever dwarf happened to still be at the academy.

And in the afternoon, he practiced Master Absin's breathing technique, trying to purify and conduct his *lorethasra*, although so far, it didn't seem to be doing him any good. In all the months since he had first learned the elven cycling technique, Cinder had only rarely seen his *lorethasra* unless he was in the Foe. Within the bizarre half-world, he could even conduct his *lorethasra*, but otherwise, it was impossible.

He recalled those moments in the Foe. In a lot of ways, it was like how the dwarves and elves described it. Sure, Cinder didn't gain an increased connection to the stone surrounding them, like the dwarves. He didn't notice the cool moistness of a distant, damp cave or the dry, ancient boulders littering the mountains. And unlike an elf, he couldn't hear the wind's voice as it blew through the trees; or feel the rain's caress as it fell on distant savannas; or know the taste of the sun's warmth on a plot of meadow.

For Cinder, it was much simpler. His awareness of the natural world increased. Every sense grew sharper, heightened, and his speed and strength were enhanced. And because of those reasons he persisted in his practices, his breathing exercises. While they often left him bored, they also served to relax his mind, soothing his restless, unnamed needs. He didn't know if this meant anything, but for now it was enough.

He spoke of this one rest day to Sriovey, who had agreed to train against Cinder in unarmed combat.

They shared a sparring ring at the Cauldron, which was quiet today. Just the two of them. Everyone else had gone to Certitude.

"Why is this so important to you?" Sriovey asked.

"I want to be the best in our class," Cinder answered.

"Didn't you beat Bones every time you faced him this week? You're already first."

Cinder shook his head. "No, I'm not. I'm sixth. I want to be first."

Sriovey chuckled. "You're an idiot. You know that? No human has ever bested a dwarf at the Directorate."

Cinder spoke quietly. "I want to best more than just the dwarves." He knew his statement would be met with ridicule.

Sriovey didn't disappoint. His eyes boggled. "Elves? You want to beat the elves?" He threw his head back and laughed.

Cinder wasn't willing to let go of his dream. "Humans were great once. Why can't we be great again?"

"Because none of you gits can cycle *prana*. Or have your months of breathing exercises taught you nothing?"

Cinder recognized the truth of Sriovey's statements. Humans were the weakest of all the races. Mede might have forged Shang Mendi, but his empire fell when he died. Otherwise, humans had to beg help from sithes and crèches whenever their villages and towns were threatened by powerful zahhacks, the spiderkin, wraiths, or *aether*-cursed beasts.

Despite this, there remained a kernel of defiance within Cinder's heart, a frustration and urgency that wouldn't allow him to accept the world as it was. He wanted to change it, work however hard was required to see his vision come to pass. And he would struggle on, even if everyone told him he was a fool railing at a pounding storm.

Besides, there were a few reasons for his hope.

"What about the *Crèche Prani*?" he asked Sriovey, referencing the dwarven book on prophets. "It also says humans were once mighty and can be again."

Sriovey coughed into a fist, appearing embarrassed. "Our holy book says a lot of things. Who knows how much of it is real? For all we know, some drunk dwarf might have written it. He might have made it all up. Holy books can be like that."

Cinder didn't believe it. "How about the troll religious text, *Revelatory Dreams*? Same with *the Lor Agni*. There are similarities in all three." Cinder knew he was right. A deep core of certainty told him so. Humans *could* conduct *lorethasra*. They could link it to *aether* or whatever the woven did. Something was holding them back, though, and Cinder was determined to overcome it.

Sriovey's brow furrowed, and he blew out what sounded like a frustrated breath. "I promised to help with your wrestling, not gossip about philosophy or the impossible."

Cinder let the matter drop. "Let's wrestle, then," he said, pointing to a nearby training circle. He grinned. "Age before beauty."

Sriovey's irritation left him. "I am more aged, but you're certainly not more beautiful."

Cinder laughed. "Maybe we should ask your sister."

"Leave my sister out of this," Sriovey growled.

Cinder kept silent, recognizing the stupidity of his statement the moment the words left his mouth.

It was a sore point for Sriovey. Sriovey's sister was supposed to be a lovely maiden who had an unfortunate penchant for easily falling in and out of love. It was a source of embarrassment for the family, who often had to rescue her from one stupid decision or another. One time, she'd even run off with a traveling band of dwarven singers.

Cinder held up his hands. "Forget I said anything. It was a bad joke."

"Don't joke about my sister."

"I won't," Cinder said. "I'm sorry. Really."

They stepped over the low line of stones marking the sparring circle's perimeter.

"Fine," Sriovey said. "Apology accepted." The glower on his face said otherwise.

Cinder considered the dwarf. "You sure? You're not going to rip my arms off or something, are you?"

Sriovey barked a single laugh, and his anger finally seemed to abate. "I wouldn't do that to you. Not for making a joke. We're supposed to be brothers, right? Aren't you always going on about that?"

"Just promise not to maim me," Cinder said, making his tone wheedling.

Sriovey rolled his eyes. "I promise, but it don't mean this lesson won't hurt. You might consider praying for wisdom next Tympany."

"I'm allowed to do that? I thought Tympany was only for dwarves. First evening of the first day of every month and all."

Sriovey winked. "I won't tell if you don't."

Cinder grinned. "My lips are sealed."

"You ready then?"

"Give me a moment." Cinder took a deep breath, seeking to center himself. He searched his core, hoping to find the liquid perfection of his unmarred *lorethasra*. He did so every time he sparred, and unsurprisingly, it didn't come. He shrugged, no longer disappointed by his failures. "Ready."

Sriovey, stout as a barn and strong as an ox, didn't bother with the careful questing he utilized when sparring against a dwarf. He rushed Cinder, who did his best to slap aside the dwarf's hands. If Sriovey got ahold of him, he'd be done for.

Cinder managed to evade Sriovey's initial charge, but not the second. Strong hands grabbed for his waist. Cinder sprawled. It was the wrong thing to do. *Damn it!* He was in trouble, and he dug for underhooks, crabbing to the side. Sriovey moved with him, pushing forward, knocking him down.

Cinder could guess what would happen next, and he desperately sought to free himself. He had to get out of his stuck position.

Sriovey didn't let him up. He locked hands behind Cinder's neck. The dwarf chained movements. Cinder tried to keep up. He knew what he had to do, but he couldn't do it. He wasn't strong enough or fast enough.

Just as Cinder predicted, Sriovey spun to his right and twisted. They were face-to-face now. Sriovey got his hands clasped around Cinder's waist, locking them.

Cinder levered himself upright, hoping his height could grant a little more time while he tried to break the lock. During all this, he continued to reach for his *lorethasra*.

With a rush, the still water reflecting an unseen sun grew visible. A wall of blue-green lightning warned him off, but Cinder reached for his *lorethasra* anyway. Burning pain immediately blossomed in his mind, and he let go of his attempted conduction.

His distraction allowed Sriovey to easily suplex him, and the air slammed out of his lungs. The dwarf pressed against him from top position. Cinder tried to get his wits about him. He had to crab. An elbow rapped him in the forehead, not hard enough to bruise, but hard enough to get his attention.

"You're done," Sriovey said.

He stood, and Cinder gasped, taking lungfuls of blessed air.

"The hell were you doing?" Sriovey asked. "You were doing alright, and then your face went . . . I don't know. Blank."

Cinder explained.

Sriovey's brows lifted. "You actually saw your *lorethasra*? That's a rare thing."

Cinder grimaced. "Rare and useless if I can't conduct it."

"Source it."

"What?"

"You source your *lorethasra*. You don't conduct it."

Cinder shrugged. It wasn't worth arguing about, but he liked using the word 'conduct' better than 'source'. "Again?"

This time it was Sriovey's turn to shrug. "Why not?"

They took their positions, and once again, Sriovey walked him down, cutting off the sparring circle.

Cinder reached again for his *lorethasra*. Maybe he couldn't conduct it but making a practice of seeing it, reaching for it had to be useful. As before the perfectly pure pond glittered just beyond his metaphorical hands.

The dwarf got an underhook, but Cinder managed to hand fight him.

Cinder hammered against the blue-green lightning barrier barring him from his *lorethasra*. He accepted the fiery agony, biting down with his will and refusing to relent. He pushed at the barrier, wanting to weep from the pain of doing so.

Sriovey got his hands around Cinder's middle. Another suplex.

With a rush, Cinder burst through the barrier. Pain continued to blaze within his mind, but it soothed to a tolerable level the moment he conducted his *lorethasra*.

Strength and speed filled him. He broke Sriovey's grip, startling the dwarf. He used the momentary surprise to his advantage, moving quickly. He managed to spin about Sriovey. His chest was to the dwarf's back. Cinder bent low, locked hands around the dwarf's abdomen, and with a grunt, he lifted Sriovey off his feet. Cinder twisted in midair and body-slammed the dwarf.

Cinder stood over Sriovey, mouth gaping in shock and losing his connection with his *lorethasra*. He'd beaten a dwarf in wrestling. Not through luck, but through skill and strength. The enormity of the accomplishment took several seconds to fully penetrate. Defeating Bones had seemed improbable but always possible. But this . . . defeating a dwarf in wrestling . . .

Wonder filled him. All these months of fruitlessly trying to cycle *prana*—maybe it hadn't been for nothing. He had touched his *lorethasra*, conducted it, and used it to make himself faster and stronger.

A way to achieve his goals presented itself, and a world of opportunities blossomed. He only had to accept the terrible agony of breaking through the lighting-like barrier locking away his *lorethasra*.

Sriovey rose to his feet he demanded with a glare. "What did you do? How did you throw me?" He appeared both confused and furious.

Cinder realized his victory might not come without a painful payment. He offered a sickly smile. "You still promise not to rip my arms off?"

Sriovey sought out Derius as soon as everyone had returned from Certitude. He had important news to relate, information that couldn't be delayed. He'd worried over it ever since Cinder had outwrestled him this afternoon. It had only been one fall, but it should have never happened. No human should be able to beat a dwarf in wrestling, at least not without trickery or fabulous luck. And neither had been the case today.

He searched the dorm for Derius and finally discovered his fellow dwarf sprawled out on his bed in his unprepossessing room.

Sriovey closed the door. "We may have a problem."

Derius cracked open an eye, a frown of irritation on his face. "Can't it wait? I'm tired. It's been a long day."

"No, it can't wait."

Derius sighed. He opened both eyes and sat up. "What kind of problem?"

"The kind in which a human defeated me in wrestling. No luck of any sort."

Derius' gaze sharpened, and his demeanor became serious. "You're sure of it?"

Sriovey nodded. "I had him wrapped up. I was about to suplex him into next week, but then it all went wrong. He broke my hold and bodyslammed *me*. I never saw it coming."

Derius' expression grew grim. "He sourced *lorethasra*?"

"He said he did. One guess on who I'm talking about."

"Cinder Shade."

"Cinder Shade," Sriovey confirmed. "You know what this means?"

"I know what it *might* mean, but more likely it was probably just dumb luck on his part. No human can intentionally source *lorethasra*."

"You want to take the chance that Cinder learns?" Sriovey asked. "You've read our scripture. Then there's this damn Genka Devesth."

Derius sighed. "What do you want to do?"

"I need you to get word to the crèche. My father needs to know about this. We need to learn everything we can about Cinder Shade."

Derius nodded agreement, but he hesitated. "Do you think he's the. . ." He trailed off.

"I don't know," Sriovey said, answering his kinsman's unvoiced question. "I hope not. Devesh save us all if he is."

Derius seemed to hesitate, as if he had something distasteful to relate.

Sriovey noticed "What is it?"

"Should we kill him?"

Sriovey sighed. It's what he'd pondered all afternoon. "No. Not yet. We need to know for sure what we're dealing with."

Cinder's rest day didn't end after his wrestling match with Sriovey. He had some reading to do, as well. He went to the library and paused at the entrance, letting his eyes adjust to the brightness within. The place was as it always was. A musty smell permeated the rooms, carrying the weight of knowledge, and there was Master Molni manning the front desk, the dispenser of said knowledge.

The old, bespectacled elf smiled when Cinder entered. "What do you plan on studying tonight?" he asked.

Cinder let his gaze wander about the illuminated space of the main reading room, and his eyes went to the second floor. The philosophical and religious texts were housed there, and so were the biographies of Shokan and Sira. Admittedly, any firsthand knowledge of those two was limited, but Cinder had found a book several weeks ago, one possibly written by the great Mythaspuri Sapient Dormant himself. In it, he claimed to have known Shokan and Sira. While others confirmed his assertion, it struck Cinder as patently absurd. Shokan and Sira had lived many thousands of years prior to Sapient's arrival to Seminal.

The book made many such fantastical claims. For example, it stated that Sapient had once been a holder, a brother in spirit to Shokan and Sira. Later, it described Sapient's transformation into a necrosed, a process leaving him in worshipful devotion to Shet. For thousands of years thereafter, Sapient had walked a different world, a place known as Urth, committing terrible acts of violence and evil. He finally found redemption in the Realms of the Rakshasas.

Cinder had smiled upon reading the account. A holder became a necrosed, who later on transformed into a figure of holy legend?

Impossible.

He might have discarded the biography as the work of fantasy, except for the book's depiction of *lorethasra*. The biography described a still water of perfect reflection. It wasn't the first time Cinder had come across such a narration, but there was more. An explanation was included about how every woven had limited weaves available to them, distinct threads by which they could use their *lorethasra*. Only humans had the full width and breadth of what was possible.

It sounded like another ridiculous claim, but the biography also referenced *Revelatory Dreams*, the holy book of trolls and holders. There was a reason for why humans were more flexible, and it was supposedly spelled out within that tome.

It wasn't. At least not the version Cinder had read.

Then again, the book he had read was a corrupted copy, a fact which he'd only recently become aware. The true version of *Revelatory Dreams* was held in a private area of the library, one requiring Master Molni's approval.

"I'm looking for a book," Cinder said in reply to Master Molni's question. "*Revelatory Dreams*. The version housed in the restricted section."

The old librarian's smile faded. "You're a Firster, Cinder. You need to be a sophomore if you want to check out any of those texts from the library."

"I don't want to borrow the book," Cinder said. "I only want to read it. Here in the library."

Master Molni continued to hesitate. "I'm not sure. Allowing you to read it here would follow the letter of the law but not the spirit."

Before coming to the library, Cinder had already considered the matter, and he had a ready response. "But the letter of the law never addresses a Firster reading the text. It only discusses not trusting us with taking them out of the library."

Master Molni slowly nodded. "That's true. I suppose you have the right of it." His decision made, his good mood was quickly restored. He smiled and clapped Cinder on the shoulder. "I'll show you where it is." He winked. "Promise not to slip it into your trousers when I'm not looking."

It was an old joke, one Master Molni said to every patron of the library. Cinder laughed. "I promise to behave myself."

They ascended to the third floor of the library and went to an area sectioned off by a folding, wrought-iron gate. Several aisles later, they reached their destination. Master Molni stood on his tip-toes and withdrew a dust-covered volume from a shelf. "Here you go." He handed the book to Cinder. "There's a reading room around the corner. If you don't mind re-shelving the book when you're finished with it, I'd very much appreciate it."

Cinder promised to do so, and after Master Molni left, he went to the reading room and cracked open the uncorrupted version of *Revelatory Dreams*. He quickly discovered that it was, in fact, very similar to the copy in the public area. He began scanning the volume, carefully flipping the brittle pages until he reached the portions describing Shokan and Sira.

Shokan was said to have been tall with dark hair and eyes, with skin the color of tea touched with milk; while Sira was green-eyed, blonde, beautiful, and nearly as tall as her husband.

Here was an interesting tidbit. Just like in Sapient's biography, *Revelatory Dreams* stated that Shokan and Sira were travelers from another world, and they had accepted the burden of saving various realms from Shet's savagery. The so-called god's children had invaded their home, wrecking it and inspiring Shokan's and Sira's mission. Also, Shokan and Sira weren't their true names.

In this small matter, *Revelatory Dreams* was as reticent as Sapient's biography.

Cinder thumbed further into the book. He reached a section on *Jivatma*, the old name for *lorethasra*.

According to *Revelatory Dreams*, there was more to it than a simple difference in name. The holy book of the trolls stated that while humans could easily separate their *lorethasra* into its component Elements of Air, Fire, Water, Earth, and Spirit, *Jivatma* had an unknown, additional property. It was the entirety of *lorethasra* combined with the nature of a person, their will, intellect, and emotional quality.

Cinder's interest quickened. The passages describing Shokan and Sira along with the nature of *lorethasra* were missing from the version downstairs.

On he read.

While elves and every other woven needed to cycle *prana* and open their Chakras in order to properly utilize *lorethasra*, humans did not. They simply wove Elemental threads to create what they required. Humans had once been able to access their *lorethasra* as easily as any woven.

In fact, their mythic forebears, the mighty *asrasins*, were the ones who'd created the woven. It was why the woven were called 'woven'. They were woven beings, created from the weaves and *lorethasra* of those ancient *asrasins*.

Everything changed when the Mythaspuris came to Seminal. Prior to defeating Shet, they created items of power, weaves meant to hobble the all-too human god and block him from the majority of his might. Later on, after the war's finale, the Mythaspuris had ascended to their final fate, and the elves and dwarves had activated those powerful constructs. Doing so somehow restricted humanity's use of *lorethasra*, forever limiting their abilities.

Electric excitement crawled across Cinder's spine when he reached the portion of prophecy. It was foretelling shared by *the Lor Agni* and *Crèche Prani*. In the distant future, Shet would rise up again. He would call for his Titans and zahhacks and unleash horror and enslavement upon Seminal. The world would descend into the dark depths of the Realms of the Rakshasas. Shet would bind Seminal to the will of the Unnamed, the Prince of Absence, forever locking its people away from the cleansing forgiveness of Devesh's singing light.

In that time of despair, the world's only hope would be the reborn paladins and their companions who would defeat Shet once and for all.

Cinder carefully shut the book. His reading spurred him to reflect on his own abilities and history. It was almost two years since he'd awoken without any memories and nearly drowned in a well in a small village in Rakesh. His right leg had been withered and weak. He had a clubfoot.

And now . . .

Cinder exhaled heavily. Now he was the finest human warrior of his class. It was a month since he'd defeated Bones and a week since he'd bested Sriovey.

And yet it still wasn't enough. Cinder had long ago vowed to protect those who couldn't protect themselves. And while he doubted the prophecies in the various religious tracts would ever come true, evil already roamed the land. Zahhacks and wraiths. *Aether*-cursed beasts and spiderkin. Someone had to defeat them.

He shook off his drifting recollections and considerations.

The future will be as it is.

29

The next week, Cinder found himself longing for a different challenge. He went to the basement of the Firemirror Hall, staring at Misery Gate in narrow-eyed determination. An ominous warning seemed to emanate off the matte-black structure, it's circular shape a mouth waiting to consume the unwary. Cinder eyed the chevrons carved into the stone.

According to Master Molni, if used correctly, the manipulation of the symbols could form a connection between Misery and other similar portals scattered throughout Seminal. It would allow for instantaneous travel between the two linked gates. Unfortunately, no one alive knew how they operated. Their nature had been a secret closely guarded by their creators, the Mythaspuris. Not even the reclusive rishis knew how to work them.

At least Misery retained its connection to the Foe, Cinder's destination. He came here often now, needing the preparation for when he had to face the spiderkin during the upcoming Grand Melee and the Unitary Trial. They were still several months away, but better to be ready now then wish he was ready when it was necessary.

Tonight, he planned on increasing the difficulty—three spiderkin and no shield. Although he was now competent in using a sword with the round bucklers favored by the elves, he wanted to face the creatures without one. He wanted to test the limits of his abilities.

Cinder went to the chevrons, twisting them as Master Absin had taught. It dictated the size and number of foes he wished to face. Once finished, he stepped back, watching for the symbols to come to life. They glowed golden, and an instant later a flash of light and the sound of waves crashing filled the basement. A watery cone blasted into the room, but not a single drop touched the floor. The cone retracted, encompassing the entirety of Misery's opening in a fluidic film.

Cinder took a steadying breath before stepping through the gate. He didn't know why he bothered. Preparing himself never did any good. The moment he came in contact with the watery film, an icy shock lanced through him, all the way to his bones. He gritted his teeth.

Less than a second later, he was in the perpetually wan realm of the Foe. At least the nausea he used to feel when traveling through Misery was no longer present.

Cinder took a moment to examine his environment. Sickly trees and thorny shrubs surrounded the meadow in which he found himself. Snowy peaks soared in all directions. The smell of rotten vegetation filled the air. At his back, a black circle squatted like a hole in the world. Misery Gate, the exit from the Foe. A chittering sound arose from the surrounding trees, and minutes later, three spiderkin pressed through the brambles. They entered the glade, standing roughly in parallel and facing him. Their chitin was matte-black like the material forming Misery Gate, and all three were the size of a dwarf. He had chosen to face young warriors.

Cinder inhaled deeply and exhaled slowly. He needed calm, and just as importantly, he needed his *lorethasra*. For whatever reason it came to him more easily in the Foe. Today, though, he couldn't seem to bring it forth.

Where is it?

The spiderkin chittered, a questioning note to their noises.

Cinder rolled his shoulders, relieving their tension. He drew his shoke, pointing it at his foes. He'd have to face them without his *lorethasra*.

One spiderkin bellowed, the high-pitched whine of an animal dying. All three charged.

Cinder dodged to the right, doing his best to face only one foe at a time. The spiderkin matched his movements. Cinder closed with one. He ducked under a forward limb, which slashed where his head had been. Cinder sent a looping cut. It amputated the spiderkin's barbed leg. The creature keened.

Cinder spun. He parried a riposte from the spiderkin now at his back. His shoke slid upward, slamming into the monster's fanged maw. Again, came the keening cry. The creature reared, impeding the progress of one of its kin.

The next spiderkin darted at Cinder. He shifted to meet its charge—

Cinder cried out, his torso a burst of agony. A spiderkin lifted him off the ground. One of its legs had impaled Cinder through the chest. Blood poured from the wound, gushing forth, soaking his shirt and streaming to the ground. The world became a whirl of colors and shapes. The monster flung him through the air. Cinder crashed to the ground.

The world of the Foe went dark and quiet.

An instant later, the world returned, and Cinder's pain was gone. He stood up with a groan, rubbing at his chest. While the pain had swiftly vanished, the memory of it remained. The horrific injury . . . He'd never get used to agony of dying.

The Foe reset.

Cinder stood once more in the center of a glade. A chittering sound heralded the advance of his enemies. He still rubbed at his chest, the recent death casting a pall on his mind. He tried to focus on what he needed to do. The spiderkin were coming. Cinder did his best to settle his jagged nerves. He hated dying in the Foe, but the unquenching force inside him wouldn't let him quit. Greatness required sacrifice.

The spiderkin exited the trees, chittering and forming a parallel line. They faced Cinder, just like the last time.

He eyed them, trying to formulate a plan. Maybe he shouldn't have gone after three spiderkin. Most nights he practiced against only one.

Frustration snarled like a growling dog. *Frag the spiderkin.* The only thing worse than dying was failing. And Cinder refused to fail. He wouldn't quit, and he wouldn't give up. The frustration transformed into anger, a single ember bursting and becoming a blazing fire.

Cinder needed more than fury. He needed his *lorethasra,* and there was only one way to reach it.

Calm.

He had a precious few seconds before the spiderkin charged, and he closed his eyes, breathing in and exhaling in perfect control.

Calm.

Somewhere in the distance, felt more than seen, a perfectly reflective pond glimmered. Cinder knew not to press. It would come.

Calm.

Another breath, and it glistened within his mind's eye, within reach, a small pond of the purest water. Cinder conducted his *lorethasra,* and it entered him just as the spiderkin charged. Cinder opened his eyes. The wan world of the Foe was brighter, his hearing sharper. Power and strength filled his muscles.

Cinder dodged right, just as he had before. A slash was coming. He blasted it aside and angled a cut into the spiderkin's maw. It reared, roaring in pain and fury. Here came another one, flanking him. Cinder twisted, keeping it to the front.

He blocked a stabbing attempt. Another parry, and he bent low. A straight thrust disabled one of the creature's limbs. The spiderkin collapsed on its side. Cinder spun away before it could right itself.

The final spiderkin was on him. Cinder met it, angling to its side. The creature tried to match his turn. *Too slow.* Cinder hammered a blow, severing a leg. The creature howled, a high-pitched chittering.

The first spiderkin, maw dripping ichor, rejoined the fray. It swung hard, a wide slash with a front leg. Cinder evaded, and the creature's own blow drove deep into the thorax of one of its fellows, killing it. The spiderkin's leg was stuck in the body of its dead brethren.

Two to go.

Cinder went after the stuck spiderkin.

It lunged for him, but the body of the dead spiderkin held it in place. Cinder amputated two limbs in quick succession.

The anticipation of success bubbled in his heart.

A blow crushed the back of his leg, breaking it and launching him skyward. A spraying fan of blood marked his flight. Cinder crashed, plowing into the ground. He slid five feet before grinding to a halt.

His body was a mass of agony—again—and the pain made his vision go gray. Everything hurt. His vision slowly returned. Cinder no longer had a connection to his *lorethasra*.

He shook off the concern. Nothing to do about it now. There were still two spiderkin to face.

Cinder struggled to his feet, unwilling to die like a crab on its back. By sheer will alone, he managed to make it to his feet just as a spiderkin crushed him like a rockslide.

He died.

The Foe went black. The world grew silent, returning an instant later.

Once again, Cinder found himself in the center of an empty glade. The spiderkin were gone, and so was his pain. He stood up, groaning more heavily this time. He could leave any time he wanted. The exit beckoned. He looked longingly to it. Glanced then toward the chittering sound coming from the forest.

No.

He came here to kill three spiderkin, and he would kill three of them.

He searched for calm. *Lorethasra* beckoned, and he embraced it.

Cinder hobbled toward Misery Gate, agony suffusing his body. It was a struggle to breathe. Several of his left-side ribs were fractured. Half his scalp was missing. Blood dripped from runnels carved into his back, chest, and abdomen—it was a wonder his intestines hadn't spilled out—and his right ankle was shattered.

The pain, however, couldn't dim his satisfaction at having finally achieved victory against the spiderkin. It had taken him five attempts, which meant four deaths, but in the end, he'd achieved his goal. He had killed three spiderkin in one go.

A dozen feet later, he exited the Foe. He immediately straightened, hissing in relief as his pains disappeared, vanishing as if they'd never existed. The injuries didn't carry over to the real world since his body had never truly been broken. The traumas he'd suffered weren't authentic, but they certainly felt that way when battling in the Foe. But the lessons learned in that strange place were worth the pain. At least he thought so. Others might have disagreed.

Cinder closed Misery Gate, and the portal resumed its normal quiescent state, exposing a dark room floored in bare stone on the other side.

Three spiderkin. He couldn't help but exult over his success. It had taken everything he had, but in the end, he'd won. His smile faded. The more important test was whether he could repeat the victory. If he couldn't, then tonight meant nothing.

Achieve success, replicate it, and advance.

With a tired sigh, Cinder left the basement, trudged up the stairs, and exited Firemirror Hall. The Quad was quiet. Crickets chirped, drawn to the world's surface by the promise of spring's warmth, a harbinger of which persisted this late evening. A soft wind carried the floral fragrance of ligustrum and honeysuckle, rustling newly bloomed leaves, shaking them like a whispering rattle. The stars shone brilliantly. It was a night of a twin new moon—Dormant and Fulsom were both absent.

Cinder made his way to Krathe House. On his way there, he noticed two others paralleling his course on the far side of the Quad, possibly headed in the same direction. He scowled when he recognized who they were. *Estin and Riyne.* They spotted him at the same time, excitedly pointing him out to one another. No one else was around, and their ugly banter murmured across the Quad.

Cinder closed his eyes, disappointed, disgusted, and angry—a turmoil of annoyance. The pleasure at his success in the Foe disappeared. *Why did I have to run into those two tonight of all nights?* He allowed the emotions to course through him for a count of five, exhaling on each number.

He opened his eyes then. The anger wasn't banished, but it was under control. He was calm, or at least calmer than before, and he needed to remain in that peaceful state. Thus far, it was the only way he could touch his *lorethasra*, and he reckoned he might soon need it.

"You chose a poor night to wander alone," Riyne said, a nasty grin on his face when he and Estin stood no more than a dozen feet away. They blocked his approach to Krathe House.

"Why is that?" Cinder asked. He looked past Riyne, not really seeing the elf. He sought the perfect purity of his *lorethasra*, but it wasn't visible.

Estin wasn't smiling. A sense of suppressed fury wafted off him. "You danced with my sister at the Winter Gala. Did you think we'd forgotten?"

"Your sister was the one who asked me to dance," Cinder reminded him, trying to delay what now sounded inevitable. His *lorethasra* wouldn't come, and he cast about for ideas. What could he do against two elven warriors? He still had a shoke at his waist, and they were unarmed. It wouldn't be the most honorable fight, but then again, they shouldn't have ambushed him at night.

"You should have refused," Estin said.

"I tried. You were—"

"And those final steps," Estin growled. "The last twirl . . . Those movements were not for you." His fists bunched. "Riyne was too kind when he tried to teach you the way of our world. You remember? He left you weeping and covered in your own vomit."

Cinder shot a glare at Riyne. That wasn't how their fight had ended.

Estin cracked his knuckles. "This time your lesson will be far more instructive."

Cinder drew his shoke, holding it at the ready. *Come on then.* He couldn't reach his *lorethasra*, but he'd fight anyway.

The elves shared a glance and burst out in laughter.

Cinder's flaring anger sputtered into confusion. *What's so funny?*

Riyne pointed at the shoke. "You think to defend yourself with that?" He sneered. "I will relish this lesson."

A vibration rumbled under Cinder's feet. He automatically glanced down. It was a mistake. He looked back to the elves, who were gone. *Where—?*

A blow to his stomach doubled him over. He hunched over in pain, struggling to breathe. The elves must have Blended. A punch or a knee clubbed him in the side of the head. He collapsed, somehow holding onto the shoke. He swung wildly. One of the elves cursed. *Riyne.* Cinder rolled, trying to regain his feet.

He sensed movement and partially blocked a kick to his face. His ears rang. His vision went black. The shoke fell from his nerveless hands. His vision returned sometime later, probably less than a second but it was blurred.

"Hold him up. He kicked me in my jewels. Only seems fair I do the same to him."

"When did he kick you?"

Cinder's consciousness faded in and out. Someone was keeping him upright. *Estin.* The prince stood behind him, gripping his arms and holding him up. Riyne faced him.

"It doesn't matter," Riyne growled. "It happened. I aim to pay him back for the affront."

Estin shouted in pain, and Cinder tumbled to the ground. Riyne cried out as well. From where he lay, Cinder realized the elves were fighting someone else. He smiled. *Sriovey, Jozep, and Nathaz.* The dwarves stood between Cinder and the elves.

"This isn't your concern," Estin said. "Move on. We have no issue with you."

"Fucking cowards," Nathaz growled. "Can't handle a single human on your own?"

Cinder's vision was still off. So was his balance, but he wasn't a bug. There was no fragging way he would lie on his back while others fought on his behalf. He rolled over with a groan, levering himself to a knee.

Sriovey spat at Estin's feet. "Your mother would be ashamed. *I* am ashamed. How far your family has fallen. You are *naaja*. Unclean filth."

Estin's visage hardened. "You'll pay for that insult."

Cinder managed to clamber to his feet.

"I'll give you payment by kicking your ass, you fucking pig," Sriovey said.

"You can't hide what you did to Cinder this time," Jozep told the elves. "You broke his nose, blackened an eye, and likely concussed him. We aren't supposed to fight outside of sparring."

"And you would tell the administration?" Riyne sneered.

"Damn right," Sriovey said.

"Now who is the coward?" Riyne asked.

"You are, you fucking moron," Nathaz replied. "You attacked him. Two-against-one. And what do you want us to do? Pretend he tripped and fell down the damn stairs?" Nathaz scoffed. "Fuck you. It's what every bully wants from their victims."

"I'm not a victim," Cinder said, addressing Estin and Riyne. Rage kept him from collapsing. Rage at how these two scions of noble houses treated those who were weaker. Rage at how those who were meant to protect were so apt to harm. Rage at the pain Estin and Riyne had inflicted on him. *Never again.* "I'll take you both on. One-on-one. Soon as I'm healed. I challenge you both. A duel. Master Absin will arbitrate."

He'd challenged the prince of the realm and the son of a high noble house to a formal duel, a fight during which the loser either begged for mercy or was rendered unable to continue. Sometimes duels ended in death, but what other choice did Cinder have? He wouldn't go on like this, having to glance over his shoulder, wondering when they would ambush him again. At least with a duel Master Absin could ensure fair play.

"I'll second him," Sriovey said, his tone unwavering, but Cinder caught him glance in his direction, appearing doubtful.

"A duel," Estin sneered. "Against him? A human?"

"A duel might keep the two of you from getting kicked out of the Directorate," Jozep reminded Estin.

Cinder struggled to understand what was being said. Wait? Estin and Riyne might be dismissed for attacking him?

"Your only hope of regaining your honor is by accepting the duel and defeating Cinder," Jozep continued. "I will not lie about what I saw. Two elves, Blended and beating on a human."

"Neither will I," Sriovey said.

"Nor I," Nathaz added.

"You'll also pay for Cinder's healing," Jozep said. "Otherwise we won't second the duel. None of us will. You pay for what you did out of your own pockets."

Estin and Riyne glared.

"Accepted," Estin growled. He spoke to Cinder. "Four weeks. We duel then." He and Riyne left the shadowed area in front of Krathe House.

Cinder slumped, and Sriovey caught him. "They might kill you, you know," the dwarf said.

"Then I'll have to kill them first."

30

The morning after he was ambushed by Estin and Riyne, Cinder still had trouble seeing straight. His head hurt, and when he moved it too quickly, nausea roiled through him, making him want to vomit. His stomach ached as well. Same with one of his shoulders. He must have wrenched it during last night's fight.

As a result, it didn't take much convincing for him to head over to the Directorate infirmary. The physicians fussed over him there, confining him to the small hospital wing, and it took them several days to repair the damage he'd suffered at the hands of the two elves. Despite all his visitors—mostly his fellow Firsters—he still had a lot of time to brood.

Until now, he'd only thought of sparring as a way for him to become the best. The desire had started as a small ember, but after the Maker's Tournament, it had flamed into a burning desire. Cinder wanted to be the best. *Had* to be the best. How else could he protect those who couldn't defend themselves? It was the reason he trained so hard. In his heart, Cinder thought of himself as a servant instead of a leader.

But being the best was meaningless. The best in a sparring match meant nothing. Cinder had forgotten what it truly meant to be a warrior, why he was actually here.

The Third Directorate trained warriors, and a warrior killed his enemies. He didn't spar with them. He destroyed them while preserving his own forces. Ambush, kill at a distance, bring overwhelming force to bear . . . anything to achieve victory as long as morality was maintained—and there was a moral undergirding to violence.

Duels, on the other hand, they were for the foolish, a waste of time, and concern about rankings was even more so.

In the Third Directorate, Cinder had been intent on the wrong things, approached his training as a dilettante.

The understanding left him nauseated. From this point forward, Cinder promised to re-dedicate himself, train as hard as possible but also focus on what was truly important: learn all he could to fight effectively and keep his brother warriors alive. Lately, he'd not given the class on Tactics and Strategy the attention it deserved.

No longer.

When Cinder finally left the infirmary a few days later, he marched out with a new sense of purpose.

He also discovered that Estin and Riyne had received a black mark in their records. In addition, the commandant had given them a severe dressing down. Estin and Riyne had exited the general's office, chastened and heads held low, but prior to reaching their dorm, they had run into Anya. The princess had lit into them as well, making no effort to hide or disguise her fury or disgust. Her outraged shouts had carried through the hallways of Firemirror Hall, all the way to the green lawn of the Quad.

Cinder didn't care about whatever punishment Estin and Riyne received. His future was more important, and he decided he needed to change how he approached his training. He vowed to learn all he could of combat as soon as his duel against the two elves was over. He would defeat them, give them a beating so they would never think to attack him again. Then he could move on.

Of course, as stupid as the duel now seemed, he was still glad he had made the offer. What Estin and Riyne had done to him would have earned any ordinary student a summary dismissal from the Directorate, but those two weren't ordinary students. One was a prince of the sithe and the other was a member of a powerful noble house. Cinder doubted Estin and Riyne would have faced any further consequences than what they had already received. However, with a duel he could administer the greater justice both of them so richly deserved.

He only had to figure out how.

Cinder left the infirmary late one morning and went to see Master Absin. The swordmaster had once told him the only way he could hope to defeat an elven warrior was by accepting a blow in order to administer one.

After the beating Estin and Riyne had administered while Blended, such advice now sounded useless, naïve, in fact. Cinder needed more information.

He found Master Absin at the Cauldron where he stood observing the warriors sent to the Directorate for specialized training. The sun beat down from a cloudless sky, muggy and hot with no breeze to moderate the warmth.

"How are you feeling?" Master Absin asked as Cinder approached.

Cinder's body remembered the aches from the punches and kicks he'd received, and even from the time lying around in the hospital. "I'll be fine in a few more days," he said, dismissing his discomfort.

"You wish to know how to battle an elf and win," Master Absin said rather than asked. Naturally, he knew Cinder's intentions. Everyone probably did.

"How do I beat them? They can Blend, make themselves faster, stronger, create heat, and so many other things." He didn't allow bitterness or defeat to enter his voice. No warrior was perfect. Everyone had a weakness. He only had to find Estin's and Riyne's.

"In a duel, elves are not allowed to Blend or use our talents on the world at large. It is a battle of shokes only."

Cinder's brows lifted in surprise. He hadn't known that. His mind raced at the options suddenly available to him. Without their *lorethasra*-inspired advantages, he could win.

Master Absin chuckled. "We can still make ourselves stronger and faster than you can handle. Our powers actually grow as we get older. Riyne and Estin are children compared to what those like Lisandre and Anya can accomplish."

Cinder didn't want to hear that. "No one is undefeatable," he said, jaw thrust out stubbornly. He wasn't willing to accept a preordained loss.

"True," Master Absin said. "Everyone has their strengths and weaknesses. It's only a matter of mitigating one and increasing the other. A balance."

There was advice in what Master Absin was saying, but Cinder was unable to deduce it. "What do you suggest?"

"What are your weaknesses?" Master Absin answered his own question. "It's your skill with the sword, your speed, your accuracy, and pure strength. Your physicality. You've spent most of your time mitigating those weaknesses. But what about your true strength?" Again, he answered his own question. "It's your predictive talent. You haven't done enough to harness it. For a while you did. When you lost to Rorian a few months ago. Then you stopped working at it, especially after you beat Bones."

Cinder exhaled heavily, seeing how he'd sabotaged his growth as a warrior. "I mitigated my weaknesses but didn't enhance my real strength?"

Master Absin nodded. "You need to do both."

"What should I do to improve my skill?"

"Talent," Master Absin corrected. "A skill is something you earn. You didn't earn this ability. You were born with it. It's a talent."

It sounded like a pedantic difference, and Cinder said so.

Master Absin shrugged. "Perhaps, but I like precision when I speak."

Cinder smiled faintly. Master Absin's sword-work, even at his advanced age, remained impeccable, and his clothes and uniform were never slipshod or covered in wrinkles. "You like precision in everything."

Master Absin grinned. "I am set in my ways."

"How do I improve my *talent*?" Cinder asked, returning to the matter at hand.

"With work. You can harness your talent, expand upon it, master it, but thus far, you haven't put in the work to harness or expand it, much less master it."

Cinder chewed his lip, unhappy when he was forced to agree with Master Absin's assessment. "What do you suggest?"

"Right now, you spend all your time sparring. You don't do enough observation. It's an oversight. Observe the others here, perpetually practice your talent while your mind is clear of the fog of fatigue." Master Absin pointed at the sparring warriors. "They would make a good start. If you can anticipate *their* plans, you can figure out Estin's and Riyne's. You can overcome their advantage of speed."

"What about accepting pain in order to administer it?"

Master Absin wore a puzzled frown. "When did I say that?"

"A few months ago. After my first run-in with Riyne. You said I should accept pain so I could give pain. Take a blow to give a blow."

Master Absin chuckled. "Sometimes that's required, but it's not what I said or the lesson I wanted you to take. I said you should accept the pain. You can tolerate it far more easily than the warriors of the Blessed Race. Embrace the grind of torturous work. Use your advantage to train harder than Estin and Riyne, push past discomfort. Do so and you'll shorten the gap between their skill and yours."

Cinder deflated. *Mitigate weaknesses and enhance strengths.* He'd done one but not enough of the other, and he'd also misinterpreted what it meant to accept pain. Part of why he went to the Foe was to inure himself to injury, teach him to fight on while hurt.

He sighed. All those wasted months, working hard but not focusing on what was important. The changes in how he approached his training would be greater than he had originally realized. "Will it be enough?"

"It might," Master Absin said. "We'll find out in a few weeks."

Cinder refused to lose to Estin and Riyne, and a vindictive part of him imagined making them suffer, hurt them like they'd hurt him.

His teeth clenched as soon as he recognized what he was doing. *No.* Justice didn't require cruelty. Victory would be enough. He recalled beating the bullies at *Our Lady of Fire.* He had been cruel then. He hadn't seen it at the time, but in hindsight, he was ashamed of how badly he'd hurt the bullies, especially Jarde.

Master Absin smiled at him in approval, as if he recognized Cinder's decision. "You've made a wise choice."

"What do you mean?" The old elf couldn't have known what he was thinking. Or was this another of their talents?

"I saw the fury leave your face," Master Absin said. "I think you've chosen a better path."

"I suppose I have, but it's the only path to take. I don't want to hurt anyone any more than what's needed. Or worse, kill someone who doesn't deserve it. Only prayer and Devesh can wash our souls clean of such a stain."

Master Absin's eyebrows rose in surprise. "The way you speak . . . you sound older than your years."

Cinder chuckled. "I'm only seventeen." He chuckled in startled realization. "Wait. I'm eighteen. I think I had a birthday a month ago."

"I hope after this duel you'll be able to witness many future birthdays."

The warning squashed Cinder's budding humor. While he didn't want to hurt Estin or Riyne any more than necessary, he didn't know if the same could be said for the two elves.

Shadion Carrend—Shadion Surent to everyone not of his crèche—was an odd dwarf. While the rest of his kind were happiest at home and hearth, snuggled in their mountainous houses and surrounded by friends and family, Shadion liked to wander the Dagger Mountains. He enjoyed traveling on his own, journeying to foreign lands with no other company but his donkey, Pretty. She was his finest friend, and she carried all his belongings, every pot, pan, and treasure . . . everything but his trusty warhammer and daggers.

Those weapons, Shadion kept on his person. Zahhacks still wandered the northern Daggers, and while the Yaksha elves prevented Shet's evil minions from penetrating south into Rakesh, it only took one to turn a beautiful near-spring day into a disaster. As Shadion reckoned matters, better safe than dead.

However, notions of zahhacks and spiderkin were far from Shadion's thoughts as he and Pretty made their way through a meadow, one soon to be lush and fragrant with spring blossoms. An afternoon sun shone high overhead, and bees were out early for the season, buzzing and flitting about. Pretty brayed, disliking it when the insects flitted around her eyes. Arguing with Pretty's braying complaint was a warm breeze. It shook the trees and leaves, a rushing sound like what Shadion imagined the sea might sound like.

He'd never seen the sea, but he wanted to. He'd simply never yet had the opportunity. Maybe one day he would. Maybe one day Shadion would be tasked to visit the sea, but until then he would go where he was told. He would travel where his people required, learn whatever information they needed.

In proper parlance, Shadion was a spy, although he preferred to think of himself as a purveyor of knowledge, like a researcher at a university. His current task was to search out the history of a boy from the backwoods of Rakesh. Cinder Shade was his name and Swallow, the name of his home.

According to his maps, Shadion was nearing his destination, and the friendly folk at a large town a dozen miles to the south had confirmed it for him.

He crested a rise and paused.

Shadion had seen much of the Daggers, visited many villages, but few were as modest as the one huddled in the nearby hollow. *Swallow.* Fifty, maybe sixty, houses clustered in a shallow bowl. Thin trails of smoke rose from some of the chimneys, drifting over the nearby fields where farmers plowed the rocky soil, laboring behind their lowing bullocks.

Shadion tugged on Pretty's halter, and they made their way down a dirt trail leading toward the village.

Children, faces smudged with dirt, ran across grassy knolls. They cackled laughter and called out boasts, but their play clattered to a halt when they noticed Shadion and Pretty. Then they stopped and openly stared.

Shadion nodded to a pair of thin lads, dark-haired and almond-eyed, wearing clothing which was frayed at the hems. Every child was similarly garbed, wearing hand-me-downs every bit as humble as the village itself.

The children's quiet spread. Shadion found himself the focus of a dozen frozen stares, intense and unwelcoming. He grimaced. Oftentimes these remote villages were insular. They took to strangers like a pack of lions did a wandering hyena. So far, the adults hadn't taken note of him, but if they had the same antipathy of their children, Shadion would have to step cautious. He kept his hands close to his weapons.

A thin man wearing a longyi and white jacket approached, and Shadion tugged Pretty to a stop.

"We don't get many dwarves here," the man said. "I'm Deepak Moral, the village priest. Can I help you?" He wore an expression of courteous curiosity, and his tone was friendly.

Shadion's anxiety eased somewhat. "I hope so. My name is Shadion Surent. I'm a merchant from Surent Crèche. I've got some dwarven goods if you're interested in purchasing them." He glanced around as if seeing the village for the first time. "By the way, what is the name of your lovely hamlet?"

"Swallow," Deepak said. "And I'm sorry to disappoint you, but this is a poor village. We don't have the coin to purchase what you're likely carrying. There's another village five miles north. Place called Inlet. They might have the money to spend on your goods."

"Five miles? Oh, no," Shadion said with a rueful shake of his head. "That's a mite too far for my short legs to want to walk in the light that remains. If you don't mind, I'll camp in a nearby field and maybe some of your folks can look over what I have to sell. Who knows? Maybe we can reach an agreement."

"There's no reason to camp in a field," Deepak said. "I have room in my house. You can stay with me."

Shadion smiled. It was more than he expected. "That's mighty generous," he said, taking on the drawl common to these parts. He found it put people at ease when he spoke in their dialect.

Deepak directed him to a single room dwelling, a rough-hewn log cabin no different than the surrounding houses. Shadion got settled in, and afterward, he went to the grassy knoll at the heart of the village. There, he met with the folk of Swallow who, unlike their children, greeted him eagerly. Strangers of any sort were likely rare here in Swallow, and the people probably wanted to know about the goings-on in the outside world.

Shadion told them what he knew of the events occurring in Gandharva, Yaksha, and his own crèche. The more he spoke, the more the villagers leaned forward, attention rapt.

Shadion also spoke of Genka Devesth, the warlord from the Sunset Kingdoms. "They say he's a genius," Shadion said. "Some even proclaim he's Mede reborn, just like it's written in the *Medeian Scryings.*"

A large villager by the name of Pitch Shade scoffed. "Reincarnation is a fable."

It was the opening for which Shadion was waiting. Pitch was Cinder's brother, and the dwarf had actually come here to Swallow just so he could speak to the man. Caution, though, was required. If Derius' father, and by extension, Derius, were correct about Cinder, it wouldn't do for anyone to learn Shadion had been snooping about here. Since some knew about his role as a spy, it might set them thinking in ways they didn't need to.

Shadion was still deliberating on what to say to Pitch when the matter was taken from his hands.

"What about Cinder?" another villager asked Pitch. "He died in a well and came back to life."

Shadion hid his rising excitement. He'd come to Swallow to learn about this exact event.

"Cinder didn't die, Simial," Pitch said.

"Well, you said he wasn't breathing when you found him in the well," the other man argued. "And when he came back to life—"

"He didn't die."

"When he came back to life," Simial persisted, "he didn't know who he was. Deepak took him to Swift Sword and said the whole time he acted like someone else."

"That's because he didn't have his memories," Pitch said, his tone patient like he was talking to a simpleton.

"What do you think?" Simial asked Deepak, who stood nearby.

Deepak took his time in answering. "I've known Cinder Shade his entire life." He snorted amusement. "I was there when he squalled his way into the world, and the boy I took to Swift Sword wasn't him—lack of memory or not. He was harder, more purposeful, driven. I even got a letter from Master Choff at the orphanage I took him to. Master Choff says Cinder was admitted to *Steel-Graced Adepts*, a warrior academy."

"A warrior academy?" Pitch sounded shocked. "You never mentioned that."

"And what kind of military academy takes in a weakling with a clubfoot and a withered leg?" Simial asked.

Deepak hesitated. "I don't know."

There was something the old priest wasn't saying, and Shadion had an idea what it was. Cinder Shade no longer had a clubbed foot or a withered leg, and Deepak knew it.

This was the same Cinder Shade about whom Derius had written to his father; not some other peasant with the same name. The stories matched. The village of Swallow. Everything was identical all the way down to the well where Cinder had awoken. Everything except for one fact. The Cinder Shade known by the folks here in Swallow had a clubfoot and a withered leg, but somewhere between the time he'd been rescued from the well, to the time he'd entered *Steel-Graced Adepts*, he no longer had either.

The only explanation was that the clubfoot and withered leg had been healed, which was impossible, unless . . .

Shadion traced the omens he'd learned. His eyes narrowed, as he recalled lessons from childhood. *The Crèche Prani.*

Understanding dawned. No wonder Derius' father had sent him here. His heart thundered in time with his fear, and it took all his training not to gasp in horror.

Cinder sat straight in his chair, paying close attention and taking notes during the class, Tactics and Strategy. Since his epiphany a few weeks ago, his recognition of what it meant to be a warrior, he had re-read the entire year's-worth of material in the course. This time, he made sure to fully understand it. This time, he gave it his full attention and effort.

The humans, elves, and dwarves still shared tables during the class, but the separation between them remained stark. The humans and dwarves slouched in their seats, at ease next to one another, while the elves sat stiff and formal, clearly unhappy. Their heads were held high, though, as if they noticed a stink in the room. Most of them anyway. A few, like Mohal who sat next to Cinder, also slouched in their chairs, relaxed and comfortable.

Master Nuhlin stood at the lectern, having to speak loudly over the gusting wind. It shook the eaves, rattled limbs and leaves, and the windows were closed against it. A late chill had sapped spring's warmth, and clouds blanketed the sky. An intermittent drizzle fell.

"Elves are supremely gifted with regards to our fighting talents," Master Nuhlin said. "No one can defeat us in single combat."

The previously uptight elves shared victorious smiles. A few, including Estin and Riyne, glanced Cinder's way, a challenging sneer on their faces.

Cinder wouldn't let their unspoken taunt go unanswered. "No one but a holder or a rakishi," he said, meeting and holding Riyne's gaze.

It wasn't easy being in the same classes with Riyne and Estin. Every time Cinder saw them, he wanted to crack the arrogant sneers off their face. A knee, fist, elbow, the hilt of his shoke—anything to pay them back for what they had done to him. It would happen. The duel. They couldn't hide from him forever.

For now, Riyne simply rolled his eyes in Cinder's direction, and the sneer remained.

"Of course," Master Nuhlin said to Cinder, "but they aren't numerous enough to form an army, and I was speaking of war. However, my contention raises a point: how did an elven army ever lose to a human one? It has happened, and the reason for it is because our skill leaves us blind to the truth. We don't comprehend the most important aspect of war." The victorious smiles from the elves faded. "Does anyone know what that is?" He glanced around to a silent room. "A hint, then. Mede once said that an army marches on its stomach."

Cinder raised his hand. "Because a starved army is a dead army. An army needs a massive amount of food for the long marches to battle."

"That only matters for humans," Riyne said. "Elves and dwarves can march for miles longer every day. We can get to the site of the battle without having to lug all that food while you humans are still floundering around the wilderness." He faced Cinder. "We'll sit and rest and eat whatever game is available while you're cooking your toes."

Cinder didn't let the elf's words get to him. "Sure, you will," he replied to Riyne's claim, yawning and stretching in an exaggerated fashion. "Because that's exactly how all battles occur."

Riyne lip curled, but he didn't answer back.

Master Nuhlin stepped out from behind the lectern, speaking to Riyne. "If you're right, then why do elves use cavalry?"

"Because we can carry more supplies that way," Riyne answered.

"But you just said that elves can carry all the food they need to the field of battle while the humans are cooking their toes."

"So," Riyne said, a mulish clench of his jaw.

"So, you're wrong," Bones said. "Admit it and move on. Horses allow you to carry your wounded, to bring in supplies, and not just food, but arrow heads, swords, pikes, weapons. Whoever shows up best equipped and rested usually wins."

"To say nothing of how armored cavalry can destroy infantry," Rorian added.

"Bones and Rorian are correct," Master Nuhlin said. "It was a large part of how Mede defeated every army sent against him."

"Mede. Mede. Mede," Estin complained. "That's all we ever hear about. He wasn't Devesh. There are other commanders we can learn from."

"Yes, but none of them are elvish," Cinder said. "The best commanders have always been human."

Estin stiffened.

"Quite so," Master Nuhlin agreed, and Cinder wasn't sure who he was talking to. Was it him or Estin? "Mede was only a human," Master Nuhlin continued, "but he set the terms of battle. He was a master of the feint and counter. He decided where the battle would occur, and he always made sure his soldiers had enough food and gear to get there intact."

"But—" Estin started.

"Your objections are unimportant," Master Nuhlin said. "Learn from Mede. The elven armies he fought were superior in conditioning and ability. They were as Riyne mentioned: able to get to the presumed site more quickly than Mede's forces. They believed Mede would join battle in a place of their choosing, but he didn't. I'm not sure what the elven generals were thinking, but Mede allowed them to settle in and never engaged. He feinted, and then the elves followed him and ran out of food." Master Nuhlin stared Riyne. "They ate all the game they could catch, and when there was none left, they starved. Then Mede attacked and crushed them."

"Sure, but it can't happen today," Estin said in airy dismissal. "We know better."

"So you believe," Master Nuhlin replied, "but recall, there were other factors at play. Mede also made sure to bring all the craftsmen he needed to maintain the equipment his army utilized. His soldiers could do most of the same. How many of you know how to carve an arrow, fletch it, repair a bow, or straighten a bent sword?"

Master Nuhlin glanced around to a room full of warriors whose hands lay in their laps. None of them knew how to do what the master asked.

"Mede's armies were full of officers and enlisted personnel who could do that. Yaksha Sithe's army is sorely lacking in that regard. It is why Gandharva claimed and kept the Sriavial Valley and Rakesh controls the Shalla Vale."

Riyne snorted. "More like we don't want anything from those backwater places. There's nothing there for us to take."

"Ashoka trees," Cinder said to Riyne.

Master Nuhlin nodded approval. "Exactly. The Ashoka trees only grow in Rakesh, in the Shalla Vale? The seeds of those trees purifies and expands *lorethasra* better than anything we can create. Gandharva supplies the cerumen gum for our *insufi* swords. They both have plenty of worth." Master Nuhlin stared at Riyne, who shifted in his seat, unable to maintain the gaze.

Cinder faced Riyne, egging him on and not caring. "Next time, do us a favor and keep your mouth shut. Spare us your stupidity."

Riyne's jaw clenched, but before he could respond, Mohal spoke. "So why not annex those places?"

"Because the cost would be too high," Rorian said. "If Yaksha attacks Rakesh, then Gandharva would join against the elves. Similarly, if Yaksha attacks Gandharva, then Rakesh enters the war. Yaksha Sithe would likely still win, but the cost would be too great. They'd then likely lose territory to Apsara Sithe or Surent Crèche."

"Exactly," Master Nuhlin said. "Yaksha would win, but at a ruinous cost. It's because our army persists in the pre-Mede way of thinking. We value warriors over soldiers, but in a battle, it isn't the best warriors who win. It's the best group of soldiers, the men who can fight as a unit. It's a different skill, to fight as part of a collective. It's something we elves, with our focus on individual martial prowess, have trouble accepting."

Estin scoffed.

What an idiot, Cinder thought.

Master Nuhlin's eyebrows rose at Estin's disbelieving expression. "You don't believe me? Then we will see how events play out during the Unitary Trial. It starts in a month. We'll see if the humans and dwarves have more spiderkin kills than the elves."

31

Spring deepened, the seasonal change highlighted by the clapping of wings from returning robins and cardinals and the singing of their songbird cousins: finches, thrushes, and swallows. Day-by-day, the sun grew brighter, more vibrant, beaming from amidst a deep, blue sky, and sending blessings of warmth and life. It banished the last lingering clouds of winter's depressing tribulations. Flowering shrubs gathered in the lush sunlight and rushed to show their wide variety of blossoms. The Quad held a suffusion of lovely aromas. Cinder knew he'd never tire of their perfume.

But right now, he had other considerations in mind. He stood in the Cauldron, well past sunset and with only Master Absin as company. Everyone else who trained here at night had returned to Krathe House or their various rooms scattered about the academy. *Diptha* lamps lit the training yards, and the moons hung low on opposite ends of the horizon, white Dormant at half, and golden Fulsom at crescent. The pleasant day, however, had given rise to an uncomfortable evening. The air held still and unmoving, an unpleasant mugginess gripping the world in an oppressive vice. No breeze to gentle the humidity.

431

Cinder's sweat-stained shirt clung to his back and chest, but he breathed smooth and unlabored. He'd swiftly recovered his fitness after his recent convalescence, and tonight—as always now—he sparred against Master Absin, training against the elven master for several hours before sunrise and several hours after sunset. In addition, during any breaks he took from sparring, he made sure to observe the others training at the Cauldron. He focused on their form and movements, using the former to predict the latter.

His talent in that regard continued to improve.

"I think you've trained enough, Cinder," Master Absin said. "I'm heading inside. I'm tired. I'm sweaty. And I need a bath."

The elven master might be old, sweaty, and in need of a bath, but as for tired, Cinder saw no evidence of it. Master Absin still breathed easy and without effort, appearing like he could go on for another hour.

"One more time?" Cinder asked. He wasn't ready to head in yet. He'd already finished his reading at the library and his requirements for Tactics and Strategy, as well as History. He wanted to keep sparring. He could have gone to the Foe for more work, but he saw no reason for it. Not now. The duel was only a week away, and if he wanted to defeat an elf, he needed to train against one; not a spiderkin.

Master Absin lifted his shoke with a sigh. "Fine. Come on then. Last one."

Cinder rolled his shoulders, loosening them in case they'd tightened during the rest period. He got his shoke in position.

Master Absin sent a probing thrust. Cinder slapped it aside and immediately got his shoke back on the centerline. Again, Master Absin probed his defenses, this time a horizontal slash he committed to half-heartedly.

He was trying to goad Cinder into coming forward. Master Absin often preferred to counter rather than initiate conflict. It didn't mean he couldn't overwhelm Cinder if he desired. He most certainly could. Cinder had seen the master fight Lisandre, Riyne's brother, the gifted warrior said to be the best the Directorate had produced in decades, other than maybe Anya. In those engagements, Master Absin had moved far more swiftly than he currently did. However, there was no learning to be gained from being disarmed inside of three strokes. The sparring session had to last longer if it was to provide instruction.

As a result, against Cinder, Master Absin's blows came more slowly. Right now, though, they were too slow. Even against his fellow human Firsters, he was pushed harder than this.

As if he sensed Cinder's thoughts, Master Absin picked up the pace. *Clack-clack.* Master Absin sent a slash followed by a lunge. Cinder parried both times. Next was a three-strike combination.

Again, Cinder defended.

The blows from Master Absin continued to increase in rapidity. Cinder kept up. Again and again, the pace grew faster. It reached a point where it was the swiftest Master Absin had sparred against him. Cinder's muscle memory showed him what was needed, and in between blows, when they broke apart, he planned, tried to guess what was to come.

Master Absin attacked, the fastest yet. Cinder parried, countered, gave ground, circled, and countered once more. All of it happened in seconds, a few heartbeats.

A distant part of Cinder realized he wasn't paying attention to Master Absin's actual strokes. It was no longer muscle memory guiding his shoke.

It was intuition.

Master Absin lunged forward. Cinder slid aside. A vertical slash. A double lunge into a short, horizontal chop.

Cinder didn't think. He followed his instincts. The blows were coming too fast for his mind to process.

A vertical slash. A thrust.

Cinder's insight showed him what to do. It set his shoke, applied the amount of force needed to parry, sent the counters, told his body when and where to slide aside or give way.

Master Absin pressed forward.

Cinder retreated, countered, falling into the rhythm of the contest.

Another brief pause.

An instant later, Master Absin was on him. They ranged across the training ring. Master Absin increased the pace even further. Cinder kept up for a few seconds, but by now sweat dripped from his brow. His heart pounded, and he panted. His arms felt heavy and sluggish. His intuition still recognized the solutions to the problems Master Absin provided, but his body couldn't take advantage of them. He was breaking, too slow and too weak to weather the storm. His form faltered.

Master Absin halted. "Break."

The elven master breathed heavily but didn't gape like Cinder, who probably looked like a fish out of water, gasping for breath.

"You did well," Master Absin said, sounding surprised and pleased.

"How fast was I?" Cinder asked. It was the only question of import.

"Fast enough to possibly hold your own."

But not fast enough to win. Cinder scowled. Holding his own wasn't enough. "Again?" Cinder asked.

"No," Master Absin said. "You can't simply push ever harder and think it will make you more effective. Overworking your body and mind will do you no good. You need to rest and recover, allow the growth to take hold. Sometimes, less is more."

It was the same advice Master Absin had offered many months ago. And as before, Cinder knew Master Absin was right, but he didn't want to hear it. He wanted to keep going, keep training until he could easily defeat Estin and Riyne. He wanted to show everyone in the Third Directorate that humans were every bit as deadly as elves. Maybe then he and everyone else from Rakesh and Gandharva would receive the respect they deserved.

Those were the lofty reasons for why Cinder wanted to keep training, but just as much was fear and loathing. Estin and Riyne had beaten him, and he'd been helpless. If not for Sriovey and the dwarves, who knew how badly the elves would have hurt him. Cinder never wanted to be so helpless again.

"Go back to Krathe House," Master Absin ordered. "Shower. Spend time with your friends. Tomorrow is another day for improvement."

Cinder bowed, giving way to the inevitable and also to what was right. "Yes, master."

Derius sat in his room at Krathe House, staring at the letter in his hand. The windows were thrown open, allowing an evening breeze to cool the room. The setting sun burnished the sky and bats darted about. The buzz of conversation from the common area carried down the hall. Sriovey's booming laughter, Ishmay's boisterous boasting, and Bones' calm surety. Others spoke as well, but those three commanded the room. They were the leaders of the Firsters.

Other than Cinder. The rest of the Firsters looked to the quiet, driven human as well, but he was often absent and therefore harder to know. Even now, Cinder was either studying in the library or off sparring against Master Absin or whoever would train against him.

He needed the work. Cinder had the duel with Estin and Riyne coming up in a few days.

What a mess the human had landed in, and Derius wished him luck. He didn't like Cinder's chances against Estin and Riyne, didn't have much hope for his victory.

But not having much hope wasn't the same as hopeless. Cinder might yet win, which was both a bizarre and terrifying acknowledgment. Before training at the Third Directorate, Derius would have thought a martial contest between a human and an elf to be a bad joke.

Not anymore.

Not since Sriovey had first told him how Cinder had defeated him in wrestling. At the time, Derius had wanted to dismiss the loss as bad luck on his cousin's part, but he no longer felt so sanguine about the matter.

Cinder had first come to the Third Directorate as a skilled but otherwise unremarkable human warrior. Small, thin, physically unimpressive but courageous were Derius' first impressions of the man, and early on Cinder had done nothing to change his opinion. He was better than some, worse than others, but overall good enough to get into the

Third Directorate. He fought hard, trained harder, but in the end, he didn't seem to be anything special in an academy of special warriors.

But as time passed, Cinder's hard work paid off. The man was a fiend, always slaving away in the Cauldron, the library, or the Foe. He steadily improved, overtaking a few of his fellow humans, but Derius had reckoned Cinder's advancement would eventually slow. Work could only carry a person so far. They also needed talent and physicality, and Derius now recognized that Cinder had both like thick veins of gold.

He'd grown since coming to the Directorate, now nearly as tall as Bones and every bit as strong and fast. His abilities had also increased, rising in startling leaps and bounds. First, he'd supplanted Ishmay and shortly thereafter, it had been Bones—and Bones *was* special—who'd fallen.

Since then, Derius had watched Cinder. The man continued to improve as a warrior, putting such great distance between himself and every other human at the Directorate, that the only ones who could now spar against him and provide him a challenge were the dwarves. And following the ambush from those cowards—Estin and Riyne—Cinder had re-dedicated himself.

Derius shook his head in disbelief. Where did he find the time? And how was he still getting better? He didn't know, but whatever the means, Cinder persisted in improving. In the last few weeks, even the dwarves were hard pressed to defeat him. It left the human Firsters in awe, and the dwarves shocked and shaken.

Cinder was an aberration, an impossibility.

Derius now knew why. He held the answer in his hands. Three letters had arrived in the mail for him today. It wasn't an unusual occurrence. Every few weeks or months, letters from home arrived.

His mother wrote to Derius all the time, generally offering advice on the importance of staying warm, eating enough food, or getting enough rest. His father's letters were usually about the crèche itself or how the family was doing, such as Derius' sister and her children. Sometimes an uncle or aunt would write, too.

However, in this packet, there had been *two* missives from his father. Both appeared innocuous, but in one of them, a discussion of crops and weather, was buried a cipher. After translating the letter's hidden meaning, Derius had sat heavily on his bed, re-reading and re-translating the letter.

His father had received word from Shadion Carrend. The wandering dwarf had visited Swallow, Cinder's home and confirmed the human's story of his past. Cinder had died and returned to life.

Derius crumpled the paper and stared out the window at the blackening night. Cinder Shade. An appropriate name.

Why did I have to live to see such times?

The morning dawned chill, a remnant of last night's icy rain. It was the kind of weather occasionally seen in the spring, the remnant of winter's final exhalation. The birds nestled in the trees, huddled and silent, unwilling to brave the cold. The skies were absent of clouds and bright sunshine promised to eventually do away with the ill weather.

Cinder's breath frosted in the air, and his feet crunched as he strode across the frost-crusted grass. The other Firsters paced alongside him, all of them silent, and he was grateful for their quiet.

Today was the day. The morning of the duel, and it captured the entirety of his focus. His disagreement with the elves might never end, but perhaps today he'd end some aspect of it. He had to first beat Riyne, and afterward perhaps Estin wouldn't want to face him. The rest of the elves who viewed him as a lesser might leave him alone, too. He hoped so.

He reached the Cauldron and discovered the elves had already arrived. Cinder's eyes went to Riyne who stood in the midst of his fellows, smiling confidently, head held high as if the outcome of today's duel was a foregone conclusion.

Cinder viewed Riyne with a flat glare. He remained angry with the elf, but over time his rage had cooled, transforming into something akin to contempt. The elf's unearned arrogance needed flattening, but by this point, Cinder considered it a job no different than cleaning a privy.

Others were in attendance, such as Master Absin, who would serve as the referee. The old master waited in the center of a sparring circle. General Arwan, Master Nuhlin, Master Capshin, and someone wearing the tabard of a healer were also present. So were the academy's administrators and instructors, who stood as a small group to one side. Princess Anya was present as well, and Cinder found her studying him. She wore an indecipherable expression, and she leaned toward General Arwan, whispering in his ear, and he nodded sharply in reply.

"You can take him," Bones said to him. "You've got this."

Cinder nodded acknowledgement, but his gaze never left Riyne. He would do whatever it took to win.

"Kick his ass!" Nathaz exhorted.

The embers of Cinder's anger crackled. It seemed his fury wasn't entirely cooled.

"Make him eat his arrogance," Ishmay said. "Shove it down his throat."

Cinder's mouth curled into a snarl. He'd beat the unholy hells out of the elf. "He'll never know what hit him," he vowed. His breathing deepened, and his exhalations shrouded him in a plume.

Master Absin gestured, and Cinder and Sriovey—his second—went to the sparring circle with Riyne and Estin arriving at the same time.

Cinder didn't bother exchanging words with the two elves. He had nothing to say to them. He simply stared at them, flat and unforgiving.

General Arwan and Anya accompanied Master Absin to the circle, and stood off to the side, silently observing the proceedings. The princess lifted a single questioning brow at her brother, and he dropped his gaze.

Master Absin addressed Cinder and Riyne. "There is no reason to review the events leading to this point. Honor demands this battle." He addressed Sriovey and Estin. "You will act as their seconds if they are unable to fight today?"

Estin merely nodded.

Sriovey growled. "I won't be needed. Cinder will break the elf."

Riyne smirked, superior and sure.

Cinder added hubris to the many reasons why he wanted to beat the elf.

"Fine," Master Absin said, sounding annoyed. "Let us review the rules first. The duel isn't to the death or even harm. You'll wield shokes. Earn four points, and the match is over. A fatal blow counts as two points; a non-fatal one as one point. Two fatal touches, four non-fatal ones, or one fatal and two non-fatal blows wins. Leaving the ring counts as a non-fatal touch. I'll make the final decisions on what constitutes a touch. Understood?"

"I heard," Riyne said.

"Understood," Cinder answered.

"In that case, everyone else leave the sparring ring. Duelists take your mark."

Cinder retreated to his starting position. He set his leather helmet on his head and shifted to settle the padded gambeson protecting his torso. He was ready.

Riyne Coushinre came from a proud family known for their unmatched martial lineage. For the past five generations along his father's side, every one of his warrior ancestors had earned an *insufi* blade. Three were titled *Sai*, and his brother, Lisandre, was expected to earn the mantle as well.

As a result, much was expected of Riyne. For him, acceptance into the Third Directorate—a fierce competition amongst young warriors of Yaksha Sithe and a high honor—was a foregone expectation. It was the first step on the road to living up to his family's heritage. He would then graduate the Directorate at the top of his class and earn an *insufi* blade within a single decade.

Those had been his brother's accomplishments, and Riyne wanted to match him, and why not? His tutors indicated he was every bit as talented, every bit as strong and fast, and every bit as fluid as Lisandre in the sourcing of his *lorethasra*.

The difference then between Riyne's current abilities and the sublime skill he desired would come down to heart, will, and want, and Riyne wanted it all. He wanted to be the best warrior of his generation. He wanted to destroy Yaksha's enemies. He wanted to live up to the fame of his name.

And there was no chance a disgusting, peasant human would steal the slightest shred of his glory, especially in the presence of the princess.

He glanced at Anya. She wasn't for him. He knew that. He was far too young for her, and besides, she was destined for Lisandre. Everyone said so. But she was beautiful and impressive, and if nothing else, he might impress her today. He smiled at the thought.

First, though, he had a match to focus upon. He set aside his wandering notions of future glory.

Master Absin called him and Cinder to the center of the sparring ring. He stared daggers at the *ghrina*, imagining the opening moves. Speed to devastate. Win with ease and humble the human. Injure for certain, cripple if necessary, although Riyne would prefer not to. All he required was for the human to remember today's agony and humiliation for the rest of his days.

Riyne would see to it. He could reclaim the honor he'd lost when he'd ambushed the human. He would still earn the title "*Sai*".

Master Absin went over the instructions, and Riyne nodded his understanding. Four points to earn the win and recover his status.

Riyne retreated to his side of the sparring ring. He put on his helmet, adjusted the straps and shifted about, making sure his leather gambeson didn't impede his arms. Once settled, he stared at Cinder, who met his gaze, unblinking and unwavering. *At least the human has courage.* Riyne centered on his *Muladhara*, his root Chakra. The red, four-petaled flower opened. Next, he sourced his *lorethasra*, ascending it as *prana* through his *Muladhara* and from there, his *nadis*. The power suffused his limbs, and they grew light.

He was ready to blur forth and smash the human.

Master Absin shouted, "Fight!"

Riyne dashed toward Cinder. He wouldn't prolong the match. He'd end it swiftly. He lunged, form and balance perfect. Riyne expected the stabbing movement to take Cinder at the level of the heart.

Cinder wasn't there. Riyne blinked in confusion, still extended in the lunge. The human had evaded his attack. *Impossible.* Cinder was moving. Riyne realized his danger. The human intended on getting inside his reach. Riyne desperately tried to straighten. He needed to—

An elbow smashed into his head. He felt it even through his helmet. Stars bloomed in his vision. The pain came an instant later. He stumbled. Another blow to the head, and he fell.

From a distance, he heard Master Absin shout, "Two points for Cinder!"

Riyne stared at the blue sky, confused. *Who got two points?* His thoughts were a muddle. He couldn't recall where he was. After a seemingly interminable time, he discovered the answer. *I'm at the Cauldron. It must be time to train. Why am I lying on the ground?*

Riyne struggled to his knees, flopped over. His limbs wouldn't work.

"Easy," a voice said to him. *Estin.* The prince peered at him, concern and suppressed outrage in his features. Riyne felt one of his arms lifted to go around Estin's shoulders. "Let me help you up," the prince said.

They rose, but Riyne could barely bear any weight. He stumbled, nearly falling again. "What happened?" Riyne asked, recognizing his words sounded slurred.

"Can you continue?" This time it was Master Absin staring at him in concern.

"Continue what?" Riyne asked.

"The duel," Master Absin told him. "Can you continue the duel?"

A duel? What duel? He blinked slowly. Blinked slowly once again. He dredged for the answer to the question, and it took him a long time to understand what Master Absin was asking. Riyne was supposed to duel the *ghrina*, Cinder Shade. Deliver a message to him and all humans. Reclaim some of his lost honor. "When do we start?" Riyne asked.

Master Absin turned away, facing others gathered at the Cauldron. Riyne saw who else was present: Master Nuhlin, General Arwan, Princess Anya . . . and a bunch of dwarves and humans.

Riyne scowled. What were they doing here?

"It's over," Master Absin said to General Arwan. "He can't continue. He's got a concussion. The victory goes to Cinder."

Victory? Riyne's mouth hung open in shock. Who did the human beat? Not Estin. The prince was a fine warrior.

"Come on," Estin said. "Let's get you out of the ring."

"Did Cinder beat you?" Riyne asked, still in shock.

"No. He beat you."

"Me?" Riyne stumbled along, held up by Estin. "Cinder beat me?" He still sounded stunned, his tone a reflection of Estin's own turbulent emotions.

After easing his friend to the ground Estin rose to his feet with a grateful sigh. Riyne was heavy, but at least he was in the hands of the healer. Estin glared at Cinder. The human stood amidst his dwarven and human friends, smiling in victory and receiving many shoulder-claps of acclaim.

How could Riyne have lost to the human? By far, Riyne was the best of the Firster elves. He should have overwhelmed the *ghrina*. But somehow, it hadn't happened.

Estin replayed the short duel in his mind. Riyne had lunged, but Cinder had moved before the attack even started. He had shifted to the side, like he already knew what Riyne intended. From there, the human had smashed Riyne in the side of his head with his elbow and followed up with the flat of his blade in the same location.

The healer spoke to Riyne, apparently telling him what had happened.

"No!" Riyne shouted. "He couldn't have won." He went silent, groaning in horror a few seconds later. "He won," he said in a stunned whisper. Riyne sounded like he wanted to weep. He must finally be remembering what happened.

Estin crouched down, facing his friend at eye level. "I won't lose to him. I'll reclaim honor for both of us."

Riyne didn't answer. He merely clutched his head, staring at the ground and appearing lost.

Estin's heart went to his friend. This would be another black mark on Riyne's record, losing to a human in a duel. Coupled with the ambush, he might not even receive an *insufi* blade, much less the title of *Sai*.

The ambush. It was shameful what they'd done. Estin knew it now, although he still thought Cinder had deserved the beating. The human had too much pride, was too brash and bold. Estin still couldn't believe the man had the temerity to dance with Anya and ended it on a dip. He snarled at the memory.

Master Absin broke him out of his thoughts. "Estin and Cinder. Approach."

Estin found himself within arm's reach of the human and glared. He'd break this man, hurt him for what he'd done to Riyne, batter him into submission for daring to think himself the equal of an elf.

"Do you have a second?" Master Absin asked.

Estin realized the question was directed to him. "I don't need one. I'm ready enough."

"As you say. You know the rules. Return to your stations."

Estin backed up to his place in the sparring ring. The entire time, he never broke gaze with Cinder. He glowered, wanting to impress on the man just how much pain he planned on delivering. Cinder stared right back, which was perfect. It would make it all the finer when Estin shattered his confidence and his pride.

He opened his *Muladhara*, sourced his *lorethasra*, and sent it spreading out as *prana* through the root-system of his *nadis*. The world grew more real. He sensed his body more acutely, grounded to the earth but ready to fly at a moment's notice.

Master Absin shouted, "Fight!"

Estin hung back, not rushing forward like Riyne had done. He would test the human, see what he could really do. Plus, only the blade could account for points, and before earning his victory, Estin planned on delivering elbows and kicks meant to break bones and will.

Cinder took the center of the ring, stalking forward.

Estin smiled, signaling him on. Let the human be the aggressor. Estin preferred to counter anyway.

Cinder took the bait, dashing across the ring.

Estin slid to the side, smacked away a weak thrust, and readied a battering elbow. Cinder leaned away from it and took a step back.

Fine. The human had evaded Estin's first move. *Let's see him evade this.* Estin sent a horizontal attack. Cinder parried. Estin rode his shoke along the human's. As expected, Cinder disengaged, taking a straight step back. Estin leaned into a thrust, one aimed at the human's heart.

Something smashed into the side of Estin's leg. *A kick.* His knee buckled. The surprise and pain caused him to lose focus. Now came a blow to his forearm. The shoke fell from Estin's nerveless hands. Tears sprung to his eyes, and he gritted his teeth to keep from screaming. He fell to the ground, clutching his forearm to his chest.

Estin barely heard when Master Absin shouted the results. "Two points for Cinder."

Shokes delivered a phantom pain, one meant to mimic the damage an edged weapon would have done, but without the actual injury. Right now, Estin felt like his forearm had been amputated.

He moaned, hating the miserable sound of his pain as he rocked back and forth, waiting for the agony to recede. A few seconds later, it did—blessed relief—but his forearm remained sore. The menacing phantom pain was thankfully gone, but he'd still been struck by a hard piece of wood. *That* discomfort lingered.

"Resume your stations," Master Absin said.

Estin shook out his arm, trying to get rid of the throbbing ache. He'd lost two points to Cinder, and he couldn't believe it. As an elf, he was the far faster, stronger warrior, supremely gifted compared to a human.

But Cinder had somehow gotten off a counter, one impossible for

Estin to see or evade. He would have to approach the rest of the duel more warily. Estin threw out notions of inflicting punishment. Victory would have to be enough.

He resumed his position, shoke in hand, a plan in place.

Seconds later. "Fight!"

Estin took the center of the ring this time. He wouldn't be the aggressor, but he also wouldn't let Cinder control the location of the fight.

Cinder eased forward, and Estin waited on him, planning his strategy and opening moves. *Careful and cautious.* As soon as the human was in range, Estin attacked. A lazy thrust, one easily parried. He wanted to gauge Cinder's timing. A slightly faster thrust. Again, parried.

Estin edged to Cinder's right. He darted toward the human, a swirling, downward strike.

Cinder evaded, not parrying this time. Estin pressed him. He mixed thrusts with questing vertical and horizontal slashes. Their shokes clashed against one another. Estin increased the pace. Faster still. Ever quicker.

He smiled to himself. Cinder could barely parry his attacks, and he'd abandoned any notion of countering. Estin knew the human's timing.

Now, to defeat him. Estin planned a series of moves. A vertical slash transitioning to a front kick to the gut followed by a hammering blow to the head. He got off the vertical slash, but his front kick met air. Expecting resistance, he found himself overbalanced.

A line of fire caused his thigh to explode in torture.

"Two points and victory for Cinder Shade!"

Cinder heard the words while staring down at Estin, who writhed on the ground. He might have felt bad for the elf, but he didn't have it in him. Estin got what he deserved. Besides, the pain would abate soon enough. It wasn't like he'd actually cut the elf's leg off at the thigh, even if that's what Estin was currently feeling.

He continued to stare down at the elf, giving him one last pitiless glance before going to his friends who greeted him with loud shouts of joy. He celebrated with them until General Arwan called for his presence along with Estin's and Riyne's.

The commandant, Anya, Master Absin, and Master Nuhlin, waited for them, all four with arms crossed.

The commandant, white-streaked blond hair gathered in a ponytail, faced them. His icy-blue eyes flashed. "Consider this the end of your disagreement," he said. "You will make peace now and accept one another as worthy members of this academy."

Cinder glanced askance at Estin and Riyne. He had no more reason to fight those two, but did they feel the same way about him?

Riyne's features were pale and unwell, except for the place where Cinder's shoke had cracked him in the head. That portion was red and swollen. It left his expression difficult to decipher.

Estin's was not. The prince was furious, red-faced and clearly angry.

The commandant noticed. So did Anya. She spoke in her brother's ear, her harsh whisper likely meant to carry. "You failed," she hissed at Estin. "You were defeated. Accept it with some modicum of grace. Take his hand, offer your apologies, and move on. You've embarrassed the family enough."

Riyne faced Cinder, surprising him by bowing low at the waist. "My apologies," he said. "I should not have done as I did."

"And what did you do?" Cinder asked. He wanted to forgive the elf, could have taken Riyne's apology on its face, but it wasn't enough. He had to express *exactly* what he had done to instigate this duel. Only then would Cinder know that the elf was sincere in his apology.

"I attacked you, but I felt I had cause. You are haughty. You are prideful enough to dance with a princess of the sithe, and you are scornful of your betters."

Cinder's desire to forgive fled, and his jaw clenched. Riyne had learned nothing, and he wasn't sorry at all for what he'd done. Cinder drew a breath. "Then you can take your apology and—"

"I suffer from those same defects," Riyne said. He flashed a sickly smile. "Except for dancing with Princess Anya. I've never done that."

Cinder viewed him in uncertainty, not sure what Riyne was trying to convey. Was he joking about not getting to dance with Anya? Was it the reason he smiled? Was he trying to lighten the mood with levity?

Master Absin shook his head, the barest hint of movement. "It's the best you can hope for," he murmured.

Cinder stared at Riyne a few seconds longer. "Apology accepted. I don't want to fight you again, and I don't expect to have to look over my shoulder because of you, Estin, or your friends and allies. I want to train and learn." He pointed to Bones, Ishmay, and the others. "Same with all of them."

"You'll have no trouble from me," Riyne said, "but I won't take it easy on you when it comes to sparring. Steel sharpens steel."

Cinder tried to hide his surprise. There sounded like there was a hidden offer in Riyne's statement. "I would expect nothing less," he said after a moment.

During all this, Estin's scowl became the pout of a child denied his favorite toy.

The commandant faced him. "You have something to say," General Arwan asked the prince.

Estin shot a glare at the commandant, his sister, and finally at Cinder. He managed to collect himself, taking a deep breath. His glower disappeared beneath a cool demeanor. He spoke in a civil tongue, facing Cinder. "I apologize as well. You need not fear anything I do regarding this unfortunate matter now or in the future. It is closed, as far as I am concerned." His cool mien fractured for an instant, and his glower returned when he faced the commandant, but he quickly recovered. "With your leave, I will withdraw now." Estin spun on his heel and left without waiting on General Arwan's approval.

The commandant wore a sour expression as Estin departed. "It is done then." He addressed Riyne. "Be off. Go to the hospital. The physicians will see to your injuries."

Cinder speculated as he watched Estin's stiff marched retreat. The commandant was wrong. This wasn't done. He sensed it was only beginning

32

The weeks following the duel passed in relative calm as Estin and Riyne left Cinder alone. So did the rest of the elves who used to cause him problems and for this, he was glad. It's all he ever wanted. He no longer had to pay attention to stupid barbs or pointless derisive laughter aimed in his direction. He could focus on his studies and his training to the exclusion of everything else.

He also had more time to spend with Fastness, the white stallion who still refused to allow anyone else to care for him. The two of them were able to train more regularly now. They galloped across the fields in cavalry charges, rode down mock bandits and zahhacks, or took part in other kinds of training missions.

It was glorious. Fastness lived up to his name, and Cinder loved the feel of the wind whipping past them as he scrunched his eyes in order to see. The stallion was incomparably swift. Intelligent, too. Fastness had taken to their training like a spindly legged foal, wobbly at first, but running with assurance in a few short hours.

In fact, at first Cinder had been the one who actually held them back. Prior to the Third Directorate, he had never ridden a horse, and it had taken him weeks to learn how. Adapting to the motion and balance of Fastness' various gaits had been a slow process, and it didn't help that he had started out months behind his classmates.

Cinder had been making up lost ground but after Riyne's first ambush, he'd set aside any extra hours aboard Fastness in favor of greater training with the sword.

But now that the duels were over, Cinder could devote more time into becoming a competent rider. Again, he was closing the gap, and his pace of improvement was accelerating. This time next year he figured he and Fastness would be the finest combination of horse and rider at the Third Directorate. Mostly because the white was simply that much better, that much swifter, stronger and smarter than any other horse at the academy.

If only Fastness wasn't such a smart-ass the rest of the time. When not training, he was a pest, nearly as irritating as the flies buzzing around his stall. Just for the fun of it, he sometimes flicked Cinder with his tail, flounced about when it was time to get saddled, or reached out to nip at Cinder when he wasn't looking. Afterward, he would nicker humor.

Such as now.

Cinder was in the midst of brushing down the stallion, scrubbing out burrs and tangled hair. They'd spent much of the afternoon in training, and he was beat.

He sweated while he worked in the shadowed stall. The exterior opening—grilled and windowless—faced east, and this late in the day, the bright afternoon sunshine didn't reach inside. Nonetheless, the warmth still beat down on the rest of the stable, leaving it sweltering. Fat flies buzzed about, their flights desultory and sluggish, lazy like a hound panting from the heat. Otherwise, the barn was relatively quiet as everyone quickly finished their work. No one wanted to be stuck indoors during this unexpected heat wave, and Cinder hoped the weather cooled down soon.

Cinder shared their mood. All he wanted was to finish brushing the white, shovel in fresh hay, refill the horse's water trough, and get some food for himself.

The stallion, however, had other ideas in mind.

"Hold still," Cinder grumbled. The stallion kept shifting about in the narrow confines of the stall, making it impossible to finish brushing him down.

Fastness shifted again, bumping Cinder into a wall this time and nickering a laugh.

"I said hold still," Cinder told his horse. He didn't know why he bothered talking to the stallion. The horse never listened, although he definitely understood what Cinder was saying. Of this, he was certain.

The white shifted around again, presenting his hindquarters.

Cinder moved to reach the stallion's withers.

The stallion moved again, flicking his tail.

Cinder's frustration grew. "Fastness. Come on!" He tried to cut the horse off.

The white was too quick, moving again and nickering his chuckle.

Cinder grabbed for Fastness's halter, trying to keep the stallion in place. The stallion responded by nearly stepping on Cinder's foot.

Cinder's annoyance boiled over, and he threw down his brush. "Enough. The *aether*-cursed cat who killed my parents would make a better mount than you."

The stallion's tail flicked about, and he neighed as if in disbelief.

"It's true," Cinder told him, tired of dealing with the stupid animal. "In fact, if I ever come across that cat again, I'll make her a deal. I'll let her have you as a meal if she agrees to be my mount."

Fastness swished his tail and nickered, low and uncertain. He faced Cinder, bumping him in the chest.

"I'm serious," Cinder said, hiding a grin. For once, the stallion was on the receiving end of a joke. "You're supposed to be a Yavana, but I swear your sire must have been a jackass. Your ears are sure long enough."

Fastness bumped him in the chest again, this time hard enough to make Cinder stumble. His nicker this time was one of deep offense. *Not funny.*

"Or maybe I should let a dragon step on your toes. We'll see how you like it when someone much bigger than you crushes your feet."

An expression in Fastness' eyes seemed to speak a question. *Dragons?*

"Yes, they're giant flying monsters the size of this barn. They breathe fire and could roast you inside of two shakes of your annoying tail."

Not real. Liar.

Cinder laughed, and the last of his annoyance faded. He never could stay angry with Fastness. "I'm not lying. Dragons are real." Or at least Cinder had read they were real. Of course, no one had seen one in decades, and people were starting to wonder if the great beasts had died out.

"You really talk to him," a voice noted from outside the stall.

Cinder glanced across the white's broad back. Sriovey stood in the corridor outside the stall, his head barely visible over the stall door.

"Sometimes he's the only one worth talking to."

Sriovey snorted. "Because the two of you have a similar intellect?"

"Intellect? Big word there." Cinder grinned. "Someone must have been spending time in the library studying their vocabulary."

Sriovey bristled. "Are you saying I'm stupid?"

Cinder turned his attention to Fastness. "What do you think? Is Sriovey stupid?"

The stallion neighed, bobbing his head up and down.

Cinder laughed. "There you have it. Straight from the horse's mouth."

"More like the ass' mouth. He's ugly enough to be a mule."

The stallion lashed out with his hind legs, hitting the side wall with a resounding smack.

Cinder rubbed the stallion's forehead. "Easy, lad. The ugly dwarf was only joking." He glanced to Sriovey. "You don't usually come down here much."

Sriovey shrugged. "I was bored and decided to go for a walk." He tilted his head as if in consideration. "He's a Yavana steed. You know they won't let you keep him after graduation, don't you Hotgate? He's too valuable to lose. They'll probably give him to someone in Yaksha's royal guard, part of the pomp and circumstance of parades and such."

Cinder realized it, too. Fastness would never ride the Daggers. Yaksha couldn't afford to lose him. He was as Sriovey said: too valuable. Cinder didn't like to think about separating from the stallion, though. As much as he found the white's behavior irritating at times, he'd bonded with the horse. He liked Fastness, warts and jackassery and all. He spoke to his stallion. "You think you'd like to wear gilded leather and a fancy saddle."

"Don't forget the prissy guard with the useless sword," Sriovey said.

Fastness shook his head. *No one else rides me. Not yet. And I'll kill cat.*

Cinder laughed. "I'm sure you would."

Anya didn't mean to stay so long at the Third Directorate, but with the weather warming, the Grand Melee and Unitary Trial only weeks away, she figured there was no reason not to. She could take up her ranger's duties in the Daggers during the summer. Plus, she had useful work to do. The commandant had asked her to help train the elves. After Estin and Riyne's loss to a human, he thought they needed the extra help. No one was pleased by how those two had treated a fellow cadet, but they also weren't happy to see them so handily defeated by a human. The commandant also wanted her opinion on a different but related matter.

"There's something odd going on with the humans and dwarves," General Arwan said. "Very odd."

Anya smiled. "Odder than a human defeating two of the Blessed Race in a duel?"

The commandant grimaced. "Maybe not that strange, but it's still bizarre. It's their small unit drills. There's someone I want you to watch. Whatever unit he's on, it always wins."

Anya had a guess who the commandant meant. "I think I know the one you mean," she said, not bothering to name him.

Cinder Shade.

Everyone at the Directorate knew him now, and to say the human warranted extra attention was an understatement. Every elf, including Anya, was watching him closely, studying his performances. Some elves feared Cinder could source his *lorethasra* at will, but they were wrong. He could at times in the Foe. At least, so he'd once told her, but nowhere else.

Anya had monitored his progress, and she never saw him moving more swiftly than his fellow humans. He simply had impeccable timing. According to Master Absin, Cinder had an innate ability to recognize an opponent's plan of attack prior to the action occurring. It was a master-level talent, rare at such a young age, but nothing worrisome like a human sourcing his *lorethasra* at will.

General Arwan continued as if she hadn't spoken, pacing now. "It doesn't matter the odds, he always finds a way to win. And there are two others who if they're matched with this individual . . ." He shook his head in disbelief. "Sometimes I think they could defeat all the other Firsters by themselves, including the elves."

Anya privately doubted it, but she supposed they'd find out during the Unitary Trial, the year-end challenge in the Daggers. Of course, prior to that would occur the Grand Melee, and the final ranking assessment. The elves always held the top positions, although every once in a while, a dwarf would achieve a top five ranking, but nothing more.

It had always been thus, and despite Cinder Shade's success against Estin and Riyne, she thought history unlikely to change.

"At least the Grand Melee might prove more interesting this year," General Arwan said. "You saw what that boy did to your brother and Riyne."

Anya flushed at the reminder, not at the loss Estin had suffered, but because of her brother's and Riyne's actions. Ambushing a fellow student? Blended while doing so? It was the action of a coward, and her heart burned, disgusted that Estin could have done such a thing. He'd shamed her, shamed the family, and his shocking loss in the duel only added to the dishonor.

"If I didn't know better, I'd think he could source *lorethasra*," the general added, his voice dark.

Anya had tried not to roll her eyes at the last. The general's assessment about Cinder was unfounded. He was only a human, and his victory against Estin and Riyne had been due to skill and a large bit of luck. Nothing more.

Nevertheless, here she stood, watching from afar as a group of five humans and one dwarf—Red Team—took on two humans and four dwarves—Gray Team. The members of Red Team: Cinder, Wark, Depth, Joria, Rorian, and Sriovey. The members of Gray Team: Bones, Ishmay, Derius, Jozep, Nathaz, and Dorcer.

It was an obvious mismatch. The Grays should overwhelm the Reds. They had four dwarves and two of the top three humans. Anya watched with arms crossed for the 'carnage' to begin.

The drill took place in a wildflower meadow amongst the low-lying hills surrounding the Directorate. A cowling of trees draped the perimeter of the field, which was warmed beneath a mid-day sun. A scattering of spring clouds lazed in a blue sky as deep as a newborn's eyes. The air held still, humid with moisture from a recent rain and the lush floral fragrance of the wildflowers.

Anya observed as the two units came closer to one another. They approached from opposite sides of the field. Her eyes narrowed. Red Team was missing a member. She could only see four humans and a dwarf. Where was Rorian? Was he injured? Or was he hiding? Some kind of ploy perhaps?

Gray Team spread out, clearly confident in the superior quality of their warriors and apparently their numbers. They grinned, shouting boastfully. The dwarves rushed toward the Reds, who appeared disorganized and incoherent.

Cinder gestured wildly, shouting while trying to bring order to his team.

Anya shook her head in disappointment. After the general's description of his prowess, she expected more of him. He might be a fine warrior, but so far, he was a terrible tactician.

The dwarves of Gray Team charged, leaving their humans far behind. Red Team fell back, sprinting in the other direction, Cinder in the lead. He stumbled, fell, and didn't rise.

Anya's frown deepened to disgust. *Cowards and klutzes.*

Yards from the treeline, Nathaz, one of the dwarves on Gray Team, shouted out in pain, rubbing at his back. Rorian rose from where he'd been crouched, hiding amongst the tall wildflowers.

Anya found herself smiling. A clever trick. She noticed Red Team's ragged line had straightened. Sriovey stood at their center and they faced the charging Grays. But where was Cinder?

Her attention returned to Nathaz, who was glaring murder at Rorian. "You Devesh-damned cheater!" Nathaz shouted. He took an aggressive step toward Rorian, hand tight on his warhammer.

Anya sourced *lorethasra*, projecting her voice. "Nathaz! You're out. No more movement."

Nathaz gave her a look of disgust before flopping to the ground. Rorian raced past him. By now the Grays realized what had happened and they slowed down, proceeding more carefully.

But not carefully enough.

Dorcer went down, clutching at his right leg. *Cinder.* The boy had also been hiding in the tall grass.

Anya didn't want a repeat of Nathaz's action. "Dorcer! You're done!" she shouted at the dwarf. She then sourced more *lorethasra*, enhancing her hearing and bringing whatever was said by the two units to her ears.

Rorian reached Cinder's side and together, they faced Bones and Ishmay.

The humans of Gray team shared an uncertain glance. They darted away from Cinder and Rorian, taking up defensive positions behind Derius and Jozep, the remaining dwarves from their unit.

Two dwarves and two humans against five humans and a dwarf.

Anya's interest perked. This was becoming interesting.

The dwarves of Gray Team went after Sriovey, trading and dodging heavy hammer blows. They sourced *lorethasra*, using it as *prana* to make themselves stronger and faster.

Sriovey defended as best he could, but against two foes, he had to give ground. He edged toward his humans, who quickly surrounded Derius and Jozep. More blows were exchanged. Joria went down. So did Depth.

Sriovey defeated Derius.

Jozep handled Wark, but somewhere during the drill, the dwarf had taken an injury. He limped, right leg clearly hurting, but he had no time to recover. Here came Sriovey. If healthy, Jozep would have provided a stiff challenge to the dwarven leader, but injured as he was, Anya didn't expect him to last very long.

She turned to where Cinder faced off against Bones while Rorian dueled against Ishmay.

"You ready for round two?" Bones asked Cinder.

"Always," Cinder said. "You haven't beaten me in months." He went on the attack. Bones defended. They came together in short bursts, neither gaining the upper hand.

Meanwhile, Rorian held his own against Ishmay, just long enough for Sriovey to enter the fray. Jozep was down, easily defeated given his injury.

Ishmay licked his lips, glancing from Rorian to Sriovey. He attacked his fellow human, but it left him open. Sriovey delivered a punishing blow to Ishmay's chest, and the young human crumpled with a groan.

Anya winced in sympathy. Even with his padded armor, Sriovey's strike had to hurt.

It was down to Cinder against Bones. They circled one another, shokes flicking, slashing and parrying. Rorian and Sriovey arrived, and Bones stepped back. He viewed his opponents for a moment, scowling.

The math was simple. Three-against-one. Bones had no chance. He dropped his shoke and went to his knees, wisely conceding the drill.

Red Team had easily won despite what on the surface should have been difficult odds.

Anya better understood the commandant's concerns. Cinder Shade was a dangerous person. A fine warrior and *possibly a better* tactician. She eyed Cinder in speculation. *Who are you?*

She and the commandant would have matters to discuss this evening. But first, she wanted to talk to Cinder in private.

"Red Team!" Anya shouted. "Congratulations on your victory. Gray Team. My compliments. Five laps around the Quad. Dismissed!"

Red Team grinned while Gray Team groaned. The humans and dwarves collected themselves, heading back to the Directorate.

"A moment of your time, Firster," Anya said, addressing Cinder. The members of both Red and Gray Teams paused. Anya waved them on. "You have your tasks. See to them."

They left with grumbles on the part of the Grays and laughter from the Reds. Anya let go of her *lorethasra*, facing Cinder and waiting on him.

He approached, relaxed and grinning. "You wanted to see me, princess?"

Anya gritted her teeth in annoyance. The way he said 'princess'. It was like a caress. No human should speak to her so.

Then again, perhaps she was reading more into his manner than actually existed. She decided to overlook his overly familiar tone even while disliking the fearless manner in which he viewed her.

It was time to throw him off his stride. "Stand still. Don't move," Anya ordered. She slowly circled him, pretending to examine him from all angles. Like any person faced with uncertainty, especially potential danger, he tensed. "I saw what you did when you fought my brother and Riyne. No human other than the rakishis of Bharat could manage what you did." She halted in front of him. "Care to explain yourself?"

Most people flinched or ducked their heads in such a situation, but Cinder did neither.

His eyes locked on hers, unwavering and unafraid. "I was lucky. They made a mistake, and I was able to take advantage of it." His mouth twisted in dissatisfaction. "Will they honor their pledges and leave me alone?"

Anya halted her pacing and viewed him through offended eyes. He hadn't properly answered her question and dared ask her one in return, challenging her brother's honor-bound oath, no less.

"General Arwan believes you can source your *lorethasra*," Anya said. "Can you?"

"Not really," Cinder said. "I can sometimes when I'm in the Foe. I've told you that before, but in the real world, I haven't been able to figure out how." His brow knitted. "I don't know what I'm doing wrong."

Anya lifted a questioning eyebrow, silently asking him to explain what he meant.

"When I'm in the Foe, I can conduct my *lorethasra*. It's like a pool of the clearest water, and it makes me faster and stronger."

Shock layered upon surprise. Anya kept her face expressionless. Cinder's description bore little similarity to what elves and dwarves could do, and for them, they could only more deeply sense their *lorethasra* once they had opened their first Chakra, *Muladhara*. Otherwise, it was simply an unusable potential, and no one actually saw their *lorethasra*. What did it mean that he could?

The possibilities left her cold but also excited. What might he be able to accomplish if he opened his *Muladhara*? He might be the first human to earn an *insufi* blade. He could be the one who broke the elves of their stagnant arrogance. She needed to talk to him about his future plans. She had ideas.

Just then, a memory sparked, one of her late husband. He moved like a stalking panther, smooth and controlled even at rest. And he could dance. How she loved dancing with him. A name she'd forgotten. *Ashoka*. Her husband's home. *Stronghold*. The home of her heart. More details, surging like waters through a broken dam. So many lost memories.

Cinder broke into her ruminations. "Are you all right, Anya?" He'd stepped into her personal space, concern written on his face.

It was a deluge of recollections, and Anya struggled to swim atop the cresting wave. "I'm fine," she managed to say, forcing a smile. "But I'd like to meet with you when you're free and discuss your future. Perhaps in a few days, after your classes."

Cinder's visage held confusion. "What did you want to talk about?"

Anya shook her head. The remembrances continued to surge. "Not now. Rejoin the others."

Cinder eyed in worry, unmoving. "Are you sure?"

Anya wanted privacy. She needed quiet in order to accept and ascertain her lost memories. "I'm fine," Anya said, her tone a bit sharper. "Rejoin the others."

This time, Cinder didn't argue. He continued to eye her in worry but withdrew, walking swiftly toward the Directorate. Anya watched him go, unseeing as her disremembered recollections washed over like a tidal wave. She'd forgotten so much.

A single tear tracked along the lines of her cheek. She remembered her husband more clearly than ever before. His image remained blurred and impossible, but she now knew his name. *Rukh.*

Devesh, how she missed him.

Several days later, as spring continued to edge toward summer with longer, warmer days, the windows in Firemirror Hall were thrown open. It allowed the entrance of a gentle wind, and the floral fragrance of gardenias swept in with the breeze. The sun shone amidst a clear sky, but to the west, clouds gathered. Cinder's table provided a view through the room's windows, and in the near distance, he saw gardeners tilling flower beds and getting small plantings in place.

"Pikes," Master Nuhlin said, his voice clear.

Cinder's drifting attention snapped back to the here and now. It was Tactics and Strategy, one of the final classes prior to the end of his first year at the Third Directorate. Next week would be the Grand Melee and the Days of Deliverance. The Firsters wouldn't have much of a chance to celebrate the latter, the festival commemorating the end of the *NusraelShev.* They'd be too busy with their testing. They would go through several days of both formal written exams and demonstrations in archery, horsemanship, and sword. Afterward, the First Years would travel to the Daggers for their final fieldwork. The Unitary Trial.

"They are an infantryman's best friend," Master Nuhlin continued. Sunshine shone off his youthful visage and the crown of his head. "At least that is what Genka Devesth is teaching us. Like all Sunset Kingdom armies, cavalry forms the core of his forces, but study how he uses pikemen. In this, you'll discover his genius."

Cinder glanced in Sriovey's direction. The dwarf wore a pursed-lipped expression, one making him appear as if he'd swallowed a solid ball of tamarind. Sriovey had an obsession with Genka, seemingly terrified of the warlord. Cinder had no idea why, but it always struck him as funny. Everyone else felt the same way.

He smiled, nudging Bones who sat to his left, gesturing toward Sriovey, indicating the fear on the dwarf's face.

Bones laughed loudly, and Mohal, seated to Cinder's right, noticed the focus of their attention and chuckled as well.

Sriovey must have reckoned the reason for their humor because he glowered in their direction.

Cinder grinned more widely.

Master Nuhlin abruptly cleared his throat. Cinder realized the instructor was staring at him. "I know it's spring, and I know your classes will soon end, and for this reason, you will only have a final paper to write."

Groans met his words. Cinder found himself the object of glares of blame.

"Have a paper done by the end of the week. Explain how Genka Devesth used his cavalry and infantry in capturing Kalesth. Class dismissed."

"Nice job, dumbass," Bones said to Cinder as they gathered their books and ledgers. "You got us stuck doing more work. We could have used that time to study or practice for next week."

Cinder didn't think it was his fault. "I'm not the one who laughed like a jackass."

"Don't blame Mohal," Bones said.

"I wasn't," Cinder replied.

"I don't laugh like a jackass," Mohal said.

"And you are to blame," Bones added to Cinder.

Cinder realized most of the Firsters were staring daggers in his direction as everyone shuffled out of the room and into the hall.

Sriovey reached Cinder out in the corridor, a scowl of disgust on his face. "Well done, getting us more work."

Nathaz reached him next, shaking his head in disbelief. "You fucking moron," he said to Cinder. "Keep your mouth shut next time."

Cinder didn't know who to address first. "I wasn't the one who brayed like a fragging donkey," he got out.

"I thought it was laugh like a jackass," Mohal said.

"Bones laughs like a jackass," Cinder explained. "You bray like a fragging donkey."

Bones eyed Cinder with pity. "When are you ever going to use a proper curse word? You're always going on with "frag this" or "frag that" or "jackhole". Sounds kind of girlish. Why not just use the right words?"

"You mean like fuck you, asshole?" Cinder shrugged. "I don't know. I like mine better."

They exited Firemirror Hall and headed toward the cafeteria in two clusters, the elves forming one group and the humans and dwarves the other. However, as a single unit, they argued over who was at fault for the homework assignment. Cinder defended himself as best he could, and thankfully, the others were soon distracted by other reasons to insult one another. Like it usually did, their conversation devolved into a competition of quips about mothers.

Cinder rolled his eyes, feeling old since he never took part in such contests.

"Devesh damn it!" Bones complained. "For the last fragging time, sisters are off limits, you jackholes."

"Fragging time? Jackholes?" Sriovey asked. He broke out into laughter. "Weren't you just going on about Hotgate using those words? You hypocrite."

"He's a bad influence, *asshole*," Bones replied with emphasis. "How's that for you?"

"Better than fragging or jackhole," Sriovey replied, smiling still.

"Yes, well, just remember sisters are off limits," Bones said.

"What is about you and sisters?" Estin asked. "You seem to have an overly protective bearing toward yours." The elf appeared to be hiding a smile.

Cinder did a double-take. In all the months he'd spent around the royal elf, only rarely did Estin address a human with a question not steeped in ridicule or haughtiness.

Estin spoke on. "Is it a human failing—"

"There it is," Cinder said, making sure the elf could hear him. "Can't have Estin speaking to us without insulting our entire race."

Estin ignored him. "To love one's sister too deeply? Like someone you wish to play court."

"I said sisters are off limits," Bones growled to the elven prince. "Or should we bring up Anya? She's a beautiful—"

Estin's easy-going demeanor vanished. Anger took its place. "Don't talk about my sister. She is not for your kind to even look upon."

"But what about if she asks us to dance?" Cinder asked, egging on the royal elf. His hostility toward Estin hadn't eased off in the slightest since the duel. He still didn't like the prince and doubted he ever would. "I'm not sure I can dance with my eyes closed."

Estin cursed him. "You have no honor, *ghrina*, but then I repeat myself."

"What's a *ghrina*?" Ishmay asked.

"An elf prince with a shoke up his ass," Cinder replied.

Estin gaped at him, apparently unable to come up with a coherent response. "Your friend is right. Sisters are off limits," he eventually said.

Bones laughed as Estin departed.

"See what I mean," Cinder said to everyone. "Laughs like a jackass."

33

Anya had sent Cinder a note earlier today to meet her after classes at the Cauldron, but it hadn't contained any hint as to why. After the small unit drills a few days back, she'd mentioned going over his future plans, but he didn't know what she meant. He always figured he'd enter the Imperial Army of Yaksha Sithe as a commander in the cavalry or fast infantry like every other human graduate of the Third Directorate. What else was there?

Cinder searched around the sparring circles for Anya, but he wasn't able to immediately locate her. The Cauldron was full of warriors, some training, others practicing balance and technique. Their voices carried as shouts, laughter, curses, and grunts. The Firsters were here tonight as well, all the humans, dwarves, and elves. They worked hard, pushing themselves and one another. The Grand Melee and the Unitary Trial were rapidly approaching, less than a week away. Everyone recognized the need to increase the intensity of their training.

That same intensity was in contrast to the soft warmth of the evening, which lingered on the sands, dirt, and grass like a mellow ale.

"Did the princess say what she wanted?" Bones asked, taking a breather from sparring against Jozep. The dwarf hadn't been easy on him either, his attacks and counters full of muscle and bad intentions. Bones had managed to stay in the fight, though, lasting longer than either he or Jozep likely thought possible.

The humans as a whole these days seemed to have a greater sureness when going against the woven, which they needed. The change had started after Cinder's duel against Estin and Riyne. Those contests had served to demonstrate that hard work, skill, and self-confidence could overcome woven advantages in physicality.

"I have no idea," Cinder said in reply to Bones' question. A breeze flickered through the boughs and branches of the surrounding trees, and the wind sent playful fingers through his hair. "She only said to wait on her."

"And you've waited patiently enough," Anya said. She strode in their direction, a shoke replacing the *insufi* sword she normally wore on her hip.

Her honey-blonde hair was tied off in a braid, and her padded clothes were as plain and nondescript as any student's, but they fit her in ways Cinder found distracting. He did his best not to notice Anya's attributes, but it was difficult, impossible really. Her gentle curves, the swell of her breasts, the elegant line of her neck, the fierce intensity of her emerald-colored eyes, the . . .

He blinked, realizing she had asked him something. Bones snickered.

"I'm sorry, princess. I missed your question."

Anya's eyes narrowed in speculation, and Cinder feigned innocence. He realized if he'd whistled nonchalantly, staring at the sky, he couldn't have done a poorer job of hiding his thoughts. Guilt also rose at his appreciation. *Coral.*

Thankfully, Anya let the matter drop, but a knowing gleam filled her eyes. "I asked if you were ready?"

"I'm off," Bones said. "Jozep wants to kick my butt again." He dipped his head to the princess. "Your highness."

"You defeated Riyne and my brother," Anya said after Bones left.

"You also did well in leading your troop in the drills I saw. The reward for your success is the opportunity to test yourself against me."

It didn't sound like much of a prize. Cinder didn't favor his chances against Anya. If he was being honest with himself, his defeat of Estin and Riyne was because of his supreme preparation and their utter lack of seriousness about the duel. He was good, but he'd also surprised them. He would have no such advantage against Anya.

In fact, sparring against her sounded like a perfect opportunity for the princess to put her boot up his ass if she wanted. And maybe she did. Maybe she wanted revenge for what he'd done to her brother. Estin would always be a prince of the sithe, but by losing to a human in a duel, his road to winning an *insufi* blade was now much longer and rockier. To say nothing of his loss of face, reputation, and honor.

"After you," Cinder said to Anya.

"So formal," Anya replied, a mysterious smile on her face. She led him to a sparring ring.

He had to remind himself not to stare at the sway of her hips, steadying himself with the image of Coral.

Thankfully, when he and Anya reached an unoccupied training ring, entering it was like a bucket of icy water. It focused Cinder's mind, pushing away thoughts of Anya's beauty or memories of Coral. He was here to train, not waste time by gawking. He settled his helmet on his head, closed his eyes, and centered himself.

Several deep breaths later, he was ready. His emotions were under control, and he opened his eyes. He scrutinized the princess, analyzing her posture, the way she held her shoke. She bounced on her toes, staring at him, brows knitted.

"Ready?" Anya asked.

A charge or possibly a feint. She was difficult to decipher. He would have to let the match progress and hope to read her movements.

"Fight!" Anya shouted.

She came at him like a bolt, but Cinder was prepared. He slid to the side fully expecting to evade her charge. An instant later, his eyes widened in shock. She matched his turn, cut him off. A slash came, too fast to block. He rolled beneath it and caught a kick to the solar plexus.

Cinder's breath blasted out. He barely noticed when Anya's shoke touched his neck. He was too busy trying to draw air into his lungs. It took a few panicked moments, but eventually his breathing came easier. He didn't immediately rise. For now, he was content to remain on the ground and stare at the darkening sky. While lying down, he tried to piece together just how he had so swiftly and spectacularly lost.

After his victory against Estin and Riyne, his self-confidence had grown, a surety that he could stand against any elf, at least for a time. Anya had just disabused him of such false belief. He was nowhere near her level.

Emotions warred within him. He was angry with himself. Angry with his easy arrogance. He'd defeated two young elves and suddenly believed himself the equal of any? *Idiot.* Didn't Master Absin tell him how elves grew more powerful as they aged? He'd forgotten the lesson.

Regardless, Cinder was also ashamed at how easily Anya had bested him. It was embarrassing. More, he was consumed with a desire to overcome. Anya had crushed him, as easily as if he'd never before trained with a sword. In doing so, she had taught him a valuable lesson, and he wouldn't let it go to waste.

Anya was fast, swifter than Lisandre, but that wasn't the key to her ability. Cinder had once thought Gorant had perfect form. Later, he'd thought the same of Bones.

He was wrong on both counts. Gorant and Bones were like ungainly toddlers in comparison to Anya's true perfection of form and technique. He now had a new target to attain, a goal to reach, and he made a promise to himself to achieve it.

His decision made, the world came into greater clarity.

Cinder rolled over onto an elbow and pushed onto his hands and knees with a hiss of pain. His abdomen ached. His padding helped, but the princess kicked as hard as Fastness.

Anya squatted on her haunches, gazing at him in concern. "Can you continue? Or do you need to stop?"

Cinder didn't answer at first. Defeating Estin and Riyne wouldn't be the summit of his achievements. It would only be the beginning. He rose to his feet. "I'm fine. I can keep going. I don't quit."

Anya stood as well and quirked a half-smile, seemingly pleased for some reason. "We shall see. I still want to talk to you about your future plans. Your next rest day. Tomorrow morning, yes? Meet me in Certitude. I'll send you the directions."

Cinder eyed her, unsure what she wanted to discuss.

They resumed their stations on opposite sides of the sparring circle, and he set aside his questions. She'd tell him tomorrow. He rolled his shoulders and neck, and once he was ready, he called out the start of their match. "Fight!"

He took the center of the ring, and Anya circled him. He twisted, keeping her directly in front. She darted forward. He gave ground, defending, trying to learn her patterns, her rhythm, and timing.

Seven moves later, Anya defeated him, a disarming maneuver with the shoke and a trip. He landed with a crash, on his back and staring at the sky.

He smiled, wanting to laugh. *Yes.* He'd train against Anya. She'd likely win plenty against him, but he wouldn't quit against her. His dreams would require no less.

Anya strode through the clogged streets of Certitude, doing her best to avoid the traffic. Today was a farmer's market and many folk were out on this lovely spring morning of sunshine. The overhanging limbs of various oaks and maple lining the streets provided shade for the vendors who quietly sold their wares. It was so unlike the raucous cries of Swift Sword or any other human city. Those of the Blessed Race preferred a more sedate sale, low-key and unpressured.

So did Anya, but sometimes the excitement of human living was bewitching, the madness and motion.

A subtle breeze tugged at Anya's hair, swaying the line of jasmines she'd woven into her braid. Every movement of her head caused the lovely fragrance to waft. She wasn't sure why she'd chosen to wear the flowers. In general, she kept her hair in a plain ponytail or at most an uncomplicated braid since she considered herself a simple warrior with simple needs such as simple clothing. She certainly wasn't someone who would willingly weave flowers into her hair. She had no use for such frivolity.

And yet she had done so, and she didn't know what might have impelled the choice. She had woken up this morning and inexplicably felt like braiding jasmines into her hair.

She mentally shrugged and set aside the question. It was of no importance.

On she strode, pushing on and leaving the farmer's market behind. A few minutes later, she reached her destination, *Chai Steep.* Awnings shaded the mullioned windows, the muntins painted white. Inside, she found a small room with a half-dozen round tables and matching chairs. The wood was darkened by age and polished to a mirror sheen. From the ceiling hung wagon-wheel chandeliers. *Diptha* bulbs lit the space.

She had asked Cinder to meet her today for chai. She had a proposition for him, and she was pleased to note he was already seated and waiting for her. It was only correct. He was a Firster, and she was his elder. He should be the one to reach the tea house first. It was a sign of respect. He rose when she entered.

The waitress, a slim elf, dark-haired and young given the guileless nature of her eyes, approached while Anya was in the midst of sitting. "May I take your order?" she asked.

Anya told her, and after the waitress departed, she faced Cinder. "Thank you for meeting me."

Cinder quirked a faint smile. "Who am I to say no to a princess?"

She comprehended her station in life, but it didn't mean she liked it. Not because of the responsibility assumed of those holding her rank, but because she found unearned titles anachronistic and distasteful. "Anya," she corrected Cinder. "I've told you that before. I'm sure you heard me."

Cinder's smile broadened. "Simply Anya."

Anya's lips split into a reluctant grin, and she rolled her eyes. What was it about this young man? He continually said what should have annoyed her, but they didn't. "Anya will do."

"Then Anya it is," Cinder said. His statement might have struck her as condescending if not for the twinkle in his eye. He was mocking himself as much as her.

The waitress arrived with Anya's order—hot chai—and Anya stirred in warm milk, cardamom, and honey. She took a sip, sighing in appreciation. She set the teacup on the accompanying saucer, vaguely noting how the color of her tea matched Cinder's skin tone. "What are your plans for the future?"

"Do well in the Grand Melee, survive the Unitary Trial, progress as a warrior, and enlist in the Imperial Army of Yaksha Sithe."

"An officer?"

He nodded.

It was a humble hope, one far beneath Cinder's potential. Anya had grown to know his abilities, and she had far greater ambitions in mind for him than simply serving in the army. He might not know it, but she did. Since observing and judging his small unit drill, she'd watched him more closely, especially at the Cauldron. Every day he seemed to improve. Another few years, and he might even match an elf bearing an *insufi* blade. His lack of speed would always limit him, but he would never lose due to lack of skill.

The truth was that every human graduate of the Third Directorate matriculated into the army as officers. They served capably and, in some cases, with distinction.

But none joined as rangers, and Anya aimed to defy the status quo. Cinder would be the first ranger. It would not only challenge him, but it would also challenge her people's views about what was possible for others to achieve. The lazy elven belief in their innate superiority needed shaking. The world was moving, and she had seen the changes. Gandharva was yearly growing in prosperity and power. It might soon challenge Yaksha for dominance in this corner of Seminal.

"You have something else in mind?" Cinder asked her, apparently picking up on her silent disapproval.

"I think you have it within you to become a ranger."

"There's never been a human ranger."

"Yet."

The word landed like a clattering stone, immediately drawing Cinder's attention. Anya could tell he was interested. He might have already been considering such an idea even prior to her suggestion, and if not, it wouldn't take much to reel him into her way of thinking.

"It's a few days to the Grand Melee," Anya said, "and after that, you ship out for the Unitary Trial. Do you know why we hold two tournaments?"

Cinder answered without hesitation. "The Grand Melee is for elven pride. It's meant to demonstrate elven superiority since your kind always wins in all the physical facets—swordsmanship, equitation, and archery. It's why it's so popular amongst the people of Certitude. They like to see the truth of the stories your kind tell about yourselves."

"That we're superior?"

"The *story* of how you're superior," Cinder corrected. "It's a myth your people like to tell themselves."

Anya left the final statement alone. He was wrong. Elves *were* superior, but Anya was more impressed by Cinder's understanding of the Grand Melee's purpose. She hadn't expected it. "What about the Unitary Trial?"

Cinder chuckled. "I know what you're doing. My father used to do it, too."

"Oh? And what do you think I'm trying to do?"

"You're asking me a series of questions. I answer them until I reach a conclusion you wanted me to arrive at all along."

Anya blinked, not expecting his insight. He was right. It was exactly what she was trying to do, and she did a quick re-evaluation of the human. He was a skilled warrior, a leader of men, and apparently quite deductive in his instincts.

She would return to that possibility, but right now, her attention caught on something else he had said. "I thought you couldn't remember your past."

Cinder's smile fell. Confusion or disappointment took its place. "I can't," he said after a few seconds of silence. "I . . ." He hesitated, staring at the table and scratching at it. His frown deepened, furrowing his brow. He ceased his scratching and met her gaze. "I sometimes remember aspects of my life. What I said sounded like it was right, but I don't know for sure."

Sympathy and understanding welled within Anya. It was a terrible thing to not recall one's past. She knew it all too well—constantly searching for hidden truths, feeling like a half-made jigsaw puzzle with pieces forever missing, always longing for completion. She still couldn't recall much of her past life. What did her husband look like?

"You can pretend I didn't ask," Anya said.

Cinder managed an easy smile in response.

Anya shook her head in disbelief. How did he manage such an unburdened grin? Her lack of remembrance filled her with frustration, and she couldn't simply will her anger away.

"In answer to the second half of your question," Cinder said, "the Unitary Trial is to teach the elves humility. Humans make better commanders. No matter how many times your kind is told this fact, young elves don't realize it until they experience the hardship, panic, and chaos of true combat."

Once again, Anya was surprised by his level of insight. He saw deeper than his eighteen years should allow. She found herself pondering who he really was. How could this orphan know so much? Speak with such confidence? She sought to test him further. "And how does this relate to what you said earlier? About how I'm asking a series of questions meant for you to reach a preordained conclusion?"

"I'm not sure," Cinder said. "You want me to become a ranger, but—"

"But you don't know how my questions might convince you of such a destiny."

Cinder nodded.

"If you do well enough in the Grand Melee, you'll know you can survive as a ranger. If you do even better in the Unitary Trial, you'll realize the best place in the army to utilize your talents will be as a ranger."

"Don't rangers require a sponsor?"

Anya nodded. "I would sponsor you."

She didn't add how doing so would scandalize her family and most of elven society. *Ghrina*, a loathsome word, might be the mildest insult she could expect.

She could take the opprobrium so long as her people recognized and reflected upon the lessons she was trying to impart. So long as they understood and confronted the dangers of their apathy and laziness.

Anya waited on his decision, perturbed when he didn't immediately say 'yes'. Instead, he stared at his teacup, as if the answer to her suggestion could be found in its contents.

"I'll think about it," he eventually allowed.

Cinder spent the next few days contemplating Anya's offer. It was generous, and he couldn't help but reflect on how it would likely hurt her own standing to sponsor a human as a ranger. It was why he hadn't leapt at her proposal. He didn't want to see her diminished in anyone's eyes.

He considered what it would mean to be the first human ranger as he strummed his mandolin in the common room, which was currently crowded. Everyone had decided to gather here after supper.

Derius, Sriovey, Bones, and Wark played euchre. Nathaz, Rorian, Dorcer, and Depth were playing darts. Others were gathered around the unlit fireplace, slouching on the couch and other assorted seating while discussing the day's events.

Cinder glanced out the window, at the sky shot with streaks of violet and red. *Twilight*. His favorite time of the day. The sun hung directly above the horizon. Only a few more minutes until it dipped below the edge of the world, and the stars and moons took command of the heavens. A gentle breeze flitted through the window, bringing a heady aroma from the gardened courtyard below and stirring his hair.

He leaned forward, glancing into the gardens. A woman weeded the flower beds.

Anya. He could tell. Not by her honey-colored hair, but by her posture, her surety of movements, her sublime grace. He would know her anywhere. He held his breath when she straightened and stretched. She lifted her face to the darkening sky, her back a bow. Something about Anya fascinated Cinder. It wasn't her appearance, her physicality, or anything he could name. It was as mysterious as the smile with which she sometimes graced him.

Cinder didn't know why she fascinated him so much. He knew she shouldn't, and his conscience reminded him of Coral. He'd promised to return to her.

Nevertheless, Cinder found himself drawn to Anya like a bee to a flower. Or more properly a moth to a flame since she was both a princess and an elf, two stations far above his meager ranking as merely human.

He sighed, turning away before Anya could notice his regard. She seemed to possess some strange ability to always know when he was staring at her. She'd caught him at it more than once, and each time, he'd had to come up with some excuse as to why he was looking her way. Thankfully, she accepted his explanations without challenge, although her wry smile indicated her disbelief in his assertions.

Cinder strummed the mandolin again. His fingers found a pattern, a playful rhythm, a song likely from his past. His eyes closed, and a smile slipped over his features. It had been a hard day of training—a hard week, really—and tomorrow morning would begin the Grand Melee.

Cinder was happy. Today, he had bested Nathaz, which meant he was now third in their class. Only Derius and Sriovey ranked higher, and perhaps he would overtake them as well; not that it mattered.

The reason for his happiness was the performance of his fellow

Firsters, all of them. Humans, dwarves and elves alike. They'd battled well today, fighting as a single unit. Even Estin and Riyne. The elves were finally learning how their remarkable skills wouldn't overcome their poor tactics. They were finally giving humans the respect they long deserved, taking heed of their advice and suggestions.

Thank Devesh.

The elven Firsters understanding of their limitations was important to all of them. The Unitary Trial allowed no falsity. The spiderkin and all manner of evil didn't care whose blood they spilled. The Dagger Mountains. Real battles. Fighting to survive. Red blood. Death imminent for the unwary or foolish.

Cinder's playing unconsciously lapsed into a melancholy pattern.

"Hotgate is playing his depressing shit again," Nathaz complained, interrupting his reverie.

Cinder opened his eyes, catching the dwarf viewing him in frustration or disgust. Nathaz only liked songs of war or derring-do. It could be tiresome, especially since there was so much more to life than just fighting. Cinder preferred songs about love, friendship, or quiet moments of introspection. "You could learn to play an instrument," he suggested to Nathaz. "Then you could play whatever you like."

Derius broke out in laughter, like Cinder's suggestion was the stupidest thing he'd ever heard. "Listening to Nathaz playing music would be like willingly eating his mother's cooking."

"More like your sister's," Nathaz replied.

"Sisters are off limits," Bones added.

"Oh, stuff your sisters," Sriovey said.

"I'm thinking his sisters have been stuffed plenty," Depth said. "Maybe that's why Bones is so sensitive about them."

Cinder laughed, and Bones viewed him in betrayal. "I thought you didn't like crude humor."

Cinder grinned at Bones, not apologetic in the slightest. "Normally not, but that was funny."

Jozep plopped down on a nearby chair, tabla in hand. "What do you want to play?"

Cinder eyed Nathaz, pitching his voice so the dwarf would hear. "Something that isn't depressing. Wouldn't want sensitive ears feeling bad."

"My ears aren't sensitive!" Nathaz complained.

Jozep drummed his fingers on the tabla. "How about "Lady the Hawke?" It's got an upbeat tempo. Plus, it's fun to play."

Cinder had never heard the song. "What's it about?"

"It's about this cursed couple in a city of surpassing beauty. The woman turns into a hawk during the day, and the man becomes a wolf at night. They can never be together."

"It's up tempo, but it's about constrained love?" Cinder asked, his voice doubtful. How could a song with those elements be fun?

"You'll like it," Jozep promised. "Trust me. It's a beautiful story. They break the curse at the end."

"Does it have lyrics?"

Jozep nodded. "I'll sing them."

Cinder shrugged. "Show me the chords."

Sriovey glanced in their direction. "Are you two finally going to stop diddling around and play something?"

Cinder shot him a rude gesture, which earned him a number of snickers.

"Something's gotten into Hotgate today," Ishmay said from where he sat at the couch. "First he laughs at a joke about sisters, and now he tells Sriovey to go frag himself."

"Fuck himself," Nathaz corrected. "I hate those made up curse words."

Cinder smiled, but the majority of his attention remained on the chord structure Jozep wanted from him. He nodded to the dwarf. "I think I got it."

Jozep set the tempo, and Cinder jumped in once he had the rhythm. His fingers found the chords, and a few seconds later, Jozep began singing in his strong tenor. Cinder fell into the music of the song. "Lady Hawk." It was beautiful and touching, just like Jozep promised.

They only played a few more songs afterward since everyone was tired and needed rest for tomorrow's tests. The Firsters soon drifted off to their rooms, and Cinder did as well. He undressed, tumbled into his bed, and was asleep in minutes.

He dreamt of a glorious city, maybe the one from "Lady Hawk" . . .

He stood upon the porch of a lovely mansion. Before him rose ornate buildings, their lintels and columns carved into fanciful figures. Enclosed courtyards and private gardens held families and couples who were gathered for meals or a stroll. Lovely homes in hues of salmon-pink, lavender, sky blue, or sunny yellow perched atop steep, verdant hills, which tumbled to the broad, blue waters of a bay. Further out to sea, rocky, green outcroppings thrust skyward like gnarled knuckles. Wide streets, paved in brick and flagstone with medians of palm trees, entered grand plazas filled with fountains spraying water. A giant stadium loomed in the distance. To the south, a park took up most of a long valley floor where several hills met, an open, spacious place, filled with trees, grassy fields, meadows, and even several small ponds. He turned toward the home to where his loving parents, brother, and sister waited.

34

On the morning of the Grand Melee, Cinder awoke refreshed and ready. He was surprised because there had been no worries or agitations to interrupt his rest. No fear of failure to keep him tossing and turning. He'd slept soundly, deep and restful, as if the morning of the tournament was one no different than any other.

It was strange, especially considering how the other Firsters had fared. They had arisen, immediately complaining of having slept fitfully. Anxiety and excitement had apparently ruined their slumber, and they rousted out of their rooms, grumbling and jittery. As a result, no one wanted to talk much at breakfast.

They had the first event of the day to occupy their minds. A race, and while it only counted for fifteen percent of the Melee's final tally, everyone wanted to do well. For the dwarves, they had a long-distance run—they rode as well as a bag of beets—while the humans and elves were to take part in an equestrian competition. Both events were to be held early in the morning with the sun barely nudged into the sky. Dew still glistened upon the fields, and the weather was crisp.

Cinder soon lost track of the dwarves when he and the other human and elven Firsters headed to the stables. They needed to prepare their mounts, and for once, Fastness didn't cause Cinder any trouble. The horse didn't play any of his usual games, and an air of gravity held over him. Hopefully it meant the white understood the day's importance.

Cinder quickly got Fastness fed, watered, and saddled, but despite his haste, by the time he got to the racecourse, it was already lined by hundreds of cheering elves. Folk from Certitude and servants at the Third Directorate. Cinder had known about the Grand Melee's popularity, but he hadn't expected so large an audience. He also noted the masters in attendance. They would be the ones to ensure a fair competition in what was reputed to be a rough and tumble race.

The riders were expected to charge their steeds through a mile-long open lawn before running into various hurdles. They'd have to make their way through an obstacle course consisting of barrels and hedges, navigate a treacherous path along the slope of a steep hill, fire arrows at set targets, and finish on a mad dash to the finish line. Cinder had ridden the route already, and during most of the race, the horses would run close to one another, bumping and shoving; every one of them pushing for position, and their riders cursing floridly.

Cinder and Fastness stood alongside the others atop a gently sloping hill where a simple chalk line demarcated the starting point. Before them stretched a long, broad swath of grass, bracketed on either side by scattered thickets of pine and cedar. In addition, along the lawn's length were strung waist-high ropes, looping from wooden pickets driven into the ground and serving to hold back the crowd.

Master Halin, the elf in charge of the overall race, paced his gray mare along the ragged line of Firsters, checking them over for a final inspection. He reined his steed to a stop, and his voice boomed, quieting the noisy crowd and causing Cinder to startle. "Welcome to the Grand Melee," he said, speaking to both the Firsters and those in attendance. He went on to describe the history of the Grand Melee, which extended to the time of Empress Swan, the founder of the Third Directorate. "This is the first event," Master Halin continued. "The equestrian competition. It is the finest challenge of horse and rider in which you will likely ever participate and the most exciting you will likely ever witness. The rules are simple. There will be no shoving. There will be no hitting one another or one another's mounts. No weapons aimed at anything or anyone other than the targets. For some of the tests, you will each have your own line to run and a task to complete. A judge will determine when you have completed that task. Only then will you be allowed back on the general racecourse. The first one who returns here after completing the circuit wins. Any questions?"

Cinder didn't have any. Everyone had been instructed in the rules during the weeks prior to the Grand Melee, and no one spoke up.

Master Halin nodded sharply. "Excellent. Then mount your horses and take your marks. You ride on the horn."

Cinder saddled up. He leaned forward and whispered to Fastness, speaking in the horse's ear. "We have to ride hard and true. Don't worry about anyone else. We run our own race, and we'll be fine." He projected confidence into his voice, hoping the stallion picked up on it.

The crowd buzzed ever more loudly, their excitement building. This was why they had come to the Third Directorate today. The Grand Melee, and the vicarious adrenaline rush of victory.

Cinder patted Fastness' withers. "Here we go, lad."

The stallion snorted, and he shook his head before settling to a tense readiness.

A few riders had to speak calming words to their spirited mounts, which neighed, whinnied, or reared. One bumped Fastness, and the white bared his teeth and shoved into the horse and rider—Estin and his high-strung stallion. The elf prince glared but didn't have a chance to do anything more as he struggled to get his mount under control.

Cinder paid them no mind. The entirety of his concentration was on the race, planning it out. A half-mile past the starting line, the long lawn of grass—the course—led into a sweeping right-hand turn. He and Fastness had an outside line, and they needed to get to the turn first to shorten it. He'd spent the past few days figuring out how to do it. Fastness was slow off the start compared to the other horses, but once he got his hooves under him, he ran like a storm. Cinder would have to trust in that speed.

There was no more time. The starting horn sounded.

Fastness bolted off the line. Cinder bent low, giving the horse his head. They thundered down the hill, the world awash in shouts, exhortations, and the pounding of hooves. Fastness got off to his typical slow start, but once he got going, he was an accelerating avalanche. The wind rushed past. Cinder squinted, his vision blurring as they tracked down the other horses. Within one hundred yards, they caught the slower mounts. Within two hundred, they had the lead. *One length.* Cinder guided Fastness in front of Estin. *Two lengths.* Cinder kept them heading to the right.

They were two horses to the outside when they reached the sweeping right hand turn. Only Riyne and Ishmay had a shorter route to run. Fastness hit the curve, digging deep, plowing into the turf, and maintaining his speed. Cinder leaned into the turn with his horse and whooped, loving his stallion's thrilling thunder of haste. They gained on Riyne and Ishmay, reeling them in.

The turn straightened, and Fastness roared past the other two horses. He had two lengths. Three. Five. Ten.

A set of thick copses on each side of the course caused it to narrow. From sunshine, they raced into shadow, a tunnel wide enough for only five horses to ride abreast. The lane narrowed further. Only two horses wide.

Fastness poured on the speed, leaving the others far in the rear.

They exploded out of the darkness and into the light. Loud cheering met their appearance. Even here, at this distant part of the course, a large crowd was gathered. They stood on a number of benches and tiered platforms surrounding the first set of obstacles, and their cheering continued as other horses rushed into view.

Cinder didn't bother glancing back to see how far behind the others were. He and Fastness had their own race to run. He reined in the stallion, slowing him to an eventual walk. The white needed a blow anyway.

"Easy, lad," Cinder said, patting Fastness' withers. "We have a lot more racing to do."

Fastness breathed deep, his flanks expanding and contracting.

They approached the first obstacles. It was a broad, flat field containing a set of barrels and a series of low-lying hedges. They needed to complete three circuits of the course, and it wouldn't be easy. Hard swings around the barrels—tight right- and left-hand turns—followed by jumping the series of hedges.

Cinder didn't like their chances here. Everything about it preyed on his weakness as a rider. He could stay in the saddle easily enough during a straight run with gentle turns, but navigating the barrels and hedges required more; a merging of horse and rider. Cinder would need to shift his balance into, during, and after the turns and jumps in perfect harmony with his mount's motions. But he lacked the skill to do so at speed. He'd have to go more carefully than the other riders, who would make up a lot of lost ground here.

Cinder got the white to the starting point, another white chalk line where a white-haired elf waited for them. He was a trainer who worked with Master Halin and today, he served as the judge for this portion of the contest.

Cinder drew Fastness to a halt. Everyone had to come to a complete stop at the starting line, pause for a beat of three seconds, and only then would the old elf let them onto the course.

The elf's mouth silently moved, and he appeared to be counting. He shouted. "Go!"

Cinder heeled Fastness into motion. They swiftly reached the first barrel, and he managed to stay in the saddle during the tight left-hand turn. Cinder heeled Fastness again, and they sprinted toward the next barrel. A right-hand turn this time. Cinder knew he wasn't shifting his balance quickly enough. His form was poor, and their slow speed reflected his lack of skill.

Riyne and his filly passed them at the third barrel. Two more horses caught Fastness by the fifth barrel. In addition, there was plenty of jostling and shoving as they completed the circuits, and by the time they exited the field, they had fallen to ninth place.

Another quarter-mile sprint regained them two of those lost positions, but now it was time to make their way down a rugged, snaking trail. It had to be taken at a careful walk, and in some places, while dismounted. There was no opportunity to make up ground here.

They finally reached the base of the rocky hill—still in seventh—and Cinder guided Fastness to the next obstacle portion of the race. It was a line of targets, and each rider had their own individual section. The objective was simple. Settle the horse on the ground and from behind the bulk of the mount, use a horsebow to land five arrows in a round target set seventy yards distant. Once more a large crowd was present to watch.

Fastness had always fought Cinder over this aspect of his training. He somehow sensed that when he was on his belly, he was being used as a living shield. It always took Cinder many minutes of shouted persuasion and shoves to get the stubborn stallion to do as required. He expected no different this time.

Cinder dismounted as soon as they reached their portion of the course and mentally prepared himself for the typical fight with the stallion. Fastness, though, surprised him. Without any guidance, the white immediately dropped to his belly. He evidently *did* understand the importance of today's race.

"Good, lad," Cinder said, patting his stallion.

He withdrew his cased bow from where it was tied off on the saddle and quickly had it strung. Archery had once been the bane of his existence, but by now, Cinder had plenty of confidence in his skill with the bow. The world without faded, and his gaze tightened to nothing more than the target in the distance. He knelt behind Fastness, breathing out any tension and relaxed. He nocked his first arrow, aimed, and fired. *Two inches off bullseye.* Four more arrows followed, a tight cluster near dead-center.

They were done, and Cinder quickly put away the bow and bag of arrows, and the elf in charge ushered them back onto the course.

Cinder was heartened when he realized they'd made up another position and were now in sixth place. Another half-mile straight-line run up and down a set of low-lying hills let them pick off another horse and rider.

They reached the final obstacle, a potentially easy sweep along a straight line of four targets, a set of human-shaped dummies nailed to bales of hay. The rider could choose to take this portion as fast as he wished. The only requirement was he had to land an arrow in each target.

Cinder reined Fastness to a walk and reached for his *lorethasra*. It seemed to heighten his concentration even when he didn't conduct it. The silvery-pool glistened beyond his reach, shielded by the usual blue-green lightning. Cinder kept his *lorethasra* in his mind but didn't reach for it as he uncased his bow and got an arrow nocked.

If his senses—his vision, hearing, and smell—became more acute, he couldn't tell, but at least his heart, which had been pounding with adrenaline, slowed. His eyes went to the target, his focus compressing to a pinpoint. Cinder heeled the stallion into motion, a quicker walk, maintaining his balance, guiding his horse with his knees. He loosed his first arrow, and the bolt slammed into the target. *Good, but we need to go faster.* Cinder clicked his tongue, and the stallion moved into a trot. He aimed another arrow, and it hit home, straight to the target's chest. Another click of his tongue, and Fastness was cantering. Cinder's concentration and balance never faltered. His next arrow was a headshot. Another click, and Fastness was galloping. The final arrow was another headshot.

Cinder recased his bow, and he and Fastness were soon thundering down the final stretch of the race. It started off as a rambling half-mile run up and down a set of low hills followed by an acute left-hand turn and then a quarter mile dash to the finish line.

Ishmay and his mare were directly ahead. Fastness reached them and surged past. They opened up a ten-yard gap, but at the left-hand turn, they had to slow to little more than a walk. Ishmay's mare caught them there and out-accelerated Fastness, taking the lead.

Once more, however, the big stallion proved up to the task, and he tracked her down. They thundered past Ishmay and his mare. Dozens of yards ahead were the race leaders—Riyne, Cariath, and Estin—running in a bunch. Only a quarter mile to the finish line. Cinder gave Fastness his head. He didn't have to tell the stallion what to do.

Fastness raced after the final three. Flecks of foam collected at his mouth and whipped away in the wind of his passage. The stallion's hooves pounded, drowning out the cheers of the crowd. His lungs worked like bellows, as the great horse gave everything he had. Cinder shouted, urging the white on. They could catch the others. They gained on them with every stride. Fastness chewed up the ground, inexorable as the tide.

They caught Estin and his Yavana stallion first. Fastness edged alongside the other horse's hindquarters, surged to his withers, past his head. *Only two more to go.* Cinder shouted more encouragement.

He cursed an instant later when Estin's steed bared his teeth and lunged at Fastness. Cinder was about to jerk them out of the way, but his horse was bigger, thicker, and unintimidated by the other mount. Fastness lowered his shoulder and plowed Estin's stallion aside.

However, the action slowed them enough to make it impossible to catch Riyne and Cariath, who crossed the finish line in first and second. Cinder and Fastness finished third, and while they might have done even better if not for Estin's high-strung mount, Cinder didn't allow disappointment to take away his overflowing pride.

Fastness had done everything he could have asked. The great horse had given it his all, and Cinder patted the stallion in affection. He leaned forward, speaking to the white. "You were magnificent, lad."

The stallion nickered acknowledgement.

After the race's conclusion, there came the ceremony honoring the victor. It took place at the starting line of the race, the grassy knoll. Riyne and his filly were surrounded by hundreds of well-wishers, all of them cheering and clapping. The applause reached a crescendo when Master Halin presented a blanket of roses and a gold-cloth bag to Riyne, who grinned proudly.

Cinder watched it with a sour lump in his stomach. *Fragging Riyne.* He hated losing to the elf, and rather than witness any more of Riyne's triumph, he led Fastness back to the stables.

"Let's get out of here," Cinder said to the stallion. "I've got some fresh apples when we get back to the stable."

The stallion's ears perked.

Cinder stood in Fastness' stall, brushing the stallion's coat and ridding it of dirt and burrs. The rest of the barn was also a beehive of activity. Everyone was back from the equestrian competition, caring for their horses as well, but in the midst of all the work, the elves called congratulations to one another, clearly jubilant. They laughed, enjoying the fact that they had won two of the race's top three positions.

Cinder watched them for a moment and shook his head in disgust. Why did the elves have to rub in their victory?

"We'll do better next year," Cinder promised Fastness. He gifted the horse an apple, and the stallion snapped it down in a single bite.

Fastness pushed his muzzle into Cinder's pockets, trying to find more treats. Discovering none, the horse gave Cinder a sad look of betrayal.

Cinder laughed. "You liar. I know you're not upset."

The stallion neighed his laughter at being caught.

Minutes later, Cinder finished brushing down Fastness and got the stallion's water and feed. "I'll check on you tonight," he promised the horse. "Get some rest. You were wonderful."

Fastness nickered in reply, head bent as he lipped his feed.

Cinder gave the stallion a final pat on the withers and left the stall. From the tack room, he picked up his bow and quiver of arrows, which he'd dropped off before the race.

He rejoined the other Firsters, and like they always did, they separated into two distinct racial groups—humans and elves—while heading for the archery field. It was where the next competition would take place, twenty percent of the final tally.

They marched toward the archery range, diverting around knots of onlookers, and the elven jubilation slowly settled. Conversations were soon measured in single word responses or mere grunts. Everyone was intent on the challenge to come.

Cinder as well. He trailed the others, reflecting on the upcoming event. *Archery.* He'd advanced far with the bow, and he had high hopes for how he would perform. He paused momentarily when they reached the range.

A ring of attendees numbering in the hundreds surrounded the field. A line of children sat toward the front, and a long set of wooden bleachers rose behind those standing. It creaked beneath the weight of even more spectators and every seat was taken. A celebratory atmosphere filled the audience, everyone smiling, laughing, or shouting to one another. The smell of candied corn and searing meat wafted. A number of vendors had brought in food carts and grills.

Wark muttered under his breath, scowling furiously while trying not to glance around. "I guess the elves want to have a party while they humiliate us."

Cinder sympathized with Wark's complaint. Some of it was true, but much of it also came from a place of fear, which was a problem. Wark was a good archer but fear would destroy his abilities. He needed to believe in himself.

Cinder stepped close to Wark, speaking quietly so no one else could hear. "Trust your training. You have all you need right here and here." He touched Wark's chest and head. "Relax. Take a breath. Don't think about the elves or anyone else." Cinder slapped Wark's shoulder in encouragement. "Come on. You'll be alright."

The words must have worked because Wark lifted his head, a newfound fire in his eyes. He nodded to Cinder in appreciation.

"Check out the dwarves," Depth said from several feet away.

He pointed to where the dwarves were throwing axes at a target. It was their portion of the ranged competition. Later on, the dwarves would have an unarmed challenge, an event no one else bothered to enter. After all, who could defeat a dwarf at wrestling? Both of those separate competitions would count for ten percent of the dwarves' final score.

Master Serwil stood in front of the Firsters and bellowed for silence. Some strange use of his *lorethasra* allowed his words to carry to all corners of the range, and the crowd quickly quieted. Master Serwil then went over the rules. "Each archer will shoot a dozen arrows." He pointed to a number of circular targets with concentric rings of differing colors. "The closer to bullseye the arrow strikes, the higher the points the archer earns, and the eight archers with the highest point total move on to the next round. Then it becomes a one-on-one competition. A dozen arrows in three volleys, four per volley. The archer having the highest point total from round one goes against the lowest. Second versus seventh, and so on. Then comes the semifinal round and the same format, and then the championship round. In addition, those who lost will continue on against one another to determine final ranking. Any questions?" Master Serwil searched out the faces of the Firsters. None were apparent. "You have your bows and arrows. Begin."

"Good luck," Cinder said to Wark.

"Good luck to you, too," Wark replied.

"Good luck to all of us," Ishmay grumbled. The Gandharvan struggled with archery, and it was clear he wasn't looking forward to this.

Cinder gave Ishmay the same advice he'd earlier given Wark, and the Gandharvan grimaced, but at least he dipped his head in acknowledgement. Cinder watched him take his place and silently hoped Ishmay would relax. He noticed the Gandharvan close his eyes and take several deep breaths. *Good.* His concern for Ishmay abated because now it was time to get ready himself.

Cinder shook out his arms, wanting them relaxed and limber. He took several deep inhalations, blowing out hard. Only then did he pull his bow out of its protective leather case. He quickly got it strung, leaned it against a hip and shook out his arms again. More deep breaths removed any lingering tension.

He was ready.

Cinder focused on the target, which was set one hundred yards away. He reminded himself to relax. He nocked an arrow. *Relax.* Sighted along it. *Relax.* Exhaled, slow and steady. *Relax.* The target sharpened, the bullseye centering in his vision.

He let loose the arrow.

Two inches off the bullseye.

Cinder didn't let the success touch him. He instantly forgot about it. The next shot was all that mattered.

Over a period of minutes, Cinder loosed eleven more arrows and managed a tight grouping. It was good enough for third place in the first round.

For round two, he was paired against Loriam Stilwen, a dark-haired elf who was generally quiet and kept to the background. Cinder might have shared a dozen words with him during his entire time at the Third Directorate.

The match was initially close. Eight arrows in, and they were tied. But the pressure must have gotten to Loriam because his next two arrows barely hit the target while Cinder's continued to slam close to center. As a result, the final result was anticlimactic.

Cinder's next match was in the semifinals. It was against Mohal. Their contest was also close, but this one came down to the final arrow where Cinder's was a half-inch closer to the bullseye than Mohal.

Cinder had to stuff down his rising excitement, which threatened to bubble over like water coming to a boil. When he'd first reached the Third Directorate, he'd been terrible at archery, and here he was making it to the finals in the Grand Melee. He had privately hoped and prayed for such an achievement, but he hadn't expected it to actually happen.

It also wasn't the end of things, though, and he did his best to ignore his sense of accomplishment. He had one more match to win. It was against Riyne, and the crowd muttered a muted response when Cinder's name was announced for the finale. It wasn't a surprise for a human to be in the archery finals. Every few years it happened, but it was clear the elves didn't like it.

Cinder didn't let the crowd's antipathy knock him off his relaxed core, and he also didn't bother saying anything to Riyne when they stepped up to the final pair of targets. No words were needed. He and Riyne had reached a detente, but they'd never be friends. It was fine by Cinder. He didn't need to be friends with everyone. Respect was enough, and he'd earned that.

Master Serwil held them from immediately starting their match. He addressed the crowd, bringing forth the two finalists, Cinder and Riyne. He had them stand in front of the audience and went over their history in greater detail. He first spoke of Riyne, telling of his warrior heritage. The audience cheered wildly, and Riyne basked in their adulation.

Next, Master Serwil spoke of Cinder. "Facing him is Cinder Shade. He's a human, and I know most of you are hoping to see Riyne win." The crowd muttered agreement at this, but Master Serwil continued on. "Cinder has no proud family lineage. He's from the Dagger Mountains and no one here would recognize the village he comes from. But he's a finalist, and that merits respect. So show him some."

The spectators cheered with a bit more enthusiasm, but it still sounded half-hearted. Cinder mentally shrugged. Their response was irrelevant. He had a final match to win.

Thankfully, Master Serwil didn't have much more to say. He went over the instructions for the finale one last time, and Cinder and Riyne got to it.

Cinder went first. He focused on the distant target, now set at one hundred and fifty yards. The bullseye swam in his vision, and he blinked, rubbing at his eyes. His eyesight cleared, and again he viewed the target. This time, the bullseye remained clear. He inhaled slowly, nocking an arrow. *Exhale. Relax.* The bullseye came sharper, and he let the arrow fly.

It slammed dead center into the target. Cinder shoved down any feelings of pleasure. He'd only be happy after the contest was over, and he'd won.

Riyne went next and managed a bullseye of his own.

Tied so far.

Seven arrows later, they remained tied. They were down to the final volley. Cinder's next shot was dragged to the left by an errant gust, which gave Riyne an opening. The elf took advantage of it. His shot landed right next to the bullseye.

Cinder didn't allow frustration to distract him. He could still pull this out. His next arrow flew straight and true, directly in the bullseye. Riyne matched him. Cinder's next shot was barely outside the bullseye. Riyne's wasn't as close, a quarter inch further out. Cinder's last arrow was another bullseye, and Riyne's next shot slammed home directly next to his second shot.

Cinder's shoulders slumped with disappointment. Riyne had won. He didn't need the final tally to tell him so.

Neither did Riyne. The elf whooped with joy. He hadn't matched Cinder's score on the final three arrows, but he hadn't needed to. Cinder's errant initial shot in the final volley proved the difference. Riyne had eked out a victory, and the crowd roared approval when the final tally was announced.

Cinder straightened his shoulders. He was a man, not a spoiled child. The match was over, and there was nothing to do about it now. He'd accept the loss with as much grace as possible, no matter how much it rankled. He offered Riyne his congratulations. "Good match. Well done on the win."

Riyne offered a triumphant, mocking grin directly in Cinder's face. "It was a good match, and you did well. But I wouldn't get used to second place. Edged weapons are tomorrow, and you won't catch any of us off guard this time. We'll kick your ass."

Cinder's jaw clenched in anger. *Jackhole.* He shouldn't have expected any better from Riyne, but a part of him had hoped otherwise. "You'll try, and you'll fail. Just like last time."

Riyne leaned in toward him, also not releasing the grip. "Keep believing that. It'll make beating your worthless hide all the sweeter."

"I already beat you once, remember? Or maybe you don't. I knocked you unconscious."

Riyne's smile soured, and the handshake tightened, but Cinder didn't break the grip. He had faced down Sriovey. He could face down any elf.

A late lunch and a short break period followed the archery competition, and then it was time for the day's final tests, which were to be held in Firemirror Hall. Everyone gathered there for their oral examinations in Tactics and Strategy as well as History—a combined fifteen percent toward their final score. Every student was tested separately in a small classroom, one after the other in a face-to-face conversation with Masters Nuhlin and Capshin. The two instructors brought up scenarios from historic battles and asked for critiques on what the commander could have done to improve the outcome.

Cinder came in third to Rorian and Joria, and he was thrilled when the scores were announced. Perhaps he could have answered Master Nuhlin's question with greater clarity and improved on his score, but overall, he was doing well in the Melee, probably the top three or four.

He hoped so, although there was no way to know for sure.

The day was done, and it had been a long one, and after the oral exams, a noisy supper ensued followed by a shared hour of relaxation in the common room. Everyone played a few games of euchre or sang a couple of songs, but the Firsters were tired, and they soon settled in for bed.

The next morning, Cinder awoke refreshed and alert. Today would be the weapons competition, which counted as a full fifty percent of their final tally, and he had high hopes for his performance. Every Firster would participate in this one, but given their uneven numbers—nineteen—the very first round would only feature three bouts, the nineteenth ranked Firster versus the fourteenth, eighteenth against fifteenth, and seventeenth facing sixteenth.

Next, would come round two, which would consist of the remaining sixteen participants. The top-ranked Firster would face the lowest ranked. The second ranked would face the next lowest, and so on. For round three, the final eight students would face off as before, and the same in the final four. The matches would continue until everyone achieved a final rank and a champion was crowned.

Cinder could now defeat most of the dwarves on most days, but the wildcard remained his performance against the elves. He would have been far more confident versus them, except for how poorly he'd done against Anya. She had defeated him with laughable ease, and his lack of success against her left him wondering if his success against Riyne and Estin had been merely a fluke.

He got dressed and wandered into the common room, but since no one else was yet out of bed, he crept out of Krathe House and headed over to the cafeteria. There, he gathered a light breakfast of fruits, upma, and eggs and settled into a quiet corner.

Shortly after his arrival, Anya wandered into the cafeteria. She gave him a brief gesture of acknowledgement, her expression cool, before collecting her own breakfast. He started when she placed her plate of food at his table and seated herself opposite him. He hadn't expected her to join him.

"You appear unsettled," she noted.

Cinder returned his attention to his food, desultorily moving his upma about. She was right. He was unsettled. He'd slept well, but now that he was awake, his worries ratcheted up his spine like icicles. "Is it so easy to tell?"

Anya chuckled, low and throaty. "No. I doubt anyone else notices, but in our short time together, I've learned to read your moods and intent."

Cinder paused in the motion of lifting a spoonful of upma to his mouth. She'd studied him during their sparring, just as he'd studied her? It shouldn't have surprised him, and yet it did. He set down his spoon. "What have you learned?"

"You're driven, but you don't know why."

"I do know why. I want to protect those who deserve it and can't protect themselves."

Anya's lips pursed. "A worthy goal, but I think there is more to it than that. You want to master all elements of combat. I know the hours you spend in the Cauldron and the Foe. Every week, you work to shore up your weaknesses. I doubt anyone else works so hard."

No one else did. Cinder knew it, and there was no reason to tell her otherwise. "I want to win."

"I thought you wanted to protect others."

Cinder found himself growing irritated. "Or maybe it's both. I want to protect others *and* win. Is that such a bad thing?"

Anya laughed, a ringing of bells. "Not at all, but you need to be honest with yourself. You need to understand the reasons for your hard work. There *can* be more than one, and when one rationale becomes uninspirational, lean on the others. Otherwise you risk faltering in your steadfastness."

Cinder considered her advice, recognizing the wisdom in it. He had multiple reasons for wanting to improve, and he needed them all if he wanted to keep advancing.

Anya finished her breakfast and rose to her feet. Before departing, she squeezed one of his shoulders in support. "Good luck today. You didn't win against Riyne and Estin due to luck alone. You have skill. Trust in it."

Several hours later, Cinder stood alongside the other Firsters on a special pavilion built just for them at the Cauldron. Master Absin was going over the instructions for the finale of the Grand Melee. It was identical to the rules Cinder had worked under during the Maker's Tournament and his duels against Estin and Riyne. *Four points to win and several ways to gain them.*

The morning sun beamed steady waves of light and warmth, drying the dew-draped fields of the Directorate. The air held still. No breeze blew, but none was needed. The weather this morning was mild and dry with no hint of mugginess. A crowd, one even larger than yesterday's, clustered around the sparring rings of the Cauldron. They held as still and unmoving as the air, rapt in their attention with nothing more than the shuffling of feet and various whispered conversations.

Cinder caught sight of his various masters and other instructors, members of the administration, and visiting dignitaries, such as Anya, standing on a set of bleachers. The position offered them a full view of the central sparring ring upon which most of the matches would take place.

The Firsters shifted about in pent up energy as Master Absin continued with his explanation. His words were likely for the crowd's benefit, and when he finally finished, he stepped aside for General Arwan. There was a collective groan from the Firsters as the commandant chose to give a speech.

Cinder listened with half an ear as General Arwan once more reviewed what was to occur. Instead, he glanced along the line, where he stood tenth amongst the nineteen irritated Firsters. The top seven positions were held by the elves. Next came Sriovey and Derius followed by Cinder, Nathaz, Jozep, and Dorcer. The other humans held the bottom six slots. It would be Bones against Rorian, Ishmay versus Joria, and Depth versus Wark for the first round.

Cinder glanced their way. Other than Bones, the rest of them appeared tight and nervous. He silently wished them the best. He next glanced toward his own first opponent, Loriam, the elf he'd defeated in yesterday's archery competition and considered him. Maybe unrelenting pressure would crack him here like it had there.

He had little opportunity for further speculation, though, because the commandant finished his speech, ending on a flourish. "And with Holy Devesh's benediction, let us begin!"

Finally. It was time to start the tournament.

"Bones and Rorian." Master Absin called forth the first participants and took a moment to address the crowd, giving a brief biography of both warriors. The match, however, proved anticlimactic. As Cinder had expected, Bones crushed Rorian, defeating him within a few minutes.

Cinder still marveled at the skills Bones possessed. His timing, speed, power, and ever improving technique. If he could only conduct his *lorethasra*, no elf or dwarf would be able to stand against him.

The next two matches followed, but Cinder paid them scant attention. He had his own fight to worry about. He barely noted the crowd—their cheers and groans; the clouds occasionally eclipsing the sun; the smells of grilled chicken on skewers, marinated meat, and fried apples from food vendors. None of it made any impact, and he only distantly noted that Ishmay and Depth had joined Bones in round two.

During it all Cinder kept himself centered, focused on what he wanted to accomplish, refusing to allow any struggling doubts to make themselves known.

He would win. Nothing less would do.

Cinder visualized his match against Loriam, and in every outcome, he was the victor. He made certain of it. It was the same as what he'd done in the Maker's Tournament. It didn't matter that today's event was far less important. Winning required a refusal to believe in the possibility of losing.

His name was eventually called, and Cinder rose to his feet and descended to the indicated sparring ring where he took his mark.

He faced Loriam, who stood on the opposite side of the ring. Master Absin introduced them, and Cinder raised his arm in acknowledgment when his name was called, eyes locked on his opponent. The crowd—ten deep now on raised platforms—might have applauded, but Cinder didn't know. His gaze never left Loriam, and he analyzed his opponent for intents and emotions.

The elf appeared calm, but several beads of sweat trickled down his temple. *Strange.* The day was mild, and even with the heavy padding and leather helmets they wore, it shouldn't be hot enough to cause perspiration. Cinder also noticed a slight quaver in the elf's sword hand. It was brief, gone in an instant, but it exposed a truth: Loriam was nervous.

Cinder immediately thought of how to make use of his opponent's weakness, recalling what he knew of the elf's fighting style. From the few times he'd seen him spar, he knew Loriam preferred to counter. Fast even for an elf, he leaned on his blistering speed to exploit any openings.

An initial plan quickly took shape, and Cinder nodded to himself. He would rush Loriam but pull up at the last instant. He wouldn't fully commit. Loriam would either retreat or counter. In either case, Cinder would press the action.

"Be ready," Master Absin said.

Cinder's breathing came smooth and easy. He relaxed, easing into the moment.

"Fight!"

Cinder dashed forward. As expected, Loriam retreated to the side. Cinder hid a frown when he noticed the elf's left foot crossed in front of his right. *Poor form, unless it was a ruse.* Loriam's speed would do him no good if he tripped over himself. Cinder lunged forward, a feint meant to test Loriam. Again, the elf's feet crossed.

Cinder crossed the distance, angling in from Loriam's left. Another shift to the elf's left, and Loriam couldn't maintain the turn. His crossed feet slowed him up, just enough. Cinder hammered home a blow to Loriam's thigh. The elf crumpled, crying out and holding his leg. It probably felt like his leg had been amputated.

"Two points to Cinder," Master Absin declared.

Cinder resumed his place, and Loriam eventually rose, a rictus of discomfort marring his elven features. The pain delivered by the shoke was abating, but Cinder's strike had been heavy. It would leave a bruise despite the thick padding.

Moments later, the call came again. "Fight!"

Cinder again shot toward Loriam. The elf retreated again, still limping heavily. This time he went straight back. Cinder kept the pressure, feinting a lunge. Loriam's feet pressed against the sparring ring's perimeter.

Cinder offered a lazy thrust. Loriam bit, seeking to counter. Cinder was already sliding to the side. He brought his weapon down on

Loriam's right forearm.

The elf's shoke fell from his hand, and he crumpled once more. This time he clutched his right arm.

"Two points and victory to Cinder!"

Cinder wanted to celebrate the easy win but doing so while Loriam still writhed in pain seemed heartless. He'd struck the elf twice, and both times pretty solid. He squatted next to Loriam. "Is the pain letting off?" he asked in concern.

Loriam glanced at him, suspicion evident on his face. "It's better," he said after a moment, shaking out his fingers. The distrust slowly faded from Loriam's visage, and Cinder offered him a helping hand. They rose together.

"How are you so good?" Loriam asked.

Cinder grinned. "Who says I'm good? I'm only human."

Loriam chuckled, appearing thoughtful. "Maybe you're human, but you're not *only* anything."

Estin nudged Riyne, who might soon have to face Cinder. Another win for both of them, and it would happen. The human had just laid a beatdown on Loriam. He wouldn't be an easy one to defeat.

The knowledge rankled, a worm of outrage born from the seeds of hatred. Estin despised Cinder Shade. The human. Unlike the rest of his debased species, he dared believe himself the equal of an elf, worthy enough to argue against his betters, to speak with a princess of the Blessed Race, and not just speak, but dance with one. His sister, no less.

Estin's teeth ground. And when brought to justice, what did the *ghrina* bastard do? He lucked into victory during a duel and now strode around like a king. Even now he did so, magnanimously lifting Loriam to his feet and waving to the crowd like a conquering hero.

Fucking prick.

"We can't let him win," Estin snarled to Riyne.

"He won't," Riyne promised.

"That's not good enough," Estin said, eyes still locked on Cinder, hatred boiling. "He humbled us. I think we should return the favor."

Riyne faced him, an intense expression on his features. "What do you want me to do?"

"Win or lose, I don't care, but bring him pain. Hurt him bad, and if he's stupid enough to face me in the finale, I'll cripple him."

Riyne was shaking his head, and Estin wanted to slap his friend. It was a good plan, and he wanted to see it done. They'd humiliate Cinder, set an example to all the other humans. The dwarves, too. Remind everyone of how low they stood in comparison to the Blessed Race. It was a fact they seemed to have forgotten.

Well, Estin would teach them, and teach them good. He didn't care if it required Cinder's corpse to impress the lesson. He didn't care how well humans did in small unit commands. So what? It didn't make them worthy of respect. Their role was to serve the Blessed Race in whatever fashion best suited their abilities.

"You can't cripple him," Riyne said. "You'll be disqualified. You'll not only lose the match, but any points you earn from the weapons competition. You'll fall out of the top three and never have a chance at the rangers."

Estin grimaced, recognizing the wisdom of Riyne's advice. "We can still hurt him without crippling him. Listen."

Riyne ignored the crowd gathered on the tiered platforms, the administrators on their raised dais, and even his brother, Lisandre, who had loomed over his life like a veritable titan.

None of them were of any import. Only one person held Riyne's attention. The man who faced him from across the sparring circle. *Cinder Shade.*

Riyne didn't hate him in the way Estin did, and he still wasn't entirely sure of his prince's plan. It struck him as somewhat honorless, cowardly, in fact. Then again, he trusted Estin's judgment. Estin was a member of the royal family, and who else would best understand the politics of this situation?

A cool breeze feathered Riyne's hair then, and bright sunshine continued to stream amidst puffy clouds. The aroma of grilled meat floated on the wind, and the day remained warm but pleasant.

It could have been a sauna for all the heed Riyne paid to it. He remained focused, standing at his place in the sparring circle, prepared and expecting to win his next bout. This was the first semi-final match, and he would do his utmost to—

He reined in his drifting considerations when he realized Master Absin had introduced him to the cheering crowd. Riyne waved to them, but he never took his eyes off of Cinder, who stared right back.

Master Absin briefly reviewed the rules of engagement. Nothing new.

Riyne adjusted his helmet and gambeson, making sure he had free range of movement. He gripped his shoke more tightly. He wouldn't lose this time. He'd crush his enemy, hurt him if possible. He studied Cinder, looking for weakness and expecting none. The human might be a barbarian, but he was tough and he wasn't a coward. He'd fight hard. Riyne bounced on his toes, feigning an explosion forward. He planned on waiting on Cinder, counteracting and crushing the human.

Riyne would then do as his prince had asked.

He breathed deeper then, reaching for his *lorethasra*, sourcing it. He'd spent last night and all day clarifying it, and his work had paid off. The locus of his power twinkled like a pond set in a beautiful glade and reflecting a perfectly blue, cloudless sky. Riyne drew upon it, channeling it as *prana* in his *nadis*.

The world grew clearer—sights, sounds, and smells—and his thoughts sharper. His muscles seemed to swell with strength and speed. He was prepared.

Master Absin shouted, "Fight!"

Riyne smiled privately when Cinder darted to the center of the ring. *Perfect. Let him come.* Riyne gestured Cinder onward. *Come on. Pain is waiting.* He held his shoke angled to the side.

Cinder pressed close. Riyne slapped aside a slow thrust, countered with one of his own. Cinder blocked, and they separated.

Again, Cinder was the one to initiate contact. Riyne drifted to the side, wanting the sun at his back. The bright light would blind Cinder. The human didn't follow. Instead, he paced back a few steps, shoke held in a relaxed grip. A ten-foot gap opened between them. Cinder rolled his shoulders, and Riyne saw his moment.

The human had misjudged. He likely didn't think Riyne could cover the space between them before he got his weapon back to the ready. *He was wrong.*

Riyne powered forward, moving with the speed of an elf, the speed to overwhelm. He arrowed his shoke, aiming to take the human in the chest.

Cinder shifted off the line of attack. Riyne's eyes widened in shock. *How did he know?* He pulled up, switching to parry an overhand chop. Cinder's shoke slid down his own. Riyne tried to disengage. *Too late.* Cinder's shoke sliced across his hand. Riyne's weapon fell from his bruised knuckles. A sharp blow followed to his armpit, dropping him to his knees.

The pain. It felt like he'd been stabbed through the heart. The world disappeared. All Riyne knew was agony. He clutched his chest, clenching his teeth, holding back a scream.

Seconds later, a short span of time that felt endless, the pain receded, and he could breathe again. Riyne took a shuddering inhalation. Awareness slowly returned.

Cinder. The human had taken two points off him. Worse, his strong hand was injured, maybe broken.

Riyne staggered to his feet, disregarding the ache in his chest where Cinder's shoke had struck and likely left a bruise. He bent to recover his own weapon, pushing past the discomfort in his hand.

"Can you continue?" Master Absin asked him in concern.

"I can go. Just give me a few minutes."

"You have two."

Riyne grimaced. *Fuck! How is this happening?* He wouldn't lose again.

He shuffled back to his starting position, finding Estin waiting for him. No one else stood close. "How are you doing?" the prince asked.

"My chest hurts, and I can barely hold my shoke."

He found Estin viewing him in worry. "Can you beat him?"

"I can beat him," Riyne avowed, although privately, doubts assailed him. He wasn't so sure anymore. Twice now the human had surprised him. *How is he doing this?*

"Your chest?" Estin asked.

Riyne took a deep breath, grimacing at a sharp twinge. "It's fine."

"And your hand?" Estin must have noticed the swelling.

Anger at Estin flared. "I can do this," Riyne snapped. "I don't need you doubting me."

Estin held up his hands in a mollifying fashion. "If you can win, then win," he said. "If you can't, then consider other options. Hurt him. You have the points in the tournament to lose."

Riyne stared at his prince. It was a hard path Estin asked of him, the craven's path, and he didn't know if he could do it.

"Do you want a human to win the Grand Melee?" Estin hissed.

Riyne shook his head.

"Then take him out. Hurt him. Teach him and all like him the error of their ways."

The force of his prince's words scattered some of Riyne's uncertainty, but he remained hesitant. In the end, he gave a half-hearted nod. He would do as Estin asked even as a small voice told him he shouldn't.

Master Absin warned them to be ready. Riyne gripped his shoke as tightly as he could, ignoring as best he could the pain and swelling. He considered what to do, and a plan swiftly formed. He breathed out the last of his reservations.

"Fight!"

Riyne took the center of the sparring ring, waiting on Cinder. He sourced his *lorethasra*, and from it, he drew a thick thread of Earth, his strongest Element. He connected it to the corresponding line of *aether*. What he was about to do was illegal, but what other choice did he have?

Cinder approached cautiously. Riyne initiated contact, sending a thrust. Cinder parried. Riyne unleashed his weave. The earth beneath Cinder's feet shifted, throwing him off-balance.

Cinder's eyes automatically went to the ground.

In that instant of distraction, Riyne attacked. Cinder had no chance to recover. Riyne's blow hammered into the human's thigh. Cinder screamed, falling to the ground.

Riyne didn't let up. He followed Cinder to the ground, landing heavy elbows to the human's face. A crunch and spurt of blood announced a broken nose. Two more blows, and he was hurled off of Cinder, flung through the air.

Riyne landed heavily. He sat up, discovering Master Absin standing protectively over Cinder and glaring in his direction.

General Arwan, Lisandre, and Anya had entered the ring as well. All of them wore disapproving glares.

"You are disqualified," General Arwan said, his tone unforgiving. "Return to your room at Krathe House."

Riyne swallowed heavily, recognizing he'd made an enormous mistake.

Not again. Cinder couldn't believe what had just happened minutes before. He waited alone in the hospital, breathing in the antiseptic aromas, seated on a cot, the silence his only companion. Everyone else was at the Grand Melee. *He* should be at the Grand Melee preparing for the finale.

Instead, here he was with his face aching and his nose broken. The pain, however, was nothing compared to the humiliation. He'd taken another beating from Riyne Coushinre.

He slapped the hospital cot in anger and frustration.

He'd promised himself this would never happen again, and yet it had. And the answer why was simple: *lorethasra.* Riyne had formed a weave of Earth, one to shake the ground and momentarily distract Cinder.

It had worked, and Riyne had managed to land a blow to Cinder's leg and follow up with unnecessary blows to the face.

It was dishonorable and Riyne had been disqualified, his points from the weapons competition stripped. He'd finish far down the rankings, but it was of little consolation to Cinder.

Here he was again, in the hospital, waiting for a physician to heal him of his injuries. As a warrior, he understood the risks inherent with his profession. This likely wouldn't be the last time he would seek the services of a physician, but he vowed this would be the last time it was because of an elf who saw him as an easy mark.

As for Riyne and Estin—and Cinder knew the prince had put the noble up to the shameful deed—he would do nothing to them for now. But he would watch them, and he would make sure neither of them had a chance to brutalize anyone else ever again.

Following Riyne's disqualification, any doubt of Estin's overall victory in the weapons tournament was put to rest. He easily won his semifinal match against Cariath Gelindum. In addition, given Cinder's inability to continue on to the finals, Estin was acclaimed the champion.

He basked in the glory of his triumph, grinning broadly. He received hearty handshakes and smiles from the administration; companionable hugs and shouts of congratulations from his fellow Firsters; and admiring glances from many comely women in attendance. Estin swelled with pride, accepting the praise as his just desserts.

Nevertheless, it didn't surprise him when he noticed Anya headed toward him, a bland expression on her face rather than a congratulatory smile.

She marched his way—and marched was the correct descriptor. His sister was martial in all her mannerisms. He loved her, respected her abilities as a warrior, but privately he sneered at the choices she had made for her life. A princess of the sithe living the life of a ranger? Ridiculous. No matter her unmatched skill, there were much better uses for her talents.

Their older sister, Enma, for instance, was a far better example of elven womanhood. Beautiful, smart, and understanding of propriety.

"Congratulations," Anya said, her features indecipherable. "You did well. The final tallies for the Grand Melee have been made. You came in third. Mother will be proud."

Estin's shoulders drew back, smiling as he imagined mother's reaction. She *would* be proud. So would father. All of Revelant would learn of his accomplishment. Maybe then Anya would finally give him the respect he deserved.

"Cariath Gelindum came in second. You couldn't overcome his lead from the earlier events."

Estin nodded understanding. "Cariath is a powerful, cunning warrior," he said. There was no shame in placing below him. His smile grew pensive, transforming into a frown as he did some quick calculations. If Cariath had come in second, then who had come in first? Riyne couldn't have. With his disqualification, he would have finished behind Estin. Who then . . .

He looked to Anya, a dawning concern on his face.

"Cinder finished first," Anya said, confirming Estin's worst fear.

Cinder? No. Horror filled Estin. It couldn't be. A human? Victorious in the Grand Melee? Fury, shame, and despair stole every last gleam of Estin's joy.

"Mother will not be proud that a human won the tournament," Anya said. "It shouldn't have happened. It need not have happened if you had the courage to face a human on your own."

"I fear no human," Estin snapped. "I would have destroyed him if Riyne hadn't done so first."

"You honestly believe that?" Anya scoffed.

Estin forced himself not to slouch under the scourge of her poor regard. "Of course I believe it."

"Then why did you have Riyne injure him? I know the plan was yours."

"Riyne's actions were his own."

"You lie. Do you suppose Mother will be proud of your work today? You dishonored Riyne. You dishonored yourself, and dishonored your name."

"I dishonored nothing," Estin replied boldly, but he couldn't help wonder if Mother would also see matters in the same fashion as Anya. It was a worrying possibility. "Riyne did as he chose. Besides, what difference does it make? He only hurt a human. Even if you have feelings for him." The last dig was a mistake, one he recognized the moment the statement left his mouth.

Anya's features, though, never changed, remaining impassive. "My feelings about Cinder Shade are immaterial. Of greater import is what you did to Riyne. General Arwan judged his actions so objectionable as to deserve another black mark. Riyne now has two. Do you understand what it means for him?"

Estin's eyes widened in comprehension. Two black marks, but then he would—

"It means he will never earn an *insufi* blade, much less the title of *Sai*. For someone from his family, do you understand how his life will be from this point on?"

"No," Estin whispered in fresh horror.

"Because of your arrogance and fear, you have stolen Riyne's future. I hope your supposed vengeance and coward's victory was worth it."

Estin's gaze wandered to nowhere as the full import of Anya's words made itself known.

A hand lashed out. His sister slapped him, rocking his head to the side. Estin's jaw ached, and he felt sure the strike would leave a bruise.

"And remember this," Anya said. "I am a princess of the sithe. I am an heir to the throne. You are merely a prince, and you will respect me. You will never again make disgusting insinuations about who I may or may not like, especially a human. Am I clear?"

Estin nodded mutely, angry at her but unable to say or do anything. Anya was right. She was an heir to the throne, and as a mere prince, he wasn't. Her standing was far above his own. He distractedly noted the excited speculation from those who remained at the Cauldron. They had seen Anya slap him. They would speak about it.

Fresh humiliation caused Estin's shoulders to hunch, but he didn't pay the tittering crowd any attention. Other concerns occupied his mind. How could he face the other Firsters once word of what he'd done reached them? Their glad smiles would transform into bitter recriminations once they realized what he'd done, what he'd asked Riyne to do for him. His thoughts spiraled, tumbling from one future problem to another.

Nothing had gone right this year, and it was all the fault of one person.

His jaw hardened.

Cinder Shade.

He was the reason. It was all his fault. If not for him, none of these disasters would have occurred. The *ghrina*. One way or another, Estin vowed to make him pay.

35

"How are you feeling?" someone asked.

Cinder sat up to answer, but agony gripped his head, and nausea made his vision swim. He lay back down with a groan, putting a hand to his forehead and trying to soothe the pain away. The adrenal rush of anger following his injuries had long since faded. "I've been better," he said, recognizing Bones and Sriovey standing at his bedside.

He was in the hospital again, recovering in a rectangular room containing cots arranged in twin rows. The beds all faced one another. Curtains hung off of rods suspended from the ceiling, maintaining a semblance of privacy. *Diptha* lights provided a calm illumination, and narrow windows marched along the room's length, allowing in more light from the late evening sun as well as a mild breeze. The aroma of jasmine and the sound of a gurgling stream carried into the hospital ward.

"We wanted to be the first to congratulate you," Sriovey said, his normally boisterous voice quiet for once.

"Congratulate me for what?" Cinder asked, still gently rubbing at his forehead. The light hurt, and he closed his eyes. Then again, everything hurt, at least from the neck up. His nose hurt. The line of his jaw hurt. His face hurt—both eyes were likely blackened. He'd look like a damn raccoon. His ears rang, and he felt certain a few of his teeth were loose.

"We wanted to congratulate you on winning the Grand Melee," Bones said.

It took several seconds for the words to penetrate Cinder's throbbing headache. Had he heard Bones correctly? He opened his eyes, blinking several times, staring in the direction of his friends. "I won the Grand Melee?"

"You won," Bones confirmed. "General Arwan announced the results right after the weapons event."

Tension that Cinder didn't realize he was holding exited him in the rush of a heavy exhalation. *I won.* A bubbling relief made its way from his stomach, up through his throat, and past his lips as a quiet chuckle. Quiet pride and a sense of accomplishment filled him. He had won. He'd managed what he intended.

"You didn't win any of the events," Sriovey said, "but you did well enough in all of them to claim overall victory."

Bones bounced on his feet, a wide grin of excitement on his face. "You realize no human has ever won the Grand Melee? Not once in the entirety of the Third Directorate. You're the first one in over twenty-five hundred years. Me and the boys are heading to Certitude later on to celebrate. We'll raise a glass for you."

"You better raise more than one," Cinder said with a soft laugh.

"We'll drink the place dry in your honor," Sriovey said, grinning as well. "But I don't think the Firster elves will be celebrating with us. They aren't taking their loss to you very well. Most of them are pissing and moaning about it, but they can go frag themselves after what Riyne pulled."

Some of the shine of Cinder's win dimmed. *Riyne.* "I owe him for what he did to me," he said, his voice flat as he struggled to tamp down his fury. If he gave vent to it, he'd probably rant and rave like a lunatic.

Bones had appropriated a pair of chairs. He offered one to Sriovey and took the other. He smirked at Cinder. "I'm guessing Riyne's not one of these brother warriors you're always going on about."

"Look at me," Cinder said, facing him. "Would my brother have done this to me?"

Bones shrugged. "I don't know. Me and my brothers went at it pretty bad sometimes. I can't tell you the number of times one of us ended up with a split lip."

"Well, Riyne's not my brother," Cinder said, scowling.

"I guess not," Bones said. His humor faded. "Are you going to be fine to come with us to the Daggers?"

It was the first question Cinder had asked the physicians when they'd started the process of healing him. His greatest fear was his injuries would keep him bound to the Directorate, shackled while the others risked the unknown on their own. "The physicians say I should be good to go in a few days. It'll depend on how quickly I recover." He prayed then, glad he didn't have a concussion and hoping the rest of his injuries wouldn't keep him out of action for too long.

"Then heal up quick," Bones said, slapping his thigh and rising to his feet. "We need you. Get some rest. Riyne might not be your brother, but we are."

"Speaking of brothers," Sriovey said, also standing, "Anya laid into hers after the weapons event. They were having a quiet discussion, and he didn't seem none too happy. Then Anya smacks him so hard, I'm surprised his head is still attached to his neck."

"What were they arguing about?" Cinder asked, curious.

"Jozep was the closest and overheard some," Bones said. "Anya thinks Estin was the one who convinced Riyne to hurt you by cheating. She didn't like what he did. It's the reason she slapped him."

Cinder had already realized the possibility, and Bones' confirmation didn't surprise him in the least. And he also figured Estin and Riyne would come after him again.

But next time, they wouldn't find him such an easy kill.

Slumber brought forth strange dreams, and in them, he knew himself. His name was Rukh, but a different world knew him as Shokan.

The titans attempted to cover Shet's retreat, but Shokan gave them no room to flee. There would be no escaping his justice. Not today. His sword burned incandescent, a reflection of his rage. Aia and Shon were gone. Sira was dead, and he would burn their murderers to ash.

Shokan had chased them here, to the Web of Worlds, and had already done away with four titans—Tomag Jury, Rence Darim, Garad Lull, and Drak Renter. He'd broken them, sending their shattered bodies flying off the anchor line in a bunched collection. Same with Sapient Dormant and Grave Invidious, the necroseds who had first attacked him and Sira. Where and when they'd wash ashore, he didn't care. Bringing vengeance to Sira's killers was all that mattered to him.

Shokan faced his remaining foes.

Fear stained Shet's arrogant visage, and he licked his lips. "You can't win," he said. "You've let your true body die in the real world."

The god was right. A silver glow emanated off of Shokan's skin. It indicated a terrible truth. He had entered the anchor line unready, letting his body die in the physical realm. No matter. If Devesh was kind, he'd obtain his vengeance and afterward, if his final death followed, so be it.

Shokan took an instant to view the place where his long life and his endless battles would at last conclude. The Web of Worlds. A blackened sky, reflective as blown glass, stretched endlessly all about him. Lights bled across the firmament like slow-motion shooting stars. Under his feet extended a rainbow bridge, the anchor line. It was immaterial as a film of water but sturdy enough to support an army on the march. Images continually changed within the bridge's structure. They formed shuddering shapes, including a few from his original home, the place of his heart, Arisa. In the near distance, he saw the anchor line's terminus, the exit to the world of Seminal.

Shokan mentally shrugged. It didn't matter that his muscles ached, that fatigue weighed his limbs, or that his Well was almost empty of Jivatma. Neither did he care about the broken ribs that made breathing a struggle, the twisted ankle limiting his mobility, or the fractured orbit hindering his vision. Multiple wounds, one across his abdomen, another to his chest, and a deep cut to his left thigh, all of them leaking a silvery light, were also immaterial.

Shokan was tired of his long life. He was ready to let it go, especially since he would face the rest of his years without Sira by his side. He couldn't imagine living another day without her. He'd face the titans and their god, and whatever the outcome, he'd finally get to set aside life's burdens.

A brief remembrance, of battling Shet in another time, one set in both their futures, flitted through his thoughts, but he snuffed out the memory. While Sira lived in that vision, Shokan had no faith that it would come to pass. After all, the future couldn't be forced. More likely today would be his final moment.

He hoped so.

Another remembrance rose to the forefront of Shokan's mind. His children. Recollections of them inspired him to pray. Maybe when he died, he would still be worthy of the singing light. Maybe he'd see his children again. Maybe he'd see Sira, too.

Shokan's breathing steadied then. He took a final few seconds to scrutinize his remaining adversaries, study them as he'd been taught long ago in the House of Fire and Mirrors.

There they stood, the last of the titans. Their commander, Sture Mael, the deadly Liline Salt, and the massive Tormak Jury. Shokan observed their worried understanding. Good. Meanwhile, Shet, the great coward, hid behind their Shields and swords.

Sture Mael ended the brief lull. He rushed forward, alone and unsupported. Shokan didn't bother to set his sword. Instead, he took Sture's vertical strike on his Shield, twisting so the blow slid off the crackling green web that surrounded and protected him. A swift kick to the side of the titan's knee crushed it and sent Sture tumbling to the ground.

Shokan pushed forward.

Liline Salt had engaged at the same time as Sture. White-hot steel slugs materialized in front of her hands, fired faster and exploding harder than force-arrows. Shokan initially accepted her attack on his Shield.

Lightning crackled. His Shield began to buckle, and he quickly adjusted. He slipped Liline's attack and rushed toward her. Her eyes widened in alarm. A slash to the arm dropped her guard. Before she could reset herself, he front-kicked her in the face. Her nose crumpled and blood bloomed, ruining her beauty, and Liline tumbled off the rainbow-colored anchor line. She screamed as she was tossed into the vast, dark unknown between worlds.

A crawling line of barbed vines shot from Tormak Jury's axe. Shokan didn't retreat. Instead he pressed forward, cutting the vines with a swirl of his sword. He reached Tormak, swatting aside a raised axe. Too slow. The hilt of his sword crunched into the titan's face, breaking a cheek. Another punch with his sword hilt sent Tormak hurling after Liline.

Shokan turned a predator's gaze to the final two enemies, Sture and Shet.

The commander had regained his feet and stood before his master, out of breath and Jivatma. His sword drooped. Shokan would deal with him shortly. But first, Shet. The so-called god wheezed for breath, every bit as spent as his titan. Blood dribbled from a scalp wound, curtaining his face in a red mask.

"Peace," Shet pleaded. "We can discuss this."

Shokan didn't bother answering. He walked Sture down. The final titan readied himself, acceptance of death flattening his visage. Shet retreated farther. The god edged toward the anchor line's exit where the safety of Seminal beckoned.

Shokan blurred forward, the speed a hallmark of the Caste to which he'd been born. Sture gathered himself, his sword rising to the ready. Shokan leapt over him, evading a wild thrust. His off-hand filled with a blistering Fireball, and he launched it at Shet from a distance of only ten feet. It screamed toward the god, who raised a hand, trying to block. He was only partially successful. The Fireball impacted against a hastily raised Shield, punching through and burning the right side of Shet's face.

The god screamed.

Shokan sensed Sture's coming attack. The titan aimed a vertical sword strike. Predictable. Shokan blocked, surprised an instant later when his *sword met no resistance. He realized his mistake a beat too late. Not a sword strike, but a fiery whip. It curled around his wrists, wrapping them in fire and pain. Shokan bit back a cry, his sword slipping from his grasp.*

His wrists and hands burned with agony. No. Shokan gritted his teeth. This wouldn't be the end. He fought on, ignoring the fiery pain encompassing his wrists. With the last of his strength, he jerked the whip forward, yanking Sture close. A spinning elbow clipped the titan in the chin. The whip wisped to nothingness, and Shokan took a relieved gasp while bending to retrieve his sword.

Sture, meanwhile, had staggered away, returning to his master's side.

Shet had managed to put out his burning face, but the right side of it still bubbled, sagging like melted candle wax. "This is not the end," the god promised. He gathered Sture close and leapt off the anchor line, chasing the rest of his titans. "My final gift," he shouted. From his hand came a line of white. It crashed into the glowing anchor line, cracking it apart like splintered glass.

Unprepared, Shokan found himself unmoored from gravity, which didn't always work as expected in the Web of Worlds. He fell toward his dissolution.

He might not have cared, but in that final moment he viewed an image in the shattered anchor line, one that caused him to surge toward life. He saw Sira, alive and healthy, on Seminal. She wasn't dead. The future with her could still be.

Hope bloomed, and Shokan hunted about desperately for a way to escape the Web of Worlds, one leading to Sira and Seminal. For frantic seconds, there was nothing. His head continued to swivel, searching.

There!

An opening. He swept toward it, using the final dregs of his Jivatma, knowing it would also empty his mind to the utter sense of self. But it would be worth it for the chance to see Sira again. Shokan remembered dancing with his wife when he'd been known as Rukh of Ashoka and she, Jessira of Stronghold.

He lunged toward a doorway, stretching to the lengths of his limits. He crossed the boundary and knew no more.

Cinder's injuries proved easy to heal, and he was grateful. It only took elven magic a few days to heal his nose and the worst of his injuries. He walked out of the hospital, left with only a few lingering bruises around his eyes to mark his damage. It gave him the appearance of a raccoon, but at least he would be able to participate in the Unitary Trial.

Shortly after his hospital discharge, it was time to set off for Revelant where they would take a ship to Swift Sword; and from there, head north into the Daggers.

He, Bones, Nathaz, and Rorian shared a carriage that took them from the Third Directorate to the elven capital, and the journey passed quickly. Cinder was glad he was able to make it, and during the trip, the last lingering effects of his injuries healed.

They reached Revelant on the third day after setting out, trundling through the capital and never slowing to a stop, always sweeping along at a relatively fast clip. Nevertheless, Cinder was able to examine some the buildings and neighborhoods, but it wasn't the same as actually walking the streets, pausing to examine new vistas, or exploring different parts of Revelant. He hadn't seen much of the elven capital the first time he was in the city, and he aimed to correct the oversight this time.

They pulled to a halt in front of a large, wrought-iron gate, and Cinder stepped out of the carriage. He arched his back, stretching out the kinks and stiffness. He straightened then, adjusting the Third Directorate academy pin on his left breast. The bronze eagle, the symbol of the school given to the students, remained bronze, but Cinder's now had ruby eyes. The difference denoted his rank as first in his class.

He took note of his surroundings.

They stood on a quiet brick road, high in Revelant's surrounding hills. Birdsong filtered through the shaded lanes. There was no other traffic to disturb this obviously wealthy neighborhood in Revelant. Along one side of the street ran a row of elegant homes. All were large and stood upon generous lots, their grounds perimetered by tall, ivy-wreathed retaining walls. Above the barriers rose palm trees, which swayed under the influence of a stiff breeze. Cinder imagined lush gardens also resided within the bounds of the manors.

Before him rose one such home, seen through a filigreed wrought-iron gate. The manor was made of rectangular blocks of stone painted a warm yellow. The building's bulk rose above the surrounding retaining wall, one painted the same hue as the house. Cinder noted that the barrier wouldn't be easily scalable on foot alone.

The smell of brine drew his gaze west.

Cinder inhaled sharply. *The sea.* Late day sunshine beamed upon the deep waters of the harbor, causing a shimmer of winking lights. Sleek, elven ships, narrow-beamed and swift, rested at anchor along the multitude of wharfs, but it was the ones further out that captured Cinder's attention. There, he saw a number of boats cutting across the blue-green water, their sails full.

"It's beautiful," Bones said, voice hushed as if he was viewing something holy.

"It's more than beautiful," Nathaz said, his voice containing a similar note. "It's humbling and inspiring at the same time."

Cinder did a double-take. It might have been the first time he'd ever heard the dwarf speak without cursing.

Another couple of carriages trundled up to theirs, and out disembarked the rest of the Firster humans and dwarves. All of them would stay here at the manor, guests of the empress until tomorrow when they'd board the ship meant to take them to Swift Sword. The elves, meanwhile, were to stay at the royal palace.

Out of the last carriage stepped Ruom Shale, the red-haired elf who had initially delivered them from Revelant to the Third Directorate. Cinder hadn't seen the man much during his time at the academy and wasn't entirely clear on his status there. Perhaps an aide of some sort?

The elf straightened his clothing, which somehow had no wrinkles, apparently remaining every bit as fussy and fastidious as Cinder remembered. Ruom cleared his throat, drawing their attention. His first words proved disappointing, eliciting a set of groans. "I know you wish to wander the city, but you cannot. It is forbidden. Those who aren't citizens of Yaksha Sithe require a minder in order to explore Revelant. We don't have enough to see to all of you. I'm afraid you'll have to remain at the manor."

The Firsters shared looks of disgust and annoyance. Like Cinder, they'd been looking forward to exploring the city, even if it was only a few hours. Revelant was a jewel, a place where the buildings were carefully designed to enhance the city's natural wonders. Cinder had read about elven philosophy when it came to constructing their homes, neighborhoods, and cities. Revelant was supposed to be the highest expression of their way of thinking.

There was also all the history. Revelant was one of the oldest cities in the world. So many momentous events had occurred here.

Cinder figured he could have spent a month in Revelant and only scratched the surface of what could be learned.

"Come along," Ruom said with a cheery smile and clap of his hands. "Let's get you settled in."

Cinder followed Ruom and the others into the grounds of the manor house. He passed through the gates bifurcating the retaining wall, taking one last longing look at the sea and the city.

From the gate, the Firsters traversed a driveway made of small pebbles. Their feet crunched as they paced behind Ruom. Gardens extended to the limits of the property. Narrow gravel paths wove amongst the beds of flowers and bushes, and large trees lorded over the domain, their boughs extending out to provide shade. Within the manor house's grounds, the retaining wall could barely be seen, camouflaged as it was by the abundance of flora and ivy. The entirety gave an impression of nature's wildness barely tamed, and Cinder reckoned the gardens might be a good representation of elven philosophy toward horticulture.

The Firsters entered the manor house through a pair of ten-foot tall, brass-braced doors that silently swung open on large wooden hinges.

Within was found an open-air foyer soaring to the ceiling of the very top floor. Centered within the space, well above Cinder's head, was a yards-wide crystal chandelier, vast and glittering like diamonds.

Ruom gave the Firsters a quick tour of the home. "This manor is owned by the imperial family and used to house visiting dignitaries," he explained. "Get yourself organized. The home is large enough for everyone to have his own bedroom. Choose one, and then come downstairs. Be quick. We'll have supper shortly."

Cinder chose a bedroom at random. He tossed his belongings in a corner, not bothering to unpack anything but a spare set of clothes. There was no need. They planned to sail on morning's first tide. He went to the bedroom's window, which was actually a pair of windowed-doors and opened them, stepping out onto a balcony.

Once more, Revelant stole his breath.

Rugged hills, crowned by dense brush and trees, ringed the city. Granite shelves pressed off the inclines, standing like sentinels. Like the last time he had been to Revelant, it took him a moment to properly see the city nestled amongst the greenery. Sculpted buildings matched the curve of the hills and hid amidst copses of trees. High-peaked roofs bearing iridescent tiles served notice that this was truly a city rather than merely a nature refuge.

As he stared about, prior recollections—dreams really—of another city on the sea flickered across his mind, a gleaming jewel set amidst nine hills. He wondered how he had come to know this other place. What book or story had inspired his imagining of it?

He shook his head. He doubted he'd ever know, and he set aside his concerns. He'd wasted enough time pondering the mysteries of his mind. Despite his best efforts, his first sixteen years of life remained a blank slate, and by now, he figured they always would be.

He turned away from the city and exited his bedroom. In the hallway, he ran into Bones and Ishmay, who were leaving their rooms as well.

"Supper?" Bones asked.

"I'm starved," Cinder said, and they set off. However, he found himself trailing his friends, and his thoughts returned to the city in his dreams and how much it reminded him of Revelant.

In that instant, a desire to truly see the elven city swept over him, and he made a decision.

He would sneak out tonight. It wouldn't be hard. He'd hop the retaining wall. There were no guards. A hooded cloak should hide his ears.

After supper, Cinder feigned fatigue and went to his bedroom, which was on the second floor. Thankfully, a small oak tree grew next to his balcony. It offered the perfect solution for reaching the ground, but before departing, Cinder gathered a hooded cloak. Wearing it now in the summer, would likely garner a number of odd glances, but he saw no other choice. He threw it over his shoulders and headed out.

He swiftly reached the ground, and from there he made his way to the corner of the lot, the area where the shadows clung heaviest. Twilight eased his travel. A few small *diptha* lamps lit the gardens, but otherwise darkness was swiftly claiming the grounds. Cinder reached the retaining wall and scrambled to the top. He paused on the lip, head peeking over as he glanced about.

In front of him stretched a park, wooded and shrouded in shadows. No one else was about. *Perfect.*

Cinder flipped over the wall, landing outside the grounds of the manor house. He crouched low behind some nearby shrubbery; senses still alert.

Silence met his examination.

He marked his location in his mind, and feeling more confident, he set out toward a pair of distant lamps. They illuminated an entrance to the park, next to a heavily traveled road he remembered seeing on his way into the city.

Cinder flicked the hood over his head before exiting the park and managed a single step onto the street when he noticed a tall woman leaning against a nearby building, arms crossed. Her features were shadowed by her golden hair, but Cinder recognized her anyway. *Anya.*

She and Lisandre had volunteered to serve as their mentors during the Unitary Trial. She moved to confront him. "I figured you'd be the one to break curfew."

Cinder cursed under his breath.

"What was that?" Anya asked. "Not a very nice thing to say in the presence of a lady."

"How did you know I'd break curfew?"

"I didn't," Anya, "but there's always someone who does, and they always head to this street. It's the closest exit from Salience Park." She smiled. "All I had to do was wait a little bit for one of you idiots to show up."

"We're not idiots," Cinder said with a sigh. "We're only curious." He flipped back his hood and faced the princess. There went his plan on exploring the city. He only hoped his small act of defiance wouldn't cost him. He thought quickly and realized there might still be a way out of this mess. Ruom had mentioned the reason why the humans and dwarves couldn't explore Revelant. "You wouldn't be willing to act as my minder, would you?"

Anya's head tilted. "Do you even know what a minder is?"

Cinder didn't, but he figured the word described the occupation. "Someone who takes care of visitors? You know, *minds* them."

"Close, but no. Like you said, a minder is responsible for a visitor. More importantly, though, a minder makes sure the visitor doesn't cause a . . . disturbance, and if he does, the minder is the one held responsible."

Cinder forced a grin. "Perfect. Then you can be my minder, I'll promise not to cause a disturbance, and you can show me the city."

Anya smiled, her teeth flashing. "You're not afraid to ask for what you want, are you?"

Cinder held onto his grin. "Is that a yes?"

Anya chuckled again. As before, Cinder liked hearing her laugh. "It's a most definite 'no'. I'll be your minder long enough to return you to the manor house."

Cinder's shoulders sagged. "Why aren't we allowed to see the city?" The question had been bothering him all evening.

"Because my people don't believe you're worthy. Once you're inducted in the army, you'll be allowed to tour Revelant, but not until then."

"Is the city really so special? And who made such a stupid rule?"

"My mother's great-grandmother made the rule," Anya said, a warning note in her voice. "And, yes, the city is 'so special'. There isn't another place like it in all the world."

"Then its loveliness should be shared, not hoarded," Cinder argued, realizing it might not be the wisest course to disagree with the princess. She hadn't yet told him if he'd face any punishment for breaking curfew.

"Come on," Anya said, her tone uncompromising yet holding a sense of understanding. "Let's get you back to the manor."

"As you wish, simply Anya," Cinder said. It was a foolish thing to say, but he liked making her laugh.

"You're both too bold and too familiar," Anya said, the warning note back in her voice along with a trace of anger. "You shouldn't speak to me like that."

Cinder frowned, wondering why she was so upset. He thought it was an old joke between them.

The trip to the manor house's entrance didn't take long, and it passed in silence.

Anya faced him. "Make sure to let the rest of your friends know not to break curfew. I don't feel like spending the entire night out here. I'll assign a guard from now on. You won't find them quite as understanding as I am."

She left him at the front door, and Cinder watched her march away. The loveliness of Revelant seemed a sad display compared to Anya's remembered smile.

The next morning, the Firsters boarded the ship which would take them to Swift Sword, and four days later, on the morning of their arrival, Cinder stood at the bow.

The sunrise was young, dawn yet to fully arrive, but a glinting on the horizon, a lightening of the sky heralded the sunrise to come. Briny spray lofted as the vessel thumped through the waves in a dull rhythm. Seagulls floated on the stiff breeze, calling incessantly, repetitiously. The birds . . . Cinder imagined them cawing a single word over and over again. Something like "mine".

Idiots.

Movement from the hatch leading down below caused him to glance back. Bones stepped onto the deck and headed his way. "Don't forget to give my best to Master Lerid and everyone at *Steel-Graced*," he said upon arriving.

"You're sure you won't have time to greet them yourself?"

Bones grimaced. "I wish I could, but you don't know my family. There are a *lot* of them. I'll be running around all day trying to see them all."

Cinder understood what Bones meant. Family was important. While Cinder couldn't recall his birth family, he had made one of his own choosing. It had started with Coral and Riner at *Our Lady of Fire*, extended to the masters and apprentices at *Steel-Graced Adepts*, and now included the Firsters of the Third Directorate. He loved them all and couldn't imagine the difficulty of trying to see every one of them during a single day visit. It would be impossible. Herding cats would be easier.

In fact, for today's short sojourn in Swift Sword, Cinder only intended on going to *Steel-Graced*. He didn't have enough time to see Riner and Coral. Guilt roiled his stomach at the notion, and he consoled himself with the knowledge that he'd see Coral and her brother on his next time through.

Nevertheless, despite the disappointment of not seeing the first friends he'd made since starting his new life, delight burbled inside him. He'd get to visit Master Lerid, Faine, Mirk, and everyone at

Steel-Graced. He couldn't wait. A quiet anticipation filled him, a soft buzzing like a distant swarm of bumblebees.

"I'll see you in a bit," Bones said, distracting Cinder from his thoughts. "I still have to gather my packs."

Cinder faced forward again after Bones left, watching the dawn slowly pink the sky. His awareness of the ship and those around him faded. The sky held his attention, and his excitement calmed as the heavens brightened. Watching the sunrise always calmed him like a meditative prayer.

Shortly thereafter, the ship slipped into Swift Sword's harbor, and word came from Farin, one of the First-year elves. Anya and Lisandre wanted to go over last minute instructions.

Cinder and Bones gathered alongside the other Firsters—humans, dwarves, and elves, near the ship's stern. They stood in a tight cluster, making sure to stay out of the way of the sailors dashing about getting the vessel ready to dock.

Anya spoke to them. "I want to make sure you all understand what happens today. The elves, dwarves, and Gandharvans are heading straight to Fort Carmine. No sightseeing. Ranger-Lieutenant Lisandre will be in charge. As natives to Swift Sword, Bones, Wark, Depth, and Cinder will visit those they wish to and arrive later." Her gaze briefly rested on Cinder. "However, everyone is to be at Fort Carmine by sunset. No exceptions. Any questions?"

"What about the horses?" Mohal asked.

Lisandre was the one who answered. Riyne's brother resembled him in an older, more self-assured fashion. Too bad Riyne didn't also have Lisandre's apparent honor and decency. The older elf had always dealt with Cinder fairly and without arrogance. "We've made arrangements for handlers to disembark your mounts and get them to Fort Carmine," Lisandre said. His expression became severe. "Don't expect this to become routine. In the future, you'll be expected to do this kind of work yourself."

Cinder wished Fastness was among the horses mentioned, but the pure-bred Yavana stallion was too precious to risk. He remained at the Third Directorate and had been none too happy about the matter. Fastness had whinnied, reared, and kicked the stall walls when Cinder told him he'd have to stay behind at the academy. It had taken a massive bribery of sugar cubes and carrots to get Fastness to calm down, and on the morning of his departure, the stallion had nuzzled Cinder's hair in worry.

"Are there any questions?" Anya asked.

No one spoke, and they were dismissed.

Their belongings were already piled near the hatch leading down below. Cinder belted on his sword, the one given to him by Master Lerid, and waited alongside the others for the ship to finish docking. As soon as the gangplank was down, they stepped ashore, making their way down the pier.

Swift Sword. It had been most of a year since Cinder had been here. The city was the closest thing he had to a home, and he viewed it with fresh eyes. The buildings were rough and brutal in comparison to Revelant's elegant melding of symmetry and nature. The miasma of filth and poverty clung to the wharfs. Children dressed in rags begged for alms, and the poor walked in a hunched over, abused manner.

But there was also life here, an energy of glad laughter, boisterous friendships, and the thrill of a new day. Cinder saw it expressed through the rough jokes shared by the dock workers; in the laughter of young, well-dressed people as they stumbled home; and merchants meeting with clients, both groups hoping to profit from the encounter.

It was a stark contrast to the quiet, reserved nature of the Yaksha elves.

At the end of the pier, the Firsters separated into two groups. The bulk of them followed Lisandre north, while Cinder, Bones, Wark, and Depth headed east.

Cinder was surprised when Anya joined him, Bones, and the others from Swift Sword. "I have business in the city," she said by way of explanation. "Close to your school, in fact. I'll join you after I'm done with my work, and we'll make the journey to Fort Carmine together."

Several blocks later, Bones left them, heading for his family's home.

Next to leave was Wark and then Depth.

Cinder continued on alone, Anya striding at his side, neither of them saying much. He imagined they made an odd couple, a human man and an elf woman. The bulk of his attention, though, remained on seeing his master and the other apprentices. As the streets became more recognizable, his anticipation built. A surge of excitement coursed through him. He grinned and felt like he was vibrating with suppressed energy. He wanted to leap straight up and shout with joy.

Anya's laughter drew him up short. "Don't hold back on my account," she said. "It's good to see someone so eager to see their home and family."

Home and family. She was right. That is what *Steel-Graced* was to him.

Soon enough, they came upon a familiar street, and a few blocks later, he reached a simple, white-washed brick building. His destination. *Steel-Graced Adepts.* Cinder paused, staring at the sign above the lintel. A warrior holding a sword, launching himself against his enemy.

His overwhelming joy dimmed into reflection and gratitude. The philosophers said a thousand-mile journey began with a single step. Cinder's had started here, and he recognized how fortunate he was to have found this place, to have found acceptance and love. *A home and family.*

"I should be done with my business in a few hours," Anya said. "If you don't mind, I'd like to meet your masters when I return."

"I don't mind," Cinder replied.

"Then go on in. They're waiting." Anya's voice and features held a gentle understanding, and she left him then.

Cinder took a deep breath, doing his best to control his spiraling emotions. When he felt ready, he pushed open the door and entered his first and most important home.

This early, the students had likely not yet arrived. At least so Cinder reckoned, but in this he was wrong. He found everyone already collected in the back, stretching and exercising under the vigorous gaze of Master Jine.

Cinder set down his bags and paused in the doorway, taking in the scene. Nothing had changed. He might as well have stepped back in time. The students and masters readying for a day of work. The familiar flagstone courtyard enclosed by a brick wall. He recalled every minute of blood, sweat, and effort he'd spent here.

What a wondrous time.

The first to take note of him was Mirk who shouted. "Look!" He pointed at Cinder, rushing over, enveloping him in a hug. "Cinder! How the fuck did you get so big? When you left, you were still a scrawny little shit." He had to look up to meet Cinder's gaze.

"Good elven cooking," Cinder said with a laugh.

"Well, I want to get me some of that food," Mirk said.

The others arrived in a gaggle of laughter and excitement. There were a couple of students Cinder didn't recognize, and they hung back.

"SILENCE!" Master Lerid shouted. The students immediately quieted. They stepped aside as Masters Lerid and Jine paced forward, their steps sedate and their features calm and controlled, the vision of monkish patience.

It was all a ruse. Cinder saw the smile threatening to spill out over Master Lerid's face, and the pride evident in the set of Master Jine's jaw.

Cinder's eyes watered.

Master Lerid reached him, gripping Cinder's arms. "You have returned to us," he said, his voice solemn. A second later, he lost control of his calm demeanor and broke into a wide grin. He drew Cinder into a hug. "Welcome home, boy."

"Thank you, Master."

Master Jine's gaze was on Cinder's pin. "Ruby eyes," he said, his hands trembling as he touched the bronze eagle. "Is this true? What I think it means?"

Cinder nodded. "I ranked first in class in the Grand Melee."

Master Jine's eyes went shiny. "I never thought I'd see the day," he whispered.

"First?" Sash asked. "As in you finally beat Bones?"

"Bones must have hated that," Gorant said with a laugh.

Cinder shook his head. "First overall." He tried to sound modest, not wanting to come across as boastful.

"First overall?" Faine said. The journeyman had another stripe on his shirt. One more, and he'd make master. "You mean like you beat the elves, too?"

Cinder nodded.

An eruption of elated questions met his statement, one the masters couldn't quell and didn't bother trying to. Cinder described the year he had experienced. He went over the different types of training to which he'd been exposed, the people he'd met, the friends he'd made.

"The dwarves actually like you?" Mirk asked. "I thought they were a bunch of prickly pricks who don't like their own mothers."

"They like me. They like all of us," Cinder said. "And all those stories about dwarves being grumpy." He waited a beat. "They're all true. A bunch of ugly, unhappy fucking bastards."

Laughter met his words.

"When did you start cursing right?" Gorant asked. "Frag and jack-hole and all that?"

"I still use them," Cinder said, "but a friend of mine, a dwarf named Nathaz, who has the filthiest mouth I've ever come across always makes fun of me when I do."

"Filthy how?" Faine asked.

"Filthy like every sentence he speaks has a curse word in it."

"Fucking cursing dwarves," Mirk replied, sounding like he was answering a challenge.

Cinder explained more about the year's events, describing the Foe, the duels he had with Estin and Riyne.

"Damn cowards, coming at you like that," Sash growled.

"Damn elves," Gorant agreed.

Cinder also described the Winter Gala and dancing with Anya. He knew the last would set their tongues wagging.

"You really danced with a princess?" one of the new students asked, a young boy named Shuman.

Cinder nodded.

"Bullshit," Mirk said.

"Bulltrue. You'll even get to meet her. She's coming here to pick me up. We're heading out to Fort Carmine together." Cinder tried not to sound too smug.

Shocked silence fell upon the students and masters of *Steel-Graced*.

Master Lerid broke the quiet. "A princess of the Yaksha Sithe is in Swift Sword, and she's coming to our school?"

"She's a ranger," Cinder explained.

Another eruption occurred, this one led by Master Lerid.

"We have work," Master Lerid said. "I want the school clean. Not a spot of dirt or a blade of grass out of place." He shouted further orders, and the students scattered. After they left, Master Lerid addressed Cinder. "I'm sorry, my boy, but a princess coming to the school is unprecedented. You understand?"

"I do. How can I help?"

"Can you still cook?"

"You want me to help Morr in the kitchen?"

"Do you mind?"

"I don't mind."

Several hours of furious work took place in *Steel-Graced*, and the place was made as clean as possible. Master Lerid called a halt to their efforts then.

They had a late lunch then and afterward, everyone filed into the courtyard. Cinder picked up on his prior conversation with the others, describing the rest of his year at the Directorate. In turn, he learned what had been going on at *Steel-Graced* during his absence.

The first item which captured his attention was the fact that Mirk and Gorant were the two who would represent the academy in the Maker's Tournament. The event would be held in a little over two months. It was a surprising turn of events. Cinder expected Sash to have been chosen for the Maker's Tournament, but he had apparently turned an ankle, an injury that had slowed him down through most of the spring.

"If it weren't for my fragging ankle, I would have taken top place here," Sash said.

Gorant snickered. "You said fragging."

Sash shrugged. "It's because of him and his bad influence." He pointed to Cinder.

Others spoke, telling of their year, and the day passed quickly. Sometime later, a ringing bell indicated someone at the front door and quieted their conversation.

"That's probably Anya," Cinder said.

"He calls her by her first name," Gorant whispered to Faine.

"I heard."

Cinder ignored the rush of hushed speculation and went to the front door. Masters Lerid and Jine along with Faine paced next to him while the students remained in the courtyard.

Master Lerid opened the door, smiling broadly when he saw Anya standing directly outside. "Your Highness. What a pleasure to meet you. I am Master Lerid. Please come in."

Anya entered *Steel-Graced* and was introduced to Master Jine and Faine, who fell over themselves, bowing and bending before her with many statements of 'your highness' dropped in. "It's a pleasure meeting you gentlemen as well," she said, "but Anya will do."

Cinder had been watching all this with amusement. "She's simple in how she wishes to be addressed," he told the others. Anya shot him a purse-lipped look of annoyance, and he smiled at her like butter wouldn't melt in his mouth.

A put-upon expression stole across her face, gone in an instant and replaced by a patient smile. She addressed the others. "Yes, I do enjoy simplicity," Anya said. "Although the student sent from here was perhaps a touch too simple, if you understand my meaning."

The others guffawed.

Cinder attempted to rally. "Bones isn't simple."

"Too late, my friend," Faine said. "We know who she meant."

Master Lerid indicated the courtyard visible through the wide-open doors. "Please meet my students. We also have a small repast prepared for you."

Anya shook her head. "I'd be happy to meet your students, but I'm afraid I can't stay to eat. Cinder and I have to leave soon."

"Perhaps another occasion," Master Lerid said, hiding his disappointment.

Cinder would have liked to stay longer, but one glance outside told him it was already late in the afternoon. The day had slipped away far too fast.

"Do you have time to show us some of your techniques?" Master Jine asked Anya. "The students would love to see a demonstration from you."

Cinder caught Anya viewing him in speculation.

"I believe I have the time," Anya said, "but I think your students would find greater benefit from a sparring match. Cinder will do for an opponent." She faced him with brows raised in clear challenge.

He eyed her in return. Anya always bested him quite easily, and today might be the same, but he didn't care. He wouldn't back down from her. She'd have to earn her victory. "As you wish," he said, accepting her challenge.

Master Jine clapped his hands together in surprised pleasure. "How wonderful! Will you need practice blades?"

"We have shokes," Cinder answered.

They exited to the courtyard where Anya met the students and Morr, who had come up from the kitchen. She spoke briefly with all of them. It was then that Master Lerid announced the sparring match to come. Excited shouts met his pronouncement.

While Anya had been talking to the students, Cinder had gone to his packs to get the shokes. He passed her one and together they went to a sparring square. He took his position, facing her from a distance of twenty feet. He stared at her, studying her posture, the clenching of her fists about the handle of her shoke, the narrowing of her green eyes . . . anything to give him a hint of her plans. What would she do this time?

Cinder didn't require anyone telling him when the match was to start. He and Anya approached one another of silent accord. Cinder shifted to the side, letting her take the center of the ring. She sent a flicking probe. He'd expected it and evaded. More flicking tests. He parried or slipped them. She increased the pace, her strikes coming harder. She was putting more force into them.

Cinder kept up. He batted aside her attacks, didn't bite on her feints, and countered when he could. Again, she increased the pace. Their shokes blurred. She came at him faster. Cinder's instincts took over. He let them. Greater surety than he'd ever before felt flowed through his nerves and muscles. He defended, responding without thought or sight. He felt he could have fought her with his eyes closed.

He sensed something else then. She was conducting her *lorethasra*. She was coming after him, ever quicker and harder. He maintained the pace. She further increased the speed of her attacks.

Finally, Cinder faltered. He blocked a thrust, was too slow to evade a kick to the side of his thigh. His leg buckled. He crashed to a knee. Only then did he feel the pain of her bruising kick and the light touch of her shoke against his neck.

Cinder held up his hands in surrender.

Anya grinned at him, offering a helping hand. "I was wondering when you'd finally let your instincts fully take over. You think too much."

The world returned, and Cinder discovered everyone at *Steel-Graced* applauding in wild jubilation. Master Jine actually had tears in his eyes. And here Cinder had always thought the usually irascible master was devoid of softer emotions. The masters and the others entered the square.

Master Lerid reached Cinder first, drawing him into a hug. "Never did I expect to see such a performance. I will forever be grateful and humbled to have had you as one of my students."

Mirk grabbed him. "You were fragging amazing."

Gorant and Sash were nodding enthusiastically.

Cinder blinked in surprise. Until now, he hadn't considered how those of *Steel-Graced* might have viewed his bout with Anya. He'd grown used to elven speed and skill and no longer thought it amazing that he could match them. He imagined what his friends here must now think after seeing what he could do, what he might have thought if he was in their position. He realized their awe-filled joy had genuine roots, and he grinned, glad to have brought them happiness and maybe a new horizon to which to strive.

"I wish we could stay longer," Anya said, breaking into their conversation. "But Cinder and I must depart."

Cinder's grin faltered. He still had so much to say to his brothers at *Steel-Graced*, so many stories to speak, words to thank them for everything they'd done for him. He wished he had more time, but the day was slipping. He nodded acceptance to Anya.

Cinder said his goodbyes to everyone, and as they gathered their belongings, Master Lerid pulled him aside.

"Be careful with your feelings," Master Lerid advised.

Cinder regarded his master, unsure what he meant.

"You are a human, but no matter how skilled, you will always be a human. She is an elf. Nothing good comes from reaching too far above your station."

Cinder's eyes widened in shock. What? He recognized Anya was beautiful—even a blind man would notice that—but anything else . . . He shook his head in disbelief. Why would Master Lerid think he had such feelings for Anya? It was ridiculous. "Anya isn't just an elf," Cinder said. "She's a princess, and I'm not a fool."

Master Lerid stared at him for a moment. "Just be careful around her."

Cinder shrugged. Of course he'd be careful. Maybe he was overly familiar with her, but he always recognized her place in the world and his. In reality, Master Lerid's warning was as useful as telling him dragons were deadly and water was wet.

36

Cinder and Anya arrived at Fort Carmine a few minutes prior to sunset, and by the time they got settled in and had supper, it was late. He never had much time to explore the fort since they left the next morning well before sunrise. They headed north toward Fort Benshire, which was in the southern Daggers. It was supposed to be a two-week journey, and initially their passage was easy. The road north from Fort Carmine was paved in flagstones. It wended along valley floors sheltered amongst steep rising hills clad in a forest of evergreens, and the trees quieted the clacking noise of their horses. They ran across a number of hamlets and villages in the foothills as well as a few larger towns, although none approached Swift Sword in terms of size.

They made fast travel until they reached the border of Yaksha Sithe. Then the road became a gravel track, rugged, narrow, and barely wide enough for a single wagon. Cinder had pulled his mare short upon seeing it. Why was the road so poorly maintained on the sithe of the border? Was it something to do with the elven philosophy of using a light touch on the land? If so, why were the roads of Yaksha proper so much finer than this? The elven home island was abundantly

532

cultivated by wide swatches of lovely fields and farms and traversed by properly built roads.

Cinder could have asked one of the elves, but he knew not to bother. Ever since his shocking victory in the Grand Melee, all of them, even Mohal, gave him the cold shoulder. They disapproved of his win and took it out on him by ignoring him if he tried to speak to them.

Frag them.

Their company's pace slowed and the foothills became craggier, the land growing steadily wilder. The track narrowed even further as shrubs and trees pressed closer, snagging at jerkins and packs. Long lines of green grass grew amongst the gravel, and ruts became commonplace. Foxes darted across their path, apparently unafraid, and there were no signs of civilization such as farms or villages. Cinder noted a family of deer—a doe and two fawns—pick their way through the thick foliage. The mother halted, meeting his gaze, but something must have spooked her because she suddenly darted away, the fawns following close behind.

Cinder halted when the family of deer left. He sensed a predator stalking the forest's deeper wilds—maybe a bear or a pack of wolves—and he searched the nearby trees. A breeze sifted amongst the branches. Leaves pattered across the ground, but otherwise nothing.

His brow furrowed.

No. Not nothing.

Something was watching him, and it wasn't a bear or a pack of wolves. Something strangely familiar. The sun burned high overhead, hotter than at the Third Directorate. The rest of the Firsters were easing past. Sweat collected on Cinder's forehead, in the small of his back, his chest, and his armpits. His heart pounded. His mouth went dry. The sensation of being watched crested. *A soft, low-throated growl.*

Anya halted her palomino. "What is it?" she asked.

The feeling of being watched went away as quickly as it had come on. Cinder sought to recapture it. He inhaled deeply—taking in the smell of the early afternoon rain, mold, and vegetation—and peered into the forest. A few more seconds passed, but there was nothing. "I thought something was watching me," he said to Anya.

"Are you sure?"

"Sure about what?"

"About something watching you?"

Cinder sighed. "I guess not."

"Then let's catch up with the others. I don't want us separated."

Cinder nodded acknowledgement and heeled his mare into motion. He glanced one more time into the forest, but still there was nothing but innocent trees and birds singing.

Early the next afternoon, they came across a large patrol of sithe warriors who were gathered in a meadow off the track. Cinder reckoned it was a company of roughly fifty.

Anya and Lisandre spoke to their commander, a tall warrior, blond and heavily built for an elf. The three of them conversed for a few minutes before another elf, slighter than the other three, joined their discussion.

"What do you think is going on?" Bones asked. The other humans and dwarves gathered close while the elves huddled on their own.

Cinder noticed a pleased expression flit across Anya's face, but he couldn't guess as to what it indicated. She and Lisandre headed back toward their group. "I don't know," Cinder said to Bones. "But we're about to find out."

"Change of plans," Anya said once she and Lisandre had rejoined their group. "Loial Company"—she pointed to the sithe warriors—"ran across a nest of young spiderkin. A mile west of here. Not too many. Less than twenty. It's a perfect test for the dangers you'll face."

"We're going to break you down into two units," Lisandre said. "Cinder will command one and Cariath will command the other."

As soon as the lieutenant finished speaking, Estin addressed the Firster elves as if he was in charge. "Everyone to me," he said. "Cariath will want us to—

"I didn't say you were in charge, Firster," Lisandre snapped. "Nor did I say every elf will serve under Cariath. Step back and shut up."

Estin's eyes flashed defiance until he saw Anya's flat glare. Then he shuffled away, head bent like a scolded child.

Cinder didn't like Estin, and he liked him less and less with every passing day. The man was a danger to the rest of them with his arrogance and his stupidity, to say nothing of his cruelty.

"Here's how it will be," Anya said. "Cinder will have Mohal, Loriam, Crail, Bones, Depth, Sriovey, Derius, and Dorcer. Cariath's group will consist of Estin, Riyne, Farin, Ishmay, Wark, Joria, Rorian, Jozep, and Nathaz."

"Fantastic," Estin muttered. "We get the dregs of both the humans *and* the dwarves."

What a jackhole.

Nathaz bristled. "You'll get my axe up your ass if you don't shut the fuck up."

"Come and try it," Estin sneered.

A part of Cinder wished Nathaz would. A brawl was very different from the formal sparring at the Directorate, and he wouldn't mind seeing Estin get his ass kicked. But he also knew a fight right now would be beyond foolish. They needed to draw together if they wanted to survive the Unitary Trial and the spiderkin.

Anya clearly felt the same way. "Enough!" she snapped, getting between the elf and the dwarf, her eyes flaring with fury. "You two, shut up. Right now. Not another fragging word. Your discipline is pathetic, and your unit cohesion non-existent. Learn both quickly, or you won't survive the Unitary Trial." Her basilisk-hard glare stayed on Estin, and she got nose-to-nose with him. "I've changed my mind. You and Riyne will serve under Cinder. And if I hear one *single* noise, sound, or expression of complaint or insult toward him, when we get back to the Directorate, you'll be cleaning latrines with your bare hands for the next month. I'll have you begging to quit the academy. Am I clear?"

"Yes, Anya," Estin replied, face flushed and unable to meet his sister's gaze.

"You address me as "captain", you idiot," Anya replied. "In the field, I am not your sister. I am your commanding officer."

Estin flush deepened.

More like an idiotic jackhole.

"I'll advise Cariath," Lisandre said. "Anya will do the same for Cinder's unit."

"We leave in fifteen minutes," Anya said. "You two"—she pointed to Cinder and Cariath—"come with me. Same with Joria and Rorian. We're going to learn everything Lieutenant Kolewin, the commander of the Loials, and his scouts know about what we might be facing up ahead. I want us to have a plan to kill something evil."

A few hours later, Cinder was crouched low beside Bones, peering through a tangle of rocks and vines toward a set of hills where the spiderkin were said to be establishing a nest. The sun climbed to its afternoon height, and humidity made the valley floor where he squatted seem like a summer swamp. Sweat trickled down the back of his neck. Barely seen gnats and mosquitoes—one of life's great irritants—buzzed about, but there were no signs of any animals. No deer, foxes, moles, squirrels, or chipmunks. There was nothing but the forest's silence.

No spiderkin, either, but Cinder didn't find the observation surprising. Spiderkin were twilight hunters. They were likely resting now, but in a few hours, they'd come out and seek prey. Over a period of weeks or months, they'd eventually denude the surrounding forest of all animal life.

The rest of the Firsters hunkered nearby, all of them studying the surrounding area. They'd already surveyed the closest hills, searching for signs of spiderkin and the entrance to their nest. The Loial scouts described it as a shadowed cave, one easily overlooked and difficult to find. They had to kill this nest before it established itself. No more than seven miles away, there were several elven villages, although Cinder hadn't seen any indication of them. He probably wouldn't even if he walked through the center of them. Elves blended their homes with the surroundings.

"I think I see something," Depth whispered.

"Where?" Cinder asked.

Depth pointed halfway up a slope, no more than a hundred yards away. "Right above those stunted trees. There's a curtain of vines. Watch."

Cinder saw the indicated area. Seconds later, a breeze blew. It brushed the tangle of vines, briefly pushing aside the hanging vegetation like a comb through unruly hair and exposing a darker area beyond.

"Good eyes," Cinder said. He glanced to Cariath. "My team will head in first. We'll take care of the guards."

Cariath nodded. "We'll protect your back. I remember the plan. Go in. Keep in close contact. Burn them out."

Anya and Lisandre remained quiet during all of this. So did the fifty members of Loial Company backing them up and their commander, Lieutenant Kolewin. Apparently, the simple smash-and-burn plan Cinder, Cariath, and Rorian had devised would still serve.

"Let's roll," Cinder said to the members of his unit.

They rose to their feet, and Cinder led them toward the hill that Depth had noted. Seconds later, Cariath's unit followed. None of them made a sound. Only a few whispered scuffing of boots against the wet dirt and the soft brush of branches carefully eased away. Whether the spiderkin were asleep or not, they all knew enough to remain as silent as possible.

Minutes later, they reached the incline, and their progress slowed. Traversing the terrain while maintaining silence was difficult. They pressed upward, and eventually reached their destination.

Cinder was heartened when they quickly located the cave camouflaged by the knot of tangled vines. The hidden entrance was easily tall enough for them to walk upright, which meant they might not have to hunch forward to get at the spiderkin. At least not the entire way.

Anya, who had paced closest to him, whispered in his ear. "The guards will be directly inside the entrance. They can be tricked."

Cinder nodded. They'd discussed this as well. He slowly drew his sword. Only the gentlest of hisses emanated.

He gestured for Crail and Riyne, and they crept forward. Cinder hated having to work with the noble elf, but he had no choice in the matter. Riyne was still a member of the Firster class in the Third Directorate. So for now, he set aside his antipathy and focused on the moment.

Meanwhile, Estin and Bones had bows strung and arrows nocked, and the rest of his unit had swords drawn and ready, too.

Riyne and Crail seemed to concentrate for a moment.

Cinder lifted his head. He inhaled. For the briefest of instances, he might have scented a sulfurous smell. He frowned. It was gone now. *No matter.*

He took up a position on one side of the cave's entrance, and with him were Depth, Sriovey, Derius, and Dorcer. Anya stood alone on the side opposite. Estin and Bones faced the entrance, arrows nocked to their bows. They nodded to Riyne and Crail, who held tiny flames in their hands. With a flick of their wrists, the two elves tossed their fires at the cave's camouflaging vines and immediately darted to join Anya. Smoke rose. Small flames crackled, but given the damp conditions, it had little chance of spreading.

Seconds later, a chittering noise holding a questioning tone approached the entrance.

Cinder's grip tightened on his sword. Estin and Bones reached full draw and their bows groaned. The sound must have carried into the cave. The spiderkin's chittering grew more excited. They burst forth from the cave. Two of them.

Bows twanged. Arrows slammed into the spiderkin, and the creatures keened. Cinder was already moving. He beheaded one monster, while Anya did in the other. The spiderkin cries lasted less than a second.

Cinder withdrew from the cave's entrance, staring at the opening with bated breath. Sometimes the spiderkin had three guards. A beat later, no more were forthcoming. *Good.* The Firsters should still have surprise on their side. Cinder immediately chided himself. Nothing righteous ever came from imagining easy success. Bones passed him a lighted torch. Estin did the same for Anya.

She pushed past the vines first—the fires were already out—Cinder right next to her. The rest of his unit trailed close behind him, and their shuffling, scraping footsteps were the only sounds Cinder heard. That, and his heavy breathing.

The darkness and air pressed against his skin, a heavy cloak of oppressiveness. Claustrophobia threatened, and Cinder did his best to disregard it. He could see. He told himself it was enough, made himself believe it as the torches lit their way. The light cast strange shadows against the dark, jagged stone. His shoulder brushed against Anya's, and on his next step, it rubbed against the sides of the narrow cavern, which showed no sign of widening.

A possible sound echoed, causing Cinder to halt.

Chittering.

He glanced at Anya, wondering if she had heard it, too. Her face was cast in shadows, but a quirked eyebrow told him she hadn't heard anything.

She held her torch to the side and whispered in his ear. "What is it?"

"Chittering," he said. "Maybe."

She nodded. "Stay frosty. They might be closer than we think."

They shuffled onward and eventually reached a place where the cavern branched. Both paths angled downward, one slightly steeper. Cinder passed the word. Cariath's unit would hold here and blockade the spiderkin from looping around and attacking the Firsters from behind.

Once Cariath's unit was properly positioned, Cinder took his group onto the right-hand path, the one inclined more shallowly. On they went into the darkness and gloom. Minutes later, the cave opened into a twenty-foot space with a ceiling rising higher than he could reach when standing on his tiptoes. Light lines of webbing crisscrossed the area, and a few long cables extended into a tunnel on the far side of the cavern.

More chittering arose from deeper down.

Cinder spoke to Anya. "I'll take Crail with me. He's the best at

Blending. We'll scout what's ahead."

"Stay close to him," Anya ordered.

Cinder signed for Crail and explained what he wanted.

The elf concentrated like he had outside. "We're good to go," he whispered.

The two of them hunched low, under the webbing and cables. Cinder carried their only torch, and they slowly belly-crawled forward. Thirty feet later, they reached a bend in the tunnel. Cinder could see a wan light illuminating the exit. He and Crail headed toward it. Fifteen more feet and they reached a point where the tunnel expanded into another cavern. This one was much bigger, a hundred feet in length and fifty in height. Chittering filled the space, and the entire volume was laced with webbing. The stench of old blood and decay permeated the air as large sacs hung from the ceiling where unfortunate animals were cocooned. They were likely food saved for a future meal and also the source of the light, a kind of wicked, distorted *diptha* bulb.

None of this was why Cinder's mouth went dry, though.

Oh, shit.

There weren't a mere twenty juvenile spiderkin in the cavern. There were hundreds of them. And most of them were adults, and most of them were awake.

Cinder quickly but quietly slapped a hand across Crail's mouth. The elf had seemed about to shout out in alarm. Crail's eyes were wide and filled with fright as he stared at the multitude of spiderkin in the cavern in front of them. After a moment, the elf appeared to have his fear under control, and Cinder removed his hand.

He whispered directly in the elf's ear. "Keep us Blended. I need to do a count. Then we ease back. Don't touch the cables. We have to get out and warn the others."

Crail nodded.

Cinder did a quick count. *Over two hundred spiderkin.* Even with

Loial Company, it might be too many to handle. It would be better to simply get out of here and call for reinforcements from Fort Benshire.

Cinder touched Crail's shoulder, indicating his readiness to leave, and they carefully edged away from the cavern. The only sound was of their soft scrabbling as they belly-crawled backward across the dirt. That and Crail's panting from either exertion or lingering terror. Maybe both. Cinder's torch lit their way, a dim beacon while Crail's Blend kept it and them hidden.

They reached a place wide enough for them to turn around and headed back to the unit, eyes forward now. Cinder's heart thudded the entire time. It wasn't exactly because of fear but more the awareness of the mortal danger confronting him and the others.

A chittering reached them, a questioning note. It sounded down the tunnel from where they'd discovered the spiderkin. He touched Crail's shoulder, and the elf froze. So did Cinder, and he lowered the torch, shielding its light with his body. He didn't know how much of its illumination bled past the Blend, and there was no reason to take any chances. Cinder glanced over his shoulder. A silhouette blocked the cavern's illumination. It stood there for a few seconds before moving on.

He breathed out in relief.

Crail gasped, shuddering in repressed fear, muscles tightening. His mouth gaped and awareness appeared to leave his eyes as panic took hold.

"We're almost out," Cinder whispered to Crail. "Keep the Blend tight. We'll reach the others and get the frag out of here." He laid a hand on the elf's shoulder, giving him an encouraging squeeze.

Crail didn't reply, but he shuddered again, muscles relaxing this time. He nodded to Cinder and they pushed on.

Minutes later, they reached the smaller cavern where their unit waited for them.

"Report," Anya ordered as soon as Cinder exited the tunnel.

"Trouble," Cinder said. "There are roughly two hundred fully formed adult spiderkin in a large cavern fifty feet down the tunnel." He addressed his unit. "I want all elves Blending as hard as you can. Link them so we can see one another. We leave now. Don't touch the cables. Stay alert. Keep your swords in their sheathes. I don't want any sound reaching the spiderkin."

Estin whined a complaint. "If we keep our swords sheathed, how are we supposed to fight the spiderkin?"

Anya answered. "We don't. Cinder's right. We need speed and stealth to get out of this. We run. Crail and Bones up front. Sriovey and Derius come next. Estin and Depth. Riyne and Dorcer. Cinder and I will bring up the rear. Go."

Seconds later, the unit was moving, hustling along, everyone with their shoulders and elbows tucked close, careful to remain as quiet as possible. They were all terrified, and fear-filled panting resounded along the tunnel. Cinder worried the sound might carry past the Blends. They soon reached Cariath's unit and explained the situation. Anya shifted to the front of the column while Lisandre drifted back to join Cinder.

They were about to get under way again.

"Oh, fuck," Nathaz whispered. He pointed. A spiderkin cable, dirt-covered and melding in with the floor and walls of the tunnel, was vibrating. Someone must have bumped it. Excited chittering arose from deeper within the cavern.

"Run," Anya said.

The column took off at a dead sprint. Cinder and Lisandre held the rear while Anya raced ahead.

"Keep your Blends taut and Linked," Lisandre said to those closest to him, speaking in a harsh whisper. "As soon as we exit the tunnel, sound the horns. Let the Loials know we're bringing trouble. They should be no more than a quarter mile east of where we left them."

Murmurs of assent met his words.

They ran flat out, not bothering with quiet. Cinder sensed lurching movement behind him. *Spiderkin.* Hundreds of scrabbling legs. Chittering. A hungry excitement to the sound. The hair on the back of his neck stood out. The noise of the spiderkin's pursuit increased. The creatures were closing fast.

The air ahead of him lightened. *The tunnel's exit.* He had no time for relief. The spiderkin were still racing forward. They sounded no more than a few dozen yards behind him. The Firsters at the front picked up sudden speed, bursting from the tunnel's mouth like bottled corks. Horns immediately blew, a strident call of warning.

Cinder blasted out of the tunnel. The others were taking a reckless course across the hill. Cinder's heart thumped. Better to be reckless than face the spiderkin. He willed himself to greater speed, chasing after the rest of his troop. No one spoke except to urge one another to run faster. Cinder risked a glance back. He and Lisandre were most of the way down the slope when a mass of spiderkin swarmed out of the tunnel, a black wave of legs and pincers. The creatures cried out in fury.

Cinder tripped, and Lisandre steadied him.

"Thanks," Cinder said.

"Eyes forward," Lisandre growled.

Cinder did as instructed. He charged on, attention straight ahead. Looking back would do no good. Besides, his feet told him what was coming. Through the soles of his boots, he could feel the pounding as the spiderkin thundering on the hunt. And they were gaining.

Anya slowed, letting them catch up with her. Her honey-gold braid bounced with every stride she took. "Don't stop," she urged. "Loial Company is only a few hundred yards away."

Cinder gritted his teeth and kept on running. He didn't need to glance back to know the spiderkin were on their heels, chasing them down like an inexorable tide.

37

Up ahead was the clearing. It appeared empty, and Cinder's heart skipped. Where was Loial Company? They should be right here.

He'd barely finished formulating the worry when the warriors of Loial Company flashed into view. They'd Linked Blends with the Firsters, and a thick knot of them had arrows nocked.

Most of the Firsters split to either side of the archers. Some continued straight ahead.

"Fire at will!" The call came from Loial Company.

Arrows blurred, passing no more than five feet above Cinder's head. Spiderkin cried out in pain.

The warriors of Loial Company loosed again, and their bows twanged like some glorious musical instrument.

Cinder dared hope.

More screams came from the spiderkin, pain mixed with rage. The pounding of their chitin covered legs told Cinder they were still coming.

The line of archers bent, forming an opening through which some of the Firsters, including Cinder, poured.

As soon as he was through the Loial's line, he turned about. He breathed heavily, but he still had enough breath to shout orders. "Firsters! Face about. Bows ready. Fire at will." The humans immediately responded; the dwarves as well, although they carried crossbows. The elves hesitated initially, but they also did as he ordered.

Cinder caught Anya and Lisandre shoot him identical expressions of surprised irritation. He knew why. They were the leaders of the Firsters. They should have been the ones to issue the commands. He disregarded their annoyance. He'd remember to keep his mouth shut, but for now, there was a battle to fight. They could rip him a new one later.

The Firsters got off a volley.

Branches swayed, and a cloud of dust heralded the spiderkin's onrushing charge. They were less than a hundred yards away.

Lieutenant Kolewin stood to the rear of his column of warriors and shouted in Anya's direction. "Get your men ready. Swords and shields! You'll plug any holes those fucking bugs manage to make."

Another member of Loial Company, the sergeant, someone who could only be described as tough and hard-bitten, stood close to the lieutenant and shouted to his warriors. "Form up. Swords and shields out!"

The warriors of Loial Company set aside their bows, drew their swords and set their shields.

Cinder drew his own blade, readied his shield. He found himself wishing he'd practiced with it more often at the Directorate.

When the spiderkin were no more than fifty feet away, lances of fire shot from the swords of Loial Company. A dozen spiderkin were instantly incinerated. The creatures roared in rage and never slowed.

The spiderkin crashed into the line of Loial Company, a smashing of armored chitin and spiked legs against sword and shield. Men cried out in pain. Spiderkin did, too. Chaos ensued. Loud chittering. Elves shouted. More lances of fire.

The spiderkin sought to overwhelm them through sheer force of mass and numbers. Loial Company was holding. An elf went down, stabbed and churned under the feet of a spiderkin. So did two more standing next to him.

An opening.

"Fill the breach!" Anya shouted.

Cinder was already there. He drew on all his experience in the Foe. Five spiderkin tried to surge through the opening. He punched one in the face with his shield, parried a stabbing leg, sliced it off. He spun under a decapitating strike. His turn completed; he aimed a strike into the neck of a spiderkin. The creature collapsed.

Other Firsters arrived. The four remaining spiderkin gave ground, one bleeding heavily from where Cinder had amputated her leg.

"Fall back," Anya ordered.

Cinder faced forward, toward the enemy, keeping his eyes on them. In passing, he grabbed an injured elf under the arm. The man lay on the ground, moaning in pain, clutching his leg, which looked broken. Blood soaked the elf's pants. Cinder dragged him to the rear of Loial Company's line. A healer took over then, and Cinder returned to the ranks of the Firsters.

He surveyed the battle. Loial Company was holding. They had lost many of their own, but the spiderkin had lost far more.

Another opening in their line formed.

Cinder disregarded his earlier admonishment to let Anya and Lisandre call the orders. "Breech!" he shouted. "On me!"

He led the Firsters to the opening, a wider one this time. Ten spiderkin faced them. Cinder cut one down, splitting its head in two. He blocked and parried. The other Firsters worked alongside him, and slowly, they turned the tide. A sharp cry suddenly cut off. Cinder didn't have time to look, but it sounded like Joria. The opening was closed, and they fell back.

Sriovey was dragging someone. *Joria.* Cinder took one glance at him, and nausea filled his stomach, a mix of sadness and fury. Joria would never again rise. He stared sightlessly at the sky.

Cinder pushed down his sorrow. While he had never gotten to know Joria as well as he had some of the others, he still counted the man a brother. For now, though, he had a battle to wage. He could grieve later.

The fight raged on. The front line was a roiling mass of spinning, stabbing spiderkin and elves seeking to repel them. More openings formed now and then. Anya or Lisandre ordered the Firsters forward as needed. Time slowed. Every blade thrust, every anguished shout and cry, the muddy mix of dirt and blood . . . none of it impacted Cinder. He noticed the events and disregarded them. He fought as needed, sometimes ordering his men to kill the spiderkin.

An interminable space of time passed. "Reset!"

It took Cinder a few seconds to understand the order. It had come from Lieutenant Kolewin. The spiderkin were retreating. They left the mangled remains of dozens of their own, some of which still twitched and stumbled about, gravely injured.

Cinder exhaled convulsively. It was over.

"Firsters! On me!" Anya ordered. "Roll call."

Cinder reached the princess, heartened to see everyone else arrive. They'd only lost Joria.

For Loial Company, the losses had been far greater. A full dozen of their men had been killed. Another five were gravely wounded and likely wouldn't survive the day. Seven more were injured but were expected to recover with time and rest, neither of which they had.

They had to get word out to Fort Benshire. The spiderkin would be back. Cinder knew it. Night would fall in a few hours. It was their natural time to hunt and kill. He was glad to see two elves sprint off after speaking to Lieutenant Kolewin.

"Are they reporting to Fort Benshire?" he asked Anya.

"Likely so," she replied.

"Not that it will do us much good," Estin muttered. "It's a two-day journey there, even at a dead sprint."

"It is not for our salvation that they'll bring the army," Lisandre chided. "It's to protect the villages."

"What happens next?" Bones asked.

"We'll retreat to one of the villages," Cinder answered. "If we're lucky, one of them will have a wall." It was the only option that made sense. They couldn't hold here. The meadow was no place to mount a defense. It was wide open, and given the stony ground, it would take them too long to dig entrenchments or build barriers.

He didn't bother adding how their retreat would be a nighttime march. How they would be slowed by their injured, and they'd face attacks the entire way. The Firsters didn't need to hear more bad news right now. Let them savor survival, mourn Joria, and then learn the hard truth of today's battle.

"They'll be back," Lieutenant Kolewin said, approaching them. "I've sent two runners to Fort Benshire. They'll bring the army to clear these bastards out of our forest." He spoke to Anya. "Get your men organized. We burn our dead and march for Fellim in fifteen minutes. The village has a wooden palisade." He swept past them, calling out more orders.

Soon, a thick plume of smoke rose from where the elves had carefully arranged their dead in a common funeral pyre. One of the healers said a prayer to Devesh before lighting the wood. Cinder watched the smoke trail upward. It felt like he'd seen something like this before, many times in the past, and a burden settled across his shoulders. It weighed of witnessing too many deaths in his life.

It was an odd sensation since this was his first battle, and he puzzled over what it meant. Maybe it was simply the shock of seeing violent death for the first time?

Soon thereafter, they collected their injured, mounted up, and left the meadow.

"Devesh save us," Bones said, riding next to him and interrupting his thoughts. "We've already lost Joria. The Unitary Trial isn't supposed to be this dangerous." He glanced at Cinder. "Do you think we'll ever see Swift Sword again?"

Cinder forced a smile. "I promise we will," he said in an utterly certain voice. Inside, he wasn't so sure.

Night fell swiftly in the foothills of the Dagger Mountains. The column consisting of the Firsters and the warriors of Loial Company pressed onward, traveling a well-trodden trail. It was one wide enough for several men to ride abreast. They pressed forward, *diptha* torches lighting their way. A tense air held over the group. All of them knew the reality of their situation. Fellim was hours distant, and while the spiderkin had yet to attack again, they would. It could come at any moment.

Cinder heard chittering and sounds of movement from amongst the trees. The noises came from dozens of yards behind, but it never ceased or fell behind.

"I wish they'd just get it over with," Ishmay said from Cinder's right. He glanced around, a worried glare on his face. "It's the waiting that's getting to me."

Cinder understood Ishmay's sentiment. He shared it. The spiderkin were shadowing the column. They were readying for their next assault, likely waiting for when tension and worry caused concentration to slacken. The creatures would attack then.

"Stay alert," Cinder said. "They'll come at us when we're least ready."

"But who knows where that might be?" Sriovey asked. He rode a sturdy pony, a dwarf's favored mount.

Cinder didn't know the answer to Sriovey's question; not exactly, but he had an idea. The column was entering the thickest parts of the forest, where the light was the dimmest and vision and hearing dulled. Where the forest would provide the spiderkin their greatest camouflage, and their dark chitin and limbs would be indistinguishable from the various branches and tree limbs. It was there that the spiderkin should attack.

He eyed the area ahead. A hundred yards or so, well beyond the illumination of their *diptha* torches, the forest appeared to thicken. The moonlight struggled to penetrate the dense brush and branches, which leaned over the trail, shadowing it. A rustle stirred along the column. A warning was passed from ahead to be wary in the heavier foliage.

Apparently, Cinder wasn't the only one expecting an attack amongst the thicker part of the forest. The column tightened their lines, hands on swords. Cinder peered about, letting his eyes drift, searching for movement. He remained alert throughout the entire passage, wishing the elves did better at maintaining their trails and paths. Brambles caught at his clothing, his saddle and bridle, but he shoved past them. He only allowed himself to relax slightly when he exited the denser foliage.

Further ahead and to the left, a dozen yards away from the path, Cinder noticed a fallen maple, a true giant of the forest. Its demise had created a small clearing, and moonlight shone down within the space. Bare tree limbs thrust at the sky like broken fingers. They moved.

Cinder cried out a warning, his mind taking in the scene, knowing the danger before conscious thought brought him true understanding. "From the left. The clearing." Spiderkin scuttled along the fallen maple. "They're coming."

Sound and movement exploded out of the clearing. Chittering and the scratching of serrated legs carried twenty spiderkin toward the column at a sprint. But Cinder's warning carried, and the column got their swords drawn. Fire streamed from their blades.

Cinder spun about. He realized what would happen. Those attacking from the clearing were a distraction. He shouted for the Firsters and anyone who could hear. "It's an ambush! They're coming from behind!"

Anya gave him a startled glance before apparently realizing the same thing. She shook off her surprise and called out instructions, getting the column faced in the right direction. Lieutenant Kolewin and his crusty sergeant were ordering the Loial to ready bows.

The spiderkin swarmed out of the forest. The creatures massed in multiple locations. *Diptha* torches were slammed into the ground, flaring brighter. The light cast the creatures and forest in strange shadows. The spiderkin forged through a sheet of arrows and lances of fire. More of their kind dropped down from the surrounding trees.

A melee broke out.

Chaos.

Horses spun about, whinnying in fear and anger. Warriors shouted, cursed, calling out warning. Shadowy figures loomed. Cinder had his sword and shield ready. Someone cried out in pain.

Rorian.

"Shit!" Rorian shouted. He cried out again.

Cinder dismounted and went to Rorian, finding the mountain Rakesh writhing in pain. Blood fountained from his severed thigh. Three spiderkin surrounded him.

"Rorian!" Cinder cried.

A spiderkin punched a leg through Rorian's chest.

Cinder saw red. He attacked a spiderkin, decapitating the creature. He eviscerated another and severed three limbs from the third one, which screeched in pain and retreated. Cinder knelt by his friend, taking Rorian's hand in his.

Rorian still lived, but not for long. Blood bubbled from his mouth. "I wish I didn't have to die." His words trailed, and Rorian's grip and features slackened.

"I wish it, too," Cinder whispered. Tears filled his eyes, and he held onto Rorian's hand and his gaze, watching the light leave his friend's eyes.

Mere seconds had passed. Cinder collected himself, shoving down the sorrow. He'd mourn later. Right now, he had more enemies to kill. He got back to his feet and—

Something slammed into him. He saw chitin and serrated legs, and he slashed out. A spiderkin keened. Cinder scrambled to his feet. He'd been knocked off the trail, and he sought to make his way back to his brothers. Five spiderkin cut him off. He gave ground. Another two dropped from the trees overhead. They surrounded him in a rough semi-circle.

"Cinder!" Nathaz shouted. He, Crail, and another dwarf, Dorcer maybe, had been cut off as well. "We have to get the fuck out of here," Nathaz said.

"To me," Cinder ordered. He backed away from the spiderkin, who for some reason weren't attacking. He didn't know why, and he didn't care. He retreated in the face of their slow advance.

Nathaz and the others reached him. The main battle raged from only a few yards away, but it might as well have been the distant sea. There was no way back to the relative safety of Loial Company and the rest of the Firsters.

Crail shot a lance of fire. It incinerated one of the spiderkin. The creature screamed in pain. The cry seemed to be a signal to attack. The spiderkin roared. Cinder punched aside one of the creatures. He sent a backslash that cut through another one's maw. Dorcer laid about with his hammer. Nathaz did the same, cursing floridly. Crail moved about the perimeter, parrying the spiderkin and sending fire into their midst. More of them burned.

But more of them also arrived. A dozen spiderkin cut them off.

"Fall back," Cinder said. They had to retreat, gain distance and regroup, come up with a plan to rejoin Loial Company and the Firsters. "Fall back!"

Nathaz retreated, facing forward, but Crail didn't. He turned and ran back toward the main battle. The spiderkin cut him down in seconds.

Dorcer tried to reach them, but he took a cut to the thigh. He crashed to his knees. A second spiderkin lunged. Dorcer smashed it aside, but a third spiderkin rushed in. It bit the dwarf in the shoulder. Dorcer cried out. He crushed the creature's head, a short blow with his hammer. The original spiderkin slashed Dorcer's chest, a deep wound. The dwarf toppled. Cinder took an unconscious step toward Dorcer. *Damn it.* Many of the spiderkin fell to feeding.

He stepped back, his gorge rising, disgusted and infuriated. He took a last glance at Dorcer before he and Nathaz took the distraction to sprint away from the battle.

They had no *diptha* torches by which to see, and Sapient's white moonlight provided dim illumination. Both struggled to keep their feet under them.

Nathaz took a hard fall. "Fucking root," he growled.

Cinder drew him back to his feet and they took off. Trees, branches, and underbrush clutched at their clothing. Cinder heard the chittering of pursuing spiderkin. He panted, sucking in great lungfuls of air. His heart pounded. He gripped his sword, seeking a place to escape.

Their path took them tumbling down an unexpected slope. Cinder fell, dragged himself to a halt. This time it was Nathaz who helped him rise. Cinder got to his feet, slipped again, but got himself steady and stumbled after the dwarf. The chittering never stopped.

On they went, a nightmare run around looming trees, and across the uncertain terrain. Sharp thorns tore at Cinder's clothing and skin. He yanked himself free of grasping brambles. He tripped again, the uneven ground. *Fragging unholy hells!* Cinder popped right back up, ignoring his throbbing ankle and plowed onward.

The sounds of combat grew faint, but the spiderkin continued to give chase. Cinder and Nathaz burst from the forest. They reached a small clearing, a rocky place where a creek had cut a narrow gorge. Without slowing, they leapt across. Cinder landed, cursing his injured ankle, but he spun about and immediately reset himself.

He had his bow ready when six spiderkin punched into the clearing. Thanks to Sapient's light, he could see, and he shot a spiderkin in the face. The creature crashed, tangling into another. They had no more time.

The other four spiderkin leapt the gorge.

Cinder threw aside his bow and drew his sword. Distantly, he noted the arrival of three more spiderkin. *Shit.*

Nathaz attacked the spiderkin on their side of the gorge. He sent a looping blow that caved in the head of the lead creature. Four more spiderkin crossed over—the three new arrivals and the one who had tangled and fallen.

Seven of them. Worry stiffened Cinder's spine like a bar of ice. He realized there was only one way out of this, and he reached inside himself. He had to push past fear and reach for hope. As before, the coruscating wall of blue and green impeded his progress. Its mildest touch was agony.

Cinder took a figurative breath and plunged into the blue-green wall.

He instantly began screaming, but he wouldn't let up. He pushed against the wall, throwing all his strength and will into the effort.

The spiderkin centered on Nathaz.

Cinder popped through the barrier with a startling suddenness. The absence of agony left him giddy, laughing hysterically with relief.

And there ahead of him lay his destination, a sparkling, perfectly reflective pond of silvery water. Cinder reached for it, conducting his *lorethasra*.

"Come on, you ugly fucks!" Nathaz shouted.

Sweet power flooded Cinder. His muscles twitched with the need for speed. The dimly lit world brightened. All senses heightened, and he breathed in the musk of spiderkin, his own sweat. He heard Nathaz's ragged breathing, and the croaking of a distant frog.

He felt a rush of wind and threw himself into a roll, ducking under a swinging leg, one which would have cut him in two. Awareness of his situation resumed. Nathaz was hard pressed by six spiderkin.

Cinder brought the relief. He attacked, jumping atop one. He balanced on the ball of one foot, pausing long enough to stab the creature in the head. He pushed off, landed on another spiderkin. His injured ankle protested, but it bore his weight long enough for him to cut his foe's face in half. He dismounted, careful to not land too heavily on his injured ankle.

Another gust of air.

Cinder parried blindly, instincts guiding his sword. He spun about, cut off a pair of serrated legs. The spiderkin trying to attack from behind collapsed and cried in pain.

He almost laughed at the ease with which he was defeating the spiderkin.

He should have known better. His cockiness did him in as karma kissed him.

A spiderkin battered him off his feet and launched him at another of its kind, which bit him deep in the shoulder. *Venom in their mandibles.* With a cry, Cinder pushed the creature away. He swung wildly. By luck, he struck the spiderkin. His sword slammed into its thorax.

Entrails or whatever they used for intestines, flopped out.

By now, only one spiderkin was still fully mobile, and Cinder backed away from it. His shoulder had gone cold. The strength was rapidly departing his arm. He snarled at the creature. *Come on, you fragger.* He wouldn't go down. Not like this.

The spiderkin waved its mandibles. She roared, rushing at him.

Cinder disregarded its threatening posture. *Kill this one, and he and Nathaz were safe.* Cinder darted forward, too fast for the spiderkin to counter. A straight thrust through her throat. He disengaged, and the spiderkin fell over with a heavy thud.

Cinder glanced around. The final spiderkin, the one missing a pair of legs, tried to hobble away. Cinder walked it down and put it out of its misery.

He looked for Nathaz, wanting to share his triumph.

But Nathaz lay on his back, holding his abdomen. The broken spar of a spiderkin's leg had impaled him, and blood seeped from between his fingers.

Cinder's connection to his *lorethasra* popped like a bubble, and he dashed to Nathaz's side. He knelt, his eyes welling.

Not Nathaz. Not another friend dying in his arms.

He took Nathaz's hand, trying to maintain his courage and composure. He reminded himself of what was needed, what he could give even as a hundred memories flitted through his mind. He recalled the first time he met Nathaz. The jokes the dwarf would tell. His bawdy sense of humor. His generosity. His protective nature. His friendship. And Nathaz, his brother, was dying.

Nathaz managed a grin. "Looks like I'll never get to show you my home like I promised."

Fresh sorrow filled Cinder, and sobs threatened, but he held them down. He had to stay strong for Nathaz. Nathaz needed him. Cinder wouldn't let him go into the long night alone. An instant later, his eyes lit with sudden hope. Maybe Nathaz's injury wasn't as bad as the dwarf thought. "Let me see it. Maybe . . ."

Nathaz shook his head. "It's too late for me. I've got a foot of spiderkin shoved inside. I think the fucker hit an artery." Nathaz stared into the dark sky. "I wouldn't mind dying if it didn't hurt so fucking much," he said, sounding philosophical.

"Nathaz," Cinder whispered, heartbroken and helpless. There was nothing he could do. No words to express his sorrow, his grief. "I'm so sorry." A pair of tears fell from his eyes, tracked down his cheek. He wouldn't allow any more to fall. If he did, he'd end up blubbering and useless.

Nathaz managed another smile. "What are you sorry about? You didn't stab me." His voice was weak.

Cinder held his friend's gaze. "You're not alone," he said, wanting his friend to understand his meaning in all its shades.

"I know," Nathaz whispered. "Neither are you." His breathing stopped.

"Nathaz?" Cinder shook the dwarf. He checked his neck for a pulse. The other side. *Nothing.*

Nathaz was gone. He'd never again see his home, walk with his family, laugh as only he could.

Cinder did what he could for his friend. He crossed Nathaz's arms over the dwarf's chest and set the handle of his axe in one hand. *A warrior's repose.* Only then did he let the tears fall.

He then also became aware of his aches and pains. The soreness in his ankle. The weakness in his shoulder and arm. *The spiderkin venom. Shit.*

His thoughts grew heavy. His vision swam. He felt himself tottering but could do nothing to stop it. Sounds faded away. The world became black.

Cinder walked a quiet street, one paved with long red bricks laid out in a herringbone pattern. Live oaks draped in wispy strands of gray moss lined both sides of the road, while the median contained an abundance of jasmines in bloom. He inhaled their perfume.

A calico cat paced at his side. The right side of her face was masked in black fur, and she stood a foot taller than him. Twenty feet at least from her nose to the tip of her tail. A powerful animal, but he didn't fear her. The cat's image dissipated like fog burning off in the sun, and Cinder walked alone.

He reached a neighborhood of large homes sitting on long, narrow lots and hidden behind large compound walls. All were multiple stories, built of cement blocks and faced with stucco. They were painted in vibrant shades of blue, red, yellow, or green and had peaked roofs tiled in slate or terra cotta. A turn of his head brought him a view of the sea and a low mountain or a tall hill rearing in the near distance.

Was this Revelant?

"He's dying," a distant voice said.

"We can still save him," another voice countered.

Cinder reached a protective wall, one with crenelated battlements soaring fifty feet in height. He passed a patrol consisting of five men. All of them were similar in appearance: tall, lean, and with dark skin. A vagrant thought touched his drifting mind: tea touched with milk. Someone had once described their skin as such.

He nodded to the warriors and entered the cool shadow of a gate. Forty feet thick and wide enough for two large wagons to pass one another with room to spare on either side. He stepped beneath a heavy ironwood portcullis, which hung like a headsman's axe.

He exited into farmlands. Gentle, rolling hills were etched in straight rows of green: wheat and soybeans, the first crops of the season. Spring. The pungent smell of turned earth, manure, and hay filled the air. In the distance, he noted the presence of another wall, one more massive than the one through which he'd just passed.

On he traveled, along a gravel road. Every so often he crossed a wooden bridge spanning a stone-lined and arrow-straight stream.

"You're pouring too much of yourself into him," the first voice from earlier admonished.

"I know my limits," she snapped.

He opened his eyes, staring at bright sunshine. Where was he?

He couldn't recall. He didn't know himself. What was his name? Impressions settled upon his dulled mind. A creek burbled. Hands pressed on his chest. A face loomed in his vision. He knew her. Concern was writ large on her features.

In her hands, he knew himself to be safe, and he closed his eyes.

Cinder crossed another bridge, and his heart lifted. He knew this place. He recognized the buildings. They were made of a mix of tan stucco and wood and possessed roofs tiled in thatch or yellow ceramic. The road grew finer, wider and was now paved in crushed stone and mortar.

He reached a turnoff, a winding lane lined by cherry trees in bloom. A final bend to the track, and he saw his destination, a small, white-clapboard farmhouse. Wind chimes jingled, and she sat on the wraparound porch, gently rocking on a swing. Her head was bent, and he couldn't see her features. Her hair draped her face like a golden flag. She lifted her head and smiled.

Cinder opened his eyes, not seeing anything. His mind's eye remained upon the dream . . . Had he been dreaming? Who was the woman? Already the image of her faded out of sight, thought, and memory. The dream itself, his recollection of it drifted away like a dandelion spiraling into the sky. The wonder of it . . .

Confusion settled upon him. Where was he? He remembered a battle. The spiderkin. *Nathaz.* Nathaz was dead. So were Joria and Rorian. His vision grew watery with tears.

"Stay with us," a voice ordered.

Cinder blinked back his tears, understanding his grief would have to wait. At this moment, he needed to attend to the now. He focused on the person whose concerned visage loomed in his vision. *Anya.*

"How are you feeling?" she asked. She knelt next to him.

His head was pillowed in her lap, and he wanted to fall asleep. His eyes drifted close.

"Don't go to sleep," she chided, shaking him gently.

Cinder's eyes opened with a snap.

"How are you feeling?" she repeated more.

Cinder noticed an elf standing over her shoulder. *Lisandre.* What was he doing here? He mentally shook his head, getting ahold of his drifting thoughts. They didn't matter. Anya had asked him a question, and he took a mental inventory. His shoulder ached. A spiderkin had bitten and poisoned him. His ankle sent flashes of pain. Same with his face and hands. He'd abraded them in the rush through the forest . . .

When was it? Was he still by the stream where he and Nathaz had made their final stand?

Cinder shook off fluttering thoughts. Anya had asked him a question. "I'm . . ." His throat was dry as a stone. He worked saliva into his mouth. "I'm fine enough."

Relief replaced the concern on Anya's face. "Then maybe you can get to your feet? I think you've spent enough time resting."

"I'll rest when I'm dead," Cinder said.

Surprise might have filled Anya's face, but if so, it was quickly masked.

38

It was only because of Anya's skill at Healing that Cinder still lived. He should have died, would have died if not for her.

Loial Company had held off the night-time spiderkin raid. It had been a running battle all the way to the walls of Fellim where they'd managed to repulse the spiderkin, who promptly retreated to their nest. Loial Company settled in to wait on the relief force from Fort Benshire to arrive, but Anya had refused to stay still.

There were warriors still missing, and Anya had left Fellim. She meant to search for injured survivors. She intended to find those who might have been cut off from the fighting and were too injured to regroup at Fellim. She had first gone back to the site of the forest ambush where the battle had started. Lisandre had accompanied her. The first set of tracks Anya had come across had been Cinder's, and she'd followed his progression.

She found the site of his last stand, a gorge carved by a gurgling stream with dead spiderkin strewn all about. Cinder lay next to Nathaz, the dwarf already fallen and Cinder hours away from passing on himself. He raged with fever. The puncture wounds from a spiderkin's fangs were clearly infected, and a portion of it was necrotic. Lisandre had believed him a lost cause, but Anya wouldn't hear of it. She'd lanced the wounds, drawing out some of the infection and Healed him.

She and Lisandre had carried him to Fellim where the relief from Fort Benshire arrived a few days later and their physicians could properly treat him.

All told, Loial Company had lost nineteen warriors, another nine would never again fight, and eight would need weeks or months to recover. As for the Firsters, they'd lost six of their nineteen: Nathaz, Joria, Rorian, Dorcer, Crail, and an elf Cinder had barely known, Farin Eshanwe.

A few more were injured, but none as severely as Cinder. He learned this later on, after recovering enough to hear of it. It had taken most of a week of convalescing before Anya had filled in the details. Cinder had closed his eyes then and said a prayer for his fallen brothers. He hoped they had found peace in Devesh's loving arms. They deserved it after the horror of their deaths. The images of Rorian and Nathaz dying . . . Cinder couldn't seem to get them out of his mind. They lingered, coming over his thoughts when he least expected it, and he wondered if they always would.

A few days later, Cinder was healed enough in body, if not mind, to join the others on the long trek back to Swift Sword. The Unitary Trial was over. The Firsters had experienced more than enough of the world's dangers, and it was time to return to the Directorate.

Cinder rode a borrowed horse, one from Fort Benshire. The Firsters had managed to recover most of their mounts, but Cinder's mare had been killed and her corpse dragged off. In some ways, she seemed like a reflection of what sorrows the Firsters suffered.

It was a slow trek, and two weeks after setting out, they entered the city in the late morning. Yards from Swift Sword's entrance, Cinder noted a nearby group of mercenaries. It was an eight-person group, a mixture of men and women, marching proudly. They carried themselves like an eight-man empire. One of them glanced in Cinder's direction, and his gaze flicked over Cinder's clothing, his weapons, and bearing, and another glance took in the line of Firsters trailing after him. The mercenary quickly looked away, respect on his face.

Cinder smirked. A few years ago, he'd been warned never to make eye contact with the mercenaries, and now they were avoiding his. The counsel had come from Deepak Moral, Swallow's priest, and Cinder wondered how the old man was doing. How was his brother doing? He hadn't thought about them in months, but then again, were they really family? He had never regained the memories of his first sixteen years of life. He wasn't the person they knew. As far as he knew, his life had begun two years ago.

Or had it? He recalled imaginings of a woman and a glorious city, recollections of a different family and a different life. The visions. What did they mean? Why couldn't he remember the details within them? He figured they must be dreams, ones remembered in a hazy fashion.

"We have a room for you to further convalesce," Anya said, intruding on his thoughts. "You're still weak. You'll have a few more days to recover before we ship out for home."

Cinder nodded understanding. "There are some things I need to take care of first." The last time he'd been to Swift Sword, he'd only had time to see his master and friends at *Steel-Graced Adepts.* He hadn't been able to visit Coral or Riner. He needed to now. There were things to tell Coral, and he feared it might be the last time they saw one another.

Her last words, the statement of waiting on him . . . he had been a coward then. He had hoped he could hold to his promise. That he would return to her.

But it was a lie. He knew it even while he'd said the vow. More importantly, his heart wasn't with Coral. He thought of her as a friend, but nothing else. He should have told her the truth back when he was readying to leave for the Directorate, not lie to her and lead her on. He had to correct his mistake.

He only hoped she didn't hate him for it.

"I'll have to go with you," Anya said. "Like I told you. You're still weak, and I don't want you passing out somewhere and dying, not after all the work I put into keeping you alive."

Cinder nodded, but he wasn't really listening to her. His thoughts were on other matters. *Coral.* Dreams were fables, and fables were stories. They weren't true. He needed to end this one.

Anya watched Cinder carefully. The other Firsters had long since split off from them, heading off to the inn where Anya had arranged for them to stay. They would hole up for the next two or three days until a boat arrived to take them back to Yaksha proper.

"We're getting close," Cinder said. It was his first words in many blocks.

Anya didn't reply. She recognized this area. She had been to Swift Sword on many occasions, and she rode silently next to Cinder along Swift Sword's streets. She didn't like this city. It was too crowded, too overwhelming with sights, sounds, and smells, and few of them comforting.

Her lips curled at the stench permeating the air. It was a miasma of grilled meat, spices, urine, and waste. Her ears twitched at the strident noise when a crowd of folk shouted, gestured, and cursed coarsely all about them. And her mind quailed in sorrow when a number of children—dirty and wearing little more than rags—raced past her mount, laughing. She shook her head, wanting to weep at their condition, unable to fathom how they found any kind of joy in their poverty-stricken lives. Worse, how could the people around them ignore the bony limbs and easily evident ribs of those poor children? Why did the folk of Swift Sword accept privation as a normal course of matters? Why did they not minister to the sick and the old? Why did they accept the filth infesting their city?

Anya had no answer, and she had long since ceased asking such questions. No one had thus far been able to answer her queries.

As for Cinder, he sat astride his horse easily enough, riding smooth and relaxed. However, by now Anya knew him too well. Cinder was clever at masking any weakness, at pressing onward despite any injuries. For him, a goal was a mission, and he refused to quit or allow failure to enter into the picture. No matter the difficulty, once he set his mind to a task, he accomplished it. Cinder was a man of will.

She wondered if he even felt such mortal emotions as fear or self-doubt. Witness his defeat of Estin and Riyne in a duel. He should have begged off the fight, but he hadn't. Instead, he'd trained like a fiend and cut a path to victory. Or what he'd done at the gorge where she'd discovered him and Nathaz.

She shied away from *how* she'd found Cinder. She had told Lisandre that she'd simply followed the trail of broken branches and torn underbrush, but the truth was she could have found Cinder with her eyes shut. She had sensed him, sensed his mortal peril. It was like a red swatch overlaying her mind, telling her where to go. No one needed to know about it, though. In fact, no one could ever know about it. She had no explanation for what the sensation meant and doubted anyone else did either. As far as she knew, it had no precedent.

At any rate, she had followed the feeling until she discovered Cinder hovering in the twilight hour between life and death. Nine spiderkin corpses lay scattered about him and Nathaz. Three were clearly killed by a dwarven hammer, one had taken an arrow in the face, but the other five had been cut down by a sword. Cinder obviously, but how?

Even an elven ranger would have found such odds daunting, but Cinder had managed it. He was a rare warrior, and she had initially feared he was too far gone to save when she had found him. But once again, his indomitable will had surprised her. Cinder had denied death's calling. He'd fought to live, and now, here he was, riding to a meeting with a young woman.

Her name was Coral. Cinder hadn't said much more beyond telling where she worked and asking for Anya's aid to arrange for a meeting, and she'd agreed. She had sent word racing ahead of them, asking the woman's employer to give her time off to meet with Cinder.

Otherwise, Cinder refused to divulge anything of his relationship with Coral. In this, he and Anya were similar. He was private in his affairs.

"We're here," Cinder said. He'd reined in his borrowed gelding and dismounted.

Anya glanced about. This wasn't the home of a wealthy merchant. Cinder had brought them to a rectangular, grassy park. Azaleas, dogwoods, and rhododendrons remained in bloom despite the lateness of the season. Same with the cherry trees planted along the winding pathways. The perfumed aroma displaced the normal stink of the city.

"I won't be long," Cinder said. He paced away from her; his gait graceful as a stalking leopard.

He'd had that manner even during her first observation of him. She remembered it. She remembered Cinder's appearance when he had first arrived at the Third Directorate. Short and slender compared to everyone else, scrawny in fact, but in the past year, he'd grown. He stood taller than her, as tall as Bones and every bit as muscular but far faster as well as stronger and with a still improving form and technique. He also possessed reflexes which were almost elf-like. And he married those attributes with his eerie way of knowing what his opponent intended, the talent he'd turned into a skill, and one that only the oldest of masters could claim. All those abilities in one person . . .

Cinder was only now tapping his potential. What could he do in another few years? Anya reckoned by then, he might be the match of nearly any elf. He could be the first human to earn an *insufi* blade.

She was determined to see it done. She would train him and make certain his skills weren't wasted in the regular cavalry or fast infantry.

Anya returned her attention to Cinder when he reached a lovely young woman seated on a bench, who stood and beamed greeting.

Coral.

It had been almost a year since he'd seen her, and she hadn't changed at all. Her clothes were somewhat finer, but they couldn't hold a candle to the woman wearing them. She remained the dark-haired, dark-eyed beauty Cinder had once known so well and thought he might marry. Her smile was welcoming and warm, and he remembered her jewel-toned laughter when he told a joke; the way her beautiful voice lifted in song, melding with his mandolin. He recalled the mother-wolverine manner in which she defended Riner. Coral was generous, loving, kind, and so very talented.

Guilt stabbed him at what he had to do, but maybe in time, she'd come to accept his decision as the best for both of them.

"You've grown so tall," Coral said. She glanced over his shoulder, obviously seeing Anya. "And you come in the company of a beautiful elf."

Cinder forced a half-hearted smile. "I accompany her. Not the other way around."

Coral quirked her eyebrows. "Should I be jealous?" she teased.

She had no reason to be jealous, but Cinder didn't say so. He continued to struggle with the same tentacled dilemma occupying his thoughts over the past week or more. So much time spent laboring over the words to tell Coral, and he still didn't know what to say.

Upon his silence, Coral's joyful smile slowly faded. Awareness took hold in her eyes along with a wise understanding. "Do you think you'll break my heart today, Cinder Shade?"

His gaze snapped to hers. His brows furrowed in confusion. How did she already know? He hadn't said anything to her yet. His surprise must have shown.

Coral took his hands. "You've been gone for a year, and in that time, I've thought about us a lot. About me. About you." She shook her head. "You and I were only ever a dream. A good dream, but we are too different."

Relieved joy bubbled in his throat. A sense of disbelief settled on him. Coral felt the same way he did. She understood why they couldn't be together. She understood and agreed. All the burdens of not wanting to hurt her faded, and he wanted to laugh. All the hours he'd wasted in worry . . . It turned out he need not have bothered.

However, the smile wouldn't come. He felt relief, yes, but there was also loss, the loss of what might have been, the loss of the woman he had once thought he'd spend his life with. "When did you realize?" he asked.

"Many months ago," Coral said, smiling again. "You are a wonderful person, Cinder, but your path isn't meant to keep you here. You aren't meant to be caged in Swift Sword."

"There is nothing wrong with living in Swift Sword, and it isn't a cage."

"No, it's not. At least not for some of us. For some of us, Swift Sword is our home, but that's not the case for you, is it? For you, Swift Sword would be a prison. You know this."

Cinder actually didn't know. He'd never considered the matter, but he did so now. And it only took a few moments for him to realize she was right. Swift Sword *was* too small. So was the Third Directorate and Revelant. The labor to which he felt a calling was vaster than any one city. He only wished he knew the actual nature of his labor.

"You have strife and war ahead of you," Coral said. "You will have to face it with all your courage."

Cinder dipped his head, overwhelmed by Coral's grace. He was unable to meet her accepting gaze, but she tilted his head up, cupping his face in her hand.

"I give you my leave," she said. "Go on with your life. Don't think about this."

Her words were brave, but when Cinder gazed into her eyes, his heart ached. Coral was courageous, but she was lying. He saw the truth. The terrible hurt and loss shadowing her eyes. The anguish of awareness, of knowing he wasn't for her. And still she courageously let him leave her life with a clear conscience.

Coral. No matter what he achieved in life, Cinder recognized he'd never be worthy of her.

She must have seen something in his face then because a sorrow-filled wistfulness overtook her features. But she said nothing. She stared at him as if to imprint every line of his face in her mind, to hoard the images away for a lifetime of memories. She brought his head down and kissed him on the mouth, soft, pressing and full of repressed longing. "Our last kiss," she whispered, smiling through her obvious grief and sorrow. A single tear traced the fine bones of her cheek, and her hands fell to her side. She took a step back. "Goodbye, Cinder Shade."

Cinder watched her go, saying nothing. He wouldn't call her back and offer false hope. He wouldn't dishonor her courage. He watched her go and felt emptier than a dried-out husk, crueler than a wicked child. He wished his life was different, that *he* was different.

War and strife.

He turned and went back to Anya.

Anya would normally have kept quiet, but the pain on Cinder's face impelled a need to speak up. And yet, she hesitated. This was merely a human. Should she bother? Her indecision lasted less than a second. "Are you going to be well?"

"I'll be fine," Cinder said, his voice flat.

Anya eyed him, wondering what was going on in his mind, and if she needed to know anything more. "It looked like it wasn't an easy conversation."

Cinder sighed. "It wasn't. Coral was—is—special to me, but we were never meant to be. I had to tell her that today. I had to tell her not to wait. To move on and find her own joy." He finished in a self-mocking chuckle. "She already knew what I had to say."

He wore such sorrow that Anya's hand was halfway to his face, seeking to console him. At the very last, she remembered her station. By a bare margin, she prevented a horrible breach and returned her hand to her side. It was not her place to bring him comfort. It was not the place of any elven woman. Cinder was human. She was not. Her true past changed nothing. She couldn't afford to forget who she was right now.

"Besides, what we might have had was only a dream," Cinder continued.

"A dream?" Anya recalled her own dreams and what they confirmed. Even as a young woman, Anya had felt like her elven skin lay poorly over her bones, and her dreams had taught her why.

This wasn't Anya's first life. Anya had been human once and in love with a human. Those memories were real, and to this day, they stalked her. She recalled part of her past from the first time she had awoken. The fever which should have killed her. But the memories only told so much. Even now, she couldn't visualize the faces of her husband, her parents, her siblings. Did she have children? She didn't know.

Only in her dreams did she feel complete.

"Sometimes a dream is all we have," she said to Cinder. "And sometimes a dream shows us the truth. Those kinds are worth everything."

Cinder smiled, faint and weary. "Those kinds most certainly are. But they can also hurt."

39

The next morning, Cinder and the rest of the Firsters left Swift Sword and journeyed back to Yaksha proper. In Revelant, as before, the humans and dwarves were housed in the yellow manor, while the elves stayed at the royal palace. And as before, it proved to be a short stay since they departed for the Third Directorate the next morning.

Their group only required three carriages this time, rather than five. There were six less of them to journey through a land at peace and with weather that was a comfortable mix of sunshine and warmth.

It felt wrong after the deaths they had experienced, and the carriages were quiet, the pleasant surroundings unable to penetrate the doleful mood. The Firsters, all of them—humans, dwarves, and elves—were bonded in shared mourning. At least enough to pass the trip in quiet contemplation. Everyone had their sorrows to bear.

They entered the grounds of the Directorate on a sunny afternoon where an aide caught them shortly after they disembarked the carriages. General Arwan wanted to address them and would meet them in the Quad.

The Firsters set their gear in a pile near the statue of Garad Lull, and

Cinder scratched at his neck, uncomfortable for some reason. Perhaps it was the warm sunshine, which felt too kind. Or the wind, which seemed too glad. The breeze carried the happy singing of songbirds, and the floral aroma of jasmine and honeysuckle. Or maybe it was the lush lawn of the Quad, so alive when so many of his brothers had died.

Maybe it was all of those things or none. Cinder didn't know, but the discomfort remained, becoming a pressure, the regard of someone's ill intentions. He turned about. *Garad Lull.* The Titan appeared to peer at them, his arrogant smirk somehow knowing and pleased at their losses.

Cinder glared at the living statue. Unreasonable anger burned within him.

General Arwan arrived then, shaking him free of his reverie. The commandant faced them silently, his demeanor sorrowful. "This has been the most disastrous Unitary Trial in memory," he said. "Never have so many died during their first expedition abroad. It tests the quality of a man." His mouth tightened, and his features set in determination. "We must not waver in our mission. Your training isn't complete. You will remain here for another three months, but then you must venture forth once again. This time as part of the regular army. Am I understood?"

A muttering of 'yes, sirs' met his question.

Cinder understood the thrust of the commandant's statements. They were meant to be a reminder and an inspiration, but it was too soon. Cinder didn't have the heart to care. *Nathaz. Rorian. Joria. Dorcer.*

He caught Anya eyeing him in worry, and he forced a tight-lipped smile for her benefit. She didn't acknowledge his expression but merely turned away to face the commandant.

General Arwan cleared his throat. "Good. We will have a memorial tonight for those who gave their last, full measure. Your friends and companions. Our students. We will hold fast and eulogize their memories. Attendance is compulsory for you and everyone here at the Directorate. You are welcome to speak on their behalf."

Cinder was glad they were having the memorial, and he wondered if he should say anything. Then again, others had held closer friendships to those who had died, so perhaps he should stay quiet.

As soon as he considered the notion, he knew it was wrong. The fallen deserved more than his silence. They required his acknowledgment. He had words to say on their behalf, and they needed to be voiced. It didn't matter if the dead could hear them or not. They were more for the living anyway.

"One other issue," General Arwan said. "There are only thirteen of you remaining. You fought together as one. Protected each other as one. Bled as one. Died as one. Your actions and courage honor your instructors." He smiled in pride. "Our teachings weren't wasted. For this reason, I've decided that you've earned the right to share quarters. The elves will move their belongings to the other dorm hall. We've already seen to the possessions of the fallen, so you need not worry on that account. See the transition done before tonight. Dismissed."

The general left, gesturing for Anya and Lisandre to join him on his way back to Firemirror Hall.

The Firsters muttered, the elves complaining about the move. Strangely, none of them whined about having to live with humans and dwarves. They simply griped about having to shift their belongings. Cinder hoped it meant that the animosity between the different species had burned to ash in the fire of battle.

"Do you need any help moving?" Cinder asked the elves.

Estin and Riyne, the leaders of the elves, didn't respond, but they stared at him like he'd sprouted a second head. The others didn't speak at first either.

It fell to Mohal to respond. "Thank you, but we can manage on our own. Perhaps when we arrive, you can direct us to the available rooms?"

Cinder nodded. "Consider it done." Their part of Krathe House had twenty total rooms, plenty of space for the elves even if no Firsters had died during the Unitary Trial. "See you in a little while."

The two groups separated then, and Cinder and the rest of the humans and dwarves went to their quarters where nothing seemed different but everything was utterly changed. Without Nathaz's forceful presence, Rorian's calming influence, and Joria's quick wit, the place felt empty.

Cinder carried his only remaining pack of belongings to his room and sorted them out. It didn't take long. At this point, he had few possessions left to his name. Most of what he owned had been lost with the mare.

But not the mandolin. He'd been wise enough to leave it here. He fingered the case, opening it, and drawing forth the instrument. He gazed at it, lost in remembrances of how Nathaz sometimes sang with them when he thought no one else was listening.

He swallowed back a lump in his throat. *Damn it. Why did they have to die?* It was a question warriors throughout the ages likely asked.

Cinder sighed, taking the mandolin with him as he rejoined the others, who had gathered in the common room. The early afternoon sunshine poured through the open windows. A bird warbled, and someone in the gardens down below chuckled briefly. A breeze drifted, carrying the scent of roses in bloom.

A lovely setting, but Cinder paid it no mind. He remained hunched over the mandolin while everyone else spoke, playing melodies as the mood struck him, but not an entire song.

"You think we'll get along with the elves?" Bones asked the room in general.

No one replied. No one likely knew the answer.

Neither did Cinder, although he had pondered Bones' question ever since the commandant had made the announcement. He strummed a chord. "I don't know," he eventually said. "I hope so, but it's going to depend on them."

"They weren't so arrogant on the journey back," Ishmay said.

Sriovey grunted. "Give it time. Their arrogance will come back."

Bones chuckled in dry humor. "Arrogance and elves," he said as if the two were one and the same.

"I don't think they'll go back to the way they were," Jozep disagreed. "Battle is supposed to forge bonds of . . ." He trailed off, apparently searching for the right word.

"Of brotherhood?" Cinder supplied, offering a faint smile as he plucked the mandolin in a hopeful set of notes.

The conversation lulled after that, and for the next few hours, it continued to rise and fall in waves until the five remaining elves in the Firster class arrived.

Cinder met them. "Welcome to our part of Krathe Hall," he said. "I don't know how it was in your area, but this is the commons. We gather here after classes and relax. We play games, gossip, listen to music. Sometimes we study. It's all yours now, too. I hope you join us." The offer made, he then led them to the available rooms.

The elves quickly stowed their belongings, and a short while later, they re-entered the common room. They paced about the space, careful and cautious as a glaring of cats entering a rival's territory. An unspoken tension permeated the space.

Cinder plucked his mandolin, waiting for the elves to break the quiet. He'd offered them welcome. It was up to them to accept it.

"So. What happens now?" Estin asked.

"What do you mean?" Cinder asked, maintaining as best he could a civil tone.

"I mean what happens now?" Estin asked. "None of you are elves, but your friends bled with ours. They died with ours. That means something to us."

"It means something to all of us," Sriovey replied.

"Which again begs the question: what happens next?"

Cinder was tired, and he didn't feel like solving whatever troubled Estin. "What happens next is we honor our dead tonight. We figure out the rest in the morning."

Estin might have said more, but Mohal touched his forearm. "He's right," the elf said to the prince. "We can't sort out everything in one day."

Cinder stood behind a podium and stared out at the gathered throng, those here for tonight's memorial. He wasn't looking forward to this. He had prepared his words, practiced them, but he feared he might break down and sob uncontrollably in the midst of delivering them. In some nations they spoke of keeping a stiff upper lip, and while Cinder could maintain a facade of control when required, tonight, he wasn't so sure.

The administration decided to hold the ceremony on the grounds beyond Firemirror Hall, in a shallow bowl surrounded by some of the cottages housing the Directorate's administrators. The Quad might have been an easier location, but no one wanted to speak in front of a sneering Garad Lull.

Twilight reigned, and crickets raised an intermittent ruckus, but their sound was somehow soothing. The chirping reminded Cinder of mythical summer days, hours spent with friends discussing what seemed wise and philosophical but was more likely foolish. A wandering breeze blew, and trees rustled under its influence like soft rattles. *Diptha* lanterns placed atop black posts ringed the grounds, lighting the setting.

Everyone had worn their best outfits, including Cinder who had left his formal uniform at the academy when he'd left for the Unitary Trial.

Cinder grabbed hold of his wandering thoughts, shaking them into control. He had a speech to give, and he cleared his throat. "When I learned of tonight's memorial, I was glad for it. It is a proper way to honor our dead brothers. They deserve our deepest respect. However, when I thought about what to say, I was struck by a question. What is respect to the dead? They aren't here to acknowledge what we say. They aren't here to accept our acclaim. They aren't here to offer forgiveness for any harm we might have done to them. Then why do it?" He paused, long enough to meet Bones' gaze. Ishmay's and Sriovey's. Anya. Master Absin. He continued. "Others have already spoken far more eloquently than I on the nature of our fallen. You've heard of their heroism and courage. Their fidelity to duty. But maybe more importantly, you've also learned of their soft moments of fellowship and caring. These were young men who laughed and loved. They were alive, searching for joy and meaning in their lives, as we all do."

Reflecting on the youth of the Firsters who had perished left him feeling old, brittle-boned and looking back on a terribly long life. It also caused his eyes to water with unbidden memories. *His friends. Nathaz and his indomitable loyalty. Rorian who didn't have a jealous bone in his body. Joria.* He missed them all. They deserved to live and laugh far more fully than what this cruel world had granted them.

Cinder's composure frayed. A wracking sigh caused him to shudder. A pair of tears tracked the lines of his face. Another shudder. It was as he had feared, and he closed his eyes, struggling to master his emotions. Seconds passed, and those in attendance remained quiet. Once he was certain of his self-control, he continued. "I wonder sometimes if we speak on behalf of our honored fallen so we can feel better for ourselves. It seems selfish, and maybe instead we should pay more attention to what we actually do with our lives. What do we do for one another now? Do we greet each other with fellowship? Acceptance? Acknowledgement? Forgiveness? We should. *That* is the greatest manner in which we can honor our brothers."

Applause broke out when he finished, and his gaze briefly rested on Estin and Riyne. In some ways, his words were mostly directed at them, but even more, they were directed inward, toward himself. He hadn't lived up to the standard he was urging for everyone else.

Cinder rejoined the Firsters, who stood at the center of the gathered folk. General Arwan took the podium, preparing to introduce the next speaker.

"You did good," Bones whispered.

Ishmay patted him on the back. "Nice."

Sriovey nodded. "Nathaz would have appreciated what you said."

"He would have *fucking* appreciated it," Bones added.

The others chuckled briefly, quieting when Master Nuhlin reached the podium. His speech only took a few minutes, and a few more spoke after him. Afterward, the memorial was finished.

Cinder prepared to join the others at Krathe Hall when Anya called his name.

"A moment of your time, Firster," she said.

His friends gave him questioning looks, and Cinder shrugged. He didn't know what Anya wanted, either. He also noticed Estin's suspicious glare, and Cinder wanted to sigh. *I guess he wasn't listening when I talked about acceptance and fellowship.*

"I'll be along," Cinder told his friends—ignoring Estin's ongoing sullen scowl.

"You spoke movingly tonight," Anya said. "It was eloquent and something we all needed to hear and heed."

"Thank you," Cinder replied, pleased at her response to his speech and puzzled over why she had asked for him.

"I hope you haven't forgotten my earlier offer," Anya said. "But before we get to that, I have a question. How did you defeat five spiderkin? At the gorge, there were five dead spiderkin who were killed by a blade."

No one had questioned what had happened at the gorge, and Cinder hadn't offered an explanation. He didn't know how the information would be received. Cinder had conducted his *lorethasra*. Would the elves think of him as a threat? He didn't know. There were accounts of humans doing as he had, but it had always been an accident occurring during times of duress, not controlled and based on clear intent. Not like what Cinder had done. And he suspected he might be able to replicate his accomplishment. That information might go over even more poorly.

He realized he'd taken too long to answer when he caught Anya's smile knowingly at him.

"It was intentional, then," she said. "Your sourcing of *lorethasra*."

Cinder merely nodded, wondering what Anya would do with the information. By force of will, he kept his heart from racing and sweat from beading.

Her smile grew gentle. "You don't have to fear what I'll do with the knowledge," she said. "I'll tell no one."

Cinder didn't yet think he was out of the woods. "You don't seem surprised."

"I'm not. You told me about it, remember? And after this encounter against the spiderkin, I recalled your duel against Riyne and Estin in greater detail. It raised suspicions. Do you know how quickly you moved against them?"

Cinder shook his head, confused now. Had he been moving quicker than usual?

"You were swifter than any human has a right to be," she explained. "Which is to say, I believe it wasn't merely your intuition which brought you victory against my brother and Riyne. It was your *lorethasra*. Whether you will it or not, I think you can source the smallest finger's width of it. Just like an elf or any other woven."

Her words landed like an anvil, and Cinder rocked on his heels. This wasn't what he had expected her to say. He could conduct his *lorethasra* intuitively? It was absurd. No human could do what she was suggesting, and he wasn't fool enough to admit to having such an ability.

"I can see you need more convincing," Anya said. "The world will need more convincing. My mother will need more convincing, which is why I want an answer tonight about my earlier offer."

Maybe it was due to the lingering emotions from the memorial, but Cinder's tension spiked again. The world? Her mother, the empress? What in Devesh's name could Anya have in mind?

Anya laughed. "Cinder, you need to relax. I'm not a wraith or some *aether-cursed* beast come to steal your soul. I'm only a woman."

Her laughter did little to calm him. "You're an elf and a princess. You'll never be *only a woman*."

A teasing grin wreathed her face. "But to you, am I not *simply Anya*?"

Cinder managed a smile, relaxing a bit. "Your offer?"

"I told it to you before, in the chai house prior to the Grand Melee, but you never gave me your answer. I want you with me for your Secondary Trial, the journey of your second year. Yes or no?"

Cinder viewed her in surprise, not sure she was being serious since she still wore a teasing grin. Vaguely, he realized Estin would be furious if he accepted. He'd be furious at the proposition itself. Many other elves would be, too. A princess of the sithe and a human traveling together would be a scandal. Was her proposal worth making so many fresh enemies? And what of her own status? He viewed her in speculation.

She noticed and somehow sensed the direction of his thoughts. "You're wise to fear my people's reaction, but you need not worry on my behalf. My title will shield me from the worst of what others might say. More importantly, consider what you may learn from me over the next year. There are fruits and food rich in *aether*. Deep in the Daggers. Places no human has ever been. Maybe they will help you. Perhaps you'll learn to source your *lorethasra* at will and teach other humans to do the same."

"Conduct," Cinder said, distractedly. "The Mythaspuris say humans conduct their *lorethasra*. Woven source it."

Anya raised a single brow. "Interesting." She viewed him in fresh assessment, concern lurking in her eyes, and strangely, so was sadness.

It wasn't new. The sadness. Cinder had long ago noticed it, and often pondered over why Anya seemed so unhappy at times.

She interrupted his considerations. "Your answer?"

Cinder took a moment longer to mull her offer. What she said made sense. He'd read of these foods she mentioned, the ones elves used to deepen and broaden their *lorethasra*. Could he use them in the same way?

Maybe he could. And maybe he could do for his people everything she suggested. Teach them to no longer bow before those who claimed to be their betters. Excitement churned. To fight so their children weren't orphaned by *aether*-cursed monstrosities. *Yes.* In the end, his decision was easy, and he nodded his head sharply. "I accept your offer."

Anya smiled, and the sun might have broken through the clouds. Cinder's breath caught in his throat.

In hindsight, Cinder knew his answer was destined to always be in the affirmative. *Anya.* She fascinated him. She always had, but it was a fascination beyond appreciation of her beauty. Anya was a puzzle, one holding an unexpected brew of sorrow and loss, but for now, she was happy, and his reply had been the cause. His heart soared at the notion, especially when she aimed her warm, joyful smile his way. She had so many types of smiles, and he wondered how many different kinds he'd see over the next year.

"I think we'll have a wonderfully adventurous time together," Anya said. "We'll discover so much."

In the bowels of a lonely mountain, one taller than any of its surrounding brothers, there stirred a being. For millennia had he laid in his prison, asleep, isolated, and impotent. In his long absence, the world had learned to forget about him, had learned to believe him a myth.

Yet, he was real.

Chains of black smoke still bound him to his living tomb, writhing about his form, holding him in place.

Chink.

An almost imperceptible sound. A link—one of a countless number—snapped. It was not the only one. Others thinned as well, frayed.

Without warning, two eyes shot open. One normal. The other aflame. Both burned with a desire for revenge, a promise of pain.

"Shokan," the being whispered. A single word before drowsing once more.

The End

A Final Note

Thank you for taking this journey with me. Without folks taking an interest in what I write, I would have no chance to do what I'm doing. I am humbled and gratified beyond measure that there are so many of you who are willing to give my words and worlds a chance.

I'd also be grateful if you decided to add a review for the book. Those social proofs are pretty much the lifeblood of an author. In addition, if you're really feeling ambitious, please consider signing up for my newsletter. It includes all of latest news, and while there's usually not a lot to tell, hey, at least you'll be up to date with what I'm doing.

As for Cinder and Anya, don't worry about them. Their story continues in *The Memories of Prophecies*.

Glossary

Absin Morewe: Weapons master at the Third Directorate.

Aether: Akin to *lorethasra*, but it is the magic imbued in the world at large. Also known as *lorasra*.

Aia: Mythical steed of Shokan. Thought to be of a species of cat called Kesarins.

Antalagore the Black: Mythical black dragon.

Apsara Sithe: An elven empire known for their agriculture and horses. They are perpetually infuriated that their horses are not a match for the Yavanas.

Anya Aruyen: Younger princess of Yaksha Sithe. She is the first and only elven woman to attend and graduate from the Third Directorate. She is also a ranger.

Avan Aruyen: Consort to Sala Yaksha, empress of Yaksha Sithe. Anya's father.

Bharat: Powerful island nation of the rishis, who claim to be direct descendants of the Mythaspuris.

Bishan: General definition means student, but in *Shevasra* it translates as *'incompetent person who has potential*

Bones Jorn: Human warrior. Cadet at the Third Directorate and in the same class as Cinder Shade. He was formerly a student of *Steel-Graced Adepts*.

Breech: A holder who protects the troll, Maize Broad.

Brow Cowl: Human warrior. Cadet at the Third Directorate and defeated by Cinder

Shade in the Maker's Tournament. A former student of the *Jasmine Water* martial academy.

Braid: Also known as a weave. A practical use of *lorethasra*.

Brilliance: An *aether-cursed* snowtiger.

Capshin Sonsing: Lieutenant and master/instructor in History at the Third Directorate.

Cariath Gelindun: Elven cadet at the Third Directorate who is in the same class as Cinder Shade.

Certitude: City in Yaksha Sithe. It is closely aligned with the Third Directorate.

Chakras: Potential loci of power, possibly within all beings, and it allows more instinctual control of weaves and braids.

Cinder Shade: Human. An unusual warrior of superlative skill. He has no recollection of his past.

Crail Valing: Elven cadet at the Third Directorate and was in the same class as Cinder Shade. Killed in the Unitary Trial.

Crèche Prani: Holy text of the dwarves.

Depth Knarl: Human warrior. Cadet at the Third Directorate and in the same class as Cinder Shade.

Derius Surent: Dwarven cadet at the Third Directorate and in the same class as Cinder Shade.

Devesth: The capital city and name of one of the Sunset Kingdoms. It is the home of the famed Yavana horses.

Dorcer Surent: Dwarven cadet at the Third Directorate and was in the same class as Cinder Shade. Killed during the Unitary Trial.

Dorr Corn: Former student at *Steel-Graced Adepts.*

Drak Renter: One of Shet's Titans.

Duchess of Certitude: Hereditary position and currently held by Duchess Marielle Cervine. Historically, the Duchess of Certitude is also a high-ranking member in the succession for the imperial throne of Yaksha Sithe.

Enma Aruyen: Elder princess and heir to the throne of Yaksha Sithe.

Estin Aruyen: Prince of Yaksha Sithe. He is also an elven cadet at the Third Directorate and in the same class as Cinder Shade.

Faine Kole: Journeyman at *Steel-Graced Adepts.*

Farin Eshanwe: Elven cadet at the Third Directorate and was in the same class as Cinder Shade. Killed in the Unitary Trial.

Fastness: A white Yavana stallion.

First Directorate: Yaksha Sithe's shadowy organization of spies.

Forever Triumphant: Elven holy text.

Gandharva Federation: A human nation. It is allied with Yaksha Sithe and Rakesh.

Garad Mull: One of Shet's Titans. Like the other known Titans, he lives in a statue-like state and is currently kept within the Quad at the Third Directorate.

Garlin Fairsent: Warrior of Rakesh. Defeated by Cinder in the Maker's Tournament.

Genka Devesth: Warlord from the Sunset Kingdom of Devesth. He believes himself the heir spoken of in the *Medeian Scryings* and intends on recreating Shang Mendi, Mede's ancient empire.

Gorant Sin Peace: Student at *Steel-Graced Adepts.*

Halin Dorund: Cavalry master at the Third Directorate.

Holder: A species of woven who are the pre-eminent warriors in all of Seminal. Little is known about them other than they have no known lands of their own and are entirely devoted to the protection of yakshins and trolls.

Indrun Agni: A Mythaspuri.

Isha: Common definition is 'instructor', but in *Shevasra*, it means 'master'.

Ishmay Sensow: Human cadet at the Third Directorate and in the same class as Cinder Shade. Originally from the Gandharva Federation.

Isthrim: A type of *aether*-infused dwarven steel that is able to kill vampires and necrosed.

Jameken Battalion: Veteran battalion of Yaksha's imperial army. Colloquially known as the 'James'.

Jasmine Water: A martial academy in Swift Sword.

Jine Kole: Master at *Steel-Graced Adepts.*

Jivatma: Supposedly the soul. Largely thought to be mythical, although some accounts of the Mythaspuris indicate it was the source of their power.

Joria Javsheck: Human cadet at the Third Directorate and was in the same class as

Cinder Shade. Killed in the Unitary Trial.

Jovick Sonsen: Unarmed combat master at the Third Directorate.

Jozep Surent: Dwarven cadet at the Third Directorate and in the same class as Cinder Shade.

Koran Yaksha: Founder and first empress of Yaksha Sithe.

Lamarin Hosh: Secret society in Yaksha Sithe. They seek to discover and aid the reborn Shokan and Sira. Founded by Duchess Sarienne Cervine of Certitude, who was a quelchon.

Lerid File: Owner/master of *Steel-Graced Adepts*.

Liline Salt: Known as Water Death. One of Shet's Titans. Along with Rence Darim, they are the only two female Titans. She is also frozen in a statue-like state and housed in a courtyard in Apsara Sithe.

Lisandre Coushinre: An elven ranger and occasional instructor at the Third Directorate. Brother to Riyne Coushinre.

Loial Company: Small unit decimated during a recent Unitary Trial.

Lor Agni: An ancient holy text centered around the proper means of righteous living and the worship of Devesh. Mostly limited in importance to Gandharva and Rakesh (translated as *the Secret Fire* in *Shevasra*).

Lorasra: Synonym for *aether*, although the term has fallen out of favor and is rarely used any longer.

Lorethasra: A mystical source of power by which woven are able to create weaves and braids that impact the world.

Loriam Stilwen: Elven cadet at the Third Directorate and in the same class as Cinder Shade.

Mahadev: The fallen city of the Mythaspuris.

Maize Broad: A troll who meets Cinder Shade at the Third Directorate and recognizes him.

Manifold Fulsom: Along with Sapient Dormant, one of the leaders of the Mythaspuris.

Marielle Cervine: Current Duchess of Certitude and the leader of the Lamarin Hosh.

Mede: Ancient warlord from Parn, who set out to conquer the world. He was largely successful, and his empire was known as Shang Mendi. However, upon his death, his empire quickly fell apart into strife and civil war.

The Medeian Scryings: Holy text written by Mede and said to be inspired by the voice of Devesh. Much of the book is a biographical account of Mede's life and conquests as well as his philosophical beliefs.

Mirk Bassang: Human student at *Steel-Graced Adepts.*

Mohal Holwarein: Elven cadet at the Third Directorate and in the same class as Cinder Shade.

Molni Cirnovain: Master librarian at the Third Directorate.

Mother Ashoka: Mother to all the Ashoka trees and yakshins on Seminal.

Mythaspuris: Powerful humans who entered Seminal during the *NusraelShev* and are thought to have turned the tide in the battle against Shet.

Naraka: Shet's ancient empire.

Nathaz Surent: Dwarven cadet at the Third Directorate and was in the same class as Cinder Shade. Killed during the Unitary Trial.

Nuhlin Genhim: Master/instructor of Tactics and Strategy at the Third Directorate.

NusraelShev: Translated as *the Disastrous Submission* in *Shevasra*. The ancient war against Shet and his forces.

Pitch Shade: Brother to Cinder Shade.

Quelchon: A rare woven who can 'recite' a person and thereby learn a hint of their future.

Quelchon Ginala: Elderly elf with the power of a quelchon. She is not what she appears.

Rakesh: A human nation. Allied with the Gandharva Federation and essentially a vassal state to Yaksha Sithe.

Recite: Rare ability that allows the practioner, known as a quelchon, to see a portion of a person's future.

Redwinth Wheat: Prince of Apsara Sithe and presumed fiancé to Enma Aruyen of Yaksha Sithe.

Rence Darim: Known as the Illwind. One of Shet's Titans. Along with Liline Salt, they are the only two female Titans.

Revelatory Dreams: A set of scrolls written by the trolls and yakshins. Translated from *Shevasra*, and there are conflicting versions.

Rishis: Rulers of Bharat, who claim to be the human descendants of the Mythaspuris.

Riyne Coushinre: Elven cadet at the Third Directorate and is in the same class as Cinder Shade. Brother to Lisandre Coushinre.

Rorian Molinking: Human cadet at the Third Directorate and was in the same class as Cinder Shade. Killed in the Unitary Trial.

Sala Yaksha: Current empress of Yaksha Sithe.

Sapient Dormant: Along with Manifold Fulsom, one of the leaders of the Mythaspuris.

Sash Slice: Human student at *Steel-Graced Adepts*.

Savage Kingdoms: Group of rival human kingdoms that were formed from the remnants of Shang Mendi, Mede's empire, in the far northeast of the world.

Seminal:

Serwil Opturund: Archery master at the Third Directorate.

Shadion Carrend: A dwarven spy from Surent Crèche. He often pretends to be a merchant and has a donkey named, Pretty.

Shalla Valley: Home of the yakshins.

Shaloce Astreas: Colonel and commander of Jameken Battalion.

Shet: A self-proclaimed god, who battled much of the world three thousand years ago in the *NusraelShev.* He was supported by seven Titans.

Shokan: A mythical human warrior. Along with his wife, Sira, they are said to be Shet's greatest foes and are collectively known as the Blessed Ones.

Shon: Mythical steed of Sira's. Thought to be of a species of cat called Kesarins.

Simone Trementh: Dowager Duchess and aunt to Marielle Cervine.

Sira: A mythical human warrior. Along with her husband, Shokan, they are said to be Shet's greatest foes and are collectively known as the Blessed Ones.

Sriovey Surent: Leader of the dwarven cadets at the Third Directorate who are in the same class as Cinder Shade.

Sture Mael: The greatest of Shet's Titans.

Sunset Kingdoms: Group of rival human kingdoms that were formed from the remnants of Shang Mendi, Mede's empire, in the far northwest of the world.

Surent Crèche: Dwarven crèche and somewhat allied to Rakesh and Yaksha Sithe. By tradition, surnames are taken from the mother's side of the family, but to everyone not of the crèche, the surnames are always told as being 'Surent'.

Swan Yaksha: Second empress of Yaksha Sithe.

Swift Sword: Capital of Rakesh.

Sylve Arwan: General and commandant of the Third Directorate.

Taj Wada: Complex of buildings that comprise the imperial palace of Yaksha Sithe.

Third Directorate: Yaksha Sithe's pre-eminent military academy.

Tomag Jury: Known as the Shield Render. One of Shet's Titans. Twin brother to Tormak Jury.

Tormak Jury: Known as the Sword Breaker. One of Shet's Titans. Twin brother to Tomag Jury.

Trolls: A species of woven known for their ability to apply Justice, a type of braid/weave by which they allow the truth of a matter to be truly known and never forgotten. They are also the only woven who procreate by parthenogenesis

Vampires: Species of woven who are beholden to Shet. They have a type of flight and gather blood slaves as a means to acquire power.

Wark Nil: Human warrior. Cadet at the Third Directorate and in the same class as Cinder Shade.

Weave: Also known as a braid. A practical use of *lorethasra*.

Woven: General name for all self-aware beings on Seminal other than humans.

Wraiths: Twisted humans, who apparently have the means to source either *lorethasra* or conduct *Jivatma*. They are universally insane and lust for flesh and brains.

Yakshins: Tree maidens. A type of woven known for their deeply held bonds to trees and nature.

Yavanas: Finest breed of horse in the world. They only breed true in the Cord Valley or Devesth, one of the Sunset Kingdoms.

Zahhack: Name given to the woven who are beholden to Shet. It is also the name of a mythical being of whom very few know, who is reputedly the son of the Empty One, Devesh's great foe.

About the Author

Davis Ashura is a legend...in his own mind. He resides in North Carolina, sharing a house with his wonderful wife who somehow overlooked Davis' eccentricities and married him anyway. As proper recompense for her sacrifice, Davis then unwittingly turned his wonderful wife into a nerd-girl. To her sad and utter humiliation, she knows *exactly* what is meant by 'Kronos'. Living with them are their two rambunctious boys, both of whom have at various times helped turn Davis' once lustrous, raven-black hair prematurely white (it sure sounds prettier than the dirty gray it actually is). And of course, there is the obligatory strange, calico cat (all authors have cats – it's required by the union). She is the world's finest hunter of socks, be they dirty or clean. When not working – nay laboring – in the creation of works of fiction so grand that hardly anyone has read a single word of them, Davis practices medicine, but only when the insurance companies tell him he can. Visit him at www.DavisAshura.com and be appalled by the banality of a writer's life.